A STEVEN SPIELBERG Film

EMPIRE OF THE SUN

WARNER BROS. Presents A STEVEN SPIELBERG Film
"EMPIRE OF THE SUN"
Starring JOHN MALKOVICH · MIRANDA RICHARDSON
NIGEL HAVERS and introducing CHRISTIAN BALE
Music by JOHN WILLIAMS
Director of Photography ALLEN DAVIAU, A.S.C
Executive Producer ROBERT SHAPIRO
Produced by STEVEN SPIELBERG ·
KATHLEEN KENNEDY · FRANK MARSHALL
Screenplay by TOM STOPPARD
Based on the novel by J. G. BALLARD
Directed by STEVEN SPIELBERG

AMBLIN
ENTERTAINMENT

SOUNDTRACK AVAILABLE ON
WARNER BROS. RECORDS, CASSETTES AND CD's

DOLBY STEREO
IN SELECTED THEATRES

EMPIRE OF
THE SUN

J.G. BALLARD

WASHINGTON SQUARE PRESS
PUBLISHED BY POCKET BOOKS NEW YORK

This novel is a work of fiction. Names, characters, places and incidents are either the product of the author's imagination or are used fictitiously. Any resemblance to actual events or locales or persons, living or dead, is entirely coincidental.

POCKET BOOKS, a division of Simon & Schuster, Inc.
1230 Avenue of the Americas, New York, N.Y. 10020

Copyright © 1984 by J. G. Ballard

Published by arrangement with Simon and Schuster
Library of Congress Catalog Card Number: 84-10630

ISBN: 0-671-64877-2

First Pocket Books printing October 1985

10 9 8 7 6 5 4 3

POCKET and colophon are trademarks of
Simon & Schuster, Inc.

Printed in the U.S.A.

FOREWORD

Empire of the Sun describes my experiences in Shanghai, China, during the Second World War, and in Lunghua C.A.C. (Civilian Assembly Centre), where I was interned from 1942 to 1945. For the most part this novel is an eyewitness account of events I observed during the Japanese occupation of Shanghai and within the camp at Lunghua.

The Japanese attack on Pearl Harbor took place on Sunday morning, December 7, 1941, but as a result of time differences across the Pacific Date Line it was then already the morning of Monday, December 8, in Shanghai. During the war, as I have recounted, the great pagoda at Lunghua was equipped with antiaircraft guns and served as a flak tower. The military airfield at Hungjao is now the site of Shanghai International Airport.

J. G. Ballard

CONTENTS

ONE

TWO

THREE

ONE

1

THE EVE OF
PEARL HARBOR

WARS CAME EARLY to Shanghai, over-
taking each other like the tides that raced up the Yangtze
and returned to this gaudy city all the coffins cast adrift
from the funeral piers of the Chinese Bund.

Jim had begun to dream of wars. At night the same
silent films seemed to flicker against the wall of his bedroom in Amherst Avenue, and transformed his sleeping
mind into a deserted newsreel theater. During the winter
of 1941 everyone in Shanghai was showing war films.
Fragments of his dreams followed Jim around the city;
in the foyers of the department stores and hotels the
images of Dunkirk and Tobruk, Barbarossa and the Rape
of Nanking sprang loose from his crowded head.

To Jim's dismay, even the Dean of Shanghai Cathedral
had equipped himself with an antique projector. After
morning service on Sunday, December 7, the eve of the
Japanese attack on Pearl Harbor, the choirboys were
stopped before they could leave for home and were
marched down to the crypt. Still wearing their cassocks,
they sat in a row of deck chairs requisitioned from the

Shanghai Yacht Club and watched a year-old *March of Time*.

Thinking of his unsettled dreams, and puzzled by their missing sound track, Jim tugged at his ruffed collar. The organ voluntary drummed like a headache through the cement roof, and the screen trembled with the familiar images of tank battles and aerial dogfights. Jim was eager to prepare for the fancy-dress Christmas party being held that afternoon by Dr. Lockwood, the vice-chairman of the British Residents Association. There would be the drive through the Japanese lines to Hungjao, and then Chinese conjurers, fireworks and yet more newsreels, but Jim had his own reasons for wanting to go to Dr. Lockwood's party.

Outside the vestry doors the Chinese chauffeurs waited by their Packards and Buicks, arguing in a fretful way with each other. Bored by the film, which he had seen a dozen times, Jim listened as Yang, his father's driver, badgered the Australian verger. However, watching the newsreels had become every expatriate Briton's patriotic duty, like the fund-raising raffles at the country club. The dances and garden parties, the countless bottles of scotch consumed in aid of the war effort (like all children, Jim was intrigued by alcohol but vaguely disapproved of it) had soon produced enough money to buy a Spitfire—probably one of those, Jim speculated, that had been shot down on its first flight, the pilot fainting in the reek of Johnnie Walker.

Usually Jim devoured the newsreels, part of the propaganda effort mounted by the British Embassy to counter the German and Italian war films being screened in the public theaters and Axis clubs of Shanghai. Sometimes the Pathé newsreels from England gave Jim the impression that, despite their unbroken series of defeats, the British people were thoroughly enjoying the war. The *March of Time* films were more somber, in a way that appealed to Jim. Suffocating in his tight cassock, he watched a burning Hurricane fall from a sky of Dornier bombers toward a children's-book landscape of English meadows that he had never known. The *Graf Spee* lay scuttled in the River Plate, a river as melancholy as the Yangtze, and smoke clouds rose from a shabby city in eastern Europe, that black planet from which Vera Frankel, his seventeen-year-old governess, had escaped on a refugee ship six months earlier.

Jim was glad when the newsreel was over. He and his fellow choristers tottered into the strange daylight toward their chauffeurs. His closest friend, Patrick Maxted, had sailed with his mother from Shanghai for the safety of the British fortress at Singapore, and Jim felt that he had to watch the films for Patrick, and even for the White Russian women selling their jewelry on the cathedral steps and the Chinese beggars resting among the gravestones.

The commentator's voice still boomed inside his head as he rode home through the crowded Shanghai streets in his parents' Packard. Yang, the fast-talking chauffeur, had once worked as an extra in a locally made film. Yang enjoyed impressing his eleven-year-old passenger with tall tales of film stunts and trick effects. But today Yang ignored Jim, banishing him to the backseat. He punched the Packard's powerful horn, carrying on his duel with the aggressive rickshaw coolies who tried to crowd the foreign cars off the Bubbling Well Road. Lowering the window, Yang lashed with his leather riding crop at the thoughtless pedestrians, the sauntering bar girls with American handbags, the old amahs bent double under bamboo yokes strung with headless chickens.

An open truck packed with professional executioners swerved in front of them, on its way to the public stranglings in the Old City. Seizing his chance, a barefoot beggar boy ran beside the Packard. He drummed his fists on the doors and held out his palm to Jim, shouting the street cry of all Shanghai: "No mama! No papa! No whiskey soda!"

Yang lashed at him, and the boy fell to the ground, picked himself up between the front wheels of an oncoming Chrysler and ran beside it.

"No mama, no papa . . ."

Jim hated the riding crop, but he was glad of the Packard's horn. At least it drowned the roar of the eight-gun fighters, the wail of air-raid sirens in London and Warsaw. He had had more than enough of the European war. Jim stared at the garish facade of the Sincere Company's department store, which was dominated by an immense portrait of Chiang Kaishek exhorting the Chinese people to ever greater sacrifices in their struggle against the Japanese. A faint light, reflected from a faulty neon tube, trembled over the Generalissimo's soft mouth, the same flicker that Jim had seen in his dreams. The whole of Shanghai was turning into a newsreel leaking from inside his head.

Had his brain been damaged by too many war films? Jim had tried to tell his mother about his dreams, but like all the adults in Shanghai that winter she was too preoccupied to listen to him. Perhaps she had bad dreams of her own. In an eerie way, these shuffled images of tanks and dive-bombers were completely silent, as if his sleeping mind were trying to separate the real war from the make-believe conflicts invented by Pathé and British Movietone.

Jim had no doubt which was real. The real war was everything he had seen for himself since the Japanese invasion of China in 1937, the old battlegrounds at Hungjao and Lunghua, where the bones of the unburied dead rose to the surface of the paddy-fields each spring. Real war was the thousands of Chinese refugees dying of cholera in the sealed stockades at Pootung, and the bloody heads of Communist soldiers mounted on pikes along the Bund. In a real war no one knew which side he was on, and there were no flags or commentators or winners. In a real war there were no enemies.

By contrast, the coming conflict between Britain and Japan, which everyone in Shanghai expected to break out in the summer of 1942, belonged to a realm of rumor. The supply ship attached to the German raider in the China Sea now openly visited Shanghai and moored in the river, where it took on fuel from a dozen lighters— many of them, Jim's father noted wryly, owned by American oil companies. Almost all the American women and children had been evacuated from Shanghai. In his class at the Cathedral School, Jim was surrounded by empty desks. Most of his friends and their mothers had left for the safety of Hong Kong and Singapore, while the fathers closed their houses and moved into the hotels along the Bund.

At the beginning of December, when school ended for the day, Jim joined his father on the roof of his office block in Szechwan Road and helped him to set fire to the crates of records which the Chinese clerks brought up in the elevator. The trail of charred paper lifted across the Bund and mingled with the smoke from the impatient funnels of the last steamers to leave Shanghai. Passengers

7

crowded the gangways, Eurasians, Chinese and Europeans fighting to get aboard with their bundles and suitcases, ready to risk the German submarines waiting in the Yangtze estuary. Fires rose from the roofs of the office buildings in the financial district, watched through field glasses by the Japanese officers standing on their concrete blockhouses across the river at Pootung. It was not the anger of the Japanese that most disturbed Jim, but their patience.

As soon as they reached the house in Amherst Avenue, he ran upstairs to change. Jim liked the Persian slippers, embroidered silk shirt and blue velvet trousers in which he resembled a film extra from *The Thief of Baghdad,* and he was eager to leave for Dr. Lockwood's party. He would endure the conjurers and newsreels, and then set off for the secret rendezvous that the rumors of war had prevented him from keeping for so many months.

By way of a happy bonus, Sunday was Vera's free afternoon, when she visited her parents in the ghetto at Hongkew. This bored young woman, little more than a child herself, usually followed Jim everywhere like a guard dog. Once Yang had driven him home—his parents were to stay on for dinner at the Lockwoods'—he would be free to roam alone through the empty house, his keenest pleasure. The nine Chinese servants would be there, but in Jim's mind, and in those of the other British children, they remained as passive and unseeing as the furniture. He would finish doping his balsa-wood aircraft and complete another chapter of the manual entitled *How to Play Contract Bridge* that he was writing in a school exercise book. After years spent listening to his mother's bridge parties, trying to extract any kind of logic from the calls of "One diamond," "Pass," "Three

Hearts," "Three No Trumps," "Double," "Redouble," he
had prevailed on her to teach him the rules and had even
mastered the conventions, a code within a code of a type
that always intrigued Jim. With the help of an Ely Cul-
bertson guide, he was about to embark on the most difficult chapter of all, on psychic bidding—all this and he
had yet to play a single hand.

However, if the task proved too exhausting, he would
set off on a bicycle tour of the French Concession, taking
his air gun in case he ran into the group of French twelve-
year-olds who formed the Avenue Foch gang. When he
returned home it would be time for the Flash Gordon
radio serial on station XMHA, followed by the record
program when he and his friends telephoned requests
under their latest pseudonyms—"Batman," "Buck Rog-
ers" and (Jim's) "Ace," which he liked to hear read out
by the announcer, though it always made him cringe with
embarrassment.

As he flung his cassock to the amah and changed into
his party costume, he found that all this was threatened.
Her head muddled by the rumors of war, Vera had decided not to visit her parents.

"You will go to the party, James," Vera informed him
as she buttoned his silk shirt. "And I will telephone my
parents and tell them all about you."

"But, Vera—they want to see you. I know they do.
You've got to think of them, Vera. . . ." Baffled, Jim
hesitated to complain. His mother had told him to be
kind to Vera, and not to tease her as he had done the
previous governess. This moody White Russian had terrified Jim as he recovered from measles by telling him
that she could hear the voice of God in Amherst Avenue,
warning them from their ways. Soon afterward Jim had
impressed his school friends by announcing that he was

an atheist. By contrast, Vera Frankel was a calm girl who never smiled and found everything strange about Jim and his parents, as strange as Shanghai itself, this violent and hostile city a world away from Cracow. She and her parents had escaped on one of the last boats from Hitler's Europe and now lived with thousands of Jewish refugees in Hongkew, a gloomy district of tenements and faded apartment blocks behind the port area of Shanghai. To Jim's amazement, Herr Frankel and Vera's mother existed in one room.

"Vera, where do your parents live?" Jim knew the answer but decided to risk the ruse. "Do they live in a house?"

"They live in one room, James."

"One room!" To Jim this was inconceivable, far more bizarre than anything in the Superman and Batman comics. "How big is the room? As big as my bedroom? As big as this house?"

"As big as your dressing room. James, some people are not so lucky as you."

Awed by this, Jim closed the door of the dressing room and changed into his velvet trousers. His eyes measured the little chamber. How two people could survive in so small a space was as difficult to grasp as the conventions in contract bridge. Perhaps there was some simple key that would solve the problem, and he would have the subject of another book.

Fortunately, Vera's pride made her rise to the bait. When she had left for her parents', setting off on the long walk to the tram terminus in the Avenue Joffre, Jim found himself still pondering the mystery of this extraordinary room. He decided to raise the matter with his mother and father, but as always they were too distracted by news of the war even to notice him. Dressed for the party, they were in his father's study, listening to the shortwave radio bulletins from England. His father knelt by the radiogram in his pirate costume, leather patch pushed onto his forehead and spectacles over his tired eyes, like some scholarly buccaneer. He stared at the yellow dial embedded like a gold tooth in the mahogany face of the radiogram. On a map of Russia spread across the carpet he marked the new defensive line to which the Red Army had retreated. He stared at it hopelessly, as mystified by the vastness of Russia as Jim had been by the Frankels' minute room.

"Hitler will be in Moscow by Christmas. The Germans are still moving forward."

His mother stood in her Pierrot suit by the window, staring at the steely December sky. The long train of a Chinese funeral kite undulated along the street, head nodding as it bestowed its ferocious smile on the European houses. "It must be snowing in Moscow. Perhaps the weather will stop them. . . ."

"Once every century? Even that might be too much to ask. Churchill must bring the Americans into the war."

"Daddy, who is General Mud?"

His father looked up as Jim waited in the doorway, the amah carrying his air gun like a bearer, this member of a volunteer infantry in blue velvet ready to aid the Russian war effort.

"Not the BB gun, Jamie. Not today. Take your aeroplane instead."

"Amah, don't touch it! I'll kill you!"

"Jamie!"

His father turned from the radiogram, ready to strike him. Jim stood quietly by his mother, waiting to see what happened. Although he liked to roam Shanghai on his bicycle, at home Jim always remained close to his mother, a gentle and clever woman whose main purposes in life, he had decided, were to go to parties and help him with his Latin homework. When she was away he spent many peaceful hours in her bedroom, mixing her perfumes together and idling through the photograph albums of her before her marriage, stills from an enchanted film in which she played the part of his older sister.

"Jamie! Never say that. . . . You aren't going to kill Amah or anyone else." His father unclenched his hands, and Jim realized how exhausted he was. Often it seemed to Jim that his father was trying to remain too calm, burdened by the threats to his firm from the Communist Labor Unions, by his work for the British Residents Association and by his fears for Jim and his mother. As he listened to the war news he became almost lightheaded. A fierce affection had sprung up between his parents, which Jim had never seen before. His father could be angry with him, while taking a keen interest in the smallest doings of Jim's life, as if he believed that helping his son to build his model aircraft was more important than the war. For the first time he was totally uninterested in schoolwork. He pressed all kinds of odd information on Jim—about the chemistry of modern dyestuffs, his company's welfare scheme for the Chinese mill hands, the school and university in England to which Jim would go after the war and how, if he wished, he could become a doctor. All these were elements of an adolescence that his father seemed to assume would never take place.

Sensibly, Jim decided not to provoke his father, nor to mention the Frankels' mysterious room in the Hongkew ghetto, the problems of psychic bidding and the missing sound track inside his head. He would never threaten Amah again. They were going to a party, and he would try to cheer his father and think of some way of stopping the Germans at the gates of Moscow.

Remembering the artificial snow that Yang had described in the Shanghai film studios, Jim took his seat in the Packard. He was glad to see that Amherst Avenue was filled with the cars of Europeans leaving for their Christmas parties. All over the western suburbs people were wearing fancy dress, as if Shanghai had become a city of clowns.

2

BEGGARS AND ACROBATS

PIERROT AND PIRATE, his parents sat silently as they set off for Hungjao, a country district five miles to the west of Shanghai. Usually his mother would caution Yang to avoid the old beggar who lay at the end of the drive. But as Yang swung the heavy car through the gates, barely pausing before he accelerated along Amherst Avenue, Jim saw that the front wheel had crushed the man's foot. This beggar had arrived two months earlier, a bundle of living rags whose only possessions were a frayed paper mat and an empty Craven A tin which he shook at passersby. He never moved from the mat, but ferociously defended his plot outside the taipan's gates. Even Boy and Number One Coolie, the houseboy and the chief scullion, had been unable to shift him.

However, the position had brought the old man little benefit. There were hard times in Shanghai that winter, and after a week-long cold spell he was too tired to raise his tin. Jim worried about the beggar, and his mother told him that Coolie had taken a bowl of rice to him.

14

After a heavy snowfall one night in early December, the snow formed a thick quilt from which the old man's face emerged like a sleeping child's above an eiderdown. Jim told himself that he never moved because he was warm under the snow.

There were so many beggars in Shanghai. Along Amherst Avenue they sat outside the gates of the houses, shaking their Craven A tins like reformed smokers. Many displayed lurid wounds and deformities, but no one noticed them that afternoon. Refugees from the towns and villages around Shanghai were pouring into the city. Wooden carts and rickshaws crowded Amherst Avenue, each loaded with a peasant family's entire possessions. Adults and children bent under the bales strapped to their backs, forcing the wheels with their hands. Rickshaw coolies hauled at their shafts, chanting and spitting, veins as thick as fingers clenched into the meat of their swollen calves. Petty clerks pushed bicycles loaded with mattresses, charcoal stoves and sacks of rice. A legless beggar, his thorax strapped into a huge leather shoe, swung himself along the road through the maze of wheels, a wooden dumbbell in each hand. He spat and swiped at the Packard when Yang tried to force him out of the car's way, and then vanished among the wheels of the pedicabs and rickshaws, confident in his kingdom of saliva and dust.

When they reached the Great Western Road exit from the International Settlement, they found a queue of cars on both sides of the checkpoint. The Shanghai police had given up any attempt to control the crowds. The British officer stood on the turret of his armored car, smoking a cigarette as he gazed over the thousands of Chinese pressing past him. Now and then, as if to keep up appearances, the Sikh NCO in a khaki turban reached down and lashed the backs of the Chinese with his bamboo rod.

Jim gazed up at the police. He was fascinated by the gleaming Sam Brownes of these sweating and overweight men, by their alarming genitalia that they freely exposed whenever they wanted to urinate and by the polished holsters that held all their manliness. Jim wanted to wear a holster himself one day, feel the enormous Webley revolver press against his thigh. Among the shirts in his father's wardrobe Jim had found a Browning automatic pistol, a jewellike object resembling the interior of his parents' cinecamera which he had once accidentally opened, exposing hundreds of feet of film. It was hard to imagine those miniature bullets killing anyone, let alone the tough Communist labor organizers.

By contrast, the Mausers worn by the senior Japanese NCOs were even more impressive than the Webleys. The wooden holsters hung to their knees, almost like rifle scabbards. Jim watched the Japanese sergeant at the checkpoint, a small but burly man who used his fists to drive back the Chinese. He was almost overwhelmed by the peasants struggling with their carts and rickshaws. Jim sat beside Yang in the front of the Packard, holding tight to his balsa aircraft as he waited for the sergeant to draw his Mauser and fire a shot into the air. But the Japanese were careful with their ammunition. Two soldiers cleared a space around a peasant woman whose cart they had overturned. Bayonet in hand, the sergeant slashed open a sack of rice, which he scattered around the woman's feet. She stood shaking and crying in a singsong voice, surrounded by the lines of polished Packards and Chryslers with their European passengers in fancy dress.

Perhaps she had tried to smuggle a weapon through the checkpoint? There were Kuomintang and Communist spies everywhere among the Chinese. Jim felt sorry for the peasant woman, whose sack of rice was probably her only possession, but at the same time he admired the Japanese. He liked their bravery and stoicism, and their sadness, which struck a curious chord with Jim, who was never sad. The Chinese, whom Jim knew well, were a cold and often cruel people, but in their superior way they stayed together, whereas every Japanese was alone. All of them carried photographs of their identical families, little formal prints, as if the entire Japanese Army had been recruited only from the patrons of arcade photographers.

On his cycle journeys around Shanghai—trips of which his parents were unaware—Jim spent hours at the Japanese checkpoints, now and then managing to ingratiate himself with a bored private. None of them would ever show Jim his weapon, unlike the British Tommies in the sandbagged blockhouses along the Bund. As the Tommies lay in their hammocks, oblivious of the waterfront life around them, they would let Jim work the bolts of their Lee-Enfields and ream out the barrels with the pull-throughs. Jim liked them, and their weird voices full of talk about a strange, inconceivable England.

But if war came, could they beat the Japanese? Jim doubted it, and he knew that his father doubted it too. In 1937, at the start of the war against China, two hundred Japanese marines had come up the river and dug themselves into the beaches of black mud below his father's cotton mill at Pootung. In full view of his parents' suite in the Palace Hotel, they had been attacked by a division of Chinese troops commanded by a nephew of Madame

Chiang. For five days the Japanese fought from trenches that filled waist-deep with water at high tide, then advanced with fixed bayonets and routed the Chinese.

The queue of cars moved through the checkpoint, carrying groups of Americans and Europeans already late for their Christmas parties. Yang edged the Packard to the barrier, hissing to himself. In front of them was a Mercedes tourer emblazoned with swastika pennants, filled with impatient young Germans. But the Japanese searched the interior with the same thoroughness.

Jim's mother held his shoulder. "Not now, dear. It might frighten the Japanese."

"That wouldn't frighten them."

"Jamie, not now," his father repeated, adding with rare humor, "You might even start the war."

"Could I?" The thought intrigued Jim. He lowered his aircraft from the window. A Japanese soldier was running the bayonet of his rifle across the windshield, as if cutting an invisible web. Jim knew that he would next lean through the passenger window, venting into the Packard's interior his tired breath and that threatening scent given off by all Japanese soldiers. Everyone then sat still, as the slightest move would produce a short pause followed by violent retribution. The previous year, when he was ten, Jim had nearly given Yang a heart attack by pointing his metal Spitfire into the face of a Japanese corporal and chanting "Ra-ta-ta-ta-ta. . . ." For almost a minute the corporal had stared at Jim's father without expression, nodding slowly to himself. His father was physically a strong man, but Jim knew that it was the kind of strength that came from playing tennis.

This time Jim merely wanted the Japanese to see his balsa aircraft; not to admire it, but to acknowledge its existence. He was older now, and liked to think of himself

18

as the copilot of the Packard. Aircraft had always interested Jim, and especially the Japanese bombers that had devastated the Nantao and Hongkew districts of Shanghai in 1937. Street after street of Chinese tenements had been leveled to the dust, and in the Avenue Edward VII a single bomb had killed a thousand people, more than any other bomb in the history of warfare.

The chief attraction of Dr. Lockwood's parties, in fact, was the disused airfield at Hungjao. Although the Japanese controlled the open countryside around the city, their forces were kept busy patrolling the perimeter of the International Settlement. They tolerated the few Americans and Europeans who lived in the rural districts, and in practice there was rarely a Japanese soldier to be seen.

When they arrived at Dr. Lockwood's isolated house, Jim was relieved to find that the party was not going to be a success. There were only a dozen cars in the drive, and their chauffeurs were hard at work polishing the dust from the fenders, eager for a quick getaway. The swimming pool had been drained, and the Chinese gardener was quietly removing a dead oriole from the deep end. The younger children and their amahs sat on the terrace, watching a troupe of Cantonese acrobats climb their comical ladders and pretend to disappear into the sky. They turned into birds, unfurled crushed paper wings and danced in and out of the squealing children, then leaped onto each other's backs and transformed themselves into a large red cockerel.

Jim steered his balsa plane through the veranda doors. As the adults' world continued above his head, he made a circuit of the party. Many of the guests had decided not to appear in costume, as if too nervous of their real roles to cast themselves in disguise. The gathering reminded Jim of the all-night parties at Amherst Avenue which lasted to the next afternoon, when distracted mothers in crumpled evening gowns wandered by the swimming pool, pretending to look for their husbands.

The conversation fell away when Dr. Lockwood switched on the shortwave radio. Glad to see everyone occupied, Jim stepped through a side door onto the rear terrace of the house. He watched the line of weeding women move across the lawn. There were twenty Chinese women, dressed in black tunics and trousers, each on a miniature stool. They sat shoulder to shoulder, weeding knives flashing at the grass, while keeping up an unstoppable chatter. Behind them Dr. Lockwood's lawn lay like green shantung.

"Hello, Jamie. Cogitating again?" Mr. Maxted, father of his best friend, emerged from the veranda. A solitary but amiable figure in a sharkskin suit, who faced reality across the buffer of a large whiskey and soda, he stared down his cigar at the weeding women. "If all the people in China sat in a line they would stretch from the North to the South Pole. Have you thought of that, Jamie?"

"They could weed the whole world?"

"If you want to put it like that. I hear you've resigned from the cubs."

"Well . . ." Jim doubted if there was any point in explaining to Mr. Maxted why he had left the wolf cubs, an act of rebellion he had decided upon simply to test its result. To his disappointment, Jim's parents had been surprisingly unmoved. He thought of telling Mr. Maxted that not only had he left the cubs and become an atheist, but he might become a Communist as well. The Communists had an intriguing ability to unsettle everyone, a talent Jim greatly respected.

However, he knew that Mr. Maxted would not be

shocked by this. Jim admired Mr. Maxted, an architect turned entrepreneur who had designed the Metropole Theater and numerous Shanghai nightclubs. Jim often tried to imitate his raffish manner but soon found that being so relaxed was exhausting work. Jim had little idea of his own future—life in Shanghai was lived wholly within an intense present—but he imagined himself growing up to be like Mr. Maxted. Forever accompanied by the same glass of whiskey and soda, or so Jim believed, Mr. Maxted was the perfect type of the Englishman who had adapted himself to Shanghai, something that Jim's father, with his seriousness of mind, had never really done. Jim always enjoyed the drives with Mr. Maxted, when he and Patrick sat in the front seat of the Studebaker and embarked on unpredictable journeys through an afternoon world of empty nightclubs and casinos. Mr. Maxted drove the Studebaker himself, a trick of behavior that seemed exciting and even faintly disreputable to Jim. He and Patrick would play the untended roulette wheels with Mr. Maxted's money, under the tolerant smiles of the White Russian bar girls darning their silk stockings, while Mr. Maxted sat in the office with the owner, moving around other piles of banknotes.

Perhaps, in return, he should take Mr. Maxted on his secret expedition to Hungjao Airfield?

"Don't miss the film show, Jamie. I rely on you to keep me up to date with the latest news in military aviation. . . ."

Jim watched Mr. Maxted sway along the tiled verge of the empty swimming pool, curious to see if he would fall in. If Mr. Maxted was always accidentally falling into swimming pools, as indeed he always was, why did he only fall into them when they were filled with water?

3

THE ABANDONED AERODROME

JIM STEPPED FROM the terrace. He ran across the lawn past the weeding women, sailing his aircraft over their heads. The women ignored him, their knives stabbing at the grass, but Jim always felt a faint shiver of horror when he strayed too close to them. He could visualize what would happen if he fainted in their path.

At the southwest corner of the estate was Dr. Lockwood's radio mast. A section of the wooden fence had been displaced by the stay wires, and Jim stepped through the gap onto the edge of an untended field. A burial tumulus rose from the wild sugarcane at its center, and the rotting coffins projected from the loose earth like a chest of drawers.

Jim set out across the field. As he passed the tumulus, he stopped to peer into the lidless coffins. The yellowing skeletons were embedded in the rain-washed mud, as if these poor peasants had been laid out on pallets of silk. Once again Jim was struck by the contrast between the impersonal bodies of the newly dead, whom he saw every day in Shanghai, and these sun-warmed skeletons, every one an individual. The skulls intrigued him, with their squinting eye sockets and quirky teeth. In many ways these skeletons were more alive than the peasant farmers who had briefly tenanted their bones. Jim felt his cheeks and jaw, trying to imagine his own skeleton in the sun, lying here in this peaceful field within sight of the deserted aerodrome.

Leaving the burial mound and its family of bones, Jim crossed the field to a line of stunted poplars. He climbed a wooden stile onto the floor of a dried-out rice paddy. The leathery carcass of a water buffalo lay in the shade under the hedge, but otherwise the landscape was empty, as if all the Chinese in the Yangtze basin had left the countryside for the refuge of Shanghai. Holding the balsa aircraft over his head, Jim ran along the floor of the paddy toward an iron building that stood on a ridge of higher ground a hundred yards to the west. Overgrown by nettles and sugarcane, the remains of a concrete road passed a ruined gatehouse and then gave way to an open sea of wild grass.

This was the aerodrome at Hungjao, a place of magic for Jim, where the air ran with dreams and excitements. There was the galvanized hangar, but little else remained of this military airfield from which the Chinese fighters had attacked the Japanese infantry columns advancing on Shanghai in 1937. Jim stepped into the waist-high grass. Like the water in the sea at Tsingtao, below the warm surface was a cool world touched by mysterious currents. The bright December wind buffeted the grass; patterns swirled around him like the slipstreams of invisible aircraft. Listening carefully, Jim could almost hear the sounds of their engines turning.

Jim launched the balsa model into the wind and caught

it as it returned to his hand. Already he was bored with this model glider. Where he now played, Chinese and Japanese pilots had stood in their flying suits, fastened their goggles over their eyes before taking off for the attack. Jim waded through the deeper grass that rose to his shoulders. The thousands of blades seethed around his velvet trousers and silk shirt, as if trying to identify this miniature aviator.

A shallow ditch formed the southern edge of the airfield. Lying in the deep nettles was the fuselage of a single-engined Japanese fighter, perhaps shot down while trying to land on the grass runway. The wings, propeller and tail section had been removed, but the cockpit remained intact, the rusting metal of the seat and controls blanched by the rain. Through the open radiator shutters Jim could see the cylinders of the engine that had pulled this aircraft and its pilot through the sky. The once-burnished metal was now as rough as brown pumice, like the hulls of the rusting U-boats beached in the cove below the German forts at Tsingtao. But for all its rust, this Japanese fighter still belonged to the sky. For months Jim had been trying to devise a way of persuading his father to take it back to Amherst Avenue. At night it could lie beside his bed, lit by the newsreels inside his head.

Jim rested his balsa model on the engine cowling, climbed over the windshield and lowered himself into the metal seat. Without the parachute that provided a cushion for the pilot, he was sitting on the floor of the cockpit, in a cave of rusting metal. He gazed at the instrument dials with their Japanese ideograms, at the trim wheels and undercarriage lever. Below the instrument panel he could see the breeches of the machine guns mounted in the windshield cowling, and the interrupter gear that ran toward the propeller shaft. A potent atmosphere hovered over the cockpit, the only nostalgia that Jim had ever known, the intact memory of the pilot who had sat at its controls. Where was the pilot now? Jim pretended to work the controls, as if this sympathetic action could summon the spirit of the long-dead aviator.

Below one of the clouded dials a metal tape bearing a row of Japanese characters had been punched into the dashboard, a list of manifold pressures or pitch settings. Jim peeled the tape from its worn rivets, then stood up and slipped it into the pocket of his velvet trousers. He lifted himself from the cockpit and climbed onto the engine cowling. His arms and shoulders were trembling with all the confused emotions that this ruined aircraft invariably set off in his mind. Giving way to his excitement, he picked up his model glider and launched it into the air.

Caught by the wind, the model banked steeply and soared across the perimeter of the airfield. It skidded along the roof of an old concrete blockhouse and fell into the grass beyond. Impressed by the model's speed, Jim jumped from the engine cowling and ran toward the blockhouse, arms outstretched as he machine-gunned the flitting insects.

"Ta-ta-ta-ta-ta. . . . Vera-Vera-Vera . . .!"

Beyond the overgrown perimeter ditch of the airfield was an old battleground of 1937. Here the Chinese armies had made one of their many futile stands in the attempt to halt the Japanese advance on Shanghai. Ruined trenches formed zigzag lines, a collapsed earth palisade linked a group of burial mounds built on the causeway of a disused canal. Jim could remember visiting Hungjao with his parents in 1937, a few days after the battle. Parties of Europeans and Americans drove from Shanghai and parked their limousines on the country roads covered with cartridge cases. The ladies in silk dresses and their husbands in gray suits strolled through the debris of a war arranged for them by a passing demolition squad. To Jim the battlefield seemed more like a dangerous rubbish dump—ammunition boxes and stick grenades were scattered at the roadside; there were discarded rifles stacked like matchwood and artillery pieces still hitched to the carcasses of horses. The belt ammunition of machine guns lying in the grass resembled the skins of venomous snakes. All around them were the bodies of dead Chinese soldiers. They lined the verges of the roads and floated in the canals, jammed together around the pillars of the bridges. In the trenches between the burial mounds hundreds of dead soldiers sat side by side with their heads against the torn earth, as if they had fallen asleep together in a deep dream of war.

Jim reached the blockhouse, a concrete fort whose gun slits let a faint light into their damp world. He climbed onto the roof and walked across the open deck, searching the nettle banks for his aircraft. The plane lay twenty feet away, caught in the rusting barbed wire of an old trenchwork. The paper was torn from its wings, but the balsa frame was still intact.

Jim was about to jump from the blockhouse when he noticed that a face was looking up at him from the trench. A fully armed Japanese soldier squatted by the broken earth wall, his rifle, webbing and ground sheet laid out beside him as if ready for inspection. No more than eighteen years old, with a passive and moonlike face, he stared at Jim, unsurprised by the apparition of this small European boy in his blue velvet trousers and silk shirt.

Jim's eyes moved along the trench. Two more Japanese soldiers sat on a wooden beam that protruded from the ground, rifles held between their knees. The trench was filled with armed men. Fifty yards away a second platoon squatted under the parapet of an earth bunker, smoking cigarettes and reading their letters. Beyond them were groups of other soldiers, their heads barely visible among the nettles and wild sugarcane. An entire company of Japanese infantry was resting in this old battlefield, as if re-equipping itself from the dead of an earlier war, ghosts of their former comrades risen from the grave and issued with fresh uniforms and rations. They smoked their cigarettes, blinking in the unfamiliar sunlight, their faces turned toward the skyscrapers of downtown Shanghai, whose neon signs flashed across the empty paddy fields.

Jim looked back to the fuselage of the fighter aircraft, expecting to see its dead pilot standing in his cockpit. A Japanese sergeant was walking through the deep grass between the blockhouse and the aircraft. His strong legs left a yellowing gulley behind him. He finished the stub of his cigarette, drawing the last of the smoke into his lungs. Although the sergeant ignored him, Jim knew that he had decided what to do next with this small boy.

"Jamie . . .! We're all waiting . . . there's a surprise for you!"

Jim's father was calling to him. He stood in the center of the airfield but could see the hundreds of Japanese soldiers in the trenchworks. He wore his spectacles, and had thrown away his eye patch and the jacket of his pirate costume. Although out of breath after running from Dr. Lockwood's house, he forced himself to stand still, in the way that least unsettled the Japanese. The Chinese, who would cry at moments of stress and wave their arms, never understood this.

Nonetheless, Jim was surprised that this small token

of deference seemed to satisfy the sergeant. Without a glance at Jim, he threw away his cigarette and jumped the perimeter ditch. He plucked the balsa aircraft from the barbed wire and threw it among the nettles.

"Jamie, it's time for the fireworks. . . ." His father walked quietly through the grass. "We ought to go now."

Jim climbed from the roof of the blockhouse. "My plane's down there. I could get it, I suppose."

His father watched the Japanese sergeant walk along the parapet of the trenchworks. Jim could see that it was an effort for his father to speak. His face was as strained and bloodless as it had be₁ ₁ when the labor organizers at the cotton mill threatened to kill him. Yet he was still thinking about something. "We'll leave it for the soldiers—finders keepers."

"Like kites?"

"That's it."

"He wasn't very angry."

"It looks as if they're waiting for something to happen."

"The next war?"

"I don't suppose so."

Hand in hand, they walked across the airfield. Nothing moved except for the ceaselessly rippling grass, rehearsing itself for the slipstreams to come. When they reached the hangar his father tightly embraced Jim, almost trying to hurt him, as if Jim had been lost to him forever. He was not angry with Jim and seemed glad that he had been forced to visit the old aerodrome.

But Jim felt vaguely guilty and annoyed with himself. He had lost his balsa plane and lured his father into a dangerous meeting with the Japanese. Solitary Europeans who strayed into the path of the Japanese were usually left dead on the roadside.

When they returned to Dr. Lockwood's house, the guests were already leaving. Rounding up the children and amahs, they climbed hurriedly into their cars and drove in convoy back to the International Settlement. Wearing the trousers of his Father Christmas suit and a beard of surgical cotton, Dr. Lockwood waved to them as Mr. Maxted drank his whiskey by the drained swimming pool and the Chinese conjurers climbed their ladders and transformed themselves into imaginary birds.

Still grieving over the loss of his plane, Jim sat between his parents in the back of the Packard. Were they frightened that he might get up to some new mischief if he sat in the front beside Yang? He had managed to spoil Dr. Lockwood's party and make it unlikely that he would visit Hungjao aerodrome again. He thought of the crashed fighter in which he had invested so much of his imagination, and of the dead pilot whose presence he had felt in the rusting cockpit.

Despite these setbacks, Jim was delighted when his mother told him that they would leave the house in Amherst Avenue for a few days and instead would stay in the company's suite at the Palace Hotel. The end-of-term examinations at the Cathedral School began the next day, with geometry and scripture. Since the cathedral was only a few hundred yards from the hotel, he would have ample time the next morning for revision. Jim was keen on scripture, especially now that he was an atheist, and always enjoyed receiving the Reverend Matthews' traditional accolade ("The first, and the biggest heathen of the lot, is . . .").

Jim waited in the front seat of the Packard while his parents changed and their suitcases were loaded into the trunk. When they set off through the gates, he looked down at the motionless figure of the beggar on his frayed mat. He could see the pattern of the Packard's Firestone tires in the old man's left foot. Leaves and shreds of newspaper covered his head, and already he was becoming part of the formless rubbish from which he had emerged.

Jim felt sorry for the old beggar, but for some reason he could think only of the tire patterns in his foot. If they had been driving in Mr. Maxted's Studebaker, the pattern would have been different, the old man would have been stamped with the imprint of the Goodyear Company. . . .

Trying to distract himself from these thoughts, Jim switched on the car radio. He always looked forward to the evening drives through the center of Shanghai, this electric and lurid city more exciting than any other in the world. As they reached the Bubbling Well Road, he pressed his face to the windshield and gazed at the pavements lined with nightclubs and gambling dens, crowded with bar girls and gangsters and rich beggars with their bodyguards. Six thousand miles away, across the International Dateline, the Americans in Honolulu were sleeping through the early hours of Sunday morning, but here, a day ahead in time as in everything else, Shanghai was ready to begin a new week. Crowds of gamblers pushed their way into the jai alai stadiums, blocking the traffic in the Bubbling Well Road. An armored police van with two Thompson guns mounted in a steel turret above the driver swung in front of the Packard and cleared the sidewalk. A party of young Chinese women in sequined dresses tripped over a child's coffin decked with paper flowers. Arms linked together, they lurched against the radiator grille of the Packard and swayed past Jim's window, slapping the windshield with their small hands and screaming obscenities. Hundreds of Eurasian bar girls in ankle-length fur coats sat in the lines of rickshaws outside the Park Hotel, whistling through their teeth at the residents who emerged from the revolving doors, while their pimps argued with the middle-aged Czech and Polish couples in neat, patched suits trying to sell the last of their jewelry. Nearby, along the windows of the Sun Sun department store in the Nanking Road, a party of young European Jews were fighting in and out of the strolling crowds with a gang of older German boys in the swastika armbands of the Graf Zeppelin Club. Chased by the police sirens, they ran through the entrance of the Cathay Theater, the world's largest cinema, where a crowd of Chinese shopgirls and typists, beggars and pickpockets spilled into the street to watch people arriving for the evening performance. As they stepped from their limousines, the women steered their long skirts through the honor guard of fifty hunchbacks in medieval costume. Three months earlier, when his parents had taken Jim to the premiere of *The Hunchback of Notre Dame,* there had been two hundred hunchbacks, recruited by the management of the theater from every back alley in Shanghai. As always, the spectacle outside the theater far exceeded anything shown on its screen, and Jim had been eager to get back to the sidewalks of the city, away from the newsreels and their endless reminders of war.

After dinner, as Jim lay in his bedroom on the tenth floor of the Palace Hotel, he tried not to sleep. He listened to the drone of a Japanese seaplane landing on the river at the Nantao naval air base. He thought of the crashed fighter at Hungjao aerodrome, and of the Japanese pilot whose seat he had filled that afternoon. Perhaps the spirit

31

of the dead aviator had entered him, and the Japanese would join the war on the same side as the British. Jim dreamed of the coming war, of a newsreel in which he stood in his flying suit on the deck of a silent carrier, ready to take his place with those lonely men from the island nation in the China Sea, borne with them across the Pacific by the spirit of the divine wind.

4

THE ATTACK
ON THE *PETREL*

A FIELD OF paper flowers floated on the morning tide, clustered around the oil-stained piers of the jetty and dressed them in vivid-colored ruffs. A few minutes before dawn Jim sat at a window of his bedroom at the Palace Hotel. He wore his school uniform and was keen to start an hour's revision before breakfast. As always, however, he found it difficult to keep his eyes from the Shanghai waterfront. Already the odor of fish heads and bean curd sizzling in peanut oil rose from the pans of the vendors outside the hotel. Tung-stained junks with eyes painted on their bows sailed past the opium hulks beached on the Pootung shore. Thousands of sampans and ferryboats were moored along the Bund, a city of floating hovels still hidden by the darkness. But between the factory chimneys of Pootung the first sunlight was diffusing across the river, illuminating the square profiles of the U.S.S. *Wake* and H.M.S. *Petrel*.

The American and British gunboats were anchored in midstream opposite the banking houses and hotels of the Bund. Jim watched a motorboat carrying two British officers back to the *Petrel* after their parties ashore. Jim had met the captain of the *Petrel*, Captain Polkinhorn, at the Shanghai Country Club, and knew all the naval ships on the river. Even in the pearly light he noticed that the Italian monitor *Emilio Carlotta*, which had been berthed beside the Public Gardens on the Bund, provocatively in front of the British Consulate, had slipped anchor during the night. Her place had been taken by a Japanese gunboat, a squat and war-stained craft with dirty guns and stark camouflage patterns on the funnel and superstructure. Rust leaked from the anchor vents on either side of her bows. The steel shutters were still locked over the bridge windows, and sandbags protected the barbettes of the forward and rear gun turrets. Looking at this powerful ship, Jim wondered if it had been damaged during its patrol of the Yangtze gorges. Sailors and officers moved about the bridge house, and a signal lamp flashed a message across the river.

Two miles upstream, beyond the naval air base at Nantao, was a boom of sunken freighters, which the Chinese had scuttled in 1937 in an attempt to block the river. The sunlight shone through the holes in their steel masts and funnels, and the incoming tide washed across their decks, swilling through the staterooms. As he rode back in the company launch after visiting his father's cotton mill, Jim always longed to climb aboard the freighters and explore their drowned cabins, a world of forgotten voyages overgrown by grottos of rust.

He watched the Japanese gunboat by the Public Gardens. The signal lamp flickered insistently from the bridge. Was this weary gun platform about to sink onto its own anchors? Although Jim had a deep respect for the Japanese, their ships were always being disparaged by the British in Shanghai. The cruiser *Idzumo*, moored alongside the Japanese Consulate at Hongkew half a mile downstream, looked far more impressive than the *Wake* and the *Petrel*. In fact, the *Idzumo*, flagship of the Japanese China Fleet, had been built in England and served in the Royal Navy before being sold to the Japanese during the Russo-Japanese War in 1905.

The light advanced across the river, picking out the paper flowers that covered its back like garlands discarded by the admirers of these sailors. Every night in Shanghai those Chinese too poor to pay for the burial of their relatives would launch the bodies from the funeral piers at Nantao, decking the coffins with paper flowers. Carried away on one tide, they came back on the next, returning to the waterfront of Shanghai with all the other debris abandoned by the city. Meadows of paper flowers drifted on the running tide and clumped in miniature floating gardens around the old men and women, the young mothers and small children, whose swollen bodies seemed to have been fed during the night by the patient Yangtze.

Jim disliked this regatta of corpses. In the rising sunlight the paper petals resembled the coils of viscera strewn around the terrorist bomb victims in the Nanking Road. He turned his attention to the Japanese gunboat. A launch had been lowered and was setting out across the river toward the U.S.S. *Wake*. A dozen Japanese marines sat facing each other, their rifles raised like oars. Two naval officers in full formal dress stood in the bows, one with a megaphone in his gloved hands.

Puzzled that they should be paying a ceremonial visit so early in the morning, Jim climbed onto the window ledge and pressed himself against the plate glass. Two picketboats had set out from the *Idzumo*, each carrying fifty marines. The three craft met in the center of the river and cut their engines. They wallowed among the paper flowers and old packing cases. A motorized junk powered past them, the bamboo cages on its deck loaded with barking dogs on their way to the Hongkew meat market. A naked coolie stood at the helm, drinking a bottle of beer. He made no attempt to alter course as the junk's wash drenched the launch from the gunboat. Ignoring the spray, the Japanese officer called to the *Wake* through his megaphone.

Laughing to himself, Jim drummed his palms against the window. None of the American officers were on board, as everyone in Shanghai well knew. All would be sleeping soundly in their rooms at the Park Hotel. Sure enough, a drowsy Chinese crewman in shorts and vest emerged from the fo'c'sle. He shook his head at the Japanese picketboat coming alongside, and began polishing the brass rail as the marines clambered onto the gangway and moved swiftly to the deck. Carrying rifles with bayonets fixed, they ran the length of the ship, searching for any American members of the crew.

Followed by the second picketboat, the motor launch approached H.M.S. *Petrel*. There was a terse exchange with the young British officer on the bridge, who dismissed the Japanese in the offhand way that Jim had seen his parents refuse to buy the Java heads and carved elephants from the dugout salesmen who surrounded the cruise ship in Singapore harbor.

Were the Japanese trying to sell something to the British and Americans? Jim knew that they were wasting their time. Standing against the window with his arms outstretched, he tried to remember the semaphore he had learned so reluctantly in the cubs. The Japanese officer in the launch was signaling with a lamp to the gunboat by the Public Gardens. As the light stuttered across the water, Jim noticed that hundreds of Chinese were running past the British Consulate. Billows of smoke and steam pumped from the gunboat's funnel, as if the ship were about to burst.

The barrel of the forward gun turret exploded in a single flash that scorched the bridge and deck. Six hundred yards away there was an answering explosion as the shell struck the superstructure of the *Petrel*. The pressure wave of this detonating round cracked against the hotels of the Bund, and the heavy plate glass hit Jim on the nose. As the gunboat fired a second shell from its rear turret, he jumped onto the bed and began to cry, then stopped himself and crouched behind the mahogany headboard.

From its moorings beside the Japanese Consulate the cruiser *Idzumo* had also opened fire. Its guns flashed through the smoke that rose from its three funnels and curled along the water like a black feather boa. Already the *Petrel* was hidden within a pall of steam, below which a series of raging fires were reflected in the water. Two Japanese fighter aircraft flew along the Bund, so low that Jim could see the pilots in their cockpits. Crowds of Chinese scattered across the tramway lines, some toward the quayside, others sheltering on the steps of the hotels.

"Jamie! What are you doing?" Still in his pajamas, his father burst barefoot into the bedroom. He stared uncertainly at the furniture, as if unable to recognize this room in his own suite. "Jamie, keep away from the window! Get dressed and do what your mother tells you. We're leaving in three minutes."

He seemed not to notice that Jim was wearing his school uniform and blazer. As they shielded their eyes from the point-blank shellfire, there was a huge explosion from the center of the river. Like rockets in a fireworks display, burning pieces of the *Petrel* soared into the air and then splashed into the water. Jim felt numbed by the noise and smoke. People were running down the corridors of the hotel; an elderly Englishwoman screamed into the lift shaft. Jim sat on the bed and stared at the burning platform that settled into the river. Every few seconds there was a steady flicker of light from its center. The British sailors on the *Petrel* were fighting back. They had manned one of the guns and were returning fire at the *Idzumo*. But Jim watched them somberly. He realized that he himself had probably started the war, with his confused semaphores from the window that the Japanese officers in the motor launch had misinterpreted. He knew now that he should have stayed in the cubs. Perhaps the Reverend Matthews would cane him in front of the whole school for being a spy.

"Jamie! Lie on the floor!" His mother knelt in the communicating doorway. In a pause between the salvos of shells she pulled him from the vibrating windows and held him to the carpet.

"Am I going to school?" Jim asked. "It's the scripture exam."

"No, Jamie. Today there'll be a school holiday. We're going to see if Yang can take us home."

Jim was impressed by her calm. He decided not to tell her that he had started the war. As soon as his parents had dressed, they set out to leave the hotel. A crowd of European and American guests surrounded the lifts. Refusing to take the stairs, they pounded on the metal grilles and shouted down the shafts. They carried suitcases, and wore their hats and overcoats, as if deciding to take the next steamer to Hong Kong. His mother joined them, but his father took her arm and forced their way to the staircase.

Knees knocking with the effort, Jim reached the entrance lobby before them. Chinese kitchen staff, guests from the lower floors and White Russian clerks crouched behind the leather furniture and potted palms, but Jim's father strode past them to the revolving doors.

All firing had ceased. Throngs of Chinese ran along the Bund between the stationary trams and parked cars, old amahs hobbling in black trousers, coolies pulling empty rickshaws, beggars and sampan boys, uniformed waiters from the hotels. A pall of gray smoke as large as a fogbound city lay across the river, from which emerged the topmasts of the *Idzumo* and the *Wake*. By the Public Gardens, clouds of incandescent soot still pumped from the funnel of the Japanese gunboat.

The *Petrel* was sinking at her moorings. Steam rose from her stern and midships, and Jim could see the queue of sailors standing in the bows, waiting to take their places in the ship's cutter. A Japanese tank moved along the Bund, its tracks striking sparks from the tramlines. It swiveled jerkily around an abandoned tram and crushed a rickshaw against a telegraph pole. Sprung loose from the wreckage, a warped wheel careened across the roadway. It kept pace with the Japanese officer who commanded the assault troops, his sword raised as if whipping the wheel ahead of him. Two fighter aircraft streaked along the waterfront, the wash from their propellers stripping the bamboo hatches from the sampans and exposing hundreds of crouching Chinese. A battalion of Japanese marines advanced along the Bund, appearing like a stage army through the ornamental trees of the Public Gardens. A platoon with fixed bayonets raced to the steps of the British Consulate, led by an officer with a Mauser pistol.

"There's the car . . . we'll have to run!" Taking Jim and his mother by the hand, his father propelled them into the street. Immediately Jim was knocked to the ground by a coolie striding past. He lay stunned among the pounding feet, expecting the bare-chested Chinese to come back and apologize. Then he picked himself up, brushed the dust from his cap and blazer and followed his parents toward the car parked in front of the Shanghai Club. A group of exhausted Chinese women sat on the steps, sorting their handbags and choking on the diesel fuel that drifted across the river from the capsized hull of the *Petrel*.

As they set off along the Bund, the Japanese tank had reached the Palace Hotel. Surrounding it was the fleeing staff, Chinese bellboys in their braided American uniforms, waiters in white tunics, and the European guests clutching their hats and suitcases. Two Japanese motorcyclists, each with an armed soldier in the camouflaged sidecar, pushed ahead of the tank. Standing on their pedals, they tried to force a way through the rickshaws and pedicabs, the horsecarts and gangs of coolies tottering under the bales of raw cotton hung from yokes over their shoulders.

Already a sizable traffic jam blocked the Bund. Once again the crush and clutter of Shanghai had engulfed its invaders. Perhaps the war was over? Through the rear window of the Packard, itself now stalled in the traffic, Jim watched a Japanese NCO screaming at the Chinese around him. A dead coolie lay at his feet, blood pouring from his head. The tank was trapped in the press of vehicles, its path blocked by a white Lincoln Zephyr. Two young Chinese women in fur coats, dancers from the nightclub on top of the Socony building, struggled with the controls, laughing into their small jeweled hands.

"Wait here!" Jim's father opened his door and stepped into the road. "Jamie, look after your mother!"

Machine-gun fire was coming from the Japanese marines who had captured the U.S.S. *Wake*. Riflemen on the bridge were shooting at the British sailors swimming ashore from the *Petrel*. The ship's cutter loaded with wounded men was sinking in the shallow water that covered the mud flats below the quays of the French Concession. The sailors slipped to their thighs in the black mud, arms streaming with blood. A wounded petty officer fell in the water and drifted away toward the dark piers of the Bund. Clinging to each other, the sailors lay helplessly in the mud as the quickening tide rippled around them. Already the first funeral flowers had found them and begun to gather around their shoulders.

Jim watched his father push through the sampan coolies who crowded the wharf. A group of British men had run from the Shanghai Club and were taking off their overcoats and jackets. In waistcoats and shirt-sleeves they jumped from the landing stage onto the mud below, arms swinging as they sank to their thighs. The Japanese marines on the U.S.S. *Wake* continued to fire at the cutter, but two of the Britons had reached a wounded sailor. They seized him under the arms and dragged him toward the mud flat. Jim's father waded past them, his spectacles splashed with water, scooping the black ooze out of his way. The tide had risen to his chest when he caught the injured petty officer drifting between the piers of the wharf. He pulled him into the shallow water, dragging him by one hand, and knelt exhausted beside him on the oily mud. Other rescuers had reached the sinking cutter. They lifted out the last of the wounded sailors and fell together into the water. They began to swim and crawl toward the shore, helped onto the mud flat by a second party of Britishers.

The cloud of burning oil from the *Petrel* crossed the Bund and enveloped the stalled traffic and the advancing

Japanese. As Jim wound up his window, the Packard was thrown forward, and then shaken violently from side to side. Broken glass fell from the windshield and showered the seats. Jim lay on the rear floor of the passenger cabin as the door pillar struck his mother's head.

"Jamie, get out of the car . . . Jamie!"

Dazed, she opened her door and stepped onto the road, taking her handbag from the swaying seat. Behind them the Japanese tank was forcing its way past the Lincoln Zephyr abandoned by the Chinese dancers. The metal tread crushed the rear fender around its wheel and then rammed the heavy car into the back of the Packard.

"Get up, Jamie . . . we're going home. . . ."

A hand to her bruised face, his mother was pulling at the buckled rear door. The tank stopped, before making a second pass at the Lincoln. Japanese marines moved between the cars and rickshaws, lunging with their bayonets at the crowd. Jim climbed onto the front seat and opened the driver's door. He jumped into the road and ducked below the shafts of a rickshaw laden with rice bags. The tank moved forward, smoke throbbing from its engine vents. Jim saw his mother pushed into the throng of Chinese and Europeans whom the marines were forcing across the Bund. A second tank followed the first, then a line of camouflaged trucks packed with Japanese soldiers.

A final rifle shot rang out from the U.S.S. *Wake*. The last of the wounded British sailors were pulled onto the mud flat below the Bund. Oil leaking from the swamped *Petrel* lay in an elongated slick across the river, calming this place of battle. The British civilians who had helped to rescue the sailors sat in their greasy shirt-sleeves beside the wounded men. Jim's father was dragging the injured petty officer onto the mud flat. Exhausted, he lost his grip and collapsed in a shallow stream that ran through the oily bank from a sewer vent below the pier.

The Japanese soldiers on the Bund were driving the crowd away from the quay, forcing the Chinese and Europeans to step from their cars and rickshaws. Jim's mother had disappeared, cut off from him by the column of military trucks. A wounded British sailor, a sandy-haired youth no more than eighteen years old, climbed the steps from the landing stage, hands outstretched like bloody Ping-Pong bats.

Straightening his school cap, Jim darted past him and the watching sampan coolies. He ran down the steps and jumped from the landing stage onto the spongy surface of the mud flat. Sinking to his knees, he waded through the damp soil toward his father.

"We brought them out—good lad, Jamie." His father sat in the stream, the body of the petty officer beside him. He had lost his spectacles and one of his shoes, and the trousers of his business suit were black with oil, but he still wore his white collar and tie. In one hand he held a yellow silk glove like those Jim had seen his mother carrying to the formal receptions at the British Embassy. Looking at the glove, Jim realized that it was the complete skin from one of the petty officer's hands, boiled off the flesh in an engine-room fire.

"She's going . . ." His father flicked the glove into the water like the hand of a tiresome beggar. A hoarse, throttling explosion sounded across the river from the capsized hull of the *Petrel*. There was a violent rush of steam from the riven decks, and the gunboat slipped below the waves. A cloud of frantic smoke seethed across the water, surging about as if hunting for the vanished craft.

Jim's father lay back against the mud. Jim squatted

beside him. The noise of the tanks' engines on the Bund, the shouted commands of the Japanese NCOs and the drone of the circling aircraft seemed far away. The first debris from the *Petrel* was reaching them, life jackets and pieces of planking, a section of canvas awning with its trailing ropes that resembled an enormous jellyfish dislodged from the deep by the sinking gunboat.

A flicker of light ran along the quays like silent gunfire. Jim lay down beside his father. Drawn up above them on the Bund were hundreds of Japanese soldiers. Their bayonets formed a palisade of swords that answered the sun.

5

ESCAPE FROM
THE HOSPITAL

"MITSUBISHI . . . ZERO-SEN . . . ah . . .
Nakajima . . . ah . . ."

Jim lay in his cot in the children's ward and listened
to the young Japanese soldier call out the names of the
aircraft flying over the hospital. The skies above Shanghai were filled with aircraft. The soldier knew the names
of only two types of plane and found it difficult to keep
up with the endless aerial activity.

For three days Jim had rested peacefully in the ward
on the top floor of St. Marie's Hospital in the French
Concession, disturbed only by the young soldier's furtive
smoking and his amateur plane spotting. Alone in the
ward, Jim thought about his mother and father, and hoped
that they would soon come to visit him. He listened to
the seaplanes flying from the naval air base at Nantao.

". . . ah . . . ah . . ." The soldier shook his head,
stumped again, and searched the immaculate floor for a
cigarette end. In the corridor below the landing Jim could
hear the French missionary sisters arguing with the Japanese military police who now occupied this wing of the

hospital. Despite the hard mattress, the whitewashed walls with their unpleasant icons above each bed—the crucified infant Jesus surrounded by Chinese disciples—and the ominous chemical smell (something to do, he surmised, with intense religious feelings), Jim found it difficult to believe that the war had at last begun. Walls of strangeness separated everything; every face that looked at him was odd.

He could remember Dr. Lockwood's party at Hungjao, and the Chinese conjurers who turned themselves into birds. But the bombardment of the *Petrel*, the tank that had crushed the Packard, the huge guns of the *Idzumo* all belonged to a make-believe realm. He almost expected Yang to saunter into the ward and tell him that they were part of a technicolor epic being staged at the Shanghai film studios.

What was real, without any doubt, was the mud flat to which his father had helped to drag the wounded sailors, and where they had sat for six hours beside the dead petty officer. It was as if the Japanese had been so surprised by the speed of their assault that they had been forced to wait before they fully grasped any sense of their victory. Within a few hours of the attack on Pearl Harbor, the Japanese armies that encircled Shanghai had seized the International Settlement. The marines who captured the U.S.S. *Wake* and occupied the Bund celebrated by parading in force in front of the hotels and banking houses.

Meanwhile, the wounded survivors of the *Petrel* and the British civilians who had helped to rescue them remained on the mud flat beside the sewer. An armed party of military police stepped from the landing stage and walked among them. Captain Polkinhorn, wounded in the head, and his first officer were taken away, but the others were left to sit under the sun. A Japanese officer in full uniform, scabbard held in his gloved hand, moved among the injured and exhausted men, peering at each in turn. He stared at Jim as he sat in his blazer and school cap beside his exhausted father, obviously puzzled by the elaborate badges of the Cathedral School and assuming that Jim was an unusually junior midshipman in the Royal Navy.

An hour later Captain Polkinhorn was taken in a motor launch to the site of the sunken *Petrel*. Before abandoning ship, the captain had been able to destroy his codes, and for days afterward the Japanese sent divers down to the wreck in an unsuccessful attempt to retrieve the code boxes.

Soon after ten o'clock the Japanese re-opened the Bund, and thousands of uneasy Chinese and European neutrals were ushered along the quay. They looked down at the wounded crew of the *Petrel*, and stood silently as the Rising Sun was ceremonially hoisted to the mast of the U.S.S. *Wake*. Shivering beside his father in the cold December sun, Jim gazed up at the expressionless eyes of the Chinese packed together on the quay. They were witnessing the complete humiliation of the Allied powers by the empire of Japan, an object lesson to all those reluctant to enter the Co-Prosperity Sphere. Fortunately, some hours later a party of officials from the Vichy French and German embassies forced their way through the crowd. They protested volubly about the treatment of the wounded British. Impelled by one of their abrupt changes of mood, the Japanese relented and the prisoners were on their way to St. Marie's Hospital.

Once there, Jim's sole thought was to leave the hospital and return to his mother at Amherst Avenue. The French doctor who Mercurochromed his knees and the sisters who bathed him saw immediately that Jim was a British schoolboy and tried to have him released. The Japanese, however, had taken over a complete wing of the hospital, cleared out the Chinese patients and installed a guard on each floor. A young soldier was posted outside the children's ward on the top floor, and passed the time asking the nuns for cigarettes and calling out the names of the aircraft overhead.

A Chinese nun told Jim that his father was with the other civilians in a ward below, still recovering from the effects of heart strain and exposure, but would be ready to leave in a few days. Meanwhile, for reasons of their own, the Japanese High Command had begun to eulogize the bravery of Captain Polkinhorn and his men. On the second day, the commander of the *Idzumo* sent a party of uniformed officers to the hospital, who paid tribute to the wounded sailors in the best traditions of *bushido*, bowing to each one of them. The English-language *Shanghai Times,* British-owned but for long sympathetic to the Japanese, carried a photograph of the *Petrel* on its front page and an article extolling the courage of its crew. The main headline described the Japanese attack on Pearl Harbor and the bombing of Clark Field at Manila. Pencil drawings supplied by a neutral news agency showed apocalyptic scenes of smoke rising from the slumped American battleships.

Now that the Japanese had won the war, Jim pondered, perhaps life in Shanghai would return to normal. When the young soldier showed him the newspaper, Jim carefully studied the photographs of fighter bombers taking off from the Japanese carriers, scenes that he seemed to remember from his own dreams in his bedroom at the Palace Hotel on the eve of the war.

Lounging on the bed beside him, the soldier pointed

to the assault aircraft, keen to impress Jim with this staggering feat of arms.

". . . ah . . . ah . . ."

"Nakajima," Jim said. "Nakajima Hayabusa."

"Nakajima?" The soldier sighed deeply, as if the subject of military aviation was far beyond the grasp of this small English boy. In fact, Jim recognized almost all the Japanese aircraft. British newsreels of the Sino-Japanese War openly derided the Japanese planes and their pilots, but Jim's father and Mr. Maxted always spoke of them with respect.

Jim was wondering how he could see his father when the guard corporal bellowed a command up the stairwell. The young private was terrified of this small and unpleasant corporal, clearly the most important rank in the Japanese Army. He put away his cigarette butt, picked up his rifle and dashed from the ward, waving a warning finger at Jim.

Glad to be alone, Jim immediately climbed out of bed. Through the window he could see a group of convalescent Chinese orphans on the balcony of the adjacent wing. In their European dressing gowns—like Jim's, donated by a local French charity—they spent all day staring at him. A metal fire escape linked the two wings, blocked by heaps of sandbags packed against the windows in 1937 to protect them from stray shells fired across the river.

Barefoot, Jim crossed the ward to its rear door. A narrow catwalk led between the sandbags, and the loose sand was littered with hundreds of cigarette ends thrown down by the bored French doctors. Picking his way through the pieces of broken glass, he set off along the fire escape. A metal staircase ran to the opposite wing, linked by a rusting bridge to the ward below Jim's.

Jim moved swiftly down the steps and crossed the

49

bridge. Somewhere on this floor were his father and the survivors of the *Petrel*. The windows of the wards over-looking the gangway had been painted with blackout tar. Watched by the wide-eyed orphans, Jim followed the gangway around the wing. The rear door into the ward was bolted, but as he pulled at the handle the Chinese children ducked below their balcony. An armed Japanese soldier stood on the roof, shouting down into the well between the wings. Soldiers with fixed bayonets ran across the courtyard of the hospital, and a motorcycle with armed sidecar swung through the entrance. Jim could hear boots and rifle butts ringing on the stone stairways, and a French nun's voice raised in protest.

Jim crouched between the sandbags outside the locked door. Soldiers were moving along the gangway of the children's ward, and sand poured through the rusting grilles. A klaxon sounded in the Avenue Foch, and he was convinced that the entire Japanese occupation forces in Shanghai were searching for him.

A bolt clattered, and the door opened into the dark-ened ward. In the brief glare of sunlight Jim saw the cavelike room crowded with bandaged men, some lying on the floor between the beds, and the nuns being pushed aside by Japanese soldiers with rifles and canvas stretchers. As the blanched faces of young British sailors turned toward the sun, a stench of sickness and wounds emerged from the dark chamber and enveloped Jim.

The Japanese corporal stared at Jim, crouching in his pajamas among the cigarette ends. He slammed the door, and Jim heard him shout as he struck one of the Japanese soldiers with his fist.

An hour later they had all gone, leaving Jim alone in the children's ward. As the klaxons sounded from the

Avenue Foch, Jim watched a military truck reverse into the hospital compound. The crew of the *Petrel* and the eight British civilians who had helped to rescue them were bundled down the staircases and loaded into the truck. Wounded men on stretchers lay under the legs of others barely able to sit.

Jim did not see his father, but the French sister told him that he had walked to the truck taking them to the military prison in Hongkew.

"This morning one of your sailors escaped. It's very bad for us." The sister stared at Jim with the disapproving gaze of the Japanese corporal. She was angry with him in that new way he had noticed in the past weeks, not for anything he had done but because of his inability to change the circumstances in which he found himself.

"You live in Amherst Avenue? You must go home." The sister beckoned to a Chinese nun, who laid Jim's freshly laundered clothes on the bed. He could see that they were eager to be rid of him. "Your mother will look after you."

Jim dressed himself, fastened his tie and carefully straightened his school cap. He wanted to thank the sister, but she had already left to look after her orphans.

6

THE YOUTH
WITH THE KNIFE

WARS ALWAYS INVIGORATED Shanghai, quickened the pulse of its congested streets. Even the corpses in the gutters seemed livelier. Throngs of peasant women packed the pavements of the Avenue Foch; outside the Cercle Sportif Français the vendors locked wheels as they jostled their carts against each other; lines of pedicabs and rickshaws ten abreast hemmed in the cars that edged forward behind a continuous blare of horns. Young Chinese gangsters in shiny American suits stood on the street corners, shouting the jai alai odds to each other. In the pedicabs outside the Regency Hotel the bar girls sat in fur coats with their bodyguards beside them, like glamorous wives waiting to be taken for a ride. The entire city had come out into the streets, as if the population was celebrating the takeover of the International Settlement, its seizure from the Americans and Europeans by another Asian power.

Yet when Jim reached the junction of the Avenue Pétain and the Avenue Haig, a British police sergeant and two Sikh NCOs of the Shanghai police force still directed the traffic from their cantilevered bridge above the crowd, watched by a single Japanese soldier standing behind them. Armed Japanese infantry sat like sightseers in the camouflaged trucks that moved along the streets. A party of officers stood outside the Radium Institute, adjusting their gloves. Pasted over the Coca-Cola and Caltex billboards were fresh posters of Wang Ching Wei, the quisling leader of the puppet regime. A column of Chinese soldiers overtook Jim in the Avenue Pétain, shouting slogans into the noisy air. They stamped away, clumsily marking time below the baroque facade of the Del Monte Casino, and then ran on past the greyhound stadium, a coolie army in pale orange uniforms and American-style sneakers.

Outside the tram station in the Avenue Haig, the hundreds of passengers were briefly silent as they watched a public beheading. The bodies of a man and woman in quilted peasant clothes, perhaps pickpockets or Kuomintang spies, lay by the boarding platform. The Chinese NCOs wiped their boots as the blood ran into the metal grooves of the steel rails. A tram crowded with passengers approached, its bell forcing the execution party aside. It clanked along, connector rod hissing and throwing sparks from the overhead power line, its front wheels a moist scarlet as if painted for the annual labor union parade.

Usually Jim would have paused to observe the crowd. On the way home from school Yang would often drive by the Old City. The public stranglings were held in a miniature stadium with a scrubbed wooden floor and rows of circular benches around the teak execution posts, and always attracted a thoughtful audience. The Chinese enjoyed the spectacle of death, Jim had decided, as a way of reminding themselves of how precariously they were alive. They liked to be cruel for the same reason, to remind themselves of the vanity of thinking that the world was anything else.

Jim watched the coolies and peasant women staring at the headless bodies. Already the press of tram passengers was pushing them aside, submerging this small death. Jim turned away, tripping over a charcoal brazier in which a pavement vendor was frying pieces of battered snake. Drops of fat splashed into the wooden bucket, where a single snake swam, thrashing itself as it leaped at the hissing oil. The vendor lunged at Jim with his hot ladle, trying to cuff his head, but he slipped between the parked rickshaws. He ran along the blood-smeared tramlines toward the entrance of the depot.

He pushed through the waiting passengers and squeezed himself onto a concrete bench with a group of peasant women carrying chickens in wicker baskets. The women's bodies reeked of sweat and fatigue, but Jim was too exhausted to move. He had walked over two miles along the crowded pavements. He knew that he was being followed by a young Chinese, probably a pedicab tout or a runner for one of Shanghai's tens of thousands of small-time gangsters. A tall youth with a dead, boneless face, oily black hair and leather jacket, he had noticed Jim outside the greyhound stadium. Kidnappings were commonplace in Shanghai—before his parents learned to trust Yang, they insisted that Jim always drive to school with the governess. Jim guessed that the youth was interested in his blazer and leather shoes, in his aviator's watch and the American fountain pen clipped to his breast pocket.

The youth stepped through the crowd and walked up to Jim, his yellow hands like ferrets. "American boy?"

"English. I'm waiting for my chauffeur."

"English . . . boy. You come now."

"No—he's over there."

The youth reached forward, swearing in Chinese, and seized Jim's wrist. His fingers fumbled at the metal strap, trying to release the watch clasp. The peasant women ignored him, chickens asleep on their laps. Jim knocked away the youth's hand and felt his fingers grip his forearm. Inside his leather jacket he had drawn a knife and was about to sever Jim's hand at the wrist.

Jim wrenched his arm away. Before the youth could seize him again, Jim hurled the wicker basket from the knees of the peasant woman on his right. The youth fell back, flailing with his heels at the squawking bird. The women jumped to their feet and began to scream at him. He ignored them and put away his knife. He followed as Jim ran through the queues of tram passengers, trying to show them his bruised wrist.

A hundred yards from the depot, Jim reached the Avenue Joffre. He rested in the padlocked entrance to the Nanking Theater, where *Gone with the Wind* had been playing for the past year in a pirated Chinese version. The partly dismantled faces of Clark Gable and Vivien Leigh rose on their scaffolding above an almost life-size replica of burning Atlanta. Chinese carpenters were cutting down the panels of painted smoke that rose high into the Shanghai sky, barely distinguishable from the fires still lifting above the tenements of the Old City, where Kuomintang irregulars had resisted the Japanese invasion.

The youth with the knife was still behind him, skipping and sidestepping through the crowd in his cheap sneakers. In the center of the Avenue Joffre was the police checkpoint, its sandbagged emplacement marking the western perimeter of the French Concession. Jim knew that neither the Vichy police nor the Japanese soldiers would do anything to help him. They were watching a single-engined bomber that flew low above the racecourse.

As the aircraft's shadow flashed across the road, Jim felt the Chinese youth snatch his cap and grip his shoulders. Jim pulled himself away and ran across the crowded street toward the checkpoint, ducking in and out of the pedicabs and shouting: *"Nakajima! Nakajima!"*

A Chinese auxiliary in a Vichy uniform tried to strike him with his stave, but one of the Japanese sentries paused to glance at Jim. His eye had caught the Japanese characters on the metal tag that Jim had taken from the derelict fighter at Hungjao aerodrome and was now holding in front of him. Briefly tolerating this small boy, he continued his patrol and waved Jim away with the butt of his rifle.

"Nakajima!"

Jim joined the crowd of pedestrians moving through the checkpoint. As he guessed, his pursuer had vanished among the beggars and loitering rickshaw coolies on the French side of the barbed wire. Not for the first time Jim realized that the Japanese, officially his enemies, offered his only protection in Shanghai.

Nursing his bruised arm, and angry with himself for having lost his school cap, Jim at last reached Amherst Avenue. He pulled his shirt-sleeve over the dark weals that marked his wrist. His mother worried constantly about the danger and violence in the streets of Shanghai and knew nothing of his long cycle rides around the city.

Amherst Avenue was deserted. The throngs of beggars and refugees had vanished. Even the old man with his Craven A tin had gone. Jim ran up the drive, looking forward to seeing his mother, sitting on the sofa in her bedroom and talking about Christmas. Already he assumed that they would never discuss the war.

A long scroll covered with Japanese characters had been nailed to the front door, the white cloth stamped with seals and registration numbers. Jim pressed the bell, waiting for Number Two Boy to open the door. He felt exhausted, as worn down as his scuffed shoes, and noticed that the sleeve of his blazer had been slashed from the elbow by the thief's knife.

"Boy, hurry!" He began to say: "I'll kill you . . ." but checked himself.

The house was silent. There was no sound of the amahs arguing over the laundry vat in the servants' quarters, or the clip-clip of the gardener trimming the lawn around the flower beds. Someone had switched off the swimming-pool motor, though his father made a point of running the filter all winter. Looking up at the windows of his bedroom, he saw that the shutters of the air conditioner had been closed.

Jim listened to the bell drill through the empty house. Too tired to reach again for the button, he sat on the polished steps and blew on his bruised knees. It was difficult to imagine how his parents, Vera, the nine servants, chauffeur and gardener could all have gone out together.

There was a muffled explosion from the bottom of the drive, the coughing exhaust box of a heavy engine. A Japanese half-track had entered Amherst Avenue, its crew standing among their radio aerials. They moved along the center of the road, forcing a Mercedes limousine from the German estate to climb the sidewalk.

Jim jumped from the porch and hid behind a pillar. A high wall faced with terra-cotta tiles ran around the house, topped with broken glass. Gripping the tiles with his fingertips, he climbed the wall below the barred cloak-room window. After pulling himself onto the concrete ledge, he crawled on his knees through the glass blades. During the past year, unknown to the gardener and the nightwatchman, he had climbed the wall a score of times, always removing a few more of the sharp spears. He lowered himself over the edge and jumped into the dark branches of the cedar tree behind the summerhouse.

In front of him was the enclosed and silent garden, even more Jim's true home than the house itself. Here he had played alone with his imagination. He had been a crashed pilot on the roof of the rose pergola, a sniper sitting high in the poplars behind the tennis court, an infantryman racing across the lawn with his air gun, shooting himself down into the flower beds and rising again to storm the rockery below the flagpole.

From the shadows behind the summerhouse Jim looked up at the veranda windows. An aircraft overhead warned him not to run too suddenly across the lawn. Although undisturbed, the garden seemed to have darkened and grown wilder. The uncut lawn was beginning to billow, and the rhododendrons were more somber than he re-membered them. Ignored by the gardener, his bicycle lay on the terrace steps. Jim walked through the thickening grass to the swimming pool. The water was covered with leaves and dead insects, and the level had fallen by almost three feet, draping a scummy curtain on the sides. Cig-arette ends lay crushed on the white tiles, and a Chinese packet floated under the diving board.

Jim followed the pathway to the servants' quarters behind the house. A charcoal stove stood in the courtyard, but the kitchen door was locked. Jim listened for any sound from within the house. Beside the kitchen steps was the enclosed hood of the garbage compactor. A chute ran from the compressor into the kitchen wall beside the sink. Two years earlier, when he was younger, Jim had terrified his mother by climbing through the chute as she arranged a dinner party menu with the houseboy.

This time there was no danger of the motor being switched on. Jim lifted the metal hood, climbed between the scythelike blades and edged his way through the greasy chute. The metal flap swung back to reveal the familiar white-tiled kitchen.

"Vera! I'm home! Boy!"

Jim lowered himself onto the floor. He had never seen the house so dark before. He stepped through the pool of water around the refrigerator and entered the deserted hall. As he climbed the staircase to his mother's bedroom, the air was stale with the smell of strange sweat.

His mother's clothes were scattered across the unmade bed, and open suitcases lay on the floor. Someone had swept her hairbrushes and scent bottles from the dressing table, and talcum covered the polished parquet. There were dozens of footprints in the powder, his mother's bare feet whirling within the clear images of heavy boots, like the patterns of complicated dances set out in his parents' foxtrot and tango manuals.

Jim sat on the bed, facing the starlike image of himself that radiated from the center of the mirror. A heavy object had been driven into the full-length glass, and pieces of himself seemed to fly across the room, scattered through the empty house.

He fell asleep at the foot of his mother's bed, rested by the scent of her silk nightdress.

7

THE DRAINED
SWIMMING POOL

TIME HAD STOPPED in Amherst Avenue, as motionless as the wall of dust that hung across the rooms, briefly folding itself around Jim when he walked through the deserted house. Almost forgotten scents, a faint taste of carpet, reminded him of the period before the war. For three days he waited for his mother and father to return. Every morning he climbed onto the sloping roof above his bedroom window and gazed over the residential streets in the western suburbs of Shanghai. He watched the columns of Japanese tanks move into the city from the countryside and tried to repair his blazer, impatient for the first sight of his parents when they returned with Yang in the Packard.

Large numbers of aircraft flew overhead, and Jim passed the hours plane spotting. Below him was the undisturbed lawn, a little darker each day now that the gardener no longer trimmed the hedges and cut the grass. Jim played there in the afternoons, crawling through the rockery and pretending to be one of the Japanese marines who had attacked the *Wake*. But the games in the garden

60

had lost their magic, and he spent most of his time on the sofa in his mother's bedroom. Her presence hung on the air like her scent, holding at bay the deformed figure in the fractured mirror. Jim remembered their long hours together doing his Latin homework, and the stories she told him of her childhood in England, a country far stranger than China where he would go to school when the war was over.

In the talcum on the floor around him he could see the imprints of his mother's feet. She had moved from side to side, propelled by an overeager partner, perhaps one of the Japanese officers to whom she was teaching the tango. Jim tried out the dance steps himself, which seemed far more violent than any tango he had ever seen, and managed to fall and cut his hand on the broken mirror.

As he sucked the wound he remembered his mother teaching him to play Mah-Jongg, and the cryptic colored tiles that clicked in and out of the mahogany walls. Jim thought of writing a book about Mah-Jongg, but he had forgotten most of the rules. On the drawing room carpet he heaped a pile of bamboo stakes from the greenhouse and began to build a man-lifting kite according to the scientific principles his father had taught him. But the Japanese patrols in Amherst Avenue would see the kite flying from the garden. Putting it aside, Jim ambled about the empty house and watched the water level falling in the swimming pool.

The food in the refrigerator had begun to give off an ominous smell, but the pantry cupboards were filled with tinned fruit, cocktail biscuits and pressed meats, delicacies that Jim adored. He ate his meals at the dining-room table, sitting in his usual place. In the evenings, when it seemed unlikely that his parents would come home that day, he went to sleep in his bedroom on the top floor of the house, one of his model aircraft on the bed beside him, something Vera had always forbidden. Then the dreams of war came to him, and all the battleships of the Japanese Navy sailed up the Yangtze, their guns firing as they sank the *Petrel*, and he and his father saved the wounded sailors.

On the fourth morning, when he came down to breakfast, Jim found that he had forgotten to turn off a kitchen tap and all the water had flowed from the storage tank. The pantry was amply stocked with siphons of soda water, but by now Jim had accepted that his mother and father would not be coming home. Jim stared through the veranda windows at the overgrown garden. It was not that war changed everything—in fact, Jim thrived on change—but that it left things the same in odd and unsettling ways. Even the house seemed somber, as if it were withdrawing from him in a series of small and unfriendly acts.

Trying to keep up his spirits, Jim decided to visit the homes of his closest friends, Patrick Maxted and the Raymond twins. After washing himself in soda water, he went into the garden to fetch his bicycle. During the night the swimming pool had drained itself. Jim had never seen the empty tank, and he gazed with interest at the inclined floor. The once-mysterious world of wavering blue lines, glimpsed through a cascade of bubbles, now lay exposed to the morning light. The tiles were slippery with leaves and dirt, and the chromium ladder at the deep end, which had once vanished into a watery abyss, ended abruptly beside a pair of scummy rubber slippers.

Jim jumped onto the floor at the shallow end. He slipped on the damp surface, and his bruised knee left a smear of blood on the tiles. A fly settled on it instantly. Watching his feet, Jim walked down the sloping floor.

Around the brass vent at the deep end lay a small museum of past summers—a pair of his mother's sunglasses, Vera's hair clip, a wineglass and an English half-crown which his father had tossed into the pool for him. Jim had often spotted the silver coin, gleaming like an oyster, but had never been able to reach it.

Jim pocketed the coin and peered up at the damp walls. There was something sinister about a drained swimming pool, and he tried to imagine what purpose it could have if it were not filled with water. It reminded him of the concrete bunkers in Tsingtao, and the bloody handprints of the maddened German gunners on the caisson walls. Perhaps murder was about to be committed in all the swimming pools of Shanghai, and their walls were tiled so that the blood could be washed away.

Leaving the garden, Jim wheeled his bicycle through the veranda door. Then he did something he had always longed to do: mounted his cycle and rode through the formal, empty rooms. Delighted to think how shocked Vera and the servants would have been, he expertly circled his father's study, intrigued by the patterns that the tires cut in the thick carpet. He collided with the desk and knocked over a table lamp as he swerved through the door into the drawing room. Standing on the pedals, he zigzagged among the armchairs and tables, lost his balance and fell onto a sofa, remounted without touching the floor, crash-landed into the double doors that led into the dining room, pulled them back and began a wild circuit of the long polished table. He detoured into the pantry, swishing to and fro through the pool of water below the refrigerator, scattered the saucepans from the kitchen shelves and ended in a blaze of speed toward the mirror in the downstairs cloakroom. As his front tire trembled against the smudged glass, Jim shouted at his excited reflection. The war had brought him at least one small bonus.

Happily Jim closed the front door behind him, smoothed the Japanese scroll and set off toward the Raymond twins in the nearby Columbia Road. He felt that all the streets in Shanghai were rooms in a huge house. He accelerated past a platoon of Chinese puppet soldiers marching down Columbia Road and swerved away showily as the NCO let loose a volley of shouts. Jim sped along the suburban pavements, in and out of the telephone poles, knocking aside the Craven A tins left behind by the vanished beggars.

He was out of breath when he reached the Raymonds' house at the German end of the Columbia Road. He freewheeled past the parked Opels and Mercedes—curious, gloomy cars that gave Jim all too much of an idea of what Europe was like—and came to a halt outside the front door.

A Japanese scroll was nailed to the oak panels. The door opened, and two amahs appeared, dragging Mrs. Raymond's dressing table down the steps.

"Is Clifford here? Or Derek? Amah!"

Jim knew both the amahs well and waited for them to reply in their pidgin English. But they ignored Jim and heaved at the dressing table. Their deformed feet, like clenched fists, slipped on the steps.

"It's Jamie, Mrs. Raymond . . ."

Jim tried to step past the amahs, when one reached out and slapped him in the face.

Stunned by the blow, Jim walked back to his bicycle. He had never been struck so hard, either in school boxing matches or in fights with the Avenue Foch gang. The front of his face seemed to have been torn from the bones.

His eyes were smarting, but he stopped himself from crying. The amahs were strong, their arms toughened by a lifetime of washing clothes. Watching them with their dressing table, Jim knew that they were paying him back for something he or the Raymonds had done to them.

Jim waited until they reached the bottom step. When one of the amahs walked up to him, clearly intending to slap him again, he mounted his cycle and pedaled away.

Outside the Raymonds' drive, two German boys of his own age were playing with a ball as their mother unlocked the family's Opel. Usually they would have shouted German slogans at Jim, or thrown stones at him until stopped by their mother. But today all three stood silently. Jim cycled past, trying not to show them his bruised face. The mother held her sons' shoulders, watching Jim as if concerned for what would soon befall him.

Still shocked by the anger he had seen in the amah's face, Jim set off for the Maxteds' apartment house in the French Concession. His whole head felt swollen and there was a loose tooth in his lower jaw. He wanted to see his mother and father, and he wanted the war to end soon, that afternoon if possible.

Dusty, and suddenly very tired, Jim reached the barbed-wire checkpoint on the Avenue Foch. The streets were less crowded, but several hundred Chinese and Europeans queued to pass the Japanese guards. A Swiss-owned Buick and a Vichy French gasoline truck were waved through the gates. Usually the European pedestrians would have gone to the head of the queue, but now they took their turn among the rickshaw coolies and peasants pushing handcarts. Gripping his cycle, Jim barely held his ground as a barefoot coolie with diseased calves labored past him under a bamboo yoke laden with bales of firewood. The crowd pressed around him, in a stench of sweat and fatigue, cheap fat and rice wine, the odors of a Shanghai new to Jim. An open Chrysler with two young Germans in the front seat accelerated past, horn blaring, the rear fender grazing Jim's hand.

Once through the checkpoint, Jim straightened the front wheel of his cycle and pedaled to the Maxteds' apartment house in the Avenue Joffre. The formal garden in the French style was as immaculate as ever, a comforting memory of the old Shanghai. As he rode the elevator to the seventh floor, Jim used his tears to clean his hands and face, half expecting Mrs. Maxted to have returned from Singapore.

The door to the apartment was open. Jim stepped into the hall, recognizing Mr. Maxted's leather overcoat on the floor. The same tornado that had whirled through his mother's bedroom in Amherst Avenue had spread in and out of every room in the Maxteds' apartment. Drawers full of clothes had been thrown onto the beds; ransacked wardrobes hung open above piles of shoes; suitcases lay everywhere as if a dozen Maxted families had been unable to decide what to pack at five minutes' notice.

"Patrick . . ." Jim hesitated to enter Patrick's room without knocking. His mattress had been hurled to the floor, and the curtains drifted in the open windows. But Patrick's model aircraft, more carefully constructed than Jim's, still dangled from the ceiling.

Jim pulled the mattress onto the bed and lay down. He watched the aircraft turning in the cold air that moved through the empty apartment. He and Patrick had spent hours inventing imaginary air battles in the sky of that bedroom above the Avenue Joffre. Jim watched the Spitfires and Hurricanes circling above his head. Their motion soothed him, easing the pain in his jaw, and he was tempted to stay there, sleeping quietly in the bedroom of his departed friend until the war was over.

But already Jim realized that it was time to find his mother and father. Failing them, any other Britons would do.

Facing the Maxteds' apartment building on the opposite side of the Avenue Joffre was the Shell Company's compound, almost all its houses occupied by British employees. Jim and Patrick often played with the children and were honorary members of the Shell gang. As Jim pushed his bicycle from the Maxteds' drive, he could see that the British residents had gone. Japanese sentries stood in the entrance to the compound behind a box fence of barbed wire. Supervised by a Japanese NCO, a gang of Chinese coolies was loading furniture from the houses into an army truck.

A few feet from the barbed-wire box an elderly man in a shabby coat stood under the plane trees and watched the Japanese. Despite his threadbare suit, he still wore white cuffs and a starched shirt front.

"Mr. Guerevitch! I'm over here, Mr. Guerevitch!"

The old White Russian was the Shell Company caretaker and lived with his aged mother in a small bungalow beside the gate. A Japanese officer now stood in the front room, cleaning his nails as he smoked a cigarette. Jim had always liked Mr. Guerevitch, although the elderly Russian remained unimpressed by him. Something of an amateur artist, in the right mood he would draw elaborate sailing ships in Jim's autograph album. His gray cupboard of a kitchen was filled with starched collars and their miniature front panels, and Jim was sorry that Mr. Guerevitch could not afford a real shirt. Perhaps he would come back to live with him in Amherst Avenue.

Jim checked this thought as Mr. Guerevitch waved him across the road with his newspaper. His mother might like the old Russian, but Vera would not—the Eastern Europeans and White Russians were even more snobbish than the British.

"Hello, Mr. Guerevitch. I'm looking for my mother and father."

"But how could they be here?" The old Russian pointed to Jim's bruised face and shook his head. "The whole world is at war and you're still riding your bicycle around. . . ." As the Japanese NCO began to abuse one of the coolies, Mr. Guerevitch drew Jim behind a plane tree. He opened his newspaper to reveal an extravagant artist's sketch of two immense battleships sinking under a hail of Japanese bombs. From the photographs beside them, Jim recognized the *Repulse* and the *Prince of Wales*, the unsinkable fortresses that the British war newsreels always claimed could each defeat the Japanese navy single-handed.

"Not a good example," Mr. Guerevitch reflected. "The British Empire's Maginot line. It's right that you have a red face."

"I fell off my bicycle, Mr. Guerevitch," Jim explained patriotically, though he disliked having to lie to defend the Royal Navy. "I've been busy looking for my mother and father. It's rather a job, you know."

"I can see." Mr. Guerevitch watched a convoy of trucks speed past. Japanese guards with fixed bayonets sat by the tailboards. Behind them, their heads resting on each other's shoulders, groups of British women and their children huddled over their cheap suitcases and khaki bedrolls. Jim assumed that they were the families of captured British servicemen.

"Young boy! Ride your bicycle!" Mr. Guerevitch pushed Jim's shoulder. "You follow them!"

"But Mr. Guerevitch . . ." The shabby luggage unsettled Jim as much as the strange wives of the British privates. "I can't go with them—they're prisoners."

"Go on! Ride! You can't live in the street!"

When Jim stood firm by his handlebars, Mr. Guerevitch solemnly patted him on the head and set off across the road. He resumed his vigil behind his newspaper, watching the Japanese strip the houses in the compound as if itemizing his lost world for the Shell Company.

"I'll come and see you again, Mr. Guerevitch." Jim felt sorry for the old caretaker, but during his return journey to Amherst Avenue he was more concerned about the two battleships. The British newsreels were filled with lies. Jim had seen the Japanese navy sink the *Petrel*, and it was obvious now that they could sink anything. Half the American Pacific Fleet was probably sitting on the bottom at Pearl Harbor. Perhaps Mr. Guerevitch was right, and he should have followed the trucks. His mother and father might already have arrived at the prison to which they were being taken.

So, reluctantly, Jim decided to give himself up to the Japanese. The soldiers guarding the Avenue Foch checkpoint waved him on when he tried to speak to them, but Jim kept his eyes open for one of the corporals in charge of everything.

For some reason, that day there seemed to be a shortage of Japanese corporals in Shanghai. Although he was tired, Jim took the long route home, along the Great Western and Columbia Roads, but no Japanese at all were there. However, when he reached the entrance to his house in Amherst Avenue, he saw that a Chrysler limousine had parked outside the front door. Two Japanese officers stepped from the car and surveyed the house as they straightened their uniforms.

Jim was about to pedal up to them and explain that he lived in the house and was ready to surrender. Then an armed Japanese soldier stepped from behind the stone gatepost. He seized the front wheel of the cycle with his left hand, his fingers gripping the tire through the spokes, and with a coarse shout propelled Jim backward into a heap on the dusty road.

8

PICNIC TIME

UNABLE TO SURRENDER, Jim returned with his broken bicycle to the Maxteds' apartment in the French Concession. From then on he lived alone in the abandoned houses and apartments in the western suburbs of the International Settlement. Most of the homes had been owned by British and American nationals, or by Dutch, Belgian and Free French residents, all of whom had been interned by the Japanese in the days after the attack on Pearl Harbor.

The Maxteds' apartment house was owned by rich Chinese who had fled to Hong Kong in the weeks before the outbreak of war. Most of the apartments had been empty for months. Although the family of Chinese janitors still lived in their two basement rooms beside the elevator well, they had been completely cowed by the squad of Japanese military police who had seized Mr. Maxted. As the uncut lawns grew deeper and the formal gardens deteriorated, they spent their time cooking small meals on a charcoal stove which they set up beside the cement statuary on the floor of the ornamental pond. The smell of bean curd and spiced noodles drifted among the disrobing nymphs.

During the first week Jim was free to come and go. He wheeled his cycle into the lift, rode to the seventh floor and let himself into the Maxteds' apartment through an unlatched mosquito window on the servants' balcony. The Maxteds' front door was fitted with a spyhole and a complex set of electrical locks—Mr. Maxted, a prominent member of the pro-Chiang China Friendship Society, an organization of local businessmen, had once been the victim of an assassination attempt. As soon as Jim closed the door he was unable to open it again, but no one called apart from an elderly Iraqi woman who lived in the penthouse. When she rang the bell Jim watched her grimacing into the spyhole, parts of her ancient face semaphoring a mysterious message. She then stood thinking for ten minutes in the stationary lift, immaculately dressed and bejeweled in this abandoned apartment house.

Jim was glad to be left alone. After being knocked from his bicycle by the Japanese soldier, he had barely managed to return to the Maxteds', and he slept on Patrick's bed for the rest of the day. He woke the next morning to the sound of trams clanking down the Avenue Foch, klaxons hooting from the Japanese convoys entering the city, and the thousands of continually blaring horns that were the anthem of Shanghai.

The bruise on his cheek had begun to subside, leaving his face thinner than he remembered it, his mouth a tighter and older shape. Looking at himself in the mirror of Patrick's bathroom, at his dusty blazer and grim shirt, he wondered if his mother and father would still recognize him. Jim wiped his clothes with a wet towel—like Mr. Guerevitch, many of the passing Chinese stared at him in a curious way. Nonetheless, Jim realized that there were certain advantages in being poor. No one could be bothered to cut off his hands.

The Maxteds' pantry was filled with cases of whiskey and gin, an Aladdin's cave of gold and ruby bottles, but there were only a few jars of olives and a tin of cocktail biscuits. Jim ate a modest breakfast at the dining-room table and then set about repairing his bicycle. He needed the machine to get himself around Shanghai, to find his parents and surrender to the Japanese.

Sitting on the dining-room floor, Jim tried to straighten the twisted forks. His hands fretted at the dusty metal, unable to clench themselves. He knew that he had been badly frightened the previous day. A peculiar space was opening around him, which separated him from the secure world he had known before the war. For a few days he had been able to cope with the sinking of the *Petrel* and the disappearance of his parents, but now he felt nervous and slightly cold all the time, even in the mild December weather. He dropped and broke the Maxteds' crockery in a way that he had never done before, and found it difficult to concentrate on anything.

Despite all this, Jim managed to repair his cycle. He unscrewed the front wheel and straightened the forks by bending them against the balcony railing. He tested the cycle in the drawing room and then took the lift down to the foyer.

As Jim rode along the Avenue Foch, he saw that Shanghai had changed. Thousands of Japanese soldiers patrolled the streets. Sandbagged sentry posts had been set up within sight of each other down the main avenues. Although the streets were filled with pedicabs and rickshaws, with trucks commandeered by the puppet militia, the crowds were subdued. The Chinese who thronged the pavements outside the department stores in the Nanking

Road kept their heads down, avoiding the Japanese soldiers who sauntered through the traffic.

Pedaling fiercely, Jim followed a heavily laden tram that clanked along the Avenue Edward VII. Morose Chinese clung to its sides, and a crop-headed youth in a black mandarin suit spat at Jim, then leaped down and ran into the crowd, nervous that even this small act would set off a train of retribution. Bodies of Chinese lay everywhere, hands tied behind their backs in the center of the road, dumped behind the sandbag emplacements, half-severed heads resting on each other's shoulders. The thousands of young gangsters in their American suits had gone, but at the Bubbling Well Road checkpoint Jim saw one youth in a blue silk suit being beaten by two soldiers with staves. As the blows struck his head, he knelt in a pool of blood that dripped from his lapels.

All the gambling parlors and opium houses in the side streets behind the racecourse had closed, and metal grilles sealed the entrances to the pawnshops and banks. Even the honor guard of hunchbacks outside the Cathay Theater had deserted their posts. Their absence unsettled Jim. Without its beggars, the city seemed all the poorer. The sullen rhythms of the new Shanghai were set by the endless wailing of the Japanese klaxons. The roads felt harder than he remembered from his previous jaunts around the city, and already he was tired. His hands felt colder than the handlebars. Trying to keep up his spirits, he decided to visit all those places in Shanghai where his parents were known, starting with his father's office. The senior Chinese staff had always made a great fuss of Jim, and would be eager to help him.

However, the Szechwan Road had been closed by the Japanese. Barbed-wire barricades sealed off both ends of the street, and hundreds of Japanese civilians moved in and out of the foreign banks and commercial buildings, carrying typewriters and boxes of files.

Jim cycled down to the Bund, dominated now by the gray bulk of the cruiser *Idzumo*. It was moored four hundred yards from the quayside, its antique funnels freshly painted, canvas awnings flared over its gun turrets. A short distance upstream was the U.S.S. *Wake*, now flying the Rising Sun, with vivid Japanese characters on its bows. An elaborate christening ceremony was taking place in front of the Shanghai Club. Scores of senior Japanese civilians in frock coats, Germans and Italians in extravagant Fascist uniforms, watched a march past of Japanese sailors and officers. Two tanks, several artillery pieces and a cordon of marines ringed the temporary parade ground on the tracks of the tramways terminal. The circling steel rails rang beneath their boots, the diagram of their victory over the British and American gunboats.

Resting his chin on the handlebars, Jim looked at the soldiers with fixed bayonets guarding the entrance to the Palace Hotel. None of them would speak any English, or have any idea that this European boy with his twisted bicycle was an enemy national. If he approached them in full view of the press-ganged Chinese audience, the sentries would throw him to the ground.

Jim pedaled away from the Bund and began the long journey back to the Maxteds' apartment. By the time he crossed the Avenue Joffre checkpoint, he was too tired to cycle and pushed the small machine through the begging peasant women and the dozing rickshaw coolies. After climbing into the apartment, he sat at the dining-room table and ate a few cocktail biscuits and olives, washed down with soda water from the siphon. He fell asleep on his friend's bed, under the endlessly circling aircraft that swam below the ceiling like fish seeking a way out of the sky.

During the next days Jim again tried to give himself up to the Japanese. Like his school friends, Jim had always despised anyone who surrendered, but surrendering to the enemy was more difficult than it seemed. By now Jim was tired most of the time as he pedaled around the uncertain streets of Shanghai. The Japanese soldiers guarding the country club and the forecourt of the cathedral were too dangerous to approach. In the Bubbling Well Road he chased the Plymouth car belonging to a Swiss driver and his wife, but they shouted at him to go away and threw a coin onto the road, as if he were one of the Chinese beggar boys.

Jim went in search of Mr. Guerevitch, but the old Russian caretaker was no longer watching the Shell compound—perhaps he, too, was trying to surrender. Jim thought of the German mother who had watched him leave the Raymonds' house. She had seemed worried for him, but when he cycled all the way down to the Columbia Road he found that the gates of the German estate were closed. The Germans were drawing into themselves, just as nervous of the Japanese as everyone else. Jim was almost knocked from his cycle in the Nanking Road by two Japanese staff cars that swerved across the street. They stopped a truck filled with Germans from the Graf Zeppelin Club on their way to beat up the Jews in Hongkew. The Japanese NCOs ordered the Germans from the truck. They took away their clubs and shotguns, ripped off their swastika armbands and sent them packing.

A week after his arrival at the Maxteds' apartment, the electricity and water supplies were switched off. Jim bumped his cycle down the stairs to the foyer, where he found the old Iraqi woman arguing with the Chinese janitor. They both turned on Jim, screaming at him to leave the apartment house, though they had known all week that he was there.

Jim was glad to go. He had eaten the last of the cocktail biscuits, and his only meal the previous day had been a musty packet of Brazil nuts which he found in the sideboard. He felt tired but curiously lightheaded—the last trickle of water from the bathroom taps had made him almost drunk, the same sensation he had known before the war when he was about to go to a party. He reminded himself of his mother and father, but already their faces were beginning to fade in his memory. He was thinking of food all the time, and he knew that there were a great many unoccupied houses in the western suburbs of Shanghai, with unlimited supplies of cocktail biscuits and soda water, enough to last him until the war ended.

Mounting his cycle, Jim left the French Concession and pedaled along the Columbia Road. Quiet residential avenues ran between the trees, and the empty houses stood in their overgrown gardens. The rain had washed the ink from the Japanese scrolls, and the scarlet streaks ran down the oak panels, as if all the Americans and Europeans had been murdered against their front doors.

The Japanese occupation forces were too busy with their takeover of Shanghai to bother with these abandoned houses. Jim chose a crescent-shaped cul-de-sac hidden from the main road, where a half-timbered house rose behind its high walls. A fading scroll hung between its brass coach lamps. Jim listened to the silence within the house and then hid his cycle in the unswept leaves beside the steps. On his third attempt he climbed the wall of the Tudor garage and scaled its gabled roof. He lowered himself into the dense foliage of the garden which clung

77

to the house like a dark dream refusing to be woken.

Carrying a loose tile from the garage roof, Jim walked through the deep grass to the terrace. He waited until an aircraft flew overhead and then broke the glass pane of a window housing the air-conditioning unit. He let himself into the house, opening the shutters of the air vent in order to hide the broken pane.

Quickly Jim moved through the shadowy rooms, a series of tableaux in a forgotten museum. The house was filled with photographs of a handsome woman posing like a film star. He ignored the framed portrait on the grand piano and the huge globe of the earth beside the bookshelf. In the past Jim would have stopped to play with the globe—for years he had nagged his father for one—but now he was too hungry to waste a moment. The house had been the property of a Belgian dentist. In his study, below the framed certificates, were white cabinets containing dozens of sets of teeth. Through the darkness they grimaced at Jim like ravenous mouths.

Jim walked through the dining room to the kitchen. He sidestepped the pool of water around the refrigerator and expertly ran his eye over the pantry shelves. To his annoyance this Belgian dentist and his glamorous companion had developed a taste for Chinese food—something his own parents rarely touched—and the pantry was hung like the storeroom of a Chinese comprador with lengths of dried intestines and shriveled fruit.

But there was a single can of condensed milk, of a richness and sweetness Jim had never remembered. He drank the milk, sitting at the desk in the dentist's study as the teeth smiled at him, and then fell asleep in a bedroom upstairs, between silk sheets scented by the body of the woman with the face of a film star.

9

AN END
TO KINDNESS

EVER SEARCHING FOR food, Jim left the dentist's house the next morning. He found another temporary home in a nearby mansion owned by an American widow whom his parents had known before her departure for San Francisco. From there he moved on, staying for a few days in each house, shielded from the distant, ugly city by the high walls and deepening grass.

The Japanese had confiscated all the radios and cameras, but otherwise the houses were intact. Most of them were far more lavish than his own home—although a rich man, Jim's father had always been Spartan—and were equipped with private cinemas and ballrooms. Abandoned by their owners, Buicks and Cadillacs slumped in the garages on their flattening tires.

Yet their pantry cupboards were bare, leaving Jim to feed on the few leftovers of cocktail food from the fifty-year-long party that had been Shanghai. Sometimes, after finding an intact box of chocolates in a dressing-table drawer, Jim would revive and remember his parents dancing to the radiogram before lunch on Sunday, and his bedroom in Amherst Avenue now occupied by the Japanese officers. He played billiards in the darkened game rooms, or sat at a card table and laid out hands of bridge, playing each one as fairly as he could. He lay on the oddly scented beds, reading *Life* and *Esquire,* and in the house of an American doctor read the whole of *Through the Looking Glass,* a comforting world less strange than his own.

But the toy cupboards in the children's rooms made him feel ever more empty. He leafed through photograph albums, filled with images of a vanished world of fancy-dress parties and gymkhanas. Still hoping to see his parents, he sat by the bedroom windows as the water drained from the swimming pools of the western suburbs, draping their white walls with veils of scum. Although he was too tired to think of the future, Jim knew that the small stocks of food would soon be exhausted, and that the Japanese would turn their attention to these empty houses—already the families of Japanese civilians were moving into the former Allied premises in Amherst Avenue.

Jim scarcely recognized his long hair and gray cheeks, the strange face in a strange mirror. He would stare at the ragged figure who appeared before him in all the mirrors of the Columbia Road, an urchin half his previous size and twice his previous age. Much of the time Jim was aware that he was ill, and often he would have to lie down all day. The main supply to Columbia Road had been turned off, and the water dripping from the roof tanks had an unpleasant metallic tang. Once, as he lay sick in an attic bedroom in the Great Western Road, a party of Japanese civilians spent an hour walking around the downstairs rooms, but Jim had been too feverish to call to them.

One afternoon Jim scaled the wall of a house behind the American country club. He jumped into a wide, overgrown garden and was running toward the veranda before he realized that a group of Japanese soldiers was cooking a meal beside the empty swimming pool. Three men squatted on the diving board, feeding sticks to a small fire. Another soldier was down on the floor of the pool, poking through the debris of bathing caps and sunglasses.

The Japanese watched Jim hesitate in the deep grass, and stirred their boiled rice in which floated a few pieces of fish. They made no attempt to pick up their rifles, but Jim knew that he should not try to run from them. He strolled through the grass to the edge of the pool and sat on the leaf-strewn tiles. The soldiers began to eat their meal, talking in low voices. They were thickset men with shaven heads, wearing better webbing and equipment than the Japanese sentries in Shanghai, and Jim guessed that they were seasoned combat troops.

Jim watched them eat, his eyes fixed on every morsel that entered their mouths. When the oldest of the four soldiers had finished, he scraped some burned rice and fish scales from the side of the cooking pot. A private first-class of some forty years, with slow, careful hands, he beckoned Jim forward and handed him his mess tin. As they smoked their cigarettes the Japanese smiled to themselves, watching Jim devour the shreds of fatty rice. It was his first hot food since he had left the hospital, and the heat and the greasy flavor stung his gums. Tears swam in his eyes. The Japanese soldier who had taken pity on Jim, recognizing that this small boy was starving, began to laugh good-naturedly and pulled the rubber plug from his metal water bottle. Jim drank the clear, chlorine-flavored liquid, so unlike the stagnant water in the taps of the Columbia Road. He choked, carefully swallowed his vomit and tittered into his hands, grinning at the Japanese. Soon they were all laughing together, sitting back in the deep grass beside the drained swimming pool.

For the next week Jim followed the Japanese on their patrols of the deserted streets. Each morning the soldiers emerged from their bivouac at the Great Western Road checkpoint, and Jim would run from the steps of the house in which he had spent the night and attach himself to them. The soldiers rarely entered the foreign mansions, and were concerned only to keep out any Chinese beggars and thieves who might be tempted into this residential area. Sometimes they climbed the walls and explored the overgrown gardens, whose ornamental trees and shrubs seemed of more interest to them than the lavishly equipped houses. Jim ran errands for them, hunting for the bathing caps that they collected, chopping wood and lighting fires. He watched silently as they ate their midday meal. Almost always they left a little rice and fish for Jim, and once the private first-class gave him a piece of hard candy which he broke from a strip in his pocket, but otherwise none of them showed any interest in Jim. Did they know that Jim was a vagrant? They would stare at his scuffed but well-made shoes, at the woollen cloth of his school blazer, perhaps assuming that he lived with some rich but feckless European family that no longer bothered to feed its children.

Within a week Jim was dependent on this Japanese patrol for almost all his food. More of the houses in the Columbia Road were being occupied by Japanese military and civilians. Several times, as he approached a deserted house, Jim was chased away by Chinese bodyguards.

One morning the Japanese soldiers failed to appear. Jim waited patiently in the garden of the house behind the American country club. Trying to calm his hunger, he broke twigs from the rhododendron bushes, ready to light a fire beside the drained pool. He watched the aircraft flying through the cool February light and counted the three liqueur chocolates in his blazer pocket, which he had saved for the emergency he knew would soon come.

The veranda doors opened behind him. Jim stood up as the Japanese soldiers stepped onto the terrace. They were waving to him, and Jim had the confused idea that they had brought his parents with them and so were making a formal entry through the house rather than climb over the wall.

He ran toward the Japanese, who were shouting at him in a surprisingly brusque way. When he reached the terrace he saw that they were members of a new patrol. The corporal cuffed Jim and pushed him around the flower beds, then made him clear away the sticks beside the pool. Shouting a few words of German, he threw Jim into the drive and slammed the wrought-iron gate onto his heels.

The houses stood around him in the sun, sealed worlds where he had briefly returned to his childhood. As he set out on the long journey to the Bund he thought of the Japanese soldiers who had fed him from their cooking pot, but he knew now that kindness, which his parents and teachers had always urged upon him, counted for nothing.

10

THE STRANDED FREIGHTER

COLD SUNLIGHT SHIVERED on the river, turning its surface into chopped glass and transforming the distant banks and hotels of the Bund into a row of wedding cakes. To Jim, as he sat on the catwalk of the funeral pier below the deserted Nantao shipyards, the funnels and masts of the *Idzumo* seemed carved from icing sugar. He cupped his hands into a pair of make-believe binoculars and studied the white-suited sailors, as busy as lice, who moved around the decks and bridge. The cruiser's gun turrets reminded him of the candied decoration on the Christmas cakes whose overripe flavor he had always hated.

All the same, Jim would have liked to eat the ship. He imagined himself nibbling the masts, sucking the cream from the Edwardian funnels, sinking his teeth into the marzipan bows and devouring the entire forward section of the hull. After that he would gobble down the Palace Hotel, the Shell Building, the whole of Shanghai. . . .

Steam throbbed from the *Idzumo*'s funnels, calmed itself and drifted across the water in a delicate veil. The cruiser had drawn its stern anchors and was swinging on the tide, bows pointing downstream. Having helped to impose Japanese rule upon Shanghai, it was about to sail for another theater of war. As if celebrating its departure, a regatta of corpses turned on the tide. The bodies of scores of Chinese, each on a raft of paper flowers, surrounded the *Idzumo,* ready to escort the cruiser to the mouth of the Yangtze.

Jim kept watch for the Japanese naval patrols. Across the river, on the Pootung shore, were the galvanized roofs and modern chimneys of his father's cotton mill. Jim vaguely remembered his visits there, embarrassing occasions when the Chinese managers paraded him under the expressionless gaze of thousands of mill girls. But it was silent, and what concerned Jim now was the boom of sunken freighters. The nearest of the wrecks, a single-funnel coaster, sat in the deep-water channel only a hundred yards from the end of the funeral pier. Its rusting bridge, like a crumbling brown loaf, still held all its mystery for Jim. War, which had changed everything in Jim's world so radically, had long since left this forgotten wreck, but he was determined to go out to the ship. Rejoining his parents, giving himself up to the Japanese, even finding food to eat meant nothing now that the freighter was at last within his reach.

For two days Jim had wandered along the Shanghai waterfront. After being discovered by the Japanese patrol, he set off for the Bund. His only hope of seeing his parents again was to find one of their Swiss or Swedish friends. Although the European neutrals drove through the streets of Shanghai, Jim had not seen a single British or American face. Had they all been sent to prison camps in Japan?

Then, as he cycled along the Nanking Road, he was overtaken by a military truck. A group of fair-haired men in British uniforms sat behind the guards.

"Speed up, lad! Let's see you look lively!"

"Faster than that, lad! We won't wait for you!"

Jim crouched over the handlebars, feet whirling on the pedals. They were cheering and waving to him, clapping their hands as the Japanese guards frowned at this absurd British game. Jim shouted at the disappearing truck, and there was laughter and a last thumbs-up when Jim's front wheel locked itself in a tramline and pitched him under the feet of the pedicab drivers.

Soon after, he lost his bicycle. He was trying to straighten the front forks when a Chinese shopkeeper and his coolie came up to him. The shopkeeper held the handlebars, but Jim knew that he was not trying to help. He stared into the matter-of-fact eyes of the two Chinese. He was tired and had been slapped enough.

Jim watched them wheel the cycle through the crowd and vanish into one of the hundreds of alleyways. An hour later he reached the Szechwan Road on foot, but the entire financial sector of Shanghai was sealed by hundreds of Japanese soldiers and their armored cars.

So Jim went down to the Bund to look at the *Idzumo*. All afternoon he wandered along the waterfront, past the mud flats where the injured sailors of the *Petrel* had come ashore and he had last seen his father, past the sampan jetties and the fish market with its pallid mullet laid out between the tramlines, to the quays of the French Concession where the Bund ran out in the funeral piers and shipyards of Nantao. No one molested Jim there. This area of creeks and waste tips was covered with the timbers of opium hulks, the carcasses of dogs and the coffins that had drifted ashore again onto the beaches of black mud. In the afternoon he watched the Japanese seaplanes moored to their buoys at the naval air base. He waited for the pilots to come out in their flying goggles and stroll down the slipway. But no one except Jim seemed interested in the seaplanes, and they sat on their long pontoons, propellers irritated by the wind.

At night Jim slept in the backseat of one of the dozens of old taxis dumped onto the mud flats. The klaxons of the Japanese armored cars wailed along the Bund, and the searchlights of the patrol boats flared across the river, but Jim fell asleep quickly in the cold air. His thin body seemed to float on the night, hovering above the dark water as he clung to the faint human odors that rose from the taxi's seats.

It was high water, and the seaplanes had begun to circle their buoys. The river no longer pressed against the boom of freighters. For a few moments the surface congealed into an oily mirror, through which the rusting steamers emerged as if from their own reflections. Beside the funeral piers the sampans swayed forward, loosened from the mud flats even as they filled with water.

Jim squatted on the metal catwalk, watching the water slap at the grille between his feet. From his blazer pocket he took one of his last two liqueur chocolates. He studied the cryptic scrolls, like the signs of the zodiac, and carefully weighed them. Saving the larger, he placed the smaller in his mouth. The fiery alcohol stung his tongue, but he sucked on the dark sweet chocolate. The brown water swelled glassily around the pier, and he remembered that his father had told him how sunlight killed bacteria. Fifty yards away the corpse of a young Chinese woman floated among the sampans, heels rotating around her head as if unsure in what direction to point her that day. Cautiously, Jim decanted a little water from one palm to the other, then drank quickly so that the germs would have no time to infect him.

The liqueur chocolate, and the swelling rhythm of the waves, made him feel giddy again, and he steadied himself against a waterlogged sampan that bumped against the pier. Looking up at the decaying freighter, Jim stepped without thinking into the sampan and pushed out into the jellylike stream.

The rotting craft was half-filled with water that soaked Jim's shoes and trousers. He tore away part of the freeboard and used the pulpy plank to paddle toward the freighter. When he reached the ship the sampan had almost submerged. He seized the starboard rail below the bridge and climbed onto the deck, as the waterlogged hulk drifted on its way to the next freighter in the boom.

Jim watched it go, then walked through the ankle-deep water that covered the metal deck. The river had begun to shift slightly, and the waxy surface was unbroken as it entered the open stateroom below the bridge and ran out through the port rail. Jim stepped into the stateroom, a rusting grotto that seemed even older than the German forts at Tsingtao. He was standing on the surface of the river, which had rushed from all the creeks and paddies and canals of China in order to carry this small boy on its back. If he stepped onto the waves by the port rail, he could walk all the way to the *Idzumo*. . . .

Towers of smoke shuddered from the cruiser's funnels as it prepared to raise anchor. Were his parents on board? Aware that he might now be alone in Shanghai, on this steamer he had always dreamed of visiting, Jim gazed from the bridge toward the shore. The tide was beginning to run, and the flower-decked corpses were following their heels to the open sea. The freighter leaned in the stream, and its rusty hull creaked and sang. The plates sawed against each other, and the trailing hawsers swung across the foredeck, the halyards of invisible sails still hoping to propel this ancient hulk to the safety of some warm sea a world away from Shanghai.

Happily, Jim felt the bridge shudder under his feet. As he laughed to himself at the rail, he noticed that someone was watching him from the shipyard beyond the funeral piers. A man wearing the coat and cap of an American seaman stood in the wheelhouse of one of three partly constructed colliers. Shyly, but captain to captain, Jim waved to him. The man ignored him and smoked the cigarette concealed in his hand. He was watching not only Jim, but a young sailor in a metal dinghy that had cast loose from the next steamer in the boom.

Eager to welcome his first passenger and crewman, Jim left the bridge and made his way down to the deck. The sailor drew nearer, rowing in strong, short movements, careful not to disturb the water. Every few strokes he looked over his shoulder at Jim and peered through the portholes as if he suspected that this rusty freighter was infested with small boys. The dinghy sat low in the water, weighed down by the sailor's broad back. He pulled alongside, and Jim saw a crowbar, spanners and hacksaw between his boots. On the bench seat were the brass rings of porthole mounts prized from the ships' hulls.

"Hello, kid—going for a run up the coast? Who else is with you?"

"Nobody." For all the hope of safety that this young

American offered, Jim was uneager to leave the ship. "I'm waiting for my mother and father. They've been . . . delayed."

"Delayed? Well, maybe they'll come later. You look like you need some help."

He reached out to climb aboard, but as Jim took his hand the sailor pulled him roughly into the dinghy, jarring his knees against the brass portholes. He sat Jim upright and fingered his blazer lapels and badge. His loose blond hair framed an open American face, but he scanned the river in a furtive way, as if expecting a Japanese naval diver in full gear to break surface alongside the dinghy.

"Now, why are you trying to bother us? Who brought you out here?"

"I came by myself." Jim straightened his blazer. "This is my ship now."

"Some kind of crazy British kid. You've been sitting on that pier for two days. Who are you?"

"Jamie . . ." Jim tried to think of something that would impress the American; already he realized that he should stay with this young sailor. "I'm building a man-flying kite . . . and I've written a book on contract bridge."

"Wait till Basie sees this."

As they drifted from the freighter, the American drew on his oars. With a few powerful strokes he pulled the dinghy toward the mud flats. They entered a shallow creek between the funeral piers, a black and oil-stained channel that wound past the shipyards. The American stared morosely at an empty coffin that had jettisoned its occupant. He spat into it for good luck and fended it off with an oar. Expertly he steered the dinghy behind the white hull of a mastless yacht lashed to a beached lighter. Hidden below the swanlike overhang of the yacht's stern, they tied up at a wooden stage. The American looped the porthole mounts onto his arm, gathered his tools together and beckoned Jim from the dinghy.

They crossed the floor of the shipyard, past stacks of steel plate, coils of chains and rusting wire, toward the shabby hulls of the three colliers. Jim scurried along, imitating the American's aggressive gait. At last he had met someone who could help him to find his parents. Perhaps the American and his companion in the wheelhouse had also been trying to surrender. The three of them together would be too many for the Japanese to ignore.

An antique Chevrolet truck was parked under the propeller of the largest collier. They stepped through a missing plate into the hull. The American lifted Jim onto a bamboo platform laid along its keel. They climbed a companionway to the next deck, walked across the wheelhouse and ducked through a narrow hatch into a metal cabin behind the bridge.

Faint with hunger, Jim swayed against the door frame. A familiar scent hung in the air, reminding him of his mother's bedroom in Amherst Avenue, the odors of face powder, cologne and Craven A cigarettes, and for a moment he was sure that she would emerge from this dark cubbyhole like the Christmas fairy and tell him that the war was over.

11

FRANK AND BASIE

A CHARCOAL STOVE burned softly in the center of the cabin, its sweet fumes lifting through an open skylight. The floor was covered with oily rags and engine parts, brass portholes and stair rails. On either side of the stove were a deck chair, with "Imperial Airways" stitched into its fading canvas, and a camp bed covered with a Chinese quilt.

The American flung his tools into the heap of metal parts. His large head and shoulders almost filled the cabin, and he slumped restlessly in the canvas chair. He peered into the saucepan on the stove and then gazed gloomily at Jim.

"He's getting on my nerves already, Basie. I don't know whether he's hungrier or crazier. . . ."

"Come in, boy. You look like you need to lie down."

A small, older man emerged from beneath the quilt and motioned to Jim with the cigarette he was holding in his white hand. He had a bland, unmarked face from which all the copious experiences of his life had been cleverly erased and soft hands that were busy powdering each other under the quilt. His eyes took in every detail of Jim's mud-stained clothes, the tic that jumped across his mouth, his pinched cheeks and unsteady legs.

He dusted the talc from the bed and counted the pieces of salvaged brass. "Is that all, Frank? That's not a lot to take to market. Those Hongkew merchants are charging ten dollars for a bag of rice."

"Basie!" The young sailor drove a heavy boot into the heap of metal, exasperated more with himself than with the older man. "The boy's been sitting on the pier for two days! Do you want the Japs in here?"

"Frank, the Japs aren't looking for us. Nantao Creek is full of the cholera—that's why we came here."

"You practically put up a sign. Maybe you want them to look for us? Is that it, Basie?" Frank dipped a rag in a can of cleaning fluid. He began to rub vigorously at the grime that covered a porthole mount. "If you want to work so hard, try going out there—with that kid watching you all the time."

"Frank, we've got my lungs, you agreed to that." Basie inhaled a little smoke from his Craven A, soothing these delicate organs. "Besides, the boy didn't even notice you. He had other things on his mind, boy's things that you've forgotten, Frank, but I can still remember." He made a warm place for Jim on the bed. "Come over here, son. What did they call you, before the war started?"

"Jamie . . ."

Frank threw down his rag. "All this scrap isn't going to buy us a sampan to Chungking! We'd need the *Queen Mary* out there." He treated Jim to a dark glare. "And we don't have enough rice for you, kid. Who are you? Jamie—?"

"Jim . . ." Basie explained. "A new name for a new life." As Jim sat beside him, he reached out a powdered hand and gently pressed his thumb against the hunger tic that jumped across the left corner of Jim's mouth. Jim sat passively as Basie exposed his gums and glanced shrewdly at his teeth.

"That's a well-kept set of teeth. Someone paid a lot of bills for that sweet little mouth. Frank, you'd be surprised how some people neglect their kids' teeth." Basie patted Jim's shoulder, feeling the blue wool of his blazer. He scraped the mud from the school badge. "That looks like a good school, Jim. The Cathedral School?"

Frank glowered over his heap of portholes. He seemed wary of Jim, as if this small boy might take Basie from him. "Cathedral? Is he some kind of priest?"

"Frank, the Cathedral School." Basie gazed with growing interest at Jim. "That's a school for *taipans*. Jim, you must know some important people."

"Well . . ." Jim was doubtful about this. He could think of nothing but the rice simmering on the charcoal stove, but then remembered a garden party at the British Embassy. "Once I was introduced to Madame Sun Yatsen."

"Madame Sun? You were . . . introduced?"

"I was only three and a half." Jim sat still as Basie's white hands explored his pockets. The watch slipped from his wrist and vanished into the haze of cologne and face powder below the quilt. Yet Basie's attentive manner, like that of the servants who had once dressed and undressed him, was curiously reassuring. The sailor was feeling every bone in his body, as if searching for something precious. Through the open hatch Jim could see a flying boat about to take off from the naval air base. A Japanese patrol boat had closed the channel, giving a wide berth to the currents that formed huge whirlpools around the boom of freighters. Jim returned to the cooking pot and its intoxicating smell of burned fat. Suddenly it occurred to him that these two American sailors might want to eat him.

But Basie had removed the lid from the saucepan. A flavorsome steam rose from a thick stew of rice and fish. Basie produced a pair of tin plates and spoons from a leather bag under the bed. Still smoking his Craven A, he served portions for himself and Jim with the deftness of a waiter at the Palace Hotel. As Jim wolfed the hot fish, Basie watched with the same wry approval that the Japanese soldier had shown.

Basie tucked into the stew. "We eat later, Frank."

Frank rubbed at a porthole, his eyes on the saucepan. "Basie, I always eat after you."

"I need to think for us both, Frank. Besides, we have to look after our young friend." He wiped a grain of rice from Jim's chin. "Tell me, Jim, have you met any other Chinese big noises? Chiang Kaishek, maybe?"

"No . . . but his name isn't really Chinese, you know." The hot food made Jim's brain swim. He remembered a word his mother had used, which he had always tried to work into his conversations with adults. "It's a corruption of Shanghai Czech."

"A corruption . . . ?" Basie was sitting up now. Having ended his meal, he began to powder his hands. "Are you interested in words, Jim?"

"A bit. And contract bridge. I've written a book about it."

Basie looked doubtful. "Words are more important, Jim. Put aside a new word every day. You never know when a word might be useful."

Jim finished his stew and sat back contentedly against the metal wall. He could remember none of his meals before the war and every one of them since. It annoyed him to think of all the food in his life that he had turned away, and the elaborate stratagems which Vera and his mother had devised to persuade him to finish his pudding. He noticed that Frank was staring at a few grains he had left in the spoon and quickly licked it clean. Jim glanced into the saucepan, glad to see that there was enough rice for Frank. He was sure now that these two merchant seamen were not going to eat him, but the fear had been sensible—there had been rumors at the country club that British sailors torpedoed in the Atlantic had taken to cannibalism.

Basie served himself a small spoonful of rice. He made no attempt to eat this second helping but played with the plate under Frank's burning gaze. Already Jim could see that Basie liked to control the young sailor and was using Jim to unsettle him. Jim's entire upbringing could have been designed to prevent him from meeting people like Basie, but the war had changed everything.

"What about your daddy, Jim?" Basie asked. "Why aren't you at home with your mother? Are they here in Shanghai?"

"Yes. . . ." Jim hesitated. All his experience of the previous two months told him not to trust anyone, except perhaps the Japanese. "They're in Shanghai—but they're sailing on the *Idzumo*."

"The *Idzumo*?" Frank jumped from his deck chair. He seized a mess tin from his haversack and helped himself vigorously to the saucepan of rice. Between mouthfuls, he shook his spoon at Jim. "Kid, who are you? Basie!"

"Not the *Idzumo*, Jim." With his white hands Basie selected a piece of charcoal from a bag under the bed. "The *Idzumo*'s heading for Foochow and Manila Bay. Jim's having you on, Frank."

"Well, I think they're on the *Idzumo*." Jim decided to fan the small doubt still in Basie's eyes. "My father often goes to Manila."

"Not on a Japanese cruiser, Jim."

"Basie!"

"Frank. . . ." Basie mimicked the sailor's voice. "Someday you'll want to trust me. I imagine Jim's folks had themselves picked up with all the other Britishers, and now Jim's looking for them. Jim?"

Jim nodded, taking the last liqueur chocolate from his blazer pocket. He unwrapped the silver foil and bit into the miniature chocolate bottle. Then, remembering what Vera had drummed into him about the need to be polite, he handed half the chocolate to Basie.

"Curacao? Well, things have been looking up, Jim, since you arrived. All these new words, and now this fancy candy; we're getting a little of that Palace Hotel style." As Basie sucked at the chocolate cup with his sharp teeth, he resembled a white-faced rat teasing the brains from a mouse. "So you've been living at home, Jim, all by yourself. Down there in the French Concession?"

"Amherst Avenue."

"Frank. . . . Before we leave Shanghai we ought to take a ride out there. There must be a lot of empty houses, Jim?"

Jim closed his eyes. He was very tired but awake, thinking of the rice he had just eaten, retasting every fishy grain. Basie talked, his devious voice circling the fume-filled air and its scent of cologne and Craven A. He thought of his mother smoking in the drawing room at Amherst Avenue. Now that he had met these two American sailors he would be seeing her again. He would stay with Basie and Frank; together they could go out to the boom of freighters; sooner or later the Japanese patrol boats would notice them.

A hot, fishy breath filled his face. Jim woke with a gasp. Frank's huge body leaned across him, heavy arms on his thighs, hands feeling in his blazer pockets. Jim pushed him away, and Frank calmly returned to his deck chair and continued to polish the portholes.

They were alone together in the cabin. Jim could hear Basie on the bamboo catwalk below. The door of the truck slammed, and the elderly engine began to throb, then stopped abruptly. There was a distant blast from the *Idzumo*'s siren. With a meaningful glance at Jim, Frank buffed the faded brass.

"You know, kid, you have a talent for getting on people's nerves. How is it the Japs haven't picked you up? You must be quick on your feet."

"I tried to surrender," Jim explained. "But it isn't easy. Do you and Basie want to surrender?"

"Like hell—though I don't know about him. I'm trying to get Basie to buy a sampan so we can sail upriver to Chungking. But Basie keeps changing his mind. He wants to stay in Shanghai now the Japs are here. He thinks we can make a pile of money once we get to the camps."

"Do you sell a lot of portholes, Frank?"

Frank peered at Jim, still unsure about this small boy. "Kid, we haven't sold a single one. It's Basie's game, like a drug; he needs to keep people working for him. Down in the yard somewhere he has a bag of gold teeth that he sells in Hongkew." With a knowing smile, Frank raised an oil-stained spanner and touched Jim's chin. "It's a good thing you don't have any gold teeth, or—" He snapped his wrist.

Jim sat up, remembering how Basie had searched his gums. The sound of the truck's motor vibrated through the metal cabin. Jim was wary of these two merchant seamen, who had somehow escaped the Japanese net around Shanghai, and realized that he might have as much to fear from them as from anyone else in the city. He thought of Basie's secret bag of gold teeth. The creeks and canals of Nantao were full of corpses, and the mouths of those corpses were full of teeth. Every Chinese tried to have at least one gold tooth out of self-respect, and now that the war had begun their relatives might be too tired to pull them out before the funeral. Jim visualized the two American seamen searching the mud flats at night with their spanners, Frank rowing the dinghy along the black creeks, Basie in the bows with a lantern, prodding the corpses that drifted past and exposing their gums. . . .

12

DANCE MUSIC

THIS FEARFUL IMAGE dominated the three days that Jim was to spend with the American sailors. At night, as Basie and Frank slept together under the quilt, Jim lay awake on his pile of rice sacking beside the charcoal stove. Reflected from the portholes and brass handrails, the embers gleamed like gold teeth. When he woke in the mornings Jim would feel his jaw, to make sure that Frank had not removed one of his molars out of cussedness.

During the day Jim sat on the funeral pier and acted as lookout while Frank rowed to the scuttled freighters. When he began to shiver, Jim returned to the cabin and lay under the quilt as Basie sat in the Imperial Airways deck chair and made wire toys from old pipe cleaners. Basie had served as a cabin steward on the Cathay-America Line, and he treated Jim to the same patter and parlor tricks with which he had amused the young children of his passengers. He made the same effort to ensure that Jim ate his morning and evening meals, while endlessly questioning him about his mother and father. To a large extent Basie had modeled himself on the women passengers he had served, forever powdering themselves in the heat as they lit a cigarette.

Every afternoon they set off together in the truck and toured the Chinese markets in Hongkew. Here Basie would haggle for a sack of rice and a few pieces of fish, trading packets of French cigarettes from the store of cartons under his bed. At times he would tell Frank to bring Jim over to the vendor's stall, where the Chinese trader would soberly inspect Jim before shaking his head.

It soon became clear to Jim that Basie was trying to sell him to the traders. Too tired to resist, Jim sat in the truck between the two Americans, like one of the chickens that the Chinese women carried beside them on the seats of the trams. Already Jim felt unwell most of the time, but his potential value at least assured him of the meals of boiled fish. Eventually the Chinese traders would realize that a few yen could be made by reporting them to the Japanese.

Meanwhile he avoided Frank's heavy hands, ransacked his mind for the unusual words that Basie liked to hear him use and regaled the cabin steward with tales of the grand houses in Amherst Avenue. Jim invented lives of wholly imaginary glamour that he claimed his parents had led. Basie never ceased to be fascinated by these accounts of Shanghai high life.

"Tell me about their swimming-pool parties," Basie asked as they waited for Frank to start the engine before their last visit to Hongkew market. "I imagine there was a lot of . . . gaiety."

"Basie, there certainly was gaiety." Jim remembered the hours he had spent alone trying to retrieve the half-crown, gleaming at the bottom of the pool like one of Basie's teeth. "They had liqueur chocolates, a white piano, whiskey and soda. And conjurers."

"Conjurers, Jim?"

"I think they were conjurers. . . ."

"You're tired, Jim." As they sat in the truck Basie put an arm around Jim's shoulders. "You've been thinking too much, all those new words."

"I've used up all my new words, Basie. Is the war going to end soon?"

"Don't worry, Jim. I give the Japs three months at the outside."

"As soon as that, Basie?"

"Maybe a little more. It takes a long time to start a war; people have a big investment to protect. Like Frank and me and this truck."

It had never occurred to Jim that anyone might want the war to continue, and he puzzled over the bizarre logic as they set out for Hongkew. They bumped along the dirt road behind the shipyards, through a desolate area of empty godowns, garbage dumps and burial mounds. Beggars lived beside the canals in hovels constructed from truck tires and packing cases. An old woman squatted by the fetid water, scrubbing out a wooden toilet. Gazing down from the safety of the truck, Jim felt sorry for these destitute people, though only a few days earlier his plight had been even more desperate than theirs. A strange doubling of reality had taken place, as if everything that had happened to him since the war was occurring within a mirror. It was his mirror self who felt faint and hungry, and who thought about food all the time. He no longer felt sorry for this other self. Jim guessed that this was how the Chinese managed to sur-

Jim heard Frank shouting and saw that the two figures were off-duty Japanese soldiers in their military kimonos. The soldiers had seen them and were bellowing at the open door. A uniformed sergeant emerged from the kerosene light that filled the hall. He stood on the top step, a Mauser holster against his stocky thigh. Frank was trying to reverse the truck when the soldiers in the kimonos jumped onto the running boards and struck with their fists at the glass. Two more soldiers carrying bamboo staves ran down the steps of the porch.

As the engine stalled, Jim felt himself pulled from the truck and hurled to the ground. Japanese in kimonos were running from the house, like a party of outraged women fresh from their baths. Jim sat on the sharp gravel between the polished boots of the Japanese sergeant, whose angry thigh rapped against his holster. The soldiers had trapped Frank within the cabin of the truck. His legs kicked out as they lunged at him with their bamboo staves, striking his bloody face and chest. Two soldiers watched from the steps of the house, taking turns to punch Basie who knelt at their feet in the drive.

Jim was glad to see the Japanese. Through the open doorway he could hear, between the heavy blows and Frank's cries, the scratchy sounds of a Japanese dance band playing on his mother's picnic gramophone.

13

THE OPEN-AIR CINEMA

HIS ARMS WARMED by the spring sun, Jim rested comfortably in the front row of the open-air cinema. Smiling to himself, he gazed at the blank screen twenty feet away. For the past hour the blurred shadow of the Park Hotel had been moving across the white canvas. After a long journey through the godowns and tenement blocks of Chapei, the shadow of the neon sign above the hotel had at last reached the screen. The immense letters, each twice the height of the young Japanese soldier patrolling the stage, moved from left to right at a brisk pace, incorporating the silhouette of this slim sentry and his rifle in a spectacular solar film.

Delighted with the display, Jim laughed behind his grimy knees, feet up on the slatted teak bench. The afternoon diorama staged in collaboration by the sun and the Park Hotel had been Jim's chief entertainment during the three weeks he had spent at the open-air cinema. Here, before the outbreak of war, cartoons and adventure serials made by the Shanghai film industry were projected at night to audiences of Chinese mill girls and dockyard workers. It often occurred to Jim that Yang, the family chauffeur, might have appeared on this very screen. Jim had already carried out a full reconnaissance of the detention center, and in a disused office above the projection room were reels of dusty film. Perhaps the Japanese corporal from the signal corps who was now trying to dismantle the projector would show one of Yang's films.

Jim's giggles brought a sour glance from the soldier on the stage. He clearly mistrusted Jim, who kept out of his way. Shielding his eyes, the soldier scanned the wooden benches, where a few detainees sat in the afternoon sun. Three rows behind Jim was the gray-haired husband of the dying missionary woman who lay on her mat in the concrete dormitory under the seats. She had not moved from the former storeroom since her arrival, but Mr. Partridge looked after her patiently, bringing water from the tap in the latrine and feeding her the thin rice gruel which two Eurasian women cooked once a day in the yard behind the ticket office.

Jim felt concerned for the old Englishman with his patchy hair and deathly skin. At times he seemed unable to recognize his wife. Jim helped him to erect a screen around Mrs. Partridge, who never spoke and had an unpleasant smell. They used Mr. Partridge's English overcoat and his wife's yellowing nightdress, suspending them from a length of electric flex that Jim pulled from the wall. If he was bored, Jim went down to the women's storeroom and chased away the Eurasian children who ran in to play.

There were some thirty people in the detention center, to which Jim had been sent after a week at the Shanghai central prison. Compared with the damp dormitory cell that he shared with a hundred Eurasian and British prisoners, the open-air cinema seemed as sunny as the resort beaches at Tsingtao. Jim had seen nothing of Basie since their capture by the Japanese and was glad to be free of the cabin steward. None of the prisoners in the central prison, most of whom were contract foremen and merchant seamen from China coasters, had heard of Jim's parents, but the transfer to the detention center was a move toward them.

Soon after Jim's capture, he had fallen ill with an aching fever, during which he vomited blood. Jim guessed that he had been sent to the detention center in order to recover. Apart from several elderly English couples, there were an old Dutchman and his adult daughter, and a quiet Belgian woman whose injured husband slept next to Jim in the men's storeroom. The rest were Eurasian women who had been abandoned in Shanghai by British husbands in the armed services.

None of them was much fun to be with—they were all either very old or sick with malaria and dysentery, and few of the Eurasian children spoke any English. So Jim spent his time in the open-air cinema, roving around the wooden seats. Despite his headaches, he tried unsuccessfully to make friends with the Japanese soldiers. And every afternoon there was the shadow film of the Shanghai skyline.

Jim watched the letters of the Park Hotel's neon sign blur and fade. Although he was hungry all the time, Jim was happy in the detention center. After the months of roving the streets of Shanghai, he had at last managed to give himself up to the Japanese forces. Jim had pondered deeply on the question of surrender, which took courage and even a certain amount of guile. How did entire armies manage it?

Jim was aware that the Japanese had seized him only because he had been with Basie and Frank. He felt frightened when he thought of the soldiers in the kimonos attacking Frank with their staves, but at least he would soon see his parents again. Prisoners were constantly coming and going at the detention center. Two British people had died the previous day, a heavily bandaged woman whom Jim had not been allowed to see, and an old man with malaria who was a retired Shanghai police inspector.

If only he could discover to which of the dozen camps around Shanghai his mother and father had been sent. Jim left his place and tried to speak to Mr. Partridge, but the old missionary was sunk inside his head. Jim approached the two Eurasian women sitting a few benches behind him. But as always they shook their heads and brusquely waved Jim away.

"Disgusting!"

"Dirty boy!"

"Go away!"

Invariably they snapped at Jim and tried to keep their children from him. Sometimes they mimicked Jim's voice during his fevers. Jim smiled at them and returned to his seat. He felt tired, as he often did, and thought of going down to the storeroom and sleeping for an hour on his mat. But a meal of boiled rice was served in the afternoon, and the previous day, when he had felt feverish, he had missed his ration. It surprised Jim how these old and sick people could manage to rouse themselves at mealtimes. No one had thought of waking Jim, and nothing was left in the brass cong. When he protested, the Korean soldier had cuffed his head. Already Jim was certain that the Eurasian women who guarded the bags of rice in the ticket kiosk were giving him less than his fair share. He distrusted them all, and their strange children, who looked almost English but could speak only Chinese.

Jim was determined to have his share of rice. He knew that he was thinner than he had been before the war, and that his parents might fail to recognize him. At mealtimes, when he looked at himself in the cracked glass panes of the ticket kiosk, he barely remembered the long face with its deep eye sockets and bony forehead. Jim avoided mirrors—the Eurasian women were always watching him through their compacts.

Deciding to think of something useful, Jim lay back on the teak bench. He watched a Kawanishi flying boat cross the river. The drone of its engines was comforting and reminded Jim of all his dreams of flying. When he was hungry or missed his parents, he often dreamed of aircraft. During one of his fevers he had even seen a flight of American bombers in the sky above the detention center.

A whistle shrilled from the courtyard by the ticket kiosk. The Japanese sergeant in charge of the detention center was holding another of his roll calls. Jim had noticed that he seemed unable to remember the prisoners' names for more than half an hour. Jim took Mr. Partridge's hand, and together they followed the two Eurasian women. A military truck had stopped outside the entrance to the cinema, whose high brick walls had concealed its films from the Chinese in the nearby tenement blocks. In the intervals between the sergeant's whistles, Jim heard the crying of a British child.

A new group of prisoners had arrived. Invariably this meant that others would leave. Jim was sure that he would be on his way within minutes, probably to the new camps at Hungjao or Lunghua. In the storeroom he and the old men still able to stand waited by their mats, mess tins in hand. Jim listened to the new arrivals being herded from the truck. Annoyingly, there were several small children, who would cry continuously and distract the Japanese from the serious task of deciding where Jim should be sent.

Followed by two armed soldiers, the Japanese sergeant stood in the doorway. All three men wore cotton masks over their faces—there was a foul smell from the young Belgian asleep on the floor—but the sergeant's eyes inspected each of them in turn and counted the exact number of mess tins. The daily ration of rice or sweet potatoes was allocated to the mess tin and not to the person attached to it. Often, when Mr. Partridge was tired after feeding his wife, Jim would collect the old man's ration for him. Once, without realizing it, he had found himself eating the watery gruel. Jim had felt uneasy and stared at his guilty hands. Parts of his mind and body frequently separated themselves from each other.

Masking the tic in his cheek, Jim smiled brightly at the Japanese sergeant, and tried to look strong and healthy. Only the healthier people tended to leave the detention center. But as usual the sergeant seemed depressed by Jim's cheerful gaze. He stepped aside as the new arrivals reached the storeroom. Two Chinese prison orderlies bore a stretcher carrying an unconscious Englishwoman in a stained cotton dress. She lay with her damp hair in her mouth, while her two sons, boys of Jim's age, held the sides of the stretcher. A trio of elderly women hobbled past, unsure of the smell and the gray light. Behind them came a tall soldier wearing lumpy boots and British army shorts. He was bare-chested, and his emaciated ribs were like a bird cage in which Jim could almost see his heart fluttering.

"Well done, lad. . . ." He gave Jim a rictus of a smile and patted his head. Quickly he sat down against the wall, his cadaverous face turned to the damp cement. A second team of orderlies lowered a stretcher onto the floor beside him. From the cradle of roped straw they lifted out a small, middle-aged man in a bloodstained sailor's jacket. Strips of Japanese rice-paper bandages were stuck to the wounds on his swollen hands, face and forehead.

Jim stared at this derelict figure and raised his forearm to his mouth to shut out the unpleasant smell. Several of the Eurasian women were leaving the detention center with their children. Looking round at the sick and dying men in the storeroom, and at the orderlies and Japanese soldiers with their cotton face masks, Jim began to grasp for the first time the real purpose of the detention center.

Mr. Partridge and the old men stood by their mats, shaking their mess tins at the guards, rattling for their evening meal. The wounded sailor beckoned to Jim with his bandaged hands, beating his empty tin with the same rhythm that the dying beggar had used outside the gates of Amherst Avenue. Even the emaciated soldier had found the lid of a mess tin. With his face pressed to the wall, he banged the lid on the stone floor.

Jim began to rattle at the Japanese watching behind their white masks. Yet, at that moment when he was about to despair of ever finding his parents, he felt a surge of hope. He knelt on the floor and took the mess tin from the injured sailor, aware of a faint scent of cologne and certain now that together they could leave the detention center and make their way to the safety of the prison camps.

"Basie!" he cried. "Everything's all right!"

14

AMERICAN
AIRCRAFT

"THE WAR'S GOING to be over soon, Basie.
I've seen American planes, Curtis bombers and
Boeings. . . ."

"Boeings? Jim you're—"

"Don't talk, Basie. I'm working for you now, just like
Frank."

Jim squatted by the American sailor, trying to remember the amahs of his early childhood. He had never looked
after anything before, except for an angora rabbit that
had died tragically within a few days. He tilted the mess
tin and tried to pour a little water into Basie's mouth,
then dipped his fingers in the murky fluid and let Basie
suck them.

For three weeks Jim had devoted himself to the cabin
steward, bringing his ration of boiled rice and sweet potatoes, fetching water from the tap in the corridor. He
sat for hours beside Basie, fanning the sailor as he lay
on his mat below the transom window. The stream of
fresh air soon revived him, and one by one he pulled

away the paper bandages fluttering on his face and wrists. Helped by Jim, he moved his mat from the English soldier dying against the wall. Within a week he had recovered enough of his strength to keep an eye on the Japanese guards and the comings and goings of the Eurasian woman who cooked for the prisoners.

As he cleaned Basie's mess tin, Jim wondered if the sailor really recognized him. Did he know that Jim had managed to trick him? Perhaps he would report Jim to the other prisoners, but there was little that they could do. Relieved that at last he had an ally in his struggle with the Eurasian women, Jim rested his head on his knees.

He felt Basie nudge him with the mess tins.

"Chow time, Jim. Get in line." As Jim sat up, hoping that he had not talked in his sleep, Basie wiped some of the dirt from his cheek. The steward's canny eyes took in every detail of Jim's shabby state. "Make yourself useful to Mrs. Blackburn, Jim. Ingratiate yourself a little. A woman always needs help with her fire."

Somehow, during his visits to the latrine, Basie had learned the Eurasian woman's name. Jim ran from the storeroom with the two mess tins. The other prisoners followed, the old men stirring from their mats. Mr. Partridge took the mess tin from the hand of the English soldier who sat in a pool of urine by the wall.

Smoke rose from the courtyard behind the ticket kiosk. The Eurasian woman fanned the briquettes in her stove, but the rice and sweet potatoes in the congs had gone off the boil. A Japanese soldier stared gloomily at the tepid swill and shook his head at the hungry prisoners. They shuffled among the teak benches of the cinema, sat down and stared at the smoke drifting across the empty screen.

Holding the mess tins, Jim hovered around Mrs. Blackburn and treated her to his keenest smile. She disliked Jim but allowed him to chop the basket of firewood. Jim pushed the spills into the stove and blew hard to ignite them. He fanned the embers until the briquettes caught light again. Half an hour later, with the Japanese soldier's approval, Jim was rewarded with his first fair ration.

Basie was satisfied but unimpressed. After finishing his meal, he propped himself on his elbows. He gazed at his fellow prisoners, some too exhausted to eat their rations, and tore the last of the paper bandages from the cuts over his eyes. Whatever had befallen him in Shanghai Central Prison—and Jim never dared to ask about Frank—he had once again become the ex-steward of the Cathay-America Line, ready to assemble a small part of a ramshackle world around himself. He surveyed Jim again, taking in his ragged clothes and scarecrow appearance, his deep-set and yellowing eyes. Without comment, he gave Jim a piece of potato skin.

"Say, thanks, Basie."

"I'm looking after you, Jim."

Jim devoured the shred of potato. "You're looking after me, Basie."

"You helped Mrs. Blackburn?"

"I ingratiated myself. I made myself very useful to Mrs. Blackburn."

"That's it. If you can find a way of helping people, you'll live off the interest."

"Like this piece of potato . . . Basie, when you were in Shanghai Central did anyone talk about my mother and father?"

"I think I did hear something, Jim." Basie cupped his

hand conspiratorially. "Good news, they're in one of the camps and looking forward to seeing you. I'll find out which one for you."

"Thanks, Basie!"

From then on Jim regularly helped Mrs. Blackburn. Every morning he was up at dawn to rake the ash from the stove, chop firewood and lay the briquettes. Long before the water in the congs began to boil, Jim had already earmarked the sweet potatoes for Basie and himself, selecting those with the least blight and fungus. He saw to it that Mrs. Blackburn served them the thicker rice, into which, at Basie's suggestion, he had been careful to stir the minimum of water. After their meal, when the other prisoners rinsed their tins at the latrine tap, Basie always sent Jim to fill their mess tins with the tepid water in the potato cong. Basie insisted that he and Jim drink only this gray, pithy liquid.

Although, like everyone else, Basie was never keen for Jim to come too close to him, he clearly approved of Jim's efforts. At the end of his second week at the detention center, Basie allowed Jim to move his sleeping mat beside his own. Lying at Basie's feet, Jim could intercept Mrs. Blackburn on her way to the kiosk.

"Always look light on your toes, Jim." Basie lay back as Jim fanned him. "Whatever happens, keep moving around the court. Your dad would agree with me."

"Actually, he would agree with you. After the war you can play tennis together. He's really good."

"Well . . . What I meant, Jim, is that I'm trying to keep up your education. Your dad would appreciate that."

"I think he'll give you a reward, Basie." Jim assumed that the notion of a reward would spur Basie in his search for his father. "Once he gave five dollars to a taxi driver who brought me home from Hongkew."

"Did he, Jim?" At times Basie seemed unsure whether Jim was having him on. "Tell me, did you see any planes today?"

"A Nakajima Shoki and a Zero-Sen."

"And American planes?"

"I haven't seen those again. Not since you came, Basie. I saw them for three days, and then they went away."

"I thought they had. They must have been a special kind of reconnaissance flight."

"To see how we all are? Where did they come from, Basie? Wake Island?"

"A long way, Jim. It must have been just about the end of their range." Basie took the fan from Jim's hand. An elderly Australian had arrived to talk to Basie about the war. "Go and help Mrs. Blackburn. And remember to bow to Sergeant Uchida."

"I always bow, Basie."

Jim hovered around the conversation, hoping to catch the latest news, but the two men waved him away. Basie was surprisingly well informed about the progress of the war: the fall of Hong Kong, Manila and the Dutch East Indies; the surrender of Singapore and the unbroken advance of Japan across the Pacific. The only good news in all this were the flights of American planes that Jim had seen over Shanghai, but for some reason Basie never mentioned them. He liked to talk out of the side of his mouth, telling the old Britishers about the other inmates at Shanghai Central Prison, who had died and who had been handed over to the Swiss Red Cross. Basie even sold information for small scraps of food. Mr. Partridge gave him his potato for news of his brother-in-law in Nanking. Inspired by this, Jim tried to tell Mrs. Blackburn about the American aircraft, but she merely sent him back to the briquettes.

Now that he felt stronger, Jim realized how important it was to be obsessed by food. Shared equally among the prisoners, their daily rations were not enough to keep them alive. Many of the prisoners had died, and anyone who sacrificed himself for the others soon died too. The only way to leave the detention center was to stay alive. As long as he ran errands for Basie, worked hard for Mrs. Blackburn and bowed to Sergeant Uchida, all would be well.

Nonetheless, some of Basie's ruses unsettled Jim. On the morning Mrs. Partridge died, Basie learned some encouraging news about the brother-in-law in Nanking and soon after was able to sell the old woman's hairbrushes to Mrs. Blackburn. Whenever anyone died Basie would be on hand with news and comfort, though death was an elastic term for the cabin steward, open to all manner of interpretation. Jim collected Private Blake's rations for two days after he lay without moving on the storeroom floor, the skin stretched across his ribs like rice paper around a lantern. Jim knew that the private had died of the same fever that he and many of the prisoners had caught. But already Jim was looking at the elderly missionaries with an expectant eye, waiting for fever to recruit the old men. Once he and Basie had admitted their part in this supplementary-ration scheme, all guilt had gone.

Jim noticed how different Basie was from his father in this respect. At home, if he did anything wrong, the consequences seemed to overlay everything for days. With Basie they vanished instantly. For the first time in his life Jim felt free to do what he wanted. All sorts of wayward ideas moved through his mind, fueled by hunger and the excitement of stealing from the old prisoners. As he rested between his errands in front of the empty cinema screen, he thought of the American aircraft he had seen in the clouds above Shanghai. He could almost summon them into his vision, a silver fleet on the far side of the sky. Jim saw them most when he was hungry, and he hoped that Private Blake, who must always have been hungry, had also seen them.

15

ON THE WAY
TO THE CAMPS

ON THE DAY of the Englishwoman's death,
a fresh consignment of prisoners arrived at the detention
center. Jim was hovering in the doorway of the women's
storeroom, as Mrs. Blackburn and the daughter of the
old Dutchman tried to comfort the two sons. The mother
lay on the stone floor in her drenched frock, like a drowned
corpse raised from the river. The brothers kept turning
toward her, as if expecting her to give them some last
instruction. Jim felt sad for the boys, Paul and David,
though he hardly knew them. They seemed much younger
than Jim, but in fact both were more than a year older.

Jim had his eyes on the mother's mess tin and tennis
shoes. Most of the Allied prisoners had far better shoes
than the Japanese soldiers, and Jim had noticed that the
bodies leaving the detention center had bare feet. But as
he sidled into the room, there was a shrill whistle from
the courtyard and a series of barked shouts. Sergeant
Uchida was working himself up to the pitch of anger that
he needed to attain in order to issue the simplest instructions. Masks over their faces, the Japanese soldiers began

to herd from the storerooms everyone who could walk. A truck had stopped outside the cinema, and its prisoners stood unsteadily in the road.

All designs on the dead woman's tennis shoes vanished from Jim's head. At last he would be leaving for the camps in the countryside around Shanghai. Pushing past the two boys, Jim dived between the guards and raced up the steps. He lined up beside his fellow prisoners— Mr. Partridge with his wife's suitcase, as if about to take his memories of her on a long journey; Paul and David; the Dutch woman and her father; and several of the old missionaries. Basie stood behind them, his white cheeks hidden behind the collar of his seaman's jacket, so self-effacing as to be almost invisible. He had erased himself from the small world of the detention center, which he had manipulated for a few weeks, and would re-emerge like some marine parasite from its shell once he reached the more succulent terrain of the prison camps.

The new arrivals appeared, two Annamese women and a group of older Britishers and Belgians, the sick and elderly carried on stretchers by the Chinese orderlies. Counting their yellow eyes, Jim knew that there would soon be extra mess tins.

His cotton mask over his face, Sergeant Uchida began to select prisoners for transport to the camps. He shook his head at Mr. Partridge and kicked the suitcase in an exasperated way. He passed the Dutch woman and her father, Paul and David, and two elderly missionary couples.

Jim licked his fingers and wiped the soot from his cheeks. The sergeant motioned Basie toward the truck. Without a glance at Jim, the cabin steward stepped between the guards, his arms around the shoulders of the two boys.

Sergeant Uchida pressed his fingers against Jim's grimy forehead. With his constant bowing and smiling, his eagerness to run errands, Jim had been a perpetual nuisance to the sergeant, who was clearly glad to be rid of him. Then he glanced at the party of new arrivals, who stared listlessly at the cold stove, at the scum of boiled rice around the rim of the cong.

The sergeant cupped his hand around Jim's neck. With a shout muffled by his cotton mask, he propelled Jim toward the stove. As Jim picked himself from his knees, the sergeant kicked the coal sacks, scattering briquettes across the stone floor.

Jim sieved the clinkers from the firebox. The new arrivals wandered among the benches and took their seats facing the empty cinema screen, as if expecting a film show to begin. Basie and the Dutch couple, Paul and David, and the old missionaries stood in the street behind the open army truck, watched at a distance by a crowd of rickshaw coolies and peasant women.

"Basie!" Jim called. "I'll still work for you!" But the steward had lost interest in him. Already he had befriended Paul and David, inducting them into his entourage. They helped Basie as he clambered on his bruised knees over the tailgate of the truck.

"Basie . . ." Jim sieved fiercely. He glared at the cinema screen, crossed by the first shadows of the Shanghai hotels. A Japanese soldier in a face mask counted out a stack of mess tins. As the injured prisoners were carried past on their stretchers, Jim knew that most of the inmates of the detention center had been sent there because they were very old or were expected to die, either of dysentery and typhoid, or whatever fever he and Private Blake had caught from the foul water. Jim was certain that many of the prisoners would soon die, and that if he stayed at the detention center he would die with them. Already the Annamese women had collected the mess tins from the soldier. They were pointing to the stove and the sacks of briquettes. When they took over the cooking of the rice and sweet potatoes, they would not give Jim his fair ration. He would see the American aircraft again, and he would die.

"Basie?" Jim threw down the sieve. The last of the departing prisoners had taken their seats in the truck. The Japanese soldier by the tailgate lowered the Dutch woman onto the wooden floor. Basie sat between the two English boys, making a toy from a piece of wire in his hand. The truck started up, moved forward a few feet and stopped. The Japanese driver shouted from his window. He waved a canvas map wallet and slapped the metal door with his fist. The guards on the pavement shouted back, eager to close the gates of the detention center and put their feet up in the orderly room. Then the engine stalled, and there was an instant clamor of angry voices, the soldiers and driver arguing over the destination of the truck.

"Woosung . . ." Sergeant Uchida lowered his cotton mask. His face was reddening, and drops of spittle formed on his lips, like pus forced from a wound. Already in a fury with the driver, he strode through the open gates. The driver had stepped from his cabin, unaware of the tornado about to engulf him. He dusted the map and spread it against the fender of the truck, shrugging hopelessly at the maze of nearby streets.

Jim followed Sergeant Uchida to the gates. He could see that neither the sergeant nor the Japanese driver had any idea of the whereabouts of Woosung, an agricultural district at the mouth of the Yangtze that lay beyond the northern suburbs of Shanghai. The driver gestured toward the Bund and Nantao, and climbed into his cabin. He sat passively when Sergeant Uchida pushed through the bored guards and began to scream abuse at him.

Standing beside the guards, Jim waited for Sergeant Uchida to reach the climax of his tirade, when he would be forced to make a decision. Sure enough, the sergeant searched the crowded skyline of tenement buildings and godowns, then pointed at random to a cobbled street with a disused tramline. Unimpressed, the driver cleared his throat. Wearily he started his engine and spat a ball of phlegm into the road, where it lay at Jim's feet.

"Straight on!" Jim called up to him. "Woosung—it's over there!" He pointed to the street with the rusty tramlines.

Sergeant Uchida cuffed Jim on the head, bruising both his ears. He cuffed him again, bringing blood from his mouth. At that moment a cloud of smoke billowed through the gates. The Annamese women had lit the stove with the rain-soaked firewood, and the smoke filled the open-air cinema, drifting across the benches as if the screen were ablaze.

Glad to be rid of Jim, Sergeant Uchida seized him in his strong hands. He swung him over the tailgate of the truck, shouting to the Japanese guard who sat with the prisoners. The soldier dragged Jim across the laps of the Dutch woman and her father. As the truck pulled away from the detention center, its wheels already locked in the tramlines, Jim clambered forward to the camouflaged driving cabin. He steadied himself against the pitching roof and ignored the stream of oaths hurled at him by the driver. He raised his bloody mouth to the wind, letting the foul odors of Shanghai flush his lungs, happy to be on the way to his parents again.

16

THE WATER RATION

WERE THEY LOST? For an hour, as they trundled through the industrial suburbs of northern Shanghai, Jim gripped the wooden bar behind the driving cabin, his head filled with a dozen compass bearings. He grinned to himself, forgetting his illness and the desperate weeks in the open-air cinema. His knees ached from the constant swaying, and at times he had to hold on to the leather belt of the Japanese soldier beside him. But at last he was moving toward the open countryside and the welcoming world of the prison camps.

The endless streets of Chapei ran past, an area of tenements and derelict cotton mills, police barracks and shantytowns built on the banks of black canals. They drove below the overhead conveyors of a steel works decorated with dragon-festival hoardings, dreams of fire conjured from its silent furnaces. Shuttered pawnshops stood outside the abandoned radio and cigarette factories, and platoons of Chinese puppet troops patrolled the Del Monte brewery and the Dodge truck depot. Jim had never been to Chapei. Before the war a small English boy would have been killed for his shoes within minutes. Now he was safe, guarded by the Japanese soldiers—Jim laughed over this so much that the Dutch woman reached out a hand to calm him.

But Jim relished the fetid air, the smell of human fertilizer from the open sewage congs that signaled the approach of the countryside. Even the driver's hostility failed to worry him. Whenever they stopped at a military checkpoint, the driver would put his head out of the cabin and wave a warning finger at Jim, as if this eleven-year-old prisoner were responsible for the absurd expedition.

Watching the sun's angle, as he had done for hours in the detention center, Jim made certain that they were moving north. They passed the ruins of the Chapei ceramics works, its kilns shaped like the German forts at Tsingtao. Its trademark stood beside the gates, a Chinese teapot three stories high built entirely from green bricks. During the Sino-Japanese War of 1937 it had been holed by shellfire and now resembled a punctured globe of the earth. Thousands of the bricks had migrated across the surrounding fields to the villages beside the works canal, incorporated in the huts and dwellings, a vision of a magical rural China.

These strange dislocations appealed to Jim. For the first time he felt able to enjoy the war. He gazed happily at the burned-out trams and tenement blocks, at the thousands of doors open to the clouds, a deserted city invaded by the sky. It only disappointed him that his fellow prisoners failed to share his excitement. They sat glumly on the benches, staring at their feet. One of the missionary women lay on the floor, tended by another prisoner, a sandy-haired Britisher with a bruised cheek who held her wrist with one hand and pressed her diaphragm with the other. The two English boys, still barely aware of their mother's death, sat between Basie and the Dutch couple.

Jim waited until Basie looked up, but the cabin steward seemed hardly to recognize Jim. His attention had turned to the two boys, and he had moved deftly into the vacuum in their lives. From the page of a Chinese newspaper he folded a series of paper animals, chuckling when the boys gave a weak laugh. Like a depraved conjurer, he slid his hands into the pockets of their school trousers and cardigans, searching for anything of use.

Jim watched him without resentment. He and Basie had collaborated at the detention center in order to stay alive, but Basie, rightly, had dispensed with Jim as soon as he could leave for the camps.

The truck struck a deep gulley in the cobbles, slewed across the road and came to a halt by the grass bank. They had left the northern outskirts of Shanghai and were entering an area of untilled fields and rice paddies. Beyond a line of burial mounds two hundred yards away, a canal ran toward a deserted village. The Japanese driver jumped from his cabin and bent over the front wheels of the truck. He began to talk to the steaming engine, now and then including Jim in his mutterings. He was only twenty years old but had clearly suffered a lifetime of exasperation. Jim kept his head down, but the driver stepped onto the running board, leveled a finger at Jim and delivered a long harangue that sounded like a declaration of war.

The driver returned to his cabin, grumbling over his map, and Basie commented: "Add that up any way you like and we're still lost." Already his attention had moved from the boys to whatever advantage could be gained from their situation. "Jim, do you know where you're taking us?"

"Woosung. I've been to the country club there, Basie."

Basie played with his paper animals. "We're going to the country club," he told the boys. "If Jim can find it for us."

"As long as we reach the river, Basie. Then it's either east or west."

"That's a big help, Jim. East or west . . ."

The sandy-haired Briton beside the missionary woman rose from his knees. There was a large, leaking bruise on his forehead and left cheekbone, as if he had recently been struck in the face by a rifle stock. In some pain, he settled himself on the bench. Long freckled legs emerged from his khaki shorts and ended in a pair of thonged sandals. In his late twenties, he carried no luggage or possessions, but he had the self-assured manner of the Royal Navy officers who cut such a dash at the Shanghai garden parties, thrilling the mothers of Jim's friends. He ignored the Japanese guard, talking across him as if he were a mess boy who would soon be dismissed to his quarters. Jim assumed that he was one of those tiresome Englishmen who refused to grasp that they had been defeated.

The man touched the bruise on his face and turned to Jim, whose ragged figure he appraised without comment. "The Japanese have captured so much ground they've run out of maps," he remarked amiably. "Jim, does that mean they're lost?"

Jim thought about this. "Not really. They just haven't captured any maps."

"Good—never confuse the map with the territory. You'll get us to Woosung."

"Can't we go back to the detention center, Dr. Ransome?" one of the missionaries asked. "We're very tired."

The physician stared at the abandoned paddy fields,

and at the prostrate old woman at his feet. "It might be for the best. This poor soul can't take much more."

The truck moved forward again, trundling at a halfhearted pace down the empty road. Jim returned to his post by the driving cabin and scanned the fields for anything that might remotely resemble Woosung. The doctor's words unsettled him. Even if they were lost, how could he want them to go back to the detention center?

Jim knew that the fury of Sergeant Uchida made it unlikely that the driver would dare to turn back. But he kept a careful watch on Dr. Ransome, trying to guess whether he spoke enough Japanese to demoralize the driver. He seemed to have difficulty with his sight, especially when looking at Jim, at whom he squinted in a curious way. Jim decided that he had entered the war at a later stage than Basie and himself. He had probably come from one of the missionary settlements in the interior and had no idea of what went on at the detention center.

But were they lost or on course? The direction of the shadows cast by the wayside telegraph poles had barely changed—Jim had always been interested in shadows, ever since his father had shown him how to calculate the height of even the highest building by pacing out its shadow on the ground. They were still heading northwest and would soon reach the Shanghai-Woosung railway line. Steam hissed from the truck's radiator. The spray cooled Jim's face, but the driver's fist drummed warningly against his door, and Jim knew that he was deciding when to stop and turn back for Shanghai.

Resigning himself to the wasted journey and to their return to the detention center, Jim studied the guard's bolt-action rifle and its imperial chrysanthemum crest. The Dutch woman pulled at his soot-stained blazer.

"Over there, James. Is that . . . ?"

A burned-out aircraft lay on the banks of a disused canal. Wild grass and nettles grew through its wings, almost invading the cockpit, but the squadron insignia were still legible.

"It's a Nakajima," he told Mrs. Hug, pleased by this shared interest in plane spotting. "It only has two machine guns."

"Only two? But that's very many. . . ."

The Dutch woman seemed impressed, but Jim had turned his attention from the aircraft. On the far side of the paddy field, hidden by the nettles, was the embankment of a railway line. A squad of Japanese soldiers rested on the concrete platform of a wayside station, cooking a meal on a fire of sticks. A camouflaged staff car was parked beside the tracks. It was loaded with coils of wire which these signals engineers were restringing between the telegraph poles.

"Mrs. Hug . . . that's the railway to Woosung!"

As steam bathed the driving cabin, the truck had stopped. It began to reverse. Beside Jim, the Japanese guard was lighting a cigarette for the return journey. Jim pulled at his belt and pointed across the paddy field. The soldier followed Jim's outstretched arm and then pushed him onto the floor. He shouted to the driver, who tossed his map wallet onto the seat beside him. Engine steaming, the truck strained at the camber, made a half-circle and set off along the dirt track to the railway station.

Dr. Ransome steadied the English boys as they slipped from Basie's grasp and swayed against the missionary woman. He helped Jim from the floor.

"Good work, Jim. They'll have water for us—you must be thirsty."

"A bit. I had a drink at the detention center."

"That was sensible. How long were you there?"

Jim had forgotten. "Quite a long time."

"So I imagine." Dr. Ransome brushed the dirt from Jim's blazer. "It used to be a cinema?"

"But they didn't show films."

"I can see that."

Jim sat back, patting his knees and beaming at Mrs. Hug. The prisoners sat weakly on the facing benches, jerked to and fro like life-size puppets that had lost their stuffing. Far from reviving them, the drive from Shanghai had made them look sallow and nervous. But Jim smiled at the rusting aircraft on the canal bank. There was now no danger that they would return to the detention center. The Japanese soldier had thrown away his cigarette and held his rifle in a military way. A signals corporal jumped from the railway platform and crossed the track.

"Mrs. Hug, I don't think we'll be going back to Shanghai."

"No, James—you must have very sharp eyes. When you grow up you should be a pilot."

"I probably will. I have been in a plane, Mrs. Hug. At Hungjao aerodrome."

"Did it fly?"

"Well, in a way." Confidences given to adults often led further than Jim intended. He was aware that Dr. Ransome was watching him. The doctor sat beside Mrs. Hug's father, whose painful breathing he was trying to help. But his eyes were fixed on Jim, taking in his stick-like legs and ragged clothes, his small, excited face. As they reached the railway line he gave Jim an encouraging smile, which Jim decided not to return. He knew that for some reason Dr. Ransome disapproved of him. But Dr. Ransome had not been to the detention center.

They stopped by the railway tracks. The driver saluted the corporal and followed him to the station, where he spread his map across the cabinet of the field telephone. The prisoners sat in the warm sunlight as the corporal pointed to the drained paddies. A haze of dust rose from the untilled earth, a white veil that screened the distant skyscrapers of Shanghai. A convoy of Japanese trucks drove along the road, a brief blare of noise that merged with the distant drone of a cargo aircraft.

Jim changed benches and sat beside Mrs. Hug, who supported her aged father against her breast. Two of the missionary women lay on the floor of the truck as the other prisoners dozed and fretted. Basie had lost interest in the English boys and was watching Jim over the blood-stained collar of his coat.

Thousands of flies gathered around the truck, attracted by the sweat and by the urine running across the wooden boards. Jim waited for the driver to return with his map, but he sat on a bale of telephone wire, talking to two soldiers who cooked the midday meal. Their voices and the clicks of the burning wood carried across the steel tracks, magnified by the dome of light that enclosed them.

Jim fidgeted in his seat as the sun pricked his skin. He could see the smallest detail of everything around him: the flakes of rust on the railway lines, the sawteeth of the nettles beside the truck, the white soil bearing the imprint of its worn tires. Jim counted the blue bristles around the lips of the Japanese soldier guarding them and the globes of mucus which this bored sentry sucked in and out of his nostrils. Jim watched the damp stain spreading around the buttocks of one of the missionary women on the floor, and the flames that fingered the cooking pot on the station platform, reflected in the polished breeches of the stacked rifles.

Only once before had Jim seen the world as vividly as this. Were the American planes about to come again? With an exaggerated squint, intended to annoy Dr. Ransome, he searched the sky. He wanted to see everything, every cobblestone in the streets of Chapei, the overgrown gardens in Amherst Avenue, his mother and father, together in the silver light of the American aircraft.

Without thinking, Jim stood up and shouted. But the Japanese guard pushed him roughly against the bench. The soldiers on the railway platform sat amid the clutter of signals equipment, cramming their mouths with rice and fish. The corporal called to the truck, and the guard stepped over the missionary women and jumped from the tailgate. He rested his rifle on the railway line and moved with his bayonet through the dried stubble of the wild sugarcane. As soon as he had gathered sufficient kindling for the fire, he joined the soldiers on the platform.

For an hour the smoke rose into the sunlight. Jim sat on the bench and brushed the flies from his face, eager to explore the railway station and the crashed aircraft near the canal. Whenever anyone moved, the Japanese shouted from the platform and pointed their cigarettes in a warning way. The prisoners had taken no rations or water with them, but there were two jerricans in the staff car from which the soldiers filled their canteens.

When Mrs. Hug's father was forced to lie on the floor, Dr. Ransome protested to the Japanese. He stood unsteadily by the tailgate, ignoring their abuse and pointing to the exhausted passengers at his feet. The bruise on his cheek had been inflamed by the sun and the flies, and had almost closed his eye. Standing there stoically, he reminded Jim of the beggars parading their wounds on the streets of Shanghai. The Japanese corporal was unimpressed, but after a leisurely stroll around the truck he allowed the prisoners to dismount. Helped by the husbands, Basie and Dr. Ransome eased the old women onto the ground, where they lay in the shade between the rear wheels.

Jim squatted on the white earth, tracing the tire patterns with a stick. How many times would each tire have to rotate before it wore itself through to the canvas? The problem, one of a host that perpetually bothered Jim, was, in fact, fairly easy to solve. Jim smoothed the white dust and made a start at the arithmetic. He gave a cheer when the first fraction canceled itself, and then noticed that he was alone in the open sunlight between the truck and the railway embankment.

Tended by a weary Dr. Ransome, the prisoners huddled in the scanty shade below the tailgate. Basie sat slumped inside his seaman's jacket, and he and the old men looked as dead as the discarded mannequins Jim had often seen in the alley behind the Sincere Company's department store.

They needed water, or one of them would die and they would all have to return to Shanghai. Jim watched the Japanese on the platform. The meal had ended, and two of the soldiers uncoiled a bale of telephone wire. Kicking a stone in front of him, Jim wandered toward the railway embankment. He stepped across the rails and without a pause climbed onto the concrete platform.

Still savoring their meal, the Japanese sat around the

cinders of their fire. They watched Jim as he bowed and stood to attention in his ragged clothes. None of them waved him away, but Jim knew that this was not the time to treat them to his brightest smile. He realized that Dr. Ransome could not approach the Japanese so soon after their meal without being knocked down or even killed.

Jim waited as the driver spoke to the signals corporal. Pointing repeatedly to Jim, he delivered what seemed to be a long lecture on the enormous nuisance to the Japanese Army caused by this one small boy. The corporal laughed at this, in a good humor after his fish. He took a Coca-Cola bottle from his knapsack and half filled it with water from his canteen. Holding it in the air, he beckoned Jim toward him.

Jim took the bottle, bowed steeply and stepped back three paces. Masking their smiles, the Japanese watched him silently. Beside the truck, Basie and Dr. Ransome leaned from the shadows, their eyes fixed on the sun-bright fluid in the bottle. Clearly they assumed that Jim would carry the water to them and share out this unexpected ration.

Carefully, Jim wiped the bottle on the sleeve of his blazer. He lifted it to his lips, drank slowly, trying not to choke, paused and finished the last drops.

The Japanese burst into laughter, chortling to each other with great amusement. Jim laughed with them, well aware that only he, among the British prisoners, appreciated the joke. Basie ventured a wary smile, but Dr. Ransome seemed baffled. The corporal took the Coca-Cola bottle from Jim and filled it to the neck. Still chuckling to themselves, the soldiers climbed to their feet and returned to the task of stringing the telephone wire.

Followed by the driver and the armed guard, Jim carried the bottle across the tracks. He handed it to Dr. Ransome, who stared at him without comment. He drank briefly and passed the tepid liquid to the others, helping the driver to refill the bottle from the canteen. One of the missionary women was sick and vomited the water into the dust at his feet.

Jim took up his position behind the driving cabin. He knew that he had been right to drink the first water himself. The others, including Basie and Dr. Ransome, had been thirsty, but only he had been prepared to risk everything for the few drops of water. The Japanese might have thrown him onto the track and broken his legs across the railway lines, as they did to the Chinese soldiers whom they killed at Siccawei Station. Already Jim felt himself apart from the others, who had behaved as passively as the Chinese peasants. Jim realized that he was closer to the Japanese, who had seized Shanghai and sunk the American fleet at Pearl Harbor. He listened to the sound of a transport plane hidden beyond the haze of white dust and thought again of carrier decks out on the Pacific, of small men in baggy flying suits standing by their unarmored aircraft, ready to chance everything on little more than their own will.

17

A LANDSCAPE OF AIRFIELDS

AS THE DRIVER filled the truck's radiator with water, Dr. Ransome settled Mrs. Hug on the seat beside the English boys. To Jim it seemed that the two missionary women on the floor were now barely alive, with blanched lips and eyes like those of poisoned mice. Flies swarmed over their faces, darting in and out of their nostrils. After lifting them into the truck, Dr. Ransome was too exhausted to help them, and rested his arms on his heavy knees. Their husbands sat side by side and stared at them in a resigned way, as if a taste for lying on the floor were a minor eccentricity shared by their wives.

Jim leaned against the roof of the driving cabin. Aware of the gap that now separated Jim from his fellow prisoners, Dr. Ransome moved forward and sat on the bench next to him. The dusty sunlight and the long journey from Shanghai had leached the pigment from his freckles. Despite his strong chest and legs, he was far more tired than Jim had realized. Blood had broken through the inflamed bruise on his face, and the first pus gathered around his eye.

He bowed and made way for the Japanese soldier who stationed himself next to Jim.

"Well, we all feel better for the water. That was brave of you, Jim. Where do you come from?"

"Shanghai!"

"You're proud of it?"

"Of course. . . ." Jim scoffed at the question, shaking his head as if Dr. Ransome were a provincial country healer. "Shanghai is the biggest city in the world. My father says it's even larger than London."

"Let's hope it can stay larger—there may be one or two hungry winters. Where are your parents, Jim?"

"They went away." Jim thought about his answer, deciding whether to invent some spoof for Dr. Ransome. There was a self-confident air about this young physician that Jim distrusted, the same attitude shown by people newly arrived from England—Jim wondered how the British newsreels were explaining away the surrender of Singapore. He could easily imagine Dr. Ransome getting into a brawl with the Japanese guards and causing everyone trouble. Yet for all his display of public spirit, Dr. Ransome had drunk more than his fair share of the water. Jim had also noticed that Dr. Ransome was less interested in the dying old people than he pretended. "They're at Woosung camp," he said. "They are alive, you know."

"I'm very glad. Woosung camp? So you might be seeing them soon?"

"Very soon . . ." Jim gazed across the silent paddy fields. The thought of seeing his mother made him smile, an act that strained the muscles of his face. His mother would have no idea of all his adventures during the past four months. Even if he told her everything, it would seem like one of those secret afternoons before the war when he had cycled all over Shanghai and come back with hair-raising stories he could never tell. "Yes, I'll be seeing them soon. I want them to meet Basie."

Basie's sallow face withdrew behind the collar of his jacket. He peered warily at the Japanese beside the railway tracks, as if suspicious of what was in store for them in these naked fields. "I'll meet your folks, Jim." To Dr. Ransome he added, without any enthusiasm: "I've been keeping an eye on the boy."

"You kept an eye on me. Basie tried to sell me in Shanghai."

"Did he? That sounds like a good idea."

"To the Hongkew merchants. But I wasn't worth anything. He looked after me as well."

"He's done a good job." Dr. Ransome patted Jim's shoulder. He slipped a hand around Jim's waist and felt his swollen liver, then raised his upper lip and glanced at his teeth.

"It's all right, Jim. I was trying to guess what you've been eating. We'll all have to take up gardening at Woosung. Perhaps the Japanese will sell us a goat."

"A goat?" Jim had never seen a goat, an exotic beast of great moodiness and independence, qualities he admired.

"Are you interested in animals, Jim?"

"Yes . . . not much. What I'm really interested in is aviation."

"Aviation? Aeroplanes, you mean?"

"Not exactly." Casually, Jim added: "I sat in the cockpit of a Japanese fighter."

"You admire Japanese pilots?"

"They're brave. . . ."

"And that's important?"

"It's a good idea if you want to win a war." Jim listened to the drone of a distant aircraft. He was suspicious of Dr. Ransome, of his long legs and his English manner and his interest in teeth. Perhaps he and Basie would team up as corpse robbers. Jim thought about the goat that Dr. Ransome wanted to buy from the Japanese. Everything Jim had read about goats confirmed that they were difficult and wayward creatures, and this suggested that there was something impractical about the physician. Few Europeans had gold teeth, and the only dead people the doctor was likely to see for a long time would be Europeans.

Jim decided to ignore Dr. Ransome. He stood next to the Japanese guard, his hands warmed by the camouflaged roof of the driving cabin. As they set off toward the highway, the soldiers were walking along the railway tracks, unwinding lengths of telephone wire. Were they about to launch a man-carrying kite? The furthest soldier was already lost in the haze of white dust, and his blurred figure seemed to rise from the ground. Jim laughed to himself, thinking that the soldier might suddenly soar into the sky over their heads. Helped by his father, Jim had flown dozens of kites from the garden at Amherst Avenue. Jim was fascinated by the dragon kites that floated behind the Chinese wedding and funeral parties, and by the fighting kites flown from the quays at Pootung, diving across each other with razor-sharp lines coated in powdered glass. But best of all were the man-flying kites that his father had seen in northern China, with a dozen lines held by hundreds of men. One day Jim would fly in a man-flying kite and stand on the shoulder of the wind. . . .

The air rushed into his watering eyes as the truck sped

along the open road. Confident of his bearings, the driver was eager to deliver his prisoners to Woosung and return to Shanghai before nightfall. Jim held tight to the cabin roof, while the prisoners huddled on the seats behind him. The two missionary husbands were already sitting on the floor, and Dr. Ransome helped Mrs. Hug to lie under the bench.

But Jim had lost interest in them. They were now entering an area of military airfields. These former Chinese bases, which once guarded the Yangtze estuary, were being occupied by the Japanese army and naval air forces. They passed a bomb-damaged fighter base where Japanese engineers were welding a new roof onto the steel shell of a hangar. A line of Zero pursuit planes stood on the grass field, and a pilot in full flying gear strode between the wings. Without thinking, Jim waved to him, but the pilot was lost among the propellers.

Two miles ahead, beyond an empty village and its burned-out pagoda, they were delayed by a convoy of trucks carrying the wings and fuselages of two-engined bombers. A squadron of the machines faced the afternoon sun, ready to take off and attack the Chinese armies to the west. All this activity excited Jim. When they stopped at the military checkpoint on the Soochow Road, he was impatient to move on. He sat next to Basie, kicking his heels as a sergeant in the *kempetai* checked the list of prisoners and Dr. Ransome protested about the condition of the missionary women.

Soon after, they left the highway and joined an unpaved secondary road that ran beside an industrial canal. Japanese tanks moved past, lashed to the decks of motorized lighters, while their gun crews slept on the canvas hatches. Usually Jim's imagination would have feasted on these battle vehicles, but by now he was only interested in aircraft. He wished he had flown with the Japanese pilots as they attacked Pearl Harbor and destroyed the U.S. Pacific Fleet, or ridden in the torpedo bombers that had sunk the *Repulse* and the *Prince of Wales*. Perhaps, when the war had ended, he would join the Japanese Air Force and wear the Rising Sun stitched to his shoulders, like the American pilots who had flown with the Flying Tigers and worn the flag of Nationalist China on their leather jackets.

Although his legs were exhausted, Jim was still standing behind the driver's cabin as they sped toward the gates of the internment camp at Woosung. In his mind, Jim had identified the Japanese aircraft of the Yangtze plain with his confidence that he would soon see his parents again. A single-engined fighter overtook them and climbed into the late-afternoon sky, lifted by the golden glaze on the undersurface of its wings. Jim raised his arms and let the sun fall on the camouflage paint that stained his hands and wrists, imagining that he too was an aircraft. Behind him the Dutch woman had collapsed on the floor of the truck. She lay at the feet of her elderly father as Dr. Ransome and the Japanese soldier tried to lift her onto the seat.

They crossed a wooden bridge over the arm of an artificial lake and passed the burned-out shell of the country club, whose mock-Tudor timbers of painted cement had alone failed to catch fire. The hull of a pleasure launch lay in the shallows, its decks penetrated by reeds that advanced up the beach to the embers of the hotel.

Ahead of them a military truck was turning through the gates of a disused stockyard, through which an even greater fire had recently swept. Bored Japanese soldiers lounged outside the guardhouse and watched a gang of Chinese laborers nailing lengths of barbed wire to a line of pine posts. Behind the guardhouse was the building contractor's store, surrounded by piles of planks and fencing timber, and a bamboo shelter where a second group of coolies dozed on their mats beside a charcoal brazier.

The truck stopped by the guardhouse, where the driver and his prisoners together gazed at this desolate site. The former stockyard was being converted into a civilian camp, but no prisoners would be interned here for months. Jim sat between Basie and Dr. Ransome, annoyed with himself for assuming that his mother and father would be at the first camp they visited.

A prolonged argument began between the Japanese driver and the sergeant in charge of the camp's construction. It was clear that the sergeant had already decided that this truck and its consignment of Allied prisoners did not exist. He ignored the driver's protests and waved his cigarette in a thoughtful manner as he paced across the wooden porch of the guardhouse. At last he pointed to a patch of nettle-covered ground inside the gates, which he had apparently deemed to be a no-man's-land between the camp and the outside world.

Dr. Ransome peered at the acres of fire-gutted stalls, a burned-out maze through which cattle had once been steered. "This can't be the camp. Unless they want us to build it."

Basie's pale ears emerged from his seaman's collar. He was barely strong enough to sit upright but could still catch the faintest scent of an opportunity. "Woosung? There might be advantages, Doctor . . . being the first people here. . . ."

Dr. Ransome began to help Mrs. Hug from the floor, but the Japanese soldier raised the stock of his rifle and waved him back to his seat. The sergeant stood in the nettles, gazing over the tailgate at the exhausted prisoners. The old women lay in the pools of urine at their husbands' feet. The English brothers huddled against Basie, while Mrs. Hug leaned on her father's knees.

Deliberately, Jim thought of his mother, and of the happy hours he had spent playing bridge in her bedroom. When the tears ran into his nose he sucked them into his parched throat. Could Dr. Ransome teach himself how to cry? He looked at the glowing end of the sergeant's cigarette and at the warm hearth of the charcoal stove in the twilight. The gang of laborers by the barbed-wire fence was walking back to the bamboo shelter.

"You're tiring everyone, Jim," Dr. Ransome warned him. "Sit still or I'll ask Basie to sell you to the Japanese."

"They wouldn't want me." Jim slipped from Dr. Ransome's grasp. He knelt on the bench beside the driver's cabin. Rocking to and fro, he watched the sergeant lead the two Japanese to the guardhouse, where the soldiers were eating their evening meal. There were bottles of beer and rice wine on the wooden table, lit by a kerosene lamp. A Chinese coolie squatted by the brazier, fanning the charcoal to a white blaze, and the smell of warm fat drifted across the air.

Somehow Jim had to catch the eyes of the soldiers in the guardhouse. He knew that far from being concerned for their unwanted prisoners, the Japanese would leave them there all night. In the morning they would be too ill to move on to the next camp and would have to return to the detention center in Shanghai.

The evening air settled over the burned-out stockyards. The Chinese coolies finished their meal and sat under the bamboo shelter, drinking rice wine and playing cards. The Japanese drank beer in the guardhouse. Hundreds of stars were coming out over the Yangtze, and with them the navigation lights of the military aircraft. Two miles to the north, beyond the lines of burial mounds, Jim saw the rigging lights of a Japanese freighter heading for the open sea, its white superstructure sailing like a castle across the ghostly fields.

A foul smell rose from one of the missionary women. Her husband sat beside her on the floor, leaning against Dr. Ransome's legs. Eager to catch sight of the freighter, Jim lifted himself onto the roof of the driving cabin. Sitting there, he watched the freighter slip away into the night and then turned to the stars over his head. Since the previous summer, Jim had been teaching himself the main constellations.

"Basie . . ." Jim felt giddy; the night sky was sliding toward him. Losing his balance, he rolled across the cabin roof, then sat up to see the driver and the Japanese soldier stride from the guardhouse. They carried wooden staves in their hands, and Jim assumed that they were coming to beat him for sitting on the cabin. Quickly he slipped onto the floor and lay beside the Dutch woman.

The driver unshackled the tailgate. As it fell with a clatter, he rattled his stave against the swinging chains. He shouted at the prisoners and waved them from the truck. Helped by Dr. Ransome, Mrs. Hug and the old men lowered themselves into the nettles. Joined by Basie and the English boys, they followed the soldier toward the timber yard. The two missionary women lay on the soiled floor. They were still alive, but the driver waved his stave at Dr. Ransome and beckoned him away from them.

Jim stepped across the damp floor and jumped onto the ground. He was about to run after Dr. Ransome when the driver held his shoulder and pointed to the sergeant in the guardhouse porch. He stood in the kerosene light, a small sack like a weighted cosh in his hand.

Cautiously, Jim walked up to the sergeant, who threw the sack onto the ground at his feet. Jim knelt in the deep ruts left by the truck's tires and treated the sergeant to his keenest smile. Inside the sack were nine sweet potatoes.

For the next hour Jim moved busily around the yard. While the prisoners rested in the timber store, he relit the charcoal stove. Under the bored eyes of the Chinese coolies he fanned the embers into a flame, then fed the blaze with shavings of waste timber. Dr. Ransome and the English boys brought him a bucket of water from the butt behind the guardhouse. Although Mrs. Hug had been drinking from the bucket, Jim decided to wait until the potato water had cooled. Dr. Ransome tried to help him with the iron cong, but Jim pushed him aside. The Eurasian women at the detention center had taught Jim that potatoes cooked most quickly in shallow water under the tightest lid.

Later, before he carried the boiled potatoes to the timber store, Jim kept the largest one for himself. He sat next to Dr. Ransome on the pine planks, while the missionary husbands lay in the sawdust, unable to eat. Jim regretted that they had been given even the smallest potato. At the same time, he needed these old people to survive, if they were to move on to the next camp. The Dutch woman seemed well, even if she had given her potato to the English boys. But Basie was already scanning the timber store, making an inventory of its possibilities inside his head, and if they stayed at Woosung camp Jim would never find his mother and father.

"Here you are, Jim." Dr. Ransome handed Jim his potato. He had taken a small bite, but most of the sweet pith was intact. "It's a good one, you'll enjoy it."

"Say, thanks. . . ." Jim swiftly devoured the second

potato. Dr. Ransome's gesture puzzled him. The Japanese were kind to children, and the two American sailors had befriended him in a fashion, but Jim knew that the English were not really interested in children.

He brought the pail of warm potato water for Basie and himself, and offered the pithy liquid to the others. He knelt beside the old missionary men, clicking his teeth and hoping that the sight of the Cathedral School badge would strike some religious spark in their minds and revive them.

"They don't look very well," he confided to Dr. Ransome. "But they'll probably eat their potatoes in the morning."

"They probably will. Rest, Jim—you'll wear yourself out looking after everyone. We'll be on our way tomorrow."

"Well . . . there might be a long way to go." The second potato had comforted Jim, and for the first time he felt sorry for the infected wound on Dr. Ransome's face. Returning the favor, he confided: "If you ever go to the funeral piers at Nantao, don't drink the water."

Jim lay on the soft sawdust with its soothing scent of pine. Through the open doors of the timber store he watched the navigation lights of the Japanese aircraft crossing the night. After a few minutes Jim was forced to admit that he could recognize none of the constellations. Like everything else since the war, the sky was in a state of change. For all their movement, the Japanese aircraft were its only fixed points, a second zodiac above the broken land.

18

VAGRANTS

"RIGHT . . . RIGHT . . . NO . . . I mean left!"

Jim leaned through the passenger window of the cabin and shouted to the driver as the truck labored onto the wooden deck of the pontoon bridge. The Japanese field engineers had built this temporary crossing over the Soochow Creek in the weeks following the Pearl Harbor attack, but already the bridge was coming apart under the heavy traffic. As the truck moved toward the first steel pontoon, the wet planking began to splay in its worn ropes.

Posted as lookout by the Japanese driver, Jim watched the front tire forcing the planks into the water. He had always enjoyed the sight of water rising through grilles or climbing the steps of a jetty. The brown stream washed the dust from the worn tire and revealed the manufacturer's name embossed on its side—befitting Jim's quest for his parents, a British company, Dunlop. The truck tilted sideways, leaning on its weak springs. Somewhere behind Jim a body rolled across the floor of the truck, but Jim was fascinated by the water sluicing across the dented hubcap, streaming through the wheel like the jets of a secret fountain.

"Left . . . left!" Jim shouted, but the soldier at the tailgate was already bellowing in alarm. With a weary sigh, the Japanese driver pulled on the handbrake, ordered Jim from the cabin and stepped onto the river-washed planks.

Jim crawled through the rear window onto the deck of the truck. He crossed Dr. Ransome's outstretched legs and knelt on the bench, ready to take a close interest in the mounting argument between the driver and the Japanese guard.

Two hundred yards downstream, the unit of field engineers was raising the central span of the old railway bridge. Jim was happy to watch them at work. Most of the morning he had felt lightheaded, and the steady flow of water through the pontoons soothed his eyes. He counted his pulse, wondering if he had caught beriberi or malaria or any other of the diseases that he had heard Dr. Ransome discussing with Mrs. Hug. Jim was curious to try out some new diseases, but then remembered the detention center and the American planes he had seen over Shanghai. The previous night, when they had camped next to a pig farm run by the Japanese gendarmerie, Jim suspected that even Dr. Ransome had seen the planes.

Certainly Dr. Ransome did not look too well. Since leaving Woosung, the wound in his face had infected the whole of his jaw and nose. He now lay on the floor of the truck, his freckled legs ominously white in the bright sun. He was asleep, but seemed to be thinking very hard about something with one-half of his head. He had last spoken to Jim before their evening meal, when he made sure that Jim received the prisoners' full ration from the

Japanese guard. By an enormous effort of will he had told Jim to strip and had washed his clothes in the pig's water trough, using a piece of scented soap he borrowed from Mrs. Hug.

Basie sat on the floor beside him, the two English boys asleep with their heads in his lap. The cabin steward was still conscious but had withdrawn into himself, his soft face like the flesh of a fading fruit. Often he was sick, and the floor of the truck was covered with vomit and urine which he nagged at Jim to clear away.

Mrs. Hug and her father also lay on the floor, rarely speaking to each other and concentrating on every bump in the road. Fortunately the two missionary couples had stayed behind at Woosung. Their places were taken by a middle-aged Englishman and his prim wife from the British Consulate at Nanking. They sat next to the Japanese guard at the rear of the truck, their faces drained of expression by some tragedy that had overtaken them. Between them was a wicker suitcase filled with clothing, which the driver and the guard searched every evening, helping themselves to the shoes and slippers. The couple stared without ever speaking at the landscape of paddy fields and canals, and Jim assumed that they had lost interest in the war.

Twice a day, when the Japanese stopped to make themselves a wayside meal, the guard ordered Jim to pass an earthenware water jar around the prisoners. For the rest of the time Jim was left to himself, free to concentrate on the task of guiding this antiquated truck toward the internment camp that held his mother and father.

For days now they had been on the road, making an erratic circuit of the countryside ten miles to the northwest of Shanghai. Jim had lost count of the exact number of days, but at least they were moving forward, and luckily the Japanese were not in any way discouraged by the worsening condition of their prisoners.

On the first day, after setting out from Woosung, a three-hour drive through the open country took them to the former St. Francis Xavier seminary on the Soochow Road, one of the first prison camps established by the Japanese in the weeks after Pearl Harbor. The seminary was already filled with military personnel. All afternoon they waited behind a queue of commandeered Shanghai Transit Company buses, which together carried several hundred Dutch and Belgian civilians. Jim peered keenly through the double wire fence. Gangs of British soldiers lounged by their huts or sat out on the assembly ground in the polished pews taken from the seminary chapel, like the congregation of an open-air cathedral. But there were no male civilians, women or children. The Japanese guards were busy taking an endless series of roll calls and had no time for the new arrivals hoping to be admitted. Jim stood on the seat, waving over the wire so that everyone in the camp could see him.

However, the hundreds of bored soldiers were not interested in these civilians and their Shanghai buses. Jim was relieved when they were turned away. As they set off toward Soochow, the driver allowed him to sit in the front cabin. In some way this restless English boy, who had so aggravated him, now offered a small measure of security. Jim was unable to read the map, printed in Japanese characters, or understand a word of the long monologues addressed to the insect-smeared windshield. But he knelt on the front seat, clicking his teeth and leaning out of the window to watch any passing aircraft. The entire Japanese Air Force seemed to be on its way to attack the Chinese armies in the west.

The flat countryside by the Shanghai-Soochow road

had been a war ground, and the miles of rotting trenches and rust-stained blockhouses reminded Jim of the encyclopedia illustrations of Ypres and the Somme, an immense museum of battle that no one had visited for years. The debris of war, and the flights of bombers and fighter planes, revived Jim. He wanted to soar like a fighting kite over the winding parapets and land on one of the massive forts built out of thousands of sandbags among the burial mounds. It disappointed Jim that none of his fellow prisoners was interested in the war. It would have helped to keep up their spirits, a task that Jim was finding more and more difficult.

In many ways, Jim liked to imagine, he was the real leader of this troupe of traveling prisoners. At times, as he carried the heavy water jar and lit the stove in the evening, he knew that he was little more than their Number Two Coolie. But without Jim to gather the firewood and boil the sweet potatoes, even Dr. Ransome and Basie would have gone the way of the missionary women. Jim noticed that after leaving the gendarmerie station at the pig farm, they all allowed themselves to become ill. During the night the Japanese had been beating a Chinese thief, and the man's voice screamed across the water-filled paddies, shaking the dark surface. The next day everyone lay on the floor of the truck, Basie with his lungs and Dr. Ransome unable to see through his infected eye.

Jim felt feverish, but he watched the Japanese planes overhead. The sound of their engines cleared his mind. Whenever his spirits flagged or he felt sorry for himself, he thought of the silver aircraft he had seen at the detention center, warning him back from his own death.

The truck was moving across the pontoon bridge, manhandled by a squad of Japanese field engineers. Unable to steady himself, Jim slipped from the bench. Dr. Ransome reached out weakly to hold him.

"Hang on, Jim. Stay up front with the driver—make sure he keeps going. . . ."

Dozens of flies festered on Dr. Ransome's face, feeding on the wound around his eye. Beside him Basie lay with Paul and David, Mrs. Hug and her father. Only the English couple with the wicker suitcase full of shoes sat beside the soldier at the rear of the truck.

Jim straightened his blazer as a Japanese corporal climbed over the tailgate. An angry man with wet boots, he shouted commands to the soldiers pushing the truck across the bridge. When they reached the opposite bank, the soldiers walked along the water's edge to their work on the railway bridge. The corporal began to abuse the driver, clearly disgusted by the condition of the prisoners. He drew his Mauser pistol and gestured to an antitank ditch on the bank they had left behind.

Jim was relieved when the corporal strode back to his bridge. However ill they were, he did not want them to rest in the tank ditch. It was an effort to sit on the bench, and he was tempted to lie on the floor next to Dr. Ransome so that he could stare straight at the sky. The landscape of paddy fields, creeks and deserted villages moved past, emerging from a white haze like the milled bones of all the dead of China. The dust cloaked the cabin and bonnet of the truck, camouflaging it for the realm it was about to enter. How long had they been on the road? The lines of burial mounds were trying to trick Jim's eyes; they moved in waves toward the lumbering vehicle, a sea of the dead. The open coffins lay empty, ready to catch the American pilots who would soon fall from the air. There were thousands of coffins, enough to take Dr. Ransome and Basie, his mother and father and Vera, Number Two Coolie and himself. . . .

The truck had stopped, the cabin striking Jim's head. A group of huts with tar-paper roofs stood beside the road, set back from a barbed-wire fence that separated them from the embankment of a canal. Idly, Jim gazed at this small internment camp built in the compound of a ceramics factory. A pair of metal lighters had capsized at their moorings, and miniature railcars still loaded with ceramic tiles stood in the yard beside the kilns. Two of the brick warehouses had been incorporated into the camp by the barbed-wire fence that divided the factory site. Men and women sunned themselves on the steps of the wooden huts; lines of washing fluttered between the windows, a cheerful spring semaphore.

Jim rested his chin on the side panel of the truck. Below him, Dr. Ransome was trying to sit up. The guard jumped from the tailgate and walked toward the entrance, where a Shanghai University bus was surrounded by Japanese soldiers. The passengers stared through the dust-stained windows. There were two nuns in black wimples, several children of Jim's age, and some twenty British men and women. Already a crowd of prisoners had gathered at the wire. Hands in the pockets of their ragged shorts, they stared silently as a Japanese sergeant boarded the bus to inspect the prisoners.

Dr. Ransome was kneeling at the rear of the truck, the wound on his face hidden behind his hand. Jim stared at an Englishwoman in a frayed cotton dress who stood by the fence, her hands clasping the wire. She looked at Jim with the same expression that he had seen on the face of the German mother in the Columbia Road.

The bus was moving into the camp through the open

gates. The Japanese sergeant stood in the passenger door, pistol in hand, waving back the crowd of prisoners. From their sullen faces it was clear that they greeted these new arrivals with little enthusiasm, more mouths to be fed from their meager rations. Jim sat up as the truck lumbered forward to the gates. Dr. Ransome fell to the floor and was helped onto a seat by the English couple with the wicker suitcase.

Jim smiled at the woman walking along the wire. When she stretched a hand to him, he wondered if she were a friend of his mother. The camp was filled with families, and somewhere among the strolling couples might be his parents. He peered at the English faces, at the gangs of boys laughing behind the Japanese sentries. To his surprise he felt a moment of regret, of sadness that his quest for his mother and father would soon be over. As long as he searched for them he was prepared to be hungry and ill, but now that the search had ended he felt saddened by the memory of all he had been through, and of how much he had changed. He was closer now to the ruined battlefields and this fly-infested truck, to the nine sweet potatoes in the sack below the driver's seat, even in a sense to the detention center, than he would ever be again to his house in Amherst Avenue.

The truck stopped by the gates. The Japanese sergeant peered over the tailgate at the prisoners lying on the floor. He pushed Dr. Ransome back with his Mauser, but the injured physician lowered himself to the ground, where he knelt at the sergeant's feet, catching his breath. Already the crowd of internees had begun to disperse. Hands in their pockets, the men strolled back to the huts and sat with the women on the steps.

Flies swarmed over the truck and settled on the damp pools that covered the floor. They hovered around Jim's mouth, feeding at the sores on his gums. For ten minutes the Japanese soldiers argued with each other, while the driver waited with Dr. Ransome. Two senior British prisoners stepped through the gates and joined the discussion.

"Woosung Camp?"

"No, no, no. . . ."

"Who sent them? In this condition?"

Avoiding Dr. Ransome, they approached the truck and stared at the prisoners through the cloud of flies. As Jim kicked his heels and whistled to himself, they watched him without expression. The Japanese sentries opened the barbed-wire gates, but the British prisoners immediately closed them and began to shout at the Japanese sergeant. When Dr. Ransome stepped forward to remonstrate with them, the British waved him away.

"Get back, man. . . ."

"We can't take you, Doctor. There are children here."

Dr. Ransome climbed into the truck and sat on the floor beside Jim. The effort of standing had exhausted him, and he lay back with his hand over his wound as the flies fought between his fingers.

Mrs. Hug and the English couple with the wicker suitcase had waited silently through the arguments. As the Japanese soldiers returned to the camp and locked the gates, Mrs. Hug said: "They won't take us. The British camp leaders . . ."

Jim gazed at the prisoners wandering across the compound. Groups of boys played football in the brick yard of the ceramics works. Were his mother and father hiding among the kilns? Perhaps, like the British camp leaders, they wanted Jim to go away, frightened of the flies and the sickness that he had brought with him from Shanghai.

Jim helped Basie and Dr. Ransome to drink, and then

sat on the opposite bench. He turned his back on the camp, on the British prisoners and their children. All his hopes rested in the landscape around him, in its past and future wars. He felt a strange lightness in his head, not because his parents had rejected him, but because he expected them to do so, and no longer cared.

19

THE RUNWAY

IN THE HOUR before dusk they entered an area of abandoned battlefields nine miles to the south of Shanghai. The afternoon light rose into the air, as if returning to the sun a small part of the strength it had cast to the indifferent fields. The terrain of trenches and blockhouses seemed to have sprung fully armed from Jim's head. A tank sat like a wheeled shack at the junction of the Shanghai and Hangchow roads, the sun's spotlights shining through its open hatches. The trenches hunted among the burial mounds, a maze lost within itself.

Beyond the crossroads a wooden bridge spanned a canal. Its white piles, from which the rain had leached all trace of resin, were as soft as pumice. The driver folded his map and fanned himself with the canvas wallet, reluctant to risk his wheels on the worn timbers. Mrs. Hug and the English couple sat at the back of the truck, their shadows reaching across the white beds of the drained paddy fields. Jim brushed the flies from Dr. Ransome's face and patted his head. He imagined that he was one of the shadows, a black carpet lying across the tired land.

A mile to the south, between the burial mounds, he could see the tailplanes of a row of parked aircraft, feathers of bone against the darkening air. Jim studied the aircraft, recognizing the plump fuselages and radial engines. They were Brewster Buffaloes, a type of American fighter that had been no match for the Japanese.

Was it here, among the burial mounds, that the American aircraft waited before taking off into his mind? However, the Japanese driver had also seen the tailplanes. He threw down his cigarette and shouted to the guard, who had jumped from the truck and was testing the rotting planks of the bridge.

"Lunghua . . . Lunghua!"

The engine started, and the driver turned east at the crossroads, setting course for this distant airfield.

"We're going to Lunghua Airfield, Dr. Ransome," Jim called between his knees. The physician lay on the floor beside Basie and the Dutch woman's father, watching Jim with his single eye. "There are Brewster Buffaloes—the Americans must have won the war."

Jim let the warm air rush into his face. They approached the military airfield, the largest grass aerodrome that Jim had seen near Shanghai. There were three metal hangars and a wooden engineering workshop built in the former car park of Lunghua Pagoda. Dozens of aircraft were drawn up on the tarmac beside the hangars, high-performance fighters of advanced design. The three Brewster Buffaloes, their American markings painted out, sat by the edge of the field. A team of engineers with a powerful crane lifted an antiaircraft gun to the upper decks of the stone pagoda.

The driver stopped at a checkpoint, where Japanese soldiers manned a fortified emplacement. As the sentries paced about in the dusk, their corporal spoke into a field telephone. They were waved through to the perimeter road. The rutted surface had been stiffened with straw matting, churned to a pith by a convoy of vehicles loaded with building stone. A truck swayed past them with a cargo of roofing tiles torn from the tenements of the Old City.

Pairs of armed guards patrolled the perimeter road, their bayonets cutting the somber air. Two single-engined transport aircraft were parked on the edge of the field. Accompanied by his ground crew, a Japanese pilot spoke to two fellow officers in uniform. The pilot pointed to the truck as it rattled past, and it occurred to Jim that perhaps he and Basie and Dr. Ransome were about to be flown from Shanghai, and that he would soon join his parents in Hong Kong or Japan.

Jim waited for the truck to stop beside the planes, but the driver pressed on to the southern perimeter of the airfield. The smooth grass fell away into a broken terrain of wild sugarcane and unleveled earth. They crossed the dried bed of an irrigation ditch and followed the truck loaded with roofing tiles into a narrow valley hidden between walls of nettles. Clouds of ashy white dust rose into the evening air as the military vehicles in front of them tipped their loads of stone and rubble onto the ground. Armed soldiers and air force police guarded the valley, rifles in hand, their uniforms blanched by the dust.

Watched by the Japanese sentries, hundreds of captured Chinese soldiers in ragged tunics were carrying the tiles and cobblestones from the dump and laying the bed of a concrete runway. Even in the dusk light, and despite all the privations of the past months, Jim could see the meager condition of these Chinese prisoners. Many were emaciated to the point of death. They sat naked in the trampled nettles, a single roof tile held in their hands like the fragment of a begging bowl. Others climbed the shallow slope to the edge of the airfield, wicker baskets laden with stones clasped to their chests.

The truck stopped by the dump. With a rattle of chains, the tailgate fell. Led by the Japanese soldier, Mrs. Hug and the English couple lowered themselves to the ground. Dr. Ransome knelt by the seats, barely able to control his clumsy body.

"Right, Jim—let's get everyone to their quarters. Help Mrs. Hug. Basie, boys . . ."

He stood unsteadily but managed to lift Basie to his feet. The cabin steward's face was already covered by a layer of talc, the delicate woman's skin that Jim had first seen near the funeral piers at Nantao. Holding Jim's shoulder, he shuffled along the damp floor of the truck.

They dismounted and stood together in the cloud of white dust beside the dump. Mrs. Hug sat with her father on a heap of cobbles, holding the English boys by the hands. The Chinese soldiers filled their baskets and spat on the stones. As they climbed the broken earth to the runway, their chalky figures seemed to illuminate the evening air.

Around them the Japanese sentries watched without moving. Fifty feet away, on the southern slope of the valley, two sergeants sat on bamboo chairs by the edge of a pit that had been freshly dug among the nettles. Their boots and the ground at their feet were covered with lime.

Jim picked up a gray ceramic tile. None of the Japanese guards appeared to care whether they worked on the runway, but Basie already held a cobblestone in his hands. Jim followed a naked Chinese soldier toward the runway. He climbed the slope and walked across the furrowed soil. The Chinese threw down their baskets and returned to the dump. Jim laid his tile on the shallow trench filled with stones and broken bricks that ran across the airfield into the night. Basie pushed past him and dropped the cobble at his feet. He swayed in the dust, trying to brush the chalky powder from his hands.

Behind them, Dr. Ransome stood at the dump with Mrs. Hug and the English couple. He was arguing with a Japanese soldier, who waved him toward the runway. Holding his rifle in one hand, the soldier picked a roof tile from the dump and handed it to Dr. Ransome.

Jim waited by the broken stones. He stared into the dusk along the white surface of the runway. He remembered the swirling grass at Hungjao aerodrome and tried to imagine the slipstreams of the Brewster Buffaloes. Jim turned to the transport aircraft parked by the perimeter road. The Japanese pilot and the uniformed officers were walking through the grass toward the runway. They stopped on the muddy verge, laughing to each other as they inspected the work. Their buckles and polished badges shone like the jewelry of the Europeans who had visited the battlefields near Hungjao before the war.

Jim stepped into the grass, leaving the dust clouds and the lines of Chinese soldiers. He wanted to see the parked aircraft for the last time, to stand under the dark span of their wings. He knew that the Chinese soldiers were being worked to death, that these starving men were laying their own bones in a carpet for the Japanese bombers who would land upon them. Then they would go to the pit, where the lime-booted sergeants waited with their Mausers. And after laying their stones, he and Basie and Dr. Ransome would also go to the pit.

The last light had faded from the fuselages of the aircraft, but Jim could smell their engines on the night air. He inhaled the odor of oil and engine coolant. Already he had begun to shut out the voices around him,

the white bodies of the Chinese soldiers and the runway
of bones. He shut out the young Japanese pilot in his
flying suit, who was pointing to Jim and shouting to the
sergeants beside the pit. Jim hoped that his parents were
safe and dead. Brushing the dust from his blazer, he ran
toward the shelter of the aircraft, eager to enfold himself
in their wings.

TWO

20

LUNGHUA CAMP

VOICES FRETTED ALONG the murmuring wire, carried like stressed notes on the strings of a harp. Fifty feet from the perimeter fence, Jim lay in the deep grass beside the pheasant trap. He listened to the Japanese guards arguing with each other as they conducted their hourly patrol of the camp. Now that the American air attacks had become a daily event, the Japanese soldiers no longer slung their rifles over their shoulders. They clasped the long-barreled weapons in both hands and were so nervous that if they saw Jim outside the camp perimeter they would shoot at him without thinking.

Jim watched them through the netting of the pheasant trap. Only the previous day they had shot a Chinese coolie trying to steal into the camp. He recognized one of the guards as Private Kimura, a large-boned farmer's son who had grown almost as much as Jim in his years at the camp. The private's strong back had burst through his faded tunic, and only his ammunition webbing held the tattered garment together.

Before the war finally turned against the Japanese,

Private Kimura often invited Jim to the bungalow he shared with three other guards and allowed him to wear his *kendo* armor. Jim could remember the elaborate ceremony as the Japanese soldiers dressed him in the metal and leather armor and the ripe smell of Private Kimura's body that filled the helmet and shoulder guards. He remembered the burst of violence as Private Kimura attacked him with the two-handed sword, the whirlwind of blows that struck his helmet before he could fight back. Jim's head had rung for days. Giving him his orders, Basie had been forced to shout until he woke the men's dormitory in E block, and Dr. Ransome had called Jim into the camp hospital and examined his ears.

Remembering those powerful arms and the quickness of Private Kimura's eyes, Jim lay flat in the long grass behind the trap. For once he was glad that the trap had failed to net a bird. The two Japanese had stopped by the wire fence and were scanning the group of abandoned buildings that lay outside the northwest perimeter of Lunghua Camp. Beside them, just within the camp, was the derelict hulk of the assembly hall, the curved balcony of its upper circle open to the sky. The camp occupied the site of a teacher-training college that had been bombed and overrun during the fighting around Lunghua Aerodrome in 1937. The damaged buildings nearest to the airfield had been excluded from the camp, and it was here, in the long grass quadrangles between the gutted residence halls, that Jim set his pheasant traps. After roll call that morning, he had slipped through the fence where it emerged from a bank of nettles surrounding a forgotten blockhouse on the airfield perimeter. Leaving his shoes on the blockhouse steps, he waded along a shallow canal and then crawled through the deep grass between the ruined buildings.

The first of the traps was only a few feet from the perimeter fence, a distance that had seemed enormous to Jim when he first crept through the barbed wire. He had looked back at the secure world of the camp, at the barrack huts and water tower, at the guardhouse and dormitory blocks, almost afraid that he had been banished from them forever. Dr. Ransome often called Jim a "free spirit," as he roved across the camp, hunting down some new idea in his head. But here, in the deep grass between the ruined buildings, he felt weighted by an unfamiliar gravity.

For once making the most of this inertia, Jim lay behind the trap. An aircraft was taking off from Lunghua Airfield, clearly silhouetted against the yellow facades of the apartment houses in the French Concession, but Jim ignored the plane. The soldier beside Private Kimura shouted to the children playing in the balcony of the assembly hall. Kimura was walking back to the wire. He scanned the surface of the canal and the clumps of wild sugarcane. The poor rations of the past year—the Japanese guards were almost as badly fed as their British and American prisoners—had drawn the last of the adolescent fat from Kimura's arms. After a recent attack of tuberculosis, his strong face was puffy and coolielike. Dr. Ransome had repeatedly warned Jim never to wear Private Kimura's *kendo* armor. A fight between them would be less one-sided, even though Jim was only fourteen. But for the rifle, he would have liked to challenge Kimura. . . .

As if aware of the threat within the grass, Private Kimura called to his companion. He leaned his rifle against the pine fencing post, stepped through the wire and stood in the deep nettles. Flies rose from the shallow canal and settled on his lips, but Kimura ignored them and stared at the strip of water that separated him from Jim and the pheasant traps.

Could he see Jim's footprints in the soft mud? Jim crawled away from the trap, but the clear outline of his body lay in the crushed grass. Kimura was rolling his tattered sleeves, ready to wrestle with his quarry. Jim watched him stride through the nettles. He was certain that he could outrun Kimura, but not the bullet in the second soldier's rifle. How could he explain to Kimura that the pheasant traps had been Basie's idea? It was Basie who had insisted on the elaborate camouflage of leaves and twigs, and who made Jim climb through the wire twice a day, even though they had never seen a bird, let alone caught one. It was important to keep in with Basie, who had small but reliable sources of food. He could tell Kimura that Basie knew about the secret camp radio, but then the extra food would cease.

What most worried Jim was the thought that, if Kimura struck him, he would fight back. Few boys of his own age dared to touch Jim, and in the last year, since the rations had failed, few men. However, if he fought back against Kimura he would be dead.

Jim calmed himself, calculating the best moment to stand up and surrender. He would bow to Kimura, show no emotion and hope that the hundreds of hours he had spent hanging around the guardhouse—albeit at Basie's instigation—would count in his favor. He had once given English lessons to Kimura, but although they were clearly losing the war the Japanese had not been interested in learning English.

Jim waited for Kimura to climb the bank toward him. The soldier stood in the center of the canal, a bright black object gleaming in his hand. The creeks, ponds and disused wells within Lunghua Camp held an armory of rusting weapons and unstable ammunition abandoned during the 1937 hostilities. Jim peered through the grass at the pointed cylinder, assuming that the tidal water in the canal had uncovered an old artillery shell or mortar bomb.

Kimura shouted to the second soldier waiting by the barbed wire. He brushed the flies from his face and spoke to the object, as if murmuring to a baby. He raised it behind his head, in the position taken by Japanese soldiers before throwing a grenade. Jim waited for the explosion, and then realized that Private Kimura was holding a large freshwater turtle. The creature's head emerged from its carapace, and Kimura began to laugh excitedly. His tubercular face resembled a small boy's, reminding Jim that Private Kimura had once been a child, as he himself had been before the war.

After crossing the parade ground, the Japanese soldiers disappeared among the lines of ragged washing between the barrack huts. Jim emerged from the damp cavern of the blockhouse. Wearing the leather golfing shoes given to him by Dr. Ransome, he climbed through the wire. In his hand he carried Kimura's turtle. The ancient creature contained at least a pound of meat, and Basie, almost certainly, would know a special recipe for turtle. Jim could imagine Basie tempting it out of its shell with a live caterpillar, then skewering its head with his jack-knife. . . .

In front of Jim was Lunghua Camp, his home and universe for the past three years, the prison of nearly two thousand British and American civilians. The shabby barrack huts, the cement dormitory blocks, the worn parade ground and the guardhouse with its leaning watchtower lay together under the June sun, a rendezvous for every fly and mosquito in the Yangtze basin. But once he stepped through the wire, Jim felt the air steady around him. He ran along the cinder path, his tattered shirt flying from his bony shoulders like the tags of washing between the huts.

In his ceaseless journeys around the camp Jim had learned to recognize every stone and weed. A sun-bleached sign, crudely painted with the words "Regent Street," was nailed to a bamboo pole beside the pathway. Jim ignored it, as he did the similar signs inscribed "Piccadilly," "Knightsbridge" and "Petticoat Lane" which marked the main pathways within the camp. These relics of an imaginary London—which many of the Shanghai-born British prisoners had never seen—intrigued Jim but in some way annoyed him. With their constant talk about prewar London, the older British families in the camp claimed a special exclusiveness. Jim remembered a line from one of the poems that Dr. Ransome had made him memorize—"a foreign field that is forever England . . ." But this was Lunghua, not England. Naming the sewage-stained paths between the rotting huts after a vaguely remembered London allowed too many of the British prisoners to shut out the reality of the camp, another excuse to sit back when they should have been helping Dr. Ransome to clear the septic tanks. To their credit, in Jim's eyes, neither the Americans nor the Dutch and Belgians in the camp wasted their time on nostalgia. The years in Lunghua had not given Jim a high opinion of the British.

And yet the London street signs fascinated Jim, part of the magic of names that he had discovered in the camp. What, conceivably, were Lords, the Serpentine and the Trocadero? There were so few books or magazines that an unfamiliar brand name had all the mystery of a message from the stars. According to Basie, who was always right, the American fighters with the ventral radiators that strafed Lunghua Airfield were called "Mustangs," the name of a wild pony. Jim relished the name; to know that the planes were Mustangs was more important to him than the confirmation that Basie had his ear to the camp's secret radio. Jim hungered for names.

Jim stumbled on the worn path, unable to control the golf shoes. Too often these days he became lightheaded. Dr. Ransome had warned him not to run, but the American air attacks and the imminent prospect of the war's end made Jim too impatient to walk. Trying to protect the turtle, he grazed his left knee. He limped across the cinder track and sat on the steps of the derelict drinking-water station. Here brackish water taken from the ponds in the camp had once been boiled by the prisoners. There was still a small supply of coal in the camp storerooms, but the work gang of six Britons who stoked the fires had lost interest. Although Dr. Ransome remonstrated with them, they preferred to suffer from chronic dysentery rather than make the effort of boiling the water.

While Jim nursed his knee the members of the gang sat outside the nearby barrack hut, watching the sky as if they expected the war to end within the next ten minutes. Jim recognized Mr. Mulvaney, an accountant with the Shanghai Power Company who had often swum in the pool at Amherst Avenue. Beside him was the Reverend Pearce, a Methodist missionary whose Japanese-speaking wife openly collaborated with the guards, reporting to them each day on the prisoners' activities.

No one criticized Mrs. Pearce for this, and in fact most of the prisoners in Lunghua were only too keen to collaborate. Jim vaguely disapproved but agreed that it was probably sensible to do anything to survive. After three years in the camp, the notion of patriotism meant nothing. The bravest prisoners—and collaboration was a risky matter—were those who bought their way into the favor of the Japanese and thereby helped their fellows with small supplies of food and bandages. Besides, there were few illicit activities to betray. No one in Lunghua would dream of trying to escape, and everyone rightly ratted on any fool about to step through the wire, for fear of the reprisals to come.

The water workers scraped their clogs on the steps and stared into the sun, moving only to pick the ticks from between their ribs. Although emaciated, the process of starvation had somehow stopped a skin's depth from the skeleton below. Jim envied Mr. Mulvaney and the Reverend Pearce—he himself was still growing. The arithmetic that Dr. Ransome had taught him made it all too clear that the food supply to the camp was shrinking at a faster rate than that at which the prisoners were dying.

In the center of the parade ground a group of twelve-year-old boys was playing marbles on the baked earth. Seeing the turtle, they ran toward Jim. Each of them controlled a dragonfly tied to a length of cotton. The blue flames flicked to and fro above their heads.

"Jim! Can we touch it?"

"What is it?"

"Did Private Kimura give it to you?"

Jim smiled benignly. "It's a bomb." He held out the turtle and generously allowed everyone to inspect it. Despite the gap in years, several of the boys had been close friends in the days after his arrival in Lunghua, when he had needed every ally he could find. But he had outgrown them and made other friends—Dr. Ransome, Basie and the American seamen in E Block, with their ancient prewar copies of *Reader's Digest* and *Popular Mechanics* that Jim devoured. Now and then, as if recapturing his

lost childhood, Jim re-entered the world of boyish games
and would play tops and marbles and hopscotch.

"Is it dead? It's moving!"

"It's bleeding!"

A smear of blood from Jim's knee gave the turtle's
head a piratical flourish.

"Jim, you killed it!"

The largest of the boys, Richard Pearce, reached out
to touch the reptile, but Jim tucked it under his arm. He
disliked and slightly feared Richard Pearce, who was
almost as big as himself. He envied Richard the extra
Japanese rations which his mother fed to him. As well
as the food, the Pearces had a small library of confiscated
books which they guarded jealously.

"It's a blood bond," Jim explained grandly. By rights
turtles belonged to the sea, to the open river visible a
mile to the west of the camp, that broad tributary of the
Yangtze down which he had once dreamed of sailing
with his parents to the safety of a world without war.

"Watch out. . . ." He waved Richard aside. "I've
trained it to attack!"

The boys backed away from him. There were times
when Jim's humor made them uneasy. Although he tried
to stop himself, Jim resented their clothes—hand-me-
downs stitched together by their mothers, but far superior
to his own rags. More than this, Jim resented that they
had mothers and fathers at all. During the past year Jim
had gradually realized that he could no longer remember
what his parents looked like. Their veiled figures still
entered his dreams, but he had forgotten their faces.

21

THE CUBICLE

"YOUNG JIM!"

An almost naked man wearing clogs and ragged shorts shouted to him from the steps of G Block. In his hands he held the shafts of a wooden cart with iron wheels. Although the cart carried no load, its handles had almost wrenched the man's arms from their sockets. He spoke to the Englishwomen sitting on the concrete steps in their faded cotton frocks. As he gestured to them his shoulder blades seemed to be working themselves loose from his back, about to fly across the barbed wire.

"I'm here, Mr. Maxted!" Jim pushed Richard Pearce aside and ran along the cinder path to the dormitory block. Seeing the empty food cart, it occurred to him that he might have missed the daily meal. The fear of being without food for even a single day was so intense that he was ready to attack Mr. Maxted.

"Come on, Jim. Without you it won't taste the same." Mr. Maxted glanced at Jim's golf shoes, those nailed brogues that had a life of their own and propelled Jim's scarecrow figure on his ceaseless rounds of the camp.

To the women he remarked: "Our Jim's spending all his time at the nineteenth hole."

"I promised, Mr. Maxted. I'm always ready. . . ." Jim had to stop as he reached the entrance to G Block. He worked his lungs until the dizziness left his head and ran forward again. Turtle in hand, he raced up the steps into the foyer and swerved between two old men stranded like ghosts in the middle of a conversation they had forgotten.

On either side of the corridor was a series of small rooms, each furnished with four wooden bunks. After the first winter in the camp, when many of the children in the uninsulated barracks had died, families with children were moved into the residence halls of the former training college. Although unheated, the rooms with their cement walls remained above freezing point.

Jim shared his room with a young English couple, Mr. and Mrs. Vincent, and their six-year-old son. He had lived within inches of the Vincents for two and a half years, but their existences could not have been more separate. On the day of Jim's arrival, Mrs. Vincent had hung an old bedspread around his nominal quarter of the room. She and her husband—a broker on the Shanghai Stock Exchange—never ceased to resent Jim's presence, and over the years they had strengthened his cubicle, stringing together a worn shawl, a petticoat and the lid of a cardboard box, so that it resembled one of the miniature shanties that seemed to erect themselves spontaneously around the beggars of Shanghai.

Not content with walling Jim into his small world, the Vincents had repeatedly tried to encroach upon it, moving the nails and string from which the bedspread hung. Jim had defended himself, first by bending the nails until, to the Vincents' horror, the entire structure collapsed one night as they were undressing, and then by calibrating the wall with a ruler and pencil. The Vincents promptly retaliated by superimposing their own system of marks.

All this Jim took in his stride. For some reason he still liked Mrs. Vincent, a handsome if frayed blonde, although her nerves were always stretched and she had never made the slightest attempt to care for him. He knew that if he starved to death in his bunk she would find some polite reason for doing nothing to help him. During the first year in Lunghua the few single children were neglected, unless they were prepared to let themselves be used as servants. Jim alone had refused, and had never fetched and carried for Mr. Vincent.

Mrs. Vincent was sitting on her straw mattress when he burst into the room, her pale hands folded on her lap like a forgotten pair of gloves. She stared at the white-washed wall above her son's bunk, as if watching an invisible film projected onto a screen. Jim worried that Mrs. Vincent spent too much of her time watching these films. As he peered at her through the cracks in his cubicle, he tried to guess what she saw—a homemade film, perhaps, or herself in England before she was married, sitting on one of those sunlit lawns that seemed to cover the entire country. Jim assumed that it was those lawns that had provided the emergency airfields for the Battle of Britain. As he was aware from his observations in Shanghai, the Germans were not too keen on sunlit lawns. Was this why they had lost the Battle of Britain? Many of Jim's ideas were hopelessly confused in a way that even Dr. Ransome was too tired to disentangle.

"You're late, Jim," Mrs. Vincent told him disapprovingly, her eyes on Jim's golf shoes. Like everyone else, she was unable to cope with their intimidating presence. Already Jim felt that the shoes gave him a special authority. "The whole of G Block has been waiting for you."

"I've been with Basie, hearing the latest war news. Mrs. Vincent, what's the nineteenth hole?"

"You shouldn't work for Basie. The things those Americans ask you to do . . . I've told you that we come first."

"G Block comes first, Mrs. Vincent." Jim meant it. He ducked under the flap into his cubicle. Catching his breath, he lay on the bunk with the turtle inside his shirt. The reptile preferred its own company, and Jim turned his attention to his new shoes. With their polished toecaps and bright studs, they were an intact piece of the prewar world that he could stare at for hours, like Mrs. Vincent and her films. Laughing to himself, Jim lay back as the hot sunlight shone through the wall of the cubicle, outlining the curious stains on the old bedspread. Looking at them, Jim visualized the scenes of air battles and armadas, the sinking of the *Petrel* and even the garden at Amherst Avenue.

"Jim, kitchen time!" he heard someone call from the steps below the window. But Jim rested on his bunk. It was a long haul to the kitchens, and there was no point in being early. The Japanese had celebrated VE-day in their own way, by cutting the already meager rations in half. The first arrivals often received less than the later ones, when the cooks realized how many of the prisoners had died or were too ill to collect their rations.

Besides, there was no obligation on Jim to help with the food cart—nor, for that matter, on Mr. Maxted. But as Jim had noticed, those who were prepared to help their fellow prisoners tended to do so, and this did nothing to stop those too lazy to work from endlessly complaining. The British were especially good at complaining, something the Dutch and Americans never did. Soon, Jim reflected with a certain grim pleasure, they would be too sick even to complain.

Jim gazed at his shoes, consciously imitating the child-like smile on Private Kimura's lips. The wooden bunk filled the cubicle, but Jim was at his happiest in this miniature universe. On the walls he had pinned several pages from an old *Life* magazine that Basie had given to him. There were photographs of Battle of Britain pilots sitting in armchairs beside their Spitfires, of a crashed Heinkel bomber, of St. Paul's floating like a battleship on a sea of fire. Next to them was a full-page color advertisement for a Packard motorcar, as beautiful in Jim's eyes as the Mustang fighters that strafed Lunghua Airfield. Did the Americans bring out a new-model Mustang every year or every month? Perhaps there would be an air raid that afternoon, when he could check the latest design modifications to the Mustangs and Superfortresses. Jim looked forward to the air raids.

Beside the Packard was a small section that Jim had cut from a larger photograph of a crowd outside the gates of Buckingham Palace in 1940. The blurred images of a man and a woman standing arm-in-arm reminded Jim of his parents. This unknown English couple, perhaps dead in an air raid, had almost become his mother and father. Jim knew that they were complete strangers, but he kept the pretense alive, so that in turn he could keep alive the lost memory of his parents. The world before the war, his childhood in Amherst Avenue, his class at the Cathedral School belonged to the invisible film that Mrs. Vincent watched from her bunk.

Jim allowed the turtle to crawl across his straw mat. If he carried it around with him, Private Kimura or one of the guards might guess that he had left the camp. Now that the war was ending, the Japanese guards were convinced that the British and American prisoners were constantly trying to escape—the last notion, in fact, to cross their minds. In 1943, a few Britishers had escaped, hoping to be sheltered by neutral friends in Shanghai, but had soon been discovered by the army of informers. Several groups of Americans had set out in the summer of 1944 for Chungking, the Nationalist Chinese capital nine hundred miles to the west. All had been betrayed by Chinese villagers terrified of reprisals, handed over to the Japanese and executed. From then on escape attempts ceased altogether. By June 1945, the landscape around Lunghua was so hostile, roamed by bandits, starving villagers and deserters from the puppet armies, that the camp and its Japanese guards offered the only security.

With his finger Jim stroked the turtle's ancient head. It seemed a pity to cook it—Jim envied the turtle its massive shell, a private fortress against the world. From below his bunk Jim pulled out a wooden box, which Dr. Ransome had helped him to nail together. Inside were his possessions: a Japanese cap badge given to him by Private Kimura; three steel-bossed fighting tops; a chess set and a copy of Kennedy's Latin primer on indefinite loan from Dr. Ransome; his Cathedral School blazer, a carefully folded memory of his young self; and the pair of clogs he had worn for the past three years.

Jim placed the turtle in the box and covered it with the blazer. As he raised the flap of his cubicle, Mrs. Vincent watched his every move. She treated Jim like her Number Two Coolie, and he was well aware that he tolerated this for reasons he barely understood. Like all the men and older boys in G Block, Jim was attracted to Mrs. Vincent, but her real appeal for Jim lay elsewhere. Her long hours staring at the whitewash and her detachment even from her own son—she fed the dysentery-ridden boy and changed his clothes without looking at him for minutes at a time—suggested to Jim that she remained forever above the camp, beyond that world of guards and hunger and American air attacks to which he himself was passionately committed. He wanted to touch her, less out of adolescent lust than simple curiosity.

"You can use my bunk, Mrs. Vincent, if you want to sleep."

As Jim reached to her shoulder, she pushed his hand away. Her distracted eyes could come to a remarkably sharp focus.

"Mr. Maxted is still waiting, Jim. Perhaps it's time you went back to the huts. . . ."

"Not the huts, Mrs. Vincent," Jim pretended to groan. Not the huts, he repeated fiercely to himself as he left the room. The huts were cold, and if the war lasted beyond the winter of 1945 many more people would die in those freezing barracks. However, for Mrs. Vincent perhaps he would go back to the huts. . . .

22

THE UNIVERSITY OF LIFE

ALL OVER THE CAMP there sounded the scraping of iron wheels. In the windows of the barrack huts, on the steps of the dormitory blocks, the prisoners were sitting up, roused for a few minutes by the memory of food.

Jim left the foyer of G Block and found Mr. Maxted still holding the wooden handles of the food cart. Having made the effort twenty minutes earlier to lift the handles, he had exhausted his powers of decision. The former architect and entrepreneur, who had represented so much that Jim most admired about Shanghai, had been sadly drained by his years in Lunghua. After arriving at the camp Jim had been glad to find him there, but by now he realized how much Mr. Maxted had changed. His eyes forever watched the cigarette butts thrown down by the Japanese guards, but only Jim was quick enough to retrieve them. Jim chafed at this, but he supported Mr. Maxted out of nostalgia for his childhood dream of growing up one day to be like him.

The Studebaker and the afternoon girls in the gambling

185

casinos had poorly prepared Mr. Maxted for the world of the camp. As Jim took the wooden handles he wondered how long the architect would have stood on the sewage-stained path. Perhaps all day, watched until he dropped by the same group of British prisoners who sat on the steps without once offering to help. Half-naked in their ragged clothes, they stared at the parade ground, uninterested even in a Japanese fighter that flew overhead. Several of the married couples held their mess plates, already forming a queue, a reflex response to Jim's arrival.

"At last . . ."

". . . that boy . . ."

". . . running wild."

These mutters drew an amiable smile from Mr. Maxted. "Jim, you're going to be blackballed by the country club. Never mind."

"I don't mind." When Mr. Maxted stumbled, Jim held his arm. "Are you all right, Mr. Maxted?"

Jim waved to the men sitting on the step, but no one moved. Mr. Maxted steadied himself. "Let's go, Jim. Some work and some watch, and that's all there is to it."

For the past year there had been a third member of the team, Mr. Carey, the owner of the Buick agency in Nanking Road. But six weeks earlier he had died of malaria, and by then the Japanese had cut the food ration to a point where only two of them were needed to push the cart.

Propelled by his new shoes, Jim sped along the cinder path. The iron wheels struck sparks from the flinty stones. Mr. Maxted held his shoulder, panting to keep up.

"Slow down, Jim. You'll get there before the war ends."

"When will the war end, Mr. Maxted?"

"Jim . . . is it going to end? Another year, 1946. You tell me, you listen to Basie's radio."

"I haven't heard the radio, Mr. Maxted," Jim answered truthfully. Basie was far too canny to admit a Britisher into the secret circle of listeners. "I know the Japanese surrendered at Okinawa. I hope the war ends soon."

"Not too soon, Jim. Our problems might begin then. Are you still giving English lessons to Private Kimura?"

"He isn't interested in learning English," Jim had to admit. "I think the war's really ended for Private Kimura."

"Will the war really end for you, Jim? You'll see your mother and father again."

"Well . . ." Jim preferred not to talk about his parents, even with Mr. Maxted. The two of them had formed a long-standing partnership, though Mr. Maxted did little to help Jim and rarely referred to his son Patrick or to their visits to the Shanghai clubs and bars. Mr. Maxted was no longer the dapper figure who fell into swimming pools. What worried Jim was that his mother and father might also have changed. Soon after arriving in Lunghua he heard that his parents were interned in a camp near Soochow, but the Japanese refused to consider the notion of a transfer.

They crossed the parade ground and approached the camp kitchens behind the guardhouse. Some twenty food carts and their teams were drawn up beside the serving hatch, jostling together like a crowd of rickshaws and their coolies. As Jim had estimated, he and Mr. Maxted would take their place halfway down the queue. Latecomers clattered along the cinder paths, watched by hundreds of emaciated prisoners. One day during the previous week there had been no food, as a reprisal for a Superfortress raid that had devastated Tokyo, and the prisoners had continued to stare at the kitchens until the late afternoon. The silence had unsettled Jim, reminding him of the beggars outside the houses in Amherst Avenue. Without thinking, he had removed his shoes and hidden them among the graves in the hospital cemetery.

Jim and Mr. Maxted took their places in the queue. Outside the guardhouse, a work party of British and Belgian prisoners was strengthening the fence. Two of the prisoners unwound a coil of barbed wire, which the others cut and nailed to the fencing posts. Several of the Japanese soldiers were working shoulder to shoulder with their prisoners, ragged uniforms barely distinguishable from the faded khaki of the inmates.

The object of this activity was a group of thirty Chinese camped outside the gates. Destitute peasants and villagers, soldiers from the puppet armies and abandoned children, they sat in the open road, staring at the barbed-wire gates being strengthened against them. The first of these impoverished people had appeared three months earlier. At night some of the more desperate would climb through the wire, only to be caught by the internees' patrols. Those who survived in the guardhouse till dawn were taken down to the river by the Japanese and clubbed to death on the bank.

As they moved forward to the serving hatch, Jim watched the Chinese. Although it was summer, the peasants still wore their quilted winter clothes. Needless to say, none of the Chinese was ever admitted to Lunghua Camp, let alone fed. Yet still they came, attracted to this one place in the desolate land where there was food. Worryingly for Jim, they stayed until they died. Mr. Maxted was right when he said that with the conclusion of the war the prisoners' real problems would not end, but begin.

Jim worried about Dr. Ransome and Mrs. Vincent, and the rest of his fellow prisoners. How would they survive, without the Japanese to look after them? Jim worried especially for Mr. Maxted, whose tired repertory of jokes about the country club meant nothing in the real world. But at least Mr. Maxted was trying to keep the camp going, and it was the integrity of the camp on which they depended.

During 1943, when the war was still moving in Japan's favor, the prisoners had worked together. The entertainment committee, of which Mr. Maxted had been chairman, had organized a nightly program of lectures and concert parties. This had been the happiest year of Jim's life. Tired of his cramped cubicle and Mrs. Vincent's nail-tapping aloofness, he spent every evening listening to lectures on an endless variety of topics: the construction of the pyramids, the history of the world land-speed record, the life of a district commissioner in Uganda (the lecturer, a retired Indian Army officer, claimed to have named after himself a lake the size of Wales, which amazed Jim), the infantry weapons of the Great War, the management of the Shanghai Tramways Company and a score of others.

Sitting in the front row of the assembly hall, Jim devoured these lectures, many of which he attended two or three times. He helped to copy the parts for the Lunghua Players' productions of *Macbeth* and *Twelfth Night;* he moved scenery for *The Pirates of Penzance* and *Trial by Jury.* For most of 1944 there was a camp school run by the missionaries, which Jim found tedious by comparison with the evening lectures. But he deferred to Basie and

Dr. Ransome. Both agreed that he should never miss a class, if only, Jim suspected, to give themselves a break from his restless energy.

But by the winter of 1944, all this had ended. After the American fighter attacks on Lunghua Airfield and the first bombing raids on the Shanghai dockyards, the Japanese enforced an evening curfew. The supply of electric current to the camp was switched off for good, and the prisoners retreated to their bunks. The already-modest food ration was cut to a single meal each day. American submarines blockaded the Yangtze estuary, and the huge Japanese armies in China began to fall back to the coast, barely able to feed themselves.

The prospect of their defeat, and the imminent assault on the Japanese home islands, made Jim more and more nervous. He ate every scrap of food he could find, aware of the rising number of deaths from beriberi and malaria. Jim admired the Mustangs and Superfortresses, but sometimes he wished that the Americans would return to Hawaii and content themselves with raising their battleships at Pearl Harbor. Then Lunghua Camp would once again be the happy place that he had known in 1943.

When Jim and Mr. Maxted returned with the rations to G Block, the prisoners were already waiting with their plates and mess tins. They stood on the steps, the bare-chested men with knobbed shoulders and bird-cage ribs, their faded wives in shabby frocks, watching without expression as if about to be presented with a corpse. At the head of the queue were Mrs. Pearce and her son, followed by the missionary couples who spent all day hunting for food.

Hundreds of flies hovered in the steam that rose from the metal pails of cracked wheat and sweet potatoes. As he heaved on the wooden handles Jim winced with pain, not from the strain of pulling the cart, but from the heat of the stolen sweet potato inside his shirt. As long as he remained doubled up no one could see the potato, and he put on a pantomime of grimaces and groans.

"Oh, oh . . . oh, my God . . ."

"Worthy of the Lunghua Players, Jim." Mr. Maxted had watched Jim remove the potato from the pail as they left the kitchens, but he never objected. Crouching forward, Jim abandoned the cart to the missionaries. He ran up the steps, past the Vincents, who stood plates in hand— it never occurred to them, nor to Jim, that they should bring Jim's plate with them. He dived through the curtain into his cubicle and dropped the steaming potato under his mat, hoping that the damp straw would smother the vapor. He seized his plate and darted back to the foyer to take his place at the head of the queue. Mr. Maxted had already served the Reverend and Mrs. Pearce, but Jim shouldered aside their son. He held out his plate and received a ladle of boiled wheat and a second sweet potato, which he had pointed out to Mr. Maxted within moments of leaving the kitchens.

Returning to his bunk, Jim relaxed for the first time. He drew the curtain and lay back, the warm plate like a piece of the sun against his chest. He felt drowsy, but at the same time light-headed with hunger. He rallied himself with the thought that there might be an American air raid that afternoon—who did he want to win? The question was important.

Jim cupped his hands over the sweet potato. He was almost too hungry to enjoy the gray pith, but he gazed at the photograph of the man and woman outside Buckingham Palace, hoping that his parents, wherever they were, also had an extra potato.

When the Vincents returned with their rations, Jim sat up and folded back the curtain so that he could examine their plates. He liked to watch Mrs. Vincent eating her meals. Keeping a close eye on her, Jim studied the cracked wheat. The starchy grains were white and swollen, indistinguishable from the weevils that infested these warehouse sweepings. In the early years of the camp everyone pushed the weevils to one side, or flicked them through the nearest window, but now Jim carefully husbanded them. Often there were more than a hundred insects in three rows around the rim of Jim's plate, though recently even their number was in decline. "Eat the weevils," Dr. Ransome had told him, and Jim did so, although everyone else washed them away. But there was protein in them, a fact that Mr. Maxted seemed to find depressing when Jim informed him of it.

After counting the eighty-seven weevils—their numbers, Jim calculated, were falling less steeply than the ration—he stirred them into the cracked wheat, an animal foodstuff grown in northern China, and swallowed the six spoonfuls. Giving himself a breather, he waited for Mrs. Vincent to begin her sweet potato.

"Must you, Jim?" Mr. Vincent asked. No taller than Jim, the stockbroker and former amateur jockey sat on his bunk beside his ailing son. With his black hair and lined yellow face like a squeezed lemon, he reminded Jim of Basie, but Mr. Vincent had never come to terms with Lunghua. "You'll miss this camp when the war's over. I wonder how you'll take to school in England."

"It might be a bit strange," Jim admitted, finishing the last of the weevils. He felt sensitive about his ragged clothes and his determined efforts to stay alive. He wiped his plate clean with his finger and remembered a favorite phrase of Basie's. "All the same, Mr. Vincent, the best teacher is the university of life."

Mrs. Vincent lowered her spoon. "Jim, could we finish our meal? We've heard your views on the university of life."

"Right. But we should eat the weevils, Mrs. Vincent."

"I know, Jim. Dr. Ransome told you so."

"He said we need the protein."

"Dr. Ransome is right. We should all eat the weevils."

Hoping to brighten the conversation, Jim asked: "Mrs. Vincent, do you believe in vitamins?"

Mrs. Vincent stared at her plate. She spoke with true despair. "Strange child . . ."

The rebuff failed to bother Jim. Everything about this distant woman with her thinning blond hair intrigued Jim, although in many ways he distrusted her. Six months earlier, when Dr. Ransome thought that Jim had caught pneumonia, she had done nothing to look after him, and Dr. Ransome was forced to come in every day and wash Jim himself. Yet the previous evening she had helped Jim with his Latin homework, matter-of-factly pointing out the distinction between gerunds and gerundives.

Jim waited until she began her sweet potato. After confirming that his own potato was the largest of the four in the room, and deciding not to save any for the turtle under his bunk, he broke the skin and swiftly devoured the warm pulp. When the last morsel had gone, he lay back and lowered the curtain. Alone now—the Vincents, although only a few feet from him, might well have been on another planet—Jim assessed the jobs ahead of him that day. First, there was the second potato to be smuggled from the room. There were his Latin homework for Dr. Ransome, errands to be run for Basie and Private

Kimura, and then the afternoon air raid—all in all, a full program until the evening curfew, when he would probably roam the G Block corridors with his chess set, ready to take on all comers.

The Kennedy primer in hand, Jim stepped from his cubicle. The second potato bulged in his trouser pocket, but for several months the presence of Mrs. Vincent sometimes gave him an unexpected erection, and he relied on the confusion to make his escape.

His spoon halfway to his mouth, Mr. Vincent stared at the bulge with an expression of deep gloom. His wife gazed in her level fashion at Jim, who sidestepped quickly from the room. Glad as always to be free of the Vincents, he skipped down the corridor to the external door below the fire escape and vaulted over the children squatting on the step. As the warm air ruffled the ragged strips of his shirt, he ran off into the familiar and reassuring world of the camp.

23

THE AIR RAID

ON HIS WAY to the hospital, Jim paused to do his homework at the ruined assembly hall. From the balcony of the upper circle he could not only keep an eye on the pheasant traps across the wire, but also bring himself up to date with any fresh activity at Lunghua Airfield. The stairway to the circle was partly blocked by pieces of masonry that had fallen from the roof, but Jim squeezed himself through a narrow crevice worn smooth by the camp's children. He climbed the stairway and took his seat on the cement step that formed the first row of the balcony.

The Kennedy propped on his knees, Jim made a leisurely meal of the second potato. Below him, the proscenium arch of the assembly hall had been bombed into a heap of rubble and steel girders, but the landscape now exposed in many ways resembled a panorama displayed on a cinema screen. To the north were the apartment houses of the French Concession, their facades reflected in the flooded paddy fields. To Jim's right, the Whangpoo

River emerged from the Nantao district of Shanghai and bent its immense way across the abandoned land.

In front of Jim was Lunghua Airfield. The concrete runway moved diagonally across its grassy table to the foot of the pagoda. Jim could see the barrels of the antiaircraft guns mounted on its ancient stone decks, and the powerful landing lights and radio antennae fixed to the tiled roof. Below the pagoda were the hangars and engineering shops, each guarded by sandbag emplacements. A few elderly reconnaissance planes and converted bombers sat on the concrete apron, all that was left of the once-invincible air wing that had flown from Lunghua.

Around the edges of the field, in the deep grass by the perimeter road, lay the wreckage of what seemed to Jim to be the entire Japanese Air Force. Scores of rusting aircraft sat on their flattened undercarriages among the trees, or lay in the banks of nettles where they had swerved after crash-landing with their injured crews. For months crippled Japanese aircraft had fallen from the sky onto the graveyard of Lunghua Airfield, as if a titanic aerial battle were taking place far above the clouds.

Already gangs of Chinese scrap dealers were at work among the derelict planes. With the tireless ability of the Chinese to transform one set of refuse into another, they stripped the metal skins from the wings and retrieved the tires and fuel tanks. Within days they would be on sale in Shanghai as roofing panels, cisterns and rubber-soled sandals. Whether this scavenging took place with the permission of the Japanese base commander, Jim could never decide. Every few hours a party of soldiers would ride out in a truck and drive some of the Chinese away. Jim watched them running across the flooded paddies to the west of the airfield as the Japanese hurled the tires and metal plates from the salvage carts. But the Chinese always returned to their work, ignored by the antiaircraft gun crews in the sandbag emplacements along the perimeter road.

Jim sucked his fingers, drawing the last taste of the sweet potato from his scuffed nails. The warmth of the potato eased the nagging pain in his teeth. He watched the Chinese scavengers at work, tempted to slip through the wire and join them. There were so many new models of Japanese aircraft. Only four hundred yards from the pheasant traps was the crashed hulk of a Hayate, one of the powerful, high-altitude fighters that the Japanese were sending up to destroy the Superfortress bombers on the fire raids over Tokyo. The long grass between the camp and the southern edge of the airfield was rarely patrolled. Jim's practiced eye searched the dips and gullies in the banks of nettles and wild sugarcane, following the course of a forgotten canal.

A second gang of Chinese coolies was at work in the center of the airfield, repairing the concrete runway. The men carried baskets of stones from the trucks parked among the bomb craters. A steamroller moved to and fro, manned by a Japanese soldier.

The sharp whistle of its valve gear held Jim to his seat. The gang of coolies reminded him that he too had once worked on the runway. During the past three years, whenever he watched the Japanese aircraft take off from Lunghua, Jim felt an uneasy pride as their wheels left the concrete surface. He and Basie and Dr. Ransome, along with those Chinese prisoners being worked to death, had helped to lay the runway that carried the Zeros and Hayates into the air war against the Americans. Jim was well aware that his commitment to the Japanese Air Force stemmed from the still-fearful knowledge that he had nearly given his life to build the runway, like the Chinese soldiers buried in their untraceable lime pit beneath the waving sugarcane. If he had died, his bones and those of Basie and Dr. Ransome would have borne the Japanese pilots taking off from Lunghua to hurl themselves at the American picket ships around Iwo Jima and Okinawa. If the Japanese triumphed, that small part of his mind that lay forever within the runway would be appeased. But if they were defeated, all his fears would have been worth nothing.

Jim remembered those pilots of the dusk who had ordered him from the work gang. Whenever Jim watched the Japanese moving around their aircraft, he thought of the three young pilots with their ground crew who had walked through the evening light to inspect the runway. But for the English boy wandering toward the parked aircraft, the Japanese would not even have noticed the work gang.

The fliers fascinated Jim, far more than Private Kimura and his *kendo* armor. Every day, as he sat on the balcony of the assembly hall or helped Dr. Ransome in the vegetable garden of the hospital, he watched the pilots in their baggy flying suits, carrying out the external checks before climbing into the cockpits. Above all, Jim admired the kamikaze pilots. In the past month more than a dozen special attack units had arrived at Lunghua Airfield, which they used as their base for suicide missions against the American carriers in the East China Sea. Neither Private Kimura nor the other guards in the camp paid the least attention to the suicide pilots, and Basie and the American seamen in E Block referred to them as "hashi-crashies" or "screwy-siders."

But Jim identified himself with these kamikaze pilots and was always moved by the threadbare ceremonies that took place beside the runway. The previous morning, as he worked in the hospital garden, he left his sewage pail and ran to the barbed-wire fence in order to see them leave. The three pilots in their white headbands were little older than Jim, with childlike cheeks and boneless noses. They stood by their planes in the hot sunlight, nervously brushing the flies from their mouths, faces pinched as the squad leader saluted. Even when they cheered the Emperor, shouting hoarsely at the audience of flies, none of the antiaircraft gunners noticed them, and Private Kimura, striding across the tomato plots to call Jim from the wire, seemed baffled by his concern.

Jim opened his Latin primer and began the homework that Dr. Ransome had set him: the entire passive tenses of the verb *amo*. Jim enjoyed Latin; in many ways its strict formality and its families of nouns and verbs resembled the science of chemistry, his father's favorite subject. The Japanese had closed the camp school, as a cunning reprisal against the parents, who were trapped all day with their offspring, but Dr. Ransome still set Jim a wide range of tasks. There were poems to memorize, simultaneous equations to be solved, general science (where, thanks to his father, Jim often had a surprise for Dr. Ransome) and French, which he loathed. There seemed a remarkable amount of schoolwork, Jim reflected, bearing in mind that the war was about to end. But perhaps this was Dr. Ransome's way of keeping him quiet for an hour each day. In a sense, too, the homework helped Dr. Ransome to sustain the illusion that even in Lunghua Camp the values of a vanished England still survived. Misguided though this was, Jim was keen to help Dr. Ransome in any way.

"*Amatus sum, amatus es, amatus est . . .*" As he recited the perfect tense, Jim noticed that the Chinese scavengers were running from the derelict aircraft. The work gang of coolies had scattered, throwing their baskets of stones to the ground. The Japanese soldier leaped from the steamroller and ran bare-chested toward the antiaircraft emplacements, whose guns were searching the sky. Already a flicker of light came from Lunghua pagoda, as if the Japanese were setting off a devotional firecracker. The sound of this lone machine gun crossed the airfield, soon drowned by the complaining drone of an air-raid siren. The klaxon above the guardhouse in Lunghua Camp took up the call, a harsh rattle that drilled through Jim's head.

Excited by the prospect of an air raid, Jim peered at the sky through the open roof of the assembly hall. All over the camp the internees were running along the cinder paths. The men and women dozing like asylum inmates on the steps of the huts scrambled through the doors; mothers leaned from ground-floor windows and lifted their children to safety. Within a minute the camp was deserted, leaving Jim to conduct the air raid alone from the balcony of the assembly hall.

Jim listened keenly, already suspecting a false alarm. The air raids came earlier each day as the Americans moved their bases forward across the Pacific and the Chinese mainland. The Japanese were now so nervous that they jumped at every cloud in the sky. A twin-engined transport plane flew across the paddy fields, its pilots unaware of the panic below.

Jim returned to his Latin primer. At that moment an immense shadow crossed the assembly hall and raced along the ground toward the perimeter fence. A tornado of noise filled the air, from which emerged a single-engined fighter with silver fuselage and the stars-and-bars insignia of the U.S. Air Force. Only thirty feet above

Jim's head, the Mustang's wings were broader than the assembly hall. The fuselage was stained with rust and oil, but its powerful engine had the smooth drive of his father's Packard. The Mustang crossed the perimeter fence and hurtled along the concrete runway of the airfield, the height of a man's head above the deck. In its wake a whirlwind of leaves and dust boiled from the ground.

Around the airfield the antiaircraft guns turned toward the camp. The tiers of Lunghua pagoda crackled with light, like the Christmas tree display outside the Sincere Company department store in Shanghai. Undeterred, the Mustang flew straight toward the flak tower, the noise of its guns drowned in the blare of another Mustang that swept across the paddy fields to the west of the camp. A third plane came in behind it, so low that Jim was looking down at the cockpit. He could see the pilots and the insignia on their fuselage blackened by oil spraying from the engine exhausts. Two more Mustangs overflew the camp, and the wash from their engines tore the corrugated iron sheets from the roof of the barrack hut beside G Block. Half a mile to the east, between Lunghua Camp and the river, a second wing of American fighters swept in from the sea, so close to their own shadows on the empty paddy fields that they were hidden behind the lines of grave mounds. They rose as they crossed the perimeter of the airfield, then dived again to fire at the Japanese aircraft parked beside the hangars.

Antiaircraft shells burst above the camp, their shadows pulsing like heartbeats on the white earth. A shell exploded in a searing flash above the assembly hall, stunning the air. Dust cascaded from the concrete roof and poured onto Jim's shoulders. Waving his Latin primer, Jim counted the dozens of shell bursts. Did the Mustang pilots realize that Basie and the American merchant seamen were imprisoned at Lunghua Camp? Whenever they attacked the airfield, the fighter pilots hid until the last moment behind the three-story dormitory blocks, even though this drew Japanese fire onto the camp and had killed several of the prisoners.

But Jim was glad that the Mustangs were so close. His eyes feasted on every rivet in their fuselages, on the gun ports in their wings, on the huge ventral radiators that Jim was sure had been put there for reasons of style alone. Jim admired the Hayates and Zeros of the Japanese, but the Mustang fighters were the Cadillacs of air combat. He was too breathless to shout to the pilots, but he waved his primer at them as they soared past under the canopy of antiaircraft shells.

The first flights of attacking planes had swept across the airfield. Clearly visible against the apartment houses of the French Concession, they flew toward Shanghai, ready to strafe the dockyards and the Nantao seaplane base. But the antiaircraft batteries around the runway were still firing into the air. Cat's cradles of tracer stitched the sky; threads of phosphorous knit and reknit themselves. At their center was the great pagoda of Lunghua, rising through the smoke that lifted from the burning hangars, its guns throwing out an unbroken flak ceiling.

Jim had never before seen an air attack of such a scale. A second wave of Mustangs crossed the paddy fields between Lunghua Camp and the river, followed by a squadron of two-engined fighter bombers. Three hundred yards to the west of the camp one of the Mustangs dipped its starboard wing toward the ground. Out of control, it slid across the air, and its wing tip sheared the embankment of a disused canal. The plane cartwheeled across the paddy fields and fell apart in the air. It exploded in a curtain wall of flaming gasoline through which Jim could see the burning figure of the American pilot still strapped to his seat. Riding the incandescent debris of his aircraft, he tore through the trees beyond the perimeter of the camp, a fragment of the sun whose light continued to flare across the surrounding fields.

A second crippled Mustang pulled away from the others in its flight. Trailing a plume of oily smoke, it rose through the antiaircraft bursts and climbed into the sky. The pilot was trying to escape from the airfield, but as his Mustang began to lose height he rolled the craft onto its back and fell safely from the cockpit. His parachute opened and he dropped steeply to the ground. His burning plane righted itself, towed its black plume in a wavering arc above the empty fields and then plunged into the river.

The pilot hung alone in the silent sky. His companions sped on toward Shanghai, their silver fuselages lost in the sun-filled windows of the French Concession. The hammering noise of their engines had gone, and the anti-aircraft fire had ceased. A second parachutist was coming down among the canals to the west of the airfield. A stench of burned oil and engine coolant filled the disturbed air. All over the camp, miniature tornados of leaves and dead insects subsided and then whirled along the pathways again as they hunted for the slipstreams of the vanished Mustangs.

The two parachutes fell toward the burial mounds. Already a squad of Japanese soldiers in a truck with a steaming radiator sped along the perimeter road, on their way to kill the pilots. Jim wiped the dust from his Latin primer and waited for the rifle shots. The halo of light that had emerged from the burning Mustang still lay over the creeks and paddies. For a few minutes the sun had drawn nearer to the earth, as if to scorch the death from its fields.

Jim grieved for these American pilots, who died in the tangle of their harnesses, within sight of a Japanese corporal with a Mauser and a single English boy hidden on the balcony of this ruined building. Yet their end reminded Jim of his own, about which he had thought in a clandestine way ever since his arrival at Lunghua. He welcomed the air raids, the noise of the Mustangs as they swept over the camp, the smell of oil and cordite, the deaths of the pilots and even the likelihood of his own death. Despite everything, he knew he was worth nothing. He twisted his Latin primer, trembling with a secret hunger that the war would so eagerly satisfy.

24

THE HOSPITAL

"JIM! ARE YOU up there! Have you been hurt?"

Dr. Ransome stood in the rubble on the floor of the assembly hall, shouting at the balcony. He had been exhausted by the effort of running from D Block, and his lungs rattled inside his chest. The years in Lunghua had made him seem taller, but his large bones were held together by little more than a rigging of tendons. Above the rusty beard his one sound eye had seen the top of Jim's head, white with dust as if aged by the air raid.

"Jim, I need you at the hospital. Sergeant Nagata says you can stay with me for the roll call."

Jim roused himself from his reverie. Uncannily, the halo cast by the burning body of the American pilot still lay over the empty fields, but he decided not to mention this optical illusion to Dr. Ransome. The all-clear siren wailed from the pagoda, a signal repeated by the guardhouse klaxon. Jim left the balcony and squeezed his way down the staircase.

"I'm here, Dr. Ransome. I think I was nearly killed. Is anyone else dead?"

"Let's hope not." Dr. Ransome leaned against the balustrade and fanned the dust from his beard with his straw coolie hat. Although unsettled by the air raid, he watched Jim in a weary but patient way. After the raids, when the Japanese guards began to abuse the prisoners, he was often short-tempered with Jim, as if he held him responsible. He ran his hand through Jim's hair, brushing away the powdered cement, and examined his scalp for any signs of blood. "Jim, we agreed that you wouldn't go up there during the raids. The Japanese have enough to contend with—they may think you're trying to signal to the American pilots."

"I was, but they didn't see me. The Mustangs are so fast." Jim liked Dr. Ransome and wanted to reassure him that all was well. "I've done my Latin prep, Doctor."

Surprisingly, Dr. Ransome was not interested in whether Jim had memorized his verbs. He strode toward the hospital, a cluster of bamboo shacks that the prisoners, in a realistic estimate of the camp's medical resources, had built next to the cemetery. The roll call had already begun, and the pathways were deserted. Japanese guards barged through the barrack huts, breaking the last panes of window glass with their rifle butts. This precaution had been insisted on by Mr. Sekura, the camp commandant, to protect the prisoners from bomb blast. In fact, it was a reprisal for the air raid, as the prisoners would know to their cost that dusk when thousands of anopheles mosquitoes rose at feeding time from the stagnant ponds around the camp.

On the steps of E Block, one of the all-male dormitories, Sergeant Nagata screamed into the face of the block leader, Mr. Ralston, the organist at the Metropole

Cinema in Shanghai. Behind the sergeant three guards stood with fixed bayonets, as if they expected a platoon of American marines to burst from the building. The hundreds of ragged prisoners waited patiently. As the war moved through its closing year, the Japanese had become unsettled and dangerous.

"Dr. Ransome, what will happen if the Americans land at Woosung?" This port at the mouth of the Yangtze controlled the river approach to Shanghai. Everyone in the camp talked about Woosung.

"The Americans probably will land at Woosung, Jim. I've always thought you should be at MacArthur's headquarters." Dr. Ransome stopped to catch his breath. He forced the air into his bony chest, staring at his reflection in the toe caps of Jim's shoes. "Try not to think about it—you've so many other things swimming about in your head. The Americans may not land there."

"If they do, the Japanese will fight."

"Jim, they'll fight. As you've loyally maintained, the Japanese are the bravest soldiers in the world."

"Well . . ." Talk of bravery embarrassed Jim. War had nothing to do with bravery. Two years earlier, when he was younger, it had seemed important to work out who were the bravest soldiers, part of his attempt to digest the disruptions of his life. Certainly the Japanese came top, the Chinese bottom, with the British wavering in between. But Jim thought of the American aircraft that had swept the sky. However brave, there was nothing the Japanese could do to stop those beautiful and effortless machines.

"The Japanese are brave," Jim conceded. "But bravery isn't important now."

"I'm not so sure. Are you brave, Jim?"

"No . . . of course not. But I could be," Jim asserted.

"I think you are."

Although offhand, Dr. Ransome's comment had an unpleasant edge. Clearly he was annoyed with Jim, as if he blamed him for the raiding Mustangs. Was it because he had learned to enjoy the war? Jim pondered this as they reached the hospital. On the ground beside the worn bamboo steps was the intact cone of an antiaircraft shell. He picked it up, curious to see if it would still be warm, but Dr. Ransome took it from him and hurled it over the barbed-wire fence.

Jim stood on the rotting steps, flexing his shoes against the bamboo rods. He had been tempted to snatch the shell back from Dr. Ransome. He was now almost as tall as the physician and in many ways stronger—during the past three years, as Jim grew, Dr. Ransome's large body had shrunk and wasted. Jim could scarcely believe his memories of the burly, sandy-haired man with heavy thighs and arms, twice the size of the Japanese soldiers. But during their first two years in the camp Dr. Ransome had given too much of his own food to Jim.

They entered the hospital, and Jim took his place outside the dispensary with Dr. Bowen, an ear, nose and throat specialist at Shanghai General Hospital, and the four missionary widows who formed the nursing staff. While they waited for Sergeant Nagata to conduct the roll call Jim peered into the adjacent wards, where the thirty patients lay on their bunks. After every air raid there were a few deaths, from shock or exhaustion. The reminder that the war was nearly over seemed to encourage some people to give up the ghost. However, for those still keen to stay alive, a death was good news. For Jim it meant an old belt or a pair of braces, a fountain pen, and once, miraculously, a wristwatch that he had

worn for three days before handing it over with everything else to Basie. The Japanese had confiscated all
watches and clocks—as Dr. Ransome said, they wanted
their prisoners to be without time. During the three days,
Jim had measured the time it took to do everything.

Most of the patients were suffering from malaria, dysentery and heart infections brought on by malnutrition.
The beriberi patients particularly unsettled Jim, with their
swollen legs and waterlogged lungs, minds so confused
that they thought they were dying in England. In their
last hours they were given a special privilege, the hospital's one mosquito net, and lay in this makeshift sep-
ulcher before being consigned to the cemetery beside the
kitchen garden.

As Sergeant Nagata approached the hospital, accompanied by two soldiers, Jim glanced into the men's ward.
For days Mr. Barraclough, the secretary of the Shanghai
Country Club, had been about to die, and Jim had noticed
his gold signet ring. It might not be gold—nothing he
offered to Basie ever was—but it would be worth something. Jim had no compunctions about stealing from the
dead. The only patients foolish enough to come to the
hospital were those without relatives or friends willing
to look after them in the huts or dormitory blocks. Apart
from the fact that it contained no medicines—the small
supply allocated by the Japanese had been used in the
first year—the hospital rarely cured anyone. The Japanese, correctly assuming that all those who entered the
hospital would soon be dead, immediately halved their
food ration. Even so, Jim thought, it could take a remarkable time before Dr. Ransome and Dr. Bowen pro-
nounced them officially dead. Jim knew that a large
number of the extra potatoes he had eaten were dead

men's rations. Dr. Ransome worked hard for the sick, and Jim was sorry that recently he had seemed to lose hope.

"They're here," Dr. Ransome called out. "Jim, stand to attention. Don't argue with Sergeant Nagata today. And don't tell him about the air raid."

Noticing that Jim's eyes were fixed on the signet ring, he turned his head to face Sergeant Nagata as he clattered up the bamboo steps. Dr. Ransome disapproved of the grave robbery, though he was aware that Jim traded the belt buckles and braces for food. However, as Jim quietly reflected, Dr. Ransome had his own sources of supply. Unlike most of the prisoners in Lunghua, who had been allowed to pack a suitcase before being interned, Dr. Ransome had entered the camp with nothing but his shirt, shorts and leather sandals. Yet his cubicle in D Block housed an impressive inventory of possessions—a complete change of clothes, a portable gramophone and several records, a tennis racket, a rugby football and the shelf of textbooks that had provided Jim with his education. These, like all the clothes that Jim had worn in the camp and the magnificent golf shoes that instantly caught Sergeant Nagata's eye, Dr. Ransome had obtained from the stream of patients who visited his D Block cubicle each evening. Many had nothing to give, but the younger wives always brought a modest *cumshaw*—a gift—for whatever mysterious service Dr. Ransome provided. Richard Pearce had even recognized that Jim was wearing one of his old shirts, but too late.

Sergeant Nagata stopped in front of the prisoners. The scale of the American air raid had clearly shaken him. His jaws clenched as he expressed a few drops of spittle onto his lips. The bristles around his mouth trembled like miniature antennae picking up an advance warning of the rage to come. He needed to work himself up into a fury, but the gleaming toe caps of Jim's shoes distracted him. Like all the Japanese soldiers, the sergeant wore rotting boots through which his big toes protruded like immense thumbs.

"Boy . . ." He paused in front of Jim and tapped his head with the roll sheet, releasing a cloud of white dust. He knew from Private Kimura that Jim was involved in every illicit activity in the camp but had never been able to catch him. He waved away the dust and, with an effort, uttered the only two consecutive words of English that the years in Lunghua had taught him: "Difficult boy . . ."

Jim waited for him to go on, fascinated by the spittle on his lips. Perhaps Sergeant Nagata would appreciate a firsthand account of the air raid?

But the sergeant strode into the men's ward, shouting in Japanese to the two doctors. He stared down at the dying men, in whom he had never shown the slightest interest, and Jim had the sudden exhilarating notion that Dr. Ransome was hiding a wounded American pilot. He wanted to touch the pilot before the Japanese killed him, feel his helmet and flight suit, run his fingers over the dust and oil on his goggles.

"Jim! Stop thinking!" Mrs. Philips, one of the missionary widows, caught him as he swayed forward, almost swooning before the image of this archangelic figure fallen among the paddies. Jim stood to attention, pretending to be weak with hunger and trying to avoid the suspicious stare of the Japanese sentry at the dispensary door. He waited for the roll call to end, reflecting on the likely booty attached to a dead American pilot. Soon enough, one of the Americans would be shot down in Lunghua Camp. Jim tried to decide which of the ruined buildings would best conceal his body. Carefully eked out, the kit and equipment could be bartered with Basie for extra sweet potatoes for months to come, and perhaps even a warm coat for the winter. There would be sweet potatoes for Dr. Ransome, whom Jim was determined to keep alive.

He rocked on his heels and listened to an old woman crying in the nearby ward. Through the window was the pagoda at Lunghua Airfield. Already the flak tower appeared in a new light.

For another hour Jim stood in line with the missionary widows, watched by the sentry. Dr. Ransome and Dr. Bowen had set off with Sergeant Nagata to the commandant's office, perhaps to be interrogated. The guards moved around the silent camp with their roster boards, carrying out repeated roll calls. The war was about to end, and yet the Japanese were obsessed with knowing exactly how many prisoners they held.

Jim closed his eyes to calm his mind, but the sentry barked at him, suspecting that Jim was about to play some private game of which Sergeant Nagata would disapprove. The memory of the air raid excited Jim. The Mustangs still streaked across the camp on their way to attack the flak tower. Jim imagined himself at the controls of one of the fighters, falling to earth when his plane exploded, rising again as one of the childlike kamikaze pilots who cheered the Emperor before hurling their Zeros into the American carriers at Okinawa. One day Jim would become a wounded pilot, fallen among the burial mounds and armored pagodas. Pieces of his flying suit and parachute, perhaps even of his own body, would spread across the paddy fields, feeding the prisoners behind their wire and the Chinese starving at the gate. . . .

"Jim!" Mrs. Philips hissed. "Practice your Latin. . . ."

Forcing himself not to blink, to the irritation of the

Japanese sentry, Jim stared into the sunlight outside the dispensary window. The silent landscape seemed to seethe with flames, the halo born from the burning body of the American pilot. The light touched the rusting wire of the perimeter fence and the dusty fronds of the wild sugar-cane, bleached the wings of the derelict aircraft and the bones of the peasants in the burial mounds. Jim longed for the next air raid, dreaming of the violent light, barely able to breathe for the hunger that Dr. Ransome had recognized but could never feed.

25

THE CEMETERY GARDEN

WHEN THE ROLL call ended, Jim rested on the hospital steps. Dr. Ransome and Dr. Bowen returned from the commandant's office and immediately shut themselves in the dispensary with the four missionary widows. Dr. Ransome seemed as nervous as the Japanese. The old scar below his eye was flushed with blood. Had Sergeant Nagata slapped him for protesting at a further cut in the food ration?

Hands in pockets, Jim sauntered down the cinder track behind the hospital. He surveyed the rows of tomatoes, beans and melons in the kitchen garden. The modest crop was meant to supplement the patients' meager diet, though many of the vegetables found their way to the American seamen in E Block. Jim enjoyed his work with the plants. He knew each of them personally and could tell at a glance if the children had stolen a single tomato. Fortunately the long lines of graves in the adjacent cemetery kept them away. Apart from its nutritional benefits, botany was an intriguing subject. In the dispensary Dr. Ransome sliced and stained the slivers of plant stems and roots, mounted them under Dr. Bowen's microscope and made Jim draw the hundreds of cells and nutrient vessels. Plant classification was an entire universe of words; every weed in the camp had a name. Names surrounded everything; invisible encyclopedias lay in every hedge and ditch.

The previous afternoon Jim had dug two fertilizer trenches for a new crop of tomato plants. Between the garden and the cemetery was a row of fifty-gallon drums which he and Dr. Ransome had buried in the ground, then filled with sewage from the overflowing septic tank in G Block. A party of prisoners in the block had decanted most of the sewage into one of the drained ponds, but Jim and Dr. Ransome made their own trips with bucket, rope and cart. As Dr. Ransome said, there was no point in wasting anything that could keep them alive for even a few days longer. The glowing tomatoes and puffed-up melons proved him right.

Jim moved the wooden hatch from one of the drums. He waited for the thousands of flies to have the first share, then picked up the bamboo ladle with its wooden cup and began to pour the manure into the shallow trenches. He worked with the slow but measured rhythm of the Chinese peasants he had watched as they fertilized their crops before the war.

An hour later, when he had covered the manure with a layer of soil, Jim rested on one of the graves in the nearby cemetery. Various people were visiting the hospital: the block leaders and their deputies, a party of Americans from E Block, the senior Dutch and Belgians. But Jim was too tired to pester them for news. It was peaceful in the kitchen garden with its green walls of beans and tomato plants. Often Jim visualized staying there forever, even after the war had ended.

He pushed this rustic fantasy to the back of his mind and listened to the drone of a Zero fighter warming up at the end of the runway. A single kamikaze plane was about to take off, all that the Japanese could muster as a reprisal for the American air raid. The young pilot, barely older than Jim, wore his ceremonial sashes, but the honor guard consisted only of a corporal and a junior private. Both turned away before the pilot had climbed into his cockpit and walked back to their repair work on the damaged hangars.

Jim watched the plane rise shakily from the runway. It climbed over the camp, engine laboring under the weight of the bomb, banked toward the river and set course for the open China Sea. Jim cupped his hands over his eyes and followed the plane until it vanished among the clouds. None of the Japanese at Lunghua Airfield had given the aircraft the briefest glance. Fires were still burning in the hangars by the pagoda, and a cloud of steam rose from the bombed engineering sheds. Already, though, the craters were being filled by the work gang of Chinese coolies, and the scrap dealers were scavenging the hulks of the derelict planes.

"Are you still interested in aeroplanes, Jim?" Mrs. Philips asked, as she and Mrs. Gilmour emerged from the hospital courtyard. "You'll have to join the R.A.F."

"I'm going to join the Japanese Air Force."

"Oh? The Japanese?" The missionary widows tittered, still unsure of Jim's sense of humor, and pushed their wooden cart. The iron wheels rang on the stony track, shaking the body that the two women were about to bury.

Jim polished the three tomatoes he had picked from the plants. None was larger than a marble, but Basie would appreciate them. Jim slipped them into his shirt pocket and watched Mrs. Philips and Mrs. Gilmour digging the grave. Soon exhausted, the two women sat on the cart and rested beside the corpse.

Jim walked over to them and took the spade from Mrs. Philips' worn hands. The body was that of Mr. Radik, the former head chef at the Cathay Hotel. Jim had enjoyed his scholarly lectures on the Atlantic liner *Berengaria* and was glad to repay his debt. He dug the soft soil. In one of their few acts of foresight, when they were still strong enough to do so, the prisoners had part-excavated the narrow graves. But the effort of removing a further spade's depth of damp soil was now too much for the missionary widows. The dead were buried above ground, the loose soil heaped around them. The heavy rains of the monsoon months softened the mounds so that they formed the outlines of the bodies within them, as if this small cemetery beside the military airfield was doing its best to resurrect a few of the millions who had died in the war. Here and there an arm or a foot protruded from the graves, the limbs of restless sleepers struggling beneath their brown quilts. Rats had burrowed deep into the grave of Mrs. Hug, the Dutch woman who had arrived at Lunghua with Basie and Dr. Ransome, and the tunnels reminded Jim of the Maginot Line he had constructed behind the rockery at Amherst Avenue for his army of lead soldiers.

He dug away, deciding to sink Mr. Radik well below the ground so that the chef would not become an instant meal for the rats. Mrs. Gilmour and Mrs. Philips sat on the cart beside the corpse and watched without comment. Whenever he paused to rest they treated him to two identical smiles, as blanched as the flowers in the patterns of their tattered cotton dresses.

"Jim! Leave that and come over! I need you here!" Dr. Ransome was shouting from the dispensary window. He had always disliked Jim digging the graves.

Hundreds of flies buzzed around the cart and settled on Mr. Radik's face. With the *Berengaria* in mind, Jim continued to spade the soil.

"Jim, the doctor's calling. . . ."

"All right—it's ready."

The women pulled Mr. Radik from the cart. Although wearied by the effort, they handled him with the same care they had shown when he was alive. Was he still alive for these two Christian widows? Jim had always been impressed by strong religious beliefs. His mother and father were agnostics, and Jim respected devout Christians in the same way that he respected people who were members of the Graf Zeppelin Club or shopped at the Chinese department stores, for their mastery of an exotic foreign ritual. Besides, those who worked hardest for others, like Mrs. Philips and Mrs. Gilmour and Dr. Ransome, often held beliefs that turned out to be correct.

"Mrs. Philips," he asked as they settled Mr. Radik into his grave, "when does the soul leave the body? Before it's buried?"

"Yes, Jim." Mrs. Philips knelt on the ground and began to scoop the earth over Mr. Radik's face. "Mr. Radik's soul has already left. Doctor's calling again. I hope you've done your Latin prep."

"Of course." Jim reflected on this as he walked to the hospital. He often watched the eyes of the patients as they died, trying to detect a flash of light when the soul left. Once he had helped Dr. Ransome as he massaged the naked chest of a young Belgian woman wasted by dysentery. Dr. Bowen had said that she was dead, but

Dr. Ransome squeezed her heart under her ribs and suddenly her eyes swiveled and looked at Jim. At first Jim thought that her soul had returned to her, but she was still dead. Mrs. Philips and Mrs. Gilmour took her away and buried her an hour later. Dr. Ransome explained that for a few seconds he had pumped the blood back into her brain.

Jim entered the dispensary and sat at the metal table facing Dr. Ransome. He would have liked to take up the matter of Mr. Radik's soul, but the doctor was curiously reluctant to discuss religious topics with Jim, although he himself went to the church services on Sunday morning. The scar on his face was still flushed with blood, and he was ominously busy with his tray of melted wax. Whenever he was tired, or annoyed with Jim, Dr. Ransome would melt a few candles and immerse squares of old cloth in the hot liquid, then hang them up to cool. The previous winter he had made hundreds of these wax panels, which the prisoners had used to replace the broken windowpanes. Although the hours of work had helped to keep out the freezing winds that swept down from northern China, few of the prisoners were grateful to Dr. Ransome. Still, as Jim observed, Dr. Ransome was not interested in their gratitude.

Jim dipped a finger in the hot wax, but Dr. Ransome brusquely waved him away. Clearly his conversation with the camp commandant had upset him—he was preparing for the winter as if trying to convince himself that they would all be there when it arrived.

Taking off his shoes, Jim began to buff the toe caps. After three years in clogs and cast-offs, he enjoyed impressing everyone with these expensive leather brogues.

"Jim, it's admirable of you to look so smart, but try

not to polish them *all* the time." Dr. Ransome stared heavily at the wax squares. "They unsettle Sergeant Nagata."

"I like them to look bright."

"They're very bright. Even the American pilots must have seen them. They probably think we have a golf course here and set their compasses to your toe caps."

"That means I'm helping the war effort?"

"In a way . . ." Before Jim could put on his shoes, Dr. Ransome held his ankle. Most of the sores on Jim's legs were infected and, given the poor diet, would never properly heal, but above the right ankle was an ulcer the size of a penny, engorged with pus. Dr. Ransome moved the tray of melted wax from the candle-lamp. He boiled a spoonful of water in a metal pail, then drained and cleaned the ulcer with a cotton swab.

Jim submitted without protest. He had formed his only close bond in Lunghua with Dr. Ransome, though he knew that in many ways the physician disapproved of him. He resented Jim for revealing an obvious truth about the war, that people were only too able to adapt to it. At times he even suspected that Jim enjoyed Latin for the wrong reasons. The brother of a games master at an English boarding school (one of those repressive institutions, so like Lunghua, for which Jim was apparently destined), he had been working up-country with Protestant missionaries. Dr. Ransome was rather like a school prefect and head of rugby, though Jim was unsure how far this manner was calculated. He had noticed that Dr. Ransome could be remarkably devious when it suited him.

"Now, Jim, I'm sure you've done your prep. . . ." Dr. Ransome opened the Latin primer. Although distracted by the prisoners who gathered outside the huts and dormitory blocks, he stared hard at the text. Hundreds of men and their wives, many with their children, were crossing the parade ground. He began to question Jim, who continued to polish his shoes under the table.

"'They were being loved'?"

"*Amabantur.*"

"'I shall be loved'?"

"*Amabor.*"

"'You will have been loved'?"

"*Amatus eris.*"

"Right—I'll set you an unseen. Mrs. Vincent will help you with the vocabulary. She doesn't mind your asking?"

"Not now." Jim reported her change of heart matter-of-factly. He guessed that Dr. Ransome had been useful with some special woman's problem.

"Good. People need to be encouraged. She may not be much use with the trig."

"I don't need her to help me." Jim enjoyed trigonometry. Unlike Latin or algebra, this branch of geometry was directly involved in a subject close to his heart—aerial warfare. "Dr. Ransome, the American bombers that flew with the Mustangs were going at three hundred and twenty miles an hour—I timed their shadows across the camp with my heartbeat. If they want to hit Lunghua Airfield, they have to drop their bombs about a thousand yards away."

"Jim, you're a war child. I imagine the Japanese gunners know that too."

Jim sat back, thinking this over. "They might not."

"Well, we can't tell them—or can we? That would be unfair to the American pilots. As it is, the Japanese are shooting too many of them down."

"But they're shooting them down over the airfield," Jim explained. "Then they've already dropped their bombs. If they want to stop them hitting the runway they should shoot them down more than a thousand yards away." The prospect excited Jim—applied to the Japanese bases all over the Pacific area, this new tactic might turn the war against the Americans and so save Lunghua Camp. Jim drummed his fingers on the table, imitating the way in which he had played the white piano in the empty house in Amherst Avenue.

"Yes. . . ." Dr. Ransome reached out and gently pressed Jim's hands to the table, trying to calm him. He submerged another cotton square in the wax tray. "Perhaps we'll leave the trig, and I'll mark up some algebra. We want the war to end, Jim."

"Of course, Dr. Ransome."

"Do you want the war to end, Jim?" Dr. Ransome often seemed doubtful about this. "A lot of the people here won't last much longer. You're keen to see your mother and father again?"

"Yes, I am. I think about them every day."

"Good. Do you remember what they look like?"

"I do remember. . . ." Jim hated lying to Dr. Ransome, but in a sense he was thinking of the photograph of the unknown man and woman he had pinned to the wall of his cubicle. He had never divulged to Dr. Ransome that these were his surrogate parents. Jim knew that it was important to keep alive the memory of his mother and father, but their faces had become hazy. Dr. Ransome might not approve of the way in which he was tricking himself.

"I'm glad you remember them, Jim. They may have changed."

"I know—they'll be hungry."

"More than hungry, Jim. When the war does end, everything is going to be very uncertain."

"So we should stay in the camp?" Jim liked the sound of this. Too many of the prisoners talked about leaving the camp without any real idea of what would happen to them. "As long as we stay in Lunghua, the Japanese will look after us."

"I'm not sure that they will. We've become an embarrassment to them. They can't feed us any longer, Jim. . . ."

So this was what Dr. Ransome had been leading toward. Jim felt a quiet tiredness come over him. His long hours spent hauling the buckets of sewage, planting and watering the crops in the hospital garden, pulling the ration cart with Mr. Maxted had been part of his attempt to keep the camp going. Yet, as he had known all along, the supply of food depended on the whim of the Japanese. His own feelings, his determination to survive, counted for nothing in the end. The activity meant no more than the movement in the eyes of the Belgian woman who had seemed to come back from the dead.

"Is there going to be any more food, Dr. Ransome?"

"We hope some will come through. The Japanese can no longer feed themselves. The American submarines . . ."

Jim stared at the polished toe caps of his shoes. He wanted his mother and father to see them before they died. He rallied himself, trying to summon his old will to survive. Deliberately he thought of the curious pleasure the corpses in the hospital cemetery gave him, the guilty excitements of being alive at all. He knew why Dr. Ransome disliked him digging the graves.

Dr. Ransome marked the exercises in the algebra textbook and gave him two strips of rice-paper bandage on which to solve the simultaneous equations. As he stood up, Dr. Ransome removed the three tomatoes from Jim's pocket. He laid them on the table by the wax tray.

"Did they come from the hospital garden?"

"Yes." Jim gazed back frankly at Dr. Ransome. Recently he had begun to see him with a more adult eye. The long years of imprisonment, the constant disputes with the Japanese had made this young physician seem middle-aged. Dr. Ransome was often unsure of himself, as he was of Jim's theft.

"I have to give Basie something whenever I see him."

"I know. It's a good thing that you're friends with Basie. He's a survivor, though survivors can be dangerous. Wars exist for people like Basie." Dr. Ransome placed the tomatoes in Jim's hand. "I want you to eat them, Jim. I'll get you something for Basie."

"Dr. Ransome . . ." Jim searched for some way of reassuring him. "If we told Sergeant Nagata about the thousand-yard range . . . the Japanese wouldn't shoot down any more planes, but they might give us some food. . . ."

Dr. Ransome smiled for the first time. He unlocked the medicine cabinet and from a steel cash box he removed two rubber condoms.

"Jim, you're a pragmatist. Give these to Basie, he'll have something for you. Now eat your tomatoes and go."

26

THE LUNGHUA SOPHOMORES

We're the Lunghua Sophomores,
We're the girls every boy adores,
C.A.C. don't mean a thing to me,
For every Tuesday evening we go on a spree. . . .

As he crossed the parade ground toward E Block, Jim paused to watch the Lunghua Players rehearsing their next concert party on the steps of Hut 6. The leader of the troupe was Mr. Wentworth, the manager of the Cathay Bank, whose exaggerated and theatrical manner fascinated Jim. He enjoyed the amateur dramatics, when everyone involved was at the center of public attention. Jim had played a page in *Henry V*, a role he relished. The costume that Mrs. Wentworth had run up for him out of purple velvet was the only decent garment Jim had worn for three years. He had offered to wear it in the Lunghua Players' next production, *The Importance of Being Earnest*, but Mr. Wentworth had declined to cast him.

. . . We've debates and lectures too,
And concerts just for you. . . .

The rehearsal was not a success. The four chorus girls in their Pierrot costumes stood on the makeshift stage of packing cases, trying to remember the song. Upset by the air raid, the women ignored Mr. Wentworth and listened to the sky. Despite the hot sunlight, they rubbed their arms to keep warm.

The audience of bored internees wandered away, and Jim decided to leave the actors to it. The Lunghua Players recruited their members from the snootiest of the English families, and there was something absurd about their high-pitched voices—as affected as the rugby match which Dr. Ransome, in a rare lapse from common sense, had arranged the previous winter. The teams of starving prisoners (husbands of the Lunghua Sophomores) had tottered around the parade ground in a grotesque parody of a rugby game, too exhausted to pass the ball and jeered at by a crowd of fellow prisoners excluded from the game because they had never learned the rules.

Jim passed the guardhouse, carrying out a quick survey of the camp. A group of prisoners had gathered by the gates, waiting for the military truck that brought the daily rations from Shanghai. No official announcement had been made that the ration was to be cut, but the news had already spread through the camp.

Significantly, there were fewer Chinese beggars outside the gates. A dead peasant woman lay on the grass verge, but the disbanded puppet soldiers and out-of-work rickshaw coolies had gone, leaving behind a circle of squatting old men and a few wan-faced children.

Jim entered E Block, the men's dormitory building, and climbed the stairway to the third floor.

Regardless of the weather, the British prisoners in E Block spent almost all their time in their bunks. A few were too ill with malaria to move and lay stretched out on straw mats soaked with sweat and urine. But others still strong enough to walk lounged beside them, examining their hands for hours or staring at the walls.

The sight of so many adult men unwilling to cope with the reality of the camp always puzzled Jim, but he recovered as soon as he reached the American dormitory. Jim liked the Americans and approved of them in every way. Whenever he entered this enclave of irony and good humor, his spirits rose.

Jim surveyed the maze of cubicles. The Britons in E Block lived in open dormitories, but each of the American seamen had constructed a small cubicle from whatever materials he could scavenge—threadbare sheets, wooden planks, straw mats and woven bamboo. Two of the former classrooms were occupied by the American merchant seamen. The partition doors had been removed, and the high-ceilinged chamber was filled by some sixty men, each in a makeshift cubicle. Now and then a party of Americans would emerge from E Block and play a relaxed game of softball, but usually they remained in their cubicles. There they lay on their bunks and entertained a steady stream of adolescent girls, single British women and even a few wives drawn to them for reasons not very different from Jim's.

By some mechanism that Jim had never understood, the sexual activity seemed to generate an endless supply of those items that most fascinated Jim. This treasure had been brought into the camp by the American sailors and now circulated like a second currency—comic books and copies of *Life, Reader's Digest* and *Saturday Evening Post;* novelty pens, lipsticks and powder compacts; gaudy tiepins, cigarette lighters and celluloid belts; fairground cuff links and Wild West buckles—a collection of gee-gaws that in Jim's eyes had the style and magic of the Mustang fighters.

"Say, it's Shanghai Jim. . . ."

"Kid, Basie's mad at you. . . ."

"You want to play chess, son?"

"Jim, I need hot water and a shave."

"Jim, bring me a left-handed screwdriver and a bucket of steam. . . ."

"Why's Basie mad at Jim?"

Jim exchanged greetings with the Americans—Cohen, the softball wizard and chess fanatic; Tiptree, the large, kindly stoker who was the comic-book king; Hinton, yet another cabin steward and philosopher; Dainty, the tele-graphist and premier cocksman of Lunghua—amiable men whose roles they played for Jim's benefit and constantly teased. When they noticed him, most of them liked Jim, who in return, and out of respect for America, ran endless errands for them. Several of the cubicles were closed as the merchant seamen entertained their visitors, but the others had their curtains raised so that the sailors could lie on their bunks and observe the passing world. Two of the older seamen were wracked by malaria, but they made little fuss about being ill. All in all, Jim felt, the Americans were the best company, not as strange and challenging as the Japanese, but far superior to the morose and complicated British.

Why was Basie angry with him? Jim stepped down the narrow corridor between the suspended sheets. He could hear an Englishwoman from Hut 5 complaining about her husband, and two Belgian girls who lived with their widowed father in G Block giggled over some object they were being shown.

Basie's cubicle was in the northeast corner of the room,

with two windows that gave him a clear view of the entire camp. As always he was sitting on his bunk, keeping an eye on the Japanese soldiers outside the guardhouse as he received the latest report from Demarest, his cubicle neighbor and chief henchman. His long-sleeved cotton shirt was faded but neatly creased—after Jim had washed and dried the shirts, Basie would fold them in a complex, origamilike package and slide them under his sleeping mat, from which they emerged with a department-store sharpness. Since Basie rarely moved from his bunk, he seemed even cooler and crisper in Jim's eyes than Mr. Sekura, and in most respects the years in Lunghua had been less of a strain for Basie than for the Japanese commandant. His hands and cheeks were still soft and unworn, though with a pallor like that of an unhealthy woman. Moving around his cubicle, as if in his pantry on the S.S. *Aurora,* he regarded Lunghua Camp in the same way that he had viewed the world beyond it, a suite of cabins to be kept ready for a succession of unwary passengers.

"Come in, kid. Stop breathing so much, you're making Basie all hot." Demarest, a former bar steward, spoke without moving his lips—either, as Jim believed, he had spent an earlier career as a ventriloquist or, as Mr. Maxted maintained, he had passed long terms in prison.

"The boy's all right. . . ." Basie beckoned Jim to sit down as Demarest returned to his cubicle. "There just isn't enough air for him in the whole of Lunghua. Isn't that it, Jim?"

Jim tried to control his panting—not enough red cells, according to Dr. Ransome, but often he and Basie meant the same thing.

"You're right, Basie. The Mustangs took it all with them. Did you see the air raid?"

"I heard it, Jim. . . ." Basie glanced darkly at Jim, as if holding him responsible for the noise. "Those Philippino pilots must have gone to flight school at Coney Island."

"Philippino?" Jim at last mastered his lungs. "Were they really Philippino pilots?"

"Some of them, Jim. There are a couple of wings operating with MacArthur's outfit. The rest are old Flying Tigers based at Chungking." Basie nodded sagely, watching Jim to make sure he appreciated his superior savvy.

"Chungking . . ." Jim was agog. This was the kind of information on which his mind feasted, even though he knew that Basie embroidered the reports for his benefit. Somewhere in the camp was a concealed radio which had never been discovered, not because it was well hidden but because the Japanese were confused by the false tips given by prisoners eager to collaborate. Despite all his efforts, Jim had been unable to track down the radio, which was inactive for long periods. Then Basie would supply Jim with news bulletins of his own, describing a parallel war. Jim always pretended to be impressed, though he could rarely separate rumor from outright fiction. It was an important way of keeping them close together.

Also, there was Basie's interest in Jim's expanding vocabulary.

"You did your schoolwork today, Jim? You learned all your words?"

"I did, Basie. A lot of Latin words." Basie was intrigued by Jim's command of Latin, but easily bored, so he decided not to recite the whole passive tense of *amo*. "And some new English words. 'Pragmatist,'" he suggested, which Basie greeted with gloom, "and 'survivor.'"

"'Survivor'?" Basie chuckled at this. "That's a useful word. Are you a survivor, Jim?"

"Well . . ." Dr. Ransome had not meant the term as a compliment. Jim tried to remember another word of interest. Basie never used the words but seemed to store them away, keeping them in reserve for a better day, as if preparing himself for a life of elaborate formality.

"Is there any more news, Basie? When are the Americans going to land at Woosung?"

But Basie was preoccupied. He rested his head against the pillow and stared at the contents of the cubicle, as if burdened by all his possessions. At first sight the cubicle seemed to be filled with old rags and wicker baskets, but it actually contained a complete general store. There were aluminum pots and pans, an assortment of women's slacks and blouses, a Mah-Jongg set, several tennis rackets, half a dozen unmatched shoes and a king's ransom of old copies of *Reader's Digest* and *Popular Mechanics*. All these had been obtained by barter, though Jim had never understood what Basie gave in return—like Dr. Ransome, he had come into the camp with nothing.

On the other hand, it had occurred to Jim that much of this equipment was useless. No one was strong enough to play tennis, the shoes were full of holes and there was nothing to cook in the saucepans. The cabin steward, for all his guile, was the same limited man whom Jim had first met at the Nantao shipyards, with the same clear but small view of the world. Basie's talents expanded to fill only the most modest possibilities of petty thievery around him. Jim worried about what would happen to Basie when the war was over.

"Jobs, Jim," Basie announced. "You set out the traps? How far did you go? Across the creek?"

"Right across the creek, Basie. I went as far as the old drill hall."

"Good."

"I didn't see any pheasants, Basie. I don't think there are any pheasants. It's too close to the airfield."

"There are pheasants, Jim. But we need to move the traps to the Shanghai road." He peered shrewdly at Jim. "Then we'll have to set up a decoy."

"We could set up a decoy, Basie." Jim guessed that there already was a decoy—himself. The whole enterprise of setting the traps had nothing to do with catching pheasants. Perhaps one of the Americans was planning to visit Shanghai, and Jim was being used to test the escape route. Alternatively, these bored sailors might be playing a game, betting among each other on how far Jim could push the traps before being shot by the Japanese sentry in the watchtower. Although they liked Jim, they were quite capable of gambling with his life. That was American humor of a most special kind.

Jim swayed with fatigue, wishing he could lie across the foot of the bunk. Basie was watching him in an expectant way. From his window he would have seen Jim at work in the hospital garden, and he was waiting for a few beans or tomatoes. Basie always demanded these tidbits, though he was generous in his own way. When Jim was younger Basie spent hours making toys for him out of copper wire and cotton reels, sewing exquisite fish flies that hung from free-floating buoys. On Jim's birthdays it was only Basie who gave him a present.

"Basie, I bought something for you. . . ." Jim took the two condoms from his pocket. Basie pulled a rusty biscuit tin from below his bunk. As he removed the lid Jim saw that the tin was packed with hundreds of the prophylactics, as the Americans called them. Once the original stock of cigarettes was exhausted, these grubby rubbers formed Lunghua Camp's main unit of currency. The number in circulation had barely fallen in three years, not because there was little sexual intercourse at Lunghua, but for the reason that the contraceptives were too valuable as units of exchange to be used for idle purposes. Playing poker, the American sailors used stacks of the condoms as chips. It was doubly ironic, as Jim had heard Dr. Ransome remark, that their value continued to rise even though almost all the prisoners in the camp were either impotent or infertile.

Basie inspected the condoms, suspicious of their pristine condition.

"Where did you get these, Jim?"

"They're good ones, Basie. That's the best type."

"Is that so?" Basie often accepted Jim's expertise in unlikely areas. "Perhaps you were looking inside Dr. Ransome's medical cabinet?"

"There weren't any tomatoes, Basie. The air raid spoiled them."

"Those Philippino pilots . . . Never mind. Tell me about Dr. Ransome's cabinet. There were medicines there, I imagine."

"Basie, there were a lot of medicines. Iodine, Mercurochrome . . ." In fact, the cupboard was bare. Jim tried to remember the medicine chest in his father's bathroom and the strange names that summed up the mysterious world of the adult body. ". . . pessaries, linctus, suppositories . . ."

"Suppositories? Lie down, Jim. You're getting tired." Basie put an arm around Jim's shoulders. Together they gazed through the window at the crowd of prisoners waiting for the overdue ration truck from Shanghai. "Don't worry, Jim, there'll be plenty to eat soon. Forget all this talk about the Japs cutting our rations."

"They might do it, Basie. We're an embarrassment to them."

"An embarrassment? Dr. Ransome is worrying you with all these words. Believe me, Jim, it's going to take more than us to embarrass the Japs." He reached under his pillow and brought out a small sweet potato. "You eat this while I work out our jobs. When you've finished, I'll give you a *Reader's Digest* you can take back to G Block."

"Say, thanks, Basie!" Jim devoured the potato. He liked Basie's cubicle. The abundance of objects, even if they were useless, was reassuring, like the abundance of words around Dr. Ransome. The Latin vocabulary and the algebraic terms were useless too, but they helped to make up a world. Basie's confidence in the future encouraged him.

Sure enough, as he licked the last pith from his fingers, saving the skin for the evening, the military truck arrived from Shanghai with the prisoners' food ration.

27

THE EXECUTION

TWO JAPANESE SOLDIERS with fixed bayonets stood behind the driving cabin of the truck, their thighs lost among the sacks of potatoes and cracked wheat. However, as he leaned from Basie's window, Jim could see that the ration had been halved. He was glad that some food had come, but at the same time he felt almost disappointed. A crowd of several hundred prisoners followed the truck toward the kitchens, hands in the pockets of their ragged shorts, their clogs clattering. How would they have behaved if the truck had been empty? None of the prisoners, not even Dr. Ransome, seemed able to rally themselves for the last stages of the war. Jim almost welcomed the hunger, when he would see again the curious light the Mustangs had brought with them. . . .

Around him the Americans were leaving their cubicles and pressing against the windows. Demarest pointed to the columns of smoke that rose from the dockyard districts of northern Shanghai. Although they were more than ten miles away, Jim could hear a hard rumble across the deserted paddy fields, a forgotten thunder that reverberated over the land long after the bombs had exploded. The sounds drummed at the windows, a vague ultimatum to the listless prisoners of Lunghua.

Jim searched the smoke clouds for any signs of American aircraft. None of the dozen serviceable Zeros at Lunghua Airfield had taken off to intercept them.

"B-29s, Basie?"

"That's it, Jim. Superfortress bombers, what we call a hemisphere defense weapon. All the way from Guam."

"From Guam, Basie . . ." Jim was impressed by the thought of these four-engined bombers making the long journey across the Pacific, in order to attack the Shanghai dockyards where he had spent so many happy hours playing hide-and-seek. The B-29s awed Jim. The huge, streamlined bombers summed up all the power and grace of America. Usually the B-29s flew above the Japanese antiaircraft fire, but two days earlier Jim had seen a single Superfortress cross the paddy fields to the west of the camp, only five hundred feet above the ground. Two of its engines were on fire, but the sight of this immense bomber with its high, curving tail convinced Jim that the Japanese had lost the war. Jim had seen captured American air crews who were held for a few hours in the Lunghua guardhouse. What impressed him so much was that these complex machines were flown by men such as Cohen and Tiptree and Dainty. That was America.

Jim thought intently about the B-29s. He wanted to embrace their silver fuselages, caress the nacelles of their engines. The Mustang was a beautiful plane, but the Superfortress belonged to a different order of beauty. . . .

"Take it easy, kid." Basie put an arm around his shaking chest. "They're a long way from Lunghua. You're going to mess yourself."

"I'm all right, Basie. The war's nearly over, isn't it?"

"That's it. Not too soon for you, Jim. Tell me, did you ever see the Hell Drivers in Shanghai?"

"Sure I did, Basie! I saw them crash right through a burning wall!"

"Okay, then. Let's calm down and get on with our jobs."

For the next hour Jim was busy with the tasks that Basie had assigned him. First, there was water to be collected from the pond behind the guardhouse. When he had carried the bucket back to E Block, Jim set about gathering fuel for the stove. Basie still insisted on boiling his drinking water, but the shortage of fuel made this difficult. After rounding up a few sticks and shreds of straw mats, Jim searched the pathways around E Block, hunting for fragments of coke embedded in the cinder track. Even the cinders gave off a surprising heat.

Having lit his stove, Jim blew on the lazy flames. He placed the pieces of coke at the neck of the clay venturi, where, as Dr. Ransome had explained, the air moved most swiftly. As soon as the drinking water had boiled, he decanted some gray fluid into the mess tin, which he carried upstairs and left to cool on Basie's window ledge. He collected Basie's clothes and washed the dirty shirts in the remaining water. These could be left for an hour, while he queued for Basie's rations. The male prisoners in E Block were the last to be fed each day, and the men queued at the kitchens. Jim always enjoyed the long wait for Basie's ration of cracked wheat and sweet potato, and felt himself a growing man in the company of men. The lines of sweating prisoners, covered with ulcers and mosquito bites, gave off a heady odor of aggression, and Jim could understand the Japanese guards being wary of them. Much of their foul language was above his head, their brutally crude talk of women's bodies and private parts, as if these emaciated males were trying to provoke themselves by describing what they could no longer perform. But there were always phrases to be catalogued away and savored as he lay in his cubicle.

By the time Jim returned to E Block with Basie's shirts and food ration, he felt entitled to push past Demarest and sit at the foot of the bunk. He watched Basie eat the cracked wheat, flicking the weevils to and fro like a Chinese shopkeeper with his abacus.

"We worked hard today, Jim. Your dad would be proud of us. Which camp did you say he was in?"

"Soochow Central. And my mother. You can meet them soon." Jim wanted Basie to be present at their reunion, so that the cabin steward could identify him if his parents failed to recognize Jim.

"I'd like to meet with them, Jim. If they're not moved up-country . . ."

Jim noticed the odd inflection in Basie's voice. "Up-country?"

"Well, it's possible, Jim. Maybe the Japs will move people from the camps near Shanghai."

"We'll be out of the war, then?"

"Yes, you'll be out of the war, all right. . . ." Basie hid the sweet potato among the saucepans under his bunk. He rummaged among the shoes and tennis rackets and then produced a copy of *Reader's Digest*. He flipped through the grimy pages, which had been read a dozen times by every resident of E Block. Layers of greasy tape, stained with dried blood and pus, held the cover to the threadbare spine.

"Jim, are you still reading the *Digest?* August '41, it has some good things in it. . . ."

Basie relished every moment of Jim's excitement. This elaborate teasing was part of the ritual. Jim waited patiently, well aware that Basie exploited him, setting him to work each day in return for the old magazines. These bored merchant seamen could see that Jim was obsessed by everything American, and in their good-natured way they kept him dangling, rationing the ancient copies of *Life* and *Collier's* that Jim needed as much as the extra sweet potatoes. The magazines fed a desperate imagination.

This unequal exchange, jobs for magazines, was also part of Jim's conscious attempt to keep the camp going, whatever the cost. The activity screened his mind from certain fears that he had tried to repress, that the years in Lunghua would come to an end, and he would find himself building the runway again. The light that emerged from the burning body of the Mustang pilot had been a warning to him. As long as he ran his errands for Basie and Demarest and Cohen, to and from the kitchens, carrying water and playing chess, Jim could sustain the illusion that the war would last forever.

Reader's Digest in hand, Jim sat on the steps outside E Block. He squinted at the sunlight, forcing himself not to glance through the pages. Groups of prisoners lounged on the balconies after their meal. The shade between the pillars was reserved for the sick internees, who squatted together like the families of beggars in the entrances to the office blocks behind the Shanghai Bund.

Next to Jim was a young man who had been a floor manager in the Sincere Company department store and was now suffering from the last stages of malaria. His body rattling with fever, he sat naked on the cement steps and watched the Lunghua Players rehearsing their concert party. His white lips, from which all iron had long been leached, repeated an inaudible phrase.

Jim wondered how to help this skeletal figure. He offered him the *Reader's Digest*, a gesture he instantly regretted. The man clasped the magazine in his hands and crushed the pages, as if the printed words inflamed his memories. He began to sing, in a harsh but barely audible voice.

> . . . *we're the girls every boy adores,*
> *C.A.C. don't mean a thing to me* . . .

A stream of colorless urine ran down his legs and trickled down the steps. He dropped the magazine, which Jim quickly retrieved before the pages could be soaked. As Jim straightened the spine, he heard the air-raid siren sound from the guardhouse. After a few seconds, before the prisoners could run for shelter, it stopped abruptly. Everyone stared at the empty sky, expecting the Mustangs to roar in from the paddy fields.

However, the siren blast signaled an altogether different display. Four Japanese soldiers, among them Private Kimura, emerged from the guardhouse. They surrounded a Chinese coolie who pulled a rickshaw which had brought one of their officers from Shanghai. Still exhausted by the long run, the coolie plodded in his straw sandals across the bare earth of the parade ground. His head was lowered as he pulled at the shafts, and he tittered in the strained way of frightened Chinese.

The Japanese soldiers strode briskly on either side of him. None of them was armed, but they carried wooden staves which they struck at the wheels of the rickshaw and at the shoulders of the coolie. Private Kimura walked behind the rickshaw and kicked the wooden seat, hurling the vehicle against the coolie's legs. At the center of the parade ground Kimura and another soldier seized the rickshaw and propelled it forward, pitching the coolie onto the ground.

The soldiers began to saunter around the upended rickshaw. Private Kimura kicked its wheels, shattering the spokes. The others stamped on the wooden handles and snapped the shafts. Together they threw the vehicle onto its back, scattering the cushions.

The coolie knelt on the ground, laughing to himself. In the silence Jim could hear the strange singsong that the Chinese made when they knew they were about to be killed. Around the parade ground the hundreds of prisoners watched without moving. Men and women sat in the makeshift deck chairs outside the barrack huts, or stood on the steps of the dormitory blocks. The Lunghua Players paused in their rehearsal. None of them spoke as the Japanese soldiers strolled around the rickshaw, kicking its seats and framework into matchwood. From the locker below the seat fell a bundle of rags, a tin pail, a cotton bag filled with rice and a Chinese newspaper, the entire worldly possessions of this illiterate coolie. He sat among the grains of rice scattered on the ground and began to sing at a higher note, raising his face to the sky.

Jim smoothed the pages of the *Reader's Digest*, wondering whether to read an article about Winston Churchill. He would have liked to leave, but all around him the prisoners were motionless as they watched the parade ground. The Japanese turned their attention to the coolie. Raising their staves, they each struck him a blow on the head, then strolled away as if deep in thought. Breathlessly now, the coolie sang to himself as the blood ran from his back and formed a pool around his knees.

The Japanese soldiers, Jim knew, would take ten minutes to kill the coolie. Although they had been confused by the bombing and the prospect of the imminent end of the war, they were now calm. The whole display, like their lack of weapons, was intended to show the British prisoners that the Japanese despised them, first for being prisoners, and then for not daring to move an inch to save this Chinese coolie.

Jim realized that the Japanese were right. None of the British internees would raise a finger, even if every coolie in China were beaten to death in front of them. Jim listened to the blows from the staves and to the muffled cries as the coolie choked on his blood. Dr. Ransome would probably have tried to stop the Japanese. But Dr. Ransome was careful never to go near the parade ground.

Jim thought about his algebra prep, part of which he had already done inside his head. Ten minutes later, when the Japanese returned to the guardhouse, the hundreds of prisoners moved away from the parade ground. The Lunghua Players continued their rehearsal. Slipping the *Reader's Digest* inside his shirt, Jim returned to G Block by another route.

Later that evening, when he had finished Basie's potato skin, Jim lay on his bunk and at last opened the magazine. There were no advertisements in the *Reader's Digest,* which was a shame, but Jim looked at the reassuring picture of the Packard limousine pinned to the wall of his cubicle. He listened to the Vincents talking in their low voices, and to the faint whoops of their son's cough. On Jim's return from E Block he had found the boy playing on the floor with the turtle. There had been a brief confrontation between Jim and Mr. Vincent, who had tried to stop him replacing the turtle in the wooden case under his bunk. But Jim had stood his ground, confident that Mr. Vincent would not try to wrestle with him. Mrs. Vincent watched without expression as her husband sat on his bed, staring in his desperate way at Jim's raised fists.

28

AN ESCAPE

"IS THE WAR over again, Mr. Maxted?"

All around Jim, as he waited by the kitchen doors, the prisoners were pushing aside the food carts, shouting and pointing to the gates. The all-clear siren sounded across the camp, the wail of a broken bird trying to hide from the American bombing. Arms on each other's shoulders, the prisoners watched the Japanese soldiers leaving the guardhouse. Each of the thirty men carried his rifle with fixed bayonet and a canvas pannier holding his personal kit. Among the straw mats and *kendo* armor there were two baseball bats, pairs of sneakers hung by their laces and a portable gramophone, all obtained from the prisoners in return for cigarettes, food and news of relations in other camps.

"It looks as if your little friends are leaving, Jim." Mr. Maxted ran his grimy fingers between his ribs, hunting for loose shreds of skin. He squinted at them in the August sun, as if concerned that he was mislaying pieces of himself around the camp. "I'll keep your place for you if you want to wave to Private Kimura."

"He knows my address, Mr. Maxted. I don't like saying good-bye. They'll probably come back this afternoon when they find there isn't anywhere to go."

Unwilling to risk his place at the head of the kitchen queue, where he and Mr. Maxted had waited since dawn, Jim climbed onto the food cart. Over the heads of the men in front of him he watched the Japanese file through the gates of the camp. They lined up along the road, their backs to the fire-gutted fuselage of a Japanese aircraft that lay in the paddy field a hundred yards away. The twin-engined aircraft had been shot down two days earlier as it took off from Lunghua Airfield, torn apart by the machine guns of the Lightning fighters that rose without warning from the deserted countryside.

As he balanced on the metal cart, Jim could see Private Kimura peering uneasily at the eastern horizon, from which the fearsome American planes emerged like pieces of the sun. Even in the warm August light, Kimura's face had the toneless texture of cold wax. He licked his fingers and wiped his cheeks with the spittle, nervous of leaving the secure world of Lunghua Camp. In front of him the group of Chinese peasants sat on the grass verge. They stared at the gates, which had rejected them for so many months and were now unguarded. Jim was sure that these starving Chinese, in their universe of death, were unable to grasp the meaning of an open gate.

Jim gazed at the untended space between the posts. He too found it difficult to accept that he would soon be able to walk through the gates to freedom. The soldier in the watchtower made his way down the ladder to the guardhouse roof, his light machine gun clipped to the webbing across his shoulders. Sergeant Nagata emerged from the guardhouse and joined his men outside the camp. Since the disappearance of the commandant in the con-

245

fusion of the previous week, the sergeant had been the senior Japanese officer in the camp.

"Mr. Maxted, Sergeant Nagata is going—the war *has* ended!"

"Ended again, Jim? I don't think we can stand it. . . ."

During the past week, when rumors of the war's end had swept the camp every hour, Mr. Maxted had found Jim's high spirits more and more tiresome. As he ran on his errands down the pathways, Jim shouted at any passersby, waved to the prisoners resting outside the barrack huts, excitedly jumped among the graves in the hospital cemetery when the American aircraft flew overhead, all part of his attempt to cover the insecurities of the coming world beyond the camp. Dr. Ransome had twice slapped him.

Yet now that the war was over, he felt surprisingly calm. Soon he would be seeing his mother and father, returning to the house in Amherst Avenue, to that forgotten realm of servants and Packards and polished parquet. At the same time, Jim reflected that the prisoners *ought* to celebrate, throw their clogs in the air, seize the air-raid siren and play it back at the incoming American planes. But too many of them were like Mr. Maxted, staring silently at the Japanese. They seemed glum and wary, the men almost naked in their ragged shorts, the women in faded sunsuits and patched cotton frocks, their malarial eyes unable to face the glare of freedom. Exposed to the light that seemed to flood into the camp through the open gates, their bodies were even darker and more wasted, and for the first time they looked as if they were guilty of a crime.

Rumor and confusion had exhausted everyone in Lunghua. During July the American air attacks had become almost continuous. Waves of Mustangs and Lightnings flew in from the air bases on Okinawa, strafing the airfields around Shanghai, attacking the Japanese forces concentrated at the mouth of the Yangtze. From the balcony of the ruined assembly hall Jim witnessed the destruction of the Japanese military machine as if he were watching an epic war film from the circle of the Cathay Theater. The apartment houses of the French Concession were hidden by hundreds of smoke columns that rose from burning trucks and ammunition wagons. Fearful of the Mustangs, the Japanese convoys moved only after dusk, and the sound of their engines kept everyone awake night after night. Sergeant Nagata and his guards had given up any attempt to patrol the camp's perimeter for fear of being shot by the military police supervising the convoys.

By the end of July almost all Japanese resistance to the American bombers had ceased. A single antiaircraft gun mounted on the upper deck of Lunghua Pagoda continued to fire at the incoming aircraft, but the batteries around the runway had been withdrawn to defend the Shanghai dockyards. In these last days of the war Jim spent hours at the assembly hall, waiting for the high-flying Superfortresses in whose silver wings and fuselages he had invested so much of his imagination. Unlike the Mustangs and Lightnings, which skimmed like racing cars across the paddy fields, the B-29s would appear without warning in the sky above his head, as if summoned by Jim's starving brain. Their rolling thunder advanced across the land from the dockyards of Nantao. A Japanese troopship leaned against the mud flats, bombed again and again until Jim could see daylight through its superstructure.

Throughout all this, the concrete runway at Lunghua Airfield remained intact. By a heroic effort, the Japanese engineers continued to fill in the craters after each raid, as if expecting a fleet of rescue aircraft to arrive from the Home Islands. The whiteness of the runway excited Jim, its sun-bleached surface mixed with the calcinated bones of the dead Chinese, and even perhaps with his own bones in a death that might have been. Impatiently he waited for the Japanese to make their last stand.

This confusion of loyalties, the fear of what would happen to them once the Japanese were defeated, affected everyone in the camp. Often there were cheers from the light-headed prisoners squatting outside the barrack huts as a stricken B-29 dropped out of its formation. Dr. Ransome had been correct to predict that the food supply to Lunghua would soon end. Once a week a single truck arrived from Shanghai with a few bags of fermenting potatoes and the godown sweepings of animal feed filled with weevils and rat droppings. Fights broke out among the prisoners queuing for their small ration. Irritated by the sight of Jim waiting all day by the kitchen doors, a group of Britons from E Block pushed him aside and overturned his iron cart. From then on, Jim recruited the help of Mr. Maxted, nagging the architect until he clambered from his bunk.

Through the last week of July they watched the Shanghai road together, hoping that the ration truck had not been attacked by a low-flying Mustang. During these hungry days Jim discovered that most of the prisoners in G Block had been quietly stockpiling a small reserve of potatoes, and that he and Mr. Maxted, who had volunteered to collect the daily ration, were among the few not to have planned ahead.

Jim sat on his bunk, empty plate in hand, and watched the Vincents share a rancid potato. They nibbled at the pith with their yellowing teeth. At last Mrs. Vincent gave him a small piece of skin. Was she afraid that Jim would attack her husband? Fortunately, Jim was fed from the modest reserve that Dr. Ransome had accumulated from his dying patients.

But by August 1 even these supplies had come to an end. Jim and Mr. Maxted roamed the camp with their cart, as if hoping that a consignment of rice or cracked wheat might materialize under the legs of the watertower or among the graves in the cemetery. Once Mr. Maxted caught Jim looking at the wrist bones of Mrs. Hug that had emerged from her grave, as white as the runway at Lunghua Airfield.

For Jim, a curious vacuum enclosed the camp. Time had ceased to exist at Lunghua, and many of the prisoners were convinced that the war was already over. On August 2, after the rumor that the Russians had entered the war against Japan, Sergeant Nagata and his soldiers withdrew to the guardhouse and no longer patrolled the fence, abandoning the camp to its inmates. Parties of British prisoners stepped through the wire and wandered around the nearby paddy fields. Parents stood with their children on the burial mounds, pointing to the watchtower and the dormitory blocks as if seeing the camp for the first time. One group of men led by Mr. Tulloch, the senior mechanic at the Packard agency in Shanghai, set off across the fields, intending to walk to Shanghai. Others gathered around the guardhouse, jeering at the Japanese soldiers who watched from their windows.

Throughout the day Jim was confused by the apparent collapse of order within the camp. He was unwilling to believe that the war was over. He climbed through the fence and spent a few minutes with the pheasant traps, then returned to the camp and sat alone on the balcony of the assembly hall. At last rallying himself, he went in search of Basie. But the American sailors no longer received their lady callers and had barricaded the doors of the dormitory. From his window Basie called to Jim, cautioning him not to leave the camp.

Sure enough, the war's end proved to be short-lived. At dusk a motorized column of Japanese troops passed the camp on its way to Hangchow. The military police returned to the guardhouse the six Britons who had tried to walk to Shanghai. Severely beaten, they lay unconscious for three hours on the guardhouse steps. When Sergeant Nagata allowed them to be carried to their bunks, they described the confused terrain to the south and west of Shanghai, the thousands of desperate peasants driven back to the city with the retreating Japanese, the gangs of bandits and starving soldiers from the puppet armies left to fend for themselves.

Despite these dangers, the very next day Basie, Cohen and Demarest escaped from Lunghua.

The prisoners pressed forward to the empty guardhouse, their clogs clacking on the cinder path. Buffeted by the almost naked men, Jim held tight to the handles of the iron cart. The other prisoners had abandoned their carts, but Jim was determined not to be caught out if the ration truck arrived. He had not eaten since the previous afternoon. Although the inmates were about to seize control of the guardhouse, he could think of nothing except food.

A group of British and Belgian women stood by the gates, calling through the wire to the line of Japanese soldiers in the road. Weighed down by their rifles and bedding rolls, they fretted in the August sunlight. Private Kimura gazed uneagerly at the desolate paddy fields, as if wishing he were back in the secure world of the camp.

Flecks of spittle brightened the dust around the soldiers' ragged boots. Venting the anger of years on their former guards, the women spat through the wire, shouting and jeering. A Belgian woman began to scream in Japanese, tearing pieces of faded cloth from the sleeve of her cotton dress and hurling them at the feet of the soldiers.

Jim clung to his cart, jerking the handles when Mr. Maxted wearily tried to sit on the wooden shaft. He felt detached from the spitting women and their excited husbands. Where was Basie? Why had he escaped? Despite the rumors that the war had ended, it surprised Jim that Basie should leave Lunghua and expose himself to all the hazards of the countryside. The cabin steward was too cautious, never the first to try anything new or gamble away his modest security. Jim guessed that he had heard some warning message on the secret radio. He had abandoned his cubicle filled with the hard-earned treasure of years, the shoes and tennis rackets and hundreds of condoms.

Jim remembered that Basie had talked about the inmates of the camps near Shanghai being moved up-country. Was he warning Jim that it was time to leave before the Japanese ran amok as they had done in Nanking in 1937? The Japanese always killed their prisoners before they made their last stands. But Basie had been wrong; at that moment he was probably lying dead in a ditch after being murdered by bandits.

Headlamps flared along the Shanghai road. Wiping their chins, the women stepped back from the wire. Necklaces of spit lay on their breasts. A Japanese staff car was approaching, followed by a convoy of military trucks, each packed with armed soldiers. One of the trucks had already stopped, and a platoon of soldiers jumped down into the road and then ran across the drained paddy field beside the western perimeter of the camp. Bayonets fixed, they took up their positions facing the wire.

Silent now, the hundreds of prisoners turned to watch them. A second platoon of air force police was wading across the canal that separated Lunghua Airfield from the camp. To the east, the long bend of the Whangpoo River completed the circle with its maze of creeks and irrigation ditches.

The convoy reached the camp, headlamps reflected in the dusty spit. Armed soldiers leaped to the ground, bayonets fixed to their rifles. From their fresh uniforms and equipment, Jim could see that these security troops were a special field unit of the Japanese gendarmerie. They moved swiftly through the gates, taking up their positions outside the guardhouse.

The prisoners drew back, bumping into each other like a herd of sheep. Caught by the retreat, Jim was knocked from his cart by the crush of bodies. A Japanese corporal, a short but strongly built man whose holstered Mauser swung from his waist like a club, seized the handles of the cart and propelled it toward the gates. Jim was about to run forward and wrestle the handles from the Japanese, but Mr. Maxted gripped his arms.

"Jim, for God's sake . . . Leave it!"

"But—it's G Block's cart! Are they going to kill us, Mr. Maxted?"

"Jim . . . we'll find Dr. Ransome."

"Is the ration truck coming?" Jim pushed Mr. Maxted away, tired of having to support this ailing figure.

"Later, Jim. Perhaps it will come later."

"I don't think the ration truck will come." As the line of Japanese soldiers forced the prisoners across the parade ground, Jim watched the guards patrolling the wire. Seeing the Japanese again had restored his confidence. The prospect of being killed excited him; after the uncertainties of the past week he welcomed any end. For a few last moments, like the rickshaw coolie who had sung to himself, they would be fully aware of their own minds. Whatever happened, he would survive. He thought of Mrs. Philips and Mrs. Gilmour and their discussion of the exact moment at which the soul left the body of the dying. His soul had already left and no longer needed his thin bones and open sores in order to endure. He was dead, as were Mr. Maxted and Dr. Ransome. Everyone in Lunghua was dead. It was absurd that they had failed to grasp this.

They stood on the grass verge behind the throng of prisoners who now filled the parade ground. Jim began to titter, relieved that he understood the real meaning of the war.

"They don't need to kill us, Mr. Maxted. . . ."

"Of course they don't, Jim."

"Mr. Maxted, they don't need to because—"

"Jim!" Mr. Maxted cuffed Jim, then pressed the boy's head to his emaciated chest. "Remember you're British."

Circumspectly, Jim eased the smile from his face. He calmed himself, then wormed his shoulders from Mr. Maxted's embrace. The moment of humor had passed, but the insight into their true situation, and his sense of being apart from himself, remained. Concerned for Mr. Maxted, who was dribbling an oily phlegm onto the ground between his bare feet, Jim put an arm around his bony hips. He felt sorry for the former architect, remembering their Studebaker jaunts around the Shanghai nightclubs, and sad that he should have been so demoralized that all he could do to reassure Jim was to remind him that he was British.

Outside the guardhouse, where the commander of the gendarmerie unit had established himself, the four block leaders were talking to a Japanese sergeant. A wan-faced Dr. Ransome, coolie hat in hand, his shoulders stooped in his cotton shirt, stood beside them. Mrs. Pearce entered the guardhouse, smoothing her hair and cheeks, already giving orders to a soldier in her rapid Japanese.

The prisoners at the front of the crowd turned and ran across the parade ground, shouting to the others.

"One suitcase! Everyone back here in an hour!"

"We're leaving for Nantao!"

"Everybody out! Line up by the gates!"

"They're holding our rations at Nantao!"

"One suitcase!"

Already the missionary couples were standing on the steps of G Block, bags in hand, as if they had somehow sensed the coming move. Watching them, Jim reassured himself that the camp was only being moved, not closed.

"Come on, Mr. Maxted—we're going back to Shanghai!"

He helped the weakened man to his feet and steered him through the hundreds of running prisoners. When Jim reached his room, he found that Mrs. Vincent was already packed. As her son slept in his bunk, she stood by the window, watching her husband return from the parade ground. Jim could see that she had begun to shed all memories of the camp.

"We're leaving, Mrs. Vincent. We're going to Nantao."

"Then you'll have to pack." She was waiting for him

to go so that she could be alone in the room for a few last minutes.

"Right. I've been to Nantao, Mrs. Vincent."

"So have I. I can't imagine why the Japanese should want us to go again."

"Our rations are in a godown there." Jim was already debating whether to carry Mrs. Vincent's suitcase. New alliances needed to be forged, and Mrs. Vincent's slim but strong-hipped body might well have more stamina than Mr. Maxted's. As for Dr. Ransome, he would be busy with his patients, most of whom would soon start dying. Jim had steered clear of Dr. Ransome, aware that he was too tired to dig any more graves.

"I'll be seeing my parents soon, Mrs. Vincent."

"I'm glad." With the mildest irony, she asked: "Do you think they'll give me a reward?"

Embarrassed, Jim lowered his head. During his illness he had mistakenly tried to bribe Mrs. Vincent with the promise of a reward, but it intrigued him that she could see the humor in her refusal to raise a finger to help him. Jim hesitated before leaving the room. He had spent nearly three years with Mrs. Vincent and found himself still liking her. Mrs. Vincent was one of the few people in Lunghua Camp who appreciated the humor of it all.

Trying to match her, he said: "A reward? Mrs. Vincent, remember you're British."

29

THE MARCH
TO NANTAO

LIKE THE MIGRATION of a shabby country carnival, the march from Lunghua Camp to the dockyards at Nantao began two hours later. Exhausted by the long wait even before they had started, Jim watched the prisoners assemble from his place at the head of the column. Under the bored gaze of the Japanese gendarmerie, the internees stepped cautiously through the gates, the men loaded with suitcases and bedrolls, the women with bundles of ragged clothes wrapped in straw panniers. Fathers carried sick infants on their backs, while mothers steered the smaller children by the hand. As he stood behind the Japanese staff car that was to lead the march, Jim was surprised by the sight of so many possessions, which had remained under the bunks throughout the years at Lunghua.

Recreation had clearly come high on the prisoners' list of priorities while they packed their suitcases before being interned. Having spent the years of peace on the tennis courts and cricket fields of the Far East, they confidently expected to pass the years of war in the same way. Dozens of tennis rackets hung from the suitcase handles; there were cricket bats and fishing rods, and even a set of golf clubs tied to the bundles of Pierrot costumes carried by Mr. and Mrs. Wentworth. Ragged and undernourished, the prisoners shuffled along the road on their wooden clogs and formed themselves into a procession some three hundred yards in length. Already the effort of carrying the baggage had begun to tell, and one of the Chinese peasant women seated outside the gates now clutched a white tennis racket.

Lounging against their vehicles, the soldiers and NCOs of the gendarmerie watched without comment. Well fed and well equipped, these security troops so feared by the Chinese were the strongest men whom Jim had seen during the war. Yet for once they seemed curiously unhurried. They smoked their cigarettes in the hot sunlight, gazed at the few American reconnaissance planes and made no attempt to abuse the prisoners or urge them along. Two of the trucks drove through the gates and made a circuit of the camp, collecting the patients from the hospital and those prisoners in the dormitory blocks who were too sick to move.

Jim sat on his wooden case, trying to adjust his mind and eye to the open perspectives of the world outside the camp. The act of walking without challenge through the gates had been an eerie experience, and Jim had been unnerved enough to slip back into the camp on the pretext of tying his shoelaces. Reassuring himself, he patted the wooden case containing his possessions—the Latin primer, his school blazer, the Packard advertisement and the small newspaper photograph. Now that he was about to see his real mother and father he had thought of tearing up the picture of the unknown couple outside Buckingham Palace, his surrogate parents for so many years.

At the last moment, as a precautionary measure, he had slipped the photograph into his box.

Jim listened to the crying of the exhausted children. Already people were sitting down in the road, trying to shield their faces from the swarm of flies that had vacated the camp and moved toward the sweating bodies on the other side of the wire. Jim looked back at Lunghua. The terrain of paddy fields and canals around the camp, and the road of return to Shanghai, which had been so real when observed through the fence, now seemed lurid and overlit, part of a landscape of hallucination.

Jim clenched his aching teeth, deciding to turn his back on the camp. He reminded himself of their food supplies in the godown at Nantao. It was important to remain at the head of the procession and, if possible, to ingratiate himself with the two Japanese soldiers beside the staff car. Jim was pondering this when an almost naked figure in ragged shorts and a pair of wooden clogs shuffled up to him.

"Jim . . . I thought I'd find you here." Mr. Maxted raised his sallow face to the sun. A fine malarial sweat covered his cheeks and forehead. He rubbed the dirt from the open spaces between his ribs, as if to expose the waxy skin to the healing light. "So this is what we've been waiting for. . . ."

"You haven't brought your luggage, Mr. Maxted."

"No, Jim. I don't think I'll be needing any luggage. You must find it strange out here."

"I don't anymore." Jim peered cautiously at the open fields, their endless perspectives broken only by the burial mounds, and at the secretive canals. It was as if these bored Japanese soldiers had switched off the clock. "Mr. Maxted, do you think Shanghai will have changed?"

A faded smile, lit by the memories of happier days,

briefly eased Mr. Maxted's face. "Jim, Shanghai will never change. Don't worry, you'll remember your mother and father."

"I was thinking of that," Jim admitted. His other problem was Mr. Maxted. Jim had come to the head of the column partly to be first in the queue for their rations when they reached Nantao, but also to free himself from all the duties that the camp had imposed upon him. Because he was alone he had been forced to do too many jobs, in return for favors that had rarely materialized. Clearly Mr. Maxted needed help and was hoping that he could lean on Jim.

Doggedly refusing to cooperate, Jim sat on his wooden case, thinking about Mr. Maxted as the architect swayed beside him. His pale hands, almost worn through by the months of pushing the food cart, hung at his sides like white flags. His bones were held together by little more than his memories of the bars and swimming pools of a younger self. Mr. Maxted was starving, like many of the men and women joining the procession. But Mr. Maxted reminded Jim of the dying British soldier in the open-air cinema.

In the ditch beside the grass verge lay the gray cylinder of a Mustang drop-tank. Looking for some way of leaving Mr. Maxted, Jim was about to cross the road when a burst of hot smoke ripped from the exhaust of the staff car. The Japanese sergeant stood on the rear seat, waving everyone on. Armed soldiers were moving down the road on either side of the column, shouting at the prisoners.

There was a clatter of clogs, as if hundreds of packs of wooden cards were being shuffled and dealt. First off the mark, Jim stepped forward, case in hand and shoes bright in the hot Yangtze sun. He waved to the Japanese sergeant and strode purposefully down the dirt road, his eyes fixed on the yellow facades of the apartment houses in the French Concession that rose like a mirage from the canals and paddy fields.

Guided by the swarm of flies that danced over their heads, the prisoners moved along the country road to Nantao. Across the burial mounds and ancient trench-works came the sounds of American planes bombing the dockyards and marshaling yards to the north of Shanghai. The thunder drummed at the surface of the flooded pad-dies. The antiaircraft fire flickered against the windows of the office buildings along the Bund and lit up the dead neon signs—Shell, Caltex, Socony Vacuum, Philco—the waking ghosts of the great international companies that had slept through the war. Half a mile to the west was the main Shanghai road, still busy with convoys of Japanese trucks and field artillery moving toward the city. The laboring noise of their engines droned like pain across the stoical land.

Jim walked at the head of the procession, listening to the men and women behind him. All he could hear was the sound of their breathing, as if the experience of free-dom had left them speechless. Jim tried to ignore his own rackety breath. Despite the ceaseless activity in Lun-ghua, he had never undertaken a task like this shuffling walk burdened by his wooden case. For the first hour he was too concerned about Mr. Maxted's exhaustion to notice his own. But soon after reaching the Shanghai-Hangchow railway line, Mr. Maxted was forced to stop, defeated by the shallow gradient that led up to the level crossing.

"We're climbing, Jim . . . feels like the Shanghai hills."

"We ought to keep going, Mr. Maxted."

"Yes, Jim . . . you're like your father."

Jim stayed with Mr. Maxted, annoyed with him but unable to help. Mr. Maxted stood in the center of the road, hands on the bowllike crests of his pelvis, nodding at the people stepping past. He patted Jim on the shoulder and waved him forward.

"You go on, Jim. Get to the head of the queue."

"I'll save your place, Mr. Maxted."

By then several hundred people had passed Jim, and it took him half an hour to return to the head of the column. Within minutes he had fallen back, lungs aching as he gasped at the humid air. Only the lengthy halt at a canal checkpoint saved him from having to join Mr. Maxted.

They had reached an industrial canal that ran westward from the river to Soochow. Two young Japanese soldiers, forgotten by the war, guarded the sandbag emplacement beside the wooden bridge. Their faces were as pinched as those of the prisoners whose clogs dragged over the scored planks.

While the trucks edged across the rotting timbers, the eighteen hundred prisoners sat on the embankment, occupying the deep grass for a quarter of a mile. Around them they settled their baggage of suitcases, tennis rackets and cricket bats. Like drowsy spectators at a rowing regatta, they stared at the algae-filled water. The current drifted past the burned-out hulk of an armored junk beached against the opposite bank.

Jim was glad to lie down. He felt sleepy in a feverish way, his brain irritated by the hot sun and the hard light reflected from the yellow grass. He could see Dr. Ransome standing in the last of the three trucks, swaying unsteadily among the patients on their stretchers. Jim thought of his Latin prep, now a week overdue, but Dr. Ransome was a hundred yards away.

Watched by the Japanese soldiers on the road above them, many of the men walked down to the water's edge. They filled their mess tins and stood drinking together in the shallows. Jim was wary of the water, remembering the black creeks at Nantao and the thousands of gallons he had boiled for Basie. Was there a crew of corpses in the armored junk? Inside the iron turret, now washed by the green waters of the canal, perhaps lay the captain of this puppet Chinese naval vessel. Jim could almost see the dead blood running out into the canal, slaking the thirst of these British prisoners, on its way to nourish the roots of the rice crops raised for another generation of Chinese turncoats.

Jim opened his wooden case and took out his mess tin. He walked down the bank between the resting women and their exhausted children. Squatting on the narrow beach, he carefully filled his mess tin with the surface water, hoping that the algae might sustain him. He drank the tepid fluid, watching the dissolving patterns of his golf shoes in the fine sand.

Filling the mess tin, Jim climbed the bank to his case. On his right was the wife of a Shell engineer in D Block. She lay weakly in the long grass, whose blades had already sprung through the rents in her cotton frock. Her husband sat beside her, dipping his fingers into his mess tin and moistening her large, carious teeth with the green water.

Lying on Jim's left was Mrs. Philips. It irked Jim that she had seen him drinking on the bank and decided to rest beside him. No doubt she had some little chore in mind, and would nag him about his Latin prep. Although he had left Lunghua, Jim felt imprisoned by the camp. Everyone he had ever helped was still clinging to him.

He almost expected to see Basie emerge from the turret of the armored junk and call out: "Jobs, Jim . . ."

But Mrs. Philips did not look as if she were about to set him a task. The walk from Lunghua had exhausted her. She lay in the bright grass with her wicker suitcase, all that survived of the decades she had spent in the Chinese hinterland. Her face was now the palest mother-of-pearl, as if she had been drowned and then lifted from the water onto this quiet bank. Her eyes were fixed on a remote point in the sky. Jim touched her cheeks, wondering if she was dead.

"Mrs. Philips—I've brought you some water."

She smiled at him and sipped the water, her small fists clinging to the handles of her suitcase like a pair of white mice. "Thank you, Jim. Are you very hungry?"

"I was this morning." Jim tried to think of a joke that would cheer Mrs. Philips. "It's air I'm short of after all that walking, not food."

"Yes, Jim. . . ." Mrs. Philips opened her case. She felt inside and produced a small potato. "There you are. Remember to pray for us all."

"Oh, I will!" Jim bit into the potato before she had a chance to change her mind. "I'll pay you back when we get to Nantao. All our rations are there."

"You've already paid me back, Jim. Many times." Mrs. Philips resumed her pinpoint scrutiny of the sky. "Could you eat the potato?"

"It was really good." As Jim finished the potato he noticed the old woman's eyes move fractionally. "Mrs. Philips, are you looking for God?"

"Yes, Jim."

"Say . . ." Jim was impressed. He was keen to repay Mrs. Philips' generosity, if only with a modest discussion of theology. He followed the angle of the old woman's gaze. "Do you mean God is right above us?"

"Of course, Jim."

"Above the thirty-first parallel? Mrs. Philips, wouldn't God be above the magnetic pole? You ought to look at the ground, under Shanghai. . . ." Intoxicated by the fermenting potato, Jim giggled at the thought of the deity trapped in the bowels of the earth below Shanghai, perhaps in the basement of the Sincere Company department store.

Mrs. Philips held his hand, trying to comfort him. Still staring at the sky, she decided: "Nantao—then they're taking us up-country . . ."

"No . . . our rations . . ." Jim turned toward the Japanese guards. The three trucks had crossed the bridge, and he could see Dr. Ransome moving among his patients with a small child in his arms. Its cries sounded through the overbright sun. The hundreds of prisoners sat in the feverish light like figures in the lurid paintings that advertised the Chinese film spectacles. The Japanese squatted beside the trucks, eating a boiled rice paste that they took from their haversacks. They made no attempt to share their food with the young soldiers defending the bridge.

Up-country? There were docks at Nantao, but why would the Japanese want to move them from Shanghai? Jim watched Mrs. Vincent paddling at the water's edge fifty yards away. Finding a portion of the current that satisfied her, she filled a mess tin for her husband and child. Dr. Ransome had recruited a human chain from the men sitting on the embankment below the trucks, and they passed pails of water up to the patients.

Jim shook his head, puzzled by all this effort. Obviously they were being taken up-country so that the Japanese could kill them without being seen by the American pilots. Jim listened to the Shell man's wife crying in the yellow grass. The sunlight charged the air above the canal, an intense aura of hunger that stung his retinas and reminded him of the halo formed by the exploding Mustang. The burning body of the American pilot had quickened the dead land. It would be for the best if they all died; it would bring their lives to an end that had been implicit ever since the *Idzumo* had sunk the *Petrel* and the British had surrendered at Singapore without a fight.

Perhaps they were already dead. Jim lay back and tried to count the motes of light. This simple truth was known to every Chinese from birth. Once the British internees had accepted it, they would no longer fear their journey to the killing ground. . . .

"Mrs. Philips . . . I've thought about the war." Jim rolled over in the grass. He was about to explain to Mrs. Philips that she was dead, but the old missionary was asleep. Jim studied her blanched eyes, her mouth open to reveal a broken dental plate. "Mrs. Philips, we mustn't worry anymore. . . ."

Headlamps flared through the dust. The gendarmerie staff car trundled along the road. Japanese soldiers strode down the bank, waving their rifles and beckoning the prisoners to their feet. The trucks at the rear of the column had started their engines. Men and women were climbing the embankment, children and suitcases in hand. Others remained in the trampled grass, unwilling to leave this placid canal.

Jim lay on his side, making a pillow of his arm. He felt drowsy after Mrs. Philips' potato, and the rumble of bombing and the voices of the British wives seemed far away. He stared at the blades of grass, trying to work out the speed at which the leaves grew—an eighth of an inch each day, a millionth of a mile per hour . . . ?

Then he noticed a Japanese soldier standing in the grass beside him. All but a hundred of the prisoners had climbed the slope and formed a procession behind the staff car. Around Jim a few people lay quietly. Mrs. Philips clasped her wicker suitcase, and the woman from D Block whimpered as her husband pressed his hands to her shoulders.

Grains of rice clung to the stubble around the Japanese soldier's lips. They moved like lice as he pondered Jim's condition. His expression was one that Jim had seen before, at the detention center in Shanghai, but for the first time Jim felt unconcerned. He would remain here beside the unhurried water and help Mrs. Philips to look for God.

"Come on, Jim! We're waiting for you!"

An emaciated figure tottered down the bank. Mr. Maxted bowed and smiled to the Japanese soldier, as if glad to recognize him. He collapsed in the grass and pulled Jim's shoulder.

"Good boy, Jim. We're moving on to Nantao."

"They're taking us up-country, Mr. Maxted. I might stay here with Mrs. Philips."

"I think Mrs. Philips wants to rest. They're holding our rations in Nantao, Jim. We need you to lead the way."

Hitching up his shorts, Mr. Maxted bowed again to the Japanese soldier and helped Jim to his feet.

The column shuffled forward, following the staff car. Jim looked back at the hundred or so prisoners left behind on the embankment. As the soldier licked the rice grains from his chin, Mrs. Philips lay at his feet in the yellow grass, beside the woman from D Block and her kneeling husband. Other soldiers moved along the bank, rifles slung while they stepped among the resting prisoners. Would they later help Mrs. Philips and the others to Nantao?

Jim doubted it. Shutting Mrs. Philips from his mind, he gripped his wooden case and placed his feet in the dusty imprints left by the man limping in front of him. Already Mr. Maxted had fallen behind. The brief rest on the embankment had fatigued everyone. Half a mile from the bridge, by the burned-out shell of an ammunition truck, the Nantao road turned at right angles from the canal and ran along a causeway between two paddy fields. The procession came to a halt. Watched by the Japanese, who made no attempt to hurry them along, the prisoners waited limply in the sun. Jim listened to the tired breathing. Then there was a shuffle of clogs, and the procession moved forward again.

Jim looked back at the ammunition truck. He was startled to see that hundreds of suitcases lay on the empty road. Exhausted by the effort of carrying their possessions, the prisoners had abandoned them without a spoken word. The suitcases and wicker baskets, the tennis rackets, cricket bats and Pierrot costumes lay in the sunlight, like the luggage of a party of holidaymakers who had vanished into the sky.

Holding tight to his case, Jim increased his stride. After so many years without any belongings, he did not intend to discard them now. He thought of Mrs. Philips and their talk together by the sunny canal, a setting so much more pleasant than the camp cemetery where he had usually questioned her about matters of life and death.

It had been kind of Mrs. Philips to give him her last potato, and he remembered his dreamy thoughts of having died. But he had not died. Jim stamped his shoes in the dust, surprised by his own weakness. Death, with her mother-of-pearl skin, had almost seduced him with a sweet potato.

30

THE OLYMPIC STADIUM

ALL AFTERNOON THEY moved northward across the plain of the Whangpoo River, through the maze of creeks and canals that separated the paddy fields. Lunghua Airfield fell behind them, and the apartment houses of the French Concession rose like advertisement hoardings in the August sunlight. The river was a few hundred yards to their right, its brown surface broken by the wrecks of patrol boats and motorized junks that sat in the shallows.

Here, in the approaches to the Nantao district, the devastation caused by the American bombing lay on all sides. Craters like circular swimming pools covered the paddy fields, in which floated the carcasses of water buffaloes. They passed the remains of a convoy that had been attacked by the Mustang and Lightning fighters. A line of military trucks and staff cars sat under the trees, as if dismantled in an outdoor workshop. Wheels, doors and axles were scattered around the vehicles, whose fenders and body panels had been torn away by the cannon fire.

Swarms of flies rose from the bloodstained windshields as the prisoners stopped to relieve themselves. A few steps behind Jim, Mr. Maxted left the procession and sat on the running board of an ammunition wagon. Still carrying his case, Jim went back for him.

"We're nearly there, Mr. Maxted. I can smell the docks."

"Don't worry, Jim. I'm keeping an eye on us."

"Our rations . . ."

Mr. Maxted reached out and held Jim's wrist. Gutted by malaria and malnutrition, his body was about to merge with the derelict vehicle behind him. The three trucks moved past, their tires crushing the broken glass that covered the ground. The hospital patients lay across each other like rolls of carpet. Dr. Ransome stood in the last truck, his back to the driver's cabin, feet hidden among the packed bodies. Seeing Jim, he gripped the sidebar of the truck.

"Maxted! Come on, Jim! Leave your case!"

"The war's over, Dr. Ransome!"

Jim watched the thirty Japanese soldiers who brought up the rear of the procession. Rifles slung over their shoulders, they strolled along at a thoughtful pace. They reminded Jim of his father's friends returning from a shooting party in Hungjao before the war. Clouds of white dust rose from the trucks, hiding Dr. Ransome. The first of the soldiers passed Jim, large men whose eyes were fixed on the ground. Their nostrils flickered at the scent of urine. As they strode through the dust, a fine film covered their uniforms and webbing, and reminded Jim of the runway at Lunghua Airfield.

"Right, Jim . . ." Mr. Maxted stood up, and Jim was aware of the odor of excrement that rose from his shorts. "Let's get you to Nantao. . . ."

Holding Jim's shoulder, he hobbled forward, clogs cracking the broken glass. Unable to overtake the trucks, they moved through the clouds of dust, joining the few stragglers at the tail of the column. A number of prisoners had given up and sat with their children on the running boards of the bombed staff cars, Gypsies about to make a new life among these partly dismantled vehicles. But Jim looked down at the powdery dust that covered his legs and shoes, like the undertaker's talc blown onto the bones of a Chinese skeleton before its reburial, and knew that it was time to move on.

By the late afternoon this layer of dust on Jim's legs and arms began to glow with light. The sun fell toward the Shanghai hills, and the flooded paddy fields became a liquid chessboard of illuminated squares, a war table on which were placed crashed aircraft and abandoned tanks. Lit by the sunset, the prisoners stood on the embankment of the railway line that ran to the warehouses at Nantao, like a party of film extras under the studio spotlights. Around them the creeks and lagoons were filled with saffron water, the conduits of a perfume factory blocked by dead mules and buffaloes drowned in its scents.

The trucks bumped forward over the wooden sleepers. Jim balanced on the steel rail and gazed through the dusk at the brick godowns beside the jetty. A concrete mole ran across the river to a derelict lighthouse. Through their binoculars a party of Japanese soldiers examined the smoking hulk of a steel collier, which had been struck by the American bombers and beached on a sandbank in the center of the stream. Scorched by the explosions, its bridge house was now as black as its masts and coal holds.

A mile downstream from the collier were the Nantao

seaplane base and the funeral piers where Jim had found refuge with Basie. Wondering if the cabin steward had returned to his old hiding place, Jim steered Mr. Maxted between the rails as the prisoners followed the railway embankment to the riverside causeway. To the west of the docks, in the waters of a shallow lagoon, lay the burned-out shell of a B-29, its tail rising into the dusk like a silver billboard advertising its squadron insignia.

Jim stared at this huge stricken plane and sat beside Mr. Maxted among the press of bodies in the dusk. Hunger numbed Jim. He sucked on his knuckles, glad for even the taste of his pus, then tore stems of grass from the bank and chewed the acid leaves. A Japanese corporal was escorting Dr. Ransome and Mrs. Pearce toward the dockyards. The wharves and godowns, which from the distance had seemed intact, had been bombed almost to rubble. The rising tide rocked the rusting hulls of two torpedo boats beached beside the mole and stirred the corpses of the Japanese sailors lying among the reeds fifty yards from where Jim was crouching. Undeterred, several of the British prisoners walked down the bank and drank at the water's edge. An exhausted woman held her child like a Chinese mother, gripping it behind the knees as it relieved itself on the oil-stained mud, then squatted and followed suit. Others joined her, and when Jim went to drink at the water's edge, the evening air was filled with the stench of defecating women.

Jim stood by the river, the wooden case at his feet. The tide swilled the white dust from his shoes. In his mess tin the water gleamed with oil washed from the sunken freighters in Shanghai harbor. Overlapping slicks covered the surface of the Whangpoo, as if trying to smother all life from the river.

Jim drank carefully, then watched the water lap around

his case. He had carried the wooden box all the way from Lunghua, holding tight to the few possessions that he had assembled with such effort. He had been trying to keep the war alive, and with it the security he had known in the camp. Now it was time to rid himself of Lunghua and face up squarely to the present, however uncertain, the one rule that had sustained him through the years of the war.

Jim pushed his case onto the greasy surface. In the last moments of the dusk the dead water came alive with roses of iridescent color. As the box floated away, like the coffin of a Chinese child, the circles of oil raced to embrace it and sent tremors of light across the river.

Jim climbed through the resting prisoners and sat down beside Mr. Maxted. He handed him the mess tin of water and then cleaned the sand from his shoes.

"All right, Jim?"

"The war must end, Mr. Maxted."

"It will, Jim." Mr. Maxted had revived briefly. "We're going back to Shanghai tonight."

"Shanghai—?" Jim was unsure whether Mr. Maxted was delirious, dreaming of Shanghai in the way that the dying prisoners in the camp hospitals had babbled of returning to England. "Aren't they taking us up-country?"

"Not now . . ." Mr. Maxted pointed through the darkness to the collier burning off the mole.

Jim watched the smoke rising from the collier's bridge and superstructure, everywhere but from its funnel. The fire in the engine room had taken hold, and the stern of the vessel glowed like furnace coal. This was the ship that would have taken them up-country, to the killing grounds beyond Soochow. For all his relief, Jim felt disappointed.

"What about our rations, Mr. Maxted?"

"They're waiting for us in Shanghai. Just like the old days, Jim."

Jim watched Mr. Maxted sink back among the exhausted prisoners. He had made his last effort to sit upright, trying to convince Jim that all was well, that the good luck and the skill of some unknown American bomb aimer, which had saved them from being shipped aboard the collier, would continue to watch over them.

"Mr. Maxted, do you want the war to end? It must end soon."

"It has almost ended. Think about your mother and father, Jim. The war has ended."

"But Mr. Maxted, when will the next one begin . . . ?"

Japanese soldiers were walking along the railway line, followed by Dr. Ransome and Mrs. Pearce. The corporals shouted to each other, their voices drumming along the rails. A faint rain fell, and the guards waiting by the trucks put on their capes. Steam lifted from the warm rails as the prisoners rose to their feet and clutched their small children. Voices murmured through the darkness, and wives grasped their husbands' hands.

"Digby . . . Digby . . ."

"Scotty . . ."

"Jake . . ."

"Bunty . . ."

A woman with a sleeping child on her shoulder seized Jim's arm, but he pushed her away and tried to steady Mr. Maxted. The darkness and the tacky river water had made them both light-headed, and at any moment they would fall across the rails. Led by the three trucks, the prisoners left the embankment and gathered on the jetty beside the ruined godowns. A hundred of the prisoners had stayed behind on the causeway, too weary to carry on and resigned to whatever future the Japanese had prepared for them. They sat in the rain below the railway embankment, watched by the soldiers in their streaming capes.

As the column of prisoners set off, Jim realized that a quarter of those inmates who had left Lunghua that morning had fallen behind. Even before they reached the gates of the dockyard, several prisoners turned back. An elderly Scotsman from E Block, a retired accountant at the Shanghai Power Company with whom Jim had often played chess, suddenly stepped from the column. As if he had forgotten where he had been for all the years of the war, he wandered across the stony yard, then walked through the rain toward the railway embankment.

An hour after nightfall they reached a football stadium on the western outskirts of Nantao. This concrete arena had been built on the orders of Madame Chiang Kaishek, in the hope that China might be host to the 1940 Olympic Games. Captured by the Japanese after their invasion in 1937, the stadium became the military headquarters for the war zone south of Shanghai.

The column of prisoners crossed the silent car park. Dozens of bomb craters had torn the tarmac surface, but the white marker lines still stretched through the darkness. Damaged army vehicles were parked in neat rows— shrapnel-torn trucks and fuel wagons, treadless tanks and armored half-tracks each pulling two artillery guns. Jim stared at the pockmarked facade of the stadium. Bomb fragments had dislodged sections of the white plaster, and the original Chinese characters proclaiming the power of the Kuomintang had emerged once again, threatening slogans that hung over the darkness like the hoardings above the Chinese cinemas in prewar Shanghai.

They entered a concrete tunnel that led into the darkened arena. With its curved stands it reminded Jim of the detention center in Shanghai, all its dangers magnified a hundredfold by the war. The Japanese soldiers formed a cordon around the running track. The rain dripped from their capes, and lit the bayonets and breeches of their rifles. Already the first prisoners were sitting down on the wet grass. Mr. Maxted dropped to the ground at Jim's feet, as if released from a harness. Jim squatted beside him, waving away the mosquitoes that had followed them into the stadium.

The three trucks emerged from the tunnel and stopped on the cinder track. Dr. Ransome climbed across his patients and lowered himself from the tailgate. Mrs. Pearce stepped from the cabin of the second truck, leaving her husband and son beside the Japanese driver. Through the rain Jim could hear Dr. Ransome arguing with the Japanese. Hidden under his cape, the senior sergeant of the gendarmerie watched him without expression, then lit a cigarette and strolled away to the stands, where he sat in the front row as if about to observe a display of midnight acrobatics.

Jim was glad when Mrs. Pearce returned to the cabin of her truck. Dr. Ransome's complaining voice, in the tones he had used so often when remonstrating with Jim over his games in the hospital cemetery, was out of place in Nantao stadium. Within a few minutes of their arrival a complete silence had come over the twelve hundred prisoners. They huddled together on the grass, watched by the guards in the stands. Dr. Ransome moved through the women and children, still trying to carry out his Lunghua inspections. Jim waited until he stumbled in the dark, prompting a surly shout from a group of men.

The rain fell across the stadium, and Jim lay back and

let it run across his face, warming his cold cheeks. Despite the rain, thousands of flies settled on the prisoners. Jim wiped the flies from Mr. Maxted's mouth, and tried to wash his face with the rain, but they festered on his lips, picking at his gums.

Jim watched the faint breath from Mr. Maxted's mouth. He wondered what he could do for him and regretted throwing away his suitcase. Pushing the wooden box into the river had been a sentimental but pointless gesture, his first adult act. He might have bartered his possessions and obtained a little food for Mr. Maxted. A few of the Japanese soldiers were Catholics and used the Latin mass. One of the guards in his rain-soaked cape might have valued the Kennedy primer, and Jim could perhaps have arranged to give him Latin lessons. . . .

But Mr. Maxted slept peacefully. A gray breath emerged through the flies on his lips, and from the other prisoners nearby. An hour later, when the rain had stopped, the flashes of an American air raid lit up the stadium, like the sheet lightning of the monsoon season. As a child, safe in his bedroom at Amherst Avenue, Jim had watched the sudden glares that exposed the rats caught in the center of the tennis court and on the verges of the swimming pool. God, Vera agreed, was taking photographs of the wickedness of Shanghai. The noiseless glimmer of the night raids, somewhere among the Japanese naval bases at the mouth of the Yangtze, cast a damp sheen over Jim's arms and legs, another reminder of that fine dust he had first seen as he helped to build the runway at Lunghua Airfield. Jim knew that he was awake and asleep at the same time, dreaming of the war and yet dreamed of by the war.

Jim propped his head against Mr. Maxted's chest. The rapid flashes of the air raids filled the stadium and dressed the sleeping prisoners in their shrouds. Perhaps they would all take part in the construction of a gigantic runway. In his mind the sound of the American planes set off powerful premonitions of death. Conjugating his Latin verbs, the nearest that he could move toward prayer, he fell asleep beside Mr. Maxted and dreamed of runways.

31

THE EMPIRE
OF THE SUN

A HUMID MORNING sun filled the stadium, reflected in the pools of water that covered the running track and in the chromium radiators of the American cars parked behind the goalposts at the northern end of the football pitch. Supporting himself against Mr. Maxted's shoulder, Jim surveyed the hundreds of men and women lying on the warm grass. A few prisoners squatted on the ground, their sunburned but pallid faces like blanched leather from which the dye had run. They stared at the cars, suspicious of their bright grilles, with the wary eyes of the Hungjao peasants looking up from their rice planting at his parents' Packard.

Jim brushed the flies from Mr. Maxted's mouth and eyes. The architect lay without moving, his white ribs unclasped around his heart, but Jim could hear his faint breath.

"You're feeling better, Mr. Maxted . . . I'll bring you some water." Jim squinted at the lines of cars. Even the small effort of focusing his eyes exhausted him. Trying to hold his head steady, he felt the ground sway, as if he and the hundreds of prisoners were about to be tipped out of the stadium.

Mr. Maxted turned to stare at Jim, who pointed to the cars. There were more than fifty of them—Buicks, Lincoln Zephyrs, two white Cadillacs side by side. Had they come to collect their British owners now that the war had ended? Jim stroked Mr. Maxted's cheeks, then reached into the cavern below his ribs and tried to massage his heart. It would be a pity for Mr. Maxted to die just as his Studebaker arrived to take him back to the Shanghai nightclubs.

However, the Japanese soldiers sat on the concrete benches near the entrance tunnel, sipping tea beside a charcoal stove. Its smoke drifted between the hospital trucks. Two young soldiers were passing pails of water to a weary Dr. Ransome, but the security troops seemed no more interested in the thousand Lunghua prisoners who occupied the football field than they had been during the previous day's march.

His legs trembling, Jim stood up and scanned the parked cars for his parents' Packard. Where were the chauffeurs? They should have been waiting by their cars, as they always did outside the country club. Then a small rain cloud dimmed the sun, and a drab light settled over the stadium. Looking at their rusting chrome, Jim realized that these American cars had been parked here for years. Their windshields were caked with winter grime, and they sat on flattened tires, part of the booty looted by the Japanese from the Allied nationals.

Jim searched the stands on the north and west slopes of the stadium. The concrete tiers had been stripped of their seats, and sections of the stands were now used as an open-air warehouse. Dozens of blackwood cabinets and mahogany tables, their varnish still intact, and hundreds of dining-room chairs were packed together as if in the loft of a furniture depository. Bedsteads and wardrobes, refrigerators and air-conditioning units were stacked above each other, rising in a slope toward the sky. The immense presidential box, where Madame Chiang and the Generalissimo might once have saluted the world's athletes, was now crammed with roulette wheels, cocktail bars and a jumble of gilded plaster nymphs holding gaudy lamps above their heads. Rolls of Persian and Turkish carpets, hastily wrapped in tarpaulins, lay on the concrete steps, water dripping through them as if from a pile of rotting pipes.

To Jim, these shabby trophies seized from the houses and nightclubs of Shanghai seemed to gleam with a show-window freshness, like the floors filled with furniture through which he and his mother had once wandered in the Sincere Company department store. He stared at the stands, almost expecting his mother to appear in a silk dress and run a gloved hand over these terraces of black lacquer.

Jim sat down and shielded his eyes from the glare. He massaged Mr. Maxted's cheeks with his thumb and forefinger, pinching his lips and hooking out the flies trapped inside his mouth. Around them the inmates of Lunghua Camp lay on the damp grass, staring at this display of their former possessions, a mirage that grew more vivid in the steepening August sunlight.

Yet the mirage soon passed. Jim wiped his hands on Mr. Maxted's shorts. The Japanese had frequently used the stadium as a transit camp, and the worn grass was covered with oily rags and the ash of small fires, strips of canvas tent and wooden crates. There were unmistakable human remains, bloodstains and pieces of excrement, on which feasted thousands of flies.

281

The engine of a hospital truck began to run noisily. The Japanese soldiers had come down from the stands and were forming themselves into a march party. Pairs of guards climbed the tailgates, cotton masks over their faces. Helped by three English prisoners, Dr. Ransome lifted down those patients either dead or too ill to continue the day's journey. They lay in the tire ruts that scored the grass, as if trying to fold the soft earth around themselves.

Jim squatted beside Mr. Maxted, working his diaphragm like a bellows. He had seen Dr. Ransome bring his patients back from the dead, and it was important for Mr. Maxted to be well enough to join the march. Around them the prisoners were sitting upright, and a few men stood beside their huddled wives and children. Several of the older internees had died in the night—ten feet away Mrs. Wentworth, who had played the part of Lady Bracknell, lay in her faded cotton dress, staring at the sky. Others were surrounded by shallow pools of water formed by the pressure of their bodies on the soft grass.

Jim's arms ached from the effort of pumping. He waited for Dr. Ransome to jump down from the hospital truck and look after Mr. Maxted. However, the three vehicles were already leaving the stadium. Dr. Ransome's sandy head ducked as the truck lumbered through the tunnel. Jim was tempted to run after it, but he knew that he had decided to stay with Mr. Maxted. He had learned that having someone to care for was the same as being cared for by someone else.

Jim listened to the trucks crossing the parking lot, their gearboxes gasping as they gathered speed. Lunghua Camp was at last being dismantled. A marching party formed itself beside the tunnel. Some three hundred British prisoners, the younger men with their wives and children, had lined up on the running track and were being inspected by a sergeant of the gendarmerie. Beside them, on the football pitch, were those prisoners too exhausted to sit or stand. They lay on the grass like battlefield casualties. The Japanese soldiers strolled among them, as if searching for a lost ball, uninterested in these British nationals who had strayed into a cul-de-sac of the war.

An hour later the column moved off, the prisoners plodding through the tunnel without a backward glance. Six Japanese soldiers followed them, and the rest continued their casual patrol of the blackwood cabinets and refrigerators. The senior NCOs waited by the tunnel and watched the American reconnaissance planes that flew overhead, making no attempt to mobilize the prisoners in the stadium. Within fifteen minutes, however, a second group had begun to assemble, and the Japanese came forward to inspect them.

Jim wiped his hands on the damp grass and put his fingers into Mr. Maxted's mouth. The architect's lips trembled around his knuckles. But already the August sun was driving the moisture from the grass. Jim turned his attention to a pool of water lying on the cinder track. He waited for the sentry to pass, and then walked across the grass and drank from his cupped hands. The water ran down his throat like iced mercury, an electric current that almost stopped his heart. Before the Japanese could order him away, Jim quickly cupped his hands and carried the water to Mr. Maxted.

As he decanted the water into Mr. Maxted's mouth, the flies scrambled from his gums. Beside him lay the elderly figure of Major Griffin, a retired Indian Army officer who had lectured in Lunghua on the infantry weapons of the Great War. Too weak to sit up, he pointed to Jim's hands.

Jim pinched Mr. Maxted's lips, relieved when his tongue shot forward in a spasm. Trying to encourage him, Jim said: "Mr. Maxted, our rations should be coming soon."

"Good lad, Jamie—you hang on."

Major Griffin beckoned to him. "Jim . . ."

"Coming, Major Griffin . . ." Jim crossed the cinder track and returned with a handful of water. As he squatted beside the major, patting his cheeks, he noticed that Mrs. Vincent was sitting on the grass twenty feet away. She had left her son and husband with a group of prisoners in the center of the football field. Too exhausted to move any further, she stared at Jim with the same desperate gaze to which she had treated him as he ate his weevils. The night's rain had washed the last of the dye from her cotton dress, giving her the ashen pallor of the Chinese laborers at Lunghua Airfield. Mrs. Vincent would build a strange runway, Jim reflected.

"Jamie . . ."

She called him by his childhood name, which Mr. Maxted, without thinking, had summoned from some prewar memory. She wanted him to be a child again, to run the endless errands that had kept him alive in Lunghua.

As he scooped the cold water from the cinder track, he remembered how Mrs. Vincent had refused to help him when he was ill. Yet he had always been intrigued by the sight of her eating. He waited while she drank from his hands.

When she had finished he helped her to stand. "Mrs. Vincent, the war's over now."

With a grimace, she pushed his hands away, but Jim no longer cared. He watched her walk unsteadily between the seated prisoners. Jim squatted beside Mr. Maxted, brushing the flies from his face. He could still feel Mrs. Vincent's tongue on his fingers.

"Jamie . . ."

Someone else was calling, as if he were a Chinese coolie running at the command of his European masters. Too light-headed even to sit, Jim lay beside Mr. Maxted. It was time to stop running his errands. His hands were frozen from the water on the cinder track. The war had lasted for too long. At the detention center, and in Lunghua, he had done all he could to stay alive, but now a part of him wanted to die. It was the one way in which he could end the war.

Jim looked at the hundreds of prisoners on the grass. He wanted them all to die, surrounded by their rotting carpets and cocktail cabinets. Many of them, he was glad to see, had already obliged him, and Jim felt angry at those prisoners still able to walk who were now forming a second march party. He guessed that they were being walked to death around the countryside, but he wanted them to stay in the stadium and die within sight of the white Cadillacs.

Fiercely, Jim wiped the flies from Mr. Maxted's cheeks. Laughing at Mrs. Vincent, he began to rock on his knees, as he had done as a child, crooning to himself and monotonously beating the ground. "Jamie . . . Jamie . . ."

A Japanese soldier patrolled the cinder track nearby. He walked across the grass and stared down at Jim. Irritated by the noise, he was about to kick him with his ragged boot. But a flash of light filled the stadium, flaring over the stands in the southwest corner of the football field, as if an immense American bomb had exploded somewhere to the northeast of Shanghai. The sentry hesitated, looking over his shoulder as the light behind him grew more intense. It faded within a few seconds, but its pale sheen covered everything within the stadium: the looted furniture in the stands, the cars behind the goal-posts, the prisoners on the grass. They were sitting on the floor of a furnace heated by a second sun.

Jim stared at his white hands and knees, and at the pinched face of the Japanese soldier, who seemed dis-concerted by the light. Both of them were waiting for the rumble of sound that followed the bomb flashes, but an unbroken silence lay over the stadium and the sur-rounding land, as if the sun had blinked, losing heart for a few seconds. Jim smiled at the Japanese, wishing that he could tell him that the light was a premonition of his death, the sight of his small soul joining the larger soul of the dying world.

These games and hallucinations continued until the late afternoon, when an air raid at Hongkew again lit up the stadium. Jim lay in his dream-wake, feeling the earth spring below his back like the ballroom floor at the Shanghai country club. The flares of light moved from one section of the stands to another, transforming the looted furniture into a series of spotlit tableaux illustrating the lives of the colonial British.

At dusk the last march party assembled by the tunnel. Jim sat by Mr. Maxted, watching the fifty prisoners form themselves into a column. Where were they going? Many of the men and women could barely stand, and Jim doubted if they could get as far as the car park outside the stadium.

For the first time since leaving Lunghua, the Japanese had become impatient. Eager to be rid of the last prisoners still able to walk, the soldiers moved across the football field. They cuffed the prisoners and pulled their shoul-ders. A corporal with a cotton face mask shone his torch into the faces of the dead, then turned them onto their backs.

A Eurasian civilian in a white shirt moved behind the Japanese, eager to help those ordered to join the march, like the courier of an efficient travel company. At the edges of the field the Japanese guards were already stripping the bodies of the dead, pulling off the shoes and belts.

"Mr. Maxted . . ." In a last moment of lucidity Jim sat up, knowing that he must leave the dying architect and join the march party into the night. "I ought to go now, Mr. Maxted. It's time for the war to be over. . . ."

He was trying to stand when he felt Mr. Maxted grasp his wrist. "Don't go with them . . . Jim . . . stay here."

Jim waited for Mr. Maxted to die. But he pressed Jim's wrist to the grass, as if trying to bolt it to the earth. Jim watched the march party shuffle toward the tunnel. Unable to walk more than three paces, a man fell and was left on the cinder track. Jim listened to the voices of the Japanese draw nearer, muffled by the masks over their faces, and heard the sergeant gag and spit in the stench.

A soldier knelt beside Jim, his breath hoarse and exhausted behind his mask. Strong hands moved across Jim's chest and hips, feeling his pockets. Brusquely they pulled Jim's shoes from his feet, then flung them onto the cinder track. Jim lay without moving, as the fires from the burning oil depots at Hongkew played across the stands, lighting the doors of the looted refrigerators, the radiator grilles of the white Cadillacs and the lamps of the plaster nymphs in the box of the Generalissimo.

THREE

32

THE EURASIAN

A RESTFUL SUNLIGHT warmed the stadium. From the cloudless sky fell a squall of hail, a flurry of frozen vapor dislodged from the wings of an American aircraft three miles above the Yangtze valley. Lit by the sun, the crystals fell onto the football field like a shower of Christmas decorations.

Jim sat up and touched the hailstones, nuggets of white gold scattered on the grass. Beside him, Mr. Maxted's body was dressed in a suit of lights, his ashen face speckled with miniature rainbows. But within a few seconds the hail had melted into the ground. Jim listened for the aircraft, hoping that it might launch another cascade of hail, but the sky was empty from horizon to horizon. A few of the prisoners in the stadium knelt on the grass, eating the hail and talking to each other across the bodies of their dead companions.

The Japanese had gone. The NCOs and soldiers of the gendarmerie had taken their equipment and vanished during the night. Jim stood in his bare feet on the icy grass, staring at the exit tunnel. The shallow sunlight veered against the concrete walls from the deserted parking lot. Already one of the British prisoners hobbled through the tunnel on his worn clogs, followed by his wife in her ragged dress, hands pressed to her face.

Jim waited for a rifle shot to throw the man at his wife's feet, but the couple stepped into the parking lot and gazed at the lines of bomb-damaged vehicles. Jim left Mr. Maxted and walked along the running track, intending to follow them, but then cautiously decided to climb one of the stands.

The concrete steps seemed to reach beyond the sky. Jim paused to rest among the terraces of looted furniture. He sat on a straight-backed chair beside a dining-room table and drank the warm rainwater from the polished blackwood. Below him, the thirty or so prisoners on the football field were rousing themselves as if from a disheveled picnic. The women sat on the grass, quietly straightening their hair among the bodies of their former friends, while a few of the husbands peered through the dusty windows at the instrument panels of the parked cars.

More than a hundred prisoners were dead, scattered on the football pitch as if they had fallen from the sky during the night. Turning his back on them, Jim climbed through the pools of water to the top tier of the stand. Now that he had left Mr. Maxted he felt guilty that he had died, a guilt in some way connected with his missing shoes. He stared at his wet footprints and told himself that he should have sold his shoes to the Japanese for a little rice or a sweet potato. As it was, by pretending to be dead he had lost both Mr. Maxted and his shoes.

Yet the dead had protected Jim and saved him from the night march. Lying with their bodies through the dark hours, both asleep and awake, he had felt closer to them than he felt to the living. Long after Mr. Maxted had grown cold, Jim had continued to massage his cheeks, keeping away the flies until he was sure that his soul had left him. During the next days he had stayed close to Mr. Maxted, despite the flies and the smell from the body of the dead architect. The prisoners resting in the center of the field waved Jim away whenever he approached. Drinking the rainwater that dripped from the furniture in the stands, he had survived on a single potato he had found in the trouser pocket of Mr. Wentworth, and on the rancid rice scattered toward him by the Japanese soldiers.

Jim leaned against the metal rail and looked down at the parking lot. The British couple were staring at the lines of derelict vehicles, alone in a silent world. Jim laughed at them, a harsh cough that spat a ball of yellow pus from his mouth. He wanted to shout to them: The world has gone away! Last night everyone jumped into their graves and pulled the earth over themselves!

Good riddance . . . Jim stared at the moribund land, at the water-filled bomb craters in the paddy fields, at the silent antiaircraft guns of Lunghua Pagoda, at the beached freighters on the banks of the river. Behind him, no more than three miles away, was the silent city. The apartment houses of the French Concession and the office blocks of the Bund were like a magnified image of that distant prospect that had sustained him for so many years.

Chilled by the river, a cool wind moved across the stadium, and for a moment that strange northeastern light he had seen over the stands returned to dim the sun. Jim stared at his pallid hands. He knew that he was alive, but at the same time he felt as dead as Mr. Maxted. Perhaps his soul, instead of leaving his body, had died inside his head?

Thirsty again, Jim walked down the concrete steps, scooping the water from the tables and cabinets. If the war had ended, it was time to look for his mother and father. However, without the Japanese to protect them, it would be dangerous for the British to set off on foot for Shanghai.

Beyond the goalposts, a British prisoner had managed to lift the hood of one of the white Cadillacs. Watched by his companions, he bent over the engine and touched the cylinders. Jim roused himself and raced down the steps, eager to be the driver's navigator. He could still remember every street and alleyway in Shanghai.

As he crossed the athletics track, he noticed that three men had entered the stadium. Two were Chinese coolies, bare-chested, with black cotton trousers tied at the ankles above their straw sandals. The third was the Eurasian in the white shirt whom Jim had seen with the Japanese security troops. They stood by the tunnel while the Eurasian inspected the stadium. He glanced at the prisoners sitting on the grass, but his attention was clearly fixed on the looted furniture in the stands.

The Eurasian carried a heavy automatic pistol tucked into the waistband of his trousers, but he smiled at Jim in an ingratiating way, as if they were old friends separated by the misadventures of war.

"Say, kid . . . You're OK?" He surveyed Jim's ragged shirt and shorts, his legs and bare feet covered with dirt and sores. "Lunghua C.A.C.? I guess you've had to tough it out."

Jim stared stolidly at the Eurasian. Despite the smile, there was no sympathy in the man's eyes. He spoke with a strong but recently acquired American accent, which Jim assumed he had learned while interrogating captured American air crews. He wore a chromium wristwatch, and the Colt pistol in his waistband was like those that the Japanese guards at Lunghua had taken from the pilots of the downed Superfortresses. His baggy nostrils quivered in the stench rising from the football field, distracting him from his scrutiny of the stands. He stepped aside for two British prisoners who hobbled through the tunnel.

"It's some setup," he reflected. "Your ma and pa here? Looks like you could use a couple of bags of rice. Ask around, kid, if they have any bracelets, wedding rings, charms. We can work together on it."

"Is the war over?"

The Eurasian's eyes lowered, eclipsed by some passing shadow. He rallied himself and smiled keenly. "That's for sure. Anytime now the whole U.S. Navy is going to tie up at the Bund." When Jim looked unconvinced, the Eurasian explained: "Kid, they dropped atom bombs. Uncle Sam threw a piece of the sun at Nagasaki and Hiroshima, killed a million people. One great big flash . . ."

"I saw it."

"Kid? Did it light up the whole sky? Could be." The Eurasian sounded doubtful, but turned his eyes from the booty in the stands and began to examine Jim. For all his easy manner he was unsure of himself, as if aware that the incoming U.S. Navy might be less than convinced by his pro-American act. He glanced warily at the sky. "Atom bombs . . . too bad for all those Japs, but lucky for you, kid. And for your ma and pa."

Jim pondered this as the Eurasian stepped to the concrete rubbish bin by the entrance tunnel and began to root around inside it. "Is the war really over?"

"Yeah, it's over, finished, we're all friends. The Emperor just announced the surrender."

"Where are the Americans?"

"They're coming, kid; they have to get here with their atom bombs."

"A white light?"

"That's correct, kid. The atom bomb, U.S. super-weapon. Maybe you saw the Nagasaki bomb."

"Yes, I saw the atom bomb. What happened to Dr. Ransome?" When the Eurasian seemed puzzled, Jim added: "And the people who left on the march?"

"Too bad, kid." The Eurasian shook his head, as if regretting a small oversight. "The American bombing, some diseases. Maybe your friend will make it. . . ."

Jim was about to walk away when the Eurasian turned from the rubbish bin. In one hand he held a pair of worn clogs which he threw onto the track. In the other he carried Jim's leather golf shoes, tied together by their laces. He was about to speak to the waiting coolies when Jim stepped forward.

"Those are mine—Dr. Ransome gave them to me." He spoke flatly and pulled the shoes from the Eurasian's hands. Jim waited for him to draw his gun or order the coolies to knock him to the ground. Though exhausted by hunger and by the effort of climbing the stand, Jim was aware that he was once again asserting the ascendancy of the European.

"That's OK, kid." The Eurasian was genuinely concerned. "I was keeping those shoes in case you turned up. Tell your ma and pa."

Jim walked past the coolies and entered the light-filled tunnel. Groups of British men and women were wandering among the tanks and burned-out trucks in the parking lot. They followed the faded marker lines, with no idea of where they were going, as if they had survived the entire war only to expire in this shabby maze. Outside the stadium, the August sunlight was made even more intense by the complete silence that lay over the paddy fields and canals. A white glaze covered the derelict land. Had the fields been seared by the flash of the atom bomb that the Eurasian had described? Jim remembered the burning body of the Mustang pilot, and the soundless light that had filled the stadium and seemed to dress the dead and the living in their shrouds.

33

THE KAMIKAZE PILOT

SECURE IN HIS SHOES, Jim stood by the concrete blockhouse that guarded the vehicles in the parking lot. The Shanghai road ran past the entrance, heading toward the southern suburbs of the city. Nothing moved in the surrounding fields, but three hundred yards away a platoon of Chinese puppet soldiers sat in an antitank ditch beside the road. Still wearing their faded orange-green uniforms, they squatted by a charcoal stove, holding their rifles between their knees. An NCO climbed from the ditch and waited, hands on hips, watching Jim as he stepped into the road.

If he approached them, they would kill him for his shoes. Jim knew that he was too weak to walk to Shanghai, let alone cope with all the dangers of the open road. Hidden behind the blockhouse, he set out toward the safety of Lunghua Airfield. Its western perimeter was little more than half a mile away, a terrain of nettles and wild sugarcane covered with fuel drums and the fuselages of abandoned aircraft. Between the rusty tailplanes Jim could see the concrete runway, its white surface almost evaporating into the heat.

The stadium fell behind him. The road was an empty

meridian circling a planet discarded by war. Jim followed the verge, stepping among the broken clogs and rags of clothing left by the British prisoners during the last yards of their march to the stadium. On either side of him were bombed-out trenchworks and blockhouses, a world of mud. On the slopes of a water-filled tank trap, among the tires and ammunition boxes, lay the body of a Chinese soldier, orange uniform split by his ballooning buttocks and shoulders, glistening with oily light like a burst paint pot. A packhorse rested beside the road, hide flayed from its ribs. Jim peered into this capacious cage, half hoping to find a rat imprisoned within it.

He left the road when it turned eastward to the Nantao docks. He crossed the flooded paddy fields, following the earth embankment of an irrigation ditch. Even here, a mile to the west of the river, fuel oil from the beached freighters leaked through the creeks and canals, covering the drowned paddies with a lurid sheen. Jim rested on the perimeter road of the airfield, then climbed through the wire fence and walked up to the nearest of the abandoned aircraft. Far across the airfield, below the massive flak tower of Lunghua Pagoda, were the bombed hangars and workshops. A few Japanese mechanics wandered among the wreckage, but the Chinese scrap dealers had yet to arrive, clearly fearful of this zone of silence. Jim listened for the noise of hacksaws or cutting equipment, but the air was empty, as if the fury of the American bombardment had driven all sound from the region for years to come.

Jim stopped under the tailplane of a Zero fighter. Wild sugarcane grew through its wings. Cannon fire had burned the metal skin from the fuselage spars, but the rusting shell still retained all the magic of those machines that Jim had watched from the balcony of the assembly hall, taking off from the runway he had helped to build. Jim touched the feathered vanes of the radial engine and ran his hand along the warped flank of the propeller. Glycol had leaked from the radiator of the oil cooler and covered the plane with a pink tracery. He stepped onto the wing root and peered into the cockpit, at the intact display of dials and trim wheels. An immense pathos surrounded the throttle and undercarriage levers, the rivets stamped into the metal fabric by some unknown Japanese woman on the Mitsubishi assembly line.

Jim wandered among the stricken planes, which seemed to float on their green banks of nettles, letting them fly once again inside his head. Dizzied by their derelict beauty, he sat down to rest on the tail of a Hayate fighter. He watched the sky over Shanghai, waiting for the Americans to arrive at Lunghua Airfield. Although he had eaten nothing for two days, his mind was clear.

". . . aah. . . aah . . ."

The sound, a deep sigh of anger and resignation, came from the edge of the landing field. Before Jim could hide, there was a scuffle in the nettles behind the Zero. A Japanese airman stood twenty feet from him. He wore a pilot's baggy flying overall, with the insignia of a special attack group stitched to the sleeves. He was unarmed but carried a pine stake he had wrenched from the perimeter fence. He thrashed at the nettles around him and gazed irritably at the rusting aircraft, sucking in his breath as if trying to inspire them to flight.

Jim crouched over his knees, hoping that the faded camouflage of the Hayate would conceal him. He noticed that this Japanese pilot officer was still in his late teens, with an unformed face, boneless nose and chin. His sallow skin and the prominent knuckles of his wrists told Jim that the schoolboy pilot was as starved as himself.

Only his guttural sighs were driven by the breath of a mature man, as if on joining his kamikaze unit he had been assigned the throat and lungs of an older pilot.

". . . uh . . ." He noticed Jim sitting on the tailplane and for a few seconds watched him across the nettles. Then he turned away and continued his bad-tempered patrol of the airfield perimeter.

Jim watched him beating the sugarcane, perhaps trying to clear a space for a helicopter to land. Had the Japanese prepared a secret weapon in answer to the atom bomb, a high-performance rocket fighter that would need a longer runway than Lunghua's? Jim waited for him to signal to the guards at the foot of the pagoda. But the Japanese was intent only on his search of the derelict aircraft. He stopped to shake his head, and Jim was reminded again of the pilot's youth. At the outbreak of war, and until a few months earlier, he would have been a schoolboy, recruited straight from the classroom to the flight training academy.

Jim stood up and walked through the nettles to the yellowing grass at the edge of the airfield. He began to follow the Japanese, fifty yards behind him, and stopped when the pilot paused to work the elevators of a damaged Zero. He waited until the Japanese moved on again and then walked after him, making no effort to hide and carefully placing his feet in the pilot's footsteps.

For the next hour they moved around the southern edge of the airfield, the young pilot with the boy in tow. The barrack huts and dormitory blocks of Lunghua Camp rose through the heat. Far away, across the airfield, the Japanese ground crews lounged in the sun beside the burned-out hangars. Although aware that Jim was following him, the pilot made no attempt to summon them. Only when they came within eyeshot of two soldiers guarding a rifle pit did the Japanese stop and beckon Jim to him.

They stood together by a rusting plane that had been stripped of its wings by the scrap dealers. The pilot sucked at the air, distracted by Jim's patient gaze like an older schoolboy forced to acknowledge an admiring junior. For all his youth, he seemed to be willing himself to the edge of an adult despair. Clouds of flies rose from the decomposing body of a Chinese coolie lying in the sugarcane among the fuel tanks and engine blocks. The flies hovered around the pilot's mouth, tapping his lips like impatient guests at a banquet. They reminded Jim of the flies that had covered Mr. Maxted's face. Did they know that this teen-age pilot should have died in an attack on the American carriers at Okinawa?

For whatever reason, the Japanese made no move to brush them away. No doubt he knew that his own life was over, that the Kuomintang forces about to reoccupy Shanghai would be eager to deal with him.

The Japanese raised his wooden stake. Like a sleeper waking from a dream, he hurled it into the nettles. As Jim flinched, he reached into the waist pocket of his flight overalls and drew out a small mango.

Jim took the yellow fruit from the pilot's callused hand. The mango was still warm from his body. Trying to show the same self-discipline, Jim forced himself not to eat. He waited while the pilot stared at the concrete runway.

With a last cry of disgust, the pilot stepped forward and cuffed Jim on the head, waving him toward the perimeter fence as if warning him away from contaminated ground.

34

THE REFRIGERATOR IN THE SKY

THE SWEET MANGO slithered around Jim's mouth, like Mrs. Vincent's tongue in his hands. Ten feet from the perimeter fence, Jim sat on a Mustang drop tank that had fallen into the grass beside a flooded paddy field. He swallowed the soft pulp and chewed at the stone, scraping away the last of the pith. Already he was thinking of the next mango. If he could attach himself to this young Japanese pilot, run errands for him and make himself useful, there might be more mangoes. Within a few days he would be strong enough to walk to Shanghai. By then the Americans would have arrived; Jim could present the kamikaze pilot to them as his friend. Being generous people at heart, the Americans would overlook the small matter of the suicide attacks on their carriers at Okinawa. When peace came, the Japanese might teach him to fly. . . .

Almost drunk on the mango's milky sap, Jim slid to the ground, his back against the drop tank. He stared at the level surface of the flooded paddy, deciding to be serious with himself. First, could he be sure that the war was really over? The Eurasian in the white shirt had been suspiciously offhand, but he was only concerned to steal the furniture and cars stored at the stadium. As for learning to fly, a kamikaze pilot might not be the ideal instructor. . . .

A familiar drone crossed the August sky, a threat of engines. Jim stood up, almost choking on the mango stone. Straight ahead, some eight hundred feet above the empty paddies, was an American bomber. A four-engined Superfortress, it flew more slowly than any American plane that Jim had seen throughout the war. Was it about to land at Lunghua Airfield? Jim began to wave to the pilot in the glass-domed cockpit. As the Superfortress swept overhead, its engines shook the ground with their noise, and the derelict aircraft at the edge of the landing field began to tremble together.

The doors of the bomb bays opened, revealing the silver cylinders ready to fall from their racks. The Superfortress drummed past, the higher pitch of one of its starboard engines cracking the air. Too weak to move, Jim waited for the bombs to explode around him, but the sky was filled with colored parachutes. Dozens of canopies floated gaily on the air, as if enjoying the August sun. The vivid parasols reminded Jim of the hot-air balloons that the Chinese conjurers sent soaring over the gardens of Amherst Avenue at the climax of the children's parties. Were the pilots of the B-29s trying to amuse him, to keep up his spirits until they could land?

The parachutes sailed past, falling toward Lunghua Camp. Unsteadily, Jim tried to focus his eyes on the colored canopies. Two of the parachutes had collided, entangling their shrouds. A silver canister dragged its collapsed parachute and plummeted to the ground, striking a canal embankment two hundred yards away.

Making a final effort, before he had to lie down for the last time among the derelict aircraft, Jim stepped through the sugarcane into the flooded paddy. He strode across the shallow water to a submerged bomb crater in the center of the field, then followed its ridge toward the canal.

As he climbed the embankment, the last of the parachutes had fallen into the fields to the west of Lunghua Camp. The murmur of the B-29's engines faded over the Yangtze. Jim approached the scarlet canopy, large enough to cover a house, which lay across the embankment. He gazed at the lustrous material, more luxurious than any fabric he had ever seen, at the immaculate stitching and seams, at the white cords that trailed into the culvert beside the canal.

The canister had burst on impact. Jim lowered himself down the slope of sunbaked earth and squatted by the open mouth of the cylinder. Around him, on the floor of the culvert, was a ransom of canned food and cigarette packets. The canister was crammed with cardboard cartons, and one had broken loose from the nose cone and scattered its contents over the ground. Jim crawled among the cans, wiping his eyes so that he could read the labels. There were tins of Spam, Klim and Nescafé, bars of chocolate and cellophaned packs of Lucky Strike and Chesterfield cigarettes, bundles of *Reader's Digest* and *Life* magazines, *Time* and *Saturday Evening Post*.

The sight of so much food confused Jim, forcing on him a notion of choice that he had not known for years. The cans and packets were frozen, as if they had just emerged from an American refrigerator. He began to fill the broken box with canned meat, powdered milk, chocolate bars and a bundle of *Reader's Digests*. Then, thinking ahead for the first time in several days, he added a carton of Chesterfield cigarettes.

When he climbed from the culvert, the scarlet canopy of the parachute was billowing gently in the air that moved along the canal. Holding the cold treasure to his chest, Jim left the embankment and waded across the paddy field. He was following the ridge of the bomb crater toward the perimeter of the airfield when he heard the leisurely drumming of a B-29's engines. Jim stopped to search for the plane, already wondering how he could cope with all this treasure falling from the sky.

Almost at once, a rifle shot rang out. A hundred yards away, separated from Jim by the open paddy, a Japanese soldier was running along the embankment of the canal. Barefooted, in his ragged uniform, he raced past the parachute canopy, leaped down the weed-covered slope and sprinted across the paddy field. Lost in the spray kicked up by his frantic heels, he disappeared among the grave mounds and clumps of sugarcane.

Jim crouched by the ridge of the bomb crater, hiding in the few blades of wild rice. A second Japanese soldier appeared. He was unarmed but still wore his webbing and ammunition pouches. He sprinted along the canal embankment and stopped to recover his breath beside the scarlet canopy of the parachute. He turned to look over his shoulder, and Jim recognized the puffy, tubercular face of Private Kimura.

A group of European men was following him along the embankment, clubs of weighted bamboo in their hands. One of the men carried a rifle, but Kimura ignored him and straightened his webbing around his tattered uniform. He kicked one of his rotting boots into the water and then walked down the slope to the flooded paddy field. He had covered ten paces when there was a second rifle shot.

Private Kimura lay facedown in the shallow water. Jim waited in the wild rice as the four Europeans approached the parachute canopy. He listened to their nervous quarreling. All were former British prisoners, barefoot and in ragged shorts, though none had been inmates of Lunghua. Their leader was an agitated young Englishman whose fists were wrapped in a pair of grimy bandages. Jim guessed that he had been imprisoned for years in an underground cell. His white skin flinched in the sunlight like the exposed flesh of a snail teased from its shell. He waved his bandages in the air, bloody pennants that signaled some special kind of anger to himself.

The four men began to roll up the parachute canopy. Despite the starvation of the past months, they worked swiftly and had soon pulled the metal canister from the culvert. They repacked its contents, lashed the nose cone in place and dragged the heavy cylinder along the embankment.

Jim watched them make their way between the burial mounds toward Lunghua Camp. He was tempted to run over and join them, but all the cautions learned in the past years warned him not to expose himself. Private Kimura lay in the water fifty feet away, a red cloud unfurling from his back like the canopy of a drowned parachute.

Fifteen minutes later, when he was certain that no one was watching from the nearby paddy fields, Jim emerged from the clump of wild rice and returned to his hiding place among the derelict aircraft.

Quickly, without bothering to wash his hands in the flooded paddy, Jim tore the key from the Spam tin and rolled back the metal strip. A pungent odor rose from the pink mass of chopped meat, which gaped in the sunlight like a wound. Jim sank his fingers into the meat and pressed a piece between his lips. A strange but potent flavor filled his mouth, the taste of animal fat. After years of boiled rice and sweet potatoes, his mouth was an ocean of exotic spices. Chewing carefully, as Dr. Ransome had taught him, drawing the last ounce of nutrition from every morsel, Jim finished the meat.

Thirsty after all the salts, he opened the can of Klim, only to find a white powder. He crammed the fatty grains into his mouth, reached through the grass to the edge of the paddy and scooped a handful of the warm water to his lips. A rich, creamy foam almost choked him, and he vomited the white torrent into the paddy. Jim stared with surprise at this snowy fountain, wondering if he would starve to death because he had forgotten how to eat. Sensibly he read the instructions and mixed a pint of milk so rich that its fat swam in the sun like the oil on the surrounding creeks and canals.

Dazed by the food, Jim lay back in the hot grass and sucked contentedly on the bar of hard, sweet chocolate. He had eaten the most satisfying meal of his life, and his stomach stood out below his ribs like a football. Beside him, on the surface of the paddy, swarms of flies festered over the cloud of white vomit. Jim wiped the mud from the second Spam tin and waited for the Japanese pilot to appear again, so that he could repay him for the mango.

Three miles to the west, near the camps of Hungjao and Siccawei, dozens of colored parachutes were dropping from a B-29 that cruised across the August sky. Surrounded by this vision of all the abundance of America falling from the air, Jim laughed happily to himself. He began his second—and almost more important—meal, devouring the six copies of the *Reader's Digest*. He turned the crisp, white pages of the magazines, so unlike the greasy copies he had read to death in Lunghua. They were filled with headlines and catch phrases from a world he had never known, and a host of unimaginable names— Patton, Eisenhower, Himmler, Belsen, jeep, GI, AWOL, Utah Beach, von Runstedt, the Bulge and a thousand other details of the European war. Together they described an heroic adventure on another planet, filled with scenes of sacrifice and stoicism, of countless acts of bravery, a universe away from the war that Jim had known at the estuary of the Yangtze, that vast river barely large enough to draw all the dead of China through its mouth. Feasting on the magazines, Jim drowsed among the flies and vomit. Trying not to be outdone by the *Reader's Digest*, Jim remembered the white light of the atom bomb at Nagasaki, whose flash he had seen reflected across the China Sea. Its pale halo still lay over the silent fields but seemed barely equal to D-day and Bastogne. Unlike the war in China, everyone in Europe clearly knew which side he was on, a problem that Jim had never really solved. Despite all the new names that it had spawned, was the war recharging itself here by the great rivers of eastern Asia, to be fought forever in that far more ambiguous language that Jim had begun to learn?

35

LIEUTENANT PRICE

BY THE EARLY afternoon Jim had rested sufficiently to turn his mind from this question and eat a second meal. The warm Spam, no longer chilled by its high-altitude flight in the bomb bays of the B-29, slipped between his fingers onto the dusty ground. Jim retrieved the block of jellied meat, scraped away the flies and dirt, and washed it down with the last of the powdered milk.

Chewing on the chocolate bar, and pondering upon the Ardennes offensive, Jim watched a B-29 soar across the open countryside two miles to the southwest. A Mustang fighter accompanied the bomber, drifting in wide circles a thousand feet above the Superfortress, as if its pilot were bored by the chore of guarding the relief plane. A flock of parachutes sailed toward the ground, perhaps aimed at an exhausted group of Lunghua prisoners abandoned by the Japanese during their march from Nantao stadium.

Jim turned to the Shanghai skyline. Was he strong enough to walk the few, dangerous miles to the western suburbs? Perhaps his parents had already returned to the house in Amherst Avenue. They might be hungry after the journey from Soochow, and would be glad of the last tin of Spam and the carton of Chesterfields. Smiling to himself, Jim thought of his mother—he could no longer remember her face, but he could all too well imagine her response to the Spam. As an extra treat, she would have plenty to read. . . .

Jim stood up, eager to begin the walk back to Shanghai. He patted his bloated stomach, wondering if there was a new American disease that came from eating too much food. At that moment, through the branches of the trees, he saw faces turn toward him. Six Chinese soldiers strode past the derelict aircraft, following the perimeter road. They were northern Chinese, tall and heavy-boned men wearing full packs and quilted blue uniforms. There were five-pointed red stars on their soft caps, and the leader carried a machine gun of foreign design, with an air-cooled barrel and drum magazine. He wore spectacles and was younger and slighter than his men, with the fixed gaze of an accountant or student.

At a steady pace, as if they had already covered an immense distance, the six soldiers stepped between the aircraft. They passed within twenty feet of Jim, who concealed the Spam and the carton of Chesterfields behind his back. He assumed that these men were Chinese Communists. By all accounts, they hated the Americans. Seeing the cigarettes, they might shoot him before he could explain that he too had once thought seriously of becoming a Communist.

But the soldiers glanced at Jim without interest, their faces free of that unsettling blend of deference and contempt with which the Chinese had always regarded Europeans and Americans. They walked swiftly and soon vanished among the trees. Jim stepped over the perimeter wire, searching for the Japanese pilot. He wanted to warn him of these Communist soldiers, who would kill him on sight.

Already Jim had decided not to walk alone to Shanghai. The Lunghua and Nantao districts were infested with armed men. He would first return to the camp and join the British internees who had shot Private Kimura. As soon as they recovered their strength, they would want to set out for the bars and nightclubs of Shanghai. Jim, with all his expertise gained in Mr. Maxted's Studebaker, would be their guide.

Although the gates of Lunghua Camp were little more than a mile from him, it took Jim two hours to cross the empty countryside. Avoiding Private Kimura, Jim waded through the flooded paddy field and then followed the canal embankment to the Shanghai road. The verges were littered with the debris of the air attacks. Burned-out trucks and supply wagons lay in the ditches, surrounded by the bodies of dead puppet soldiers, the carcasses of horses and water buffalo. A glimmer of golden light rose from the thousands of spent cartridge cases, as if these dead soldiers had been looting a treasury in the moments before their death.

Jim walked along the silent road, watching an American fighter cruise in from the west. Sitting in his open cockpit, the pilot circled Jim, engine throttled back so that the silver machine whispered through the air. Then Jim saw that its guns were cocked, their ejection ports open, and it occurred to him that the pilot might kill him for fun. He raised the carton of Chesterfields and the

*Reader's Digest*s, displaying them to the pilot like a set of passports. The pilot waved to him and banked the aircraft, setting course for Shanghai.

The presence of this American aviator cheered Jim. He confidently strode the last hundred yards toward the camp. The sight of the familiar buildings, the watchtower and barbed-wire fence, warmed and reassured him. He was going back to his real home. If Shanghai was too dangerous, perhaps his mother and father would leave Amherst Avenue and live with him in Lunghua. In a practical sense it was a pity that the Japanese soldiers would not be there to guard them. . . .

As Jim reached the camp, he was surprised to find that the Chinese peasants and army deserters had returned to their plot beside the gates. They squatted in the sun, staring patiently at the bare-chested Briton who stood inside the wire, a holstered pistol strapped to his bony hips. Jim recognized him as Mr. Tulloch, the chief mechanic at the Packard agency in Shanghai. He had spent the entire war playing cards in D Block, pausing once to have a brisk row with Dr. Ransome for refusing to help with the sewage detail. Jim had last seen him lying outside the guardhouse after his abortive attempt to walk to Shanghai.

He now lounged against the gates, picking at an infected bruise on his lip and watching the activity on the parade ground. Two Britons were dragging a parachute canister and its canopy through the door of the guardhouse. A third man stood on the roof, scanning the countryside with a pair of Japanese binoculars.

"Mr. Tulloch . . ." Jim pulled at the gates, rattling the heavy padlock and chain. "Mr. Tulloch, you've locked the gates."

Tulloch stared distastefully at Jim, clearly not recognizing this ragged fourteen-year-old and suspicious of the carton of cigarettes.

"Where the hell did you come from? Are you British, boy?"

"Mr. Tulloch, I was in Lunghua. I lived here for three years." When Tulloch began to wander away, Jim shouted: "I worked at the hospital with Dr. Ransome!"

"Dr. Ransome?" Tulloch returned to the gates. He peered skeptically at Jim. "Doctor shit-stirrer?"

"That's it, Mr. Tulloch. I stirred shit for Dr. Ransome. I have to go to Shanghai and find my mother and father. We had a Packard, Mr. Tulloch."

"He's stirred his last shit. . . ." Tulloch took Sergeant Nagata's key ring from the ammunition pouch of his holster. He was still unsure whether to admit Jim to the camp. "A Packard? Good car . . ."

He unlocked the gates and beckoned Jim inside. Hearing the clatter, the Englishman with the bandaged hands who had shot Private Kimura strode from the guardhouse. Although emaciated, he had a strong, nervous physique and a pallor that was heightened by his bloodied knuckles. Jim had seen the same chalklike skin and deranged eyes in those prisoners released after months in the underground cells of the police headquarters. His chest and shoulders were covered with the scars of dozens of cigarette burns, as if his body had been riddled with a hot poker in an attempt to set it alight.

"Lock those gates!" He pointed a bloody hand at Jim. "Throw him out!"

"Price, I know the lad. His people bought a Packard."

"Get rid of him! We'll have everyone with a Packard in here. . . ."

"Right, Lieutenant. Hop it, lad. Look sharpish."

Jim tried to hold the gates open with his golf shoe, and Lieutenant Price punched him in the chest with a bandaged fist. Winded, Jim sat down hard on the ground beside the watching Chinese. He held on to the Spam and the carton of Chesterfields, but the six *Reader's Digest*s inside his shirt spilled onto the grass and were instantly seized by the peasant women. The small, starving women in their black trousers sat around Jim, each holding a magazine as if about to take part in a discussion group on the European war.

Price slammed the gates in their faces. Everything around him, the camp, the empty paddy fields, even the sun, seemed to anger him. He shook his head at Jim, and then caught sight of the Spam in Jim's hand.

"Where did you get that? The Lunghua drops belong to us!" He screamed in Chinese at the peasant women, suspecting them of complicity in this theft. "Tulloch! They're stealing our Spam!"

He unlocked the gates, intending to wrest the can from Jim, when there was a shout from the watchtower. The man with the binoculars stepped down the ladder, pointing to the fields beyond the Shanghai road.

Two B-29s appeared from the west, their engines droning over the deserted land. Seeing the camp, they separated from each other. One flew toward Lunghua, its bomb doors opening to reveal their canisters. The other altered course for the Pootung district to the east of Shanghai.

As the Superfortresses thundered over their heads, Jim crouched beside the Chinese peasants. Armed with the rifle and bamboo clubs, Price and three of the Britons ran through the gates and set off across the nearby field.

Already the sky was filled with parachutes, the blue and scarlet canopies sailing down into the paddies half a mile from the camp.

The engine noise of the B-29 softened to a muffled rumble. Jim was tempted to follow Price and his men, and offer to help them. The parachutes had landed behind a system of old trenchworks. Losing their bearings, the Britons ran in all directions. Price climbed the parapet of an earth redoubt and waved his rifle in a fury. One of the men slipped into a shallow canal and waded in circles through the water weed, while the others ran along the mud walls between the paddies.

As Tulloch watched them despairingly, Jim stood up and stepped past him through the gates. The Packard mechanic loosened the heavy pistol in his holster. The sight of the falling parachutes had aroused him, and the stringlike muscles of his arms and shoulders trembled in a cat's cradle of excitement.

"Mr. Tulloch, is the war over?" Jim asked. "Really over?"

"The war . . . ?" Tulloch seemed to have forgotten that it had ever taken place. "It better be over, lad—anytime now the next one's going to begin."

"I saw some Communist soldiers, Mr. Tulloch."

"They're everywhere. You wait till Lieutenant Price gets to work on them. We'll park you in the guardhouse, lad. Keep out of his way. . . ."

Jim followed Tulloch across the parade ground, and together they entered the guardhouse. The once-immaculate floor of the orderly room, polished by the Chinese prisoners between their beatings, was covered with dirt and refuse. Japanese calendars and documents lay among the empty Lucky Strike cartons, spent ammunition clips and the tatters of old infantry boots. Against the rear wall of the commandant's office were stacked dozens of ration boxes. A naked Britisher in his late fifties, a former barman at the Shanghai Country Club, sat on a bamboo stool, separating the canned meat from the coffee and cigarettes. He packed the bars of chocolate on the commandant's desk, and brusquely threw aside the bundles of *Reader's Digest*s and *Saturday Evening Post*s. The entire floor of the office was covered with discarded magazines.

Beside him, a young British soldier in the rags of a Seaforth Highlander's uniform was cutting the nylon cords from the parachutes. He tied the ropes into neat coils, then expertly folded the blue and scarlet canopies.

Tulloch gazed at this treasure house, clearly awed by the fortune that he and his companions had amassed. He pushed Jim from the door, concerned that the sight of so many bars of chocolate would derange the boy.

"Don't dwell on it, son. Eat your Spam in there."

But Jim was staring at the magazines heaped on the floor at his feet. He wanted to tidy them up and hoard them for the next war. "Mr. Tulloch, I ought to go back to Shanghai now."

"Shanghai? There's nothing there except six million starving coolies. They'll cut off your foreskin before you can say Bubbling Well Road."

"Mr. Tulloch, my mother and father—"

"Lad! Nobody's mother and father are going to Shanghai. All those FRB dollars chasing a hundred bags of rice? Here it's falling out of the sky."

A rifle shot rang out across the paddy fields, followed by two more in quick succession. Leaving the naked barman to protect their treasure store, Tulloch and the Seaforth Highlander ran from the guardhouse and climbed the ladder of the watchtower.

Jim began to straighten the magazines on the floor of the commandant's office, but the barman shouted at him and waved him away. Left to himself, Jim stepped into the cell yard behind the orderly room. The warm Spam in his hand, he peered into the empty cells, at the dark blood and dried excrement that stained the concrete walls.

In the cell at the far end of the yard, shaded by a straw mat hung from the bars, was the body of a dead Japanese soldier. He lay on the cement bench that was the cell's only furniture, his shoulders lashed to the remains of a wooden chair. His head had been bludgeoned to a pulp that resembled a crushed watermelon, filled with the black seeds of hundreds of flies.

Jim stared through the bars at the soldier, shocked that one of the Japanese who had guarded him for so many years should have been imprisoned and then beaten to death in one of his own cells. Jim had accepted Private Kimura's death, in the anonymity of the flooded paddy field, but this reversal of all the rules governing their life in the camp at last convinced Jim that the war might be over.

Jim left the cell yard and returned to the orderly office. He sat behind Sergeant Nagata's desk, a luxury he had never once been allowed, and began to read the discarded copies of *Life* and *Saturday Evening Post*. For once the lavish advertisements, the headlines and slogans—"When Better Cars are built, Buick will build them!"—failed to touch him. Despite the food he had eaten, he felt numbed by the task of finding a way to Shanghai, and by all the confusions of the arbitrary peace imposed on the settled and secure landscape of the war. Peace had come, but it failed to fit properly.

Through the broken windows Jim watched a B-29 cross the river two miles away, searching the warehouses of Pootung for any groups of Allied prisoners. The peasants outside the gates of Lunghua ignored the bomber. Jim had noticed that the Chinese never looked up at the planes. Although they were nationals of one of the Allied powers at war with Japan, they would not share in these relief supplies.

He listened to the angry voices of the Britons returning from their foray across the paddy fields. Despite all their efforts, they had seized only two of the parachute canisters. While Lieutenant Price stood guard by the gates, rifle trembling in his hands, the others dragged the canisters into the camp. The sweat dripped from their bodies onto the scarlet silk. The remaining parachutes had vanished into the countryside, spirited from under Price's nose by the secret tenants of the burial mounds.

As large as bombs, the canisters lay on the floor in the commandant's office. The naked barman sat astride them, the sweat from his buttocks dulling the silver, while the Seaforth Highlander struck off the nose cones with the rifle butt. The men tore the cartons apart, loading their emaciated arms with cans of meat and coffee, chocolates and cigarettes. Lieutenant Price hovered among them, the bones in his shoulders shaking like castanets. He was excited and exhausted at the same time, eager to work up his irritation again and put to good use all the violence he had found within himself on beating the Japanese to death.

He noticed Jim quietly reading his magazines behind Sergeant Nagata's desk. "Tulloch! He's here again! The boy with the Packard . . ."

"The lad was in the camp, Lieutenant. He skivvied for one of the doctors."

"He's roaming around everywhere! Lock him up in one of the cells!"

"He isn't the talkative type, Lieutenant." Tulloch held Jim's arm, reluctantly pulling him toward the cell yard. "He's walked all the way from Nantao Stadium."

"Nantao? The big stadium?" Price turned to Jim with interest, gazing at him with all the guilelessness of the fanatic. "How long were you there, boy?"

"Three days," Jim replied. "Or I think it was six days. Until the war ended."

"He can't count."

"He must have had a good look, Lieutenant."

"I bet he had a good look. Roaming around all the time. Boy, what did you see in the stadium?" Price treated Jim to a roguish grimace. "Rifles? Stores?"

"Cars, mostly," Jim explained. "At least five Buicks, two Cadillacs and a Lincoln Zephyr."

"Forget about the cars! Were you born in a garage? What else did you see?"

"Just a lot of carpets and furniture."

"Fur coats?" Tulloch interjected. "There was no ordnance there, Lieutenant. What about scotch whiskey, son?"

Price pulled the copy of *Life* from Jim's hands. "For God's sake, you'll ruin your eyes. Listen to Mr. Tulloch. Did you see any scotch whiskey?"

Jim stepped back, keeping the silver canisters between himself and this unstable man. As if excited by the booty in Nantao Stadium, the lieutenant's hands were bleeding through their bandages. Jim knew that Lieutenant Price would have liked to get him alone and then beat him to death, not because he was cruel, but because only the sight of Jim's agony would clear away all the pain that he himself had endured.

"There might have been scotch whiskey," he said tactfully. "There were a lot of bars."

"Bars?" Price stepped across the cartons of Chesterfields, ready to slap him. "I'll give you bars. . . ."

"Cocktail bars—at least twenty of them. There might have been whiskey there."

"Sounds like a hotel. Tulloch, what sort of war did you people have here? Right, boy, what else did you see?"

"I saw the atom bomb drop at Nagasaki," Jim said. He spoke in a clear voice. "I saw the white flash! Is the war over now?"

The sweating men put down their cans and cartons. Lieutenant Price stared at Jim, surprised by this statement but prepared to believe it. He lit a cigarette as an American aircraft flew over the camp, a Mustang returning to its base on Okinawa.

Through the noise Jim shouted: "I saw the *atom bomb!*"

"Yes . . . you must have seen it." Lieutenant Price fastened the bandages around his bleeding fists. He sucked fiercely at his cigarette. Gazing hungrily at Jim, he picked up the copy of *Life* and left the commandant's office. As the Mustang's engine faded across the paddy fields, they could hear Price striding up and down the cell yard, striking the doors of the cells with the rolled magazine.

36

THE FLIES

DID LIEUTENANT PRICE believe that he had been poisoned by the atom bomb? Jim walked across the parade ground, looking up at the empty barrack huts and dormitory blocks. The windows hung open in the sunlight, as if the tenants had fled at his approach. The mention of the Nagasaki raid, and its confusion with the booty waiting for Price in Nantao Stadium, had calmed this former officer in the Nanking police. For an hour Jim had helped the men to unpack the parachute canisters, and Price had not objected when Tulloch gave their young recruit a bar of American chocolate. Images of hunger and violence fused in Price's mind, as they had done during the years of his imprisonment by the *kempetai*.

Holding his tin of Spam and a bundle of *Life* magazines, Jim climbed the steps into the foyer of D Block. He paused by the notice boards with their fading camp bulletins and commandant's orders. In the dormitories he strolled along the lines of bunks. The homemade lockers had been looted by the Japanese after the departure of the prisoners, as if there was still something of value to be found in this rubbish of urine-stained mats and packing-case furniture.

322

Yet despite the emptiness of the camp, it seemed ready for instant occupation. Outside G Block he looked at the baked earth, at the worn ruts of years left by the iron wheels of the food cart, pointing their way to the camp kitchens. He stood in the doorway of his room, barely surprised to see the faded magazine cuttings pinned to the wall above his bunk. In the last minutes before joining the march, Mrs. Vincent had torn down the curtain of his cubicle, satisfying a long-held need to occupy the whole room. Neatly folded, the curtain lay under Jim's bunk, and he was tempted to pin it up again.

A marked smell hung in the room, one he had never noticed during all the years of the war, at once enticing and ambiguous. Jim realized that it was the odor of Mrs. Vincent's body, and for a moment he imagined that she had returned to the camp. Jim stretched out on Mrs. Vincent's bunk and balanced the tin of Spam on his forehead. He surveyed the room from this unfamiliar angle, a privilege he had never been allowed during the war. Tucked behind the door, his cubicle must have resembled one of those ramshackle hutches that the beggars of Shanghai erected around themselves out of newspapers and straw mats. Often he must have seemed to Mrs. Vincent like a beast in a kennel. It was no wonder, Jim reflected as he perused a copy of *Life*, that Mrs. Vincent had been intensely irritated by him, wishing him away even to the point of hoping he would die.

Jim lay on her straw mattress, smelling the scent of her body, fitting his hips and shoulders into the shallow mold she had left behind. Seen from Mrs. Vincent's vantage point, the past three years appeared subtly different; even a few steps across a small room generated a separate war, a separate ordeal for this woman with her weary husband and sick child.

Thinking with affection of Mrs. Vincent, Jim wished that they were still together. He missed Dr. Ransome and Mrs. Pearce, and the group of men who sat all day on the steps outside the foyer. It occurred to Jim that they might also miss Lunghua. Perhaps one day they would all return to the camp.

Jim left the room and walked down the corridor to the rear door where the children had played. The marks of their games—hopscotch, marbles and fighting tops—still covered the ground. Jim kicked a small stone into the hopscotch court and deftly flicked it around the squares, then set out on a circuit of the deserted camp. Already he could feel Lunghua gathering itself around him again.

As he approached the hospital, he began to hope that Dr. Ransome would be there. By the entrance to Hut 6 a rain-soaked Pierrot costume of the Lunghua Sophomores lay in a muddy pool. Jim stopped to clean the Spam tin. He wiped the label with the ruff of the costume, remembering Dr. Ransome's lectures on hygiene.

The bamboo shutters were lowered across the windows of the hospital, as if Dr. Ransome wanted the patients to sleep through the afternoon. Jim climbed the steps, aware of a faint murmur within the building. When he pushed back the doors, a cloud of flies enveloped him. Maddened by the light, they filled the narrow entrance hall, as if trying to shake off the foul odor that clung to their wings.

Brushing the flies from his mouth, Jim walked into the men's ward. The decaying air streamed down the plywood walls, bathing the flies that fed on the bodies piled across the bunks. Identifiable by their ragged shorts and flowered dresses, and by the clogs embedded in their swollen feet, dozens of Lunghua prisoners lay on the bunks like sides of meat in a condemned slaughterhouse.

Their backs and shoulders glistened with mucus, and the splayed mouths in their ballooning cheeks still gaped as if these bloated men and women, dragged from a banquet, were gripped by a ravenous hunger.

Jim walked through the darkened ward, the tin of Spam held tightly to his chest, breathing through the magazines cupped over his mouth. Despite their caricature faces, Jim recognized several of the prisoners. He searched for Dr. Ransome and Mrs. Vincent, assuming that the bodies were those of the Lunghua internees who had fallen behind during the march from the stadium. The flies festered over the bodies, in some way aware that the war had ended and determined to hoard every morsel of flesh for the coming famine of the peace.

Jim stood on the steps of the hospital, looking out at the deserted camp and the silent fields beyond the wire. The flies soon left him and returned to the ward. Jim set out for the kitchen garden. He walked among the fading plants, wondering whether to water them, and plucked the last two tomatoes. He raised the berries to his lips but stopped before eating them. He remembered his fears that his soul had died in the stadium at Nantao, even though his body had survived. If his soul had been unable to escape and had died within him, would feeding his body engorge it like the corpses in the hospital?

Thinking about his last night in Nantao Stadium, Jim sat on the balcony of the assembly hall. In the late afternoon a Chinese merchant arrived at the gates of the camp, accompanied by three coolies. They carried earthenware jars of rice wine suspended from bamboo yokes across their backs. Jim watched the barter of goods take place outside the guardhouse. Wisely, Lieutenant Price had closed the door of the treasure chest in the commandant's office. Cartons of Lucky Strikes and a single parachute canopy were exchanged for the jars of wine. When the merchant left, followed by his coolies with their bale of scarlet silk, the Britons were soon drunk. Jim decided not to return to the guardhouse that evening. Lieutenant Price's white body lurched through the dusk, the cigarette burns on his chest inflamed by the wine.

From the balcony Jim gazed across Lunghua Airfield. Carefully he opened his tin of Spam. It was a pity that Dr. Ransome would not be sharing it with him. As he raised the warm meat to his mouth, he thought of the bodies in the hospital. He had not been shocked by the sight of the dead prisoners. In fact, he had known all along that those who fell behind during the march from Lunghua would be left to die or killed where they rested. Nonetheless, he associated the chopped ham with those fattened corpses. Each was enveloped in the same mucus. The living who ate or drank too quickly, like Tulloch and the police lieutenant with his bloody hands, would soon join the overfed dead. Food fed death, the eager and waiting death of their own bodies.

Jim listened to the drunken shouts from the guardhouse and the volley of rifle shots as Price fired over the heads of the Chinese at the gates. With his dungeon pallor and bandaged hands, this albino figure frightened Jim, the first of the dead to rise from the grave, eager to start the next world war.

Jim rested his eyes on the reassuring geometry of the airfield runway. Four hundred yards away, the young Japanese pilot walked among the derelict aircraft. Bamboo stick in hand, he searched the nettles. His baggy flying suit, lit by the evening air, reminded Jim of another pilot of the dusk who had saved him three years earlier and opened the doors of Lunghua.

326

37

A RESERVED ROOM

SOON AFTER DAWN Jim was awakened by the first reconnaissance flights of the American fighters. He had spent the night sleeping in Mrs. Vincent's bunk, and from the windows of G Block he watched the pairs of Mustangs circle the pagoda at Lunghua Airfield. An hour later the air drops began to the prisoner-of-war camps near Shanghai. The squadrons of B-29s emerged from the hazy light over the Yangtze and cruised over the empty paddy fields with their open bomb doors, an armada for hire of vacant limousines.

Now that the war was over, the American bombardiers seemed either unwilling, or too bored, to concentrate on their sights. Much to the annoyance of Tulloch and Lieutenant Price, they dropped their cargoes into the open fields around the camp, rolled their wings and set off in a leisurely way for home, the day's work done.

When were the American army and navy coming to Shanghai? From the roof of G Block, Jim examined the calm surface of the river three miles to the north. No doubt the Americans were wary of sailing up the Yangtze, fearing that the Japanese submarine commanders might have decided not to surrender. But until they arrived it was too dangerous for Jim to set out in search of his mother and father. The whole of Shanghai and the surrounding countryside was locked into a zone where there was neither war nor peace, a vacuum that would soon be filled by every warlord and disaffected general in China.

After waiting for Price and his men to leave the camp in search of the parachute canisters, Jim went down to the guardhouse. The wash from the engines of the relief Superfortress had driven the stench of rotting meat from the hospital, a pall that hung over the camp for hours. But Tulloch appeared not to notice. Once Lieutenant Price was out of the way, a specter hunting other specters among the burial mounds, Tulloch was prepared to admit Jim to the commandant's office. Jim helped himself to the cans stacked against the wall. He made a quick meal of Spam and powdered milk, then sat behind Sergeant Nagata's desk in the orderly room, chewing a chocolate bar and sorting out the copies of the American magazines.

Later, when Tulloch went off to abuse the growing crowd of starving Chinese outside the gates, Jim climbed the ladder of the watchtower. He could see Price and his raiding party searching the creeks to the west of the camp. They had joined forces with a group of Allied prisoners from Hungjao, and the armed men were running along the embankments of the antitank ditches, firing across the flooded paddy fields.

Already it was clear that the former British internees were not the only scavengers roving the countryside. The Chinese peasants were returning to the villages they had abandoned in the weeks before the war's end. Gangs of coolies roamed the area, stripping the tires and body panels from the burned-out Japanese vehicles. Squads of renegade Kuomintang soldiers who had deserted to the Chinese puppet armies wandered the roads, well aware of their fate if they fell into the hands of their former Nationalist comrades, but drawn toward Shanghai by the American air drops. As Jim stood in the observation box of the watchtower, a company of these demoralized troops straggled past the gates of Lunghua. Still fully armed, in ragged uniforms from which they had torn their badges, they passed within a few feet of the solitary Packard mechanic guarding his treasure of chocolate bars and *Saturday Evening Posts*.

At noon, when Lieutenant Price appeared, dressed like a corpse in the scarlet canopy of the parachute canister dragged by his men, Jim gathered together his bundle of magazines and returned to G Block. He spent an hour sorting them into their correct order and then set out on a tour of the camp. Avoiding the hospital, he climbed through the wire and explored the overgrown terrain between the camp and Lunghua Airfield, hoping to find the turtle that he had released in the last weeks of the war.

But the canal beside the fence contained only the body of a dead Japanese airman. Sections of Lunghua Airfield—the pagoda, barracks and control tower—were now occupied by an advance brigade of Nationalist troops. For reasons of their own, the Japanese aircraftsmen and ground crews made no attempt to escape, and lived on in the gutted hangars and workshops. Each day the Nationalist soldiers took a few of the Japanese and killed them in the waste ground to the south and west of the airfield.

The sight of this dead Japanese airman, floating face-down in the canal among the Mustang drop tanks, unsettled Jim as much as the bodies of the Britons in the camp hospital. From then on he decided to remain within the safety of the camp. He slept at night in Mrs. Vincent's bed, and spent the days sampling the American canned food and chocolate, and sorting out his collection of magazines. By now he had assembled a substantial library, which he stacked neatly on the spare bunks in his room. The copies of *Time, Life* and the *Reader's Digest* covered every conceivable aspect of the war, a world at once familiar and yet totally removed from his own experiences in Shanghai and Lunghua. At moments, as he studied the dramatic accounts of tank battles and beachheads, he wondered if he himself had been in the war at all.

But he continued to collect the magazines from the floor of the commandant's office, concealing within them a few extra cans of Spam and powdered milk, part of a long-term reserve that he had sensibly begun to stockpile. Already it was clear to Jim that the American air drops were becoming less frequent, and sooner or later they would stop. Now that his strength had returned, Jim was able to scavenge busily around the camp and was never more pleased than when, under a bunk in D Block, he found a tennis racket and a tin of balls.

On the third morning, as Price and his men stood with the binoculars on the roof of the guardhouse, waiting impatiently for the American relief planes, an ancient Opel truck arrived at the gates of the camp. Two bare-chested Britons, sometime Lunghua prisoners, sat in the driving cabin, while their Chinese wives and children rode in the back with their possessions. Jim had last seen the men, foremen at the Moller Line dockyards, in the stadium at Nantao, lifting the hoods of the white Cadillacs on the morning the war had ended. Somehow they had made their way to Shanghai and collected their families, who had not been interned by the Japanese. Finding themselves destitute in the hostile city, they had decided to return to Lunghua.

Already they had collected their first booty. A silver parachute canister lay like a bomb on the floor of the truck, dwarfing the dark-eyed children in their Chinese tunics. Jim watched from Basie's window in E Block, smiling contentedly as Tulloch and Lieutenant Price climbed down from the roof of the guardhouse. They strolled over to the gates but made no attempt to unlock them. A rambling argument ensued between Price and the former Lunghua prisoners, who pointed angrily at E Block, deserted now except for the fourteen-year-old boy laughing to himself at the top-floor window.

Jim drummed his fists on the concrete sill, and waved to the men and their glowering Chinese wives. After three years of trying to leave the camp they were now back at its gates, ready to take up their stations for World War III. At long last they were beginning to realize the simple truth that Jim had always known, that inside Lunghua they were free.

The gates were opening; a bargain had been struck. Lieutenant Price had taken a fancy to the Opel. Within a minute the two Britons and their families sped across the parade ground toward D Block, followed by the first Mustangs of the morning. As they soared over the camp, the wash from their engines drove a foul wind through the empty buildings, a reek of offal borne on a plague of thousands of glutted flies.

The Chinese beggars sitting by the gates shielded their faces. But Jim inhaled the heady stench, shutting out his thoughts of the hospital and the dead Japanese airmen in the canal beyond the wire. The time had come to forget the dead. In its way the camp was coming alive again.

The days of powdered milk and chocolate bars had made him stronger, but not yet equal to the long walk back to Shanghai. Other people would be returning to the camp, and perhaps his mother and father would join him there. Even with the reduced American air drops, there would be a constant supply of food. Jim looked down at the silent kitchens behind the guardhouse and the rusting collection of metal carts. Already he was thinking of a sweet potato. . . .

His shoes rang through the empty corridors and down the stone steps. As he raced from the foyer, he heard the throbbing engine of the Opel. Tulloch and the Seaforth Highlander were loading parachute canopies and cartons of canned food over the tailgate.

"Jim! Hold it!" Tulloch beckoned to him. "Where do you think you're going?"

"G Block, Mr. Tulloch . . ." Gasping for breath, Jim leaned against the Opel's shaking fender. In the doorway of the guardhouse, Lieutenant Price was feeding cartridges into the ammunition clip of his rifle, the ritual of a man counting his secret gold. "I want to reserve a room for my parents—they might be coming to Lunghua. I'll reserve a room for you, Mr. Tulloch."

"Jim . . . Jim . . ." Tulloch placed his hand on Jim's head, trying to steady the overexcited boy. "It's time you found your father, lad. The war's over, Jim."

"But the next war, Mr. Tulloch. You said it's going to begin soon."

The Packard mechanic helped Jim onto the floor of the truck. "Jim, you need to get the last war over before you start the next. We'll give you a lift—you're going back to Shanghai!"

38

THE ROAD
TO SHANGHAI

THE TRUCK CAREENED from one side of the Shanghai road to the other, throwing Jim onto the agitated bundle of parachute silk. He clung to the cartons of K-rations stacked around him, and listened to Tulloch and Lieutenant Price shouting to each other above the bellowslike roar of the engine.

Through the fading camouflage on the rear window, Jim could see the policeman's bandaged hands, deliberately raised from the wheel as he allowed the speeding truck to wobble and drift from the center of the road. The tires reached the verge, ripping up a storm of dust and leaves. Tulloch sat in the passenger seat beside the jar of rice wine, holding the rifle through the open window. He pounded on the dented hood as the apartment blocks of the French Concession appeared between the bomb-torn trees.

For all the dangers of Lieutenant Price's driving, Jim was glad that the two men were in such high spirits. For the first mile the lieutenant had been unable to find second gear, and they had labored along the Shanghai road at a noisy walking pace that threatened to boil the water from the radiator. Then an air drop at Hungjao brought back Price's driving skills. They hurtled along the farm tracks and canal embankments, following the parachutes toward the landing ground, cheered by the prospect of even more American merchandise to be sold in the black markets of Shanghai.

Others, however, had reached the treasure before them. For half an hour they trundled around the deserted paddy fields, unable to find a single parachute canister. Price waved his rifle, threatening an entire world of silent canals.

Fortunately, Price's anger soon abated. After returning to the Shanghai road, the lieutenant steered the truck toward the body of a dead Japanese dispatch rider lying beside a motorcycle. The dead man's head burst in a spray of bloodied maggots and brain tissue that drenched the roadside trees. This feat of steering put Price in an excellent mood, which Jim hoped would last long enough for him to reach Shanghai and jump from the truck at the first traffic lights.

Jim looked back at the distant rooftops of the camp. It was strange to be leaving Lunghua, but he realized that once again he had been imprisoned by the camp as he had been during the war. At a single word from Tulloch, the apparently secure world he had begun to rebuild for himself out of one small room and a few tins of Spam had collapsed at his feet.

They passed Lunghua Pagoda at the northern edge of the airfield, the barrels of its antiaircraft guns still pointing to the sky. Jim searched the ruined hangars for any sight of the young kamikaze pilot, sorry that he had never been able to repay him for the mango. A mile to the east was the Olympic stadium at Nantao. The Chinese characters on the shell-pocked facade, celebrating the generosity of Generalissimo Chiang, rose ever more vividly above the parking lot, as if China's feudal past had returned to claim its time.

The truck swerved, skidding across the camber. On a whim, Lieutenant Price had turned onto a mud track that ran toward the stadium. Jim heard Tulloch protest, but then the wine jar was passed across the steering wheel. They sped between the first of the earth bunkers and rifle pits that guarded the former Japanese headquarters. Lines of crumbling tank ditches crossed the fields, their slopes strewn with webbing and ammunition boxes.

Jim lay back on the bale of parachute silk. He had known all along that the sight of the Olympic stadium would prove too large a temptation. Since his arrival at Lunghua camp, the group of Britons had never ceased to question him about the looted furniture in the stands. Jim had been forced to embroider his memories, in order to ensure his supplies of canned goods and magazines from the commandant's office. By now his make-believe had seized Price's imagination, and it was too late to turn back.

A hundred yards from the parking lot, they left the road and stopped in a culvert between two tank-trap embankments. Price and Tulloch, both drunk on the rice wine, stepped from the driving cabin. They lit cigarettes, staring slyly at the stadium.

Price tapped the side of the truck with his rifle. In a mocking voice, he called out: "Shanghai, Jim . . ."

"Just a detour, Jim," Tulloch assured him boozily. "We'll pick out a case of scotch, and a few fur coats for the girls in the Nanking Road."

"I didn't see any fur coats, Mr. Tulloch, or any scotch. Lots of chairs and dining tables."

Lieutenant Price pushed Tulloch aside. "Dining tables? Do you think we came here to have lunch?" He stared at the facade of the stadium, as if its shabby chalk challenged his own pallid skin.

Jim avoided the rifle barrel aimed at his head. "There were cupboards and wardrobes."

"Wardrobes?" Tulloch swayed between them. "That could be it, Lieutenant."

"Right . . ." Price calmed himself. He touched the cigarette burns on his chest, tapping out a secret code of pain and memory. "I told you the boy had his eyes open."

The two men crossed the road and entered the parking lot. Price leaned against a trackless tank and spat the prison phlegm from his lungs through an open hatch. Jim hung back among the lines of trucks, thinking of Mr. Maxted. Was he still lying on the bloodstained grass? Having eaten so much, Jim felt guilty and remembered that he might have sold his shoes. For all the looted cocktail bars it contained, the Olympic stadium seemed somber and threatening, a place of omens. Here he had seen the afterglow of the atomic flash at Nagasaki. Its white glare still lay over the road of their death march from Lunghua, the same pale light that he could see in the chalky facade of the stadium and in Lieutenant Price's lime-pit skin.

Fanning away the flies with a copy of *Life*, Jim sat on the running board of a truck. He studied a photograph of American marines raising the flag on the summit of Mount Suribachi after their battle for Iwo Jima. The Americans in these magazines had fought an heroic war, closer to the comic books that Jim had read as a child. Even the dead were glamorized, the living's idea of the dead. . . .

Two Mustang fighters flew overhead, leading a Superfortress that lumbered in from the west, its bomb doors open, ready to scatter its Spam and *Reader's Digest*s across the empty fields. The engines drummed at the ground below Jim's feet, shaking the lines of derelict vehicles.

Jim lowered the magazine and noticed that armed men were running from the entrance tunnel of the stadium, their voices drowned in the noise of the aircraft. The Superfortress ambled through the sky, but the men scattered in panic from the tunnel, as if expecting the stadium to be bombed. A bearded European in the leather jacket of an American pilot raced across the parking lot, followed by two more men carrying shotguns. A bare-chested Chinese with a pistol belt around his black trousers scuttled along at a crouch, leading a group of coolies with bamboo staves.

Pursuing them through the tunnel was a platoon of Nationalist soldiers, rifles raised to the strong sunlight. They stopped to fire at the fleeing men, letting off a ragged volley of shots. Jim opened the door of the truck and climbed into the driving cabin. Fifty feet from the entrance tunnel, Tulloch lay in the white dust that had fallen from the facade of the stadium. Lieutenant Price ran past him toward the line of trucks, his face like a lantern scanning the ground. Shaking off his bandages, he leaped the perimeter wall of the parking lot and plunged into the flooded paddy field beyond the road.

The Chinese officer fired a last pistol shot at Price's splashing figure, then knelt in the stadium entrance. Rifles raised, his men approached the rusting vehicles. They made a token show of flushing out any wounded members of the raiding party, turned and retreated to the safety of the stadium. Tulloch lay dead in the sun, his blood leaking into the chalky dust.

Blue and scarlet parachutes were falling over Hungjao. Jim slid across the seat, opened the door on the far side of the cabin and slipped onto the ground. Screened by the ammunition wagons and field guns, he ran toward the perimeter wall.

Lieutenant Price had abandoned the Opel and its cargo of silks and K-rations. When Jim reached the culvert, he found the truck standing alone among the antitank embankments. On the ground beside the passenger door a faint smoke still rose from the butt of Tulloch's last Lucky Strike.

Jim stared through the window at the instrument panel. Could he drive the vehicle to Shanghai? It was too dangerous to give himself up to the Nationalist soldiers at the stadium—they would shoot him on sight, taking for granted that Jim was a member of the raiding party.

Thinking of Tulloch, who had died before seeing the white Cadillacs of Nantao, Jim decided to walk to Shanghai. He was climbing over the tailgate of the Opel, about to select several cans of food and copies of the *Reader's Digest,* when he heard footsteps beside the truck. Before he could turn, someone seized him by the shoulders. Hard fists punched the back of his head and hurled him to the floor.

Sitting among the cartons of cigarettes, Jim felt the blood run from his nose and mouth, dripping through his hands onto the parachute canopy. He looked up at the bare-chested Chinese with the pistol belt who had raced from the stadium. He stared at Jim with the expressionless gaze he had often seen on the cook's face at Amherst Avenue before he killed a chicken. Behind him, impatient to get his hands on the truck's cargo, was a Chinese coolie with a bamboo stave.

On both sides of the culvert armed men were walking

down the embankment, led by the bearded European in the leather flying jacket. Half the members of this bandit group were Chinese, some of them coolies with staves, others in Nationalist and puppet uniforms, still with their rifles and webbing. The others were Europeans or Americans, wearing an assortment of clothes and ammunition belts, holsters and Shanghai police pouches hung over Chinese tunics. From their starved bodies, Jim assumed that most were former internees.

When the coolie raised the bamboo stave, Jim sucked back the blood and swallowed the hot phlegm. "I'm going to Lunghua Camp . . . I'm a British prisoner." He pointed to the southwest. Through his swollen nose his voice sounded strangely bass, as if his body were aging in the few moments of life left to it. "Lunghua Camp . . ."

Ignoring him, the armed men sat on the embankment and smoked their cigarettes. The European in the flying jacket paced around the truck. A coolie picked up Tulloch's cigarette butt and inhaled the smoke. Everyone watched the sky and the deserted road past the stadium. They had brought with them the slow, empty time of the prison camp. Their faces were drawn and colorless, and they seemed to have emerged from a deep lair below the ground.

"Lunghua . . ." Jim repeated. The coolie with the stave still had his eyes on Jim. At the smallest signal, Jim knew, the coolie would step forward and crush his skull. The bare-chested Chinese who had struck him was examining the truck, peering at the rear tires. Hoping somehow to catch the attention of the Europeans, Jim pointed to the stadium. "Lincoln Zephyrs—in Nantao. Buicks, white Cadillacs . . ."

"What's this talk about Cadillacs?" A small man with silvery hair and an effeminate American voice walked toward the truck, rifle slung over his shoulder. No one listened to him, and he lit a cigarette to cover the lack of response. The flame trembled in his powdered cheeks, exposing a familiar pair of wary eyes, with their sharp but modest focus.

"Basie!" Jim wiped the blood from his nose. "It's me, Basie—Jim! Shanghai Jim!"

The cabin steward stared at Jim. After a moment's thought he shook his head in an almost formal way, as if recognizing the fourteen-year-old but no longer interested in him. He scanned the cartons of K-rations and fingered the silk of the parachute. He stepped aside to give the coolie more room to swing his stave.

"Basie!" Jim picked up the scattered magazines and cleaned the blood from their covers with his fingers. He held them up before the angry gaze of the bare-chested Chinese with the pistol. *"Life* magazine, Basie, *Reader's Digest!* I kept the latest copies for you. . . . Basie, I've learned hundreds of new words—Belsen, von Runstedt, GI Joe. . . ."

39

THE BANDITS

THE CAR SPED along the shore of an oil-filled lagoon, past the rusting hull of a beached torpedo boat. Squeezed between Basie and the bearded Frenchman in the rear seat, Jim watched the spray leap from the wheels of the Buick. The lurid rainbows opened like peacock tails, transforming the distant office blocks of Shanghai into the towers of a paint-box city. The same gaudy light veiled the torpedo boat and cloaked the bodies of the dead Japanese lying in the shallows.

Jim tried to look over his shoulder at the receding skyline of Shanghai, but the bruises on his neck made it difficult for him to turn his head.

"Hey, boy . . ." The Frenchman struck Jim's arm with the carbine held between his knees. "Settle down. You want some more bloody nose?"

"Jim, there's no room to wrestle in here. We'll just sit quiet and learn our words." Basie put an arm around Jim. "Keep an eye on that *Digest* so you stay awake."

"Right, Basie. I'll stay awake."

Staying awake was all-important, as Jim knew. He

propped his feet against the ammunition boxes on the floor of the car, then pinched his bruised lips until his eyes brightened. Next to the Frenchman, against the right-hand passenger door, sat the coolie with the bamboo stave who had been about to kill Jim before Basie intervened. In the front seat, beside the Chinese driver, were two Australians from Siccawei Camp.

The seven of them were packed into the mud-spattered Buick. Its windows were still adorned with the insignia and rice-paper stickers of the puppet Chinese general whose staff car this had been throughout the war. Dried vomit, blood from Jim's nose and from the wounds of injured men stained the seats. Along with the staves and weapons, the car was crammed with ammunition boxes, cartons of American cigarettes, earthenware jars of rice wine and beer bottles into which the men continually urinated as they sped along the country roads to the south-west of Shanghai.

They came to a halt, and the oily water of the lagoon swilled around the Buick's wheels. Ahead of them was the Japanese truck carrying a dozen members of this bandit gang. The top-heavy vehicle swayed up a narrow ramp of gray bricks that led from the beach to the em-bankment road. It was loaded with parachute canisters, Japanese stores seized that morning from the military godowns at Nantao, and a collection of mattress rolls, bicycles and sewing machines looted from the villages in the open country south of Lunghua.

The Buick climbed the ramp of crumbling bricks and followed the truck through the clouds of dust that swirled from its wheels. The road ran inland from the lagoon, soon losing itself in a maze of paddy fields and canals. Jim wondered if this bandit group had any idea where it was going, a poisonous shuttle that flicked to and fro across the quilted land. Yet eight hundred yards away, along a parallel road, a second truck sped through the deserted paddies. The antique Opel captured at the Olympic stadium carried the remaining five members of the gang. They had left the seaplane base at Nantao soon after dawn but somehow had managed to rendezvous within a few minutes of their next objective.

As the roads converged, Jim could see the bare-chested figure of the Chinese gunman with the black trousers and revolver belt. He stood behind the driving cabin, shouting commands to the coolie at the wheel. Jim feared this former officer in the Chinese puppet army, whose iron knuckles he could still feel in the bruised bones at the back of his neck. Only Basie's presence had saved Jim, but the reprieve might be short-lived. Captain Soong paid little attention to Basie, or to the other European members of the bandit gang, and regarded Jim as no more than a dog to be worked to death if necessary. Within an hour of his capture by the bandits, Jim was crawling among the burial mounds that overlooked a village near Hungjao, sent on ahead like a beagle to sniff out the land and draw any surprise fire. Still half stunned, the blood from his nose dripping onto the *Reader's Digest* in his hand, he waited among the rotting coffins until the shooting subsided and the bandits returned from the village with their looted bicycles, bedrolls and sacks of rice. Recognizing that Captain Soong was the real leader of this bandit group, Jim had tried to make himself useful to the Chinese. But Captain Soong did not want Jim to run any errands for him. The war had changed the Chinese people—the villagers, the wandering coolies and lost puppet soldiers looked at Europeans in a way Jim had never seen before the war, as if they no longer existed, even though the British had helped the Americans to defeat the Japanese.

The trucks stopped at a crossroad. Captain Soong jumped from the Opel and strode over to the Buick. Without thinking, Basie held Jim's arm. Basie had been prepared to see him die, and only Jim's lavish descriptions of the booty waiting for the bandits in the stadium at Nantao sustained Basie's interest in Jim.

A tornado of dust seethed around the three vehicles as they reversed and set off along a disused canal. Within half a mile they stopped on a stone bridge above a deserted village. Captain Soong and two of his men dismounted from their truck, joined by the Frenchman in the Buick and the coolie with the stave. The Australians sat in the front of the car, drinking from a wine jar and ignoring the shabby dwellings. Usually Captain Soong would have called Jim and sent him to ferret through the buildings, but the village was clearly abandoned, looted many times over by the bandit groups in the area.

"Are we going back to Shanghai, Basie?" Jim asked.

"Soon, Jim. First we have to pick up some special equipment."

"Equipment you stored in the villages? Equipment for the war effort?"

"That's it, Jim. Equipment the OSS left here for us while I was working undercover with the Kuomintang. You wouldn't want the Communists to get it, would you, Jim?"

Both of them went along with this pretense. Jim stared at the empty village, its single mud street divided by an open sewer. "There must be a lot of Communists here. Is the war over, Basie?"

"It's over, Jim. Let's say it's effectively over."

"Basie . . ." A familiar thought occurred to Jim. "Has the next war effectively begun?"

"That's a way of putting it, Jim. I'm glad I helped you with your words."

"There are still a lot of words I haven't learned, Basie. I'd like to go back to Shanghai. If I'm lucky, I might see my mother and father today."

"Shanghai? That's one dangerous city, Jim. You need more than luck in Shanghai. We'll wait till we see the U.S. Navy tie up alongside the Bund."

"Will Uncle Sam soon be here, Basie? Every gob and GI Joe?"

"He'll be here. Every GI Joe in the Pacific area . . ." Basie sounded unenthusiastic at the prospect of being reunited with his fellow countrymen. Jim had questioned him about his escape from Lunghua, but Basie was sly and evasive. As always, whatever had happened after the escape had long since ceased to interest him. He remained the same small, finicky man worrying about his hands, ignoring everything but the shortest-term advantage. His one strength was that he never allowed himself to dream, because he had never been able to take anything for granted, whereas Dr. Ransome had taken everything for granted. However, Dr. Ransome had probably died on the death march from Lunghua, while Basie had survived. Yet now, for the first time, the prospect of the treasure store in the Olympic stadium had sprung the safety catch of Basie's caution. Jim assiduously fed the cabin steward's vision of enough wealth to return him in luxury to the United States. He assumed that Basie had heard on the camp radio of the imminent march to the killing grounds and had bribed a nightwatchman to conceal him in one of the Nantao godowns.

Sitting beside Basie as he polished his nails, Jim realized that the entire experience of the war had barely touched him. All the deaths and starvation were part of a confused roadside drama seen through the passenger window of the Buick, a cruel spectacle like the public stranglings in Shanghai which the British and American sailors watched during their shore leaves. He had learned nothing from the war because he expected nothing, like the Chinese peasants whom he now looted and shot. As Dr. Ransome had said, people who expected nothing were dangerous. Somehow, five hundred million Chinese had to be taught to expect everything.

Jim nursed his bruised nose as the armed men squatted on the bridge with their jars of rice wine. Despite the years of malnutrition in the camps, few of the former prisoners bothered to eat the canned food heaped on the back of the trucks. They drank alone in the hot sun, rarely speaking to each other. Jim knew almost none of their names. At dusk, when they returned to the seaplane base at Nantao, most of them dispersed with their share of the day's booty to their hideouts in the tenements of the Old City, reassembling the next morning like factory workers. Jim slept in the Buick parked on the concrete slipway, surrounded by the hulks of the burned seaplanes, while Basie and the bearded Frenchman drank through the night in the pilots' mess.

The Frenchman wandered back from the village and leaned against Basie's window. "Nothing—not even one piece of shit."

"They could have left us that," Basie said in disgust. "Why don't the Chinese come back to their villages?"

"Do they know the war's over?" Jim asked. "You ought to tell them, Basie."

"Maybe . . . We can't wait forever, Jim. There are big guns moving up to Shanghai, about six different Kuomintang armies."

"So it might be difficult to collect your equipment?"

"That's it. We'll go now to this Communist village. Then I'll take you back to your dad. You can tell him how I looked after you through the war, taught you all your words."

"You did look after me, Basie."

"Right . . ." Basie gazed thoughtfully at Jim. "You stay with us. It would be too bad if you got yourself kidnapped."

"Are there a lot of kidnappers here, Basie?"

"Kidnappers *and* Communists. People who don't want to know the war is over. Remember that, Jim."

"Right . . ." Trying to distract the cabin steward with some more cheerful topic, Jim asked: "Basie, did you see the atom bomb go off? I saw the flash over Nagasaki from Nantao Stadium."

"Say, kid . . ." Basie peered at Jim, puzzled by the calm voice of this bloody-nosed boy. He took a gun rag from the rear windowsill and wiped Jim's nose. "You saw the atom bomb?"

"For a whole minute, Basie. A white light covered Shanghai, stronger than the sun. I suppose God wanted to see everything."

"I guess He did. That white light, Jim. Maybe I can get your picture in *Life* magazine."

"Say, could you, Basie?"

The thought of appearing in *Life* exhilarated Jim. He wiped the blood from his mouth and tried to straighten his ragged shirt, in case a photographer were to appear suddenly on the scene. At a signal from Captain Soong, the bandits returned to their vehicles. As they left the village and set out toward the river, Jim imagined his photograph among the pictures of Tiger tanks and U.S. Marines. He had now spent four days with Basie's bandit group, and it occurred to him that his parents might think that he had died in the death march from Lunghua. Perhaps they would be sitting by the swimming pool at Amherst Avenue, leafing through the latest issue of *Life*, when they would recognize their son's face among the admirals and generals. . . .

They were passing the eastern perimeter of Lunghua Airfield. Jim leaned across Basie and hung from the window. He scanned the creeks and paddy fields for the bodies of Japanese air crews. The Kuomintang units that had seized part of the airfield were still killing the Japanese in batches.

"You like those airplanes, Jim?"

"I'm going to be a pilot, Basie, one day. I'll take my mother and father down to Java. I've thought a lot about that."

"A good dream to have . . ." Basie pushed Jim aside and pointed to the derelict aircraft among the trees. "There's a Jap pilot over there—no one's got him yet."

Basie cocked the bolt on his rifle. Jim craned through the window, searching the line of trees. Beside the tailplane of a Zero fighter he saw the pallid face of the young pilot, lost among the upended wings and fuselages.

"He's a hashi-crashi," Jim said quickly. "A screwysider. Basie, do you want me to tell you about the stadium? There might be fur coats, I think Mr. Tulloch saw them before he was shot, and hundreds of crates of scotch whiskey . . ."

Fortunately, Basie was winding up the window. A pungent grit filled the Buick. It rose from the chalky surface of the road, joining the haze of dust that climbed from the bleached fields, the tank ditches and burial mounds, the same light that Jim had seen from the Olympic stadium, heralding the end of one war and the beginning of the next.

Shortly before dusk they reached the Communist town on the river two miles to the south of Lunghua. The shabby, single-story houses huddled against the walls of a ceramics factory, like the medieval dwellings Jim had seen in his childhood encyclopedias, clustering around a Gothic cathedral. The domed kilns and brick chimneys drew the last of the day's sunlight toward them, as if advertising the warmth and benefit that Communist rule had brought to this collection of hovels.

"Right, Jim, never mind the word power. You're going in."

Before Jim could place his *Reader's Digest* on the windowsill, Captain Soong had flung open the door. The bare-chested officer bundled Jim from the Buick. Handling the bloody-nosed boy like a drover with a truffling pig, he propelled Jim across the road with a series of whoops and grunts, prodding him sharply with his automatic pistol. The two trucks and the Buick had stopped beside the embankment carrying the Shanghai-Hangchow railway line. Three hundred yards ahead, a spur of the line ran in a wide arc toward the ceramics works, concealing them from the town. The armed men stepped down onto the drained paddy that followed the embankment. Some opened their ammunition pouches and cleaned the breeches of their rifles. Others smoked cigarettes and drank wine from the earthenware jars they placed on the hood of the Buick. Each man on his own, they stood silently in the fading light.

As the whoops and whistles of Captain Soong faded behind him, Jim trotted across the hard surface of the paddy. He pinched his nose, hoping to stop the bleeding, then let the blood smear his cheeks in the wind. With luck, any Communist sentry stationed on the embankment would think that Jim was already wounded and turn his fire on the gunmen behind him.

Jim reached the foot of the embankment and crouched among the clumps of wild rice. He wiped the blood from their stems and licked his fingers. Already he had served his purpose. Fifty yards away, Captain Soong had crossed the paddy and was scuttling up the soft soil of the embankment. Armed with their staves, his coolies followed, accompanied by Basie and the Frenchman. Two groups of gunmen were moving across the next paddy field. The Australians and a Kuomintang deserter sat on the running board of the Buick, drinking their wine.

Jim climbed the talclike slope. Rain had washed away parts of the embankment, and he crawled below the rusting rails and their rotting sleepers. Several sections of the line had recently been replaced, presumably by the Communist troops who had made the town their base. The jetty of the ceramics factory, the railway line and the reserve of bricks in the fabric of the old kilns and chimneys, together with the proximity to Lunghua Airfield, had drawn the Communist garrison to this modest backwater. According to Basie, however, they had left two days earlier, continuing their advance on Shanghai, and the town's few hundred inhabitants were undefended. Apart from their possessions, there might be stores of Communist arms, and collaborators to be traded for the goodwill of the Kuomintang generals approaching Shanghai.

Concealed by the railway sleepers, Jim crouched on the edge of the embankment. Below him lay a plain of unworked paddies, separated by a navigation canal from the patchwork of vegetable plots that encircled the town.

The narrow streets were empty, but a weak smoke rose from several chimneys.

Across the river, a naval gun fired a single booming round. Two Nationalist Chinese gunboats were moored in midstream. The shell landed in the storeyard of the ceramics works, throwing up a cloud of red dust. The sound of small-arms fire came from the beaches of the river to the south, where a company of Kuomintang soldiers disembarked from a wooden lighter.

Its diesels thudding, an armored junk motored up the canal below the railway embankment. Chinese officers in smart American uniforms and steel helmets stood on the bridge, scanning the town and its vegetable plots through binoculars. The nearer of the two gunboats fired a second shell, which exploded among the gray-tiled rooftops, sending up a shower of debris. Immediately there was a flurry of movement. Like ants escaping from a broken flowerpot, hundreds of Chinese ran from the narrow alleys into the surrounding fields. Over their heads they carried bedrolls and bundles of clothing. They raced down the pathways between the vegetable plots. An old woman in black trousers and jacket waded waist-deep in a creek beside the road, shouting to her relatives who clambered down the bank.

The motorized junk sailed along the canal, its engines drumming like fists against the wooden hull. Jim could see clearly the fresh pleats in the uniforms of the senior Chinese officers and their elegant American combat boots. Even the platoons of private soldiers on the deck below the bridge were lavishly equipped with weapons and radios. Parked across the midships of the junk was a black Chrysler limousine, the pennant of a Kuomintang general flying from its chromium mast.

351

The metal barbette of an automatic cannon was mounted in the bows of the junk. Without warning, the gunners opened fire at the town. The tracers soared over the heads of the fleeing villagers and burst against the roofs of the houses. At a signal from the bridge, the gunners swung the barrel, setting their sights on a small hamlet a few hundred yards to the west of the town. Already the first shells from the gunboats were landing on the dusty road beside the single-story hovels. The company of Nationalist soldiers who had disembarked from the wooden lighter were now running across the paddies, hunting down the fleeing townspeople.

Then the first shell of the next salvo tripped off an immense explosion. The group of mud dwellings vanished, sucked into the air by the boiling cloud of its own debris. The cache of detonating ammunition continued to erupt, throwing towers of smoke into the sky. On the road approaching the hamlet, dozens of villagers lay among their bundles and bedrolls, as if the inhabitants of this town had decided to spend the night sleeping in the fields.

Jim cupped his hands over his nose and mouth, trying to stop himself from shouting. He watched the plain of fire below him, the smoke-covered fields lit by the flashes of the naval guns and by the burning houses beside the ceramics factory. The kilns and chimneys glowed in the sunset as if the ancient ovens had been lit again, to be fueled by the bodies of the villagers lying in their vegetable gardens. Jim listened to the engines of the motorized junk as it moved down the canal, an ugly heart bearing the beat of its death across China, while immaculate generals masked their eyes with binoculars, calculating their astronomy of guns.

"Basie . . ." The bandits were withdrawing from the

railway line. Captain Soong and his coolies had climbed down the embankment and were returning to the trucks. "Basie, can we go back to Lunghua?"

"Back to the camp?" The cabin steward squinted through the dust falling from the air. He had been stunned by the concussion wave of the exploding ammunition store and stared at the landscape below him as if waking from a dream. "You want to go back to the camp, Jim?"

"We ought to get ready, Basie. When are the Americans coming?"

For the first time Basie seemed lost for an answer. He lay back among the wooden sleepers, and then pointed to the north and gave a whistle of triumph. Ten miles away, across the somber surface of the river, the sunlit masts and superstructure of an American cruiser had taken their place beside the office blocks and hotels of the Shanghai Bund.

40

THE FALLEN
AIRMEN

ALL MORNING THE sound of artillery fire had crossed the river from Pootung. A column of incendiary smoke, broader than the group of burning warehouses, leaned over the water and darkened the Nantao shore. From the front seat of the Buick parked on the mud flat, Jim watched the flashes of gunfire in the dusty windshield. The American artillery pieces brought up by the Nationalists emitted a harsh and wet noise, as if their barrels were filled with water. Hidden from the sun, a gloomy air lay over the slack tide that swilled against the beach. The glowing barrel of the Kuomintang howitzer behind the Pootung mole flickered against Jim's knuckles as he held the steering wheel of the Buick, and lit up the conning tower of the beached submarine a hundred yards away.

Jim noticed a reconnaissance aircraft emerge from the smoke cloud, shaking off the wisps of black vapor that streamed from its wings. A flight of three American bombers approached from the southwest. The gunfire ceased, and a torpedo boat fortified with sandbags set out across the river, ready to collect any stray canisters.

A dozen parachutes fell from the B-29s and streaked swiftly to the ground. The canisters were loaded, not with Spam, Klim and the *Reader's Digest*, but with ammunition and explosives for the Kuomintang troops. The battalion, with its artillery support, was rooting out the last of the Communist units that still hung on among the ruins of the Pootung warehouses. On the mole, the corpses of dead Communist soldiers were stacked like firewood.

In the silence after the bombers had passed, Jim could hear the aching rumble of artillery barrages from Hungjao and the open country to the west of Shanghai. At least three Nationalist armies were closing around Shanghai, jockeying among themselves for control of the airfields, dockyards and railway lines, and above all for the stocks of weapons and munitions left behind by the Japanese. Collaborating with the Nationalists, though sometimes fighting against them, were the remnants of the puppet armies, groups of renegade Kuomintang driven back to the coast, and various militia forces recruited by the local warlords who had returned to Shanghai.

Swept in front of these rival armies, like dust before a set of colliding brooms, were tens of thousands of Chinese peasants. Columns of refugees wandered the countryside, trying to shelter in the fields and looted villages, turned away from the gates of Shanghai by advance units of Nationalist armies.

It was these refugees, the bands of starving coolies armed with knives and hoes, whom Jim most feared. Avoiding them at all costs, Basie and his bandit group stayed close to any battle that was taking place. On the eastern fringes of Nantao, between the dockyards and the seaplane base, was a no-man's-land of wharves, warehouses and deserted barracks which the Kuomintang militias and the peasant refugees found too near to the fighting across the river at Pootung. Here Basie and the remaining six members of the gang camped out in the bunkers and concrete forts, with little left to them but the prewar Buick and the vague hope of selling themselves to a Nationalist general.

Now even the car was proving too obvious a target for the Kuomintang gunners.

"You sit behind the wheel, Jim," Basie had told him as the bandits left the Buick on the mud flat. "Pretend you're driving this fine car."

"Say, can I, Basie?" Jim held the steering wheel as the men stood on the black beach beside the car and prepared their weapons. Their faces flinched at the sound of the explosions that crossed the water. "Are you going to the stadium, Basie?"

"Right, Jim. Remember those years in Lunghua—we have an investment to protect. The Nats want to take over Shanghai and keep out any foreign business interests."

"Is that us, Basie?"

"That's you, Jim. You're part of the foreign business community. When we get back you'll have a fur coat and a case of scotch whiskey for your dad."

Basie stared at the ruined warehouses and the corpses stacked on the mole, as if seeing them loaded with all the treasure of the East about to be freighted back to Frisco. Jim felt sorry for Basie and was tempted to warn him that the stadium was probably empty, stripped by the Kuomintang troops of the few valuables that had survived the sun and rain. But Basie had taken the hook and was now running eagerly toward the gaff. With luck, if he survived the attack on the stadium, he would throw away his rifle and walk back to Shanghai. Within a few days he would be a wine waiter at the Cathay Hotel, serving with a flourish all the American officers who stepped ashore from the cruiser moored by the Bund. . . .

When Basie and the men had gone, vanishing among the ruined warehouses on the quay, Jim studied the magazines on the seat beside him. He was sure now that the Second World War had ended, but had World War III begun? Looking at the photographs of the D-day landings, the crossing of the Rhine and the capture of Berlin, he felt that they were part of a smaller war, a rehearsal for the real conflict that had begun here in the Far East with the dropping of the atom bombs. Jim remembered the light that lay over the land, the shadow of another sun. Here, at the mouths of the great rivers of Asia, would be fought the last war to decide the planet's future.

Jim wiped his blood from the steering wheel as the shelling began again from the Pootung shore. His nose had been bleeding on and off for two weeks. He swallowed the blood and watched the open road that ran from the wharves toward the distant stadium. A hundred yards from the Buick, two Chinese militiamen had climbed onto the bows of the beached submarine. Rifles slung over their shoulders, they ignored the battle across the river and walked along the deck to the conning tower.

Jim unlatched the driver's door. It was time to leave, before the militiamen noticed the Buick. From the heap of cans, cigarette cartons and ammunition clips on the floor of the car he selected a chocolate bar, a tin of Spam and a copy of *Life*. When the two Chinese were behind the conning tower, he stepped onto the mud flat. Crouching below the embankment wall, he ran toward the stone ramp of a Shanghai River police jetty. Little more than two miles to the north were the tenements and godowns of the Old City, and beyond them the office blocks of downtown Shanghai, but Jim ignored them and set out again for Lunghua Airfield.

Smoke rose from the Olympic stadium, a thin white plume fed by a single flame, as if Basie and his gang had lit a bonfire of furniture in the stands. The artillery barrages from Pootung and Hungjao had fallen silent, and Jim could hear the brief bursts of rifle fire from the stadium.

Searching for shelter, Jim left the exposed country road. He walked through the wild sugarcane that covered the waste ground beside the northern perimeter of Lunghua Airfield. A screen of trees and rusting fuel tanks separated him from the open plain of the landing field, the ruined hangars and pagoda. Cartridge cases lay on the narrow path at his feet, chips laid in a brassy trail. Jim followed the straggling wire, avoiding the swarms of flies that clustered over the miniature bowers in the banks of nettles.

On either side of the pathway the bodies of dead Japanese lay where they had been shot or bayonetted. Jim stopped by a shallow irrigation ditch, in which an air force private lay with his hands tied behind him. Hundreds of flies devoured his face, enclosing it in a noisy mask. Unwrapping his chocolate bar and fanning the flies from his face with the magazine, Jim walked through the sugarcane. Dozens of dead Japanese lay in the nettles as if they had fallen from the sky, the members of a youthful armada shot down as they tried to fly to their home airfields in Japan.

Jim stepped over a collapsed section of the perimeter fence and moved through the derelict aircraft that lay among the trees. Their fuselages had wept rivers of rust in the summer rain. The flies raged at the morning light, a vast anger about nothing. Leaving them, Jim set out across the grass expanse of the airfield. Inside one of the ruined hangars a group of Japanese waited in the shade, listening to the rifle fire from the stadium, but they ignored Jim as he walked across the field.

Jim stared at the concrete runway below his feet. To his surprise, he found that the surface was badly cracked and stained with patches of oil, scored by the marks of tires and wheel struts. But now that World War III had begun, a new runway would soon be laid. Jim reached the end of the concrete strip and strode through the grass toward the southern perimeter of the airfield. The ground rose to the overgrown hillocks left by the original earthworks, then shelved into the valley where the Japanese trucks had once delivered their loads of building rubble and roof tiles.

Despite the deep nettles and the hot September sunlight, the valley seemed filled with the same ashy dust. The banks of the canal were as pale as the conduit of a mortuary stream in which the dead were washed. The burst casing of an unexploded bomb lay in the shallow water, like a large turtle that had fallen asleep trying to bury its head in the mud.

Aware that the vibration of a low-flying Mustang might trip its detonator, Jim pressed on into the valley, parting the nettles with his magazine. He tossed the tin of Spam into the air, caught it with one hand, but on the second throw lost it among the reeds. Hunting about in the thick grass, he at last found it near the water's edge, and decided to eat the chopped ham before it slipped through his hands for good.

Sitting on the bank of the canal, he washed the dirt from the lid. A drop of blood fell from his nose into the water and was instantly attacked by myriads of small fish no longer than a match head. As a second drop struck the surface, there was a violent struggle that seemed to involve entire nations of minute fish. They swerved through the water, unaware of the sunlit surface, ferociously attacking each other. Clearing his mouth, Jim leaned over and released a ball of pus from his infected gums. It fell like a depth charge among the fish, driving them into a frenzy of panic. Within a second the water was empty except for the dissolving pus.

Losing interest in the fish, Jim stretched out among the reeds and studied the advertisements in his magazine. He listened to the deeper sound of the artillery fire. The guns of Siccawei and Hungjao were louder, as the rival Nationalist armies closed their grip on Shanghai. He would eat his Spam and then make a last effort to return to Shanghai. He was certain that Basie and the bandit gang never intended to return to the Buick and had left Jim on the mud flat to draw away any Chinese soldiers who might have followed them to the river.

In the grass nearby, a head nodded twice, approving this strategy. Jim lay rigidly, the last of the chocolate trapped in his throat, startled by this intimate apparition. Someone was lying in the reeds a few feet from him, his knees almost touching the water's edge. As if trying to reassure Jim, the head nodded again. Jim reached out one hand and parted the grass, carefully examining the figure's face. The round cheeks and soft nose, pinched by the privations of a wartime childhood, were those of a teen-age Asiatic, some villager's son come here to fish. The boy lay on his back, surrounded by a wall of grass and reeds, as if sharing a four-poster bed with Jim and quietly listening to his thoughts.

Jim sat up, the rolled magazine raised above his head. Through the swarming flies he waited for the sound of footsteps in the long grass. But the valley was empty, its bright air devoured by the flies. The figure moved slightly, crushing the grass. Too idle to stop himself, the lazy youth was sliding down the bank into the water.

With all the caution learned during the long years of the war, Jim climbed to his knees, then stood up and stepped through the reeds. Calming himself, he looked down at this dozing figure.

In front of him, wearing a bloodstained flying overall with the insignia of a special attack group, was the body of the young Japanese pilot.

41

RESCUE MISSION

JIM DESPAIRED. FLATTENING the grass with his hands, he made a small place for himself beside the Japanese. The pilot lay in his overall, one arm under his back. He had been thrown down the slope toward the canal, and his legs were caught beneath him. His right knee touched the water, which had begun to soak the thigh of his overall. Above his head Jim could see the chute of bruised grass down which he had fallen, the stems straightening themselves in the sun.

Jim stared at the pilot, for once glad of the swarm of flies interceding between himself and this corpse. The face of the Japanese was more childlike than Jim remembered, as if in his death he had returned to his true age, to his early adolescence in a provincial Japanese village. His lips were parted around his uneven teeth, as if expecting a morsel of pork to be placed between them by his mother's chopsticks.

Numbed by the sight of this dead pilot, Jim watched the youth's knees slide into the water. He squatted on the sloping earth, turning the pages of *Life* and trying to concentrate on the photographs of Churchill and Eisenhower. For so long he had invested all his hopes in this young pilot, in that futile dream that they would fly away together, leaving Lunghua, Shanghai and the war forever behind them. He had needed the pilot to help him survive the war, this imaginary twin he had invented, a replica of himself whom he watched through the barbed wire. If the Japanese was dead, part of himself had died. He had failed to grasp the truth that millions of Chinese had known from birth, that they were all as good as dead anyway, and that it was self-deluding to believe otherwise.

Jim listened to the artillery barrages at Hungjao and Siccawei, and to the circling drone of a Nationalist spotter plane. The sound of small-arms fire crossed the airfield, as Basie and the bandits tried to break into the stadium. The dead were playing their dangerous games.

Deciding to ignore them, Jim continued to read his magazine, but the flies had swarmed from the corpses further along the creek and soon discovered the body of the young pilot. Jim stood up and seized the Japanese by the shoulders. Holding him under the armpits, he pulled his legs from the water, then dragged him onto a narrow ledge of level ground.

Despite his plump face, the pilot weighed almost nothing. His starved body was as light as the children in Lunghua with whom Jim had wrestled when he was young. The waist and trousers of his flying overall were thick with blood. He had been bayonetted in the small of his back, and again through the thighs and buttocks, then thrown down the bank with the other air crew.

Squatting beside the body, Jim snapped the key from the Spam tin and began to wind off the lid. Once he had eaten, he would use the can to dig a grave for the Japanese. When he had buried the pilot he would walk to Shanghai, regardless of the games the dead were playing. If he saw his parents, he would tell them that World War III had begun and that they should return to their camp at Soochow.

That hot jelly of chopped ham bulged within its mucilage of melted fat. Jim washed his hand in the canal and used the lid to cut a modest slice. He raised the meat to his mouth but spat the fragment into the water. The greasy flesh was still alive, as if carved from the body of the breathing animal. Its lungs and liver quivered in the can, still driven by a heart. Jim cut a second slice and placed it in his mouth. He could feel its pulse between his lips and the fear of the creature in the moments before its slaughter.

He picked the slice from his lips and stared at the oily meat. Living flesh was not meant to feed the dead. This was food that would devour those who tried to eat it. Jim spat the last shred into the grass beside the Japanese. Leaning across the corpse, he patted the blanched lips with his forefinger, ready to slip the morsel of ham into its mouth.

The chipped teeth closed around his finger, cutting the cuticle. Jim dropped the can of meat, which rolled through the grass into the canal. He wrenched his hand away, aware that the corpse of this Japanese was about to sit up and consume him. Without thinking, Jim punched the pilot's face, then stood back and shouted at him through the swarm of flies.

The pilot's mouth opened in a noiseless grimace. His eyes were fixed in an unfocused way on the hot sky, but a lid quivered as a fly drank from his pupil. One of the bayonet wounds in his back had penetrated the front of his abdomen, and fresh blood leaked from the crotch of his overall. His narrow shoulders stirred against the crushed grass, trying to animate his useless arms. Jim gazed at the young pilot, doing his best to grasp the miracle that had taken place. By touching the Japanese he had brought him to life; by prizing his teeth apart he had made a small space in his death and allowed his soul to return.

Jim spread his feet on the damp slope and wiped his hands on his ragged trousers. The flies swarmed around him, stinging his lips, but Jim ignored them. He remembered how he had questioned Mrs. Philips and Mrs. Gilmour about the raising of Lazarus, and how they had insisted that far from being a marvel this was the most ordinary of events. Every day Dr. Ransome had brought people back from the dead by massaging their hearts.

Jim looked at his hands, refusing to be overawed by them. He raised his palms to the light, letting the sun warm his skin. For the first time since the start of the war, he felt a surge of hope. If he could raise this dead Japanese pilot he could raise himself, and the millions of Chinese who had died during the war and who were still dying in the fighting for Shanghai, for a booty as illusory as the treasure in the Olympic stadium. He would raise Basie when he had been killed by the Kuomintang guards defending the stadium, but not the other members of the bandit gang, and never Lieutenant Price or Captain Soong. He would raise his mother and father, Dr. Ransome and Mrs. Vincent, and the British prisoners in Lunghua hospital. He would raise the Japanese air crew lying in the ditches around the airfield, and enough ground staff to rebuild a squadron of aircraft. . . .

The Japanese pilot made a small gasp. His eyes tilted, as if trying to revolve like those of the patients whom Dr. Ransome revived. He was barely clinging to life, but

Jim knew that he would have to leave him beside the canal. His hands and shoulders were trembling, electrified by the discharge that had passed through them, the same energy that powered the sun and the Nagasaki bomb whose explosion he had witnessed. Already Jim could see Mrs. Philips and Mrs. Gilmour rising politely from the dead, listening in their concerned but puzzled way as Jim explained how he had saved them. He could imagine Dr. Ransome shrugging the earth from his shoulders, and Mrs. Vincent looking back disapprovingly at the grave. . . .

Jim sucked the blood and pus from his teeth and quickly swallowed them. He slipped on the damp grass and slid into the shallow water of the canal. Steadying himself, he washed his face. He wanted to look his best when Mrs. Vincent opened her eyes and saw him again. He wiped his wet hands on the cheeks of the young pilot. He would have to leave him, but like Dr. Ransome he had only a few seconds to spare for each of the impatient dead.

As he ran through the valley toward the camp, Jim noticed that the artillery guns at Pootung and Hungjao had fallen silent. Across the airfield a column of trucks had stopped by the hangars and armed men in American helmets were climbing the staircase of the control tower. Flights of Mustangs circled Lunghua in close formation, their engines roaring at the exhausted grass. Waving to them, Jim ran to the perimeter fence of the camp. He knew that the American planes were coming in to land, ready to take away the people he had raised. By the burial mounds to the west of the camp three Chinese stood with their hoes among the eroded coffins, the first of those aggrieved by the war now coming to greet him. Jim shouted to two Europeans in camp fatigues who climbed from a flooded creek with a homemade fishing net. They stared at Jim and called to him, as if surprised to find themselves alive again with this modest implement in their hands.

Jim climbed through the fence and ran down the cinder track to the camp hospital. Men with spades stood in the cemetery, shielding their eyes from the unfamiliar daylight. Had they dug themselves free from their own graves? As he neared the steps of the hospital, Jim tried to control his trembling. The bamboo doors opened, and a swarm of flies fled through the air, their feast days done. Brushing them from his face, over which he wore a green surgical mask, was a sandy-haired man in a new American uniform. In his hand he carried an insecticide bomb.

"Dr. Ransome!" Jim spat the blood from his mouth and ran up the rotting steps. "You came back, Dr. Ransome! It's all right, everyone's coming back! I'm going to get Mrs. Vincent!"

He stepped past Dr. Ransome into the dark, but the physician's hands gripped his shoulders.

"Hold on, Jim . . . I thought you might be here." He removed his mask and pressed Jim's head to his chest, inspecting the boy's gums and ignoring the blood that stained the crisp fabric of his U.S. Army shirt. "Your parents are waiting for you, Jim. Poor fellow, you'll never believe the war is over."

42

THE TERRIBLE CITY

TWO MONTHS LATER, on the eve of his departure for England, Jim remembered Dr. Ransome's words as he walked down the gangway of the S.S. *Arrawa* and stepped onto Chinese soil for the last time. Dressed in a silk shirt and tie, and a gray flannel suit from the Sincere Company's department store, Jim waited politely for an elderly English couple to make their way down the wooden ramp. Below them was the Shanghai Bund, and all the clamor of the gaudy night. Thousands of Chinese filled the concourse, jostling among the trams and limousines, the jeeps and trucks of the U.S. military, and a horde of rickshaws and pedicabs. Together they watched the British and American servicemen moving in and out of the hotels along the Bund. At the jetties beside the *Arrawa*, hidden below its stern and bows, American sailors came ashore from the cruiser moored in midriver. As they stepped from their landing craft the Chinese surged forward, gangs of pickpockets and pedicab drivers, prostitutes and bar touts, vendors hawking bottles of home-brew Johnnie Walker, gold dealers and opium traders, the evening citizenry of Shanghai in all its black silk, fox fur and flash.

The young American sailors pushed past the sampan men and shouting military police. They tried to stay together and fight off the crowd so eager to welcome them to China. But before they reached the first set of tram tracks down the center of the Bund they were swept away in a convoy of pedicabs, their arms around the bar girls screaming obscenities at the sleek Chinese pimps in their prewar Packards, down from the blocks in the back-alley garages of the Nanking Road.

Dominating this panorama of the Shanghai night were three cinema screens which had been set up on scaffolding along the Bund. In collaboration with the U.S. Navy, the Nationalist general who was the military governor of the city had arranged this continuous screening of newsreels from the European and Pacific theaters, in order to give the population of Shanghai a glimpse of the world war that had recently ended.

Jim cleared the last step of the swaying gangway and looked up at the trembling images, which were barely strong enough to hold their own against the neon signs and strip lighting on the hotel and nightclub facades. Fragments of their amplified sound tracks boomed like guns over the roar of the traffic. He had begun the war watching the newsreels in the crypt of Shanghai Cathedral and was now ending it below the same repetitive images: Russian machine gunners advanced through the ruins of Stalingrad; U.S. Marines turned their flame-throwers on the Japanese defenders of a Pacific island; RAF fighters strafed an ammunition train in a German railyard. Promptly at ten-minute intervals, Chinese characters filled the screens, and vast Kuomintang armies saluted the victorious Generalissimo Chiang on his reviewing podium in Nanking. The only forces not to be celebrated were the Chinese Communists, but they had been cleared out of Shanghai and the coastal cities. Whatever contribution their troops had made to the Allied victory had long been discounted, lost under the layers of newsreels that had imposed their own truth upon the war.

During the two months since his return to Amherst Avenue, Jim often visited the reopened cinemas in Shanghai. His parents recovered only slowly from their years of imprisonment in the camp at Soochow, and Jim had ample time to tour Shanghai. After calling at the White Russian dentist in the French Concession, he would order Yang to drive him in the Lincoln Zephyr to the Grand or the Cathay, those vast and cool palaces where he sat in the front row of the circle and watched yet another screening of *Bataan* and *The Fighting Lady*.

Yang was puzzled why Jim should want to see these films so many times. In turn Jim wondered how Yang himself had spent the years of the war—as a valet to a Chinese puppet general, as an interpreter for the Japanese or as a Kuomintang agent working on the side for the Communists? On the day of his parents' arrival Yang had appeared with the limousine, promptly sold the car to Jim's father and re-enrolled himself as its chauffeur. Yang was already performing in small roles in two productions of the renascent Shanghai film studios. Jim suspected that while he sat through another double feature at the Cathay Theater the car was being rented out as a film prop.

These Hollywood movies, like the newsreels projected above the crowds on the Bund, endlessly fascinated Jim. After the dental work to his jaw, and the healing of the wound in his palate, he soon began to put on weight. Alone at the dining-room table, he ate large meals by day and at night slept peacefully in his bedroom on the top floor of the unreal house in Amherst Avenue, which had once been his home but now seemed as much an illusion as the sets of the Shanghai film studios.

During his days at Amherst Avenue, he often thought of his cubicle in the Vincents' room at Lunghua Camp. At the end of October he ordered the unenthusiastic Yang to drive him to Lunghua. They set off through the western suburbs of Shanghai and soon reached the first of the fortified checkpoints that guarded the entrances to the city. The Nationalist soldiers in their American tanks were turning back hundreds of destitute peasants, without rice or land to crop, trying to find refuge in Shanghai. Shantytowns of mud dwellings, walls reinforced with truck tires and kerosene drums, covered the fields near the burned-out Olympic stadium at Nantao. Smoke still rose from the stands, a beacon used by the American pilots flying across the China Sea from their bases in Japan and Okinawa.

As they drove along the perimeter road, Jim stared at Lunghua Airfield, now a dream of flight. Dozens of U.S. Navy and Air Force planes sat on the grass, factory-new fighters and chromium-sheathed transport aircraft that seemed to be waiting delivery to a showroom window in the Nanking Road.

Jim expected to see Lunghua Camp deserted, but far from being abandoned the former prison was busy again, fresh barbed wire strung along its fences. Although the war had been over for nearly three months, more than a hundred British nationals were still living in the closely guarded compound. Entire families had taken over the former dormitories in E Block, in which they had built suites of rooms within the walls of American ration cartons, parachute canisters and bales of unread *Reader's*

*Digest*s. When Jim, searching for Basie's cubicle, tried to pull one of the magazines from its makeshift wall he was brusquely warned away.

Leaving the inmates to their treasure, Jim signaled Yang to drive on to G Block. The Vincents' room was now the quarters of a Chinese amah working for the British couple across the corridor. She refused to admit Jim or open the door more than a crack, and he returned to the Lincoln and ordered Yang on a last circuit of the camp.

The hospital and the camp cemetery had vanished, and the site was an open tract of ash and cinders, from which a few charred joists protruded. The graves had been carefully leveled, as if a series of tennis courts was about to be laid. Jim walked through the empty drums of kerosene that had fueled the fire. He gazed through the wire at the airfield, and at the concrete runway pointing to Lunghua Pagoda. The dense vegetation covered the wrecks of the Japanese aircraft. As Jim stood by the wire, tracing the course of the canal through the narrow valley, an American bomber swept across the camp. For a moment, reflected from the underside of its silver wings, a pale light raced like a wraith between the nettles and stunted willows.

While Yang drove uneasily back to Amherst Avenue, annoyed in some way by the visit to Lunghua, Jim thought of the last weeks of the war. Toward the end, everything had become a little muddled. He had been starving and perhaps had gone slightly mad. Yet he knew that he had seen the flash of the atom bomb at Nagasaki even across the four hundred miles of the China Sea. More important, he had seen the start of World War III, and realized that it was taking place around him. The crowds watching the newsreels on the Bund had failed to grasp that these were the trailers for a war that had already started. One day there would be no more newsreels.

In the weeks before he and his mother sailed to England in the *Arrawa,* Jim often thought of the young Japanese pilot he had seemed to raise from the dead. He was not sure now that this was the same pilot who had fed him the mango. Probably the youth had been dying, and Jim's movements in the grass had awakened him. All the same, certain events had taken place, and with more time perhaps others would have returned to life. Mrs. Vincent and her husband had died on the march from the stadium, far from Shanghai in a small village to the southwest. But Jim might have helped the prisoners in the camp hospital. As for Basie, had he died during his attack on the stadium, within sight of the gilded nymphs in the presidential stand? Or were he and Lieutenant Price still roving the landscape of the Yangtze in the puppet general's Buick, waiting for a third war to bring them into their own?

Jim had told his parents nothing of all this. Nor had he confided in Dr. Ransome, who clearly suspected that Jim had chosen to stay on at Lunghua after the armistice, playing his games of war and death. Jim remembered his return to the house in Amherst Avenue, and his mother and father smiling weakly from their deck chairs in the garden. Beside the drained swimming pool, the untended grass grew around their shoulders and reminded him of the bowers of nettles in which the dead Japanese airmen had lain. As Dr. Ransome stood formally on the terrace in his American uniform, Jim had wanted to explain to his parents everything that he and the doctor had done together, but his mother and father had been through their own war. For all their affection for him, they seemed older and far away.

Jim walked across the quay from the *Arrawa,* looking up at the newsreels projected above the evening crowd. The second of the screens, in front of the Palace Hotel, was now blank, its images of tank battles and saluting armies replaced by a rectangle of silver light that hung in the night air, a window into another universe.

As the army technicians on their tower of scaffolding repaired the projector, Jim walked across the tramlines toward the screen. Noticing it for the first time, the Chinese stopped to look up at the white rectangle. Jim brushed the sleeve of his jacket as a rickshaw coolie blundered into him, pulling two bar girls in fur coats. Their powdered faces were lit like masks by the weird glimmer.

However, the heads of the Chinese were already turning to another spectacle. A crowd had gathered below the steps of the Shanghai Club. A group of American and British sailors had emerged through the revolving doors and stood on the top step, arguing with each other and waving drunkenly at the cruiser moored by the Bund. The Chinese watched as they formed a chorus line. Provoked by their curious but silent audience, the sailors began to jeer at the Chinese. At a signal from an older sailor, the men unbuttoned their bell-bottomed trousers and urinated down the steps.

Fifty feet below them, the Chinese watched without comment as the arcs of urine formed a foaming stream that ran down to the street. When it reached the pavement the Chinese stepped back, their faces expressionless. Jim glanced at the people around him, the clerks and coolies and peasant women, well aware of what they were thinking. One day China would punish the rest of the world and take a frightening revenge.

The army projectionists had rewound their film, and an air battle started again over the heads of the crowd. As the sailors were carried away in a convoy of rickshaws, Jim walked back to the *Arrawa*. His parents were resting in the passenger saloon on the upper deck, and Jim wanted to spend a last evening with his father before he and his mother sailed for England the next day.

He stepped onto the gangway, conscious that he was probably leaving Shanghai for the last time, setting out for a small, strange country on the other side of the world that he had never visited, but that was nominally "home." Yet only part of his mind would leave Shanghai. The rest would remain there forever, returning on the tide like the coffins launched from the funeral piers at Nantao.

Below the bows of the *Arrawa* a child's coffin moved onto the night stream. Its paper flowers were shaken loose by the wash of a landing craft carrying sailors from the American cruiser. The flowers formed a wavering garland around the coffin as it began its long journey to the estuary of the Yangtze, only to be swept back by the incoming tide among the quays and mud flats, driven once again to the shores of this terrible city.

About the Author

"One of the most important, intelligent voices in contemporary fiction," according to Susan Sontag, J. G. Ballard is the author of many novels, including *High-Rise, Crash* and *Concrete Island. Empire of the Sun,* which is based on Ballard's childhood experiences during the Second World War, was nominated for Britain's premier fiction award, The Booker Prize. His previous novel, *The Unlimited Dream Company,* was selected by Anthony Burgess in *99 Novels* as one of the best English novels since 1939, and will be forthcoming from Washington Square Press, along with *The Best Short Stories of J. G. Ballard.* Ballard lives in Shepperton, England.

WÓJT

JEDZIEMY Z FRAJERAMI!

JANUSZ WÓJCIK   PRZEMYSŁAW OFIARA

WÓJT

JEDZIEMY Z FRAJERAMI!

Całe moje życie

KRAKÓW 2014

WÓJT
JEDZIEMY Z FRAJERAMI. CAŁE MOJE ŻYCIE

Redakcja – Joanna Mika-Orządała
Redakcja merytoryczna – Jakub Kuza
Korekta – Kamil Misiek / Editor.net.pl
Opracowanie typograficzne i skład – Joanna Pelc
Okładka – Paweł Szczepanik / BookOne.pl

Front cover photgraph – Monika Wrzesińska / Studio MMP

Zdjęcia w środku książki, jeśli nie zostały podpisane inaczej, pochodzą z prywatnego archiwum trenera Janusza Wójcika. Wydawnictwo SQN serdecznie dziękuje trenerowi i jego bliskim za ich udostępnienie. Autor i wydawca dołożyli wszelkich starań, by dotrzeć do wszystkich właścicieli i dysponentów praw autorskich do ilustracji zamieszczonych w książce. Osoby, których nie udało nam się ustalić, prosimy o kontakt z wydawnictwem.

Wydanie I, Kraków 2014
ISBN: 978-83-7924-275-7

www.wydawnictwosqn.pl

Szukaj naszych książek również w formie elektronicznej

DYSKUTUJ O KSIĄŻCE

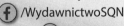
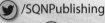
/WydawnictwoSQN

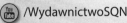
/SQNPublishing

/WydawnictwoSQN

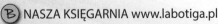
NASZA KSIĘGARNIA www.labotiga.pl

Wspieramy środowisko! Książka została wydrukowana na papierze wyprodukowanym zgodnie z zasadami zrównoważonej gospodarki leśnej.

PROJEKT BARCELONA
1989–1992

– Panowie, kiełbachy do góry, rąbiemy ich w kakao! Siekać frajerów, do piachu z nimi! Wślizg, wślizg, wślizg! – krzyczałem do chłopaków.

Dla mnie i dla nich była to najważniejsza chwila w życiu – przerwa meczu finałowego igrzysk olimpijskich w Barcelonie. Prowadziliśmy z Hiszpanami 1:0, ale moi piłkarze chcieli rywali pożreć. A ja ich jeszcze podpuszczałem.

– Wskakujemy im na garby, nosami mają ryć po glebie. Nie popuszczamy ani metra! Zapomnijcie, kurwa, o tym, że prowadzicie. Jest 0:0. Wychodzimy do nich i łapiemy za gardła. Nie pozwalamy nawet pierdnąć! Ty, Kowal, też. – Skinąłem w kierunku mojego ulubieńca Wojtka Kowalczyka.

– Trenerze, do upadłego będę walczył. Padnę, ale będę zapierdalał! – odpowiedział nabuzowany. W życiu, ani wcześniej, ani później, go takiego nie widziałem.

Prowadziliśmy, ale darłem się wniebogłosy, jakby rzeczywiście było 0:0. Akcja motywacyjna przebiegała w najlepsze. Nie cackałem się, od razu jechałem ostro. Musiałem pobudzić im mózgi. Nie pałą baseballową, ale słowem.

Było gorąco, kurewsko gorąco. Pot spływał mi po skroni, a chusteczka, którą się wycierałem, przypominała namokniętą gąbkę. Z kolei piłkarze byli okładani lodem, wachlowani, ale w ogóle im to nie pomagało. Jakby w szatni był lekarz, toby powiedział, że zaraz pierdolną na zawał, jeden po drugim, albo dostaną wylewu – tak byli nakręceni. Musiałem szybko decydować, co robimy z kontuzjowanymi: czy zakładamy blokady, czy jednak zmienimy. Niestety, do zmiany był Piotrek Świerczewski, jednak w ogóle nie chciał schodzić. Szykował się na zwieńczenie tej pięknej barcelońskiej masakry.

– Panie trenerze, a może przyjebać któremuś? – zapytał.

– Czy ciebie, Świerszczu, popierdoliło? Jucha pójdzie mu z ryja, pokaże sędziemu i dostaniesz czerwoną kartkę, zanim wyjdziesz na boisko – opierdoliłem go lekko, ale czułem też satysfakcję, że chłopaki są mocno nabuzowane. – Poza tym ty jesteś kontuzjowany, nie wiem, czy dasz radę wyjść na drugą połowę.

– Trenerze, niech masażysta robi, co chce, wali mi jakieś zastrzyki! Kulawy, ale wyjdę! – zarzekał się.

Został w szatni. Nie miałem wyjścia, musiałem go zmienić. Ale jego koledzy wcale nie byli łagodniejsi. Kiedy ustawili się w tunelu, przeraźliwie głośno tupali korkami w podłogę. Był półmrok, cokolwiek widać było tylko dzięki lekkim, zielonym światełkom. A oni tłukli, jak ZOMO pałami w tarcze. Hiszpanie byli przerażeni, patrzyli na siebie i dziwili się, co za pojeby z tych Polaków. Jeden z naszych chłopaków podłożył nawet nogę Hiszpanowi, a tamten się wypierdolił jak długi. A Kowal jak złapał jednego za ucho, to mało mu tego ucha nie urwał! Chłopcy szukali zaczepki, chcąc wyprowadzić przeciwników z równowagi. Liczyli, że któryś odda na boisku.

– I o to, kurwa, chodzi! Wszystkie chwyty dozwolone – krzyczałem do Pawła Janasa, mojego asystenta.

To nie był podwórkowy meczyk. Żadne tam dziesięć tysięcy kibiców na trybunach, ale ponad sto tysięcy! Piłkarze zapierdalali, jakby byli nafaszerowani najlepszymi prochami na świecie. A na boisko wychodzili jak gladiatorzy na arenę. I mieli dwie możliwości. Albo ich ściągną jak ścierę z placu boju, albo będą tak ściągać rywali. To była walka na śmierć i życie. 45 minut, które miało wprowadzić ich do piłkarskiego raju. Ostatnie 45 minut podczas najważniejszego turnieju w życiu.

KIERUNEK: HISZPANIA

Zanim jednak opowiem o naszym występie na igrzyskach, winien jestem wyjaśnienie, jak właściwie się to zaczęło. Otóż w grudniu 1989 roku, podczas rozmów z Wydziałem Szkolenia i Wydziałem Młodzieżowym PZPN, stwierdziliśmy, że mamy zdolnych chłopaków i trzeba spróbować przygotować ich do igrzysk olimpijskich w Hiszpanii. Wzorowałem się na krajach zachodnich, które z takim właśnie wyprzedzeniem zaczęły myśleć o starcie w tej imprezie.

Miałem szczęście, bo w tamtym czasie w PZPN-ie było z kim podyskutować, pracowali tam ludzie, z którymi dało się robić pozytywne rzeczy. Wcześniej – a także teraz – związek był zbieraniną beztroskich i zabawowych misiów. Człowiek prędzej oszaleje, niż się z nimi dogada. Nie chcę źle mówić o nieżyjących, ale Ryszard Kulesza czy Edmund Zientara, obaj z PZPN-u, nie byli przychylni reprezentacji olimpijskiej. Tak samo ówczesny wiceprezes PZPN-u Marian Dziurowicz, któremu kiedyś zagroziłem nawet, że jak się nie uspokoi to „zajebię mu w łeb". Na szczęście dla niego ostatecznie tego nie zrobiłem. Bo ta śląska łepetyna chybaby mu odpadła.

Jako teren przygotowań postanowiłem wybrać Niemcy albo Śląsk. Wszyscy się dziwili, dlaczego akurat ten Śląsk, a nie Warszawa. Ano dlatego, że wszedłem w komitywę z ministrem Janem Szlachtą, który na Śląsku mógł robić wszystko, co chciał. Co tylko powiedział, było absolutnie święte. Marian Dziurowicz meldował się u niego jak w wojsku, waląc obcasami, a Szlachta tak go opierdzielał, że aż przykro było słuchać. Cóż, taki mieli już sposób rozmowy. Ja natomiast, dzięki ministrowi Szlachcie właśnie, również mogłem robić na Śląsku, co tylko chciałem.

– O której chciałbyś trenować na Górniku? – pytał na przykład.

– O 17.00, panie ministrze.

– Łączyć mnie z prezesem Górnika – mówił do sekretarki, a po chwili już ustawiał nieszczęsnego prezesa: – O 17.00 przyjeżdża Wójcik ze swoją reprezentacją, proszę mu wszystko udostępnić.

I wszystko było udostępnione, dosłownie wszystko. Miałem telefon kontaktowy, dzięki któremu zawsze mogłem się ze Szlachtą połączyć. Często się spotykaliśmy, zawsze późnym wieczorem i zawsze na neutralnym gruncie. Wychodziliśmy na spacery, bo minister bał się, że ktoś może go podsłuchiwać.

– Janusz, coś złego może się ze mną wydarzyć – dał mi do zrozumienia podczas jednego z takich spotkań.

Przyjechał do mnie specjalnie, żeby mi o tym powiedzieć. Niecały tydzień później przyszła informacja, że zginął w wypadku samochodowym w dziwnych okolicznościach. Od razu wiedziałem, o co chodzi, wiedziałem, że wcale to nie był wypadek, tak samo jak w przypadku „samobójstwa" polityka Ireneusza Sekuły. Przecież Sekuła sam do siebie nie strzelał. Po prostu w to nie wierzę.

Wiadomość o śmierci Szlachty spadła na wszystkich jak grom z jasnego nieba, ale machina przygotowań do igrzysk rozpędzała się i zamiast opłakiwać zmarłego, trzeba było skupić się na treningach. Wszystko ruszyło z kopyta po losowaniu grup eliminacyjnych. Oczywiście mieliśmy pecha – trafiliśmy do najsilniejszej grupy w Europie. Mieliśmy grać z Anglią, Irlandią i Turcją. Każdy z rywali teoretycznie był silniejszy od nas. Gdybyśmy teraz trafili do takiej grupy, to moglibyśmy od razu iść się wykąpać, a z szatni nie wychodzić, żeby się nie ośmieszać.

Zacząłem budować drużynę olimpijską. Rzecz jasna postanowiłem skorzystać z zawodników, którzy grali u mnie w reprezentacjach juniorskich, ale na przykład takiego Wojtka Kowalczyka dołączyłem do drużyny dopiero w trakcie eliminacji, z okazji meczu z Irlandią. Wcześniej moimi faworytami byli inni, na przykład Juskowiak i Grad.

Pierwszy mecz eliminacyjny graliśmy z Anglikami, na White Hart Lane, czyli stadionie Tottenhamu. Zwyciężyliśmy 1:0 po golu Adamczuka. W rewanżu Anglicy po raz kolejny dostali łupnia, tym razem 2:1. Potem odbyły się mecze z Turcją. Przed wyjazdem do Turcji udaliśmy się do Izraela, żeby złapać trochę ciepła, bo w Polsce była wtedy zima. I jak nam poszło z Turkami? No orżnęliśmy ich 1:0!

Przy okazji wyjazdu do Turcji miałem trochę problemów z Juskowiakiem. Zaczęli wokół niego biegać menedżerowie, między innymi pan Kopa, który przyjechał za nim do Stambułu. Wziąłem więc Andrzeja na rozmowę.

– Józiu, ja nie chcę, żebyś ty się spotykał z dziennikarzami i menedżerami, bo zaraz gramy mecz. I gramy z Turcją, a nie z Republiką Czadu. Żadnych meetingów w hotelu – zapowiedziałem stanowczo i udałem się do polskiej ambasady, gdzie byłem zaproszony.

Po jakimś czasie dostaję telefon z jasnym przekazem: „Józio działa". Samochód z ambasady dowiózł mnie pod sam hotel. Wchodzę cichaczem i widzę, że Juskowiak siedzi sobie na środku lobby, a wokół niego mnóstwo dziennikarzy – telewizja, prasa, radio, co tylko chcecie. Wkurwiłem się, podszedłem i zacząłem rozpędzać towarzystwo.

– Koniec dnia medialnego, żegnam państwa – pogoniłem dziennikarzy i zwróciłem się do Józia: – A ty natychmiast na górę i tam czekasz na mnie. Pogadamy na odprawie.

Dzień przed meczem, o 22.00, zawodnicy mieli odprawę, podczas której mówiłem, jaki mamy plan, niejednokrotnie też zdradzałem, w jakim składzie zagramy. Tym razem też zacząłem czytać szesnastkę meczową. Nagle konsternacja – w drużynie nie ma Józia. Kapitan, Jurek Brzęczek, zagaił:

– Trenerze, a Józio? Co z nim?

– No co Józio? On już miał swój mecz, na dole. Skończył grać.

– Ale co z nim będzie?

– Pójdzie na trybuny.

Piłkarze zbaranieli. W końcu to podstawowy zawodnik, a graliśmy przecież z silną Turcją. Ja jednak miałem plan: po zakończeniu odprawy wziąłem na rozmowę Adama Grada, takiego niesfornego misia, który kilka razy mi podpadł.

– Słuchaj, Adam, jutro najprawdopodobniej będziesz grał, szykuj się. Gotowy jesteś?

– Trenerze, oczywiście, jestem gotowy!

– To jest dla ciebie szansa – podkręcałem go. – Albo z niej skorzystasz, albo rano skocz do Bosforu i śmigaj na drugi brzeg, szukać szczęścia w Azji.

I Adaś Grad strzelił bramkę na 1:0, dzięki której wygraliśmy mecz! A Juskowiak? Oglądał pojedynek z trybun z miną kota srającego w sieczkę. Porozmawiałem z nim oczywiście o całej sytuacji, już na spokojnie. Potem jeszcze kilka razy musiałem lekko go wyprostować, ale na szczęście to ten typ człowieka, który bierze do siebie wszystkie rady i polecenia. Był posłuszny, nie popełniał dwa razy tego samego błędu.

Życie jest zresztą przewrotne, co pokazuje przykład Juskowiaka i Grada. Józio na igrzyska pojechał i, jak wiecie, był ich gwiazdą, a tego drugiego gagatka odpaliłem. Dlaczego? Na zgrupowaniu w Bydgoszczy podpadł mi niemiłosiernie. Zamiast wrócić na czas do hotelu, wolał się zabawić z kolegami. Był po alkoholu.

– W Turcji wygrałeś swoją szansę, a teraz ją straciłeś – nie patyczkowałem się.

– Ale, ale tre… trenerze, ja się poprawię, obiecuję.

– Chłopcze, poprawić to się możesz teraz na wadze. Ja już cię ostrzegałem, bo zdarzały ci się lekkie zakręty.

Grada więc nie było, a do drużyny wskoczyli inni, między innymi Kowal, którego wziąłem do Irlandii. Przyglądałem mu się i w lidze, i w meczach pucharowych. Wiedziałem od razu, że to jest chłopak do grania, do pierwszego składu. Zresztą ślepy by to nawet zauważył – Kowalczyk to był talent czystej wody. Pamiętam do dziś, jak po meczu z Sampdorią Genua w ćwierćfinale Pucharu Zdobywców Pucharów zszedłem do szatni Legii, by z nim porozmawiać.

Ej, ty, kundlu! Będziesz grał u mnie w reprezentacji! – zakomunikowałem.

– Trenerze, oczywiście! Tu i teraz mogę zagrać! – zapalił się.

No i byliśmy dogadani. Problemów z nim nie miałem żadnych. I jego, i innych trzymałem twardą ręką. Zawiązała się zresztą tak zwana grupa ostrzegawczo-porozumiewawcza w osobach Jurka Brzęczka i Tomka Wałdocha. To oni mieli rozmawiać z delikwentami, którym coś nie pasowało. Bo jeśli chłopcy nie umieliby sami rozwiązywać problemów, to trzeba byłoby całe towarzystwo rozgonić i budować na nowo. Zadbałem jednak, by odpowiednio budować napięcie: jeżeli Brzęczek i Wałdoch nie dawali rady, do akcji wkraczał agent do zadań specjalnych – Alek Kłak. Starcia z tym wielkim chłopiskiem nie życzyłbym nikomu.

– Aluś, ty masz po prostu podejść walnąć w cymbał takiego klienta. Tylko krzywdy mu nie zrób. Jeżeli powie, że zrozumiał, to ja już nic nie muszę wiedzieć. A jeśli dalej będzie podskakiwał, to przyjdź do mnie – tłumaczyłem Kłakowi, a on załapał w lot. Wiem, że kilku delikwentów dostało porządnie w łeb od naszego bramkarza.

Grupę eliminacyjną rozbiliśmy doszczętnie – jako jedyny zespół w Europie wygraliśmy wszystkie mecze. Dawałem chłopakom taki wycisk, że wieczorami nie mieli siły, żeby nawet pomyśleć o dupach czy balowaniu – po prostu padali i szli spać jak przedszkolaki na leżakowaniu. To procentowało na boisku. Awans był w zasięgu ręki, teraz przyszedł czas na ćwierćfinałowe starcie z Danią. Zwycięstwo dałoby nam ten awans, ale uzyskaliśmy go także za sprawą korzystnych rezultatów w innych meczach ćwierćfinałowych. W jaki sposób? Otóż wszystko dzięki zawiłemu regulaminowi. Przewidywał on awans nawet w przypadku odpadnięcia w 1/4 finału. Moja drużyna miała najlepszy współczynnik punktów oraz zdobytych bramek wśród wszystkich europejskich drużyn. Do wyjazdu na igrzyska niezbędny był tylko brak porażki w jednym z dwóch meczów przeciwko Duńczykom oraz wygrana Szkocji z Niemcami.

Byliśmy przekonani, że każdego na świecie jesteśmy w stanie zlać, i trochę zlekceważyliśmy rywali. Do Aalborga przyleciała delegacja prominentnych działaczy i polityków z Polski, którzy liczyli, że przejedziemy się po Duńczykach jak walec. I wszyscy, łącznie ze mną, przeżyli szok – przegraliśmy 0:5. Nie dlatego, że Duńczycy byli mocni, w końcu na igrzyskach nie mieli nic do powiedzenia. Szczęście im jednak dopisywało i strzelali gola za golem, a moi chłopcy byli totalnie bezradni. Po każdej bramce rzucali się odrabiać straty, jednak po prostu im nie wychodziło. W rewanżu w Polsce padł remis 1:1. W mistrzostwach Europy dalej przeszli Duńczycy, ale my i tak mogliśmy otwierać szampany! Wynik zapewnił nam taki współczynnik UEFA, że bez względu na wszystko mogliśmy już być pewni gry w Barcelonie. Wprawdzie przeskoczyli nas Szkoci, którzy pokonali Niemców, ale chłopcy w kraciastych spódnicach nie mogli wystawić drużyny w Barcelonie, bo przecież Szkocja była częścią składową Wielkiej Brytanii. W taki sposób my, kuchennymi drzwiami, dostaliśmy się na wymarzone igrzyska olimpijskie.

Cieszyliśmy się niebywale, ale na krótko przed wyjazdem niewiele brakło, żeby nasz zespół został z imprezy wycofany! Chcieliśmy samodzielnie zrobić zawodnikom badania antydopingowe. Poprosiliśmy ludzi z Centralnego Ośrodka Sportu, aby wytypowali grupę, która mogłaby je przeprowadzić.

Zebrałem całą drużynę w Warszawie i ulokowałem w hotelu Solec niedaleko stadionu Legii. Teraz ten hotel nazywa się Ibis. To zresztą w Solcu właśnie w latach 1980–1891 chlała Solidarność przed rozmowami z rządem. Kadra zawsze spała tam przed meczami – bo i monopol był blisko, i o dziewki portowe trudno nie było…

Ekipa, która przyjechała, nadawała się jednak wyłącznie do cyrku albo programu o patologiach społecznych. Panowie ci na wejściu zapowiedzieli, że trzeba nakupić piwa, aby piłkarze szybciej sikali do probówek. Przystałem na to. Załatwiliśmy parę skrzynek i chłopcy wypili po jeden–dwa browarki. Niestety członkowie ekipy przechylili kropelkę więcej złocistego trunku niż zawodnicy i kiedy piłkarze zobaczyli, że mogą zrobić, co tylko chcą, rozwinęli skrzydła. Zaczęli sikać raz do jednej, raz do drugiej probówki i powstały mieszaniny moczu. Stwierdziłem, że skoro nikt tego nie pilnuje, to i ja nie będę swoich piłkarzy dyscyplinował. A „ekipa badawcza" tak się narąbała, że musieliśmy zamówić jej taksówki, żeby mogła wrócić w to smutne miejsce, z którego przybyła. Za jakiś czas przyszły wyniki. I szok – u trzech zawodników wykryto ślady niedozwolonych środków! Chodziło o Aleksandra Kłaka, Piotra Świerczewskiego i Dariusza Koselę. W zespole konsternacja. Potem oczywiście okazało się – co za zaskoczenie! – że wszystkie zasady przeprowadzania badań i przechowywania probówek zostały złamane. Mimo to w PZPN-ie stwierdzili, że trzeba odsunąć tych trzech piłkarzy i mnie jako trenera. Dziś uważam to za bezczelny i chamski zamach na tę drużynę. Całe szczęście, że w Komitecie Olimpijskim pracowali rzetelni ludzie, którzy zlecili kolejne testy. Wyniki jasno wykazały: piłkarze są czyści. Oczywiście pojawiły się rozmaite teorie spiskowe, między innymi taka, że zawodnicy zdążyli już wypłukać ten koks, co było totalną bzdurą, bo wszystkie środki wypłukujące są również substancjami niedozwolonymi! Jaki był finał całej sprawy? Otóż władze PKOl-u po zbadaniu okoliczności uznały, że należy nas puścić na igrzyska w normalnym składzie, razem z feralną trójką. Nie udało się misiom z PZPN-u udupić tej drużyny, która była zadrą w ich paznokciach. Nie chcieli jej dofinansowywać, a kiedy już sama zarabiała jakieś pieniądze, to żądali, by cała kasa przechodziła przez związek. A podział byłby jasny – sobie kupiliby diamenty, a nam daliby kamienie z bruku. Ja się na to nie zgadzałem, co strasznie ich wkurwiało. Na tyle, że zaczęli robić nam pod górkę. I, co ciekawe, już podczas samych igrzysk po każdym meczu robiono nam badania antydopingowe. Piłkarzy wybierano losowo – na tyle losowo, że niezmiennie padało na... Świerczewskiego, Kłaka i Koselę! Chłopcy byli nieprawdopodobnie zestresowani, ja również cały się trząsłem. Wyniki zawsze jednak były jednoznaczne: brak zakazanych substancji we krwi. Banda z PZPN-u, Zientara, Kulesza,

Dziurowicz czy Bugdoł, pokazała, na co ją stać, ale nie udało jej się ukręcić nam głów.

– Śmierdziele, kutasy, topicie polski futbol! Ale mojej drużyny nie zatopicie, nie pozwolę – darłem się na nich.

I na zatopienie nie pozwoliłem. Pojechaliśmy do Barcelony i graliśmy jak z nut, jakby przeciw działaczom. Ci niech się cieszą, że po powrocie z turnieju piłkarze nie obili im mord za to, że chcieli nas potopić.

PRZEDOLIMPIJSKI CYRK

Moja droga do Barcelony była długa i kręta, ale przede wszystkim wesoła. Załapałem się na przykład na dwie barwne wyprawy – do Włoch i Albanii. Najpierw, dwa lata przed igrzyskami, wraz z Andrzejem Strejlauem, selekcjonerem pierwszej reprezentacji, pojechaliśmy na obserwację mistrzostw świata we Włoszech. Mnie miało to pomóc w ukształtowaniu warsztatu trenerskiego, a Andrzejek towarzyszył mi jako ten bardziej doświadczony. Cały ten wyjazd to był taki, za przeproszeniem, kabarecik – gdyby mi ktoś powiedział wcześniej, tobym nie uwierzył. Piłka piłką, ale najciekawsze działo się, że tak powiem, po godzinach.

Wybraliśmy się na Sardynię, gdzie grała grupa, której mieliśmy się przyglądać. Dolecieliśmy na miejsce, a tam dupa – nie mamy nic: ani transportu, ani hotelu, tak się ładnie misiaczki z PZPN-u postarały. Siedzieliśmy godzinę na lotnisku i zastanawialiśmy się, co robić. Strejlau zaczął się pruć:

– Janusz, poczekamy jeszcze trochę, złapiemy jakiś samolot do Warszawy i wracamy. Co my tu będziemy robić? Gdzie tu się podziejemy? Pod most pójdziemy?

Tak, kurwa, i jeszcze rozbijemy namiot pod gwiazdami.

– Damy sobie radę, nie przejmuj się – powiedziałem, po czym zagaiłem po angielsku jednego z taksówkarzy, czy mógłby zawieźć nas do jakiegoś spokojnego hoteliku.

Taksówkarz odparł, że owszem, mógłby, i tak właśnie zrobił. Wylądowaliśmy w starszej dzielnicy Cagliari, gdzie, jak się okazało, mieliśmy spędzić prawie całe mistrzostwa. W hotelu bardzo ładnie nas ugościli, mimo to Strejlau cały czas był wystraszony, jakby zaraz mieli nas stamtąd wyrzucić.

Wieczorem wyszedłem na przechadzkę i poznałem ciekawych ludzi, oczywiście zakochanych w piłce nożnej. Pokażcie mi zresztą Włocha, który nie kocha futbolu! Kiedy powiedziałem, że ja i kolega jesteśmy trenerami, od razu zaprosili nas na winko. Na drugi dzień przyjechali po nas i zapoznali ze swoimi znajomymi, bardzo bogatymi ludźmi. Mieli wielką farmę ze stadniną koni i uznali, że koniecznie musimy ich odwiedzić. Wybraliśmy się tam więc kilka razy, a gospodarz bardzo mnie polubił – prosił nawet, żebym zawsze siadał po jego prawej stronie. Pewnego dnia mnie zaskoczył:

– Janusz, może byś się na koniu przejechał?

– A czemu nie, przejadę się – odpowiedziałem, pewny siebie i doskonale nieświadomy tego, co mnie czeka.

Wsadzili mnie na jakiegoś dziwnego konia. Na początku kroczył sobie spokojnie, ale nie po to się jeździ konno, żeby się snuć jak chłop na kacu. Lekko dotknąłem go piętami, a on jak pierdzielnął do przodu, to myślałem, że już po mnie! Tak się go trzymałem, jakbym za chwilę miał się oderwać od Mount Everestu i jebnąć w przepaść! Wywiózł mnie gdzieś na pustkowie, nie wiedziałem kompletnie, gdzie jestem. Bałem się dzióbnąć go jeszcze raz, bo jakby pocwałował jeszcze dalej, to już na pewno nikt by mnie nie znalazł. Wreszcie, po półgodzinie zwiedzania w siodle włoskiego zadupia, słyszę krzyki: „Janusz, Janusz!". Strasznie się ucieszyłem, że mnie szukają, i zacząłem się wydzierać, machać, generalnie robić wszystko, żeby mnie zobaczyli. Konno nadjeżdżało dwóch gości z grupy poszukiwawczej. Odetchnąłem z ulgą, ale wystraszony byłem nie na żarty! W Polsce mieliby używanie: pojechał Wójcik mecze oglądać, a pocwałował w stronę zachodzącego słońca i tyle go widzieli.

No ale przynajmniej spróbowałem. Strejlau koniki oglądał z daleka.

Tak nam się spodobało na tej farmie, że jeździliśmy tam dzień w dzień. W końcu pewnego dnia najdroższy gospodarz orzekł, że już dość nasiedzieliśmy się w domu jak jakieś ciule, że zarżną świniaka na naszą cześć i zabiorą nas w góry, do „banditos". Pomyślałem: dobra niech będą banditos. Zapakowali nas w jeepy i pojechaliśmy. Balanga była taka, że klękajcie narody. Wypiliśmy kilka gąsiorów wina, zjedliśmy świniaka i tak sobie kulturalnie biesiadowaliśmy, kiedy zauważyłem, że zjawiła się policja.

– Czego oni tutaj chcą? – zapytałem naszego organizatora.

– Spokojnie, Janusz, przyjechali nas pilnować. Pojadą sobie jeszcze z 500 metrów wyżej, postawią swoje auto w poprzek drogi i będą stali, dopóki nie skończymy. Na dole jest kolejna ekipa, która pilnuje drugiego wjazdu.

„Jeśli mamy taką obstawę, to musi być tu ciekawie!", pomyślałem. Jakiś czas później policjanci podjechali do nas, przywitali się z naszymi kompanami, a ja, że byłem leciutko wstawiony, zacząłem przymierzać ich policyjne czapki. W końcu prawie cały przebrałem się w uniform, tylko spluwy nie chcieli mi dać.

Z taką obstawą jeździliśmy później na wszystkie mecze mistrzostw świata. A Andrzejek Strejlau nie mógł wyjść z podziwu.

– Kurwa, Janusz, co ja bym tu bez ciebie zrobił? Jednego dnia bym sam nie wytrzymał. A teraz mi się nie chce stąd wyjeżdżać! – emocjonował się.

„Nic byś nie zrobił, Andrzejku – pomyślałem. – Poczekałbyś parę godzin na lotnisku, rozpłakał się i wrócił do Polski".

Z żalem musieliśmy opuścić Sardynię i polecieliśmy do Mediolanu na dalszą obserwację. Oczywiście znów nie mieliśmy gdzie się zatrzymać. Załatwiłem więc w niemieckiej federacji piłkarskiej, byśmy mogli nocować tam, gdzie ich reprezentacja. Zgodzili się i nawet przyjechali po nas na lotnisko, po czym zawieźli do hotelu. Wszystkie koszty pokrywała DFB, a nie PZPN, który nas tam wspaniałomyślnie wydelegował.

Niemcy od razu zaprosili nas na imprezę. A następnego dnia na kolejną. I tak dzień w dzień. Piłkarze przychodzili na mały browarek i wychodzili, nie mogli za bardzo się znieczulić przed ważnymi meczami. Natomiast my, żeby nie urazić naszych miłych gospodarzy, karnie stawialiśmy się na każdej popijawie. Strejlau się pilnował: to znaczy żłopał browary jak król Oktoberfestu, ale wstydu nie przyniósł. A kiedy wracaliśmy, był mi bardzo wdzięczny.

Mnie też ten wyjazd bardzo wiele nauczył. Bo imprezy imprezami, ale dzięki niemu na pewno stałem się lepszym trenerem, co dwa lata później pomogło mi na igrzyskach.

Jakiś rok przed Barceloną wybraliśmy się też do Albanii, na mecz towarzyski. Przepiękny kraj, ale co 100 metrów bunkier, na ulicach pełno zakapiorów, jednym słowem: bandziorstwo i mafia. Pojechał z nami taki dziennikarz, radiowiec Zbigniew Wojciechowski, wyjątkowy „gorzelnik", a wyróżniało go to, że miał protezę zamiast ręki.

Walczyliśmy z niemalże pierwszą reprezentacją Albanii, ale bez problemu wygraliśmy to spotkanie. Po meczu była kolacja w pięknej restauracji. Po pewnym czasie wszyscy się rozglądają, a tu zaginął dziennikarz! Znaleziono tylko jego... protezę. Zaglądamy pod długi stół, faceta nie ma. Zrobiło się groźnie nie na żarty. W końcu znaleźliśmy go na zapleczu, narąbanego jak stodoła. A dlaczego był akurat tam? Ano ci, którzy sprzątali w restauracji, zobaczyli, że dżentelmen ów zwalił się z krzesła i zażywa odpoczynku pod stołem. Chcieli go wyciągnąć, ale niestety złapali za protezę i oczywiście ją wyrwali. Zaciągnęli go jakoś na zaplecze, a sztuczną rękę odłożyli na stół. W rezultacie proteza była, a klient zaginął.

W Albanii i ja, i drużyna doceniliśmy walory przyrodnicze tego kraju. Były tam na przykład piękne gaje mandarynkowe, a w Polsce, jak wiadomo, taką egzotykę można było znaleźć co najwyżej w Peweksie. Wziąłem więc chłopaków i poszliśmy sobie pozrywać trochę tych smakołyków. Oto reprezentacja Polski wybrała się na tak zwaną dzierżawę! Oczywiście gospodarze nas pogonili i trzeba było spierdalać, ale z innego miejsca wróciliśmy do hotelu już z pełnymi torbami. A potem chłopcy mieli co pojeść.

Kapelanem reprezentacji olimpijskiej był świętej pamięci prałat Henryk Jankowski. Zaproponował mi, żebym zabrał drużynę do Rzymu na audiencję u papieża Jana Pawła II. Rzecz jasna nie mogłem i nie chciałem odmówić – to była wielka sprawa zarówno dla mnie, jak i dla wszystkich moich piłkarzy. Cała ekipa była podekscytowana wyjazdem. Wcześniej jednak udaliśmy się do kościoła Świętej Brygidy w Gdańsku, którego proboszczem był prałat Jankowski. Msza niesamowita... W świątyni nie było wolnych miejsc, również dlatego, że ludzie dowiedzieli się o tym, że w nabożeństwie będzie brała udział reprezentacja. Później prałat zaprosił nas na specjalnie przygotowaną ucztę. Czego tam nie było... Wykwintne przystawki, mięsa, sery, owoce, no i popitka z najwyższej półki. Raj na ziemi.

Na początku jednak było dość grzecznie.

– Janosik, przejdź no się i zobacz, czy jest coś mocniejszego do napicia się – poinstruowałem Pawełka Janasa, mojego asystenta.

Pawełek chodził, szukał, ale nie mógł znaleźć. Pomyślałem, że w sumie to w miarę normalne, że u księdza nie ma alkoholu. Ale Jankowski szybko wyprowadził mnie z błędu.

– W lodówce szukajcie, w lodówce! – wskazał, a Janosik szybko pobiegł po skarby. Wrócił uśmiechnięty od ucha do ucha.

– No i co żeś zobaczył, że tak się szczerzysz? – zapytałem.

– Janusz, tam jest wszystko! Co tylko chcesz! Dwie lodówki pełne gorzały i whisky – relacjonował podekscytowany.

– Dobra, to przynieś co nieco. Tylko pod żadnym pozorem nie mów o tym piłkarzom, bo zaraz jeden z drugim się napierdoli – zastrzegłem.

Podczas biesiady omówiliśmy ostatnie szczegóły wyjazdu do Rzymu, który zbliżał się wielkimi krokami. Głównym celem było oczywiście spotkanie z papieżem, ale oprócz tego mieliśmy zagrać tam towarzyski mecz z olimpijską reprezentacją Włoch.

Wkrótce potem polecieliśmy. Zatrzymaliśmy się ni to w hotelu, ni to domu pielgrzyma, ale muszę podkreślić, że warunki były bardzo dobre. Zresztą gdyby nawet nie były – nie wybraliśmy się do Italii pławić się tam w luksusach, tylko spotkać z Ojcem Świętym.

W przeddzień audiencji wielu działaczy, którzy wybrali się z nami, chciało się zabawić. Ja oczywiście zasiadłem do nocnych rozmów razem z nimi. Najpierw kosztowaliśmy włoskiego wina, a jak już humory zaczęły dopisywać, towarzystwo przerzuciło się na whisky i wódeczkę. Impreza tak się rozkręciła, że potrwała do rana. A przecież kilka godzin później mieliśmy rozmawiać z papieżem!

Niektórzy mieli spore problemy z organizmem. Jeden nieszczęśnik jeszcze przed spowiedzią, a podczas imprezy, nie wytrzymał ciśnienia. Wziął klucz, pobiegł do pokoju i padł jak nieżywy. Kiedy go znaleźliśmy, leżał zaszczany, zarzygany i skromnie odziany jedynie we własny kał. Na drugi dzień musiał opłacić czyszczenie pościeli i materaca, ale dużo więcej kosztowało go pokazanie nam się na oczy. Bo smród ciągnął się za nim podczas całego tego wyjazdu.

W międzyczasie pojawił się mały problem. Prałat Jankowski zarządził spowiedź, by każdy mógł udać się na audiencję z duszyczką czystą jak łza. Razem z piłkarzami w kolejce do konfesjonału ustawili się również kompletnie napierdoleni działacze. Z minuty na minutę prałat krzywił się coraz bardziej, bo musiał wdychać alkoholowe wyziewy wydzielane przez kwiat PZPN-u.

Tuż po spowiedzi towarzystwo poszło na śniadanie, które pijaków trochę postawiło na nogi. Potem podziemnymi korytarzami udaliśmy się do komnat, w których miał przyjąć nas papież. Sala była wypełniona po brzegi – mnóstwo ludzi, a każdy chciał być jak najbliżej Ojca Świętego. My jednak nie musieliśmy się przepychać. Po oficjalnej części audiencji zaprowadzono nas do tajemnej sali, w której odbyło się nasze prywatne spotkanie z papieżem Polakiem. Tam już każdy mógł spokojnie podejść i z bliska popatrzeć na wspaniałego rodaka.

– Proszę, tylko nie róbcie żadnych zdjęć ani nie proście o autografy – powiedział nam ksiądz Stanisław Dziwisz, najbliższy współpracownik Jana Pawła II.

Ja w międzyczasie musiałem zająć się jeszcze inną, poważniejszą rzeczą. Trzeba było poprzestawiać na koniec sali tych, którzy najbardziej odczuli trudy imprezy z poprzedniego wieczoru.

– Panowie, schowajcie się trochę. Chcecie zadusić papieża swoim odorem? – prosiłem, a patrzyłem głównie w kierunku Mariana Dziurowicza, który ledwie trzymał się na nogach.

Niestety, nie bardzo chcieli mnie słuchać, bo każdy chciał być jak najbliżej papieża i otrzymać błogosławieństwo. Teraz im się przypomniało! Szkoda, że parę godzin wcześniej błogosławili się nawzajem czystą!

Zawodnicy ustawili się w trzech rzędach, by papież mógł wszystkich dobrze widzieć. Kiedy wyszedł, pozdrowił nas. Jako trener reprezentacji przedstawiłem Ojcu Świętemu każdego z osobna, a na końcu siebie.

Po części oficjalnej przyszedł czas na rozmowy indywidualne z papieżem. Wyjąłem zdjęcie kadry, by mu je zaprezentować. Ni stąd, ni zowąd Ojciec Święty poprosił Stanisława Dziwisza o długopis i podpisał się na fotografii, dołączając życzenia. Nie miałem żadnej podkładki, więc Jan Paweł II położył mi fotografię na piersi i dopiero w taki sposób podpis.

– Jakie macie plany? Zostajecie jeszcze trochę w Rzymie? – zapytał mnie papież.

– Ojcze Święty, od razu po audiencji wsiadamy do autokaru i jedziemy na mecz z reprezentacją Włoch – wyjaśniłem.

– Powodzenia, koniecznie wygrajcie. I życzę sukcesu na igrzyskach olimpijskich – zakończył Jan Paweł II, po czym pobłogosławił ekipę. A my, kompletnie spontanicznie, odśpiewaliśmy mu polski hymn, co go ogromnie wzruszyło.

Mecz z Włochami zakończył się remisem, ale już na igrzyskach odnieśliśmy sukces. Czyli stało się tak, jak chciał Ojciec Święty.

NA IGRZYSKACH

Wreszcie nadszedł Wielki Dzień. Przylecieliśmy do Saragossy, gdzie mieliśmy stacjonować. Od razu było widać, że coś jest nie tak, bo z lotniska jechaliśmy pod eskortą policji, a wokół naszego hotelu było tyle radiowozów, jakby na naszą cześć ściągnęli funkcjonariuszy z całej Hiszpanii. Nawet budynki rządowe nie są tak chronione, jak był ten hotel!

Rozdzielono pokoje, ja z ulgą udałem się do swojego. Podchodzę do balkonu i widzę, że na dachu budynku naprzeciwko ktoś leży na dachu i celuje we mnie z karabinu! Padłem. Kiedy to zobaczył, podniósł się, a karabin miał już przy nodze. Patrzę, a ten skurwysyn do mnie macha! Ze strachem, ale też się podniosłem. Okazało się, że to nie żaden zamachowiec, ale jeden z ochroniarzy, mających zapewnić bezpieczeństwo uczestnikom igrzysk. O całym zdarzeniu opowiedziałem szefowi hotelu.

– Panie Wójcik, pan się nie boi, my nad wszystkim panujemy – uspokajał mnie.

– No wszystko fajnie, dziękuję, ale mogliście mi wcześniej o tym powiedzieć. Szkoda, że jeszcze do pokoju mi ten snajper nie wszedł! – odpowiedziałem.

Wsiedliśmy do autokaru, patrzę na zawodników, a oni nie mniej przestraszeni ode mnie. Pojazd był obstawiony z każdej strony, eskortowali nas policjanci na motocyklach w cywilu. Jedno ich łączyło – mieli takie czarne, nieduże plecaki. Jak się później okazało, trzymali w nich krótkie, szybko strzelające karabiny maszynowe. Poza tym cały czas leciał nad nami policyjny helikopter – krążył nad nami nawet podczas treningu! Z taką obstawą nie spotkałem się nigdy wcześniej i później.

Zawodnicy codziennie trenowali, więc nie mieli czasu na głupoty, nie piłowałem ich jednak cały czas. Kilka razy pozwoliłem im pójść na plażę, a także na basen, by trochę się popluskali. Zawsze okazywało się, że ci, którzy są z nami na tym basenie, to również policjanci! Nie mogli mieć spluw na wierzchu, ale siedzieli sobie dookoła, tacy smutni, z tymi swoimi plecaczkami. Ci dżentelmeni towarzyszyli nam dosłownie cały czas. Naprzeciwko hotelu była taka fajna kafejka, do której często chodziłem z Pawłem Janasem i innymi ludźmi ze sztabu szkoleniowego. Tam popijaliśmy kawkę albo hiszpańskie brandy. Kiedy tylko przekraczaliśmy próg, zaraz pojawiali się „turyści" z plecakami. Może i dobrze, że nas tak pilnowali – jeśli oczywiście były jakieś podstawy do obaw. W końcu wszędzie są jacyś „banditos"!

Warunki hotelowe mieliśmy bardzo dobre. Pokoiki były skromne, ale nam w zupełności wystarczały. Ja na przykład byłem razem z Pawłem Janasem. Piłkarze nie narzekali na nieklimatyzowane pokoje, zresztą wiedzieli doskonale, że przyjechali tutaj grać w piłkę, a nie pławić się w luksusach. Jedynymi, którym to nie pasowało, byli amerykańscy koszykarze ze słynnego Dream Teamu. Stwierdzili oni, że nie będą mieszkali w wiosce olimpijskiej, i zatrzymali się w innym hotelu. Poza tym mało kto wie, ale oni jako jedyni nie poddawali się badaniom antydopingowym. Zapowiedzieli, że jeśli ktoś będzie chciał to na nich wymusić, spakują się i opuszczą Hiszpanię. Oznacza to oczywiście, że koksowanie było tam nieprawdopodobne. Nikt jednak nie zamierzał im podpaść, bo przecież koszykówka bez Amerykanów straciłaby zainteresowanie kibiców.

Spaliśmy na trzecim piętrze w budynku w wiosce olimpijskiej. Śniadania zarządziłem o 9.30, nie chciałem chłopaków zrywać zbyt wcześnie. Wiedzieli też, że nie mogą za bardzo się najeść, bo będą zbyt ociężali na treningu. Ser, miód, dużo soków – to im było wolno.

– Tylko mi, kurwa, kiełbasy nie żreć! – zastrzegałem.

Pewnego razu jednak masażysta wraz z innym misiem nawalili sobie pełen talerz wędlin i innych niezbyt zdrowych rzeczy. Rozsierdziło mnie to strasznie.

– Kurwa, tak to sobie w domu kładź! Tutaj masz dawać chłopakom przykład! Wypierdalać z tym albo zabiorę wam te talerze i na łbach rozbiję! – zagroziłem, co oczywiście przyniosło pożądany skutek, bo panowie w popłochu odłożyli tłuste żarcie.

Na obiad jedli zwykle makaron, jakieś dobre kluski. Ale też kazałem im brać przykład z innych sportowców.

– Popatrzcie sobie na nich, popatrzcie, jak są zbudowani. To rekordziści świata, wielcy mistrzowie. Idźcie i nałóżcie sobie to samo co oni. Wpierdalajcie to w tych samych proporcjach! Czy oni żrą tak, żeby się od razu zesrać? Nie! Więc wy też miejcie umiar – radziłem moim misiaczkom.

Po obiedzie i między treningami mieli czas na odpoczynek. Niektórzy prosili o zgodę na wyjście na plażę.

– Dobra, tylko się nie opalać, bo potem będziecie zdychać. Popływajcie, odpocznijcie przed treningiem, bo dam wam ostro w pizdeczkę – zapowiadałem.

Potem oczywiście była kolacja, jakieś odprawy, na których mówiliśmy o rywalach. Mieli też czas wolny – chłopcy mogli spokojnie wyjść na dyskotekę, w której bawili się olimpijczycy. Zawsze wracali punktualnie.

O 22.00 wszyscy mieli być w pokojach. Nie musiałem tego sprawdzać, nie robiłem ani jednego obchodu – panowie dokładnie wiedzieli, co mają robić. Byli niczym oddział wojskowy, zdyscyplinowany i gotowy do ataku.

Najwięcej czasu spędzaliśmy oczywiście w wiosce olimpijskiej. To były takie trzy-, czteropiętrowe budynki, wystylizowane na hotel. Poza tym jakieś ścieżki spacerowe, kafejki (głównie można było napić się tam coca-coli), mnóstwo zieleni, kwiatów, palm. Na plażę, ku naszej radości, były dosłownie dwa kroki.

Z drużynami z innych krajów raczej nie mieliśmy kontaktów. Nie za bardzo zgadzałem się na to, bo nie chciałem, by moi piłkarze przy jakimś zgrzycie musieli kogoś znokautować. Za dziewczynami się jednak cały czas oglądali, bo spaślaków żadnych tam nie było. Najładniejsze były oczywiście te „beżowe". Za naszych chłopaków z kolei brały się...

polskie dżudoczki. Szczególnie potężna Beata Maksymow, która miała ciekawy sposób na łapanie kontaktu z piłkarzami. Otóż przygotowywała takie specjalne woreczki z wodą i czekała na nich na balkonie. Kiedy przechodzili, rzucała w nich tymi pociskami. Chłopaki wkurwiały się niesamowicie i szukały sposobów na rewanż. Wiedzieli, że z Beatą szarpać się nie mogą, bo jakby którymś pierdolnęła o ziemię, toby zakończył udział w igrzyskach. Ale na przykład jak przyniosła sobie do stolika jedzenie, to wystarczyła chwila nieuwagi, żeby jej to zapierdolili i gdzieś schowali. Innym razem oblali ją całym kubłem zimnej wody.

Moi piłkarze nie bardzo mieli czas, żeby wychodzić na imprezy. Oczywiście jak byliśmy już w Barcelonie, wybrali się na dyskotekę, taką zorganizowaną specjalnie dla olimpijczyków. Kontakty z dziewczynami mieli, ale raczej żadnego seksu, bo po prostu nie było gdzie. Na imprezy od czasu do czasu im zezwalałem, bo siedząc cięgiem przez prawie miesiąc w hotelu, po prostu dostaliby szajby. Kilka razy postanowiłem ich sprawdzić: wiedziałem, gdzie w mieście są te dyskoteki, więc zabierałem któregoś ze współpracowników i wychodziliśmy z wioski olimpijskiej. Od razu obok materializował się radiowóz. Szybko się z niebieskimi dogadałem i zamiast w taksówkę wsiadaliśmy w radiowóz właśnie, który dowoził nas na miejsce imprezy. Policjanci grzecznie czekali, aż opuścimy lokal. W samej dyskotece nie działo się nic budzącego niepokój, moi chłopcy byli grzeczni jak harcerze. Zresztą uważałem, że należy im się chwila wyluzowania, bo ciągle jechali na stresie. Ale szeptali między sobą cały czas. Dziwili się, jak ja sobie to załatwiłem, że zawsze czeka na mnie transport, tymczasem oni muszą sobie zorganizować powrót na własną rękę.

Nie miałem żadnych problemów z dyscypliną, ale inni polscy sportowcy nie byli już tak wzorowi. Na przykład bokser Dariusz Snarski, pseudonim „Snara" lub „Małpka". Wiąże się z nim niezła historia. W naszym sztabie zadzwonił telefon, a człowiek po drugiej stronie poinformował, że „Snara" trafił do... olimpijskiego aresztu! Zapytano, czy ktoś może przyjść i go odebrać. Zgłosiłem się na ochotnika. Poszło o to, że Snarski został oszukany w jednej z walk. Rozżalony wypił trochę za dużo brandy i zaczął rozrabiać, próbował walczyć na terenie wioski. Dali mu odpocząć w areszcie. Poszedłem po niego, spokojnie odprowadziłem do pokoju. Był mi potem bardzo wdzięczny, zresztą jest do dziś, i na pewno się nie obrazi, że wspominam tę historię.

A co do brandy: waliliśmy często i chętnie! Wiadomo, że nie można było doprowadzić się do stanu upodlenia, ale dwóch albo trzech szklaneczek sobie nie odmawialiśmy. Nie przesadzaliśmy zbytnio, ale członkowie innych ekip – jak najbardziej. Tacy Skandynawowie na przykład naprawdę ostro dawali w palnik. Raz o 8.00 rano zobaczyłem pod hotelem trzech kompletnie zdojonych gości. Leżeli obok siebie na chodniku idealnie równo, cholerne pedanciki. To, zdaje się, byli jacyś żeglarze, widać złapali dobre wiatry i popłynęli za daleko. W każdym razie pojawił się ktoś z obsługi, pobudził delikwentów i zaprowadził do hotelu.

Na igrzyskach zawsze rano, na naradzie, spotykaliśmy się z Kaziem Górskim. Schodziłem z nim do takiego pokoiku, gdzie siedzieli lekarze. Wyjmowaliśmy flaszeczkę i na dobre rozpoczęcie dnia piliśmy po kieliszeczku. Popijaliśmy to napojem Isostar – pięknie kopało! Zaciekawiło mnie raz, co jeden z lekarzy ma w takiej walizeczce, z którą się nie rozstawał. Otworzył ją, wysypały się jakieś papierki. Okazało się, że walizka była wypchana… prezerwatywami! Ważyło to z 30 kilo! Chodziło o to, żeby olimpijczycy, jak będą chcieli podymać, mieli zabezpieczenie.

– Panowie, to myśmy przyjechali tutaj na konkurs dymania czy grać w piłkę?! – zapytałem Kazia i lekarza.

– W piłkę pogramy tak czy siak, a dymanie rzecz ważna – odpowiedział Kazio.

Zresztą gdy zaglądaliśmy porankami na plażę, to cała zasypana była opakowaniami po kondomach. Okazało się, że wieczorami sportowcy schodzili na tę plażę i regularnie się dymali. Cóż, jak widać, dla chcącego nic trudnego. Po prostu barceloński burdel.

„Jestem tutaj, jestem na otwarciu igrzysk olimpijskich. Ja, Janusz Wójcik, dotarłem do pierdolonej Barcelony, więc możecie mnie w trąbę pocałować" – tak w duchu mówiłem do wszystkich, którzy we mnie i w moją drużynę nie wierzyli. A takich było sporo – niech za przykład posłuży informacja, że kondomy z PZPN-u zaplanowały start polskiej ligi jeszcze w trakcie igrzysk!

Nie było jednak tak, że ucieszyłem się samym wyjazdem do Barcelony. Nie należę do skromnych ludzi i od początku mówiłem, że jedziemy po medal. Wbijałem chłopakom do łbów, że mamy walczyć o najwyższe trofea.

Podczas ceremonii otwarcia szedłem w pierwszym szeregu, zaraz za chorążym. Panowała podniosła atmosfera, wszystkie ekipy zebrały się na środku stadionu. A na koniec był taki pokaz sztucznych ogni, że zdawało się, że stadion zaraz pierdolnie. Taki Pierwszy Maja, tylko do potęgi. W polskiej ekipie doszło do zgrzytu, bo miśki z PZPN-u, czyli Heniek Loska i Kazio Górski, bardzo pragnęły iść razem z defiladą sportowców, kiedy jednak się dowiedzieli, że ja będę w pierwszym rzędzie, to dosłownie chuj ich strzelał. Starym dziadom lansu się zachciało! Na szczęście przytomnie zareagował Piotr Nurowski, czyli ówczesny szef Komitetu Olimpijskiego, który kazał cwaniaczkom wypierdalać na trybuny – tam, gdzie ich miejsce!

Igrzyska otworzył król razem z szefem MKOL-u. Później nastąpiła wymiana pamiątek. Ja oddałem komuś swój kapelusz, a jakiemuś śniademu zabrałem myckę. Chodziłem w niej do końca ceremonii otwarcia. Na szczęście nie musiałem wracać w slipach, na oddaniu kapelusza się skończyło.

Piłkarze trzymali fason i twardo bratali się z zawodnikami z innych narodów. Udzieliłem im specjalnej dyspensy:

– Dziś możecie. Ale pamiętajcie, że od jutra będziecie musieli ich napierdalać! Nie będzie litości. I golimy frajerów!

No a potem przyszło najważniejsze, czyli mecze. Niedojdom z obecnej reprezentacji Polski mówię: czytajcie uważnie i płońcie ze wstydu.

To, co działo się w Barcelonie, przeszło do historii. I wy przejdziecie do historii, ale za sprawą własnej nieudolności.

– Panowie, kiełbasy do góry i golimy frajerów!

– Tak jest, panie trenerze!

Właśnie wtedy zacząłem używać tego słynnego już teraz zdania motywacyjnego. Zawodnikom to pomagało, a podczas igrzysk okazało się znakomitym kopem do walki.

Moje przygrywki na skrzypcach są wam doskonale znane. A piłkarze nauczyli się ich niemal na pamięć. Wiedzieli, że nie będzie tak, że otworzymy paszczę, żeby przyjąć kiełbasę. To oni mają nam zrobić dobrze! Do dziewczyn mówi się często po kilku głębszych: „Córa, zakisić ci ogóra?". No to ja to wykorzystywałem w dopingowaniu chłopaków.

– Chcecie, żebyśmy wam zakisili ogóry? – tak kazałem, żeby mówili do rywali. Nawet jeśli nie znali polskiego, to na pewno wiedzieli o co chodzi. A nasi kisili każdego.

Zaczęliśmy od meczu z Kuwejtem i nie było możliwości, żebyśmy go nie wygrali. Jedyną niewiadomą było to, ile razy będę podbiegał do linii i poganiał chłopaków, żeby dalej strzelali. Ale nic złego nie mogło się nam przydarzyć, mimo że graliśmy w temperaturze ponad 40 stopni. Raz tylko się wkurzyłem nie na żarty. W ostatniej minucie mieliśmy karnego, a do piłki wyrwał się Mirek Waligóra, choć nie był do tego wyznaczony. No i przestrzelił. Zawołałem go do siebie.

– Miruś, tak to możesz strzelać, ale z procy w wujka – grzmiałem, choć mecz już był rozstrzygnięty.

Ostatecznie wygraliśmy go 2:0 po dwóch trafieniach Józia.

Problemy miały zacząć się później. Kolejnym meczem grupowym było starcie z Włochami. Wiedzieliśmy, że ten, kto wygra to spotkanie, na pewno awansuje do fazy pucharowej. Włosi, mistrzowie Europy w tej kategorii wiekowej, wraz z Hiszpanami byli faworytami igrzysk, przymierzano ich do meczu finałowego. Ich trenerem był słynny Cesare Maldini. Grali pod ogromną presją.

Zdarzało się, że graliśmy w temperaturze ponad 40 stopni Celsjusza

Przed meczem powiedziałem chłopakom, że mają cały czas wywierać presję.

– Macie zawinąć im ten makaron na uszach i przejechać się po nich! Kiełbasy do góry i golimy ich!

Piłkarze wyszli więc na boisko tak naładowani, że od początku siedli na rywali. Szybko padł pierwszy gol dla nas, po atomowym strzale Juskowiaka. Józio tak kropnął, że włoski bramkarz tylko się schował, żeby mu łba nie urwało.

– Jedziemy z nimi dalej! – krzyczałem do chłopaków, a oni idealnie się do tego stosowali.

Włosi przez długie minuty nie wychodzili ze swojej połowy. Zaraz po przerwie walnęliśmy im kolejnego gola, a oni obalili się na murawę tak, jakby ich Tyson strzelił! Wkurzał mnie tylko Grzesiek Mielcarski, który zmarnował dwie setki.

– Grzesiek, kurwa, jeszcze raz nie trafisz, a wygonię cię z tego boiska! – darłem się na Mielcarskiego, co przyniosło skutek, bo chłopak się w końcu opamiętał i pod koniec strzelił gola na 3:0.

Jak ci Włosi płakali! Trenerzy i dziennikarze łapali się za głowę. Kazałem tłumaczowi, by im powiedział, że to najmniejszy wymiar kary, bo mogliśmy wygrać z 6:0. Kiedy ochłonęli, zaczęli nam gratulować.

W szatni zapanowała radość, ale też bez przesady, bo przed nami były kolejne mecze. Wyjście z grupy mieliśmy już pewne, ale nie myśleliśmy nawet o tym, że możemy przegrać najbliższe spotkanie z USA. Tym bardziej że jeśli zajęlibyśmy drugie miejsce w grupie, to w dalszej fazie trafilibyśmy na Hiszpanów, a tego chciałem uniknąć.

– Słuchajcie no, misie – zacząłem odprawę przedmeczową – jak przegracie, to całą noc będziecie za mną biegać. A ja będę jeździł rowerem.

Doskonale wiedzieli, jak to jest, bo już im się zdarzyło zasuwać za mną truchcikiem. Od Czesia Langa dostałem rower, kolarzówkę, więc wpadłem na pomysł, że będę na nim jeździł, a piłkarzom kazał biec za sobą. Tempo było szybkie, ale żaden nie zostawał w tyle – mojej reakcji się obawiali!

Zaczyna się więc ten mecz z USA, moi chłopcy zmotywowani, jakbyśmy już byli w finale, a tu dupa – 1:0 dla Amerykanów. Oczyma wyobraźni musieli dostrzec mnie pędzącego kolarzówką po ulicach Barcelony, więc szybko wzięli się do roboty. Zaraz gola strzelił Juskowiak, potem Koźmiński i prowadziliśmy 2:1. I mimo że Amerykanie wyrównali, nie narzekałem – wygraliśmy grupę i już wkrótce mieliśmy ogolić kolejnych frajerów.

W ćwierćfinale mieliśmy się zmierzyć z Katarem. Przerośnięte chłopy, na moje oko z przerobionymi dokumentami, poza limitem wiekowym. Wygraliśmy 2:0 po golach Kowala i Jałochy, ale mogliśmy spokojnie obić ich ze 4:0. Nie napierałem jednak na wyższe zwycięstwo – liczył się awans.

Przyszedł półfinał i zrobiło się naprawdę ciekawie. Następną drużyną, której mieliśmy skopać dupę, była Australia. Zapamiętałem, że do Barcelony jechaliśmy razem, autokar obok autokaru. Pewne siebie „Kangury" pokazywały nam na palcach, że rozwalą nas czwórką, piątką do zera. Myśleli, że jak wyeliminowali Szwedów, to siłą rozpędu rozjadą i nas. A takiego!

Sami zostali rozjechani – boleśnie i na miazgę. W 27. minucie Kowal przejął piłkę, wyszedł na sam na sam z bramkarzem, Bosnichem, położył go na tak zwaną dupę i strzelił tak, że biedny Bosnich ani się zorientował, a piłka już była w siatce. Chłopaki złapały wiatr w żagle i pod koniec pierwszej połowy Józio dołożył drugiego gola. „Kangury" miały pełne portki, aż żal było patrzeć. A tego Bosnicha to później kupił Manchester United i miał z nim siedem światów. Chyba byli tam ślepi – przecież od kopa dało się zauważyć, że to bezużyteczny pajac.

W przerwie przykazałem moim zawodnikom:

– Bez kombinowania, panowie, robicie to, co umiecie najlepiej, czyli szukacie kontry, a będziemy to mieli!

Wyszli na drugą połowę i pokazali, na co ich stać. To była poezja! Padały kolejne gole, jeden za drugim, a publiczność szalała. „Co – myślałem – nie spodziewaliście się, że moje chłopaki tak zatańczą? No

„Ja, Janusz Wójcik, dotarłem do pierdolonej Barcelony, więc możecie mnie w trąbę pocałować" – tak w duchu mówiłem do wszystkich, którzy we mnie i w moją drużynę nie wierzyli

Od Czesia Langa dostałem rower, więc wpadłem na pomysł, że będę na nim jeździł, a piłkarzom kazał biec za sobą. Tempo było szybkie, ale żaden nie zostawał w tyle – mojej reakcji się obawiali!

to patrzcie!" W sumie Józio strzelił trzy bramki, Kowal dwie, a jeden z tych nieszczęsnych Australijczyków dołożył swoim samobója.

– Dalej, jechać ich, pozarzynać! – kipiałem przy linii bocznej. – Nie dajcie im złapać oddechu!

Po ostatnim gwizdku Australijczycy, którzy mieli być rewelacją turnieju, pokładli się na murawie i z wściekłością walili pięściami w ziemię, a ich trener się popłakał. Gigant, który miał zdobyć złoto, padł. Jak kawka. Przegrał aż 1:6!

Nadszedł wielki dzień. Chwila prawdy. Godzina zero. Jednym słowem: finał. Wielkie Camp Nou, a na nim my naprzeciwko gospodarzy i faworytów – Hiszpanów. Na trybunach znakomici kibice – Fidel Castro, Silvio Berlusconi i inni. Zabrakło niestety prezydenta Lecha Wałęsy. Stwierdził, że istnieje ryzyko zamachu, że podobno ETA się na niego szykuje, no i nie przyjechał. Dziwnym trafem tylu gości zapowiedziało przyjazd na mecz, a terroryści szykowali się akurat na niego.

Ale przejdźmy do meczu. Powiedziałem chłopakom, że to Hiszpanie mają się bać nas, a nie my ich. – To nie obrona Częstochowy, ale przejmowanie piłki i szybkie kontry. Zrozumiano?

Na początku wszystko było tak, jak sobie zaplanowaliśmy. Kowalczyk zabawił się z Hiszpanami jak z młodymi kotami i strzelił gola na 1:0. Na przerwę schodziliśmy, prowadząc, co było wielką sensacją. Wkurzałem się, bo tuż za ławką ustawili się jacyś Hiszpanie z bębnami i dudnili mi przez cały mecz jak jakieś dzikusy. Nie dość, że głowa mnie rozbolała przez ten łomot, to na dodatek zagłuszali wszystko, co mówiłem do piłkarzy. A przecież musiałem mieć z nimi kontakt, tym bardziej że wiedziałem, że po przerwie będzie znacznie trudniej. W drugiej połowie miało zabraknąć Jałochy, który doznał kontuzji. Do tego przed gwizdkiem na trybunach pojawił się król Hiszpanii, co zawsze było prognostykiem tego, że drużyna się podniesie i wygra.

I rzeczywiście, podnieśli się. Abelardo i Quico błyskawicznie strzelili nam po golu i zrobiło się 1:2. Wtedy jednak błysnął Rysiu Staniek, który w fantastyczny sposób doprowadził do remisu. Mecz zbliżał się ku końcowi, a mnie wydawało się, że sędzia zaraz gwizdnie. Masażysta i kierownik pytali, czy mają iść już po wodę dla piłkarzy, żeby napili się przed dogrywką. Jak ja czekałem na tę dogrywkę! Czułem, że właśnie wtedy ogramy tych południowców, bo jesteśmy lepiej przygotowani fizycznie, a oni – zbyt pewni siebie.

Nie dostaliśmy jednak nowej szansy – doszło do tragedii! Sprawę zawalił Marek Koźmiński, który w prostej sytuacji zagrał na rzut rożny, zamiast wywalić piłkę przed siebie. Po rogu i zamieszaniu w polu karnym piłka trafiła do Quico, który strzelił gola. Jestem pewien, że gdyby chciał to powtórzyć, nie udałoby mu się.

To był koniec. Ostatni gwizdek. Chłopaki pokładały się na ziemi. Płakały. Wpadłem na boisko i zacząłem ich uspokajać, potem zgoniłem ich z murawy do szatni. Kiedy już trochę opanowali emocje, wrzucili mnie w garniturze do takiego minibasenu, który mieliśmy do dyspozycji. Wtedy wiedziałem, że już doszli do siebie.

– Teraz zdejmować gacie i wymoczyć się trochę – przykazałem. – Zaraz będziecie wzywani na dekorację.

W szatni odwiedził nas działacz FIFA Władimir Kołoskow, prominentna postać, i pogratulował nam fantastycznej walki w całym turnieju.

Kiedy potem przechadzałem się po korytarzach Camp Nou, widziałem, jak hiszpańscy piłkarze, jeden po drugim, wchodzą do stadionowej kaplicy. Zapewne dziękowali Bogu za cudownego gola, który dał im złoto olimpijskie.

Wieczorem udaliśmy się całą drużyną na bankiet do jednego z hoteli. Potem pojawiły się głosy, że moich zawodników trzeba było stamtąd wynosić. Bzdura! Było naprawdę spokojnie. Przecież oni jeszcze cały czas mieli w głowach to Camp Nou – ten gwar, tumult, tych ludzi na trybunach. Przecież przyszło ich obejrzeć 110 tysięcy kibiców! Na tym jednym finale było więcej widzów niż na każdej innej imprezie tych igrzysk! Oczywiście, na tym bankiecie chłopaki wypiły sobie trochę alkoholu, ale wszystko było pod kontrolą, bez żadnych ekscesów.

Zaraz po igrzyskach powstało słynne hasło: „Zmieniamy szyld i jedziemy dalej", czyli z reprezentacji olimpijskiej robimy pierwszą, co nie spodobało się w PZPN-ie. Nie bardzo wiem dlaczego, przecież to byli w tamtej chwili najlepsi polscy piłkarze. Tak to się robi za granicą, a u nas uważa się za jakiś zamach stanu. Mówili, że to bezczelność, że próba przejęcia reprezentacji Polski. Chłopcy zobaczyli jednak, że potrafią grać w piłkę, doceniali ich także piłkarze z pierwszej reprezentacji. Normalnym krokiem byłoby więc przemianowanie kadry olimpijskiej na narodową. Wiele razy próbowałem zorganizować mecz: olimpijska kontra pierwsza, ale nikt się na to nie godził. Nawet zawodnicy z kadry A.

– Trenerze, nie chcemy grać – mówili z obawą. – Przecież te pana harpagany by nas zjadły, zajechały na śmierć.

Nie ma co płakać nad rozlanym mlekiem, w każdym razie igrzyska olimpijskie w Barcelonie to z pewnością mój największy sportowy sukces. O podobnym teraz możemy pomarzyć. Niektórzy piłkarze grający obecnie w reprezentacji mogą co najwyżej kartofle kopać, a nie piłkę na wysokim poziomie. Nawet nie chcę porównywać mojej reprezentacji olimpijskiej do obecnej kadry. Przecież moi chłopcy by ich zmietli z powierzchni ziemi. Przeważali pod każdym względem: fizycznym, technicznym, zespołowym. Ogoliliby ich bez żadnego problemu, a tamci nawet nie wiedzieliby, kiedy mieliby parówy pozasadzane w dupy. To byłaby przepaść. Moja drużyna olimpijska była naprawdę wielka.

MOJA SREBRNA DRUŻYNA

Nie byłoby mowy o żadnym sukcesie, gdyby nie grupa fantastycznych ludzi, z którymi pracowało mi się wspaniale. Mam na myśli moich chłopaków, tych wspaniałych zawodników, z którymi miałem zaszczyt współdziałać i którzy zrobili dla polskiej piłki więcej niż niejeden za-

Igrzyska olimpijskie w Barcelonie to z pewnością mój największy sportowy sukces. O podobnym teraz możemy pomarzyć

Po finale udaliśmy się całą drużyną na bankiet do jednego z hoteli. Potem pojawiły się głosy, że moich zawodników trzeba było stamtąd wynosić. Bzdura! Było naprawdę spokojnie

służony działacz. Chcę podziękować każdemu z osobna, a wam trochę o nich opowiedzieć. Dowiecie się, jacy byli i na boisku, i prywatnie.

DARIUSZ ADAMCZUK

Drużynie olimpijskiej zawdzięcza bardzo wiele – to dzięki występom w tej ekipie zwrócono na niego uwagę za granicą. Pamiętam, że już kiedy przygotowywaliśmy się do meczów w Niemczech, zachodni sąsiedzi dostrzegali w nim dobrego piłkarza. To człowiek niezwykle ambitny, miły, ale też bardzo agresywny w grze. Można było na niego stawiać wszystko, co się miało – bardzo jasna postać reprezentacji. Absolutnie nie był typem rozrabiaki, nie miałem z nim żadnych kłopotów. Na boisku wypracowywał mnóstwo korzystnych dla drużyny sytuacji, sam także strzelał wiele goli. Mimo wszystko uważam, że mógł osiągnąć o wiele więcej. Wówczas nie było żadnych menedżerów, którzy by poprowadzili takich zdolnych piłkarzy, no i Adamczuk poniekąd poszedł na zmarnowanie.

MAREK BAJOR

To chłopak, który kiedy pierwszy raz przyjechał na trening reprezentacji, był totalnie wystraszony. Zagadnąłem o niego kierownika drużyny, Krzysztofa Rolę-Wawrzeckiego.

– Krzysiu, co on ma za buty? – zapytałem zdziwiony.

I Krzysiu wzruszył ramionami:

– Trampkokołki.

– Ale jak to? Nie ma chłop normalnych butów?

– Marek ma tak złą sytuację finansową, że nie ma pieniędzy, żeby je kupić – wyjaśnił Wawrzecki.

Aż się we mnie zagotowało.

– Natychmiast weź od niego numer buta i leć mu po jakieś! Nie będzie chłopak w korkach chodził po hotelu!

Bajora zrobiło mi się zwyczajnie żal. Trzeba było mu przecież jakoś pomóc.

Dla niego reprezentacja była jak bajka, cieszył się z niej jak dziecko. Wyrósł na zawodnika, który dałby się pokroić za tę drużynę. Był to człowiek twardy, ale i dobrze wychowany, absolutnie nie można go było nazwać rozpieszczonym. Nigdy nie miałem do niego żadnych zastrzeżeń.

JERZY BRZĘCZEK

Wołaliśmy na niego Brzękol. Kreowałem go na kapitana drużyny ze względu na charakter i sumienne podejście do pracy. Dał się poznać jako chłopak inteligentny, uczynny, oddany drużynie. Wszyscy błyskawicznie zaakceptowali go jako boiskowego i pozaboiskowego przywódcę – i to pomimo tego niewysokiego wzrostu. Dlaczego mu się nie udało, dlaczego nie zrobił wielkiej kariery? Bo nikt go nie promował, bo nie miał prężnego menedżera. Nikt go wtedy nie wyhaczył, a on sam nie miał siły przebicia, może charakteru. Nie strzelał gola za golem, więc nie czytało się o nim na pierwszych stronach gazet. Ludzie dziwili się, że powołuję Brzęczka do reprezentacji. A przecież to był bardzo pożyteczny zawodnik środka pola, zarówno jeśli chodzi o odbiór, jak i o konstrukcję gry. Idealny gość od czarnej roboty na boisku. Nie za wysoki, trochę karzełek, ale mocno trzymał się na nogach. Doskonale wiedział, od czego jest. Pełnił funkcję mojej prawej ręki. Inni byli od walenia po łbie, a on od myślenia. Na co dzień raczej spokojny, ale kiedy padała komenda, że idziemy na browarek, to karnie szedł i pił równo z pozostałymi. Cieszy, że bardzo pomógł w karierze Kubie Błaszczykowskiemu, którego jest wujkiem. Fajnie, że tak się angażował w wychowanie tego piłkarza, bo wyrósł z niego bardzo porządny chłopak.

DARIUSZ GĘSIOR

Gąska to wyjątkowo spokojny człowiek i w rozwoju talentu przeszkodziło mu jedno – właśnie ten brak agresji w grze. Czasami potrafił zagrać ostro, ale nie było to jego stałą cechą. Chłopaki z kadry za nim przepadały. Pomimo pokaźnego wzrostu nie wywyższał się.

MARCIN JAŁOCHA

Ważne ogniwo drużyny – mógł grać zarówno na prawej, jak i na lewej stronie, a także jako defensywny pomocnik. Przeciwnik nie do przejścia. Zabrakło go w drugiej połowie finału, ponieważ nabawił się kontuzji. Nie był łatwy w kontakcie, ale szybko się dogadaliśmy. Miał taki trochę krakowski charakter, nie dawał sobie w kaszę dmuchać. Ograć Marcina w środku pola było naprawdę wielką sztuką, prawie niemożliwą nawet dla takich zawodników jak Luis Enrique. W dużej mierze taktyka zespołu była budowana właśnie pod niego.

ANDRZEJ JUSKOWIAK

W kadrze miał różne momenty. Zdarzało się, że odsyłałem go do Poznania, gdzie wówczas grał, bo czymś mi podpadał. Kiedyś pogoniłem go, bo myślał, że w reprezentacji będzie mógł robić takie same figle jak w Lechu. Jak mu się chciało, to biegał, jak nie – to brał się pod boki i sobie stał. Uważał, że jeśli pójdzie na miasto, to może sobie wrócić, o której mu się podoba. Indywidualista za dychę.

– Józiu, albo się zmienisz, albo niestety, ale wypierdalasz – dałem mu wybór.

On jednak najwyraźniej zapomniał o tej rozmowie, bo dalej robił swoje.

– Dobra. Pakuj się i wydupiaj do Poznania. A jak ci się we łbie poukłada, to zadzwoń i wrócimy do rozmowy – stwierdziłem.

I rzeczywiście. Za jakiś czas dostałem sygnał z Lecha, że Józio zmienił się nie do poznania. Jurek Brzęczek przyszedł i powiedział, że Juskowiak chce ze mną porozmawiać.

– Ty z nim gadaj, ja go pierdolę – uciąłem.

Brzęczek, jako kapitan, porozmawiał z Andrzejem, a ten zarzekał się, że się zmienił, i błagał o wybaczenie. Obiecał, że jeśli przyjmę go do drużyny, to się podporządkuje. Jurek długo mnie przekonywał, żebym zmienił zdanie i pozwolił mu wrócić do kadry. W końcu się zgodziłem:

– Niech przyjeżdża. Tylko koniec, kurwa, numerów!

Dawałem mu kolejne szanse, a on je wykorzystywał. Nie można więc powiedzieć, że był odporny na wiedzę. Przełknął wszystkie gorzkie pigułki i zaczął robić to, czego od niego wymagałem. Był o krok od zrobienia wielkiej kariery. Widocznie zabrakło mu szczęścia, bo spokojnie mógł grać w wielkim klubie za wielkie pieniądze.

Dziwiłem się matołkom z zachodnich klubów, że nie kupili pary Juskowiak – Kowalczyk! Dla bogatego klubu to pierdnięcie finansowe, a zyskaliby parę napastników na lata. To byli wówczas najgroźniejsi napastnicy na świecie, taki Alan Shearer był ich cieniem. Mogli go przeciągnąć nitką przez kakao i wyciągnąć nosem. Dosłownie!

Juskowiak mógł więc grać w każdym klubie europejskim – włoskim, hiszpańskim, nawet w lidze angielskiej by się sprawdził, bo był z niego zdrowy cham. Popełnił jednak błąd i już przed igrzyskami podpisał kontrakt ze Sportingiem Lizbona. Po tak fantastycznym występie na turnieju w Barcelonie mógł trafić jeszcze lepiej, za znacznie większe pieniądze.

ALEKSANDER KŁAK

Nieprawdopodobny charakter. Twardziel, człowiek, na którego ja i inni członkowie ekipy mogliśmy liczyć w każdej sytuacji. Oddany drużynie całym sercem.

To był w tamtym okresie najlepszy bramkarz w Polsce, a na linii jeden z najlepszych w Europie. Powinien zrobić zdecydowanie większą karierę. Gdybym po igrzyskach objął pierwszą reprezentację, stawiałbym właśnie na niego. Poza boiskiem skromny i cichy, za to na murawie – ogień.

Fakt, że nie odniósł sukcesu, to wina ludzi rządzących polskim futbolem. Ten piłkarz nie został odpowiednio poprowadzony, wypromowany, nikt mu nie podał ręki. Przeszkodziła mu kontuzja, bo w Belgii uszkodził sobie bark. Tylko dzięki wielkiej zaciętości wrócił do piłki, ale nie zdołał niestety dostać się do świata wielkiego futbolu.

ANDRZEJ KOBYLAŃSKI

– Panowie, wymienię wam nazwisko zawodnika, którego powołam na igrzyska, i mogę się założyć, że nie będziecie wiedzieli, gdzie on gra – powiedziałem pewnego razu Andrzejowi Zientarze i Ryszardowi Kuleszy. – I to mimo że szefujecie komisji młodzieżowej.

– No co to za piłkarz? – zapytali z zainteresowaniem.

– Andrzej Kobylański.

Oczywiście obaj zrobili wielkie oczy i nie byli w stanie wymyślić klubu, w którym grał Andrzej (Siarka Tarnobrzeg).

Znakomita lewa noga. Charakterny, ale zamknięty w sobie. Nie chciał się wyróżniać poza boiskiem, ale na nim – jak najbardziej. Największa niespodzianka w moim zespole. Wspominam go ogromnie ciepło.

DARIUSZ KOSEŁA

Zapowiadał się ciekawie. Dobry zawodnik, jeśli chodzi o rozegranie piłki, choć na boisku był trochę za spokojny. Nie znalazł u mnie więc zbyt wielkiego uznania. W każdej chwili był jednak gotowy, by wejść na murawę, i za to go ceniłem.

WOJCIECH KOWALCZYK

Ach, ten Wojtuś! Łączyła nas szczególna nić sympatii. Na pewno nie był człowiekiem łatwym w obyciu, wręcz przeciwnie. Mimo to znakomicie się rozumieliśmy, wystarczyło, żebyśmy się na siebie spojrzeli. Nie musiałem przeprowadzać z nim tak zwanych rozmów wychowawczych czy tym bardziej karać. Choć przyznaję, zawsze wolałem łobuziaków od lalusiów – takich szybciej można poukładać. I w olimpijskiej, i w Legii, i w pierwszej reprezentacji piłkarze śmiali się z Wojtka, z tych naszych bliskich relacji. Kiedy przychodziłem na trening, koledzy krzyczeli w jego kierunku: „Kowal, popatrz, tatuś przyjechał!". Ale nie było tak, że traktowałem go lepiej niż innych. Jedno jest pewne: z takimi zawodnikami jak on można przenosić góry!

MAREK KOŹMIŃSKI

Pierwszy raz spotkałem go, kiedy miał jakieś 13 lat. Znałem jego ojca, Zbyszka, i odwiedziłem go kiedyś w domu w Nowej Hucie. Żona zrobiła kolację, wypiliśmy po parę kieliszeczków. Nagle przyleciał Marek, jeszcze mały kajtek.

– Grasz w piłkę? – zahaczyłem młodego.

– Taaak, panie trenerze. W grupie juniorów starszych!

– Dobrze, dobrze.

– A lekcje odrobiłeś?! – wtrącił się Zbyszek, chcąc pogonić synka od stołu.

– Tato, zaraz odrobię, obiecuję. – Mareczek aż się spocił, tłumacząc się ojcu.

– Zbychu, zostaw dzieciaka w spokoju. A ty, Marek, słuchaj i zapamiętaj, co ci powiem: graj dobrze w piłkę, a jak przy okazji będziesz miał czas, to się trochę poucz. Kiedy zostaniesz gwiazdą futbolu, nie będziesz musiał być naukowcem.

Tak też się stało. Na boisku zawsze można było na niego postawić. Silny jak koń, wyróżniał się w każdym meczu, grał bardzo nowocześnie jak na tamte czasy. Biegał od jednej linii końcowej do drugiej i tym zabijaliśmy rywali. Poza boiskiem był spokojny i wyważony, a na murawie widać było, że liczy się dla niego tylko mecz. Prezentował przykład poważnego, bardzo solidnego podejścia do dziedziny, która tak naprawdę jest zabawą, ale która wymaga pełnego zaangażowania, jeżeli chce się w niej osiągnąć coś więcej. Życzyłbym sobie więcej takich zawodników.

TOMASZ ŁAPIŃSKI

Był duszą tej drużyny, bez dwóch zdań. Nieprawdopodobnie nie lubił latać samolotami, kiedy jednak ja go poprosiłem, zaciskał zęby i leciał. W szatni czasami miał momenty omdlenia, bo przypominało mu się, jak siedział na pokładzie... Kiedyś, już w pierwszej reprezentacji, mieliśmy grać mecz ze Słowacją i szykowaliśmy się do lotu do Bratysławy.

– Trenerze, ja nie polecę – zapowiedział.

– Łapa, nie denerwuj mnie. Wsiadaj do tego samolotu.

– Dojadę samochodem, będę godzinę po was. Proszę mi tylko podać nazwę hotelu.

Jak powiedział, tak zrobił. Nie dziwiłem się jednak do końca Łapińskiemu, bo niewiele wcześniej przeżyliśmy trudne chwile podczas lotu z Paragwaju do Chile. Samolot spadł o kilkaset metrów i cudem nie rozbił się o skały. Od tego czasu Łapa miał uraz związany z lataniem. Jako zawodnik mógł stać się filarem defensywy każdego zespołu. W tamtym czasie był na swojej pozycji w czołowej trójce Europy. Miał niebywałą umiejętność przewidywania tego, co wydarzy się na boisku, a także kapitalny start do piłki i niebywałą szybkość na kilku pierwszych metrach biegu. Potrafił prześcignąć wszystkich napastników, z którymi się mierzył – nieważne, czy to byli Anglicy, czy Włosi, wystarczyło, żeby zrobił kilka ruchów, a już był przy piłce. Obrońca praktycznie nie do przejścia, natomiast poza boiskiem cichutki. Co ciekawe, pochodzi z takiej wioski na Podlasiu, która nazywa się Łapy, bo tam wszyscy są Łapińscy. Mógłbym o nim mówić jeszcze długo. Wspaniały chłopak i wielki zawodnik.

GRZEGORZ MIELCARSKI

Typ wojownika. Duży chłop, który szukał wyzwań. Kiedy trzeba było komuś przywalić, to był gotowy. Zawsze pomocny i na boisku, i poza nim. Nigdy nie miałem z nim problemów wychowawczych, był spokojny, lubił też pożartować.

Pogodził się z rolą rezerwowego. Nie było tak, że ktoś mi przyniósł deser i potem grał w meczu. Na boisko wychodzili najlepsi, bezwzględnie.

ARKADIUSZ ONYSZKO

Zastępca Alka Kłaka. Twardziel. Wygrał rywalizację z Radkiem Majdanem. Charakterny gość, podobny w pewnym sensie właśnie do Kłaka. Miał bardzo dobre serce. Po meczach lubił się zabawić – nie zabraniałem mu, dopóki nie przekraczał granic, a to mu się raczej nie zdarzało.

A że potem coś się z nim działo, że podobno bił żonę? Nie moja sprawa. A poza tym ponoć każdy bramkarz ma nierówno pod kopułą.

RYSZARD STANIEK

Niedoceniony, a obdarzony nieprawdopodobnym talentem. Powinien był zrobić wielką karierę. Miał wszystko, co trzeba: odbiór, świetną grę głową, grę kombinacyjną. Poza boiskiem cichy, skryty, nawet trochę zamknięty w sobie, za to na murawie – petarda. Mogłem go wykorzystywać do najrozmaitszych zadań. Problemów nie sprawiał, chociaż piwka lubił się napić, ale zawsze po meczu.

Często wypomina mu się rzekomą nadwagę. Na igrzyskach nie był jednak za gruby, ważył tyle, ile trzeba. Później, kiedy nasze drogi się rozeszły, trochę mu się przytyło, pewnie przez piwko i nieodpowiedni trening, ale na boisku zawsze był twardy jak skała. Zderzyć się z nim na boisku, to jakby przypierdolić w słonia. Leciał, leciał i nie wiedział, kiedy wyląduje. Nie ustępował nikomu w środku pola. Uważam, że również jego kariera nie potoczyła się tak, jakby sobie tego życzył. Było go stać na więcej.

DARIUSZ SZUBERT

Znów: piłkarsko bardzo dobry, ale niespełniony talent. Lubił nocne rozrywki i chyba to mu zaszkodziło w zrobieniu większej kariery. Och, jak on uwielbiał panienki!

PIOTR ŚWIERCZEWSKI

Kolejny wojownik. Z nim miałem trochę problemów, musiałem mu tłumaczyć, na czym polega gra w reprezentacji. Prostowałem go przez kilka lat, ale w końcu mi się udało. Zmienił się, dojrzał i stał się podporą drużyny. Również był bardzo uniwersalny, mógł grać z prawej, z lewej, w środku. Bardzo dobry w destrukcji i trudny do przejścia ze względu na swoją ambicję i charakter. Był krnąbrny, lubił czasem coś odburknąć pod nosem. Szybko sprowadzaliśmy go jednak z kosmosu na ziemię, czasem miał twarde lądowanie. Kiedyś mnie mocno wkurzył, jeszcze w reprezentacji do lat 18. Pojechaliśmy grać mecz do Szkocji. W hotelu kierownik rozdawał klucze do pokojów, a Świerszczu jak zwykle zaczął filozofować – nie podobało mu się to, nie podobało tamto…

– Trenerze, Świerszczu opowiada jakieś dyrdymały, nie chce iść do pokoju – relacjonował kierownik, a ja szybko zawołałem szalonego Piotrusia do siebie.

– Świerszczu, albo weźmiesz te klucze i zaraz będziesz spierdalał mi sprzed oczu, albo tu przed recepcją dostaniesz ode mnie kopa i pójdziesz jeszcze szybciej. Wybieraj, co chcesz!

Nadąsał się niewiarygodnie, ale z bólem wziął ten klucz i poszedł do pokoju. Na drugi dzień jednak grał bardzo dobrze i byłem z niego zadowolony.

MIROSŁAW WALIGÓRA

Typowy krakusik. Skryty, spokojny, na pewno nie wybuchowy, jak Świerczewski. Czasem wydawał się za grzeczny, może dlatego nie zrobił większej kariery. Gdybym wcześniej miał go w drużynach juniorskich, mógłbym go wyszkolić na lepszego piłkarza. Zwykle mi nie podpadał, raz tylko dostał zjebę za niestrzelonego karnego, o czym już wspominałem. Dobiegłem do linii, Miruś usłyszał kilka jobów i tyle. Dobrze mi się z nim pracowało.

TOMASZ WAŁDOCH

Był członkiem grupy specjalnej, która miała wyjaśniać kwestie sporne. Przydzieliłem go do niej ze względu na wzrost, posturę, ale także umiejętności czysto piłkarskie. Nie był to wariat; typ raczej spokojny, ale na boisku bardzo konsekwentny. Dlatego można było mu zaufać w stu procentach. Zrobił karierę, choć mógł zrobić jeszcze większą. Bardzo ważne ogniwo naszego zespołu.

TOMASZ WIESZCZYCKI

Jako piłkarz miał prawie wszystko, jednego mu jednak zabrakło – charakteru. Nie był twardzielem jak Kowal, Świerczewski, Jałocha czy

Brzęczek. Nie był to też Messi, który mógł ograć pięciu, ośmiu rywali. Pomimo dobrego wyszkolenia technicznego miał różne braki. Tłumaczyłem mu to, ale nie potrafił się przełamać. W związku z tym nie pograł u mnie za wiele.

Taki obrazek w Barcelonie wcale nie był rzadki. Mecz po meczu, runda po rundzie, aż do finału…

KARIERA PIŁKARSKA I PODRÓŻE
1967–1980

W tamtych czasach wszyscy zaczynali przygodę z piłką od gry na podwórku. Pierwszym moim klubem, w którym grałem jako trampkarz, była Gwardia Warszawa. Z tym że tam nieładnie się zachowywałem i musiałem zrobić sobie małą przerwę. Co zrobiłem? Napyskowałem trenerowi i pobiłem jakiegoś kolegę, więc musiało się to tak skończyć.

Później trafiłem do Agrykoli, a następnie do młodzieżowej reprezentacji Warszawy. Doceniali mnie, bo grałem na całej długości boiska. Byłem twardy, zdecydowany i nie pozwalałem, by ktokolwiek spuścił mi łomot. Niestety, odniosłem w tym czasie liczne kontuzje, w tym uraz łąkotki, które przeszkodziły mi w zrobieniu kariery piłkarskiej.

Po jakimś czasie na szczęście udało mi się wrócić do Gwardii; miałem wtedy niecałe 18 lat. Przeżyłem tam mnóstwo fantastycznych chwil. Funkcję głównego trenera pełnił świętej pamięci Ryszard Koncewicz. Pierwszym meczem, na który mnie wystawiono, był pojedynek z ŁKS-em Łódź. Kazano mi kryć niezwykle groźnego zawodnika, niejakiego Sadka, wielokrotnego reprezentanta kraju. Uprzykrzałem mu życie w najrozmaitszy sposób. O, a innym razem wkurzyłem nawet Włodka Lubańskiego! Graliśmy mecz z reprezentacją Polski, która przygotowywała się do jakiegoś ważnego spotkania, i miałem kryć właśnie jego. Tak go wymęczyłem, że kiedy w przerwie podszedł do naszej ławki, aż kipiał z wściekłości.

– Panie trenerze – zwrócił się do Koncewicza. – Kto to jest? Czy może go pan trochę uspokoić? Przecież ja mam przed sobą jeszcze ważny mecz o punkty! Ja rozumiem, że młody, ambitny, ale niech się trochę opanuje!

Oczywiście usłyszałem te słowa. Ograniczałem się potem, nie faulowałem przesadnie ostro, ale wcale łatwiej ze mną nie miał.

Innym znowu razem graliśmy z reprezentacją NRD, która też szykowała się do ważnych spotkań. Mecz odbywał się w Poczdamie. Kryłem na przemian Joachima Streicha i Eberharda Vogla, czyli wielkie gwiazdy tej reprezentacji. Dochodziło do spięć, dostałem nawet żółtą kartkę za faul na Voglu. A później, kiedy raz po raz poniewierałem Streicha, wzbudziłem prawdziwą wściekłość niemieckich kibiców. Chcieli przeskoczyć przez siatkę okalającą boisko i mnie zlinczować – dosłownie! Śmiałem im się w twarz.

Po przygodzie z Gwardią grałem w Ursusie, a potem króciutko w Zagłębiu Sosnowiec, wspólnie z Władkiem Grotyńskim z Warszawy. Mojej gry nie można jednak nazwać karierą, bo już wówczas dokuczały mi kontuzjowane kolana. W końcu dotarło do mnie, że wielkiej kariery to ja nie zrobię.

Trafiła mi się też fajna przygoda piłkarska – grałem bowiem w Pakistanie, w zespole Rawalpindi. Pojechałem tam… ożenić się. Moja ówczesna narzeczona, Wisława Janas, przez wiele lat związana była potem z PZPN-em. Jej rodzice pracowali w Islamabadzie na placówce dyplomatycznej. Spytali, czy ślub nie mógłby się odbyć właśnie tam, a ja oczywiście na to przystałem.

Ślubu udzielał nam sam ambasador. Ależ była uroczystość! Nie to co u nas, czyli kicz i bieda. Wszystko w przepięknych kolorach, ślicznych kwiatach… Później bawiliśmy się w ogrodach ambasady.

Ożenek ożenkiem, ale trzeba było coś robić. Grałem więc sobie w miejscowym, wojskowym klubie. Pakistańczycy raczej bawili się piłką, trudno było zresztą normalnie grać, skoro temperatura dochodziła

PAKISTAN

do 50 stopni Celsjusza. Biegaliśmy po piachu, wzniecając mnóstwo pyłu, którym można było się udusić. Stadiony były tam nieduże, takie na dwa–trzy tysiące kibiców. Miejscowi notable siedzieli pod daszkiem, a reszta prażyła się na słońcu jak skwarki.

Inną korzyścią związaną z wyjazdem do Pakistanu była dla mnie możliwość zebrania materiałów do pracy magisterskiej z dziedziny antropologii. Moje pomiary, cóż, polegały na badaniu młodzieńców nago. A wiadomo, jakim problemem dla muzułmanów jest obnażanie się przed obcymi. Podczas jednej z takich sesji nagle dopadło do mnie dwóch gości. Ręce trzymali pod tymi swoimi sukienkami, więc oczyma wyobraźni widziałem, jak wyciągają broń i wymierzają mi sprawiedliwość. Nic takiego na szczęście się nie stało, mieli jednak pretensje, że obnażam ich dzieci. Na szczęście dyrektor szkoły załagodził sprawę.

Wróćmy do początku – muszę przecież opowiedzieć, w jaki sposób w ogóle dotarłem na ten Daleki Wschód. Otóż najpierw, przez Taszkent, poleciałem do Kabulu, stolicy Afganistanu. Sytuacja była akurat bardzo napięta, bo tego samego dnia do Kabulu wkroczyły wojska rosyjskie. Zaraz po wylądowaniu wszyscy zostali wyprowadzeni z samolotu i skierowani do sali lotniskowej. Usłyszeliśmy jakże filmową komendę „ręce do góry", a potem w mało uprzejmy sposób zażądano od nas okazania paszportów. Ja miałem oczywiście to szczęście, że posiadałem paszport kraju będącego sojusznikiem ZSRR, po krótkiej chwili mogłem więc opuścić ręce i puszczono mnie wolno. Polski konsul już na mnie czekał. Wyjechaliśmy z lotniska. Po drodze widziałem mnóstwo trupów – mężczyzn, kobiet, dzieci. Zmasakrowane zwłoki leżały wszędzie, na poboczach, czasem na drodze. Makabra i prawdziwie wstrząsające doświadczenie. To wtedy po raz pierwszy w sposób bezpośredni i namacalny zetknąłem się z wojną.

W Kabulu zostałem na trzy noce. Spałem na podłodze, bo cały czas trwała strzelanina. Podnosząc się, można było przypadkowo dostać kulkę, nie wiedząc nawet z której strony. Nie ukrywam, że aby w ogóle zasnąć, wieczorami wypijałem po kropelce whisky.

Jednego dnia wraz z konsulem udaliśmy się do ambasadora Czechosłowacji. Było późno, na pewno trwała już godzina policyjna. Mieliśmy oczywiście specjalną flagę na samochodzie, ale jak wiadomo, kawałek chorągiewki przed śrutem chroni umiarkowanie skutecznie. Proszono nas nawet, żebyśmy poczekali do rana, ale poczuliśmy się na tyle odważni, że postanowiliśmy podjąć ryzyko. Witaj, przygodo! Jedziemy więc sobie spokojnie, kiedy nagle na drodze przed nami wyrasta tak zwany wojskowy szperacz, czyli wielki reflektor o średnicy około półtora metra. Najdrożsi radzieccy „towarzysze" wpatrywali się w nas podejrzliwie i całe szczęście, że zauważyli flagę, bo pewnie otworzyliby ogień. Podjechali. Trzymali naładowane, gotowe do strzału karabiny. Sprawdzili nasze dokumenty, coś pomruczeli, a potem… odstawili nas do ambasady. Przyjaźń polsko-radziecka nigdy nie wydawała mi się tak piękna jak wtedy!

Mimo licznych niebezpieczeństw jakoś mnie potem jeszcze ciągnęło do Kabulu i wracałem tam kilka razy – głównie w celach zakupowych, bo można tam było znaleźć bardzo fajne rzeczy. – Lubiłem tam kupować starą broń, rzeczy ze srebra, można było dostać tanie kożuchy. Tylko trzeba było zwiać się o 18.00, bo jak zapadał zmrok, zaczynała się regularna strzelanina.

Raz podczas takiej podróży widziałem coś, co normalnym ludziom nie pomieściłoby się w głowie. Jedziemy sobie z konsulem, kiedy nagle widzę, jak stojący kilkaset metrów dalej pastuch, opierając się o osła, wykonuje dziwne ruchy, podobne do kopulacyjnych. Podjechaliśmy i potwierdziło się – obrzydliwy pastuch dymał osiołka! Konsul wyjaśnił mi, że to częste w tym kraju, bo biedni ludzie nie mogą sobie pozwolić na zakup żony. A że mają swoje potrzeby, to czasami wyładowują je na zwierzętach. Ów pastuch był bardzo zadowolony i nawet strzał w powietrze, który oddaliśmy, nie odgonił go od osiołka.

– Dymaj na zdrowie! – zawołałem po polsku i pojechaliśmy dalej.

Po tych trzech dniach w Kabulu ruszyliśmy na granicę afgańsko--pakistańską. Tam miał czekać na mnie samochód, którym miałem się udać do Islamabadu. Konsul cały czas miał przy sobie broń. Jechaliśmy przez Himalaje, bardzo wąską, dość niebezpieczną drogą: po jednej stronie skały, po drugiej przepaść. Powiedziano mi, że jeszcze przed wojną grasowały tam bandy, które napadały na podróżnych. Ludzie byli zarzynani, okradani z cennych przedmiotów, a samochody ze zwłokami spychano w dół.

Udało nam się na szczęście takich ludzi nie spotkać, ale za to już na samej granicy czekała na nas pewna ciekawostka. Stał tam mianowicie Rosjanin z karabinem na... sznurku. Na szczęście nie palił się specjalnie do strzelaniny, więc po prostu spokojnie przejechaliśmy. W samochodzie po drugiej stronie czekał człowiek z polskiej ambasady, który zabrał mnie do Islamabadu.

Kiedy już zadomowiłem się w Pakistanie, przekonałem się, że wcale nie jest tam szczególnie bezpiecznie. Pewnego razu odwiedziłem Alego Bhutto, ówczesnego premiera. Wówczas w kraju rozpoczynały się zamieszki. Do wspaniałej willi, do której zaprosił mnie brat premiera, wpadło dwóch misiów, którzy nie wyglądali na pokojowo nastawionych. Gospodarz pomacał się po klapie marynarki, sprawdzając tylko, czy broń jest na swoim miejscu. Przeprosił mnie i zaczął nalegać, byśmy czym prędzej zakończyli rozmowę. Wyprowadzono mnie bardzo kulturalnie i bezpiecznie odwieziono do domu. Później się dowiedziałem, że te misie przyjechały, żeby go zaaresztować. Co się z nim później stało – nie wiem.

Zwiedziłem Pakistan wzdłuż i wszerz. Raz cudem udało mi się uniknąć śmierci. Tego dnia udałem się do Karaczi, poopalać się, wykąpać i zwiedzić imponujące miejscowe groty. To cudowne miejsce, ale jak się później okazało, nieprawdopodobnie niebezpieczne. Wspiąłem się wraz z moimi towarzyszami na dość wysokie, ukształtowane przez wodę skały. Niżej też były skałki, kilka takich specyficznych stopni. Na nich odpoczywali miejscowi. Ni stąd, ni zowąd zerwał się wiatr. I nagle jak nie pieprznie kilkunastometrowa fala! Zmiotła tych ludzi w kilka sekund. Nikt się nie uratował, żywioł zabrał wszystkich. Nam jedynie zmoczyło ubrania. A przecież jeszcze pół godziny wcześniej byliśmy na dole i staliśmy tam, gdzie ci nieszczęśnicy! Gdybyśmy zabawili tam, dłużej, nie mielibyśmy szans na przeżycie… Po przyjeździe do ambasady od razu wypiliśmy po whiskaczyku na odstresowanie.

Muszę też wspomnieć o tym, że byłem w Islamabadzie podczas wizyty generała Jaruzelskiego, kiedy to przeprowadzono nieudany zamach na jego życie, za którym stała zapewne jakaś grupa, która bardzo chciała go zlikwidować, bo tam przyjaciół Rosjan za bardzo się nie lubiło. Kiedy wylądował samolot z generałem, zamachowcy próbowali wjechać w niego samochodem dostawczym. Plan wziął w łeb i doszło do potwornej strzelaniny. Nikt nie pukał z korkowców, tylko strzelał tak, żeby zabić, a ludzie na moich oczach padali jak muchy. Staliśmy w pewnym oddaleniu, więc nie groziło nam bezpośrednie niebezpieczeństwo. To chyba jednak był ten moment, w którym stwierdziłem, że chciałbym z powrotem znaleźć się w Polsce.

Do kraju musiałem wrócić, żeby dokończyć studia, ciągnęło mnie też do futbolu. Przyjechałem już oczywiście z żoną. Dostałem zatrudnienie na warszawskim AWF-ie na wydziale biomechaniki. Równolegle obroniłem pracę magisterską w dziedzinie antropologii. Co ciekawe, proponowano mi nawet podjęcie studiów doktoranckich, bo przywiozłem unikalny materiał z Dalekiego Wschodu, ale mnie już nosiło, chciałem znów gdzieś wyjechać i pograć w piłkę.

Szybko nadarzyła się ku temu okazja. W 1979 roku teść przeniósł się z placówki w Islamabadzie do Kanady, a ja dostałem informację, że mam szansę na grę w kanadyjskim Toronto Falcons. Wyjechałem więc i związałem się z tym zespołem, występując między innymi u boku Janusza Żmijewskiego. Zostałem tam ponad rok. Goliliśmy frajerów bez litości, ale trzeba podkreślić, że była to liga półamatorska.

W tak zwanym czasie wolnym pracowaliśmy fizycznie, codziennie rano przez kilka godzin. Wraz ze Żmiją i dwoma innymi kolegami zatrudniliśmy się w fabryce okien – Sherwood Windows, pamiętam jak

KANADA

W 1979 roku teść przeniósł się z placówki w Islamabadzie do Kanady, a ja dostałem informację, że mam szansę na grę w kanadyjskim Toronto Falcons. Zostałem tam ponad rok. Goliliśmy frajerów bez litości

W fabryce okien – Sherwood Windows – zatrudniliśmy się wraz ze Żmijewskim i dwoma innymi kolegami. Składaliśmy okna, a potem montowaliśmy je na budowach

dziś. Składaliśmy okna, a potem montowaliśmy je na budowach. Po robocie szliśmy oczywiście na trening. Po całym dniu ciężkiej fizycznej roboty nie bardzo chciało nam się ćwiczyć, ale nie mieliśmy wyjścia. Wstawaliśmy o 5.00 rano, żeby na 7.00 być w fabryce. Niech te francuskie pieski, które teraz grają w piłkę, z uwagą raz jeszcze przeczytają ten akapit. Gdyby przeszły taką szkołę, może zrozumiałyby, czym jest ciężka praca.

Z Januszem Żmijewskim miałem trochę przygód – czasem śmiesznych, czasem strasznych. Kiedyś zgłosili się do mnie ludzie spod Toronto, żebym wybrał kogoś jeszcze ze swojej drużyny i związał się z ich zespołem, Hamilton, cały czas pozostając w Falcons. Człowiek miał wtedy zdrowie, więc mógł biegać, choć oczywiście nie za darmo. I jeździliśmy tam ze Żmiją, a właściwie to po nas przyjeżdżali, żebyśmy nie musieli wydawać na paliwo. Co ciekawe, graliśmy na lewo, pod innymi nazwiskami – w papierach był misio, a na boisko wychodził niedźwiadek. Na mnie wołali Johnny. Pamiętam, jak kiedyś rąbnąłem jednego rywala. Sędzia chce mi dawać czerwoną kartkę, a ja go za rękę i z powrotem wkładam mu kartkę do kieszeni! Podbiegł jeden z moich kolegów z drużyny i zaczął tłumaczyć, że to ostatni raz i że teraz Johnny będzie już grzeczny. Ogólnie byli z nas bardzo zadowoleni, bo większość meczów wygrywaliśmy. Dla nas natomiast gra w Hamilton i dawała możliwość zarobienia, i stanowiła formę dodatkowego treningu. A rywale? Jeśli ciemne kanadyjskie masy nie wiedziały, o co chodzi, to trzeba je było wyrąbać i tyle. Po meczach organizowali nam imprezy w sali kościelnej – czasem odstawialiśmy taki jazz, że trudno było o własnych siłach wrócić do domu. No ale dawaliśmy radę, bo człowiek miał wtedy wydolność zwierza i mógł na drugi dzień grać jak złoto.

Wszystko, co dobre, szybko się jednak kończy. Niebawem trzeba mi było wracać do Polski, bo żona na to bardzo nalegała. Wówczas postanowiłem zakończyć przygodę z kopaniem piłki nożnej.

MOJA JAGIELLONIA
1986–1987

„Kurwa, gdzie ja trafiłem? To jakaś Syberia!", pomyślałem, wysiadając na dworcu w Białymstoku. Był środek piekielnie mroźnej zimy 1986 roku, a ja miałem zostać trenerem Jagiellonii Białystok. Szefowie klubu przyjechali po mnie zdezelowanym żukiem, takim blaszakiem, w którym temperatura oscylowała w granicach -18 stopni Celsjusza. „Chcą mnie chuje zamrozić!", pomyślałem, ale już w klubie zmieniłem zdanie, bo podali coś mocniejszego na rozgrzewkę. Jednak mimo wszystko na myśl, że spędzę na tym wygwizdowie najbliższe lata, cierpła mi skóra. W końcu jednak – szybciej, niż przewidywałem – przyzwyczaiłem się do panujących tu niskich temperatur. A Białystok na długi czas stał się moim drugim domem.

W skrócie wyglądało to tak: zespół, kiedy go przejmowałem, był na dnie tabeli drugiej ligi, drugi od końca. Nikt tak naprawdę nie chciał jeździć do Białegostoku ze względu na zbyt długi czas podróży. Ja jednak postanowiłem wyprowadzić tę drużynę na prostą, jako że widziałem w niej olbrzymi potencjał. Poza tym: jeśli nie ja, to kto? I udało się – tym, czego dokonaliśmy, uciszyliśmy niedowiarków, bo nie tylko się utrzymaliśmy, ale też awansowaliśmy do czołówki! W kolejnym sezonie postanowiłem zagrać naprawdę ostro i powiedziałem, że interesuje mnie tylko awans do Ekstraklasy. Zawodnikom dawałem taki wycisk (jeszcze o tym opowiem), że jakbym spróbował tak w tym klubie dzisiaj, to sraliby na miękko. Ale to były twarde chłopaki, awans osiągnęliśmy, i to z ogromną przewagą nad resztą zespołów.

Zdarzyła mi się w tym czasie interesująca przygoda, posłuchajcie. Parę razy, kursując między stolicą a Podlasiem, przysnąłem za kierownicą. Było ciepło, to i się oczy zamykały. I pewnego razu obudziłem się sto metrów od ulicy, w jakimś życie. Popatrzyłem na te drzewa, które cudem ominąłem swoim wysłużonym maluchem, i pomyślałem, że Opatrzność musiała nade mną czuwać, inaczej byłoby już po mnie. Wylazłem z auta, podszedłem do drogi i zacząłem machać na przejeżdżające auta. Zatrzymał się facet w samochodzie marki Żuk.

– Wyciągnij mnie pan, proszę, z tego żyta – zagadałem uprzejmie.

– Wie pan, ale to dla mnie kłopot…

– Pan się nie przejmuje, ja zapłacę.

– No dobra, pomogę panu, ale niech pan najpierw zobaczy, co mam w samochodzie – zaproponował.

Podeszliśmy razem do tego auta, otworzył tylne drzwi, patrzę, a tam… trumna.

– Pełna? – zapytałem ogarnięty przerażeniem.

– Oczywiście, ze zwłokami w środku – oświecił mnie uprzejmy kierowca.

– Kurwa, jedź pan stąd! Dam sobie radę!

Uciekłem czym prędzej od tego żuka, a potem pomyślałem sobie, jak blisko było, bym nie miał okazji tych moich wspomnień wam opowiadać. W każdym razie te wszystkie mrożące krew w żyłach wypadnięcia z trasy miały miejsce, kiedy jeździłem maluchem. Potem dostałem od ministra budownictwa talon na fiata 125p z pięciobiegową skrzynią. Jak na tamte czasy – luksusowa fura!

Wróćmy do Jagiellonii. Zajmowałem się tam nie tylko trenowaniem piłkarzy, ale również pozyskiwaniem pieniędzy dla tego biednego klubu. Kasy nie było bowiem na nic. Zdarzało się na przykład, że na zgrupowania jeździliśmy zwykłymi autobusami, zatrzymującymi się na każdym przystanku, takimi z kasownikami w środku. Jechaliśmy kawał drogi z Białegostoku do Wisły, a że była zima, to w autobusie temperatura oscylowała w granicach minus ośmiu stopni Celsjusza. Między drzwiami były ogromne dziury, więc mróz w pełni dało się odczuć w środku. Jechaliśmy opatuleni, jakbyśmy po górach chodzili. Mimo to od razu po przyjeździe zarządzałem intensywny trening. Ciekaw jestem, jak zachowaliby się piłkarze z obecnej Ekstraklasy, gdyby mieli jechać w takim zimnie. A właściwie nie jestem ciekaw – doskonale wiem, że wysiedliby na pierwszym przystanku i z płaczem wrócili do domu.

Gościnność w Białymstoku była niesamowita. Ale też bardzo oryginalna. Przed jednym z pierwszych meczów w roli trenera Jagiellonii chciałem jakoś miło ugościć sędziów, tym bardziej że już jakiś czas przed spotkaniem doskonale wiedziałem, kto będzie go prowadził. Przecież będą głodni, spragnieni... A muszą mieć siłę, żeby porządnie nam posędziować.

– Panie trenerze, restauracja to za drogo. Nie stać nas – zakomunikowano mi w klubie.

– To zróbcie coś w budynku klubowym!

– Oczywiście, będą ugoszczeni – usłyszałem, ale obawiałem się, czego mogę się spodziewać.

Kiedy przyjechali sędziowie, oczywiście byłem dla nich niezwykle miły – w końcu Wujo słynął z gościnności.

– Panowie, chodźcie za mną. Przekąsicie coś, pierdolniecie na rozgrzewkę – zaproponowałem i nie usłyszałem słowa sprzeciwu. Mecz był dopiero na drugi dzień.

Poprowadził nas klubowy „pan Stasiu" – ale nie do lokalu, tylko obskurnymi schodami, gdzieś do piwnic. Jebie pleśnią, ciemno jak w dupie u murzyna – po prostu cudownie!

– Może tam jest jakaś sala VIP-owska – zastanawiałem się.

Wchodzimy, a tam zamiast pięknej sali – kotłownia. Rury, piece, ciepło jak cholera. Pod ścianą dwa stoły przykryte śnieżnobiałym obrusem. Na nich kotlety, ziemniaki, przekąski i dużo mięsa. No i białostocka zapojka! Najmilsi goście weszli zniesmaczeni, za to wyszli bardzo za-

„Kurwa, gdzie ja trafiłem? To jakaś Syberia!" pomyślałem, wysiadając na dworcu w Białymstoku. W końcu jednak – szybciej, niż przewidywałem – przyzwyczaiłem się do panujących tu niskich temperatur dowoleni. Ich nazwisk już nie pamiętam, ale to nie byli przypadkowi sędziowie – to było widać po tym, jak spożywali wódeczkę. Tak dobrze się bawili, że jednego z nich koledzy musieli wnosić po schodach. I o to chodziło!

Na odpowiednie przyjęcie sędziów pieniądze się znajdowały, gorzej było z wyposażeniem zaplecza klubowego. Nie mieliśmy się gdzie przebierać, bo nawet szatni porządnej nie było. W tejże „szatni" poustawiane były drewniane ławki, a na środku stały metalowe wieszaki. Trzeba było usiąść sobie na rozwalającej się ławie, zdjąć gacie i powiesić je na wieszaku. O żadnych szafkach dla piłkarzy nie było nawet mowy, wszystko wspólne. Najczęściej woda była zimna, a jak zdarzała się letnia, to tylko od święta. Kiedy natomiast chciało mi się do kibla, to nie miałem się gdzie, za przeproszeniem, wysrać. Kibel był „carski", na lotnika. Raz mi noga wpadła w tę dziurę i nie mogłem jej wyciągnąć. Teraz brzmi to śmiesznie, ale wtedy nie byłem skory do żartów. Musiałem zawołać ludzi z klubu, żeby pomogli mi wyjść. Jeśli noga wpadłaby mi głębiej, chyba całkiem bym tam ugrzązł. W każdym razie zaraz po tym incydencie pojechałem do prezesa i powiedziałem:

– Przecież w tym klubie nie ma nawet normalnej szatni ani kibla! Gdzie ci chłopcy mają zmieniać ciuchy albo walić kloce? Na murawie?

Tym razem podziałało, ale tak było ze wszystkim, musiałem walczyć o każdą najmniejszą pierdołę. Zaczynaliśmy dosłownie od zera. Nawet nie da się tego porównać do współczesności. Teraz w Białymstoku otworzyli piękny stadion ze znakomitym zapleczem, a za moich czasów to była bida z nędzą.

Fajnie, że szefem Jagiellonii jest teraz Czarek Kulesza, mój dawny podopieczny. Mam do niego wielki sentyment, on do mnie również. Pamięta, że dzięki mnie nie został kaleką. Kiedyś podczas jednego z meczów Jagi rywal tak wjebał mu się w nogi, że złamał mu dwie kości – piszczelową i strzałkową. Otwarte złamanie z przemieszczeniami, noga wisiała tylko na skórze. Gdyby ktoś lekko ją ruszył, toby się urwała. Dramat. Zobaczyłem, że obok boiska jest płot z drewnianych sztachet.

– Wyrwijcie szybko te dechy! I przynieście mi, raz-raz! – krzyknąłem do piłkarzy. Pobiegli do płotu szybciej niż do prostopadłego podania. Czarek wył z bólu, potem nawet zemdlał. A ja pogoniłem któregoś misia, żeby zapierdalał do telefonu i zadzwonił po karetkę. Kierowałem całą akcją ratunkową. Założyłem fachowy ucisk, a nogę umieściłem na desce, przymocowując ją gaciami jednego z zawodników. Wkrótce przyjechał ambulans. Poskładali Czarka na tyle udanie, że potem grał jeszcze w piłkę. A teraz może zarządzać klubem, który kocha tak samo jak ja.

Kuleszy i jego kolegom wbijałem do głów, że pieniądze pojawią się, jeśli będą wygrywać, bo wtedy kibice zaczną przychodzić na mecze. Poskutkowało – po kolejnych zwycięstwach na stadionie pojawiało się coraz więcej fanów, a z czasem frekwencja stała się znakomita – bywało, że kluby pierwszoligowe nie miały takiej publiki, mówię bowiem o 30-, 40-tysięcznym tłumie! Ludzie zjeżdżali nawet spod granicy, zimą najczęściej saniami, po 10–15 osób na jednych. Po drodze pili gorzałę, a kiedy docierali na miejsce, „parkowali" sanie pod stadionem. Pokażcie mi teraz taki klub!

„Kto to jest ten młody, ten Janusz Wójcik? Jak on to zrobił, że na Jagiellonię tyle ludzi przychodzi?", pytał w PZPN-ie legendarny Kazimierz Górski. A ludzie przychodzili, bo moi chłopcy grali niesamowitą piłkę. Większości rywali nie ogrywaliśmy – myśmy ich wręcz zgniatali jak wszy.

„Do tych ludzi z puszczy nie ma co jechać, bo to dzikusy. To tak, jakby dzikich wypuścić, tylko zamiast skór i maczug mają stroje piłkarskie. Nikt za nimi nie nadąży, bo narzucają takie tempo i są tak agresywni, że nie ma na nich siły" – takie słowa z ust piłkarzy i trenerów drużyn przeciwnych słyszałem niejednokrotnie. Bo też dokładnie tak było. Rywale czasami wytrzymywali tylko do połowy, a potem opadali z sił. Przypominali dziurawy balon, z którego uchodzi powietrze. To była tylko kwestia tego, ile dostaną. Czasem przed meczami prosili, żeby za dużo

Obywatel

Janusz WÓJCIK

Z okazji awansu Zespołu Międzyzakładowego Klubu
Sportowego Budowlanych "JAGIELLONIA" do I ligi piłkarskiej
składamy Wam najserdeczniejsze gratulacje.

Kierując słowa uznania i podziękowania za wkład
wniesiony w rozwój sportu Białostocczyzny, życzymy Wam dalszych
sukcesów we współzawodnictwie sportowym oraz dużo zdrowia
i pomyślności w życiu osobistym.

Marian GAŁA
Wojewoda Białostocki

Włodzimierz KOŁODZIEJUK
I Sekretarz KW PZPR

Białystok, 1987-06-22

WOJEWÓDZKI ZAKŁAD TRANSPORTU MLECZARSKIEGO
„TRANS—MLECZ"

TRANS MLECZ

15-727 BIAŁYSTOK, ul. Hetmańska 38
telex: 3359 WZTM tel. dyr. 511-107, c. 512-825; 512-712
konto bankowe: Nr 805012-6086 B.G.Ż. Białystok

„Transport —
— krwioobiegiem gospodarki"

WYKONUJE
USŁUGI
przewozowo-spedycyjne
artykułów mleczarskich
na terenie województwa
i kraju przez swoje
jednostki terenowe.

1. Oddział Białystok
   ul. Zwycięstwa 28
   tel. 510-833

2. Oddział Bielsk Podlaski
   ul. Wojska Polskiego 20
   kod 17-100 tel. 29-52

3. Zajezdnia Dąbrowa B-stocka
   ul. 22 Lipca 37
   kod 16-200 tel. 62

4. Zajezdnia Łapy
   ul. Brańska 8
   kod 18-100 tel. 22-23 w. 35

5. Zajezdnia Mońki
   ul. Mickiewicza 44
   kod 19-100 tel. 25-30

6. Zajezdnia Hajnówka
   ul. Warszawska 108
   kod 17-200 tel. 24-95

7. Zajezdnia Siemiatycze
   ul. Kościuszki 72
   kod 17-300 tel. 24-13

8. Zajezdnia Sokółka
   ul. Głowackiego
   kod 16-100 tel. 24-46

Nasz znak: Białystok, dnia 1987.07.29

Wasz znak:

KLUB OLIMPIJCZYKA i KIBICA
przy
Wojewódzkim Zakładzie
Transportu Mleczarskiego
„TRANS—MLECZ"
w Białymstoku

BIAŁOSTOCZANIN ROKU

Janusz WÓJCIK

Trener I ligowej "Jagiellonii"

Z ogromną satysfakcją, zadowoleniem,
radością i przyjemnością kibice naszego zakładu
przyjęli fakt zwycięstwa Obywatela w plebiscycie
"Kuriera Podlaskiego" i otrzymanie tytułu

BIAŁOSTOCZANINA ROKU

Kto jak kto, ale te zaszczytne wyróżnienie
mógł otrzymać tylko ten człowiek, który doprowadził
Jagiellonię do ekstraklasy, zrobił sympatykom piłkarstwa
największą frajdę i niespodziankę, spełnił długo
oczekiwane marzenia o I lidze.

Gratulujemy, pozdrawiamy i życzymy
Białostoczaninowi Roku dalszych sukcesów - jakich?
Oczywiście Mistrza Polski. A nasze odczucie niech
odda ten oto wierszyk:

"Jagiellonia" Pany - Twoja to zasługa
Prawda to jest piękna - oby była długa !
Z Kopciuszka na króla chłopcy wyskoczyli
Chociaż nie tak dawno w okręgówce byli

Natomiast w plebiscycie choć rywale z klasą
Wójcik ich pokonał właśnie ekstraklasą
Żyj nam w grodzie długo, w "Jagiellonii" kręgu
Bo Mistrzostwo Polski w Twoim jest zasięgu !

Prezes Klubu
Olimpijczyka i Kibica

Tadeusz Borys

DYREKTOR

mgr inż.

Do wiadomości:

-Redakcja "Kuriera
          Podlaskiego"
-MKSB "Jagiellonia"

im nie dokładać. A publika szalała, rozwalała płoty, milicja natomiast uciekała i nawet próbowała nie reagować. Cały Białystok zakochał się w piłce. Nawet niektórzy cinkciarze opodatkowali się, żeby do klubu przynosić pieniądze! A przecież mogliby pochować je po kieszeniach, a na Jagiellonię się wypiąć. Moi chłopcy natomiast grali coraz lepiej, byli nawet powoływani do reprezentacji narodowych, czy to juniorskich, czy nawet pierwszej. Cinkciarze widzieli, jak pracują, i to doceniali.

Czy miałem jakieś kłopoty z drużyną? No cóż, to jest wschód, a na wschodzie ludzie lubią sobie łyknąć. Zawodnicy nie raz i nie dwa przekonali się jednak, że ponieważ na treningach codziennie jest taki jazz, to od razu bez majtek widać, kto poprzedniego dnia dał w rurę. Taki delikwent od razu biegł w krzaki i puszczał pawia za pawiem. Był taki bramkarz, Sowiński, nazywaliśmy go „Suwa". Lubił sobie ciachnąć, ale raz na treningu obrzygał się z pięć razy i na dłuższy czas miałem z nim spokój. Zatańczyć lubił też Darek Czykier, ale również się uspokoił, kiedy trochę pohaftował.

Mimo wszystko byłem przygotowany na to, że takich będę miał piłkarzy, bo chciałem drużyny złożonej właśnie z mieszkańców tamtej części Polski, nie przyjezdnych. To ludzie twardzi, ambitni, i choć lubili dać w szyję, zdawali sobie sprawę, że na drugi dzień mają wyjść na trening i zasuwać tak, że aż dym z dupy pójdzie! Do tamtej drużyny należał dzisiejszy prezes Jagiellonii, Czarek Kulesza, który wspomina, że gdyby teraz zawodnicy mieli tak trenować, toby poumierali, a karetki nie nadążyłyby przyjeżdżać. Ma rację, bo ja się ze swoimi chłopakami nie pieściłem – wywoziłem ich do Suwałk, gdzie było jeszcze zimniej, i kazałem biegać po lesie albo po zamarzniętych jeziorach. Obserwowałem ich z brzegu i mierzyłem czas. Ubrany byłem ciepło i żadnej piersióweczki nie miałem, rozgrzewałem się dopiero po zajęciach. A piłkarze wydeptywali sobie ścieżki w zaspach i tak zapierdalali w mrozie, że aż im łby odskakiwały. Nikt jednak nawet nie szepnął, że może byśmy przerwali, bo już mamy dosyć. Prawdziwi sportowcy, proszę państwa, nie miękkie pizdy, tak jak dziś.

Piłkarze liczyli się także z tym, że będą ostro karani za spóźnienia. Raz miałem interesującą przeprawę z Czykierem. Na jednym z treningów asystenci zameldowali mi, że go nie ma. Zjawił się pięć minut po rozpoczęciu zajęć.

– Darek, co się stało? – zapytałem bardzo spokojnie, przyglądając się, czy nie jest czasem dziabnięty. O dziwo nie: był trzeźwiutki jak niemowlę.

– Panie trenerze, przepraszam bardzo – wydukał. – Wstydzę się nawet mówić, dlaczego nie przyszedłem na czas…

– Dobra, wal prosto z mostu i nie marudź – przerwałem.

– Musiałem zaczekać na brata.

– Ale dlaczego? – Wszystko trzeba było z niego wyciągać jak na torturach.

– Bo mamy tylko jedne dżinsy i buty. Brat się spóźniał i nie miałem w co się ubrać. Przecież nie przybiegłbym w samych spodenkach i klapkach…

Zamilkł i patrzył na mnie wyczekująco, a mnie zamurowało. Na początku nie chciało mi się wierzyć, ale później dowiedziałem się, że u niego w domu faktycznie się nie przelewa. Oczywiście wyjątkowo odstąpiłem od kary.

Większość piłkarzy pochodziła z ubogich rodzin. To nie były dzieci biznesmenów, tylko naprawdę biednych ludzi. Gra w piłkę była dla nich sposobem na odbicie się od dna. Sodówka im jednak nie uderzała do głów, ba!, mogliby stanowić wzór dla dzisiejszych rozpuszczonych gnojków, którym się wydaje, że jak raz uda im się strzelić bramkę, to powinni z automatu dostać milion dolarów i lukratywny kontrakt reklamowy.

Zawodnicy mojej Jagiellonii potrafili korzystać z pieniędzy, ale nie trwonili ich w głupi sposób. Znali ich wartość i szanowali je, zdając sobie sprawę, że doszli do nich katorżniczą pracą.

Kiedyś na meczu Hetmana Białystok spodobał mi się bardzo Jacek Bayer – zapuszczony, z nadwagą, ale świetny pod względem technicznym i skuteczny zawodnik. Od razu chciałem sprowadzić go do Jagiellonii, w której zresztą pracował jako... elektryk. Nadawał się do tej roboty, bo był wysoki.

– Trenerze, mam chorą mamę, nie mogę teraz przejść do Jagiellonii, chcę być blisko niej i pomagać – tłumaczył, kiedy usłyszał moją propozycję. Widać było, że czuje się niezręcznie.

– Słuchaj – zniecierpliwiłem się – chcesz całe życie żarówki wkręcać?

– Wolałbym nie, no ale jeśli będzie trzeba, to będę...

Ręce mi opadły. Nic jednak nie powiedziałem i w dalszym ciągu delikatnie na niego naciskałem, aż w końcu udało mi się go przekonać. I całe szczęście!

Rozpoczął z nami treningi. Tak dostał w dupę, że po niedługim czasie był już całkiem innym zawodnikiem i zaczął strzelać gole jak na zawołanie. Został królem strzelców i Wojtek „Baryła" Łazarek powołał go do reprezentacji Polski.

Popularność moich chłopaków była ogromna. Gdzieśmy się nie pojawili, ustawiały się do nas takie kolejki, jakby ktoś bimber albo kiełbasę za darmo rozdawał. Ale podkreślam, żadnemu z chłopaków palma nie odbijała. Oczywiście od czasu do czasu musiałem niektórych wyprostować, ale tak jest w każdej rodzinie. Czasami dowiadywałem się od miejscowej policji, że moi piłkarze coś nawywijali i trzeba ich wyciągać z tarapatów. Czasem kogoś pobili, czasem rozbili jakiemuś delikwentowi kufel na łbie... a jeśli ktoś za bardzo machał rękami, to szybko go pacyfikowali. Na szczęście nie zdarzyła się sytuacja, żebym musiał któregoś wyciągać z pierdla.

Darek Czykier miał takiego kumpla od baletów, Lisowskiego, wołaliśmy na niego „Lis". Obrońca, brzytwa taka, że daj Boże zdrowie. Jak powiedziałem mu: „Lis, kasacja", to on niszczył napastnika błyskawicznie, zmiatał go z boiska. Nie miał też oporów, żeby walnąć kogoś w łeb.

Czarny charakterek, trudny w obyciu, ale mnie tacy piłkarze odpowiadali. W każdym razie tej dwójce zdarzało się parę razy nieźle pobalować. Gdy jednak przychodził dzień bitwy, także oni zakładali bagnety na broń i rzucali się do walki.

Piłkarze nie tylko grali, lubili również pohandlować. Sprzedawali, co się dało. Wyjeżdżali do ZSRR, na dzisiejszą Białoruś i Litwę, przywozili papierosy, alkohol czy złoto i spieniężali je w Polsce. Mieli swoich zaufanych odbiorców, wszyscy ich szanowali. W żaden sposób nie przeszkadzało im to w dobrej grze. Nie miałem więc problemu z tym, że po treningach zajmują się swoimi sprawami.

Chłopaki zaciągały w charakterystyczny sposób, było to tak zwane „śledzikowanie". Rozmawialiśmy jednak zupełnie normalnie – ja, mokotowianin z Warszawy, i oni, mieszkańcy głębokiej puszczy, posługujący się własnym narzeczem. Na początku nie każdy mnie zresztą akceptował, byłem traktowany trochę jak obcy. Miałem takiego zawodnika, którego wziąłem z Hutnika Warszawa, króla strzelców w drugiej lidze. Nazywał się Jasiukiewicz. Zaczął się opierdzielać na treningach. Myślał, że skoro jest z dalekiego świata, to będzie wiódł prym wśród chłopaków. Na jego nieszczęście nie było tego widać na boisku, a ja zauważyłem, że chłopaki trochę się buntują. Pewnego dnia po skończonych zajęciach zakomunikowałem:

– Słuchaj. Żegnamy się, to był twój ostatni trening.

Piłkarze, z Jasiukiewiczem na czele, zgłupieli. Trochę nie dowierzali, ale na drugi dzień rzeczywiście delikwenta na treningu nie było.

– Myśleliście, że on będzie przeze mnie faworyzowany, a wy rąbani po dupie i po łbie? Widzicie, co się stało. Ale tak, jak z nim się szybko uporałem, tak z każdym z was mogę się uporać. Przemyślcie sobie własne postępowanie, bo jak widzicie, reaguję w sposób szybki i zdecydowany – zapowiedziałem.

Piłkarze milczeli, rozglądając się po ścianach. Choć starali się nie dać tego po sobie poznać, bardzo poruszył ich ten incydent. To jednak nie przeszkodziło, a wręcz pomogło w budowaniu drużyny. Moi zawodnicy wierzyli we wszystko, co im mówiłem, a za swój klub poszliby w ogień. Jeśli naprzeciw nim wyszłyby niedźwiedzie z puszczy, toby się na nie rzucili i podusili gołymi rękami.

Pewnego dnia do Białegostoku przyjechał Waldek Marszałek, słynny motorowodniak, a prywatnie mój przyjaciel. Miał startować w jakichś zawodach. Zabrałem chłopaków na te wyścigi, wygrał je oczywiście Waldek. Poprzedniego dnia daliśmy w szyję, ale byliśmy przyzwyczajeni do działania na niewielkim kacu. Waldek na podwójnym gazie jeździł znakomicie, a potem tylko cmokał z zachwytu i mówił: „Dobra nafta, oj dobra". Po zawodach od razu pojechaliśmy na stadion, bo tego samego dnia graliśmy mecz. Zaprosiłem Waldka na ławkę rezerwowych. Był zachwycony drużyną, a chłopaki nim jeszcze bardziej – taki mistrz, a siedzi razem z nimi!

– Wygramy na twoją cześć – zagaiłem Waldka.

– Janusz, co ty opowiadasz? – nie dowierzał.

– Zobaczysz, chłopaki chcą zwyciężyć specjalnie dla ciebie.

Przeciwnikiem była Korona Kielce, ale rzecz jasna wygraliśmy, bodajże „trójasia" albo „czwórasia" do zera, dokładnie nie pamiętam. Waldek został jeszcze na jedną noc, więc trzeba było uczcić nasze i jego zwycięstwo kilkoma flaszeczkami. Do tego chłopcy porobili sobie zdjęcia z mistrzem, a on był zachwycony ich otwartością.

Bo takie właśnie były te moje chłopaki, typowi ludzie ze ściany wschodniej – bardzo bezpośredni, szczerzy, oddani, uczciwi. Wymagający uczciwości i szacunku, ale odpłacający w dwójnasób. Do dziś, kiedy tylko pojadę na Podlasie, jestem witany z wielkimi honorami. I bardzo mi z tego powodu miło.

Mimo sukcesów postanowiłem rozstać się z Jagiellonią. Nie ze względu na wyniki – po prostu objąłem w tym czasie reprezentację juniorską, poza tym zdecydowałem osiąść w Warszawie. Urodził mi się syn i chciałem spędzać więcej czasu z rodziną. Nieraz zdarzało się tak, że bezpośrednio po treningu wsiadałem w samochód, jechałem do Warszawy, przespałem się i wracałem do Białegostoku. Szaleńcze życie, na dłuższą metę nie do wytrzymania. Zakończył się więc krótki, lecz ogromnie ważny etap mojego życia. W stolicy Podlasia zostawiłem cząstkę siebie i zawsze, kiedy odwiedzam to miasto, czuję się trochę jak w domu. Dziękuję całemu Białemustokowi za piękne chwile.

„CAŁA LEGIA ZAWSZE RAZEM!"

1992–1993

Legia to mój ukochany klub. Dla rodowitego warszawiaka, mokoto-wianina, Łazienkowska była, jest i będzie miejscem świętym. Przeżyłem w Legii wiele chwil wesołych i wiele strasznych. Przytrafiło mi się tam też parę rzeczy, których do dziś nie mogę darować ówczesnym władzom PZPN-u. Mam tu oczywiście na myśli bezprawne i bezpodstawne ode-branie Legii mistrzostwa Polski.

Ale o tym później. Najpierw opowiem, jak w ogóle zostałem trene-rem klubu, który do dziś na sportowej mapie mojego serca zajmuje ważne miejsce.

Po igrzyskach olimpijskich PZPN, w osobach Edmunda Zientary i Ry-szarda Kuleszy, zaproponował mi, bym dalej był trenerem młodzieżów-ki – czyli jeszcze raz przeszedł tę samą drogę. Niedoczekanie, kurwa. Oczywiście się nie zgodziłem, bo dalej chciałem pracować z chłopaka-mi z olimpijskiej, tylko po zmianie szyldu na „Reprezentacja A". Nie chcieli o tym słyszeć.

Wiedziałem, że z zakutymi łbami z PZPN-u się nie dogadam, więc podpisałem kontrakt z Legią, która wówczas miała duże kłopoty, ale też mocno o mnie zabiegała. Od razu postawiłem kilka warunków, które przekazałem prezesowi Januszowi Romanowskiemu. Postawiłem spra-wę jasno:

– Nie chcę, żeby przy drużynie kręcili się jacyś pseudomenedżerowie i wciskali mi piłkarzy.

– Nic się nie martw, Janusz, nie będą się kręcić.

Nie do końca się to udało, bo był na przykład świętej pamięci Benek Blaut, ale szybko ustawiłem go do pionu – a w zasadzie pogoniłem, bo miałem już na oku Pawła Janasa i to jego chciałem na asystenta. Przeszedł ze mną cały olimpijski szlak, nie sprawiał większych problemów, więc nie widziałem przeszkód, żeby nie pracował ze mną dalej. Oj, było z nim w Legii wesoło!

Wiecie, co to jest mazut? To taka pozostałość po ropie naftowej, koloru zwykle ciemnobrązowego. W Legii natomiast mazucikiem nazywaliśmy po prostu whisky z colą, którą przygotowywał nasz barman, Paweł Janas – po raz pierwszy przy okazji pewnej imprezy. Otóż jednego razu byliśmy na takim krótkim zgrupowaniu w hotelu Solec niedaleko Legii. Wieczorem wypiliśmy po małej whisky z colą. Siedzimy sobie, jest przyjemnie, a tu nagle patrzę, a Pawła wcięło. Od razu za nim posłałem masażystę Zbyszka Korolkiewicza.

– Szukaj, Zbysiu, Janosika, żeby go ktoś jeszcze nie napadł – poprosiłem.

Korol ruszył, otwiera drzwi i kto wpada do pokoju – Janas we własnej osobie, cały poobijany. Właściwie to wpełzł do środka w pozycji półsiedzącej.

– Przyjacielu, jak z tobą będą takie problemy, to jak niby mamy współpracować? Mam ci ochroniarza znaleźć? – spytałem dobrotliwie.

Otrząsnął się i spojrzał na mnie spode łba. Sprawiał wrażenie człowieka, który nie ma pojęcia, kim jest ani gdzie się znajduje – tak go ten mazucik pogrążył.

MOJE GAGATKI

Jak myślicie, co to jest wiejski zwód? Otóż ten sposób dryblingu opatentował w Legii Wojtek Kowalczyk. Łapał się na to każdy bez wyjątku. A ja się z Wojtusiem podśmiewałem:

Paweł Janas przeszedł ze mną cały olimpijski szlak, a nasze drogi przecinały się potem wielokrotnie, m.in. w Legii

– Na ciebie to trzeba wystawić chyba chłopa ze wsi – on nie będzie reagował na te twoje zwody, po prostu stanie w miejscu, a ty rąbniesz w niego. A profesjonalni obrońcy chcą cię wyczuć, więc ich mijasz tym swoim chamskim zakosem.

– Czego pan trener chce ode mnie? – denerwował się.

– Wojtuś, jakbyś trafił na mnie za dawnych lat, tobym ci zajebał kopa i skończyłoby się twoje machanie nogami – obśmiałem go, a mój kochany Kowal aż kipiał ze złości.

To prawda, uwielbiałem się z nim droczyć. Ale to z sympatii, bo Wojtek Kowalczyk to był jeden z moich ulubionych piłkarzy, szczególnie z Legii. Czy miałem z nim problemy? Zdarzało się, ale żeby z każdym takie były… Chociaż muszę przyznać, wkurwiał mnie regularnie. Czasem nawet starał się podbierać mi panienki! Kowal to był chart na blondynki, uwielbiał jasne włosy. Kiedy mnie spodobała się jakaś kobitka, on zaraz próbował ją wyrwać.

– Kurwa, Kowal, do budy! Nie dla psa kiełbasa! – goniłem gnojka, ale ten nie dawał za wygraną. Zawzięta bestia.

Kowalczyk dał się lubić, chłopak z charakterem. Oczywiście uwielbiał też wypić. Na Bródnie miał ulubiony pub, w którym stawiał kumplom. Był tam powszechnie znany i bardzo lubiany. Zawsze zaczynali w knajpie, ale często kończyli w parku. Walili zdrowo, ale Wojtek nigdy nie przyszedł najebany na trening. No, może na lekkim kacu. Zresztą wiedział, że większa imprezka może zakończyć się dla niego tragicznie. Nieraz go ostrzegałem:

– Możesz się w trupa uchlać, wypić litr, dwa, ja nie będę cię sprawdzał. Ale jak zobaczę, że na drugi dzień nie masz zdrowia, bo jesteś przechlany, to dobiję cię na treningu, a kierownik będzie musiał dzwonić po karetkę. I powtórz to kolegom, to się tyczy także ich.

Wiecie jednak, co wam powiem? Kowal wyciągnięty z baru był lepszy niż niejeden z Orłów reprezentacji Smudy, Nawałki czy Fornalika!

Zwykle był posłuszny, ale pewnego razu wkurwił mnie nie na żarty. Kiedyś pojechaliśmy do Budapesztu na mecz z Honvedem i Ujpestem. Wojtek ze swoim podopiecznym Krzysiem Ratajczykiem pewnego pięknego wieczoru zniknęli. Dostałem informację od policji, że mają ich na posterunku, bo gdzieś narozrabiali. Od razu wiedziałem, że musiało pójść za dużo procentów i chłopaki postanowiły sprawdzić się z Węgrami również poza boiskiem. Musiałem pojechać do aresztu i wyciągnąć ich za łby. Oczywiście dostali makabryczny opierdol, żeby długo tę sytuację popamiętali.

– Jak, kutasy, nie potraficie pić, to pijcie oranżadę – rozpocząłem. – Myślicie, że jutro będziecie mogli odpocząć i dostaniecie wolne? Nie, kurwa. Zagracie od początku i będziecie zapierdalać. A jeśli się nie zmęczycie, to po meczu, gnojki, będziecie biegać wokół boiska.

Kowal z Ratajem nie na żarty się wystraszyli i wszystko odpokutowali na boisku następnego dnia. Zagrali wspaniale! Odpuściłem im, sprawa poszła w zapomnienie. Poza mną zresztą nikt o tym nie wiedział – do tej pory, wspominam teraz o tym po raz pierwszy.

Zaszaleć Kowalczyk lubił także w Polsce, oczywiście w duecie z Ratajem. Pewnego razu pod jedną z restauracji pod Pałacem Kultury pobili taksówkarza. Facet zgłosił sprawę na policję i chłopcy mieli poważne problemy. Musiałem wszystko zamiatać pod dywan, korzystając z moich znajomości. Ale poprosiłem też kolegów z policji, by przyjechali pod stadion i przed treningiem pokazowo zgarnęli Wojtka i Rataja.

– Panowie, zatrzymam ich trochę dłużej w szatni, tak by na boisko wyszli ostatni. Zakujcie obu – poleciłem.

– I co dalej? – W oczach funkcjonariuszy narastało przerażenie, ale też zaciekawienie.

– Podprowadźcie ich w kajdankach pod radiowóz. Ja do was za chwilę podejdę i ich puścicie.

Cała drużyna na boisku, a szalona dwójka skuta przez psy! Niespiesznym krokiem ruszyłem w kierunku moich gagatków.

– Panie trenerze, ale już przecież wszystko załatwione, facet wycofał zeznania, więc dlaczego chcą nas zamknąć? Obiecujemy, to się nie powtórzy – błagali.

– Czy są z nimi jeszcze jakieś problemy? Mamy ich aresztować? – zapytał policjant, który pięknie nauczył się scenariusza mojego przedstawienia.

– Nie, panowie, już wszystko dobrze. Poza tym muszą dołączyć do pozostałych piłkarzy na treningu – stwierdziłem.

Policjanci rozkuli Kowala z Ratajem, ale chłopcy ani drgnęli, gapili się tylko. Na przemian: na siebie, na mnie i na gliniarzy.

– Na co się, kurwa, jeszcze patrzycie? Zapierdalać na boisko! – wydarłem się.

Ależ ruszyli przed siebie! Popierdalali jak Usain Bolt na 100 metrów albo jak kot, którego poleje się wodą. A potem tylko przyglądali mi się podczas treningu. Do tej pory jednak nie wiedzieli, że im zrobiłem takiego psikusa. A więc chłopaki – niespodzianka! Co wy na to?

– Daruś, pamiętaj, nie będzie żadnego pobłażania. Będziesz traktowany jak inni zawodnicy – zapowiedziałem Dziekanowskiemu, kiedy zacząłem z nim pracować w Legii.

– Oczywiście, trenerze, będę spokojny jak dziecko! – przysięgał.

Lubiłem tego Dziekanowskiego. Wkurwiał mnie czasami, potrafił tak zajść za skórę, że się z nim nie dało wytrzymać, ale potem zawsze przyszedł, przeprosił i mydlił oczy, że już będzie grzeczny. Specjalnie mu nie wierzyłem, bo wiedziałem, że Dareczek w spokoju nie jest w stanie spędzić choćby kilku godzin. Szybko okazało się, że moje obawy były słuszne.

Pojechaliśmy na zgrupowanie do Zakopanego, zatrzymaliśmy się w miejscowym ośrodku COS. Bardzo dobre warunki, górskie powietrze – nic tylko skupić się na treningu, a i pobalować, kiedy trener pozwoli. Jednak Dziekan nie chciał czekać na moje przyzwolenie. Jednego z pierwszych wieczorów w Zakopanem okazało się, że w hotelu są wszyscy oprócz Darka, który wziął i przepadł.

Co się stało? Otóż Dziekanowski, znudzony samotnym wieczorem w pokoju hotelowym, postanowił zejść po piorunochronie na dół i ruszyć na miasto. Zamiast być królem Legii, został królem Krupówek. Za bardzo się znieczulił, a na drugi dzień mieliśmy intensywny trening biegowy. Wszyscy jakoś dawali radę, a Darek nie wytrzymywał tych obciążeń. Zamiast normalnie biegać, człapał z wywalonym jęzorem. Wiedząc, co działo się w nocy, specjalnie dawałem mu w pizdeczkę.

– Darek, chodź no tu – zawołałem w końcu.

– Słucham, trenerze – wydukał zdyszany.

– Nie ma sensu, żebyśmy się ze sobą męczyli, bo tylko denerwujemy siebie nawzajem. Nie będę za tobą chodził, pilnował, czy nie spadniesz z piorunochronu i nie rozjebiesz łba, czy też cię dupy na mieście czymś nie zarażą. Wróć do Warszawy i baw się dobrze. Widać, że ci tego brakuje.

Dawno nie byłem taki grzeczny. Powinienem był zjebać go przy wszystkich, ale postanowiłem, że porozmawiam z nim na osobności. Dostał propozycję nie do odrzucenia. Musiał spakować walizki i opuścić zgrupowanie.

– Weź się, chłopie, w garść. Potrenuj indywidualnie na Legii, przemyśl sobie wszystko. Jak wrócę z drużyną, to porozmawiamy – dodałem.

Za kilkanaście dni zgodnie z umową spotkaliśmy się. Ukorzył się i obiecał, że takie zachowanie więcej się nie powtórzy. Przywróciłem go co prawda do drużyny, ale stuprocentowym pewniakiem do gry w pierwszym składzie to u mnie już nie był. Talentu i umiejętności odmówić mu nie mogłem, ale jak już ktoś mnie wkurwi, to pamiętam mu to długo.

Do dziś wspominam jeszcze inną historię z Dziekanem. Zaprosiłem go kiedyś do domu i Darek przyjechał już lekko trafiony. Chciał powspominać stare, nie zawsze dobre czasy. Wyjąłem flaszkę, potem drugą. Niestety dla Dziekana okazało się, że stary materiał jest trwalszy i wytrzymalszy. Po wyżłopaniu wszystkiego, co miałem w domu, ja wciąż byłem rześki, a Dareczek był napierdolony jak szpadel. Zrobiło mu się gorąco, więc... zdjął spodnie. Siedział w samych bokserkach i koszuli. No i dalej rozglądał się za naftą.

– Tre... trenerze, ja pójdę na stację po flachę – wybełkotał z na wpół zamkniętymi oczami.

– No dobra, idź, tylko nie zgiń gdzieś.

Zasiadłem spokojnie na kanapie, relaksowałem się. Nagle zauważyłem, że na podłodze leżą spodnie Darka – poszedł na stację benzynową w samych majtkach! Jedna sprawa, że paradował po mieście z prawie gołą dupą, a druga – była akurat zima. „Kurwa, zamarznie debil", pomyślałem, ale nie wiedziałem, co robić. Iść za nim? Fajnie, tylko gdzie? Nie miałem pojęcia, na którą stację poszedł.

Czekam i czekam, a Darusia nie ma. Po 20, może 30 minutach pojawia się. Roznegliżowany, ale szczęśliwy. I co najważniejsze – z butelką.

– Baranie jeden, jakby ktoś zrobił ci zdjęcie w tych majtach, to znalazłbyś się na pierwszych stronach gazet!

– Trenerze, spokojnie, nikt mnie nie widział.

– No dobra. To dawaj tę flaszkę.

Piliśmy sobie spokojnie, a dzięki wódeczce Darek w ogóle nie poczuł zimna. Sączyłem, słuchałem, opowiadałem, przede wszystkim zaś myślałem o tym, że to miłe, że były podopieczny się pofatygował, żeby mnie odwiedzić. Tak jak Kowal – wkurwiał mnie niemiłosiernie, ale go uwielbiałem.

Chłopaki często robiły sobie żarty z masażysty Zbyszka Korolkiewicza. A to schowali mu walizkę, a to zmoczyli gacie czy nawkładali czegoś do skarpetek. Kiedyś nawet Kowal podłączył szlauch pod hydrant i oblał biednego Zbysia lodowatą wodą. Biedak wyglądał jak zmokła kura i zaczął gonić gówniarza, ale Wojtek młody, szybki, więc z łatwością zwiał. Cała drużyna, i ja też, wyła z radości. Przeważnie jednak piłkarze bali się Korola jak ognia. Nic dziwnego, skoro facet ważył 150 kilo i miał rękę jak patelnię. Dlatego często używałem go jako rozjemcy.

– Zbyszek, idź ich uspokój, bo jak ja wkroczę do akcji, to ich zapierdolę. Nie chcę słyszeć nawet szmeru – zwracałem się do niego, kiedy piłkarze zaczynali dymić.

A Korol wpadał do szatni i grzecznie prosił:

– Debile, zamkniecie się? Jak trener przyjdzie, to wam jaja pourywa!

Skutek był natychmiastowy.

Uwielbiałem Korola. Raz jednak byłem wobec niego bezlitosny, ale sam był sobie winien. Wyzwał mnie bowiem na oryginalny pojedynek. A przecież z Wójtem nikt nie może wygrać!

– Janusz, ty to szybki jesteś? – zagaił.

– Do wódeczki pierwszy – odburknąłem. – A czego chcesz?

– Może byśmy się ścignęli na długość boiska?

– Korol, co ty pierdzielisz za głupoty? Ze mną chcesz się ścigać?

– A co, boisz się?

– W życiu. O co chcesz się założyć?

– Skrzynka wódki, pasuje?

– Świetnie. Jeszcze większa motywacja.

Ruszyliśmy, wystartowały nas chłopaki z drużyny. Biegliśmy równo. Specjalnie mu nie odskakiwałem, żeby mieć trochę zabawy. Na 15 metrów przed środkiem boiska przyspieszyłem. Za sobą słyszałem tylko jęki i sapanie Korolkiewicza. Jakby słoń biegł do zbiornika z wodą. „Żeby na mnie tylko nie wpadł, bo mnie zgniecie!", pomyślałem.

Nagle słyszę – pierdut! Leży! Zbysiu nie miał siły, wywalił się tak ślicznie, że aż salto zrobił. Zadudniło tak, że wydawało się, jakby kopalnia się zawaliła. Leżał jednak dłużej, niż powinien, więc chłopaki podbiegły, bo myślały, że nie żyje. Tak źle nie było, ale pechowiec złamał sobie obojczyk.

– Będziesz, kurwa, jedną ręką masował! – zapowiedziałem mu, bo liczyłem, że jakoś to będzie. Ale nie dał rady. A przegraną wódkę dostarczył tego samego dnia. I od razu część wypiliśmy, bo Zbycha tak bolało, że chciał się znieczulić.

Zbyszka wspominam bardzo dobrze. Mogłem mu zaufać. Współpracowaliśmy przez wiele lat, a wiecie przecież, że gdy ktoś mi się nie spodobał, to zbyt łatwo u mnie nie miał. Z Korolem nadawaliśmy jednak na tych samych falach.

W Legii zawsze było wesoło. Trafiłem na grupę, która za kołnierz nie wylewała, lubiła się też obejrzeć za dziewczynkami. Wiadomo – w Warszawie piłkarze zawsze byli traktowani niczym półbogowie. Lubili bawić się w baraku obok Legii. Piwo lało się strumieniami, wódeczka również. Oczywiście doskonale wiedziałem, kiedy imprezowali. Miałem dwa sposoby na odgonienie ich od butelki i wysłanie do roboty. Czasami puszczałem informację, że nadciąga Wujo, a wtedy oni spierdalali aż miło, zdarzało się, że nawet przez okna, w pobliskie krzaki. Niekiedy też lubiłem zrobić im niespodziankę i nagle przerwać biesiadę.

– No to teraz, niedźwiadki, kończycie imprezę, dopijacie, co macie, i spierdalacie – nakazywałem, a potem spokojnie wychodziłem. Wiedziałem, że moje wojsko jest na tyle posłuszne, że zaraz odstawi napitek i ruszy na poligon.

Ekipa to była zresztą zacna, pełna oryginałów. Przykład? Pierwszy z brzegu – Marek „Beret" Jóźwiak.

– Dlaczego to ja zawsze muszę grać na prawej obronie?! Zawsze w pierwszej połowie biegam koło naszej ławki rezerwowych i najwięcej jobów zbieram od trenera. Opierdala mnie i każe przekazywać reszcie. Już nieraz chciałem uciec gdzieś do środka, żeby tego nie wysłuchiwać – narzekał pewnego razu Jóźwiak.

– Bereciku kochany, powinieneś być dumny! To do ciebie pierwszego trafiają ważne informacje taktyczne. I możesz je przekazać dalej.

– Panie trenerze, jakbym miał to dosłownie przekazywać, to samymi kurwami musiałbym rzucać! – uśmiechnął się gorzko.

No, trochę racji to miał.

Mareczek lubił zabawę. Często kręcił się wokół Leszka Pisza, bo lubili się wspólnie mocno upodlić. Poza tym był bardzo oddany zespołowi i waleczny. Pamiętam mecz z Cagliari w Pucharze Polonii w 1993 roku, który wygraliśmy 2:1. Rywal był wówczas bardzo mocny, miał w składzie kilku reprezentantów Włoch. Mimo że był to mecz towarzyski, piłkarze młócili się, aż miło, bo mieli obiecaną solidną premię od organizatorów. Beret był jednym z prowodyrów walk na boisku – rąbał przeciwników po kościach, aż trzeszczało. Na pięści się bił, chciał dusić. Nie wytrzymał też Kowal, który kręcił, kiwał niemiłosiernie Włochów, a oni wkurwieni go wycinali.

– Na co czekasz, Wojtek? On cię rąbie, a ty co? – naskoczyłem na niego.

Jak to usłyszał, długo się nie zastanawiał. Jebnął gościowi tak, że tamtego musieli znieść. Kowalczyk zszedł o własnych siłach – z czerwoną kartką. A Beret rąbał makaronów do końca!

Znakomicie wspominam również sympatycznego Jacusia Kacprzaka. Pochodził z podradomskich Białobrzegów i cieszył się sympatią chłopaków. Nie był podstawowym graczem, ale jak już wchodził na boisko, to nie zawodził. Raz jednak nieźle mnie zaskoczył.

– Trenerze, mam prośbę. Udałoby się naszą drużynę ściągnąć do mojej miejscowości i tam zagrać pokazowy mecz? – zapytał.

– Jacusiu kochany – westchnąłem. – Myślisz, że pojedziemy tam, pogramy, pouśmiechamy się, a oni przyniosą nam wodę mineralną, zjemy kiełbasę z rożna i pojedziemy z powrotem? Nie mamy czasu na takie przejażdżki.

– Ale mnie tak na tym zależy… Już wszystkim obiecałem – nie dawał za wygraną, a mnie wpadł do głowy kolejny szatański pomysł.

– W tej twojej miejscowości coś wytwarzają? Mają jakąś fabrykę?

– Robią buty! – wystrzelił.

– Jakie te buty? Oficerki czy do wspinaczki? Konkretnie mi tu mów!

– Trenerze, normalne buty! Eleganckie – zachwalał.

– No to przywieź parę pudełek, obejrzymy, wypróbujemy.

Dwa dni później Jacek zameldował się z kilkoma parami butów. Całkiem mi się spodobały.

– Chcesz, żebyśmy zagrali ten mecz? To pozbieraj od chłopaków numery butów. Nie tylko ich – także tatusia, mamusi, dziadka, babci! Powiedz w fabryce, że jak nam przygotują obuwie, to zagramy najśliczniej na świecie!

I Kacper stanął na wysokości zadania. Chłopcy wypili piwko, zjedli kiełbaski i wywieźli niezliczone ilości butów. A mecz? Wygraliśmy 6:1, a gola straciliśmy tylko dlatego, że... ja tego chciałem. Krzyknąłem do Jacka Zielińskiego, żeby wyciął ich napastnika w polu karnym. Niech zobaczą, że Wujo i Legia mają gest! Jacuś Kacprzak chodził taki dumny, że mało nie pękł.

Kto poza Jóźwiakiem i Kacprzakiem. Cóż, kilku innych niedźwiadków również zasługuje na to, żeby ich wyróżnić. Na przykład Marcin Jałocha, na którego wołałem Jałoszkin. Na początku był grzeczny i spokojny, ale potem się rozkręcił. Chłopcy go polubili i zabierali na wszelakie imprezy. Na boisku był niezawodny, wycinał wszystkich jak kombajn. Kolejny do golenia był Grzegorz Wędzyński. W Legii nauczył się grać w piłkę, bo wcześniej nieszczególnie umiał. Zawzięty, silny, zdrowy, ambitny. Zawsze słuchał tego, co mówiłem, nie pajacował, tylko strzelał kopytami jak oficer. Na początku nazwałem go Bendzyński, co go denerwowało.

– Panie trenerze, jestem Wędzyński! – protestował.

– Dla mnie jesteś Bendzyński i koniec dyskusji.

Chłopakom tak się to spodobało, że przerobili ten przydomek na „Benzyna" i tak już zostało. Przestał nawet protestować, bo wiedział, że nic nie wskóra. Mógł jedynie spalić się ze wstydu – jak benzyna.

– Trenerze, kłócą się! Pomocy! – krzyczał przerażony Paweł Janas.

– Ale kto się kłóci?

– Szczęsny z Kowalem. Nie daję sobie z nimi rady. Zaraz się pozabijają! – histeryzował.

– Już ja im, kurwa, dam kłótnie – stwierdziłem i jak chmura burzowa ruszyłem w stronę szatni.

Nie było wyjścia, musiałem załatwić to sam. Wpadłem do środka i rzeczywiście – warczeli na siebie, jeszcze chwila, a pięści poszłyby w ruch i rąbaliby się po pyskach.

– Ty prymitywie, nieuku! Żadnej szkoły nie skończyłeś, debilu! – wydzierał się Szczęśniak.

– A z ciebie jest pizda nie fotograf! Intelektualista z kiszką w torbie! – ripostował Wojtek.

Jeden siedział w jednym rogu szatni, drugi w drugim. Piłkarze stali po stronie Kowala, bo Szczęsnego nie lubili. Kiedy tylko mnie zobaczyli, lekko przystopowali.

– Słuchajcie no, intelektualiści. Zakładać gacie na obsrane dupy i buty na koślawe kopyta, a potem na trening. I dosyć tej dyskusji. Jakby wam obu zliczyć wszystkie klasy, to ledwie byście razem skończyli podstawówkę! Wybitni naukowcy – rozpocząłem od przemówienia do obu, a potem przeszedłem do indywidualnych opierdoli: – Dziwię ci się, Maciek. Po chuj wyskakujesz z takimi tekstami? Co chcesz osiągnąć? Obaj wybitni naukowcy jesteście, tylko twój problem polega na tym, że on gra i strzela. A ty co? – zapytałem Szczęsnego. – Kowal, ty też się nie wpierdalaj. Może byś coś poczytał? Książki jeszcze nikomu nie zaszkodziły. A ty jesteś wyjątkowo odporny na wiedzę. Nic do baniaka ci nie wchodzi – dołożyłem Wojtkowi, a potem wygoniłem ich na trening. – Za minutę będę na boisku, ma was tu nie być! Leszek – zwróciłem się do Pisza – zrozumiano?

– Panie trenerze, oczywiście! – wykrzyczał nasz kapitan jak w wojsku, po czym wziął się do roboty.

– Na co czekacie? Wypierdalać z tej szatni! Nie słyszeliście, co trener powiedział? – wrzasnął.

Kiedy wyszedłem na boisko, od razu zagadnął mnie Lucek Brychczy.

– I jak, Janusz, nie kłócą się już?

– A jak myślisz, Lucusiu?

– Janusz, jak ty się za to wziąłeś, nie ma szans, żeby chociaż słowo powiedzieli.

Tak było. Awantura się zakończyła, a Kowalczyk ze Szczęsnym trenowali bez gadania. To oczywiście nie znaczy, że pozostali piłkarze o całej sytuacji zapomnieli – cały czas dokuczali obu gagatkom.

– Kowal, ile jest dwa razy dwa? Jak tam tabliczka mnożenia, nauczyłeś się już? – tak Leszek Pisz drwił z Wojtusia, a wtórowała mu cała drużyna.

Oczywiście intelektualista Szczęsny wcale nie miał łatwiej. W ogóle Maćka w klubie mało kto lubił. Ciągle chodził obrażony, że broni Zbyszek Robakiewicz, a nie on. Drużyna bardziej była za Robakiewiczem, zawodników wkurwiały durne wywiady Szczęśniaka, głupie zachowanie i kolegowanie się z dziennikarzami. Nie może być tak, że piłkarze z pola nie mogą patrzeć na bramkarza. A w tym przypadku tak było. Zastanawiałem się tylko, kiedy mu wpierdolą, a parę razy się o to prosił. Później spuścił z tonu, bo wiedział, że nie wygra, ponieważ większość drużyny jest przeciwko niemu.

– Trenerze, proszę mi powiedzieć, dlaczego nie gram – pewnego razu zdobył się na odwagę i zadał mi to kluczowe pytanie.

– A na chuj się pytasz? Idź na boisko i pokaż mi, że jesteś lepszy od Robakiewicza. Raz byłeś – jak Kowala wkurwiłeś, co się Robakiewiczowi nigdy nie udało. Już mi wtedy pokazałeś, jaki jesteś dobry.

Szczęsny nie był zawodnikiem, za którym piłkarze w trudnej sytuacji stanęliby murem. Za Robakiem nogi by połamali, a za Szczęsnym nie. Czasem chciał się popisać wiedzą, to wyczytał w słowniku wyrazów obcych jakieś słowo, a koledzy oczywiście się z niego nabijali. Jak szli na piwo, to w tajemnicy przed nim. Nie chcieli go między sobą, bo ich drażnił.

Dlaczego właściwie na niego nie stawiałem? Przecież Szczęsny miał znacznie lepsze warunki fizyczne od Robakiewicza. Był szybszy, sprytniejszy. Ale jednak lepiej bronił Zbyszek.

– To twoja decyzja, ale ja uważam, że bronić powinien Robakiewicz. Bardziej mu ufam – radził mi Lucek Brychczy.

I najczęściej się z nim zgadzałem. Robak nie bał się gry na przedpolu, był też świetny na linii. Wszystko przemawiało za nim. Mimo to Maciek miał dużo czasu, by wygryźć Zbycha ze składu. Nie tępiłem go, nie wywaliłem z zespołu, a na treningach dawałem szanse.

Teraz Maciej jest ekspertem telewizyjnym – oglądałem jego opinie po meczach reprezentacji. Wszystko fajnie, to były reprezentant Polski i solidny ligowiec. Ale dlaczego bramkarz wypowiada się o piłkarzach z pola? Niech o bramkarzach mówi! Nigdy nie był ani trenerem, ani pomocnikiem, ani napastnikiem. W jednym był za to dobry – po mistrzowsku wkurwiał Kowala.

NEGOCJACJE Z GANGSTERAMI

– Panie trenerze, dwóch dziwnych panów przyszło. Chcą rozmawiać o jednym z naszych – wydukał zestresowany kierownik drużyny.

Zacząłem się zastanawiać, o co chodzi. Może coś nawywijał i policja chce go zgarnąć? Kiedy zobaczyłem moich gości, od razu wiedziałem, że to nie policja – raczej chłopcy „z miasta". Świetnie ubrani, czarne płaszcze, po kilka kilo złota, te sprawy. Nie byli to dresiarze z Pragi, ale poważni biznesmeni. Tacy nie przyjeżdżają, by napić się kawki i porozmawiać o pogodzie.

– Janosik, rozpocznij trening, trochę się spóźnię. Niech chłopaki pograją sobie w dziadka z dziesięć minut – zakomunikowałem Janasowi i przeszedłem do rozmowy z dżentelmenami. Jeden lekko zaciągał po rosyjsku, drugi mówił płynnie po polsku. Przedstawili się. Jeden miał na imię Borys.

– Słucham, o co chodzi? Tylko szybko, bo jak widzicie, zaraz mam trening – zacząłem oschle.

– Jeden z pana zawodników widział coś, o czym powinien zapomnieć. Nie może zeznawać. Zbliża się rozprawa i jeżeli coś powie, zrobimy krzywdę jego rodzinie, a jemu urżniemy łeb – zagrozili.

– Panowie, bardzo dobrze, że przyszliście – posłałem im najpiękniejszy ze swoich uśmiechów. – Jutro wyjeżdżamy na mecz do Dębicy, zapraszam, porozmawiamy. Macie moje zapewnienie, że nie piśnie słowa, póki nie ustalimy szczegółów. A na razie nie straszcie, bo wy też różnie możecie skończyć.

– Szto, kurwa?! – krzyknął Borys. Chyba nie rozumiał po polsku.

– Sro. Groźby działają w obie strony. Weźcie to pod uwagę, chłopaki. To co, przyjedziecie do Dębicy?

– Dobra, niech ci będzie, przyjedziemy. Ale gówniarz ma być ustawiony!

Pożegnałem się i poszedłem na boisko, a od razu po treningu wziąłem tego gagatka na rozmowę.

– Jakieś ruskie chcą cię skrócić o głowę. Coś ty widział? – zacząłem. Facet zrobił się siny ze strachu. Nie wykluczam, że się zsikał, albo i coś gorszego.

– Trenerze, bo ja… Za dużo widziałem – dławił się.

– Dobra, mów wreszcie.

– Widziałem, jak ci ludzie kradną auta i tłuką człowieka do nieprzytomności. Przyjechała policja, więc opisałem, jak wyglądali – wyjaśnił.

– No dobra, teraz mnie posłuchaj uważnie: siedź na razie cicho, żadnych zeznań. Rodzinie i tobie nic się nie stanie, nie bój się – klepnąłem go w ramię.

– Panie trenerze, oni mnie zabiją… – rozpaczał.

– Jak nie będziesz opowiadał, co widziałeś, to będziesz miał spokój. A jeśli będzie trzeba, to ja uruchomię swoich ludzi na mieście. I zrobimy wojnę gangów. Nie martw się, najwyżej my ich zawiniemy i będziemy przetrzymywać w piwnicy – podkręciłem.

– Trenerze, dziękuję, nie wiem, co by ze mną było, gdyby nie pan – Jacek wyraźnie się uspokoił.

– Tylko nie kręć się nigdzie po nocy, żeby ich nie kusić – poradziłem.

– Oczywiście. Nosa z domu nie wystawię! – przysiągł.

Od razu po rozmowie odezwałem się do moich przyjaciół „z miasta". Dowiedziałem się tego i owego o misiach, którzy straszyli mojego piłkarza. Jak się okazało, mieli na koncie rozboje, pobicia, wymuszenia i inne cuda. Tak, morderstwa również. Oprychy, które kiedy groziły, to na poważnie. Policja chciała ich zgarnąć, ale potrzebowała zeznań. Dzięki pierwszym zeznaniom jeden z ich kolegów trafił za kratki, niestety pozostali mieli wtyki w policji i dowiedzieli się, kto udupił ich kolegę.

Na drugi dzień pojechaliśmy do Dębicy. Wieczorem pojawili się nasi przemili gangsterzy. Przywieźli koniaczek, co od razu bardzo mi się spodobało. „Wiedzą, że do trenera z pustymi rękami się nie przychodzi, chłopcy z manierami!", pomyślałem. Od razu z jednym z nich, tym mówiącym dobrze po polsku, walnąłem po kilka luf.

– Gdzie on jest? – szybko przeszedł do meritum.

– W pokoju. Nie będzie z wami rozmawiał, bo jutro ma mecz i musi się skupić. Ale możecie być spokojni, ustawiłem go. Nie piśnie ani słówka.

– Oby tak było. Jeśli będzie cicho, włos mu z głowy nie spadnie.

– Nic nie powie. Tylko nie próbujcie go straszyć, bo całe nasze ustalenia szlag trafi. Do żadnego sądu nie pójdzie. Ale wy odpierdolcie się od niego i jego rodziny – zażądałem.

„Polak" był usatysfakcjonowany, ale ten drugi coś tam jeszcze dogadywał po rusku.

– Weź się lepiej z nami napij – zaproponowałem.

– Jestem na odtruciu. Tylko woda – odpowiedział.

„Nawiedzony albo pierdolnięty, z takimi rozmawia się najgorzej", pomyślałem. Ale że z drugim dyskutowało mi się znacznie lepiej, to pierdolnęliśmy jeszcze po kilka kielichów.

– Powtarzam wam jeszcze raz – będzie cisza. Ale jeśli się dowiem, że coś mu zrobiliście, to was odnajdę. Albo moi ludzie to zrobią – wypaliłem.

Niedźwiadki spojrzały na siebie, potem na mnie. Zapewne nikt w ciągu całej ich gangsterskiej kariery tak się do nich nie zwrócił. Szczęśliwie doszliśmy do porozumienia. Po jakimś czasie poczłapali do wyjścia i więcej ich nie widziałem. I najważniejsze, że dali chłopakowi spokój, bo rzeczywiście nie poszedł na rozprawę i nie zeznawał.

– Trenerze, to wszystko pana zasługa, dziękuję! Jak mogę się odwdzięczyć?

– Na boisku się odwdzięcz. Żebyś nie strzelał do własnej bramki –
klepnąłem go w policzek i pogoniłem na trening. A on zrobił to, o co
go prosiłem. Odwdzięczył się za uratowanie mu dupy wyśmienitą grą.

„CAŁA POLSKA WIDZIAŁA"

Chyba każdy kibic zna te słowa. Użył ich ówczesny członek prezydium
Zarządu PZPN-u, świętej pamięci Ryszard Kulesza. Niech mu ziemia
lekką będzie, ale ja nie mam dla niego szacunku. Chodzi oczywiście
o legendarną końcówkę sezonu 1992/93, kiedy mojej Legii w skurwy-
syński sposób odebrano mistrzostwo Polski, bezpodstawnie oskarżając
o ustawienie ostatniego meczu. Zdaniem Kuleszy „cała Polska widzia-
ła", jak Legia kupiła mecz od Wisły. Bzdura, bzdura, bzdura!
Prowadzona przeze mnie Legia walczyła o mistrzostwo z ŁKS-em.
Przed ostatnim meczem sezonu mieliśmy tyle samo punktów co ŁKS
i o trzy bramki lepszy bilans (a w bezpośrednich starciach ograliśmy ich
dwa razy). Klub z Łodzi, którego prezesem był wtedy mój przyjaciel,
obchodził 75-lecie i chciał je uczcić zdobyciem majstra.

Przyszła ostatnia kolejka. Oni grali z Olimpią Poznań, a my jechaliśmy do Krakowa, na mecz z Wisłą. W Olimpii występowało wielu
zawodników, którzy kiedyś grali w ŁKS-ie. Wiedziałem, że dotarli do
piłkarzy z Poznania i że wszystko jest już załatwione. Mieli stać w miejscu, a ŁKS – strzelać kolejne bramki. Potwierdził mi to prezes Olimpii,
a także jej bramkarz, Alek Kłak, który obiecał, że będzie się starał wy-
bronić, co się da.

– Weź wypierdol wszystkich tych starych byłych ełkaesiaków – powiedziałem przez telefon prezesowi. – Wstaw zawodników z drugiej
drużyny, którzy chociaż będą przeszkadzać – prosiłem.

Zapewnił mnie, że tak właśnie zrobi.

To, że rozjedziemy Wisłę, nie budziło moich wątpliwości. Bałem
się za to, że ŁKS wygra w Poznaniu 15:0 lub lepiej, wysłaliśmy więc
do PZPN-u wniosek, prosząc, żeby ostatnia kolejka nie decydowała

o mistrzostwie, żeby zorganizować dodatkowy mecz, pomiędzy Legią a ŁKS-em. Oczywiście nie przyniosło to żadnego efektu. Pojechaliśmy do Krakowa na mecz z Wisłą, a delegacja z PZPN--u udała się do Łodzi. W jej skład wchodzili prezes Kazimierz Górski oraz Michał Listkiewicz. Zawieźli tam medale mistrza Polski dla ŁKS--u, nie czekając na to, jakie będą wyniki! Pomyślałem: „Takiego wała, nie uda wam się". Chłopaki porozumiały się między sobą, nikt nie chciał, żeby ŁKS został mistrzem. Piłkarze Legii i Wisły namawiali się i przekonywali siebie nawzajem: „Co, chcecie, żeby tamci wygrali ligę?".

Zaczęły się mecze. My strzelaliśmy gole Wiśle, a ŁKS Olimpii. Wygraliśmy 6:0, a łodzianie – 7:1. Takie wyniki dawały nam mistrzostwo Polski. Świętowaliśmy na stadionie Wisły, szczęśliwi piłkarze podrzucali mnie do góry – euforia. Niestety nie potrwała zbyt długo. Niewiele później oskarżono Legię o kupienie meczu z Wisłą. Nad nami rozpoczął się sąd.

W siedzibie PZPN-u przy Alejach Ujazdowskich punktualnie o 9.00 wystartowało posiedzenie Zarządu, który miał zdecydować o przyszłości mistrzostwa Polski. Oczywiście się tam udałem, ale nie chcieli mnie wpuścić do środka. Kręciłem się więc po związku i niecierpliwie czekałem.

Chłopcy przy dobrym napitku zastanawiali się, czy zabrać Legii tytuł mistrzowski. Wiedziałem, że coś się szykuje, ale kompletnie zaskoczyły mnie pracownice związku, które przybiegły do mnie zmieszane.

– Janusz! Coś się dzieje, tu się dzikie tłumy zbierają! – krzyczały jedna przez drugą.

Wyjrzałem przez okno. Na Alejach Ujazdowskich stało mnóstwo kibiców, z flagami i szalikami. Wstrzymali ruch, nie można było dojechać do placu Trzech Krzyży. Cała ulica była wypełniona tłumem. Policja odpuściła, bo wiedziała, że może dojść do ostrej bijatyki. Kiedy tylko pokazałem się kibicom, od razu oszaleli ze szczęścia, skandowali na przemian moje nazwisko i „Legia! Legia!".

W tym czasie w PZPN-ie cały czas trwały gorące dyskusje. Raz panowie byli za pozostawieniem Legii tytułu, innym razem za jego odebraniem. Cały czas swoje głupoty opowiadał Rysiu Kulesza. Krętacze pierdoleni.

Posiedzenie się przedłużało, stwierdziłem więc, że nie będę dłużej siedział w tym cholernym PZPN-ie, bo jak się w końcu wkurwię, to wpadnę na tę salę i ich baranów powyzywam. A jak mnie poniesie, to i przyjebię. Wyszedłem, przekroczyłem bramę i... to by było na tyle. Kibice złapali mnie za ręce i za nogi i podnieśli. Całymi Alejami Ujazdowskimi, a potem aż do stadionu Legii, nieśli mnie na barkach! Po drodze oczywiście sparaliżowali cały ruch uliczny. Gdybym tylko krzyknął: „Panowie, wracamy i rozpierdzielamy ten PZPN", zrobiliby to. Byli gotowi na wszystko.

Postawili mnie na nogi dopiero na murawie stadionu przy Łazienkowskiej. Cała impreza trwała kilka godzin, aż do późnego wieczora. Była jednym wielkim pokazem siły kibiców Legii. Na przemian śpiewali piosenki o klubie, skandowali moje imię, była też oczywiście jakże urocza przyśpiewka: „PZPN, PZPN, jebać, jebać PZPN".

Na decyzję trzeba było trochę poczekać. Niestety była ona dla nas negatywna. Odebrali nam mistrzostwo Polski i przekazali je Lechowi Poznań. Do dziś nikt nie udowodnił, że Legia załatwiła tytuł przez szwindel. Może w którymś momencie ktoś z Wisły zwolnił, nie dobiegł do piłki, ale tylko dlatego, że nikt nie chciał, by mistrzem został ŁKS. To była ustawka, od początku do końca chciano Legię ujebać, bo nie pasowała tym dżentelmenom z bożej łaski. Nie ma co szukać kwadratowych jaj i mówić, że na boisku wykopano diamenty. Mamy kopać dalej? To się przekopiemy przez całą kulę ziemską!

Po co niby mieliśmy kupować mecz z Wisłą? Przecież laliśmy ją bez problemu – i u siebie, i na wyjeździe. To, że wpadło aż sześć goli, było świadectwem słabości Wisły. Stworzyliśmy dobre sytuacje, a te cienkie fiutki z Wisły nie wiedziały, jak się bronić przed naszym naporem. Zobaczcie sobie te gole raz jeszcze. Co tam było ustawione? Co kupiłem?

Wszystkie bramki były poprawne, nie było tam żadnej reżyserii. Krótko po meczu krakowska prokuratura wszczęła zresztą śledztwo w tej sprawie. I wiecie co? Zostało umorzone! Przesłuchano wszystkich zawodników i działaczy Wisły, żaden nic nie powiedział. To co, mieli ich jeszcze przypalać, torturować? Ludzie, bądźmy poważni! Nie kupiliśmy tego meczu! Nie chce mi się nawet słuchać pierdolenia, że wiślacy potykali się o własne nogi, że nam puścili ten mecz. Nie było żadnego samobója, żadnego ewidentnego dowodu na ustawienie tego meczu. A więc, proszę państwa, o czym tu w ogóle mówić? Reżyseria oczywiście była, ale z innej strony. Dlaczego nikt nie przyczepił się do meczu ŁKS-u z Olimpią Poznań, który łodzianie wygrali 7:1? Tam wszystko było w porządku? Taki chuj!

– Możemy was ograć nawet o 6.00 rano, w Pułtusku, Poniatówku, kiedy i gdzie tylko będziemy chcieli. Zerżniemy wam dupę – mówiłem do ełkaesiaków.

Gdybyśmy wtedy zostali mistrzami Polski, dominowalibyśmy w kraju przez lata, ale nie wszystkim to by się podobało. W tamtym mitycznym sezonie rywale przyjeżdżali do nas i błagali, żebyśmy nie strzelali im za dużo goli, bo w klubie będą ich karać.

Pracowałem w wielu różnych miejscach na świecie, ale to w Legii czułem się jak w domu. Warszawa to było i jest moje miejsce na ziemi. Chyba każdy trener pochodzący ze stolicy marzy, by kiedyś popracować w Legii. Spotkałem tam wspaniałych ludzi: Leszka Pisza, „profesora nad profesory", Darka Dziekanowskiego, który ciągle dawał mi się we znaki, a także Marka Jóźwiaka, Berecika, którego ciągle opierdalałem, bo za blisko stał. A także wielu innych, którym bardzo dziękuję. Panowie, „cała Legia zawsze razem!".

POŚRÓD SZEJKÓW
1994–1997

EMIRATY PO RAZ PIERWSZY

– Spakuj mnie, bo dzisiaj wylatuję – zakomunikowałem żonie.

– Gdzie?

– Do Emiratów Arabskich.

Popatrzyła na mnie jak na debila.

– Ale o której godzinie? Zaraz, Janusz, co ty w ogóle mówisz?!

– Jakoś po dwudziestej.

– Ale jak to: lecisz? Po co? Nie rozumiem.

– No normalnie. Spakuj mnie i tyle.

W ten oto sposób poinformowałem kochaną małżonkę, że na najbliższe kilka lat wyprowadzam się na Bliski Wschód. Zanosiło się na to już od jakiegoś czasu, ale siedziałem cicho, nikomu się nie chwaliłem. Emiratczycy namawiali mnie na pracę u nich już podczas igrzysk w Barcelonie. Jeden z nich, menedżer imieniem Abdul, otwarcie mówił, że jeśli podpiszę z nim umowę, załatwi mi kontrakt u Arabów. Wymieniliśmy się namiarami i od tego czasu byliśmy w stałym kontakcie.

Kiedy po igrzyskach wróciłem do Polski, wciąż wydzwaniał. W końcu przysłał mi bilet na samolot, a ja poleciałem. Nikt nie miał o tym pojęcia. Nie musiałem załatwiać żadnych wiz, tylko wziąłem paszport i już – po paru godzinach znalazłem się w Dubaju. Na miejscu czekał na mnie komitet związku piłkarskiego Emiratów Arabskich, który po wylewnym powitaniu przewiózł mnie do superhotelu. Tam odpocząłem po locie, a na drugi dzień zaczęliśmy rozmawiać o warunkach mojej pracy.

– Chcemy, żeby pan objął reprezentację olimpijską. Kiedy mógłby pan rozpocząć pracę? – przywalił od razu prezes.

– O tym jeszcze porozmawiamy. Jutro muszę wracać do Polski. Przemyślę waszą propozycję.

Udawałem, że jestem średnio zainteresowany ofertą, żeby podbili stawkę. Poza tym byłem umówiony na rozmowy z szefem Legii, Januszem Romanowskim. Pożegnaliśmy się, a ja zapewniłem drogiego prezesa, że pozostaniemy w kontakcie.

Nazajutrz faktycznie wróciłem do kraju. Z Ramonowskim dogadaliśmy się błyskawicznie i zamiast uczyć Arabów, jak się kopie piłkę, zostałem trenerem Legii. Ale Emiratczycy bynajmniej o mnie nie zapomnieli – już jako pracownik Legii wiele razy potajemnie latałem na Bliski Wschód. Podczas jednej z takich wizyt podpisałem (lekko znieczulony koniaczkiem) nawet jakieś dokumenty – jak się później okazało, był to kontrakt na objęcie reprezentacji olimpijskiej Zjednoczonych Emiratów Arabskich. Powiecie, że Wójcik nieświadomie coś skrobnął i wpierdolił się w cyrk, którego tak naprawdę nie chciał. Gówno prawda! Zapewniam, że jeśli ktokolwiek z was dostałby taką propozycję, poleciałby do ZEA pierwszym samolotem. A jeśli ktoś zapyta: „Trenerze, dlaczego?", to odpowiem krótko: „Kasa, misiu, kasa!". Tak właśnie mówiłem każdemu: piłkarzom i znajomym, którzy twierdzili, że Wujowi odjebało, bo emigruje do Emiratów.

Wróciłem do Warszawy, prowadziłem Legię, ale wiedziałem, że będę musiał z niej odejść. Nie spodziewałem się jednak, że stanie się to aż tak szybko. Zaraz miała wystartować runda wiosenna, więc liczyłem, że jeszcze na pół roku zostanę w Warszawie, a dopiero potem ruszę podbijać świat.

W pewnym momencie Emiratczycy zaczęli mnie trochę straszyć. Grozili, że jeśli nie przyjadę, to zaskarżą mnie do FIFA. Chcieli wysłać podpisane przeze mnie dokumenty i pożalić się, że choć mam kontrakt, to go nie realizuję. Przysłali nawet po mnie człowieka.

– Popatrz, to są podpisane przez ciebie dokumenty. Lepiej jedź do Emiratów, bo oni nie żartują. Mają dobre układy w FIFA i mogą narobić ci problemów – straszył, ale w końcu miał ku temu podstawy. Lekko się wystraszyłem, bo wyglądało na to, że jestem na przegranej pozycji. Umówiłem się na telefon z Emiratczykami. Zadzwonili raz, drugi, trzeci… Na przemian błagali i grozili.

– Dobra, misie. Przyjadę – zgodziłem się jak dobry wujek.

Dla Emiratczyków było to chyba święto państwowe, tak się cieszyli. Błyskawicznie przysłali mi bilet na samolot.

Był środek zimy, a ja zaczynałem już z Legią przygotowania do rundy wiosennej. Piździło jak chuj, ale pogoniłem swoje orły nad Kanałek Piaseczyński. Zawsze tam zaczynały się nasze treningi zimą, zresztą chyba do dzisiaj tak jest. Zaraz po zajęciach zwołałem spotkanie mojego sztabu.

– Panowie, to był ostatni poprowadzony przeze mnie trening. Odchodzę, jutro mnie tu nie będzie – zakomunikowałem. Na sali konsternacja. Wieść spadła na nich jak grom z jasnego nieba.

– Janusz, co ty opowiadasz? Nie rób sobie jaj! – zaatakował mnie Paweł Janas.

– Janosik, to nie jaja. Rezygnuję z prowadzenia Legii – powtórzyłem, a kierownika drużyny wysłałem na Torwar po flaszkę i kotlety mielone. Zanim wrócił, udałem się do biura i zadzwoniłem do prezesa Romanowskiego, by poinformować go o mojej decyzji.

– Ale co, podwyżkę chcesz? Mamy zmienić ci kontrakt? – dopytywał.

– Prezesie, dziękuję, wszystko jest dobrze. Ale muszę lecieć, podpisałem dokumenty. Może jeszcze kiedyś los nas połączy – mydliłem oczy, bo wiadomo: „Kasa, misiu kasa!". A takiej kasy jak Arabowie, Romanowski zapewnić mi nie mógł.

– Proszę to jeszcze na spokojnie przemyśleć. Jest pan potrzebny drużynie! – prosił Romanowski.

Po rozmowie z nim zszedłem na dół. Zjedliśmy ze sztabem kotlety, wypiliśmy wódeczkę. Poprosiłem Janasa, by zatrzymał piłkarzy po treningu, bo i im chciałem zakomunikować tę informację. Nie bardzo wiedzieli, o co chodzi, bo nigdy wcześniej nie zwoływałem pogadanek po kąpieli.

– Panowie, dziękuję wam za współpracę. Dziś wieczorem wylatuję do Zjednoczonych Emiratów Arabskich. To był nasz ostatni trening – poinformowałem, po czym każdemu z osobna podałem rękę i udałem się w kierunku wyjścia. Drogę zagrodził mi jednak Leszek Pisz.

– Panie trenerze, a czy możemy z chłopakami dzisiaj do pana wpaść?

– Przyjeżdżajcie, Lesiu, oczywiście – ucieszyłem się. Naprawdę chciałem się z tymi moimi niedźwiadkami jakoś czulej pożegnać.

Prosto z Legii pojechałem na Rakowiecką do kolegów z UOP-u. Poszliśmy do restauracji, dobrze zjedliśmy, wypiliśmy też po parę szybkich. Podwieźli mnie do domu. Zacząłem się pakować, przyjechał też brat, który o wszystkim się dowiedział. Pół godziny później pojawili się piłkarze. Z jedenastu. Przywieźli mi butlę whisky, piękną, taką wielką i jak się później okazało – bardzo smaczną. Żegnaliśmy się bardzo sympatycznie i procentowo.

Niestety, wszystko co dobre, szybko się kończy. Nieubłaganie nadchodził czas wylotu do Emiratów. Piłkarze oczywiście pojechali na lotnisko razem ze mną. Na miejscu czekali już dziennikarze, którzy jakimś cudem o wszystkim się dowiedzieli. Byli też kumple z UOP-u – pięknie przekazali mnie kolegom ze Straży Granicznej. Z nimi też trzeba było się pożegnać, a tu przelewek nie było, bo chłopaki wypić lubiły. Wsiadłem do samolotu, a moja przygoda z Legią ostatecznie dobiegła końca. Oto zostałem trenerem olimpijskiej reprezentacji Zjednoczonych Emiratów Arabskich.

W Polsce wszyscy zastanawiali się, dlaczego Wujo tak niespodziewanie spierdolił do Arabów. Powstała jedna niedorzeczna teoria. Otóż dziennikarze, którzy pojawili się na lotnisku, usłyszeli, jak wypytywałem, gdzie jest UOP. Oczywiście szukałem moich kolegów, którzy obiecali wpaść i mnie pożegnać. A te barany napisały potem, że musiałem uciekać, bo UOP mnie ścigał. Przecież to można tylko z rozpaczy tłuc łbem w ścianę, powiedzcie sami...

PRZYGODA SIĘ ZACZYNA

No i wylądowałem w ZEA. Zostałem zakwaterowany w luksusowym hotelu w Szardży, czyli jednym z emiratów. Widok na morze, żarcie i warunki jak w raju. Przydzielono mi kierowcę, który 24 godziny na dobę był do mojej dyspozycji. Po dwóch dniach aklimatyzacji pojechałem do federacji, gdzie spotkałem się z sekretarzem generalnym związku i ludźmi, którzy mieli się mną opiekować. Kontrakty były podpisane, więc zacząłem przygotowywać się do prowadzenia drużyny i organizowania planu gier moich olimpijczyków.

Krótko po przylocie do mojego apartamentu zadzwonił Paweł Janas. Akurat nie było mnie w pokoju, więc słuchawkę podniosła żona.

– Czy mógłbym rozmawiać z Januszem? – poprosił Janosik.

– Ale po co, czego od niego chcesz? – dopytywała.

– Potrzebuję rad. Nie wiem, jak mam prowadzić tę drużynę. Nie radzę sobie – skamlał.

– Paweł, daj spokój. Janusz wszystko ci nakreślił. Ustawił drużynę, ty nic nie musisz robić. Nie będzie z tobą rozmawiał – ucięła.

Rzeczywiście, było dokładnie tak, jak powiedziała. Janas dostał ode mnie zeszyt, w którym miał dokładnie rozpisane, co trzeba robić z drużyną. Nie trzeba było nic zmieniać. To, jak ustawiłem zespół, poskutkowało tym, że niedługo później Janas awansował z Legią do Ligi Mistrzów. Nie muszę dodawać, że ogromna w tym zasługa Wuja.

Ale wróćmy do mojej nowej pracy. Trenerem pierwszej reprezentacji ZEA był wówczas Antek Piechniczek, a pomagał mu Józek Młynarczyk. Później dołączył do nich Zdzisiek Podedworny. Pewnego dnia dostaliśmy z Piechniczkiem informację, że mamy razem jechać do Abu Zabi na spotkanie z szejkiem Abdullahem, synem prezydenta i szefem związku piłkarskiego w Emiratach, a dziś ministrem spraw zagranicznych.

Ruszyliśmy, ale nie wiedzieliśmy, czego od nas chce. Najpierw spotkanie miał Antek. Kiedy wyszedł, miał nietęgą minę. Potem przyszedł czas na mnie. Wszedłem do gabinetu, oczywiście pełnego przepychu. Zasiadłem w fotelu, tak miękkim i wygodnym, że można było w nim zasnąć. Normalnie porozmawialiśmy, w bardzo sympatycznej atmosferze. Aż zastanawiałem się, co takiego szejk powiedział Antkowi, skoro ze mną tak miło rozmawiał.

Niedługo musiałem czekać, by się dowiedzieć, że Antka zwolnili, a jego miejsce zajął ukraiński legendarny trener Walery Łobanowski. Z Łobanowskim szybko złapaliśmy wspólny język i zostaliśmy dobrymi druhami. Walery uwielbiał koniak i chętnie mnie nim częstował. Mimo że w Emiratach nie można było dostać alkoholu, to kochany Walery nie miał z tym żadnych problemów. Zażądał, by wpisano mu do kontraktu prawo do otrzymywania koniaku, który – jak twierdził – świetnie działał na jego serce. Wprawdzie nieraz na własne oczy widziałem, że to lekarstwo wcale mu nie pomaga, ale szkodzi, jednak nie był w stanie wyzbyć się miłości do koniaczku – pił go codziennie, z zapamiętaniem godnym wytrawnego amatora złotych trunków. Ja oczywiście nie odmawiałem. Opowiadał mi o swojej służbie w KGB, gdzie był pułkownikiem.

Dość szybko znalazłem sobie apartament. Mieścił się parę kroków od Łobanowskiego, co pod względem towarzyskim było znakomite, ale dla zdrowia już nie najlepsze. W środku miałem luksusy, jakie zwykłym śmiertelnikom się nie śniły – marmury, prześliczne, designerskie meble, które sprowadzono na moje życzenie, złote klamki. W ZEA – tak, dobrze się domyślacie – miałem mnóstwo znajomości, czy to z polskiej ambasady, czy też instytucji państwowych. Wszyscy doskonale wiedzieli, że mam dobre relacje z szejkiem Abdullahem, wiele osób otwarcie prosiło, bym umożliwił im spotkanie z nim. Byłem ich jedyną szansą, bo normalni ludzie nie byli dopuszczali choćby w pobliże szejka. Dzięki mnie polski ambasador mógł się spotkać z szejkiem, z czego był bardzo dumny.

Pewnego razu pojechałem z jednym z sekretarzy szejka szukać miejsca na letnie zgrupowanie dla mojej drużyny. Ruszyliśmy do Europy, gdzie było chłodniej niż w Emiratach – temperatura znacznie przekraczała tam 40 stopni Celsjusza. Zaproponowałem Niemcy albo Szwajcarię. I tu ciekawostka – po drodze mój kompan zaproponował mi, zapewne na rozkaz swoich szefów, bym został... jednym z nich! Tak, miałem przyjąć ich obywatelstwo i zostać muzułmaninem! Przekonywał mnie, że islam to wspaniała religia. Ot, wymyślił! Wujo klęczący na kocyku parę razy dziennie, wyobrażacie to sobie? Mało tego – miałbym wybrać sobie nowe imię. Już nie byłbym Januszem, a jakimś Abdullahem czy innym Mohamedem. Wiedziałem, że wystarczyło tylko, bym kiwnął głową, a wszystkie formalności zostałyby załatwione.

– Powiedz tylko „tak", nic więcej cię nie będzie interesowało. Dostaniesz paszport i wszystkie inne dokumenty na tacy – przekonywał.

Trochę zamętu mi to w głowie narobiło. Jako ich rodak, Abdullah Wójcik, opływałbym w luksusach do końca życia! Mimo to odmówiłem. Głównie ze względu na rodzinę i bliskich, którzy czekali w Polsce.

Mogłem sobie odmawiać i odmawiać, ale Arabowie nie dawali za wygraną. Naciski nasiliły się, kiedy w eliminacjach do igrzysk olimpijskich wylosowaliśmy Iran i Turkmenistan. Chcieli, żeby drużynę prowadził ich rodak, czyli... niejaki Abdullah Wójcik. Fakt, że trafiliśmy na Iran, przeraził wszystkich w Emiratach. Po pierwsze dlatego, że sytuacja dyplomatyczna pomiędzy tymi krajami była napięta, a po drugie Irańczycy, którzy dobrze grali w piłkę, regularnie tłukli Emiratczyków. Gdyby trzeba było, to i polskiej reprezentacji by wpierdolili.

Zaczęły się więc eliminacje, a ja wybrałem się do Turkmenistanu na obserwację meczu z Iranem. Leciałem specjalnym szejkowskim samolotem, odpicowanym tak, że błyszczał się jak psu jajca. Ale to jeszcze nic! Nie bardzo wiedziałem, o co chodzi, bo każdy z ubranych na biało szejków miał klatkę, a w niej – potężnego sokoła. Nosili grube, czarne rękawice i od czasu do czasu wyjmowali ptaki z klatek. Serce podchodziło mi do gardła, bo to piekielnie niebezpieczne zwierzęta, ale ci Arabowie panowali nad nimi w sposób niesamowity. Dość powiedzieć, że nigdy w życiu nie widziałem, żeby jakiekolwiek zwierzę było tak posłuszne swojemu właścicielowi. W pewnym momencie nawet panom było mało wrażeń, więc postanowili wymienić się sokołami. I tak potężne ptaszyska przeleciały sobie najpierw na jeden koniec samolotu, a potem na drugi.

Gdy dotarliśmy na miejsce, na szejków czekała ekipa z emirackiej ambasady w Turkmenistanie, a mnie przewieziono do najlepszego hotelu w kraju – co prawda, nie wiedzieć czemu, tylko na godzinę. W każdym razie ktoś po 60 minutach zapukał do hotelowych drzwi i zakomunikował, że mam jechać do ambasady. Tam też zabawiłem tylko chwilę – pojęcia nie mam, po co mnie tam zawieźli.

– Teraz, trenerze, pojedziemy do hotelu, w którym będzie pan mieszkał – usłyszałem od jednego misia.

No dobra, to jedziemy. Na początku zareagowałem ochoczo, bo byłem już zmęczony i liczyłem, że się trochę prześpię. Tymczasem droga zaczęła się dłużyć i nim się zorientowałem, byliśmy… w górach! Mimo to postanowiłem, że na razie nie będę zadawał pytań.

Zza gór zaczęły się w końcu wyłaniać jakieś szlabany, a potem żołnierze i wozy bojowe. Kurwa, gdzie ja jestem!? Miałem mecz oglądać, a oni mnie na jakąś wojnę przywieźli! Przypatrzyłem się dobrze – cholera, byliśmy na granicy.

– Gdzie jesteśmy? – zdobyłem się na odwagę.

– Przy granicy z Iranem, w specjalnej strefie – odparł kierowca.

Jakiej, kurwa, strefie?! No to się wpierdoliłem po same uszy. Jeśli mnie wwiozą do Iranu, to chyba do Polski wróci tylko mój zakuty łeb… Zachciało mi się Azji, to teraz skończę w dwóch kawałkach. Po kilkunastu minutach zatrzymaliśmy się przy jakimś budynku – kilka pięter, wielki basen. Jest dobrze, może będę żył. Moi towarzysze wysiedli, ale mnie nakazali pozostać w aucie. Niebawem wrócili z kluczem do pokoju i jakimś dżentelmenem, który przedstawił się jako Abdella.

– Chcesz teraz coś zjeść, czy od razu przyjdziesz do mojego apartamentu? – zwrócił się do mnie. – Musimy porozmawiać.

– Pójdę do ciebie – wymamrotałem.

Nie macie pojęcia, jaki byłem zesrany. Gorączkowo zastanawiałem się, czego ten beżowy ode mnie chce. Wydymać mnie czy od razu łeb urżnąć? Bagażowi zanieśli moją walizkę do pokoju, a ja szedłem krok w krok za człowiekiem, który za chwilę miał się okazać moim przyjacielem albo oprawcą. Weszliśmy w końcu. Wielki, przepiękny apartament. Siadłem w fotelu.

– W jakim języku chcesz rozmawiać? Po angielsku czy rosyjsku? – zapytał na wstępie, po czym przeszedł do przechwałek: – Byłem ambasadorem w Rosji, więc znam ten język doskonale.

– To ci ciekawostka, ważny gość jesteś – palnąłem po rosyjsku.

Gdy to powiedziałem, schylił się do torby. Nawet nie zastanawiałem się, co tam może mieć, pogodziłem się już bowiem, że zapewne odstrzeli mi łeb. Grzebie, szuka, znaleźć nie może. W końcu znalazł. Mnie pot ściekał po skroni, zgrzałem się jak skacowany Dziekan na treningu, a ten co wyjmuje z torby? Maskowskaja! Gorzała! No to albo jesteś swój chłop i zaraz się razem najebiemy, albo to jakaś cholerna prowokacja.

– Wyluzuj. Jak można być ambasadorem w Rosji i nie pić? Polubiłem wódeczkę – uspokoił.

– No, przyjacielu, to teraz możemy pogadać jak brat z bratem! – ucieszyłem się, a kilka sekund później już przechylałem pierwszą szklankę ruskiej wódki, którą uraczył mnie mój nowy przyjaciel. On nie ustępował nawet na krok. Więcej! Wciągał tę wódkę jak niemowlę mleko matki. Widać było, że przeszedł dobrą, rosyjską szkołę. Powalczyliśmy trochę, potem zjedliśmy kolację.

– Jedziemy teraz na spotkanie – zakomunikował.

Jakie, kurwa, spotkanie? Już mam dosyć spotkań i niespodzianek na dzisiaj. No ale nie miałem wyjścia. Pojechaliśmy specjalnym samochodem z ambasady. Jak się okazało, czekał na nas sam premier Turkmenistanu, kraju przecież mocno zależnego od Emiratów. Prawie każdy z jego świty – on zresztą też – miał złotą szczękę. I przez te złote zęby tego wieczoru przelało się wiele litrów wódki. Kiedy już towarzystwo było mocno podpite, premier zaczął przemawiać.

– Ja już nie chcę być premierem. Nie chcę być też prezydentem – wybełkotał.

– A kim chcesz być? – zaciekawił się jeden z jego kompanów.

– Szejkiem!

Myślałem, że się przewrócę ze śmiechu. Ładnie wam się we łbach zakręciło, chłopaki. Posiedzieliśmy jeszcze chwilę, walnęliśmy kilka bomb i ruszyliśmy z powrotem.

W drodze zauważyłem niewielkie, ale kapitalnie oświetlone osiedle u podnóży gór.

– Co to jest? – zainteresowałem się.

Kompan na początku się wykręcał, widać było, że to dla niego trudny temat. W końcu się jednak przełamał:

– Baza CIA. Agenci mają tu obóz wypadowy – wyjaśnił.

Ho, ho, nieźle! Ciekawe, co jeszcze tu zobaczę. I zobaczyłem: na drugi dzień obejrzeliśmy mecz Turkmenistanu z Iranem. Wiedziałem już, na co stać naszych rywali, a więc i pod jakim kątem powinienem przygotować drużynę. Zdawałem sobie sprawę, że łatwo nie będzie, ale byłem dobrej myśli. No bo kto jak nie Wujo?

Wieczorem wróciłem do Dubaju.

SUKCESY Z REPREZENTACJĄ ZEA

Oba mecze z Turkmenistanem wygraliśmy – i wygralibyśmy nawet jako zgraja najebanych paralityków, taki poziom prezentował ten Turkmenistan. Zabawa miała się zacząć później – czekał nas pojedynek w Iranie. To był mecz podwyższonego ryzyka. Odczuwało się duże napięcie, także polityczne. Od razu dostałem obstawę w postaci kilku ochroniarzy.

Wczesnym popołudniem ruszyliśmy na Stadion Narodowy w Teheranie, wybudowany przez Rezę Pahlaviego, ostatniego szachinszacha Iranu. To potężny obiekt, mieszczący ponad 100 tysięcy kibiców. Wjeżdżamy, spoglądam – stadion jest pełny. Wypchany po brzegi! Od razu udaliśmy się do szatni, chociaż szatniami bym tych lochów nie nazywał… W każdym razie zostawiliśmy rzeczy, rozłożyliśmy się, a ja pomyślałem, że zobaczę, jak wygląda murawa. Wychodzę, rozglądam się, a 100 tysięcy ludzi zaczęło przeraźliwie na mnie gwizdać. To akurat specjalnie mnie nie ruszyło, bo w Polsce przyzwyczaiłem się do gwizdów. Ale pomyślałem, że skoro na mnie gwiżdżą, to ja się im ukłonię. Chwilę potem… zamilkli. Akurat gdy wróciłem do szatni, nadszedł czas modlitwy. Piłkarze modlili się w szatni, a kibice na trybunach. „Allah Akbar, Allah Akbar!" – to był jeden wielki ryk. Chyba nie muszę mówić, że te słowa wykrzykiwane przez 100 tysięcy Arabów robią kolosalne wrażenie. Miałem regularne ciarki.

Zastanawiałem się, co mam zrobić, żeby moi piłkarze nie zesrali się po wyjściu na boisko.

– Panowie, ruszamy trochę wcześniej – zarządziłem, a potem rozrysowałem im na tablicy ustawienie: na całym obwodzie środkowego koła boiska, twarzami do publiczności. – Kiedy kibice zaczną gwizdać, macie im się ukłonić.

No więc wychodzimy. Jest oczywiście przeraźliwy gwizd, bębenki pękają. Zgodnie z moim rozkazem chłopaki ustawiły się w kole. Kibice na chwilę się wyciszyli, jakby zaciekawieni, co się dzieje. Ale po chwili znowu – gwizd gigant.

– Kłaniajcie się! – krzyknąłem.

Jak powiedziałem, tak zrobili. Irańczycy od razu się zamknęli, kompletnie oniemiali… i zaczęli bić brawo!

– Pomachajcie im jeszcze, uśmiechajcie się jak do przyjaciół! – dodałem, a potem zarządziłem powrót do szatni.

Odprowadzały nas owacje irańskiej publiczności. Sekretarz szejka uwiesił się na moim ramieniu.

– Coś ty zrobił? Jak ujarzmiłeś te diabły?

– Nie z takimi diabłami w Polsce dawało się radę – uśmiechnąłem się szelmowsko, ale nie kontynuowałem rozmowy, bo zaraz rozpoczynał się mecz.

No i jak sobie poradzili moi waleczni beżowi rycerze? Zremisowaliśmy z faworyzowanymi Irańczykami 1:1! W Emiratach zostało to odebrane jako sukces narodowy.

Od razu po meczu wypuściłem się na zakupy. Generalnie było to zabronione, ale po takim sukcesie Emiratczycy nie umieli mi odmówić i dali mi ochronę. Co więcej – ochronę otrzymałem również od Irańczyków! Zastanawiałem się jednak, czy mi nie zarekwirują zakupów.

– Nie bój się, akurat ty możesz kupować – zapewnił mój irański ochroniarz. Skoro mogę, to co będę się szczypał! Kupiłem kilka takich rzeczy, których w normalnych warunkach nikt nie mógłby z Iranu wywieźć. Były to stare, przepiękne, zabytkowe pamiątki.

Ci sami irańscy ochroniarze odprowadzili mnie na lotnisko. Podczas odprawy szepnęli coś celnikowi do ucha, a ten pro forma poprosił mnie o otworzenie walizki, ale nawet do niej nie zajrzał. A była pełna nielegalnie wywożonych przedmiotów.

Po kilku tygodniach graliśmy rewanż z Iranem, tym razem u siebie. Zjechała cała świta emiracka, a także od cholery jakichś ważnych ajatollahów z Iranu. Goście liczyli, że zrewanżują nam się za stratę punktów w pierwszym meczu. A my pokazaliśmy im wała – wygraliśmy 2:1! Irańczycy siedzieli wkurwieni, a szejkowie szaleli ze szczęścia jak dzieci. Prezes federacji zaprosił nas do siedziby związku, by wręczyć piłkarzom nagrody. Zwrócił się też do mnie.

– Daję ci dwa tygodnie urlopu. Leć do Polski, odpocznij, bilety oczywiście ci opłacimy. Dostaniesz też premię, z której – zapewniam – będziesz zadowolony.

Tak oto w Emiratach rozpoczął się festiwal Wójta. Kraj ogarnęło szaleństwo. Nieustannie zapraszano mnie na obiady i kolacje z najrozmaitszymi szejkami, w nieprawdopodobnie luksusowych warunkach. Szczególnie pamiętam jedno z takich spotkań – szejk zaprosił mnie na bankiet do namiotu przed jego rezydencją. Wszystko wyłożone było kobiercami jak z baśni tysiąca i jednej nocy, dookoła stały i leżały cuda – rzeźby, wazony, pozłacane poduszki. Na dywanach, w misach i na paterach, porozkładano jedzenie. Siedziałem obok jakiegoś Araba i przyglądałem się, co robi. A facet brał do tych swoich ciemnych rąk jedzenie z różnych misek i kleił je w kulki.

– Proszę, skosztuj – zachęcił, podając mi jedną. – No, zrób mi tę przyjemność.

Wszyscy nagle przestali jeść i skierowali wzrok w moją stronę. Wiedziałem już, że jeśli odmówię, obrażę gospodarzy. Ale jak niby miałem to zjeść? Skąd miałem wiedzieć, czy on się wcześniej po dupie albo jajach nie drapał? Wymiętolił brudnymi łapskami jakąś kulkę i podetkał mi pod nos. Cywilizacja, kurwa. „Odpierdol się, bambusie", pomyślałem, posyłając mu najpiękniejszy z Wójtowych uśmiechów. Kilkunastu beżowych przyglądało nam się z zainteresowaniem.

Przeanalizowałem sytuację. Wyrzucić tego nie ma jak, bo patrzą. Odłożyć nie mogę, bo potraktują to jako zniewagę. Chcąc nie chcąc, musiałem zjeść, choć zbierało mi się na wymioty. Gdy przełknąłem, stwierdziłem, że skoro on mi ukleił taką obrzydliwą kulkę, to ja mu też taką zrobię! Nabrałem żarcia i wymiętoliłem.

– Masz, żryj – powiedziałem po polsku, wyciągając dłoń w jego kierunku i szczerząc się od ucha do ucha.

Ach, jaki był dumny! Jak paw. Wziął tego mojego kotlecika i przyglądał mu się jak najważniejszej relikwii. A potem zjadł niczym najsmaczniejszą potrawę świata. Ale nie od razu. Pomału, kęs po kęsie. Celebrował, delektował się smakiem. W ten sposób poczuł się przeze mnie doceniony. A mnie tak się spodobała ta zabawa, że za chwilę wymacałem kulkę kolejnemu arabskiemu misiowi. Skoro lubicie jeść Wójtowi z ręki, chłopaki, to jedzcie na zdrowie!

KRAKSA

W wolnych chwilach spotykałem się z przyjacielem, mieszkającym w Szardży. Z żoną i synem, których ściągnąłem do Emiratów, żyliśmy w Dubaju, więc musieliśmy pokonać spory kawałek. Jedna z takich wizyt była mocno zakrapiana. Wracaliśmy dziwną drogą z betonowymi zaporami po bokach. Zapadła noc. Jak wiadomo, chłopcy w Emiratach na brak kasy nie narzekają, więc jeżdżą po tej drodze porsche, ferrari i innymi cudami. I zapierdalają jak szaleni.

Byłem dość poważnie narąbany – do tego stopnia, że musiała prowadzić żona. Nagle obok nas świsnęły dwa ferrari. Krystyna się wzdrygnęła, a ja, durny, złapałem za kierownicę. Krysia straciła panowanie nad samochodem i z ogromnym impetem walnęliśmy w betonową ścianę. Na szczęście jechaliśmy dużą i bezpieczną toyotą crown, dzięki czemu uderzenie zostało w pewnym stopniu zamortyzowane. Mimo to z połowy samochodu została miazga, a ja głową rozwaliłem przednią i boczną szybę. Nie miałem zapiętych pasów bezpieczeństwa, więc fruwałem jak Żyd po pustym sklepie.

Obok nas zatrzymali się jacyś ludzie, potem przyjechała policja. Poczuli ode mnie alkohol, co, umówmy się, trudne nie było. Zażądali, byśmy pojechali z nimi na komisariat, usytuowany gdzieś na granicy emiratów szardżyjskiego i dubajskiego. Pokazałem im kwitki, które potwierdzały, że jestem trenerem reprezentacji, ale niewiele to dało. Mnie i żonę odseparowali. Ja się ich w ogóle nie bałem, bo wiedziałem, że wszystko będzie załatwione, martwiłem się natomiast o Krystynę, ponieważ gliniarze zaczęli ją straszyć. To mnie wkurwiło, więc zaczątem do nich startować.

– Kutasy jebane, jadę z żoną, chuj mnie obchodzi, co wy sobie postanowiliście – wydarłem się na nich.

Zrozumieli, że nie ma co się ze mną kłócić, i mogłem pojechać z żoną. Wymogłem, żeby zadzwonili do moich znajomych w służbach. Krystyny w ogóle to nie uspokoiło.

– Zamkną mnie na pewno. Ty się wyplączesz, ale ja tu trafię za kraty – mówiła przez łzy.

– Spokojnie, nie będzie tak źle – uspokajałem ją, choć przyznaję, że miałem jednak sporego pietra.

Po przesłuchaniu zawieźli nas do szpitala w Dubaju. Zaczęli sprawdzać, czy jestem pijany, jakby, durnie, nie umieli trzeźwego od naprutego odróżnić. Kazali mi chodzić po jakiejś linii. Chodziłem więc, jak jakiś linoskoczek, ale kiedy zrobiłem zwrot w tył, runąłem jak długi. Uderzenie o podłogę zabolało mnie jeszcze bardziej niż wypadek! Stwierdziłem jednak, że skoro kazali mi odstawiać ten cyrk, to niech mnie teraz podnoszą. Patrzyli, a ja udawałem zabitego! W szpitalu wielkie poruszenie, szybko sprowadzili lekarza z Polski, mojego kolegę, który akurat miał wtedy dyżur.

– Janusz, co ci jest? – zapytał przerażonym głosem.

– Cicho bądź, wszystko dobrze. W chuja ich robię – wyjawiłem.

Połknął haczyk i zaczął udawać, że ratuje mi życie. Policjanci jak to zobaczyli, to po prostu zbaranieli. Patrzyli to na mnie, to na siebie nawzajem i drapali się po tych swoich beżowych łbach. W końcu znudziła mi się ta zabawa.

– Krzysiu, podaj mi rękę i mnie podnieś, nie będę tu wiecznie udawał. Daj mi tylko może jakiś zastrzyk, bo chyba żebra mam złamane – poprosiłem.

– Nie przejmuj się, stary, opatrzymy cię – zapewnił.

Postawili mnie na nogi, więc policjanci stwierdzili, że trzeba zawieźć mnie z powrotem na komisariat. Po czterech czy pięciu godzinach przesiadywania tam, kiedy na zewnątrz robiło się już widno, przyjechali panowie w bieli.

– Kochana, to już jest dobrze – szepnąłem żonie do ucha, wiedząc, że ważni panowie nie zostawią w potrzebie swojego ukochanego trenera.

Wszyscy stanęli na baczność. Goście w bieli porozmawiali chwilę z policjantami, po czym zaprosili nas do luksusowego lexusa i bezpiecznie zawieźli do naszego domu do Dubaju.

Sprawę przejęła komenda główna w Szardży. Nikomu o tym nie mówiłem, postanowiłem, że wszystko załatwię sam. Spotykałem się z policjantami i ustalaliśmy plan działania. Niedługo później odbyłem rozmowę z pracownikami służb.

– Zbierze się sąd i pana żona usłyszy wyrok.

– Mam wziąć prawnika?

– Przestań, jaki prawnik. Wszystko wam powiemy. Gdy przyjdzie dzień rozprawy, to ważne, by żona była ubrana na czarno, jak Arabka. Musi mieć twarz zasłoniętą chustką. Powiemy, co ma mówić.

No, skoro tak, to już byłem spokojny. Klocki zostaną odpowiednio poukładane.

W końcu przyszedł dzień rozprawy. Krystyna, zgodnie z wytycznymi moich znajomych, miała tylko dwa razy wypowiedzieć „tak". To ją bardzo zastanawiało.

– Skąd mam wiedzieć, o co oni mnie pytają?

– A co cię to obchodzi? Mówią, żeby tak odpowiedzieć, to tak masz zrobić. I koniec. Chcesz z nimi rozmawiać? Ciekawe po jakiemu? Po chińsku? – zdenerwowałem się.

Rozprawa odbyła się po naszej myśli. Żonie zasądzono grzywnę, około 200–300 dolarów, którą mogłem zapłacić właściwie od ręki. Zabrano też jej prawo jazdy, które im od razu... rąbnąłem. Leżało sobie na biurku jednego z policjantów, więc kiedy się odwrócił, zwinąłem je i schowałem do skarpety. Biegali potem jak wariaci i szukali.

– Macie tu taki bałagan, tyle papierów, że normalne, żeście zgubili. Szukajcie teraz, bo prawo jazdy jest nam potrzebne! – darłem się na nich, powstrzymując wybuch śmiechu.

Potem już nikt nie czepiał się żony, gdy prowadziła, bo czuli się winni, że zgubili jej „poprzednie" prawko. Ot, słynna arabska solidność i porządek!

WSPÓŁPRACOWNICY

W Emiratach współpracowałem także z Polakami. Pomagał mi na przykład Józio Młynarczyk, którego „odziedziczyłem" po zwolnionym Piechniczku. Wiedziałem, że daje sobie lekko w szyjkę, ale raz przegiął pałę, bo zniknął – całkowicie straciłem z nim kontakt. Dzwonię – nic. Pukam do drzwi – cisza. Przepadł.

– Co z tym Młynarczykiem? – zaczęli pytać w federacji.

– A skąd mam wiedzieć? Co ja, jego rodzina?

W końcu zacząłem się trochę martwić. Myślałem, że może wrócił do Polski, ale pracownicy lotniska utrzymywali, że nikogo o takim nazwisku nie było w ostatnim czasie na liście pasażerów. Wspólnie z ludźmi z federacji uradziliśmy, że trzeba wyważyć drzwi do jego mieszkania. Postaraliśmy się o oficjalną zgodę na taki proceder i razem z policją zabraliśmy do dzieła. Fachowiec, który grzebał coś przy zamku, z twarzą tuż przy dziurce od klucza, zaczął dziwnie się krzywić.

– Co ci jest? – zapytałem.

– Tak śmierdzi stamtąd łychą, że nie da się oddychać! – prychnął.

Pogrzebał jeszcze trochę i wreszcie otworzył drzwi. Wchodzimy, a tu ciekawostka: Józio usłyszał, że ktoś włamuje mu się do mieszkania, wziął nóż, schował się za drzwiami i czekał na bandziorów, by wbić kosę w karczycho!

– Józiu! Odłóż ten nóż! – wydarłem się.

Popatrzył, ucieszył się, że to ja, odetchnął i posłusznie wykonał polecenie. Zaopiekowano się nim potem, odkażono go, a mieszkanie dokładnie wywietrzono. Wkrótce Józio wrócił do pracy. Potem współpracowało nam się znakomicie.

Kiedy skończył się mój kontrakt z reprezentacją, działacze klubu Al--Khaleej Chur Fakkan namówili mnie, bym poprowadził ich piłkarzy w lidze. Chur Fakkan to przepiękne miasto w emiracie Szardża nad Oceanem Indyjskim. Z jednej strony jest woda, z drugiej góry. Pracował tam ze mną taki masażysta, Andrzejek, który miał dwie pasje – wódę i wędkarstwo. Często więc byliśmy zapraszani przez prezesa klubu i jednocześnie szefa służb specjalnych Szardży, z którym się zakolegowałem, na wypady rybackie w ocean, 15–20 kilometrów od brzegu. Łowiło się przeróżne ryby, w tym rekiny. Pewnego pięknego dnia wypłynęliśmy z Andrzejem i kilkoma Arabami, ale przydarzył nam się pech – z łódki wypadła nam jakaś ważna walizka. Na pokładzie konsternacja, nikt nie chciał płynąć po zgubę, ze względu na rekiny.

– Jędruś, na co czekasz, wskakuj do wody! – nakazałem współpracownikowi. – No szybko, bo walizka odpływa!

– Janusz, kurwa, chcesz mnie zabić! Przecież te rekiny mnie tu zeżrą!

– Dobra, nie marudź, skacz. Powąchają, uznają, żeś niesmaczny, i sobie odpłyną. Wskakuj albo w drodze powrotnej będziesz płynął za łódką. Chłop nie miał wyjścia. Prawie się zesrał, ale skoczył. Błyskawicznie podpłynął po naszą zgubę i z prędkością światła wrócił na pokład. Był tak zasapany, jakby właśnie odwalił pływacki maraton! Nasi arabscy towarzysze na przemian śmiali się i cmokali z uznaniem – w końcu mało kto wyskoczyłby z łodzi na środku oceanu wypełnionego rekinami.

W Al-Khaleej współpracowałem również z wiceministrem oświaty, który pracował u nas jako kierownik drużyny. Szybko się z nim skumałem, głównie dlatego, że nieprawdopodobnie lubił whisky. Nazwałem go nawet „Shark", czyli „rekin", bo połykał łychę tak, jak rekiny mięso. Facet często przyjeżdżał do mnie ze swoją świtą i urządzaliśmy bankiety. Była whisky, było piwo, a także takie wielkie gary ze specjalnie po arabsku doprawionym ryżem. Muzyka, tańce, harce, impreza na całego. Mój przyjaciel Shark podczas jednej z takich balang myślał, że przepije wszystkich, ale się przeliczył. Spadł z fotela i tak zaległ na dywanie, że z trudem go podniosłem. Na kolejną imprezę przyjechał więc z żoną, aby pozbierała go z podłogi i odwiozła do domu. Jego małżonka, imieniem Zakija, była oczywiście gorliwą muzułmanką – wiecie, zakryta twarz, wstydliwość, posłuszeństwo, te sprawy. W pewnym momencie wyciągnęła moją żonę do kuchni. Tam nalała sobie pół szklanki whisky, dolała coli i walnęła na raz! Kiedy żona mi to opowiedziała, zacząłem się martwić, że może chcą mnie w coś wkręcić i wsadzić do arabskiego pierdla za rozpijanie muzułmanów. To by dopiero było! Wujo w więzieniu w Emiratach za spożywanie rudego trunku w towarzystwie Arabów!

Pokochałem Emiratczyków i ich zwyczaje. Z wzajemnością! Mogłem zostać Abdullahem Wójcikiem i żyć w luksusach do dziś, leżąc i popijając whisky wśród wachlujących mnie Arabek. I może zrobiłem błąd, może powinienem był tam zostać na zawsze. Wtedy jednak czułem, że mam coś jeszcze do zrobienia w Polsce. Bo kasa kasą, luksus luksusem, ale trzeba było przypomnieć pewnym misiom, że żyję i mam się dobrze. Chciałem zostać trenerem kadry. A wiecie, że jeśli ja czegoś chcę, dopinam swego. I tak też było tym razem.

Aha, na koniec jeszcze słowo o mistrzostwach świata, które w 2022 roku mają się odbyć w Katarze. Słyszę głosy ekspertów, którzy twierdzą, że to będzie klapa, że mundial zakończy się porażką organizatorów. Bzdury! Jak ci wszyscy mądralińscy zobaczą na własne oczy tę imprezę, to zakochają się w arabskiej piłce i w arabskiej gościnności. Tak samo jak ja zakochałem się podczas mojego pobytu w ZEA. Bo Wujo żył tam jak pączek w maśle. Nie inaczej zostaną przyjęci piłkarze, trenerzy, dziennikarze i kibice podczas mundialu. No a nasze orzełki niech też się szykują! Warto nawet już teraz kupić jakieś winko. Trochę poleży i za parę lat będzie jak znalazł!

Idealne, by popijając, obejrzeć przed telewizorem popisy prawdziwych piłkarzy.

REPREZENTACJA POLSKI
1997–1999

WÓJCIK NA SELEKCJONERA

Reprezentacja, ta pierwsza. Zawsze o niej marzyłem – lecz chyba każdy trener tak ma. Większość musi obejść się smakiem, ale ja wiedziałem, że kiedyś zostanę selekcjonerem. Kampanię, bym to ja poprowadził kadrę, rozpoczął poniekąd Zbyszek Boniek, który nawoływał, by zorganizować w telewizji głosowanie audiotele, w którym kibice mieliby wybrać trenera reprezentacji.

Oczywiście wygrałem ze znaczną przewagą, ale głos kibiców nie miał w tym przypadku decydującego znaczenia. Towarzysz Marian Dziurowicz, czyli prezes PZPN-u, i jego banda wymyślili sobie, że po tymczasowym trenerze Krzysztofie Pawlaku nowym selekcjonerem będzie kapuściana głowa, a mianowicie Edward Lorens. To człowiek Dziurowicza ze Śląska. Dziura chciał mieć na selekcjonerskim stołku kogoś zaufanego, przydupasa. I takiego znalazł.

Kiedy wróciłem z Bliskiego Wschodu, dowiedziałem się, że Edek jest już właściwie namaszczony na trenera. Podobno nawet został przez tych półgłówków wysłany na objazd po Europie, a także do... Singapuru i Malezji. Nie wiem po co – miał tam zbierać doświadczenie czy po prostu sobie odpocząć? W każdym razie odniosłem wrażenie, że na tę drużynę położono laskę, że wybrano byle jakiego trenera, aby tylko ktoś poprowadził tę drużynę za niezbyt duże pieniądze.

Akurat zbliżał się finał Pucharu Polski, który rozgrywano w tej łódzkiej ruderze, czyli na stadionie ŁKS-u. Dowiedziałem się, że na meczu obecny będzie prezydent Aleksander Kwaśniewski, więc nie zastanawiając się długo, ruszyłem do Łodzi. Nie spodziewałem się emocji piłkarskich, ale chciałem spotkać się z dawno niewidzianym kolegą z polityki. Traf chciał, że dostałem miejsce pod lożą, w której zasiadł Kwaśniewski ze swoją świtą. Siedział tam też prezes Dziurowicz i inni palanci z PZPN-u.

Kiedy zobaczyłem prezydenta, z szacunkiem należnym jego stanowisku ukłoniłem się. Kwaśniewski machnął do mnie ręką i się uśmiechnął. Oglądam więc sobie spokojnie mecz, mija jakieś 15–20 minut i nagle ktoś stuka mnie w ramię.

– Panie trenerze, pan prezydent zaprasza do siebie – mówi mi na ucho postawny mężczyzna w ciemnych okularach. Od razu wiedziałem, kim jest. Był to oficer Biura Ochrony Rządu.

– Oczywiście, z wielką chęcią – odpowiadam i od razu się podnoszę. Pan prezydent wskazuje mi miejsce. Jest to krzesełko zaraz obok niego, oddzielające go od... Dziurowicza!

Zaczęliśmy rozmawiać, na początku oczywiście o meczu (Legia wygrała z GKS-em Katowice 2:0). Ale nie za bardzo było o czym gadać, bo gra wyglądała totalnie przeciętnie. Kwaśniewski oczywiście pytał kurtuazyjnie, jak mi się pracowało na Bliskim Wschodzie, i chwilkę o tym pogawędziliśmy. Potem ni stąd, ni zowąd przeszedł do rozmowy na temat nowego selekcjonera. „Dziura" się nie odzywał. Wiedział, że zaraz mogą pojawić się problemy. Namaścił już Lorensa, wysyłał go w świat, ale prezydent nic o tym nie wiedział. Nie zastanawiając się długo, postanowiłem... podkablować Dziurowicza.

– Panie prezydencie, przecież prezes już wybrał selekcjonera. Swojego ziomka ze Śląska, Edka z fabryki kredek. I wysłał go, żeby zwiedzał sobie Azję – wyjaśniłem.

Dziurowicz zrobił się czerwony, kipiał ze złości, palił się ze wstydu i nikł ze strachu. A prezydent aż się skrzywił – był zdziwiony i mocno zniesmaczony. Chwilę pomyślał, a potem zaczął się znęcać nad przerażonym Dziurką.

– Kogo pan jeszcze szuka? Przecież ma pan trenera. Tutaj siedzi, obok pana. Jeszcze pan szuka? – zaatakował. – Trenerze, czy byłby pan gotów objąć kadrę? – zwrócił się do mnie.

– Panie prezydencie, ku chwale Ojczyzny! Po to tu wróciłem! – mówiłem głośno, żeby Dziurowicz to usłyszał. Wyglądał, jakby go ktoś bejsbolem przez łeb walnął. Totalnie zgłupiał. Nawet nie wiedział, co ma odpowiedzieć. Siedział tylko zielony ze złości. Natomiast ja czułem się w towarzystwie prezydenta jak ryba w wodzie. Wszyscy na nas patrzyli i nie mogli się nadziwić.

– No, Janusz, skoro ty cały mecz obejrzałeś w towarzystwie Kwaśniewskiego i Dziurowicza, to już wiadomo, kto będzie selekcjonerem – zagaił mnie po spotkaniu Leszek Jezierski, legendarny trener i mój przyjaciel.

– Masz rację, Napoleon – tak prywatnie go nazywałem. – Ale wiem doskonale, że ty, kurwa, byłeś jednym z tych, którzy przyklasnęli namaszczeniu Lorensa! – przywaliłem z grubej rury.

– Przestań, Janusz. Dziura go faworyzował. Znasz mnie dobrze, nie zrobiłbym tego. Ale tu już wszystko jest jasne: będziesz selekcjonerem. A rozmawialiście o tym?

– Prezydent lekko to zasugerował Dziurowiczowi.

– Kurwa, to nad czym ty się jeszcze zastanawiasz?! Dziura dziś nie zaśnie bez wypicia paru butelek. I będzie musiał postawić na ciebie. Spodziewaj się zaproszenia do jego gabinetu i konkretnej oferty.

Jak przepowiedział Jezierski, tak było. Całkowicie ucichły głosy, jakoby Lorens miał pracować z kadrą. Zgodnie z przewidywaniami Napoleona dostałem zaproszenie do PZPN-u na rozmowę z prezesem Dziurowiczem.

– Widzę, Janusz, że spokorniałeś ostatnimi czasy – wypalił na początek drogi pan prezes. Oczywiście gdybym mu puścił jakąś wiąchę, szybko zmieniłby zdanie, ale postanowiłem za bardzo nie szaleć.

Prezydent
Rzeczypospolitej Polskiej

Warszawa, 12 czerwca 1996 roku

Pan
Janusz Wójcik
Dubai - U.A.E.

Szanowny Panie Januszu!

Dziękuję za pozdrowienia i wyrazy pamięci. Miło mi, że chciałby Pan spotkać się ze mną i podzielić swoimi doświadczeniami z pracy z reprezentacją Zjednoczonych Emiratów Arabskich. Zapraszam zatem - przy okazji wizyty w Warszawie - do odwiedzenia Pałacu Prezydenckiego. Szczegóły proszę ustalić z szefem mojego Gabinetu, ministrem Markiem Ungierem.

Serdecznie pozdrawiam, życząc zadowolenia i sukcesów w pracy trenerskiej.

Łączę wyrazy szacunku

Aleksander Kwaśniewski

– No tak, panie prezesie, uspokoiłem się, człowiek się starzeje. A i daleki wyjazd do pracy uczy pokory – lałem wodę do jego młyna.

– To dobrze. Szczególnie że mam dla ciebie pewną propozycję.

– Ciekaw jestem jaką – odparłem, choć przecież doskonale wiedziałem, o co chodzi.

Właściwie w tym momencie wszelkie negocjacje zostały zakończone. Zamknięto drzwi przed Lorensem, a otworzono je przede mną. Dziura kipiał ze złości, ale nie miał nic do powiedzenia. Mógł tylko iść i przynieść mi dobrą kawę na początek pracy z reprezentacją.

Postanowiłem, że moim asystentem będzie Lorens. Chodziło o to, by nikt z PZPN-u nie kopał pode mną dołów. Chcieli promować Lorensa, no to będą go mieli w reprezentacji. Zresztą Dziurowicz mocno naciskał, bym postawił właśnie na niego:

– Janusz zgódź się, on ci nie będzie przeszkadzał. Przecież i tak go do niczego nie dopuścisz.

Tak, to mnie przekonało. Jakby Edzio zaczął mi się mieszać w robotę, tobym go zwolnił bez mrugnięcia okiem, z dnia na dzień. W końcu oczywiście doszło do takiego momentu, ale o tym zaraz.

Dziurowicz porozmawiał więc z Lorensem, który propozycję oczywiście przyjął. Jednak już na jednym z pierwszych zgrupowań Edziu mocno mnie wkurwił. Zaczął się dzielić swoją nikomu niepotrzebną filozofią, mówił, jak on by zrobił to, a jak tamto. Mnie się to nie podobało, więc postanowiłem pognębić go psychicznie. Rozmiękczyć. A on nie wytrzymywał. Darłem się na niego strasznie, dostał jeden z największych, a może nawet największy opierdol w życiu. Nic jednak nie odpowiedział. Stał, słuchał i płakał. Tak – po jego twarzy ciekły łzy! Najpierw pojedyncze, a potem miał już mokre policzki. Przejął się, biedak, tym, jak pojechał go trener Wójcik.

– Ooo, Edziu, ty jesteś jednak miękkim chujem robiony. Za dużo razem nie porysujemy – zakończyłem.

Był więc Edek z fabryki kredek, ale się kredka złamała. Za dwie godziny wytarł łzy, trochę mu przeszło i poprosił mnie o rozmowę.

– Janusz, daj spokój, jak ty mnie traktujesz… – jęczał.

Ja jednak wcale nie zluzowałem. Przeciwnie – dostał powtórkę. Znowu lekko zrosiły mu się oczęta, więc nie próbował dyskutować. Wiedział, że lepiej ze mną nie zadzierać. Co gorsza, nie mógł liczyć na pomoc kogokolwiek ze sztabu, bo wtedy i on by dostał po łbie. Tu nie było przeproś. Jak uruchamiałem młockarnię, to wciągała każdego, kto mi się nawinął.

Piłkarze też nie traktowali Lorensa z przesadnym respektem. Oczywiście, kiedy do nich mówił, słuchali, bo wypowiadał się w moim imieniu. Wiedzieli, że to moje wytyczne, bo nikt nie miał prawa wymyślać swoich teorii, to nie było laboratorium doświadczalne. Ale Kowal i reszta patrzyli na niego z politowaniem.

Edek niby był płaczliwy i niedorobiony, ale potem zaczął kopać pode mną dołki i robić krecią robotę. Również dzięki niemu na jednym z posiedzeń zarządu PZPN-u doszło do głosowania na mój temat – chodziło o zawieszenie mnie w prawach selekcjonera reprezentacji. Edek nie wiedział jednak, że ja mam wtyki również tam. Wiceprezesem był wówczas Andrzej Pawelec, który zdecydowanie stanął w mojej obronie, i pozostałem na stanowisku. A kilka dni później zadzwoniłem do kolegi Edwarda.

– Edziu, nie pokazuj się już na kadrze, to się dla ciebie źle skończy. Bo może być nie tylko opierdziel, ale i wpierdziel – zapowiedziałem.

W taki sposób Edward Lorens zakończył swoją karierę w reprezentacji Polski. Nigdy potem nie mieliśmy dobrych relacji, choć normalnie się witaliśmy. Czy ma do mnie żal? Nie obchodzi mnie to. Facet dostał ode mnie szansę zaistnienia w reprezentacji i nie wykorzystał jej, nie był lojalny. Taki, jaki powinien być asystent. Dlatego odpłynął.

RELACJE Z PREZESEM PZPN-U

Dziurowicz oczywiście płakał po Lorensie, ale nie miał wyjścia – musiał zaakceptować moją decyzję. Choć nie przyszło mu to łatwo i mocno się o to pożarliśmy. Z Dziurowiczem miałem przeróżne relacje. Na pewno nie byliśmy typowym duetem pracodawca – pracownik. Normalności w tym związku prezesa z selekcjonerem nie zaznaliśmy. Muszę jednak przyznać, że Dziura przyjmował mnie zawsze, kiedy chciałem. Najczęściej rozpoczynaliśmy spotkania od bardzo ostrej kłótni, a kończyliśmy, żegnając się na niedźwiadka, oczywiście po wypiciu buteleczki koniaku. Kiedy zaczynaliśmy się kłócić, wszyscy uciekali, bo bali się, że jak się Dziurze napatoczą, to wylecą na pysk. Ja zawsze mogłem się z nim dogadać, choć często szło na ostro. Prezesem był jednak bardzo dobrym. Wzorcowo trzymał wszystkich za mordę, potrafił zorganizować każdą sprawę.

Z Dziurowiczem wiąże się ciekawa historia. Mieszkaliśmy jeszcze z żoną na Stegnach. Późny wieczór, leżymy sobie już w łóżku. Nagle ktoś dzwoni do drzwi. Była chyba 23.00, zdziwiłem się więc, kogo niesie o tej porze. Nawet się nie podnosiłem, to Krystyna poszła otworzyć. A tam Dziura z Rudolfem Bugdołem.

– Jaaanusz, Jaaanusz – krzyczą. Od razu widać, że są na poważnej bani.

„Widocznie już w PZPN-ie mocno się zaszczepili", pomyślałem i oczywiście poszedłem po flaszkę. Miałem jedną butelczynę. Wypili ją jak głodne niemowlę grysik. Mało im było, ale nie miałem skąd załatwić kolejnej flaszki, było już po północy… Żona wpadła na pomysł, żeby podjechać do teściów. I pełny sukces – wróciła z trzema czy czterema butelkami. Oni zadowoleni – od razu wzięli się do picia.

– Januszku, ty wiesz, ty wiesz! – bełkotał Dziura.

– Ale co wiem, panie prezesiku?

– Wiesz, że cię kocham jak brata! – wykrzyczał i przykleił się do mnie na misiaka.

Nie chcielibyście być na moim miejscu – przytulał mnie przepocony, śmierdzący, nachlany Dziurowicz, a mnie wypadało udawać, że jestem najszczęśliwszym trenerem na świecie. „Dziś mnie kochasz, jutro będziesz chciał wypierdolić z roboty", pomyślałem. I polałem jeszcze po jednym.

Dziurowicz i Bugdoł byli już tak najebani, że nie wiedzieli, o co chodzi. Opuścili mnie dopiero nad ranem, a biedny kierowca czekał na nich w samochodzie przez całą noc.

– Co to miało być, prezesie, kontrola? – zapytałem na drugi dzień Dziurowicza.

– Nie, Janusz, takie normalne odwiedziny, mam nadzieję, że wszystko w porządku.

– Spokojnie, prezes przychodzi, kiedy tylko chce – zbajerowałem go.

PO GODZINACH

– No co się patrzycie? Idźcie do baru, zamawiajcie! – strofowałem moich piłkarzy, kiedy podczas zgrupowań schodziłem do restauracji i widziałem konsternację chłopaków.

Niektórzy uciekali, inni chowali kufle pod stołem. A ja miałem zasadę – jeśli pozwalam pić, to nie robię im awantur. Niektórzy walnęli po jednym, inni dochodzili do czterech. A byli też i tacy, jak Świrek czy Kowal, którzy chowali się gdzieś po kątach i walili coś mocniejszego. Zdarzało mi się ich na tym przyłapać, a wtedy mieli przejebane.

Była jedna taka sytuacja, w której zdenerwowałem się nie na żarty. Pojutrze gramy kluczowy mecz w eliminacjach do Euro 2000, a tu przy jednym z pokojów ruch jak na Marszałkowskiej. Spojrzałem w rozpiskę – zakwaterowani byli tam Kowalczyk i Ratajczyk. Aha, czyli szykuje się coś ekstra! Te małe fiutki na pewno chleją! A przecież mają pojutrze wygrać, a nie leczyć kaca. Postanowiłem ich sprawdzić, tylko musiałem zastosować pewien podstęp. Nie mogłem się oczywiście ujawnić, bo jeżeli mieliby jakieś alkohole na stole, to z pewnością by je pochowali. Dlatego stanąłem cichaczem za filarem i podsłuchiwałem. Szybko zorientowałem się, że piłkarze pukają do drzwi specjalnym kodem, żeby uchronić się przed wizytą osób niepożądanych. Zapamiętałem go, poczekałem na odpowiedni moment i wkroczyłem do akcji. Pukam, mija chwila, a przede mną staje Kowal w samych bokserkach.

– A co tu tr… tre… trener robi? – wydukał.

– Co się, Kowal, jąkasz? Nie wpuścisz trenera do środka?

– Oczywiście, trenerze, proszę. – Spuścił łeb, a ja już wiedziałem, że coś jest grubo nie tak.

Miałem rację. Na stole stała jedna butelka łychy, na szafie druga. Chłopcy bawili się w najlepsze.

– Panowie, ja teraz stąd wyjdę i wrócę za jakieś 20 minut. Wtedy te butelki mają być już opróżnione. Sprawdzę to – zapowiedziałem. Wojtek i Krzysiek skonsternowani, a ja usatysfakcjonowany udaną prowokacją udałem się do swojego pokoju. Wróciłem pół godzinki później. Patrzę – rzeczywiście butelki puste.

– I jak się, kutasy, czujecie? Zakręciło się w główkach? Dobrze, to teraz spierdalać spać. I o 8.00 rano na trening! – poinformowałem.

Oczywiście nie miałem pewności, czy nie wylali whisky do zlewu, ale wielką przyjemność sprawiło mi przyłapanie ich na gorącym uczynku. A następnego dnia tak dostali w pizdeczki, że na długo to zapamiętali! Dali jednak radę i później już tego tematu nie ciągnąłem.

Skoro już zacząłem mówić o alkoholu, to pociągnę ten temat. Jak pewnie powszechnie wiadomo, w reprezentacji czystej i kolorowych nie brakowało. Mecze, które prowadziłem, często były ogromnie stresujące, więc przed pierwszym gwizdkiem trzeba było się odrobinkę znieczulić. W grę najczęściej wchodził koniaczek, który wypijałem ze sztabem szkoleniowym. To nie wszystko – masażysta Zbigniew Korolkiewicz miał za zadanie przygotować specjalny roztwór alkoholowy do napełnienia bidonów, by nie zabrakło napitku podczas meczu. Raz jednak Zbysiu się pomylił i podczas jakiegoś meczu podał nasz bidon piłkarzowi. Ten wypił na raz, chrząknął i ślicznie spurpurowiał.

– Kurwa, co to jest?! – wycharczał.

– Zbyszek, baranie, coś ty mu, kurwa, rzucił?! – wydarłem się na naszego masera.

– Przepraszam, Janusz, to nasz roztwór, pomyliłem się! – nie owijał w bawełnę.

Na pewno nie byliśmy pionierami w przygotowywaniu takich koktajli w reprezentacji Polski. Świętej pamięci Waldek Obrębski opowiadał mi, w co oczywiście nietrudno uwierzyć, że kiedy prowadził kadrę młodzieżową, przygotowywał sobie wraz z współpracownikami specjalne drinki w wiadrach z lodem. Kto chciał, podchodził do takiego kubła i nabierał chochlą kilka łyków. Przypadek sprawił, że podczas jednego z meczów towarzyskich pragnienie ogarnęło Mirka Okońskiego. A że niepowtarzalny smak mikstury ogromnie mu się spodobał, to zaczerpnął ze źródełka jeszcze kilka razy.

– Panowie, co wyście tutaj wlali?! Ja już jestem najebany! – wykrzyczał i chwiejnym krokiem wrócił na boisko. Pobiegał kilka minut, ale nie dał rady. Był bardzo ciepły dzień i Okonka rozebrało. – Jestem do zmiany, już nie mogę – wybełkotał i udał się w kierunku linii bocznej.

Za kołnierz nie wylewali również działacze, którzy jeździli z nami na mecze wyjazdowe. W październiku 1997 roku graliśmy dwa spotkania przegranych już eliminacji do mistrzostw świata 1998 – najpierw z Mołdawią w Kiszyniowie, a potem z Gruzją w Tbilisi. Pierwsze wygraliśmy 3:0, a drugie – dla odmiany przegraliśmy 0:3. Działacze spisywali się tam znakomicie, jazzu dawali non stop. Trzeźwego działacza nie widziałem. Koncert rozpoczęli już zresztą na lotnisku, bo niektórych trzeba było wnosić do samolotu. Ale to nic! Jeden z pilotów (a było ich trzech), prawie spierdolił się ze schodów prowadzących na pokład, taki był napruty. W ogóle artystów poniosła fantazja i startowali pionowo, jakby lecieli helikopterem. Aż nam uszy rozsadzało z przeciążeń.

Jakoś na szczęście dolecieliśmy, ale w Tbilisi pojawiły się kolejne problemy. Odebraliśmy bagaże i wsiedliśmy do podstawionego autokaru, jednak świętej pamięci Leszek Jezierski był tak nawalony, że wpierdzielił się do innego autobusu, który – jak się później dowiedzieliśmy – wywiózł go do centrum miasta! Dopiero przy kolacji dowiedziałem się, że trwają poszukiwania, bo Napoleon miał fantazję ruszyć na podbój Gruzji. Szukała go policja i wszelkie służby. Nam nie było do śmiechu, obawialiśmy się, że całkiem nam Lesiu zaginął. Na szczęście odnaleziono go w jednym z lokali, gdzie spokojnie sączył sobie piwko. Policja przywiozła go do hotelu i jakoś przetrwał zgrupowanie.

Niewiele za to brakowało, by cała nasza wesoła wycieczka nie przetrzymała powrotu do Warszawy. Otóż, jak wspomniałem, kiedy lecieliśmy do Tbilisi, jeden z trzech pilotów był nawalony. Ale jak wracaliśmy, ledwo się poruszała cała trójka! Stewardessy musiały ich podtrzymywać, bo zaliczyliby kompletny zgon i spadli ze schodów prowadzących na pokład. „To z nami już koniec", pomyślałem przerażony. Okazało się jednak, że niepotrzebnie się martwiłem, bo panowie chyba przyzwyczajeni byli do pilotowania w takim stanie. Na miejsce dotarliśmy cali i zdrowi.

Było już o pijących piłkarzach, działaczach, trenerach. No to teraz czas na samego selekcjonera! Pamiętacie Walerego Łobanowskiego? Nieżyjący już niestety legendarny ukraiński trener doprowadził mnie do takiego upojenia, że nie mogłem trafić na ławkę rezerwowych. Ale po kolei.

W 1998 roku byłem na obserwacji mistrzostw świata we Francji, kiedy nagle dowiedziałem się, że prezes Marian Dziurowicz postanowił, iż mamy zagrać mecz z Ukrainą w Kijowie. Ostro zaprotestowałem, bo to był czas urlopów i nie sposób było zebrać silnej jedenastki.

– Masz zagrać! – pieklił się Dziura przez telefon.

– Jak ja mam piłkarzy ściągnąć? Skąd? Nie będę grał tego meczu – zapowiedziałem i rozłączyłem się. Na drugi dzień Dziurowicz zadzwonił raz jeszcze.

– Masz zagrać! Jeśli nie, to cię zwolnię, a drużynę przejmie Paweł Janas albo Edward Lorens – zagroził.

– Jeżeli już się zgodzili, to niezłe z nich dupki. Podtrzymuję to, co powiedziałem: nie gram.

Nazajutrz zadzwonił do mnie Leszek Jezierski, który wówczas był bardzo bliskim doradcą prezesa.

– Janusz, nie wygłupiaj się, zagraj. Nikt nie będzie zwracał uwagi na wynik – przekonywał.

– Lesiu, ale jaki to sens? Rozpierdzielą nas w pył, jeśli wystąpią w najlepszym składzie. Zagrają i Andrij Szewczenko, i Serhij Rebrow. Nie będzie co zbierać. No, ale zadzwoń za godzinę, jeszcze to sobie przemyślę – poprosiłem.

Odłożyłem słuchawkę, po czym zamówiłem dwie butelki wina. Nie byłem w stanie analizować tego na trzeźwo. Po godzinie Jezierski znów zadzwonił.

– No dobra, pies was drapał, zagram. Ale na konferencji prasowej powiem, że mnie do tego zmusiliście – zaznaczyłem.

Trzeba było zacząć wysyłać powołania. Ale nie do klubów, bo piłkarze byli na urlopach – musiałem wydzwaniać do chłopaków na komórki i ściągać ich z wczasów. Na przykład Tomek Wałdoch przyleciał z Malediwów! Dał żonie buzi i ruszył w drogę.

Inni wykazali się podobnym zdyscyplinowaniem – w Warszawie stawiło się 99 procent tych, z którymi się skontaktowałem. Odbyliśmy jeden trening i na drugi dzień polecieliśmy do Kijowa. Na miejscu też potrenowaliśmy, zwiedziliśmy ośrodek treningowy. A wieczorem – bankiet. I to taki, że daj Boże zdrowie… Ledwo się udało do pokojów wrócić.

Trenerem reprezentacji Ukrainy był właśnie Walery Łobanowski, mój przyjaciel z czasów pracy w Emiratach Arabskich. Na godzinę przed meczem do naszej szatni przyszedł jego asystent i zapytał, czy mógłbym odwiedzić Łobanowskiego w ukraińskiej szatni. Oczywiście przystałem na tę propozycję. Piłkarzy wysłałem na rozgrzewkę, a sam ruszyłem do starego druha. Walery od razu przywitał mnie bardzo serdecznie, po czym ryknął na swojego asystenta, by otworzył barek. Tyle tam było różnych różności, że dwie drużyny by się mocno zgrzały. Postawił szklaneczki, polał po radziecku. Jedna, druga, trzecia, czwarta bomba…

– Walery, żebyśmy tylko na mecz zdążyli, bo zaraz zaczynamy grać – zagaiłem nieśmiało.

– Dobra, jeścio raz – uciął dyskusję.

Rzeczywiście, było „jeścio raz" i skończyliśmy. Walery opuścił szatnię chwilę wcześniej, bo ja jeszcze musiałem skorzystać z toalety. Wychodzę potem i ja, patrzę, a Łobanowskiego nie ma. W międzyczasie od wódy trochę zaszumiało mi w głowie i ni cholery nie wiedziałem, w którą stronę mam iść! Lewo, prawo czy prosto? Zdecydowałem – poszedłem w prawo. Nagle słyszę moje imię wypowiadane z wschodnim akcentem.

– Jaaanusz, Jaaanusz! Dawaj!

„Co za chuj na mnie krzyczy?!", pomyślałem i obróciłem się, rozglądając się za gagatkiem. Okazało się, że to Walery! Wyszło na to, że zamiast na boisko, skierowałem się do wyjścia ze stadionu. Łobanowski w porę mnie zatrzymał, bo jeszcze chwila, a wyszedłbym na miasto! Złapałem oddech, przyspieszyłem kroku i udałem się na ławkę. Zaczął się mecz. W pierwszej połowie jeden gol dla nas, po przerwie drugi. Na trybunach konsternacja. Polacy przyjechali prosto z urlopów i ogrywają miejscowych tytanów murawy. Sędzia wywalił nawet nam zawodnika z boiska, chcąc ratować Ukraińcom wynik. Nie udało się, bo gospodarze wepchnęli tylko jednego gola i wygraliśmy 2:1.

Po meczu unikałem wzroku Walerego, ponieważ obawiałem się, że spotkanie z nim może się skończyć zwałką. Jednak z łatwością mnie odnalazł.

– Janusz, chodź, odprężymy się. – Komunikat Łobanowskiego był jasny.

– Żadne, kurwa, odprężymy, ty chcesz mnie zabić! Nie udało ci się na boisku, to próbujesz przy kieliszku!

– Jaaanusz, troszeczkę się napijemy, dawaj! – nie odpuszczał.

Wypiliśmy na szybko po jednym, podziękowałem za więcej, chociaż Walery szykował się na ostre radzieckie bombardowanie. Dla mnie z pewnością skończyłoby się ono kapitulacją, musieliby mnie z tej szatni wynosić! Szczęśliwie na lotnisko mogłem się udać o własnych siłach i bez przeszkód wróciliśmy do Polski.

Gdy byłem już w Warszawie, zadzwonił do mnie Dziurowicz.

– Widzisz, Janusz, a tak się wzbraniałeś przed tym wyjazdem – puszył się.

– Nie zmieniam zdania, wciąż uważam, że ten pomysł był niedorzeczny – nie dawałem za wygraną.

– No, ale przecież wygraliśmy.

– Prezes, wygraliśmy, bo masz dobrego trenera!

Co sądzę o piciu alkoholu przez piłkarzy? Sam, jak wiecie, nigdy za kołnierz nie wylewałem, więc nie zdziwi was, jeśli powiem, że przeciwnikiem alkoholu nigdy nie byłem. Jeśli zawodnik jest wytrenowany, to wieczorny browarek czy łycha naprawdę nic złego mu nie zrobi. Gorzej, kiedy nawali się tak, że traci kontakt z rzeczywistością. Ale w takiej Anglii piłkarze lubią się napić i w niczym im to nie przeszkadza.

Chcecie przykładu? To to już! Najlepszy jest mecz Polska – Anglia w eliminacjach do mistrzostw świata 2014, który rozegrano na Stadionie, albo lepiej – Basenie Narodowym. Został, jak wiadomo, przełożony o jeden dzień, bo na murawie można się było najwyżej wykąpać, granie nie wchodziło w rachubę. Nasi pojechali do hotelu, a Anglicy – jak to oni – rozpoczęli balangę, o czym dowiedziałem się od pracowników hotelu. Zakwaterowano ich w Hiltonie, ale nie chcieli tam imprezować, bo bali się, że wytropią ich dziennikarze. Przy samym hotelu na Woli są świeżo wybudowane apartamentowce i bogaci Anglicy postanowili wynająć sobie kilka pokojów na dwóch piętrach. Wiadomo po co – żeby ściągnąć sobie dupy i walić whisky. Były więc i zakąseczki, i panieneczki.

Bawili się całą noc. Rano dostali od lekarzy glukozę i potas, co miało postawić ich na nogi, ale mimo wszystko przystąpili do meczu z Polakami na dużym kacu. Nasi spali grzecznie, przygotowali się jak należy, a okazało się, że nie są w stanie pokonać najebanych i wycieńczonych po dymaniu Anglików! Co by było, gdyby nasze orły usiadły do stołu razem z Anglikami? Skończyłoby się pogromem.

O szalonej nocy Anglików opowiedziałem jednemu z dziennikarzy, który puścił tę bombę do internetu. Niedługo potem dzwoni do mnie angielski dziennikarz z „The Sun". Pytał o szczegóły: kto pił, kto załatwiał dupy i alkohol.

– Słuchaj, mogę ci powiedzieć tylko tyle, że nie pili w hotelu, wyszli na miasto. Dokąd? Nie powiem, bo nie jestem oficerem Scotland Yardu, takie wiadomości kosztują. Co mi zaoferujecie? – zapytałem.

Oczywiście doskonale wiedziałem, kto rozkręcał całą imprezę – było to dwóch czołowych angielskich piłkarzy, nazwiska z pierwszych stron gazet. Jakby dobrze chuchnęli tuż przed meczem, to jeszcze byłoby czuć. Tym bardziej przerażające jest to, że nasi nie potrafili pokonać na wpół przytomnych Angoli.

UKŁADY POZASPORTOWE

No dobra, była dygresja alkoholowo-przyrodnicza, a teraz wróćmy do mojej pracy w reprezentacji. Jedną z pierwszych moich decyzji było przeniesienie zgrupowania kadry z Wisły – gdzie Antek Piechniczek odpoczywał przy kominku, a jego piłkarze jedli przeterminowaną kiełbasę – do hotelu Sobieski w Warszawie. Świetne warunki, wszystko po to, by piłkarzom mieszkało się dobrze. Działało to też w drugą stronę – zrobiliśmy przecież hotelowi świetną reklamę. Menedżer Sobieskiego powiedział mi wówczas, że obroty wzrosły o kilkadziesiąt procent! Każdy chciał potem spędzić czas w hotelu, w którym śpi reprezentacja Polski. No i oczywiście Wujo. Wykreowaliśmy też kolegę Roberta Sowę, który teraz jest gwiazdą kuchni. Dzięki pracy w reprezentacji miał szansę błysnąć ze swoimi potrawami przed opinią publiczną.

Od początku mojej pracy w kadrze wokół drużyny kręciło się mnóstwo dziennikarzy. Byli wszędzie. Chcieli miło spędzić czas, najeść się i oczywiście nieźle zatankować. Dobrze z nimi żyłem, zawsze mieli możliwość rozmowy – z piłkarzami albo ze mną. Bardzo często nas odwiedzali, a wybrani mogli korzystać z takich samych dobrodziejstw co piłkarze. Oczywiście nie pozwalałem na to wszystkim, bo ustawiłaby się kolejka do koryta, jak do kina na najlepszy film. A poza tym jak mi ktoś nie pasował, nie mógł przekroczyć nawet progu hotelu. Kiedy jednak się pojawiali, nie odmawialiśmy im jedzenia, by nie obciążali swojego budżetu. Oprócz tego mogli napić się czegoś z procentami i jeśli tylko mogli, to korzystali. Czasem wręcz dzwonili z pytaniem, czy mogą wpaść na kolację i porozmawiać. Co się przed nimi postawiło, to wciągali. Często ledwo udawało im się wytoczyć z hotelu, bo byli już całkowicie napompowani wódeczką. Nie powiem, ja też przechylałem z nimi kieliszki, święty nie jestem. Czasem odwiedzali mnie ważni ludzie ze świata pozasportowego, między innymi mój przyjaciel Marek Papała. Kiedy dziennikarze widzieli, że do pokoju wchodzi komendant główny policji, uciekali w popłochu, bo obawiali się, że przyjechał po nich!

À propos, przypomniał mi się niezły numer. Pewnego razu przyniosłem sobie do pokoju wielki talerz kanapek wysmarowanych majonezem z kolacji. Wyszedłem na chwilę do toalety, wracam – a pół talerza wyparowało! W pokoju siedziało dwóch czy trzech czołowych dziennikarzy sportowych, członków ekipy, o której wcześniej wspomniałem.

– Kto to zjadł? Niemożliwe, żebyście w tak szybkim tempie to wciągnęli! – powiedziałem, choć oczywiście jedzenia nikomu nie żałuję.

Gdy im się przyjrzałem, spostrzegłem, że jeden z nich ma kieszenie urąbane majonezem. Okazało się, że podczas pakowania kanapek do kieszeni te barany pomazały sobie całe ubranie. Tak oto ich misterna kradzież żywności wyszła na jaw.

– Jak chcesz, to zamówię słoik majonezu i posmarujesz sobie, ile ci będzie potrzeba – wypaliłem do smakosza. Facet wyglądał żenująco.

Innym razem zauważyłem, że ktoś buchnął mi reprezentacyjne dresy. Wkurzyłem się strasznie. Koledzy z miasta pytali, kto to mógł zrobić, obiecywali, że zajmą się sprawą. Dres wróciłby szybko, bo chłopaki miałyby małe Guantanamo. Ostatecznie machnąłem na to ręką.

– Dobra, chłopcy. Nie dość, że głodni, nie napici, to jeszcze nie macie w co się ubrać. Nie musicie oddawać tych dresów, chociaż w zasadzie nie powinniście mieć prawa ich noszenia – stwierdziłem zrezygnowany.

Tych dziennikarzy lubiących się zabawić naprawdę dobrze było trzech. Jeden już niestety nie żyje, zdradzę, że miał na imię tak jak ja. Pisali różne dziwne rzeczy, i prawdziwe, i nieprawdziwe. Po meczu z Anglią miałem ostrą utarczkę słowną z jednym z nich – w przeszłości

Kiedy wygraliśmy z Rosją 3:1, czekały na mnie w hotelu dwie pannice. Żałowałem trochę, że nie jestem młodszy, bo ledwo dawałem sobie z nimi radę

pracował między innymi w „Przeglądzie Sportowym" i „Super Expressie". Na konferencji prasowej powiedziałem, że powinniśmy ten mecz wygrać, bo mieliśmy więcej sytuacji, a on zaczął porównywać obecne realia z czasami Kazia Górskiego. Zdenerwowałem się i doszło do ostrej spinki, ale szybko wszystko wróciło do normy. Szczególnie, że byłem przyzwyczajony, że w prasie często znajdują się rozmaite bzdury.

Prowadzenie reprezentacji Polski to nie tylko profity finansowe i wielki prestiż. Bywa też często całkiem... przyjemnie. Otóż wszystkie mecze towarzyskie starałem się organizować na stadionie Legii, jako że byłem kiedyś jej trenerem, a poza tym jestem rodowitym mokotowianinem, więc jakże by inaczej? Szybko złapałem kontakt z panami, którzy opiekowali się stołecznymi klubami ze striptizem. Jeden z kolegów, z którym się wychowałem na podwórku, a który był właścicielem jednego z takich przybytków, wziął mnie pewnego razu na bok:

– Janusz, po każdym twoim wygranym meczu w hotelu będzie czekało na ciebie tyle pań, ile twoi chłopcy strzelą bramek!

Spojrzałem na niego z powątpiewaniem, ale ciekaw byłem, czy tak rzeczywiście będzie. Tym bardziej że mecze towarzyskie to my raczej wygrywaliśmy. Po pierwszym ze zwycięskich spotkań z ciekawością udałem się do hotelu, żeby sprawdzić, czy czeka na mnie specyficzna nagroda. Wchodzę do lobby, a moi przyjaciele już na mnie czekają. Walnęliśmy symboliczną bombę, by uczcić wynik, ja jednak już myślałem o tym, czy w pokoju będę miał towarzyszki. Idę. Docieram na miejsce, po cichu otwieram drzwi. I faktycznie! Spod kołdry wychylają się dwie niunie, jedna czarna, druga ruda! Podziękowałem przyjacielowi, że nie rzucał słów na wiatr. W każdym razie to był dodatkowy element mobilizacyjny dla trenera reprezentacji. I dodatkowy trening, bo selekcjoner również musi być w formie. Kiedy na przykład wygraliśmy z Rosją 3:1 i czekały na mnie dwie pannice, to żałowałem trochę, że nie jestem młodszy, bo ledwo dawałem sobie z nimi radę. A jurne były, że hej! A piłkarze? Oni takich przyjemności nie mieli, żadnych panienek! Pozwalałem za to wypić po dwa piwka, żeby nie było żadnego walenia wódy po kątach.

PRACA Z DRUŻYNĄ

„Jak się nie będą ciebie bali, to się będą śmiali" – takie słowa powtarzałem moim zawodnikom w reprezentacji. Chodziło o to, żeby przeciwnik, obawiając się zderzenia z moim graczem, oddał piłkę albo wybił ją na aut. Uczyłem też ich faulować, brałem na takie specjalne korepetycje. Bo przecież faul to też element futbolu. Po naukach u mnie piłkarze nie łapali zbyt często czerwonych kartek, za to w piękny sposób odbierali przeciwnikom chęć do gry.

Jeśli nie pasowała mi gra zespołu, to opierdol dostawali wszyscy, nie pojedynczy piłkarze – trudno, żebym w szatni znęcał się tylko nad jednym, pozwalając reszcie śmiać się z delikwenta. Oczywiście zdarzały się sytuacje, że jakiś grajek mnie dokumentnie wkurwił. Wówczas wołałem go do siebie podczas meczu – nawet gdy akurat znajdował się po drugiej stronie boiska. Formacja przesuwała się o jednego zawodnika, a ja rozpoczynałem dyskusję.

– Jeszcze jeden taki numer zrobisz, a długo nie powąchasz boiska! A teraz wypierdalaj z powrotem na swoje miejsce!

Takie rozmowy musiały być krótkie i rzeczowe. Żaden nigdy nie próbował wejść ze mną w polemikę, a jeśli po powrocie na murawę powtarzał swoje błędy, zarządzałem zmianę. Każdy z chłopaków doskonale wiedział, że jeśli zostanie w taki sposób zmieniony, to drogo go to będzie kosztowało.

Podczas meczów eliminacyjnych musiałem zachować ostrożność, bo stawką były ważne punkty, w spotkaniach towarzyskich nie ograniczałem się za to w ogóle. Marek Jóźwiak biegał w Legii, a Wojtek Kowalczyk w prawie każdej mojej drużynie – w kadrze, a wcześniej w reprezentacji olimpijskiej. Trzy czwarte piłkarzy dotykała ta wątpliwa przyjemność.

– Chodź no tu! – krzyknąłem kiedyś do „szczęśliwca", który mnie wkurwił. To był właśnie Wojtuś albo Marek.

– Ale trenerze, trwa mecz – usłyszałem. Ta odpowiedź doprowadziła mnie do wrzenia. Poinformowałem sędziego technicznego, że piłkarz na chwilę schodzi z murawy.

– Zapierdalaj pięć okrążeń dookoła boiska. I to w odpowiednim czasie. Jak wrócisz, zbadam ci puls. Jeśli będzie dobry, wracasz do gry, jeśli nie, będziesz biegał dalej – zarządziłem.

Ludzie byli zdziwieni takimi akcjami, nieraz słyszałem, jak wołali z trybun:

– Kurwa, co tu się dzieje, czemu ten gość biega wokół boiska?! To jakieś nowe przepisy?

Zdarzało się też, że i dwóch naraz biegało! Reszta musiała dwoić się i troić, żeby nie stracić gola, bo mieliby naprawdę przesrane. Patrzyłem sobie na takich biegających delikwentów i jak zauważyłem, że któryś się snuje, to tak przy czwartym okrążeniu krzyczałem:

– No, to misiu, jeszcze trzy!

– Panie trenerze, ale za co? – pytali nieraz.

– Za jajco. Dla zdrowotności! – uśmiechałem się zawadiacko.

Takiemu piłkarzowi język opadał aż do kolan, ale co miał zrobić? Zasuwał! Nie mówię już o pompkach, które robili na okrągło. Jeśli podczas strzeleckiego treningu któryś nie wcelował w bramkę, robił dziesięć pompek. U żadnego trenera nie napompowali się tyle co u mnie.

Oprócz kar fizycznych zawodników dotykały również kary finansowe. Przed meczami towarzyskimi określałem, iloma bramkami mają wygrać. Jeżeli nie wygrali dwoma, trzema golami, to nie dostawali nawet złotówki. A jeśli, nie daj Boże, przegrali, wówczas wszystko zależało od mojego humoru. Albo wychodzili na zero, albo musieli dopłacać! Wszystko sobie dokładnie zapisywałem i przy okazji następnych wypłat egzekwowałem należną kwotę.

Groźnie to wszystko brzmi? Spokojnie, to i tak było przedszkole! Pierwszej reprezentacji nie trzymałem bowiem tak krótko jak olimpijskiej. Tam to było, kurwa, jak w obozie koncentracyjnym. Z pierwszą postępowałem dużo spokojniej, piłkarze wiedzieli, że zrobię dla nich wszystko i nie dam ich skrzywdzić. Jednak jeśli nie chcieli się dostosować do moich reguł, nie miałem litości.

Zawsze denerwował mnie Tomek Łapiński, nałogowy palacz. Ciągle się chował i tylko wynosił po sobie te pety. Wiadomo, że zawodowy sportowiec nie może sobie pozwolić na nałóg, dlatego ostro go ustawiałem. Moje wysiłki zdawały się jednak na nic, bo Łapa palił i palił. Poza tym był bardzo grzeczny – wypił piwko, wypalił fajeczkę i siedział cicho.

Czasami jednak Tomcio potrafił zaskoczyć. Pewnego razu wziął mnie na bok na pół godziny przed meczem. Już to mnie zdziwiło, bo takie rzeczy rzadko się zdarzają.

– Panie trenerze, ja nie będę dzisiaj grał – oznajmił.

– Łapa, co ty pierdolisz?!

– Źle się czuję, trenerze, chyba zaraz zemdleję…

– Ja ci, kurwa, zemdleję. Dostaniesz przez łeb, to ci się poprawi – uciąłem dyskusję i zawołałem lekarza.

– Zobacz no szybko, co mu jest. Coś żeście mu dali?! – wypytywałem.

– Nic, Janusz, wszystko jest w porządku! Przed chwilą mierzyliśmy mu ciśnienie, wszystko jest pod kontrolą! Nie wiem, może on się boi zagrać? – zastanawiał się doktor.

Wkurwiłem się. Wziąłem Łapę za łeb i prowadzę go na boisko.

– Czego ty się boisz? Pierwszy raz będziesz, kurwa, grał? Musisz grać! Jebnięty jesteś, że mi takie rzeczy mówisz! Mnie twoje samopoczucie nie interesuje. Kulawy, ale będziesz grał. Jesteś podstawowym obrońcą! Jak chcesz zemdleć, to wywal się podczas meczu, na boisku, karetka po ciebie przyjedzie. A ja cię wtedy kopnę w dupę i z powrotem wbiegniesz na murawę. – Moje groźby wydawały się robić na nim spore wrażenie.

– No dobra, to już może wyjdę – zaczął się łamać.

– Powtarzam ci jeszcze raz: jak chcesz, to mdlej na murawie, nie mam nic przeciwko.

Łapiński wystraszył się nie na żarty, błyskawicznie się przebrał i rzeczywiście rozegrał ten mecz. Mało tego – był jednym z najlepszych na boisku. W ogóle uważam, że to w tamtym czasie był czołowy europejski stoper. Świetnie się ustawiał, kapitalnie przewidywał grę, miał nieprawdopodobne przyspieszenie. Na kilku początkowych metrach był szybszy niż najszybsi napastnicy.

MOJA REPREZENTACJA

Wspomniałem o Łapińskim, byłbym niesprawiedliwy, gdybym zapomniał o reszcie piłkarzy. Dlatego teraz opowiem wam po kilka słów o swoich najważniejszych podopiecznych, tworzących kadrę narodową. Niektórych pochwalę, a niektórych uszczypnę. Nie obrażajcie się jednak, panowie, to z wielkiej sympatii! Pomijam tu piłkarzy, którzy grali u mnie również w reprezentacji olimpijskiej i o których już opowiadałem.

JACEK KRZYNÓWEK

Pamiętam, jak wyłowiłem i powołałem tego „Rudolfa Valentino" z wy-
suniętą szczęką. Tak na niego mówiłem, miał w końcu niepowtarzalną
buźkę. Na to jednak nie patrzyłem, bo facet nie musi być przystojny,
żeby grać dobrze w piłkę. No, powinien być trochę przystojniejszy od
małpy. Ale mówiąc serio, to pasował mi do zespołu – i jeśli chodzi o grę,
i o charakter. Bo gdyby nie miał jaj, to nawet gdyby był żonglerem
z Rio, u mnie by nie grał. Po pierwszym zgrupowaniu musiałby wrócić
do siebie na sianokosy.

RAFAŁ SIADACZKA

Było z nim kilka numerów, bo bardzo lubił się zaprawić. Kilka razy nakry-
łem go na piciu wódki. Za każdym razem odbywaliśmy trudną rozmowę,
a ja odstawiałem go od drużyny. Mówiłem, że jest idiotą, bo nie korzysta
ze stojących przed nim szans. Ściągnąłem mu lejce i prowadziłem jak
konia w powozie. Oczywiście, był charakterny, potrafił grać w piłkę, ale
miał ciągoty do napojów pędzonych na drożdżach. Był, moim zdaniem,
trochę leniuchowaty, dlatego wielkiej kariery w kadrze nie zrobił.

TOMASZ IWAN

Największy wpływ miał na niego Piotrek Świerczewski – jeśli mu coś
nie pasowało, za grdykę łapał go właśnie Świr. Lubił się napić whisky
albo browarka, ale tylko po meczach. Nigdy przed ważnym spotkaniem nie szukał okazji, by schować się w tataraku i coś przechylić. Bardzo spokojny i stateczny gość.

ADAM MATYSEK

Duży, ale spokojny facet. Był trochę jak Alek Kłak – gotów, by zareago-
wać w każdej chwili i ustawić niegrzecznego kolegę. Superlojalny gość,
dałby się pokroić za drużynę. To mój błąd, że wstawiłem do bramki na
mecz ze Szwecją Kazia Sidorczuka, a nie Matyska właśnie. Dziś posta-
wiłbym na Adama.

RADEK MICHALSKI

Mój wychowanek – kiedy przyszedłem do Legii, grał w drugiej drużynie. Wybrałem się na kilka treningów, zobaczyłem, co potrafi, i byłem wściekły na tych baranów, którzy nie dali mu grać z najlepszymi. Razem z Leszkiem Piszem tworzyli niesamowitą parę. Potrafili we dwóch rozmontować każdą obronę. Właśnie dzięki temu, że tak świetnie się rozumieli. I na boisku, i poza nim. Radek, jeśli było trzeba, przegryzłby komuś nogę, by ten nie przeszedł. Wypić lubił. Z kolegami chodził do tak zwanego kontenera, gdzie ładowali browary albo whisky. Aniołkiem nie był – i na boisku, i poza nim. Zasłynął jednak ze swej solidności.

TOMASZ KŁOS

Ełkaesiak, bardzo spokojny chłopak. Obawiałem się, że będzie to „łódzka rozrywka", ale miło się rozczarowałem. Oczywiście kiedy piłkarze dostawali trochę luzu, to także lubił pobrykać, ale nie do przesady. Zrównoważony, na boisku zawsze można było na niego liczyć. Dał się poznać jako zawodnik uniwersalny, ostry, zdecydowany.

JACEK BĄK

Kiedy pierwszy raz powołałem go do reprezentacji U-16, miał chyba 15 lat. Od razu umiał się wkomponować w drużynę. Zawsze chudy jak patyk, opowiadał kawały, każdy go lubił. Zaczął od 16-latków i doszedł aż do prowadzonej przeze mnie pierwszej reprezentacji. Typowy zawodnik środka pola, na bok kompletnie się nie nadawał, bo był za wysoki.

Bardzo szybko zaprzyjaźnił się z Piotrkiem Świerczewskim. Razem się bawili, razem też próbowali robić jakieś biznesy, ale zwykle wychodziły im bokiem. Wyróżniał się ubiorem, lansował modę na przebierańca. Jakieś dziwne futra, kosmiczne buty, porwane na dupie spodnie. No cudak. Chłopaki z niego żartowały, ale on to lubił.

KRZYSZTOF NOWAK

Bardzo solidny chłopak. Skryty, spokojny, lubił pozostawać na uboczu. Poza boiskiem nie było go widać, za to na murawie był agresywny, zdecydowany, ostry. No i przede wszystkim potrafił dobrze grać w piłkę! Kiedy tylko go potrzebowałem, przyjeżdżał na zgrupowanie, nawet płacąc kary w swoim klubie w Bundeslidze. Za wszelką cenę chciał reprezentować kraj. Ogromna szkoda, że akurat on zmarł na skutek ciężkiej choroby. Zawsze bardzo ciepło o nim myślę.

SŁAWOMIR MAJAK

Widzewiak. Piłkarsko nic nie można było mu zarzucić – silny jak koń, trzeba było kilku piłkarzy naraz, żeby zwalić go z nóg. Gdzie tylko grał, wyróżniał się bardzo wysokimi umiejętnościami, znakomitą szybkością i wydolnością. Powinien był zrobić większą karierę. Na mecze kadry przylatywał nawet z wakacji. A prywatnie? Lubił zabawę, nigdy nie odmawiał piweczka.

SYLWESTER CZERESZEWSKI

Wołaliśmy na niego Cygan. Chłopak mocno niedoceniany, wiedziałem, że drzemie w nim mnóstwo energii. Był z niego kawał chłopa. Wyżyłowany, z sercem do walki, idealny, by zapierdalać po boisku na całego. Postawiłem na niego i się nie zawiodłem. Spełniał wszystkie moje oczekiwania. Trzymał z legionistami, ale nie szukał na siłę rozrywki. Nie miałem z nim żadnych problemów wychowawczych. Jako pierwszy powołałem go do kadry, więc był w stanie za mnie oddać serce. Jeśli trzeba było nadstawić głowy, to nie zastanawiał się długo. Doskonale zagrał w meczu z Bułgarią w Burgas, strzelił wówczas dwa gole. Szkoda, że nie zrobił kariery za granicą. Myślę, że gdybyśmy awansowali do mistrzostw Europy, toby na nich zabłysnął.

ARTUR WICHNIAREK

Następne dziecko łódzkiej piłki i kolejny zmarnowany talent. Fajny był z niego Artek, ale zbyt zabawowy, zdecydowanie wolał figle od piłki nożnej. Wiedziałem, że w klubie bryka nagminnie, ale i na zgrupowaniach kadry łeb mu się kręcił jak radar wojskowy na poligonie. Tylko szukał, gdzie by się tu zabawić, panienkę zaliczyć czy jakąś bombę wypić. Mógł zrobić znacznie większą karierę – dostał szansę w Niemczech, mógł ją wykorzystać o wiele pełniej.

KAZIMIERZ SIDORCZUK

Skryty facet. Nie miał specjalnych warunków, ale w austriackim Sturmie Graz bardzo się z nim liczono. Zawodowiec, u mnie zachowywał się wzorowo, choć lubił wypić browarek. Wszystko popsuła mu ta szmata, którą wpuścił w meczu ze Szwecją w Chorzowie. Wiedział, że zarówno ja, jak i koledzy z drużyny mamy do niego o to pretensje. Bronił się, że Ljungberg nie powinien być dopuszczony do takiej sytuacji, no ale jednak ja połowę winy przypisuję jemu. Kazek to taka cicha woda. Raz byliśmy na zgrupowaniu w Austrii i miał mnóstwo zachcianek – a to piwko, a to inne przyjemne rzeczy. Wpadł więc pod moją młockarnię i momentalnie udało mi się go wyprostować.

TOMASZ FRANKOWSKI

Kiedy jeszcze pracowałem w Jagiellonii Białystok, to Franio razem z Markiem Citko biegał wokół boiska i podawał piłki. Bardzo związany z Jagą, w której się wychował, jako dzieciak podawał przecież piłki w prowadzonej przeze mnie Jagiellonii. Nie miał żadnych warunków, taki piłkarski przedszkolak.

Dał się poznać jako zawodnik niezmiernie trudny do upilnowania. Pamiętam mecz kadry z Austrią na wyjeździe, za kadencji Pawła Janasa. Drużynie nie szło, a polscy kibice, których przyjechało do Wiednia mnóstwo, skandowali, by Janosik wpuścił Frankowskiego. Tak też się stało, a Tomcio strzelił gola i Polska wygrała 3:1! Problemów z nim nigdy nie miałem. Ale jak usiadł do stołu – to jak ludzie z Podlasia nie odmówił. Puszcza wzywała.

PAWEŁ KRYSZAŁOWICZ

Świetna lewa noga. Mógł odnieść większy sukces – miał coś w sobie, ale podobnie jak Wichniarek był bardzo niesfornym zawodnikiem. Do większych zgrzytów między nami nie dochodziło. Nie pograł jednak u mnie zbyt wiele, na więcej po prostu nie zasłużył.

MIROSŁAW TRZECIAK

Mówiliśmy na niego „Trzeci", „Franek", ale mało kto wie, że nazywaliśmy go także „Szafa" i „Waliza". A to dlatego, że miał nieziemsko szeroką dupę. Był taki trochę ścichapęk, ale potrafił się odgryźć, jak chłopaki go atakowały, że rusza się jak żółw. To nie był osiołek, który nie potrafił się odezwać. Umiał pokazać swoją inteligencję, bo to był bardzo mądry chłopak. Poza tym miał w nogach manianę, potrafił się kiwać.

Kiedy powoływałem go do reprezentacji, bardzo dobrze grał w ŁKS-ie Łódź, potem przeniósł się do Osasuny Pampeluna. Potrafił się uwolnić spod opieki rywali, uciec dwóm–trzem obrońcom. Umiał zagrać mądrą, fajną piłkę do kolegi. W jakimś sensie przypominał Mirka Okońskiego. Oczywiście z zachowaniem wszelkich proporcji, bo Okoń był piłkarzem znacznie lepszym technicznie. Takie żywe srebro, czego o Trzeciaku powiedzieć nie można. Natomiast Franio mógł na swoją walizę przyjąć dwóch rywali i ich przepchnąć, odegrać piłkę, i dlatego znalazł się w reprezentacji. Nigdy natomiast nie był wyjątkowym snajperem. No i to dupsko… Trzeba było zamknąć go gdzieś na miesiąc i zaordynować jakąś dietę wodną, cztery litry dziennie i nic więcej. Wtedy miałby lepszą sylwetkę i grałby jeszcze lepiej.

Kto jeszcze tworzył prowadzoną przeze mnie reprezentację? Oczywiście wymienieni w rozdziale pierwszym Dariusz Adamczuk, Marek Bajor, Jerzy Brzęczek, Dariusz Gęsior, Marcin Jałocha, Andrzej Juskowiak, Aleksander Kłak, Andrzej Kobylański, Wojciech Kowalczyk, Marek Koźmiński, Tomasz Łapiński, Grzegorz Mielcarski, Ryszard Staniek, Piotr Świerczewski, Mirosław Waligóra, Tomasz Wałdoch, Dariusz Koseła, Arkadiusz Onyszko, Dariusz Szubert, Tomasz Wieszczycki. Każdy z nich był dla mojej kadry ważny, jedni w większym stopniu, inni w mniejszym. Muszę natomiast podkreślić, że jako całość, jako drużyna prezentowali się wyśmienicie. I omal nie awansowali do Euro 2000. Od tego wielkiego sukcesu dzieliła nas długość paznokcia. Ale niestety się nie udało. Przeczytajcie, jak do tego doszło.

EURO 2000

Solą mojej pracy w reprezentacji były eliminacje do mistrzostw Europy 2000 organizowanych w Holandii i Belgii. Zaraz po losowaniu wszyscy zaczęli mówić, że trafiliśmy do grupy śmierci. I rzeczywiście – mieliśmy zagrać z Anglią, Szwecją, Bułgarią i Luksemburgiem. Teoretycznie nie mieliśmy prawa z takiej grupy wyjść, ale ja zapowiedziałem, że to zrobię. I od pierwszego meczu chciałem rozpocząć nasz marsz do Euro 2000.

Pierwszy mecz eliminacji graliśmy w Bułgarii, w Burgas. Jechaliśmy tam na pewno nie w roli faworyta, bo przecież Bułgarzy mieli mocną drużynę, która kwalifikowała się do wielkich imprez. Mimo to wierzyliśmy, że będzie można ich puknąć.

Na miejscu odbyliśmy dwa treningi – pierwszy na dość nieciekawym boisku, natomiast drugi przysługiwał nam na tym głównym, w przeddzień meczu. Doszło jednak do wyjątkowej awantury, bo nie chcieli nas tam wpuścić! Dowiedziałem się, że klub i stadion należą do ludzi z miasta, którzy gdzieś mają jakąś reprezentację Polski. Wypowiedziałem więc prawdziwą wojnę. Chodziłem z miejsca w miejsce i awanturowałem się z każdym, kto mi się nawinął. Również z delegatem UEFA, który chyba bał się Bułgarów. Nagle w klubie pojawił się jakiś ważny gość. Okazało się, że to jeden z właścicieli klubu. Od razu poszedłem z nim pogadać.

– Słuchaj, ja dobrze znam Christo Stoiczkowa, na pewno byłby niezadowolony, że nie pozwalacie nam potrenować na waszym stadionie – zacząłem, licząc na to, że magia wielkiego Stoiczkowa zadziała.

– A skąd go znasz? – dopytywał, a po chwili odszedł na bok, by zadzwonić do Christo. Szybko wrócił. – Jak długo chcecie trenować? – zapytał od razu.

– Najwyżej 50 minut. To przecież tylko rozruch przedmeczowy – wyjaśniłem.

– Dobrze, możecie trenować. Tylko nie zniszczcie murawy – zastrzegł, co mnie rozsierdziło.

„Już ja wam, kurwy, pokażę zrytą murawę", pomyślałem. Trening odbył się normalnie, a na jego koniec zarządziłem starty i sprinty.

– Ostatnie pięć metrów każdy jedzie na dupie, wślizgiem! – wykrzyczałem, a tu nagle z budynku klubowego wypadło dwóch ochroniarzy!

– Chłopaki, idźcie w ich stronę – nakazałem drużynie.

A kiedy kilkunastu chłopa ruszyło w kierunku dwóch Bułgarów, ci w pośpiechu ukryli się za drzwiami, bo myśleli, że dostaną wpierdol, i już był spokój. Potem zarządziłem jeszcze ze dwie serie wślizgów, które chłopcy ochoczo wykonywali. Ale nawet wśród nich dało się wyczuć duże napięcie. Bo gdyby nas rzeczywiście na ten stadion nie wpuścili, to nie wiem, gdzie byśmy trenowali. Chyba na plaży.

Problemy, choć już zupełnie innego rodzaju, pojawiły się na drugi dzień. Na popołudnie mieliśmy wyznaczoną odprawę – było to na dobre kilka godzin przed rozpoczęciem meczu. Przyszedłem i wraz z asystentami zaczęliśmy spokojnie przygotowywać się do rozpracowania Bułgarów. Nagle patrzę, a tu brakuje jednego piłkarza – Juskowiaka! Po pięciu czy dziesięciu minutach zjawia się rzeczony Józio, a za nim kryje się kucharz Robert Sowa.

– Gdzie, kurwa, byliście? Na placach ziemniaczanych? Coś mu gotowałeś? – zdenerwowało mnie to nie na żarty.

– Byliśmy na spacerze relaksacyjnym – wypalił Sowa.

– A to co, kurwa, na wczasy sobie przyjechaliście, debile?!

Dobrze, że chociaż powiedzieli prawdę, ale i tak opierdziel dostali niesamowity. Słuchali mnie z opuszczonymi łbami. Potem pomyślałem, że to mimo wszystko był dobry element motywacyjny, bo po raz kolejny wszyscy piłkarze zobaczyli, że nie ma litości. Juskowiak oczywiście zagrał w tym meczu. Drużyna spisała się wybornie, aż miło było patrzeć. Nawet nie musiałem za często podbiegać do linii i ich opierdzielać, co było dla mnie pewną nowością. Rozjechaliśmy ich gładko 3:0 (po dwóch golach Sylwestra Czereszewskiego i jednym Tomasza Iwana), a mogliśmy jeszcze wyżej. Prezes Dziurowicz mało się nie zesrał ze szczęścia. Oczywiście pojawiły się głosy, że ja ten mecz ustawiłem. Nawet chłopaki w samolocie zastanawiały się, jak to się stało, że tak łatwo im poszło z tymi Bułgarami. Ale z tym ustawieniem to jakieś kompletne bzdury były. W każdym razie to zwycięstwo sprawiło, że wzięliśmy na swoje barki jeszcze większą presję. Kibice mieli w głowie już tylko jedno – awans do mistrzostw Europy.

Kolejny mecz eliminacyjny graliśmy w Warszawie, z Luksemburgiem. Co ciekawe, nasi piłkarze byli ubrani w czarne stroje, co wzbudziło w kraju wielkie oburzenie. Chodziło o to, że nasi rywale grali w strojach białych, a my, żeby się od nich odróżniać, musieliśmy wystąpić w trzecim zestawie. A że innego nie było, to zagraliśmy na czarno. Nie chciałem, żebyśmy w takich grali, ale zostałem zaskoczony tuż przed meczem i właściwie już nic nie dało się zmienić. Oczywiście największy opierdol zebrał Wiesiu Ignasiewicz. Przeczytacie o tym w ostatnim rozdziale.

Mówiłem chłopakom, że trzeba tym Luksemburczykom wpierdolić, ale nie na siłę, żeby nie narazić się na kontuzje. Wiedziałem, że jak spokojnie pogramy, to trzy punkty będą pewne. I były. 3:0 po golach Brzęczka, Juskowiaka i Trzeciaka to najmniejszy wymiar kary. A rywale pokopali rowy przed bramką, żeby nie dostać więcej.

Zaraz po meczu dowiedziałem się, że mamy pojechać do pałacu prezydenckiego, na zaproszenie prezydenta Aleksandra Kwaśniewskiego. Wjechaliśmy na dziedziniec, a rzadko się zdarza, żeby ktokolwiek mógł przekroczyć autokarem bramę pałacu. Rysiu Kalisz, który wtedy współpracował z prezydentem, przyjął mnie dobrym napitkiem. Drużynę po jakimś czasie wygoniłem, a sam jeszcze trochę zostałem. Popiliśmy, porozmawialiśmy. Było bardzo miło.

W Wielkiej Brytanii zatrzymaliśmy się w świetnym ośrodku Arsenalu Londyn. Było to idealne miejsce, żeby spokojnie przygotować się do meczu. Meczu dla nas arcyważnego – i ze względu na walkę o awans do mistrzostw Europy, i dlatego, że spotkania z Anglią w Polsce zawsze są traktowane wyjątkowo. Niestety umiarkowanie przejął się tym Jacek Bąk, który odwalił wyjątkową kaszanę. Dwa razy dał się oszukać Paulowi Scholesowi, który przy nim był wzrostu siedzącego psa. Oczywiście, faktem było to, że rudzielec Scholes swoje dwa gole strzelił ręką. Zaraz po pierwszym trafieniu zerwałem się z ławki i zacząłem się wydzierać w kierunku portugalskiego sędziego Vítora Pereiry, natomiast liniowy kazał mi natychmiast wracać na miejsce. Gdybym zacząłem jechać swoimi tekstami, pewnie od razu trafiłbym na trybuny. Trochę nawyzywałem arbitrów, ale oczywiście nic to nie pomogło – główny, którego nazwałem „pedałem" ze względu na sposób poruszania się, wskazał na środek boiska. Nie wiem, co Anglicy z nim zrobili i w jakim pedalskim klubie spędził czas przed meczem, ale ewidentnie sędziował na ich korzyść. Zaraz po zakończeniu pierwszej połowy podbiegli do mnie dziennikarze i zapytali, czy widziałem, że Scholes strzelił gole ręką. Odparłem, że tak, tylko szkoda, że tamten pedał na boisku tego nie dostrzegł.

W przerwie w szatni byłem spokojny. Ba, to ja musiałem uspokajać wściekłych piłkarzy! Powiedziałem, że teraz nie ma wyjścia i trzeba się trochę otworzyć, by powalczyć o choćby punkt, zdecydowanie wyżej ich atakować i kontrować. Liczyłem na wyrównanie, szczególnie że mieliśmy przecież kontaktowego gola, którego w 28. minucie strzelił Jurek Brzęczek.

Taka sytuacja szybko się pojawiła. Wyszliśmy z kontrą trzech na dwóch, przy dobrym rozegraniu moi piłkarze mogli wjechać z piłką do bramki. Jednak Mirek Trzeciak, nie wiedzieć czemu, zdecydował się

Anglia – Polska. Przyznaję, że popełniłem w tym meczu jeden błąd – nie puszczając wcześniej na boisko Kowala. Przynajmniej na 45 minut. On pokazałby swój charakter, poustawiałby tych Angoli. Wojtuś był taki, że zasuwałby, dopóki nie padłby na ryj

Zaraz po meczu z Luksemburgiem dowiedziałem się, że mamy pojechać do pałacu prezydenckiego, na zaproszenie prezydenta Aleksandra Kwaśniewskiego. Wjechaliśmy na dziedziniec, a rzadko się zdarza, żeby ktokolwiek mógł przekroczyć autokarem bramę pałacu

na strzał z 30 metrów! Od razu dałem mu mocno do wiwatu, ale co to mogło pomóc? Gola nie było.

Przyznaję, że popełniłem w tym meczu jeden błąd – nie puszczając wcześniej na boisko Kowala. Przynajmniej na 45 minut. On pokazałby swój charakter, poustawiałby tych Angoli. Wojtuś był taki, że zasuwałby, dopóki nie padłby na ryj. Zresztą miał do mnie trochę pretensji, wyczuwałem to.

Po przerwie dostaliśmy trzeciego gola od rudego Scholesa. Później zaatakowano mnie, że ustawiłem drużynę zbyt defensywnie z sześcioma obrońcami, z czym się kompletnie nie zgadzam. Być może jednak moi piłkarze samozachowawczo trochę zbyt głęboko się cofnęli, przez co nie mogli odbierać piłki w odpowiedniej odległości od bramki. Dzięki temu Anglicy mieli możliwość, żeby spokojnie rozgrywać sobie piłkę i dośrodkowywać ją w nasze pole karne. Wybrałem niby najlepszy skład, ale mi się ten skład zesrał.

Na konferencji prasowej powiedziałem otwarcie, że sędzia nie nadaje się do niczego, skoro puszcza dwie takie bramki. Pogratulowałem Anglikom i tyle.

Przed meczem ze Szwecją mieszkaliśmy w pałacyku w Świerklańcu, co załatwiłem dzięki moim śląskim układom. Chłopcy byli przed tym meczem bardzo dobrze zmotywowani. Zabroniłem im się murować i nastawiać na kontry, kazałem walczyć o zwycięstwo! Choć ostrzegałem też przed siłą szwedzkiej drużyny, która potrafi grać piłkę twardą, zdecydowaną, siłową.

Atmosfera przed meczem była emocjonująca – mnóstwo ludzi, kapitalny doping na Stadionie Śląskim oraz pod nim. Na stadionie było 30 tysięcy kibiców. Przyszli nawet mimo porażki z Anglią kilka dni wcześniej. Wszystko jednak zepsuł świętej pamięci Dziurowicz. Chodziło o niemieckiego sędziego Markusa Merka. Ale po kolei.

Jakiś czas przed pojedynkiem miałem okazję porozmawiać z arbitrem i trochę poprzekonywać go, by był przychylny naszej reprezentacji.

– Nie będę wam przeszkadzał – zapewnił mnie Merk.

– Markusiku, ale gramy u siebie, może byś coś pomógł…

– Jeśli będzie taka możliwość, to pomogę, ale na pewno nie pójdę na żadne cuda.

– No dobra, ale przydałoby się, żeby szala tak w 25 procentach przechyliła się w naszą stronę.

Sędzia był urobiony. Na pewno nie zrobiłby nam żadnej krzywdy, a i trochę pod nas gwizdał, niestety pierdolnięty Dziurowicz wymyślił największą głupotę w dziejach. Chciał robić karierę w UEFA, więc zaprosił na mecz Szweda Lenarta Johanssona, czyli ówczesnego prezydenta europejskiej federacji piłkarskiej. Ugościł go znakomicie, spoił wódką, widziałem, że napierdoleni byli jak koziołki matołki. Wszystko fajnie, ale dla mnie i drużyny miało to opłakane skutki. Jak się Merk dowiedział, że na trybunach jest Szwed Johansson, a gramy właśnie ze Szwedami, to poruszał się po boisku przestraszony jak przepiórka. Na nic ekstra nie mogliśmy liczyć.

Przegraliśmy 0:1 po golu tego małego śmierdziela Fredrika Ljungberga. Ewidentny błąd Jurka Brzęczka, który zamiast urżnąć kundla w środku pola, biegł za nim jak głupek dobre 40 metrów i kompletnie nic z tego nie wynikło. A krzyczałem do Brzękola kilka razy: „Rżnij go!". Nie urżnął i ten mały Szwed pokonał Kazka Sidorczuka, który też bronił tak, jakby chciał, a nie mógł. Szwedzi poza tą sytuacją nie mieli jakichś klarownych momentów, byliśmy bardzo dobrze na nich ustawieni. Juskowiak miał setkę, to samo Tomek Wałdoch, który zamiast pierdolnąć piłkę głową prosto w bramkę po stałym fragmencie gry, walnął po koźle. Kiedy piłka dolatywała do głowy Tomka, pomyślałem sobie, że na pewno będzie gol. Nie miałem co do tego wątpliwości. Nie wiem, dlaczego stało się inaczej. Przyłożył tak mocno, że piłka odbiła się od murawy i przeleciała ponad poprzeczką. Bramkarz nie wiedział nawet, o co chodzi. Stał jak dupa, wmurowany, i tylko patrzył jak cielę.

Szwedzi dowieźli zwycięstwo 1:0 i skakali jak szaleni. Bo to nie był ich mecz, na pewno nie zasłużyli na wywiezienie z Polski trzech punktów. A sędzia Merk zagadnął mnie tylko po spotkaniu:

– I coście, kurwa, narobili?!

Chodziło oczywiście o zaproszenie Johanssona. Dziurowicz kariery w UEFA nie zrobił, a my przerżnęliśmy ze Szwedami. Takie to sukcesy przyniosła jego działalność.

Następny był pojedynek z Bułgarią i wiedziałem, że musimy go wygrać. Panowały bardzo ciężkie warunki, ponieważ przez cały dzień padał rzęsisty deszcz. Nam to jednak nie przeszkadzało. Bułgarzy tworzyli co prawda silną drużynę, ale widać było, że po porażce u siebie nie czują się pewnie. Mieli oczywiście kilku świetnych zawodników ze Stoiczkowem na czele, ale tamtego dnia nie mogli nic zrobić. Na tej wodzie świetnie czuł się Tomek Hajto – zawodnik z gór, któremu nie była straszna żadna pogoda ani żadni rywale.

Pamiętam, że przed meczem długo dyskutowałem z Christo Stoiczkowem. Spotkałem się z nim zresztą już na lotnisku. Przywitaliśmy się „na misia", jak druh z druhem. No i potem usłyszałem, że ja ten mecz z sympatycznym Christo załatwiłem. Totalna bzdura! Znaliśmy się od dawna, więc to dla mnie normalne, że zamieniłem z nim kilka słów. Po meczu jednak pseudoeksperci zaczęli głosić, że wynik był ustawiony. Fachowcy od siedmiu boleści.

Z Luksemburgiem graliśmy z pełną kontrolą – potem się okazało, że z aż za dużą! Prowadziliśmy 3:0 (gole strzelili: Siadaczka, Wichniarek, Iwan) i wydawało się, że z łatwością wygramy. Już nawet przestałem opierdzielać piłkarzy, pozwoliłem im spokojnie robić swoje. Nagle na kilkanaście minut przed końcem spotkania któryś Luksemburczyk dołożył łeb i wpadł gol. Za chwilę kolejne trafienie! Przypadkowe, ale gol to gol. Wszyscy myśleli, że zaraz walną trzecią i zrobi się remis. Wyskoczyłem do linii i zacząłem ich tak jebać, że chyba z kilometra było mnie słychać. Wykorzystałem całą artylerię, jaką dysponowałem. To pomogło, bo chwilę później chłopaki kompletnie zgniotły Luksemburczyków. Trafiała się sytuacja za sytuacją. Rywale mieli szczęście, że skończyło się tylko 3:2. Ale po meczu pochwał nie było.

– Barany jesteście! Macie 3:0, możecie grać sobie z debilami w dziada. A wy dajecie sobie dwa gole strzelić? – opierdalałem ich. – Chcieliście się po meczu zabawić, napić piwa? Teraz, kurwa, dostaniecie, ale po szklance wody. I to niech wam wystarczy do rana.

– Panie trenerze, prosimy, przecież wygraliśmy… – kajały się barany jedne.

– No i co, kurwa, z tego, że wygraliście? Gdyby zabrakło kogoś, kto złapie was za łby i każe wziąć się do roboty, to gdzie wtedy będziecie?!

Zamilkli. Zarządziłem wymarsz do autokaru, gdzie oczywiście też ich zjebałem. Dostawali po łbach, dopóki nie posnęli w hotelowych pokojach. Ale należało im się. Skoro wygrywamy ze stokrotnie lepszą Bułgarią na wyjeździe, to frajerstwem jest pozwolenie Luksemburgowi na wbicie dwóch goli.

Czy zlekceważyliśmy rywali? Nie sądzę. Raczej mieliśmy sporo pecha. No i fakt, że rywal był na dechach, trochę nas uśpił. Chłopaki nie przewidziały, że jak ktoś potrafi się choć trochę bić, to nawet z desek może przywalić kopa w łeb. No i tak było.

Kolejny mecz z Anglią prezes Marian Dziurowicz koniecznie chciał rozegrać na Stadionie Śląskim w Chorzowie. Ja się nie zgodziłem i zażądałem, byśmy grali na Legii. Postawiłem sprawę jasno:

– Jak pan chce, niech pan mnie wypierdoli, ale ja w Chorzowie grał nie będę.

Wymusiłem też, żeby poustawiać trybuny na kilka tysięcy miejsc na zakolach boiska, do normalności trzeba było doprowadzić też toalety i szatnie. Mimo to Anglicy potem powiedzieli, że takiego pierdolnika to w życiu nie widzieli, że u nich nawet w czwartej lidze jest lepiej. Dla nich nasz stadion był jak slumsy. No ale to był nasz stadion i mieli grać, gdzie wyznaczyliśmy, kręcenie nosem zdało się na nic. Jakby teraz przyjechali, to pewnie wszystko by im się podobało. Stadion Legii jest piękny i z wielką radością zawsze go odwiedzam. I trochę żałuję, że za moich czasów był tam taki burdel…

Z całą pewnością był to mecz podwyższonego ryzyka i wielkiego napięcia. Zapotrzebowanie było na ponad 200 tysięcy biletów, a na Legię wchodziło raptem kilkanaście tysięcy osób. To pokazuje, jakim zainteresowaniem cieszyło się to spotkanie.

– Janusz, ty chcesz grać na Legii, ale jak ci ludzie przyjadą, to bramy porozwalają! – ostrzegały mnie dziewczyny z PZPN-u.

– Może nie przyjadą... – mydliłem im oczy, ale wiedziałem, że będzie inaczej. Przyjechali. I było ich tyle, że nie dało się wcisnąć szpilki. Siadali po dwóch na jednym miejscu, wieszali się na płotach, słupach, nikt nie był w stanie tego kontrolować.

W szatni przed meczem dawało się odczuć, jak ważny mecz jest przed nami. Dla mnie był w jakimś sensie wyjątkowy. Zanim się rozpoczął, wiedziałem, że czeka nas szczególnie ostre starcie. Krew, pot, zacięta walka i emocje na pełnej piździe. Krążyłem po szatni z dłońmi splecionymi za plecami. Jedno kółko, drugie, trzecie... Paweł Janas wielokrotnie widział mnie przed meczem, ale potem powtarzał, że tak nakręconego – nigdy. Przysięgam, w tamtej chwili sam bym wyszedł na to boisko z chłopakami i zrobił kilka wślizgów na wysokości kolan.

Patrzyłem raz w ziemię, raz na piłkarzy i byłem zadowolony z poziomu ich wkurwienia i sportowej złości. Nienawidzili tych Anglików. Chcieli ich zniszczyć, zabić, obedrzeć ze skóry. Byli jak głodne wilki, chcieli ich pożreć. Jeśli kiedykolwiek panowie policjanci wlepili wam niezasłużony mandat, z pewnością życzyliście im wszystkiego najgorszego. Tak samo było z moimi piłkarzami. Anglicy tego wieczoru byli niczym te parszywe kundle, które zamiast pójść sobie w pizdu, chcą wam wlepić punkty za jakąś pierdołę. Wy pewnie burknęlibyście pod nosem kilka niemiłych słów, a moi piłkarze dołożyliby jeszcze soczystego kopa w dupę. Kilka takich ciosów mieli na Łazienkowskiej przyjąć Anglicy.

Postanowiłem ich jeszcze ponakręcać. Podszedłem do Mirka Trzeciaka i z całej siły przypierdoliłem mu otwartą dłonią w plecy. Ślad mojej ręki na jego łopatce stawał się coraz bardziej widoczny, jakby ktoś wytatuował mu na czerwono Wujową dłoń. Na twarzy Walizy najpierw dostrzegłem grymas bólu, a potem wściekłość – za wszelką cenę starał się nie wybuchnąć.

– Co, Miruś, zdenerwowany jesteś? Stało się coś? – zapytałem.

– Tak – wycedził, ale miałem pewność, że chce powiedzieć więcej. Dużo więcej.

– Dobrze, a chciałbyś może mi oddać? – kontynuowałem.

Milczał. Zacisnął wargi niemal do krwi.

– To oddaj, kurwa, ale Angolom! I wy pozostali też! Macie tych fiutów zajebać! – darłem się wniebogłosy, a piłkarze wyglądali jak koguty wypuszczone po miesiącu z ciasnej klatki. Żeby jednak czerwona plama przed oczami do reszty nie przysłoniła im świata, pozwoliłem sobie na merytoryczne podsumowanie: – Musimy ich opierdolić, panowie, i tyle. Wychodzimy i golimy frajerów, nie ma, że Premiership, Scholesy-srolesy. Rękoma wam strzelali gole, to teraz wy im tak samo strzelajcie. A jak nie będziecie mogli sięgnąć, to fujarami wpakujcie do bramki! Tego meczu nie można przegrać. Jak was ograją, nie pokazujcie mi się na oczy.

To jednak nie koniec. Tomek Iwan wyszczerzył się, a ja zauważyłem, że ma sporą szparę pomiędzy zębami.

– Tomcio, chodź no tu – poleciłem. – Podejdziesz do Beckhama i strzykniesz mu trochę ślinki do jego paszczy. Podkurwimy gwiazdorka. Tylko pamiętaj, nie odchodź od niego, czekaj na odwet.

Do meczu pozostawało tylko kilkanaście minut. Chłopcy byli nakręceni i tak spoceni, jakby właśnie rozegrali pierwszą połowę. Jedni walili łapami po szaflach, inni z całej siły kopali piłką o ścianę. Amok. I w końcu jest! Gwizdek sędziego, nawołujący do wyjścia do tunelu. Kiedy się w nim pojawiliśmy, Anglicy już czekali. Wpatrywali się w tych moich zbójów jak Rzymianie w Kartagińczyków. A oni byli wściekli, naładowani jak nowiutkie akumulatory. Z niecierpliwością czekałem na jakąś zadymę: lekkie nadepnięcie, uszczypnięcie czy też zdrowe przyjebanie po kopytach – oczywiście wszystko w ramach przepisów.

– Rozjebmy ich, panowie! Jeden za wszystkich, wszyscy za jednego! – krzyczeli.

Gdybym stał na miejscu tych wszystkich „Becksów", srałbym w gacie na samą myśl o boiskowej walce z takimi piłkarzami, którzy zachowują się jak kryminaliści wypuszczeni na spacerniak, a jedyną szansą na wyjście na wolność jest wygranie tego meczu. Za wszelką cenę. Wszelkimi możliwymi sposobami. Zabić, zniszczyć. Ogolić frajerów. Tak – to właśnie były moje chłopaki. Byłem z nich dumny.

Na stadionie istne szaleństwo – włosy stawały dęba, jaja furczały. Ani przez moment nie było widać, że to wielka Anglia, która jeszcze niedawno z łatwością ograła nas 3:1. Polacy byli tak zawzięci, że gdyby mogli, toby rywalom tętnice przegryźli. Nawet Jacek Zieliński, zawodnik na co dzień łagodny, wycinał ich równo z trawą. To bardzo denerwowało trenera Anglików Kevina Keegana, który co chwila podbiegał do sędziego liniowego z pretensjami.

– Siadaj, kundlu, nie zasłaniaj ludziom widoku! – krzyknąłem do niego po polsku i poprawiłem kilkoma angielskimi epitetami.

Byłem w swoim żywiole. Cały czas zagrzewałem chłopaków do walki. Nie mogło być mowy o odpuszczaniu, nawet na centymetr! Atakowaliśmy, graliśmy tak, jak sobie wymarzyłem. To samo miało być w Londynie. Tam się nie udało, ale w Warszawie rozpętało się piekło! Już przy środkowej linii boiska Anglicy byli kasowani. W jednej z sytuacji Tomek Hajto trafił w poprzeczkę, wydawało się, że zaraz ich ukłujemy. Dwie setki zmarnował Juskowiak, no a do szewskiej pasji doprowadził mnie ten Radosław „wzrostu siedzącego psa" Gilewicz. Wyjechał sam na sam z frajerem, spieprzył setkę, a nawet dwusetkę, a potem tylko przepraszał i przepraszał.

– Kurwa, co mnie przepraszasz? Jesteś właśnie od tego, żeby takie sytuacje wykorzystywać! Jak chcesz przepraszać, to idź do programu *Wybacz mi* – opierdzieAłem go już po meczu.

– No przepraszam, trenerze… Pośliznąłem się.

– Weź już się zamknij, zejdź mi z oczu – pogoniłem go.

Niestety, dostało mu się także od kolegów z drużyny, którzy zwyzywali go od kundli. Chcieli go nawet bić, tacy byli sfrustrowani i wściekli. Tomek Hajto i Kazek Sidorczuk wzięli go za łeb. Nie ma się co dziwić – zabrał kolegom pieniądze i awans do mistrzostw Europy... – Zostawcie go już. Ma dosyć. – Odciągnąłem najbardziej krewkich. Wynik mógł był przeróżny: i oni mogli nas puknąć, i my ich. My w zasadzie nie tyle mogliśmy, co powinniśmy, bo mieliśmy cztery takie sytuacje, że żal było z nich nie skorzystać. Anglicy mieli jedną, ale też bardzo dobrą – uratował nas słupek. Aż dziw bierze, że nie padł żaden gol. A angielskie gazety potem pisały, że my byliśmy zdecydowanie lepsi. Tylko cóż z tego, że nas chwalili, skoro wynik był niekorzystny.

Całkiem inny mecz rozegrał się na trybunach. Pijani angielscy kibice, którzy siedzieli na łuku od strony Kanałku Piaseczyńskiego, zaczęli rzucać race i butelki w kierunku sektora naszych fanów. Kibice z Żylety się wkurwili i zaczęli tłuc Angoli po łbach. Tyle się mówiło o niebezpiecznych angielskich kibicach, a kiedy do akcji wkroczyli nasi, to okazało się, że goście są co najwyżej harcerzami. W każdym razie musiała zainterweniować policja, ale co Anglicy dostali, to zapamiętali z pewnością na długo. Spierdzielali do Kanałku, woleli kąpiel niż lanie od polskich kibiców!

Jeśli chodzi o kolejny pojedynek, ze Szwecją, zdawałem sobie sprawę, że remis i nasze zwycięstwo eliminowały Anglików, a nam dawały grę w barażach. Szwedzi natomiast nie musieli z nami wygrywać, bo mieli już pewny awans. Dochodziły do mnie jednak sygnały, że Anglicy straciliby nieprawdopodobne pieniądze, gdyby nie awansowali, i że po prostu dofinansowali Szwedów, by ci mieli większą ochotę do walki. Nie widzę w tym zresztą nic złego – mieli kasę, to ich zmotywowali.

– Jak liczycie na to, że Szwedzi będą sobie tylko spokojnie biegać, to jesteście w błędzie. Anglicy na pewno się postarają, by nas ograli – ostrzegałem chłopaków przed meczem.

Wydaje mi się, że tak właśnie było. Ale my też w pewnym sensie jesteśmy sami sobie winni. Już na początku Tomek Hajto zaczął tych

Szwedów rżnąć po łydkach, co ich tylko mocno wkurwiło. Wpierdzielał się w nich po swojemu, zupełnie niepotrzebnie. Szwedzi strzelili dwa gole, ale my też mieliśmy swoje sytuacje.

Cholernie szkoda mi było tego meczu, bo moim zdaniem Szwedzi zagrali nawet gorzej niż w Polsce. Kiedy prowadzili, nie było już czego bronić, odsłoniliśmy się i atakowaliśmy. Stwarzaliśmy sytuacje, ale ci, którzy je mieli, zesrali się, nasmrodzili, a na boisku pozostawiali placki jak krowy na pastwisku. W meczu o taką stawkę nie można sobie pozwolić na niewykorzystywanie okazji.

W szatni panowała grobowa cisza. A ja wpadłem tak wkurwiony, że przez jakieś trzy minuty nie mogłem słowa wypowiedzieć. Potem dopiero rozpoczął się mój koncert. Wstąpiło we mnie szaleństwo.

– Jak można było takiego meczu przynajmniej nie zremisować? Po co, głupki, ich prowokowaliście?! – prawie lałem ich po łbach.

Żaden nie odezwał się słowem.

Strasznie szkoda było mi tych eliminacji. Trafiliśmy do silnej grupy, być może nawet najsilniejszej. Wystarczyło zdobyć punkt więcej, żeby z niej wyjść i awansować do baraży. Wcześniej mogliśmy pokonać Anglię, zremisować ze Szwecją u siebie. A na rewanż do Szwedów jechalibyśmy napić się piwa i poprawić gorzałą.

Żałowałem też meczów z Luksemburgiem. Skoro wygraliśmy z Bułgarami na wyjeździe 3:0, to Luksemburczykom powinniśmy nałobzować z sześć, i to w obu meczach. Choć wygraliśmy, pozostał niedosyt.

Poniekąd winny jest też PZPN. Bodajże przed rewanżowym meczem ze Szwecją spotkałem się z wiceprezesem Zbigniewem Bońkiem i prezesem Marianem Dziurowiczem.

– Zdopingujcie chłopaków finansowo. Nie liczcie tylko na to, że będę ich motywował swoimi sposobami. Anglicy na pewno, na sto procent zaproponują kasiorę Szwedom, zróbmy coś, chociaż obiecajmy coś tym chłopakom za awans. Dajcie im do powąchania kiełbachę – apelowałem.

Bonias nie zareagował na to dobrze. Pamiętam, że nawet żeśmy się trochę pożarli na tym spotkaniu. Nie palił się, żeby cokolwiek zapłacić.

– To trener jest od motywowania – powtarzał.

– Patrz, kurwa, z kim my gramy! Gdzie my jesteśmy, a gdzie oni! Pod każdym względem! – denerwowałem się. – Kasa, misiu, kasa!

– Co ty pierdolisz, jaka kasa? – wtrącił się Dziurowicz.

– No kasa, podrzućcie coś! – cisnąłem.

Niestety, nic nie dali. Za bardzo obawiali się o swoje portfele. Zabrakło tej dodatkowej motywacji dla chłopaków, tego włączenia dopalaczy. Być może dlatego właśnie przegraliśmy ten mecz i całe eliminacje. To na pewno nie pomogło. Przegraliśmy eliminacje, a mędrcy w PZPN-ie stwierdzili, że trzeba nowego trenera, i nie zdecydowali się przedłużyć ze mną kontraktu. Zresztą jeszcze w przeddzień meczu ze Szwecją wiedziałem, że chcą się mnie pozbyć. I tak też się stało. Zatrudnili uzdrowiciela polskiego futbolu, czyli Jerzego Engela. I znów świat stał się odrobinę gorszy.

POGOŃ SZCZECIN
2000

Słyszałem, że sympatyczny Radek Majdan to teraz wielki celebryta. Jak dla mnie to taki celebryta jak z koziej dupy trąba. Kiedy pracowałem w Pogoni Szczecin, lansować mógł się jedynie przed lustrem. Oczywiście już zanosiło się na to, że uderzy mu woda sodowa, ale trochę ten syfon przyblokowałem. Uważam, że w jakimś stopniu uratowałem Majdana przed wdepnięciem w celebryckie gówno. Choć wówczas nieszczególnie mu się to podobało.

Kibice go kochali, bo był szczecinianinem, ale ja nic sobie z tego nie robiłem i nie zawsze na niego stawiałem. Chuj mnie obchodziło, że ludzie go lubią. Miałem drugiego bramkarza, Rosjanina Siergieja Szypowskiego, który był lepszy od Majdana i to on zwykle grał. A Radzio błyszczał nie na boisku, ale w lokalach, już po zmroku. Lubił balangi, a że Szczecin jest miastem rozrywkowym, to często dawał czadu. Szlajał się po mieście z dziewczynkami. Niestety nie wpadł na to, że tak od ręki będę dostawał informacje, jak i gdzie się bawi.

– Radeczku, gdzie to się było w nocy? Imprezka udana? – pytałem go w klubie.

Majdan nic nie odpowiadał. Jąkał się, dostawał zeza i czkawki, wszystkiego naraz. Nagle zapominał, jak się języka używa.

– Może popij, bo się udusisz – drwiłem.

Nie będę oszukiwał. Znacie mnie – sam często odwiedzałem te same kluby co piłkarze. Ale co wolno wojewodzie, to nie tobie, smrodzie, prawda? W każdym razie tancerki niejednokrotnie mówiły mi, że chłopcy z Pogoni odwiedzają je i proszą o coś do picia, bo są spragnieni. Raz postanowiłem zrobić wjazd do jednego z klubów, bo dowiedziałem się, że najprawdopodobniej balują tam piłkarze. I bingo! Spojrzałem, a na kanapach siedziało kilku moich niedźwiadków, wszyscy idealnie poprzedzielani cycatymi blondynami. Pięknie się bawili. Trzymali dziewczynki za nóżki i gasili pragnienie wódeczką. I przyglądali się, jak dupeczka tańczy na rurze. No kurwa, bogowie miasta! Gdy mnie zobaczyli, nie wiedzieli, którędy spierdalać. Przerażeni pochowali buteleczki, a ja spokojnie rozsiadłem się na kanapie obok, mając ich na celowniku. Od razu przysiadły się do mnie miłe panie – wiedziały widocznie, co dobre. Posiedziałem 10–15 minut, wypiłem drineczka, porozmawiałem z dziewczynkami i cały czas czekałem, co zrobią moje misiaczki.

– Trenerze, czy możemy jeszcze trochę posiedzieć? – zapytał w końcu najodważniejszy.

– Siedźcie, skoro zapłaciliście za te wszystkie atrakcje – odburknąłem. – Tylko nie za długo. Ja zaraz wychodzę, a kiedy się podniosę, nie chciałbym już was tutaj widzieć. Jeszcze raz was tu spotkam, to nie będę rozmawiał. Od razu wyjebię z zespołu.

Wystraszyli się. Posiedzieli jeszcze parę minut i się zmyli. Na drugi dzień musieli zapierdalać na treningu jak konie pociągowe. Nie było mi ich ani trochę żal. W końcu wpadłem na pomysł, jak do minimum ograniczyć imprezowanie piłkarzy na dzień przed meczem. Za jedną z bramek na stadionie Pogoni postawiliśmy kontener, z którego stworzyliśmy hotel, w którym zawodnicy musieli przebywać przed meczami. Takie zgrupowania, oczywiście w cudzysłowie. Jak pewnie łatwo się domyślić, i tam chcieli się zabawić, ale zrobiłem im małe Guantanamo – ochrona, szlaban na wyjścia do monopolowego, dupeczkom wstęp wzbroniony. Radzio i inni znali zasady: łapki na kołderkę i lulu.

A jak któryś kombinował, to wiedziałem od razu – moja siatka szpiegowska działała doskonale.

Jak właściwie trafiłem do Pogoni? Dzięki pośrednictwu przyjaciół skontaktowałem się z właścicielem klubu, Turkiem Sabrim Bekdasem, biznesmenem, który inwestował w Polsce. Działał między innymi w Warszawie, gdzie akurat wtedy powstawało jego centrum handlowe Blue City. Błyskawicznie porozumieliśmy się w sprawie mojego kontraktu z Pogonią. Wiecie, gdzie rozmawialiśmy? W kontenerze, na placu budowy! Cóż, prawdziwi profesjonaliści dogadają się wszędzie, w każdych warunkach. Zgodnie z umową miałem być menedżerem klubu, czyli przede wszystkim zajmować się sprowadzaniem zawodników, co przy moich kontaktach nie było trudne. Co ciekawe, kiedy już selekcjonowałem piłkarzy, zapraszałem ich do kontenerów. Byli zdziwieni warunkami, ale żaden nie odmawiał. Niechby tylko spróbował.

Nie chciałem mieć w drużynie pizdeuszów, dlatego zacząłem sprowadzać graczy z Legii czy Wisły. To nie podobało się piłkarzom Pogoni, którzy w pewnym momencie zaczęli nawet strajkować – bali się, że tamci zabiorą im miejsca i będą pierdzieć w ławkę, zamiast grać. Burzyli się również dlatego, że były pewne opóźnienia w płatnościach. Postawili sprawę na ostrzu noża i stwierdzili, że nie będą ani grać, ani trenować. Wzywałem więc do siebie każdego z osobna i rąbałem w łeb.

– Masz ochotę na wygłupy? Drzwi są otwarte. Wypierdalać i więcej mi się nie pokazywać. Ten wasz strajk tylko pomoże mi w selekcji. Skoro nie chcecie grać w piłkę, możecie zatrudnić się na kutrze i poławiać ryby!

Bardzo aktywny wśród tych strajkujących był Radek Majdan i to za nim poszła część drużyny. Później jednak się dogadaliśmy i Radzio diametralnie zmienił swoje podejście. Natomiast insekty, które dalej chciały kąsać, po prostu wytępiłem. Trzeba było wypierdolić tych, którzy puszczali bąki i zasmradzali drużynę. To było konieczne – Pogoń była w czarnej dupie i musiałem ją ratować. Pomagać mi chciał jeden

SELEKCJA

z tureckich doradców Sabriego, ale w końcu zaczął mnie już wkurwiać, bo za bardzo wpieprzał się w sprawy zespołu. Gdy rozmawialiśmy, to dym mieszał się z ogniem. Wszystko fruwało.

– Masz zrobić tak, jak ja chcę! – rozpoczynał.

– Odpierdol się! Ja prowadzę zespół i chuj ci do tego. Ty idź kozy pasać w Turcji. W tym na pewno jesteś dobry!

– No to będziemy ze sobą walczyć – zapowiedział.

I oczywiście gówno zdziałał – sprowadzałem sobie, kogo chciałem. Pewnie wielu trenerów, widząc tę moją selekcję, złapałoby się za głowy, ale mnie zwisało i powiewało to, co ktoś o mnie myśli. Tylko podczas jednego krótkiego zgrupowania w Wiśle przez drużynę przewinęło się kilkudziesięciu piłkarzy. Menedżerowie poczuli tureckie pieniądze Bekdasa i przysyłali najrozmaitszych grajków. Nie spodziewali się jednak, że będę aż tak surowy. Niektórych odpalałem już po jednym meczu sparingowym.

– Powiedz temu, temu i temu – mówiłem do rzecznika – że nie muszą już wychodzić na popołudniowy trening. Skończyliśmy współpracę. Zapraszam na kolację, ewentualnie nocleg, ale rano nie chcę ich widzieć.

Turka mi nawet zaproponowali, Gokmen Kore się zwał, ale na wejściu tak go opierdoliłem za jakieś zagranie, że struchlał. Siny się zrobił. Jak mu potem przetłumaczyli moje słowa, to powiedział, że w życiu nie słyszał czegoś takiego. Potem grał już lepiej, w sumie był niezłym piłkarzem, ale i tak nie chciałem go w drużynie. Raz, że nic nie rozumiał po polsku, a dwa – po prostu wolałem rodaków, ludzi sprawdzonych.

Z Legii Warszawa wziąłem między innymi Jacka Bednarza i Piotra Mosóra, a z Wisły Kraków Kazka Węgrzyna. Kazik miał pseudonim „Odważnik", bo w torbie sportowej zawsze nosił ciężarki do ćwiczeń. Często zdarzało się, że po treningu piłkarze uciekali jak najszybciej do domu, a Węgrzyn wyciągał swoje odważniki i sobie machał. Ambitny chłopak! W pełni wykorzystywał swoje warunki fizyczne, czyścił pod bramką wszystko, co się dało. Jeśli było trzeba, potrafił też ustawić niepokornych kolegów z drużyny – a to złapał jakiegoś za ucho, a to walnął w cymbał i było po sprawie. A kiedy i on nie dawał rady, to do delikwenta podchodzili ochroniarze Bekdasa i pytali, kiedy chce dostać wpierdol: rano, w południe czy wieczorem.

Jednym z takich, którzy czasami zasługiwali na spotkanie z chłopakami Bekdasa, był niejaki Brazylijczyk Brasilia. Świetna lewa noga, generalnie jak na polską ligę bardzo dobry gracz. Walił z wolnych niemal tak celnie jak Leszek Pisz. Ale był też z niego niesamowicie rozrywkowy misio, taki wiercipięta. Na piłce skupiał się, kiedy mu się chciało. Całkowite przeciwieństwo pracusia Węgrzyna.

Z Sabrim Bekdasem do dziś mam świetny kontakt. Kiedy do mnie dzwoni, nazywa mnie „przyjacielem". Ten gość naprawdę chciał zbudować w Szczecinie wielką Pogoń. Wyciągnął klub z piłkarskiego niebytu, pospłacał długi. Planował stworzyć kompleks piłkarski, łącznie z centrum handlowym. Nie udało mu się, bo władze miasta nie chciały sprzedać mu terenów wokół stadionu. Do dziś zresztą toczy się w tej sprawie postępowanie sądowe, ale to nie moja sprawa – ja miałem się zająć wyłącznie sferą sportową i to na szczęście poszło już znacznie lepiej. Przejmowałem rozbity zespół, który zdołałem doprowadzić do wicemistrzostwa Polski.

Na początku pracy mieszkałem jeszcze w Warszawie, a do Szczecina co jakiś czas latałem – nieraz w towarzystwie Sabriego i jego uzbrojonych po uszy ochroniarzy. Bardzo często się widywaliśmy, nie tylko w celach służbowych. Spędzaliśmy dużo czasu w szczecińskim hotelu Radisson, głównie w tamtejszym kasynie. Turek uwielbiał hazard, więc i mnie namawiał, żebym pobawił się w ruletkę. Dostawałem w prezencie całe stosy żetonów. Nie pierdoliłem się – stawiałem wszystko na jeden kolor.

– Janusz, może to rozłóż jakoś, pokombinuj – radził Sabri.

– Pierdolę to. Albo wygram i będziemy bawić się dalej, albo idę do pokoju. Rozumiem, że wszystko już tam przygotowane? – dopytywałem, wiadomo co mając na myśli.

– Januszku, wszystko gotowe, będziesz zadowolony – zapewniał.

I tak było. W pokoju czekało pełne wyposażenie i towarzystwo. Czy damskie? No a jak, kurwa, inaczej, przecież chłopców nie dymałem! Mój serdeczny przyjaciel Sabri dbał o to, bym nie czuł się samotny. Widzicie więc, że z Bekdasem zawsze było miło i sympatycznie. Wypić lubił, ale nie do przesady – wychylał dwie–trzy szklaneczki i na tym kończył. Bardziej ciągnęło go do towarzystwa, które czekało w pokoju.

Taki właśnie był Sabri. Serdeczny, pracowity, ale i zabawowy. Rozstaliśmy się, ale pozostaliśmy przyjaciółmi. Odszedłem, bo klub przegrał walkę o mistrzostwo z Wisłą Kraków i nie wydawało się, żeby w przyszłym sezonie miało być lepiej. Po prostu nie porozumieliśmy się z Sabrim w sprawie dalszej współpracy. Zostawiłem jego Pogoń, a za chwilę okazało się, że mam się brać do ratowania kolejnego zasłużonego, ale pogrążonego w kryzysie klubu – Śląska Wrocław. Przed meczem z takimi zespołami mówiłem piłkarzom, żeby ogolili tych frajerów. Teraz takich frajerów sam miałem uratować przed spadkiem…

ŚLĄSK WROCŁAW
2001

– No, pięknie to trener poukładał! – rzucił w moją stronę Wojtek Kowalczyk.

– Co jest, misiaczku, co ci się nie podoba?

– No, kurwa, przecież te nasze barany nie wiedziały, o co chodzi! Zamiast do przodu, grały do tyłu! – denerwował się mój ulubieniec.

– Kowal, trzeba było złapać piłkę, opierdzielić czterech czy pięciu i strzelić gola. Ktoś ci bronił? Czego ty ode mnie chcesz? Rozmawiaj z kolegami – pogoniłem młodziana.

Chodziło oczywiście o mecz prowadzonego przeze mnie Śląska Wrocław z Legią. Zremisowaliśmy, co było ogromną sensacją. Ten punkt bardzo nam się przydał. Kowal był zły, że przegrał z kumplami Szamotulskim i Piszem, których ściągnąłem do Śląska, a także byłym trenerem Wójcikiem. Coś mu nie pasowało, nie był chyba w stanie pogodzić się z tym, że Legia nie ograła swobodnie słabego wtedy Śląska. Potem awanturował się, że ja ten mecz niby ustawiłem. Pewności, że tak właśnie się stało, nabrał, kiedy pomyliłem się i najpierw wparowałem do szatni Legii, a potem do pokoju sędziów. Oczywiście zrobiłem to przez pomyłkę, ale w obieg poszła jednoznaczna wiadomość: Wójcik załatwił mecz.

– Nie no, trener już działa! – pieklił się Kowalczyk.

To mnie mocno wkurwiło i musiałem mu posłać parę jobów:

– Kowal, trzeba było strzelać gole, nikt ci tego nie bronił. Trzeba było opierdalać tych swoich baranów! A teraz zamknij gębę i zjeżdżaj do szatni.

Rzeczywiście, posłusznie się zawinął, ale pod nosem wymruczał jeszcze parę słów od serca. Trochę go rozumiałem, bo ambitna była z niego bestia, zawsze chciał tylko wygrywać, a w tym przypadku czuł się zupełnie bezradny.

W Śląsku dostałem zadanie uratowania klubu przed spadkiem, do czego remis z Legią oczywiście mnie przybliżył. Jak tam trafiłem? Było to w 2001 roku. Dostałem telefon od Ryśka Sobiesiaka, głównego sponsora i właściciela klubu. W pobliżu plątało się jeszcze kilku innych frędzli, którzy udawali, że coś dla Śląska robią, ale nie mieli nic do powiedzenia. Zostałem zaproszony na koszt klubu i przyjechałem.

Dostałem od Ryśka willę na obrzeżach Wrocławia do swojej dyspozycji – w pełni umeblowaną, z kortem tenisowym na zewnątrz. Mieszkałem tam samotnie. Obok stał pusty dom, który wcześniej zajmował jeden z grubszych wrocławskich gangsterów, ale musiał spierdzielać przed policją i teraz siedział w RPA. Z kolei jakieś 200 metrów dalej Polsat kręcił swój *reality show* – uczestników zamknięto w wielkiej willi, ale bardzo często mnie odwiedzali, czasem też ja wpadałem do nich.

Jak już wspominałem, miałem utrzymać klub w lidze – klub, który całkowicie się sypał. Nie było kasy, zespół miał braki kadrowe, o miejscu do treningów mogliśmy pomarzyć. Szatnia była kompletnie do dupy, musiałem ostro walczyć, żeby została wyremontowana. Jednym słowem pełne dziadostwo. Poza Ryśkiem Sobiesiakiem wielkiego wsparcia Śląsk nie miał. Zresztą Ryśka za bardzo w Śląsku nie lubili, raczej tolerowali. Najchętniej pewni ludzie przejęliby klub, ale nie wydając na to złotówki. Rysiek oczywiście się na to nie zgadzał.

Podjąłem się walki, ale z miejsca zapowiedziałem, że trzeba będzie wzmocnić skład. Zacząłem od Grześka Szamotulskiego. Szamo, kiedy tylko się dowiedział, że to ja trenuję Śląsk, nie zastanawiał się ani chwili. Spakował toboły i zaraz był we Wrocławiu. Uwielbiałem go. Był świetny nie tylko na boisku, ale również poza nim. Dlaczego? Jak trzeba było kogoś pacnąć, to nie musiał tego robić trener, tylko sprawy w swoje silne ręce brał właśnie Szamo. Miał duży wpływ na funkcjonowanie drużyny, motywował chłopaków przed wyjściem na boisko niemal tak dobrze jak ja. Był wykonawcą moich poleceń od strony fizycznej.

– Coś ci się nie podoba? Zaraz przyjdzie Szamo i sobie to załatwicie – to słyszeli zawodnicy, którzy odważyli się kręcić na coś nosem.

I rzeczywiście – Szamo reagował bardzo ostro, ale ja z nim żadnego problemu nie miałem. Nie tylko opierdalał zawodników, ale również potrafił rozładować atmosferę. Kiedy ja kończyłem w szatni swoją „suszarkę", a piłkarzom pot aż spływał po skroniach, on zawsze powiedział coś wesołego, dzięki czemu nawet najbardziej wystraszeni się uśmiechali. I o to chodziło! Szamotulski był moją lewą ręką. Prawą był Leszek Pisz. Jak możecie sobie wyobrazić, i jedna, i druga mogła porządnie przypierdolić frajerowi, który się stawiał. Wszyscy ich szanowali, a mnie to pasowało, bo pomagali mi w prowadzeniu drużyny. Dlatego bardzo ich ceniłem. Podchodzili z wielką ambicją do każdego spotkania. Takich zawodników uwielbiałem!

Jednym z piłkarzy Śląska był wówczas niejaki Piotr Stokowiec, dziś znany trener. Miał ksywę Rudy – i faktycznie był rudy, nie tylko z wyglądu, ale i z charakteru. Chodził, nadawał, obgadywał po kątach. Uzdrowiciel, kurwa. Miałem kłopoty kadrowe, więc nie mogłem, ot tak, się go pozbyć, ale pewnie w innej sytuacji bym go wypierdolił na zbity pysk. Postanowiłem za to nasłać na niego Szamo. Temu długo nie trzeba było mówić. Poszedł do Stokowca, sprzedał kilka klapsów, a potem wytargał za uszy. Dosłownie. Ja też dołożyłem swoje na jednej z odpraw przedmeczowych.

– Posłuchaj no. Może i gdziekolwiek indziej twoje wybryki i teksty uchodziłyby płazem, ale nie u mnie. Jeszcze chyba dobrze mnie nie poznałeś, nie słyszałeś o mnie zbyt wiele. To coś ci powiem: skasuję cię, chłopcze, tak że się już nie odrodzisz. Będziesz się czuł, jakbyś musiał zejść do głębokich kanałów – podkręcałem go, a ten siedział ze spuszczonym łbem. A ja wcale nie zamierzałem kończyć. – Jeśli będzie potrzeba, jeśli się nie wyprostujesz, to ja mam na ciebie inny sposób. Dostaniesz w cymbał i tak się zakończy twoja kariera w tym klubie. W Śląsku jest trudna sytuacja, jeśli chcesz, to zostań i pomagaj, a jeśli nie, to pakuj się i wypierdalaj. I nie pokazuj mi się na oczy. Wybieraj. Teraz. Nie ma, że będziesz się zastanawiał. Masz się zdecydować podczas tego spotkania. Chcę jasnej deklaracji, albo w tę, albo w tę stronę. Będę tu jeszcze przez dziesięć minut i w tym czasie chcę decyzji.

Po szatni przeszedł tylko szmer. Ale taki pozytywny, szmer uznania. Piłkarze nie lubili rudego cwaniaka, więc cieszyli się, że wreszcie dostał po łbie. Po dziesięciu minutach Stokowiec zapowiedział, że postanowił zostać w klubie. W sumie to nie miał innego wyjścia. A ja takim stanowczym wyprostowaniem nieposłusznego gnojka sprawiłem, że zawodnicy przekonali się, że ze mną nie ma żartów. Że nikomu nie przepuszczę i jeśli trzeba będzie, to każdego z nich mogę wypierdolić.

Stokowca spotkałem niedawno w Białymstoku, był wtedy trenerem Jagiellonii. Bardzo grzecznie się zachowywał, ale jakże mogłoby być inaczej, skoro przecież nic złego mu nie zrobiłem, a opierdol zawsze dostawał w pełni zasłużony. Trener jednak z niego moim zdaniem był marny, znacznie agresywniejszy był jako piłkarz. Wydał mi się wtedy taki trochę zaszczuty. To się zresztą przekładało na wyniki.

– Czarek, ty nie będziesz miał z niego wiele pożytku – mówiłem prezesowi Jagiellonii.

Kulesza podrapał się w głowę.

– No, nie bardzo jestem z niego zadowolony.

– Obsra się parę razy i będziesz musiał go zmienić – zawyrokowałem.

Było, jak rzekłem, Stokowiec się obrał i po dosłownie kilku meczach Kulesza go pogonił. Nic mi jednak do tego. On u mnie nie terminował, nie uczył się ode mnie trenerki. Nie ten rozmiar kapelusza.

Wróćmy do Śląska. Szatnię miałem podporządkowaną, teraz trzeba było dalej wzmacniać zespół. Z drugiej drużyny wyciągnąłem pomocnika Dariusza Sztylkę, który potem przez lata grał w Śląsku. Przydawał mi się też do czarnej roboty w środku. Od myślenia był Pisz, a ten miał po prostu zapierdalać.

Problemy kadrowe nie były moją jedyną bolączką we Wrocławiu. Klub bronił się przed spadkiem, więc działacze szukali możliwości, żeby tego uniknąć. Rozglądali się za możliwością kontaktu z sędziami i mieli już w klubie takiego człowieka do zadań specjalnych. Powiedziano mi wprost, że to właśnie on będzie załatwiał „sprawy".

– Jeśli tak, to go bierzcie, płaćcie mu. Niech sobie robi, co chce, w dupie to mam. Ale pamiętajcie, jak się raz wpierdoli w rzeczy związane z piłkarzami, to pożałuje, że się urodził. Mam w drużynie takiego, który jak mu raz przyjebie, to będzie tydzień bez muzyki tańczył – oznajmiłem.

Za cholerę nie wierzyłem w tego kolesia, jednak działacze zapewniali mnie, że jest skuteczny. Machnąłem ręką, ale awantura z szefami klubu przez cały ten czas wisiała na włosku. I oczywiście w końcu do niej doszło. Miało to miejsce przed przedostatnim meczem ligi, z Groclinem na wyjeździe, bardzo dla Śląska ważnym w kontekście walki o utrzymanie. Przypuszczałem, że oni ten mecz ułożą. No i rzeczywiście – Śląsk wygrał 2:1 i uratował się przed spadkiem. Moim zdaniem mecz został ustawiony. Ja oglądałem go z trybun, bo byłem świeżo po rzeczonej awanturze z działaczami.

– Janusz, może byś sobie odpoczął, może ktoś inny by poprowadził drużynę? – wypalił przed meczem któryś z szefów.

– Tak postępujecie? To pierdolcie się. Mam was w dupie – uciąłem i trzasnąłem drzwiami.

I już, moja przygoda ze Śląskiem się skończyła. Trochę żałowałem, ale taki już jestem – wolę odpuścić, niż szarpać się z debilami. Poszedłem do jednego z moich wrocławskich kolegów, zrobiliśmy grilla na tarasie, wypiliśmy butelkę whisky. Byłem oczywiście wściekły, ale nie chciałem się kopać z koniem. Noc po meczu spędziłem jeszcze we Wrocławiu, ale nazajutrz poleciałem do Warszawy. Problemy jednak się nie skończyły, bo działacze oczywiście nie chcieli się rozliczyć z wszystkich pieniędzy. Po tygodniu skontaktowałem się z Ryśkiem Sobiesiakiem, który poprosił, bym na jego koszt przyleciał do Wrocławia. Poszliśmy na obiad, potem kolację w jednym z kasyn. W międzyczasie Rysiek oczywiście wszystko uregulował. Do dziś trochę mi go szkoda. To bardzo poważny facet, który niestety musiał zarządzać cholernie niepoważnym klubem.

CYPR JEST NASZ!
2001–2002

„Pobawiłem się już z tymi misiami w Polsce, może by znów spróbować sił za granicą?", pomyślałem, kiedy zakończyła się moja krótka przygoda w Śląsku Wrocław. Zacząłem się rozglądać za jakąś fuchą na południu Europy. Zamarzył mi się Cypr – bo i ciepło, i kaska dobra, i wino zapewne smaczne. A więc zacząłem rozpuszczać wici. Długo nie musiałem czekać na pierwsze reakcje.

Bardzo pomocny okazał się przede wszystkim szef firmy Sportfive Andrzej Placzyński, który skontaktował mnie z najprężniejszą na Cyprze agencją menedżerską. Wysłałem CV, które spasowało tym wszystkim misiakom. Trudno zresztą, żeby nie spasowało! W każdym razie panowie menedżerowie obiecali, że znajdą mi klub na Cyprze, i słowa dotrzymali. Anorthosis Famagusta – tam miałem pracować. Klub formalnie był wprawdzie z Famagusty właśnie, ale z racji, że to miasto przejęli Turcy, graliśmy w cypryjskiej Larnace. Jednak po kolei.

Szczegóły kontraktu ustaliłem w Grecji, na spotkaniu z przedstawicielami klubu. Potem na chwilę wróciłem do kraju, by rozejrzeć się za asystentem. Po dłuższym namyśle postawiłem na świętej pamięci Andrzeja „Czyżyka" Czyżniewskiego, niegdyś świetnego bramkarza i sędziego. Trochę się wahał:

– Bramkarz ma być trenerem piłkarzy z pola…? Janusz, sądzisz, że sobie poradzę?

– Masz robić to, co powiem, i wystarczy. Będziemy golić tych cypryjskich frajerów – dodałem, po czym wyjaśniłem mu, jak będzie wyglądała nasza współpraca.

Zapakowaliśmy się więc z Czyżykiem do samolotu i polecieliśmy na Cypr. Tego samego dnia spotkaliśmy się z właścicielem klubu w jego luksusowej posiadłości. Tam podpisaliśmy kontrakty, wypiliśmy trzy butelki wina, zjedliśmy trochę pysznych owoców i udaliśmy się do hotelu w Larnace. Później, kiedy już mieliśmy własne wille, przepiękne zresztą, to Andrzej i tak najczęściej przesiadywał u mnie – już od samego rana. A to zrobił śniadanie, a to posprzątał. Chciał się najwidoczniej wykazać i w taki sposób podziękować, że dałem mu szansę na fajny zarobek. Czyżyk był bramkarzem, ale ja potrzebowałem człowieka, który będzie robił rozgrzewki. W związku z tym przed każdym treningiem dokładnie wszystko Andrzejowi rysowałem. Nie musiał się więc, specjalnie wysilać, po prostu działał według rozpiski. Początkowo mieliśmy parę problemów, ale potem wszystko wyglądało niemal podręcznikowo. Niemal, bo zdarzało się, że Andrzejek coś spierdolił, i wtedy wkraczałem do akcji. Najpierw ustawiłem drużynę, a już po treningu fundowałem lekką zjebkę swojemu asystentowi. Zawsze potulnie słuchał, nie robił mi żadnych wyrzutów. Cóż, był mi wdzięczny za dobrą fuchę, ale przede wszystkim to był bardzo uczciwy, spokojny i porządny człowiek – godzien zaufania i wart tego, by mu pomóc.

Z Czyżykiem mieliśmy jedną ciekawą przygodę. Otóż na Cyprze, tak jak w Wielkiej Brytanii, obowiązuje ruch lewostronny. Dali mi samochód, bez żadnych egzaminów dostałem też cypryjskie prawo jazdy, ale i ja, i Czyżyk trochę obawialiśmy się jeździć.

– Janusz, przecież my się porozbijamy. Co tu robić? – lamentował Andrzej.

– Wyobraź sobie, Andrzejku, że doskonale wiem co. Przede wszystkim chodźmy się napić, bo na trzeźwo to my się tu jeździć nie nauczymy – postanowiłem.

Ruszyliśmy do Larnaki, do znajomego restauratora, który miał i dobre żarcie, i nie żałował alkoholu. Zabalowaliśmy uczciwie, aż się wywracaliśmy. Tymczasem nieuchronnie zbliżał się czas testowej jazdy.

– Januszku – wybełkotał Czyżyk. – Ty pojedziesz czy ja?

– Jedź, nie bój się, Cypr jest nasz! Jesteśmy królami tej drogi! – ekscytowałem się.

Andrzejkowi udzielił się mój pijacki entuzjazm – ruszył z piskiem opon! Pędzimy więc, obaj porządnie trafieni i bezgranicznie szczęśliwi. Aby wyjechać z miasta, trzeba było pokonać duże rondo. Oczywiście należało je objechać, kierując się w lewo, a nie w prawo, jak w Polsce. Najebany Czyżyk nie pojechał jednak ani w lewo, ani w prawo, lecz prosto! Śmignął przez skrzyżowanie jak zawodowy rajdowiec, prawdopodobnie nie zaprzątając sobie głowy czymś tak błahym jak przepisy. Byłem posrany ze strachu. Błyskawicznie otrzeźwiałem.

– Kurwa, jak tak masz jeździć, to może ja będę prowadzić? – krzyczałem. – Ty nas zaraz, debilu, do morza wpierdolisz! Pozabijać nas chcesz?

Czyżykowi udało się jednak nas nie zabić i kiedy wreszcie się zatrzymaliśmy, wiedzieliśmy, jak będzie wyglądała dalsza nauka jazdy. W kolejnych dniach, siadając za kółkiem, niezmiennie mieliśmy więc za sobą dłuższe posiedzenie z cypryjskim winem, pysznym, ale i mocno uderzającym do głowy. Z każdą kolejną próbą szło nam coraz lepiej, a po miesiącu czy dwóch ruch lewostronny był już dla nas niczym bułka z masłem. Oczywiście obficie popijana.

Z Czyżykiem mieliśmy nieograniczony dostęp do wina oraz najbardziej znanego cypryjskiego piwa – KEO – których właściciel klubu był producentem. Muszę przyznać, że o nasze wątroby dbali tam znakomicie. Któregoś dnia usłyszałem pukanie do drzwi.

– Wejść! – krzyknąłem, wylegując się na leżaku jak sułtan.

– Janusz! – darł się Czyżyk od progu. – Jakieś paczki nam tu przywieźli!

Razem z nim wlazł kurier i po angielsku tłumaczył mu, co jest zawartością przesyłki.

– Nie wiem, co on pierdoli! – biadolił Andrzej.

– Ucz się języków, debilu! Przecież facet mówi, że to wino!

– Kurwa, ja tyle wina w życiu nie widziałem…

Okazało się, że szefostwo klubu po prostu chciało zrobić nam przyjemność, więc przysłało, bagatela, kilka palet wina. Zajęły pół pokoju, nie dało się przejść. Poupychałem butelki po całym domu, gdzie tylko się dało. Wyszło tego dwie pełne szafy, a i tak trochę musiało zostać na podłodze. Mroczne szaleństwo.

Któregoś dnia odwiedził nas jeden z zaprzyjaźnionych dziennikarzy, Jacuś Kmiecik, wówczas współpracownik „Przeglądu Sportowego". Oczywiście został podjęty z honorami. Najpierw więc wydoił pół butelki koniaku, a później dwie butle wina. Doił tak, jakby się po raz pierwszy w życiu do alkoholu dorwał, aż mu się z ust wylewało. Smakosz, kurwa.

Siedział u mnie ten Kmieć przez kilka dni, popijał moje wino i pisał do gazety te swoje bzdury. Opowiadałem mu przeróżne rzeczy, między innymi o tym, jak budowałem z Czyżykiem drużynę Anorthosisu. Co nie było wcale takie proste.

Już na początku mocno się wkurwiłem, bo okazało się, że jeszcze przed moim przyjazdem Cypryjczycy porobili zakupy i stwierdzili, że ja mam stawiać na tych sprowadzonych przez nich graczy. Wśród nich był jakiś niedojda z Niemiec. Obejrzałem sobie go raz, drugi, trzeci… aż żal dupę ściskał.

– Słuchajcie – zawyrokowałem – możecie go sobie na wursty przerobić, do niczego się nie nadaje. Może w kuchni się przyda, na zmywaku.

Oprócz niego miałem w drużynie też Greka, który pasował mi do koncepcji – szybki, mocny, silny. Zdrowy chłopak jednym słowem. Grał albo w środku pola, albo na skrzydle. I jakoś tam się sprawdzał, pozostali też, ale jako drużyna sprawdzali się mocno umiarkowanie. Mówiąc wprost: brakowało mi prawdziwych piłkarzy! Postanowiłem więc ściągnąć do klubu jakichś Polaków. Przekręciłem do Radka Michalskiego, Sławka Majaka i oczywiście mojego ulubieńca – Wojtka

Kowalczyka. Przekonałem ich bardzo szybko, z szefami klubu też nie było problemów.

– Takiego piłkarza jak Kowal jeszcze na Cyprze nie widzieliście. Lecę po niego do Polski, wrócimy razem – obiecałem. I dotrzymałem słowa. W Warszawie dogadałem się z władzami Legii, wziąłem Wojtusia i ruszyliśmy na Cypr. Mniej więcej w tym samym czasie dotarli Radek i Sławek. Jak Cypryjczycy na nich patrzyli, to przecierali oczy ze zdumienia – byli zachwyceni. Mieli ku temu podstawy, Kowal został później królem strzelców ich ligi i wybrano go najlepszym ligowym obcokrajowcem. Michalski i Majak także błyszczeli. A ja puchłem z dumy.

Problemem było to, że nawyki imprezowe z Polski w znakomity, nienaruszalny sposób przenieśli na Cypr. Spotykali się na swoich balkonikach i ładowali gorzałę. Nie będę wam mydlił oczu – zdarzało się, że do nich dołączałem. Nawet czasem zainicjowałem jakąś imprezkę. Otwarte chłopaki, ja też zabawowy, więc świetnie czuliśmy się w swoim towarzystwie. I towarzystwie procentów. Niejednokrotnie jednak musiałem interweniować i świecić oczami, bo było tak głośno, że przyjeżdżała policja. Ale niech Cypryjczycy spierdalają na swoje drzewa. Jak się „Wujo" z „Kowalem" bawi, to musi być głośno! Taki już był urok moich chłopaków. Oni nawet po grubej imprezie grali tak, że można było tylko cmokać z zachwytu. Taki Kowal po wieczorze spędzonym w barze grał lepiej niż niektórzy dzisiejsi „profesjonalni" piłkarze.

Ja na Cyprze trochę popracowałem, a odszedłem po porażce 0:2 z Olympiakosem Nikozja. Moim zdaniem szefostwo klubu trochę zbyt pochopnie się ze mną pożegnało, ale cóż – takie już ich prawo. Zresztą życie trenera jest przewrotne, jednego dnia pracujesz i cię chwalą, a drugiego – chcą zwalniać. Jedno jest pewne: takiego trenera jak Wujo już nie znaleźli! Miałem oczywiście oferty z innych klubów, pół ligi mnie chciało. Ale wolałem wrócić do Polski. Wiecie, rodzina, własne śmieci, Warszawa. Tam czuję się najlepiej. W domu. W tamtym momencie dość miałem wojaży.

„W DAMASZKU SIEDZIAŁ
DIABEŁ NA DASZKU"
2003

Znacie to przysłowie? Kiedy miałem zacząć pracę w Syrii, pomyślałem, że takiego diabła jak Wujo to oni tam jeszcze nie widzieli! Choć sami aniołkami nie są. Coś zresztą w diabelskości tego kraju jest. Nie wiem, czy wiecie, ale w Damaszku swoje rezydentury mają podobno wszystkie wywiady świata, a te najważniejsze to na pewno. W końcu więc musiałem tam trafić – ja, agent, jakich mało.

Wyjazd załatwił mi Michał Listkiewicz. To on skontaktował mnie z prezesem Syryjskiego Związku Piłki Nożnej, wcześniej wystawiwszy mi bardzo dobrą opinię. Ów prezes nazywał się Buzo i był jednocześnie generałem syryjskiej armii – szefem sił lotniczych – a wcześniej sędzią piłkarskim i działaczem związkowym. Dużo udzielał się też w FIFA i UEFA. Listek również współpracował (i nadal współpracuje) z FIFA, dobrze znał Buzo, więc bez problemu mógł załatwić mi tę robotę.

– Byłby pan gotów na pracę z naszą reprezentacją? – zapytał mnie Buzo, czego rzecz jasna się spodziewałem.

– Oczywiście, panie prezesie, biorę waszą kadrę tu i teraz. Osiągnę z nią liczne sukcesy – zapewniłem. W końcu lepszego trenera ode mnie nie miał.

Do Damaszku ruszyłem sam, dopiero później dołączyła do mnie żona. Wylatywałem z Polski w dniu, kiedy niewielu ludzi się na to decydowało, bowiem tego wieczoru Amerykanie zaczęli inwazję na Irak. Na miejscu napięcie spowodowane konfliktem zbrojnym było bardzo wyczuwalne. Nic dziwnego! Nieustanny huk bomb i widok przelatujących samolotów amerykańskich zrobiły na mnie kolosalne wrażenie. Chłopaki prezydenta Busha waliły bardzo ostro.

Na lotnisku przywitano mnie z wszelkimi honorami. Czekali na mnie przedstawiciele związku i… wojska. Jeden generał, jeden pułkownik. Weszli po mnie do samolotu, a stamtąd przetransportowali do hotelu. Nie musiałem przechodzić żadnych odpraw czy zbierać pieczątek. Byłem przepuszczany poza kolejnością. Spokojnie spędziłem noc w hotelu wojskowym, a rano udałem się do starej części Damaszku, gdzie mieściła się siedziba Syryjskiego Związku Piłki Nożnej. Potem zaglądałem tam niemal codziennie i spotykałem się z najważniejszymi działaczami.

Pierwsze dni w Syrii poświęciłem na organizację. Przede wszystkim musiałem podpisać kontrakt, jako że nie zrobiłem tego wcześniej. Końcowe negocjacje prowadziłem nie tylko z generałem Buzo, ale również z przedstawicielami partii rządzącej. Zatrudnienie mnie musiało klepnąć kilku ważnych misiów, ale w końcu się dogadaliśmy i mogłem zacząć pracę.

Zanim wziąłem się do poważnej roboty, poznałem mój… cień. Miał na imię Ali i był na oko 50-letnim, krępym, nieco zmarnowanym przez życie człowiekiem. Został mi przydzielony jako kierowca, jednak jego prawdziwą rolą było szpiegowanie mnie. Otwarcie zresztą przyznawał, że jest szpiclem. Woził mnie starym, niezawodnym mercedesem, a przepisy miał w nosie. Częściej niż kierunkowskazu używał klaksonu, bo w krajach arabskich, jeśli ktoś mało trąbi, to jest uważany za debila. Często odstawiał mnie na jakieś spotkanie czy bankiet. Wiedziałem doskonale, że ma rodzinę, więc mówiłem mu, żeby wracał do domu i przyjechał po mnie o konkretnej godzinie, jednak nie słuchał. Obawiał się, biedak, że coś mi się stanie, a wtedy jego odstrzelą za niedopełnienie obowiązku.

Kiedyś chciałem wejść do sklepu, przed którym kłębił się tłum. Bałem się, szczególnie że w Syrii raczej nie warto rozmawiać z ludźmi po angielsku, gdyż ten język działa na miejscowych jak płachta na byka. Nienawidzą Amerykanów i wszystkiego co amerykańskie. Już chciałem zrezygnować, ale Ali wkroczył do akcji.

– Załatwię to – wydukał po angielsku z jak zawsze ponurą miną.

Ruszył, zamienił z kimś parę słów, wrócił i zakomunikował:

– No, już może pan iść na zakupy.

Wyszedłem, czując się niczym Ojciec Chrzestny, któremu wszystko wolno. Zza drzew i płotów wyglądały beżowe twarze, w których błyszczały wytrzeszczone ślepia. Do dziś nie wiem, czym Ali ich postraszył. I chyba nie chcę wiedzieć.

Gdy tylko miałem sposobność, chętnie zawierałem znajomości z wysoko postawionymi misiami. Z tym, jak wiecie, nigdy nie miałem problemów. Pewnego razu spotkałem się nawet z synem prezydenta Syrii, wielkim sympatykiem futbolu. Utrzymywałem też bliskie kontakty z generałami, czyli *de facto* ludźmi zarządzającymi tym wojskowym krajem. Uwielbiali mnie, a ja okręciłem ich sobie wokół palca. Jeśli czegoś potrzebowałem, wystarczał jeden telefon. Dodatkowy sprzęt dla drużyny? Proszę bardzo, od ręki. Zgrupowanie w fajnym miejscu? Jak najbardziej. Jedynie na mieszkanie musiałem czekać półtora miesiąca, ale to dlatego, że byłem wybredny – odwiedziłem aż kilkanaście willi, zanim się na jedną zdecydowałem. Do tego czasu mieszkałem w hotelu, oczywiście najlepszym w Damaszku.

Trochę się po tej Syrii bujałem. Na przykład urządzałem sobie wycieczki krajoznawcze – bywałem po stronie irackiej, ale częściej jeździłem do Libanu. Bejrut to Paryż Bliskiego Wschodu. Piękne miasto i prawdziwy raj dla takiego rozpustnika jak ja! Wszystkiego było tam pod dostatkiem – i rozmaitych alkoholi, i dupeczek. No właśnie, panienki. Bejrut był otwartym miastem, jego znakiem rozpoznawczym były kobiety, wino i śpiew. Arabki są tam bardzo ładne, niezwykle mi się podobały. Piękne twarze, wielkie oczy, lśniące czarne włosy…

W tamtym czasie już zaczęły dbać o siebie, dlatego przyciągały swoim wyglądem. Libanki były bardziej nowoczesne, w większości chodziły bez chust zakrywających twarz.

Ali podwoził mnie na granicę, gdzie przejmowali mnie pracownicy tamtejszej polskiej ambasady. Kiedy tylko miałem okazję, robiłem sobie wypad do Bejrutu. Ludzie często pytali, czy się nie boję. Cóż, to prawda, oberwać tam to nie sztuka, bowiem w Bejrucie działa Hezbollah, groźna organizacja terrorystyczna. Wójt nie byłby jednak Wójtem, gdyby nie wlazł do jaskini lwa. Znajomi z Damaszku załatwili mi zaproszenie na spotkanie z prawdziwą szychą w Hezbollahu.

Jak takie spotkanie wygląda? Tak, że można się zesrać ze strachu. Po drodze trzeba przejść przez kilka kontroli. Należy się zatrzymać, a do samochodu podchodzą terroryści – najczęściej dwóch, czasem więcej. Zawsze mają przy sobie kałasznikowy. Jeden celuje w głowę kierowcy, natomiast drugi sprawdza, kim są pasażerowie. Jeśli nic nie wiedzą o spotkaniu, trzeba się czym prędzej wycofać, póki nie zaczną strzelać. A proszę mi uwierzyć, że przychodzi im to łatwo jak pstryknięcie palcami. W moją stronę na szczęście nigdy nie otworzyli ognia, bo zawsze byłem umówiony. Za pierwszym razem musiałem przejść przez trzy kontrole. Cała operacja zajęła jakieś pół godziny. Kiedy jednak wchodziłem do willi, czułem na sobie wzrok tych jego psów z kałachami. No i lufy karabinów wycelowane w moją głowę.

– Imię? – zapytał oschle dwumetrowy ochroniarz przy drzwiach. Kątem oka widziałem, jak poprawił sobie palec na spuście. Mógł mnie odstrzelić w ciągu sekundy.

– Janusz – wyjąkałem. Serce podchodziło mi do gardła.

– Oczywiście! Zapraszam pana do środka! – niemal wykrzyczał, promieniejąc z radości. Nie miał żadnej listy, komputera czy rozpiski. Miał za to kałacha i wszystko pamiętał.

Niepewnym krokiem ruszyłem do środka. Rozejrzałem się. Po lewej piękny obraz, po prawej rzeźba ze złota. Misternie tkane dywany. I służba, uwijająca się jak w ukropie. Podziwianie przepychu przerwał mi mój sympatyczny rozmówca sprzed drzwi, który nie rozstając się z karabinem, poprosił, bym poszedł za nim. Prowadził mnie przez różne zaułki i zakamarki i już po drugim zakręcie zapomniałem, jak wygląda droga powrotna. W końcu dotarliśmy do apartamentu szefa. Ochroniarz wskazał mi miejsce na tarasie. Zasiadłem w miękkim fotelu, przy suto zastawionym stole. Nie minęła minuta, a pojawił się facet, z którym miałem się spotkać. Zupełnie niepozorny, ale o groźnym wyrazie twarzy. Od razu zaczęliśmy rozmawiać, oczywiście przez tłumacza. Ochroniarze gdzieś się rozpierzchli, ale nie miałem wątpliwości, że gdyby tylko mój nowy kolega kiwnął palcem, przybiegliby jak psy. Spotkanie potrwało kilkadziesiąt minut i przebiegło w bardzo sympatycznej atmosferze. Wypiliśmy po dwie kawy, trzy herbaty. Zapewnił, że jak będę czegoś potrzebował, on pomoże mi w każdym zakresie. Miły pan terrorysta zaprosił mnie jeszcze kilka razy.

Byłem w oku cyklonu, a nie zostałem nawet draśnięty. Niewiele jednak zabrakło, bym został przypadkiem odstrzelony podczas niewinnego towarzyskiego spotkania. Otóż ze znajomym z Polski poszliśmy do pewnej kafeterii w Bejrucie, żeby trochę się napić i zapalić sziszę. Ot, wyjście jakich wiele. Problem w tym, że dzielnica, do której się udaliśmy, była opanowana przez Hezbollah. Zajęliśmy miejsca w ogródku, blisko wejścia. Nagle do knajpy weszło dwóch gości. Trzask, prask – pistoletami z tłumikami zarąbali dwóch facetów siedzących w rogu. Egzekucja. Jeden nieszczęśnik zwalił się na ziemię, cały we krwi, drugi zawisł na krześle z przerażająco wybałuszonymi oczami. Zamachowcy sprawdzili, czy delikwenci rzeczywiście nie żyją, po czym nie zatrzymywani przez nikogo opuścili lokal. Ot, jakby wypili sobie po espresso i poszli do domu. Ja też nie chciałem tam długo zostawać. Przecież do tej przyjemnej kafejki za chwilę mogła wpaść banda terrorystów i walić do ludzi jak do kaczek! Od pracowników ambasady dowiedziałem się, że zamordowani tam zostali agenci Mosadu, izraelskiej grupy wywiadowczej, którzy do Bejrutu przylecieli na przeszpiegi. Po głowie tłukła mi się pełna zadumy refleksja: „Co ja tu, kurwa, robię?!".

To jeszcze nie wszystko! Na jednym ze spotkań z urzędnikami państwowymi oprócz kielicha dostałem taką oto propozycję:

– Janusz, może wybrałbyś się z nami na patrol na Wzgórza Golan?

– Ale po co? Myślicie, że mi życie niemiłe?

– Z nami będziesz bezpieczny.

Rozmowę przerwał jednak inny wojskowy, jeszcze ważniejszy, który wrócił właśnie z takiego patrolu.

– Lepiej tam trenera nie zabierajmy. Niech się skupi na pracy z kadrą – stanowczo uciął dyskusję.

Jak się potem okazało, dobrze zrobiłem, że nie pojechałem, bo akurat podczas tego patrolu Izraelczycy urządzili sobie ostrzał strefy syryjskiej. Trochę się wzdrygnąłem, ale jakoś cały czas byłem ciekaw, jak tam jest.

Pewnego dnia prosto z mostu zapytałem zaprzyjaźnionego generała, czy jego oferta jest aktualna. Stwierdził, że owszem, tak więc pojechałem na Wzgórza Golan. Po drodze nic ciekawego nie wypatrzyłem – ot, pustynia, jakieś rudery, bezpańskie psy. Kiedy jednak dotarliśmy na miejsce, zaparło mi dech. Ta przestrzeń, ten bezkres, ta dzika i bezludna kraina przyprawiały o zawrót głowy. Wszędzie góry, wokół pojedyncze krzewy i ciągnące się aż po horyzont druty kolczaste. Spojrzałem przez lornetkę na terytorium Izraela – żołnierze, setki żołnierzy! Niektórzy spokojnie przemieszczali się pomiędzy stanowiskami, inni stali i dyskutowali w podgrupach. Wokół oczywiście mnóstwo sprzętu wojskowego. Przecież w ciągu minuty mogli wywołać prawdziwe piekło!

– No dobra, napatrzyłem się, wracajmy – poprosiłem, a w drodze nie odezwałem się nawet słowem. Popatrzy sobie człowiek przez lornetkę i od razu wraca mu świadomość klasowa.

Chcąc poprowadzić reprezentację, musiałem ją najpierw wyselekcjonować, bo drużyna praktycznie nie istniała. Szybko się zorientowałem, że tamtejsza liga to przedziwne połączenie socjalistycznych praktyk z zachodnią nowoczesnością. No bo było i wojsko, które trzymało nad wszystkim pieczę, ale też prywatni sponsorzy, pompujący w futbol wielką kasę. Wbrew pozorom Syria wcale nie była wtedy takim biednym krajem.

Jeden z pierwszych meczów, dość ważnych, graliśmy na Stadionie Narodowym w Damaszku. Czytam skład: w obronie jakiś Ahmed, w ataku inny Alibaba. Jeśli jednak myślicie, że wybierałem piłkarzy na chybił-trafił, to jesteście w błędzie. Selekcja była dokonywana w podobny sposób jak w reprezentacji Polski – czy to pierwszej, czy olimpijskiej. Jeździłem na mecze ligowe, z uwagą obserwowałem piłkarzy i wybierałem najlepszych. Takich, jacy pasowali do mojej koncepcji. Doskonale wiedziałem, że Ahmed to Ahmed, a Alibaba to Alibaba.

Ale wróćmy do naszego meczu. Zaczęło się nietypowo. Nagle do szatni wpada jeden z miejscowych pułkowników, prezes klubu z Damaszku, i pierdoli coś po swojemu. A drze się tak, że już wiadomo, że coś jest nie po jego myśli.

– O co mu, do chuja, chodzi? – zwróciłem się do Adama, mojego tłumacza.

– Mówi, że nie wystawił trener zawodnika z jego drużyny i bardzo mu się to nie podoba – wyjaśnił mi kompletnie zesrany.

– Coach, coach! – ryknął pułkownik w moją stronę. Było to chyba jedyne angielskie słowo, które znał. – Dlaczego nie gra Murat? Wystaw go!

Zapewne liczył, że się wystraszę. Oj, misiu syryjski, a wiesz, z kim ty rozmawiasz? W Polsce nikomu do łba by nie przyszło, żeby mi kazać wystawić zawodnika, bobym go wypierdolił na kopach z szatni. Nie znałem syryjskich przekleństw, więc użyłem naszych.

– Wypierdalaj stąd, frajerze! Jedyne, co mogę wystawić na twoje życzenie, chuju złamany, to dupę na słońce!

Zapadła grobowa cisza. Piłkarze popatrzyli na tłumacza, a gdy dowiedzieli się, co powiedziałem, ryknęli śmiechem. Brawo, chłopaki, macie być po mojej stronie. Intruz kompletnie zgłupiał.

– Adam – zwróciłem się do tłumacza – nie musisz dokładnie przekładać, ale powiedz temu dziadowi, żeby stąd wyszedł. Widzi przecież, jak chłopaki reagują, i dobrze by było, żeby ktoś go przez przypadek nie kopnął w dupę.

Adaś powiedział kilka słów w tym barbarzyńskim języku, a pułkownik popatrzył na mnie tak, jakbym był jego największym wrogiem. Odpowiedziałem podobnym spojrzeniem, lecz gryzłem wargi, bo śmiać mi się chciało z tego durnia.

Nie obawiałem się, bo wiedziałem, że po mojej stronie są generałowie, którzy mogą go zmieść z powierzchni ziemi. On miał tego świadomość, więc odwrócił się na pięcie i odmaszerował. Jak szeregowiec, a nie pułkownik. Kiedy wyszedł, piłkarze zaczęli bić mi brawo. Byłem ich bohaterem.

– Adam, powiedz im, że jak nie wygrają tego meczu, to usłyszą takie same teksty jak ten pułkownik! Albo i jeszcze gorsze! – zagroziłem.

Grajkom opadły szczęki. Zobaczyli, że z Wujem nie ma żartów!

Jak myślicie, jaki był wynik? Pojechaliśmy frajerów „czwórasiem" do zera!

Sądziłem, że mój kochany pułkownik zapadł się pod ziemię i już nigdy go nie zobaczę. Nie minął jednak tydzień, a dowiedziałem się, że mam zaproszenie do siedziby klubu, którego prezesem jest właśnie ten wojskowy. Zastanawiałem się już, jaką artylerię wyprowadzić na tego gagatka, ale gdy dotarłem na miejsce, okazało się, że mój niedawny wróg stał się wielkim przyjacielem! Uznał, że po tej awanturze w szatni jestem dla niego godnym partnerem do rozmowy.

– No i to jest trener! Wszyscy przede mną srają po nogawkach, a ty mnie opierdoliłeś i wyrzuciłeś za drzwi. Tak ma działać szef drużyny – piał z zachwytu. – Czego się napijesz? Kawki, może piwka?

– Piwo? Zawsze chętnie! – rozochociłem się.

Pułkownik posłał służącego po alkohol i po kilku minutach rozmawialiśmy jak starzy kumple. Pozostaliśmy nimi aż do końca mojego półtorarocznego pobytu w Syrii. A koledzy z ambasady nadziwić się nie mogli, skąd ja znam takich ludzi.

– Panowie, jestem trenerem reprezentacji Syrii, a nie miejscowego przedszkola. Jak chcecie, to was umówię z moimi przyjaciółmi – puszyłem się.

Wiedzieli, że nie przesadzam. Bo co to za problem dla Wuja wkręcić się do wyższych sfer?

Skład już wyselekcjonowałem, trzeba było jeszcze umówić jakieś mecze. Korzystając ze swoich znajomości, załatwiłem towarzyskie spotkania z Jordanią i Arabią Saudyjską. Pierwsza z tych reprezentacji dotychczas Syryjczyków regularnie tłukła. Jordańczycy prezentowali lepszą kulturę gry, taką europejską. Pojechaliśmy tam więc na pożarcie, wszyscy spodziewali się, że dostaniemy bańki. Przed meczem zmotywowałem jednak chłopaków w swoim stylu, więc na boisku tak fruwali, że opędzlowali Jordańczyków 2:0! Jeszcze tego samego dnia jordańscy działacze próbowali mnie namówić, bym został trenerem ich reprezentacji. Odmówiłem i zabrałem się z drużyną na drugi mecz – z Saudyjczykami. Udaliśmy się do miasta Dżeda w Arabii Saudyjskiej; spaliśmy oczywiście w wypasionym, luksusowym hotelu. W tym samym budynku zatrzymali się również nasi rywale, którzy byli zdecydowanym faworytem tego starcia. To tak, jakby reprezentacja Polski miała się spotkać z Niemcami, Holandią czy Hiszpanią. W saudyjski futbol pompowano wielkie pieniądze.

„Zobaczymy, cwaniaczki, czy pójdzie wam tak łatwo", pomyślałem, a chłopakom natłukłem do głów, co mają robić. Wspomniałem też rzecz jasna o goleniu frajerów za pomocą tępej żyletki.

I ogolili – 2:1! Absolutna sensacja, wieść rozniosła się na cały Półwysep Arabski. Byliśmy na ustach wszystkich, Saudyjczycy łapali się za głowy.

– Czym ty ich nafaszerowałeś? – wypytywali.

– Co wy pierdolicie? Przecież jedliśmy to samo co wy. A nawet gorsze, bo wy te lepsze kąski wyłapywaliście. Może za bardzo się nażarliście? – drwiłem.

Syryjska telewizja piała z zachwytu, działacze nie przestawali poklepywać mnie po plecach. Wszyscy oczekiwali kolejnych zwycięstw. Akurat w Dżedzie przebywała reprezentacja Jemenu, która również grała z Arabią Saudyjską, więc szybko umówiliśmy się na sparing. Skoro byliśmy na fali, to aż żal było się z nimi nie zmierzyć. Mecz bardzo przypominał mi starcie mojej olimpijskiej drużyny z Barcelony w półfinale z Australią. Wtedy Polska wygrała 6:1, a teraz Syria z Jemenem – 7:1. Po każdym golu dopadałem do linii i zamiast chwalić, darłem się:

– Więcej! Trzymajcie ich za jaja!

Słuchali mnie jak rudy kujon belfra, więc strzelali, aż tamtych do łez doprowadzili. Fajnie się na to patrzyło. Jemeńczycy byli załamani, ale wieczorem zaprosili mnie na kolację.

– Bez ciebie nie wracamy do Jemenu, ty już jesteś naszym trenerem. Zgodzimy się na wszelkie twoje warunki. – Przedstawiciel jemeńskiego związku napalony był nieprawdopodobnie, aż przykro było słuchać.

– Zaraz, zaraz. Gdzie ten wasz Jemen jest? Dajcie jakąś mapę! – odparłem. – Dobra, spotkajmy się jutro, obgadamy to na spokojnie.

Nazajutrz dopadli mnie na śniadaniu. Zakomunikowali, że już wszystko jest ustalone z prezesem związku, a dotychczasowy trener został zwolniony, by zrobić miejsce dla mnie.

Powiem szczerze, że wolałbym, by to Saudyjczycy wypierdolili swoich Holendrów i zaproponowali mi robotę, wówczas nie zastanawiałbym się nawet chwili. A tego Jemenu to nie byłem pewien… Zostałem więc w Syrii i w sumie nie żałowałem, bo spędziłem tam bardzo miło czas, a i trochę kasy natłukłem. Piłkarze i działacze byli zapatrzeni we mnie jak w obrazek.

Pewnie się zastanawiacie, dlaczego mnie z tej Syrii wyjebali. I tu was zaskoczę – sam odszedłem! Zrezygnowałem, kiedy doszło do wewnętrznej wojny o stanowisko prezesa związku piłkarskiego. Jedni mnie chcieli, inni nie. Atmosfera zaczęła się zagęszczać, a ja otwarcie okazywałem niezadowolenie. Stojący po mojej stronie generał o nazwisku Surya pytał wprost, kto mi przeszkadza. Gdybym kogoś wskazał, bezwzględnie wsadziliby faceta do pierdla. Miałem już jednak trochę dosyć tego kraju i nie chciałem się dalej w to bawić. Poprosiłem o wypłacenie mi reszty pieniędzy, co zrobiono błyskawicznie, bo Syryjczycy to bardzo honorowi ludzie. Wróciłem do kraju, ale potem wiele razy odbierałem telefony od Suryi i kochanego pułkownika, którzy wprost pytali, kiedy do nich wrócę. Ja jednak nie chciałem. Diabeł znudził już się Damaszkiem i postanowił znów pogrzeszyć trochę we własnym, polskim piekiełku.

PIŁKARSKI POKER

MECHANIZM KORUPCYJNY

„Tu nie ma co trenować, tu trzeba dzwonić" – tak podobno miałem powiedzieć, kiedy objąłem stery w Świcie Nowy Dwór Mazowiecki. Pierdolenie o Szopenie, takiej sytuacji nie było, ale od tematu korupcji w polskiej piłce uciec się nie da. Mówiło się, że szefem mafii piłkarskiej był pewien dżentelmen spod Wronek o pseudonimie Fryzjer, ale to kompletna bzdura. Mafię to on mógł tylko w telewizji zobaczyć, jakiś film o Cosa Nostrze czy coś takiego, ale za mały był z niego Kazio, żeby zostać dopuszczonym do głównej rozgrywki. Przy piłkarskim pokerze nawet do stołu nie podchodził, kart nie mógł tasować, a co dopiero mówić o rozdawaniu! A że podłączył się pod jednorękiego bandytę, który posypał pieniążkami, to całkiem inna sprawa.

Rzeczonego Fryzjera poznałem we Wronkach, przy okazji jakiegoś meczu, kiedy trenerem Amiki był Paweł Janas. Wcześniej nie dążyłem do kontaktu z nim, bo nie był mi do niczego potrzebny. Jego wsparcia szukali ci, którzy mniej potrafili. O, a w ogóle to niedawno dostałem wiadomość, że Fryzjer jest zły, bo za dużo o nim opowiadam. Nie wiem, o co mu chodzi – niech lepiej sobie powspomina, ile nawywijał, i zrobi rachunek sumienia.

Fryzjer lubił mówić szyfrem. Często używał metafory muru. Czyli jeśli na przykład mecz miał kosztować 50 tysięcy złotych, to przekazywał kupcom następujący komunikat: „Przed wami stoi wielki mur. W nim jest 50 cegieł, które ważą trzy tony". Obeznani w temacie bez kłopotów byli w stanie rozwikłać tę zagadkę. „Wielki mur" to wysoka cena. „50 cegieł" to początek kwoty, a te „trzy tony" to trzy zera tworzące w sumie 50 tysięcy. Proste. Dziwiłem się, bo nigdy budowlańcem nie był, więc raczej powinien o fryzjerstwie pierdolić, ale tak już się przyjęło, że mówił o cegłach. To były takie durne próby kamuflażu. Bo Fryzjer to był wieśniak. Rozkręcenie machiny korupcji na pewno było nie na jego głupi łeb. On nie bardzo nawet wiedział, jak piłka nożna wygląda, mylił ją z piłką do rugby! Namierzyli mnie, że ileś tam razy z nim rozmawiałem, ale spokojnie, byli ode mnie lepsi. Po co dzwoniłem do Fryzjera? Żeby dowiedzieć się, kto ustalił, że jeszcze przed końcem rozgrywek jesteśmy skazani na spadek. Bo to nie była sprawka Rysia. On miał chuj do gadania, mógł co najwyżej nożyczki naostrzyć albo wymoczyć grzebienie w płynie, żeby mu się wszy na łbie nie zalęgły. Na pewno nie mógł mi pierdolić koszałów-opałów, bo ja doskonale wiedziałem, jak działa ten mechanizm. Nie mógł mi powiedzieć, że kapusta rośnie tam, gdzie żyto.

Z Fryzjerem częściej rozmawiałem telefonicznie, twarzą w twarz spotykaliśmy się rzadziej. My, czyli Świt Nowy Dwór. Nie byliśmy jednak dla niego partnerem ze względu na brak kasy. Ci panowie od kręcenia lodów przecież nie prowadzili swojej działalności charytatywnie, to nie była fundacja Ratuj Się Kto Może, ale sklep, w którym trzeba było płacić. Fryzjer dowiadywał się o cenę, a potem przekazywał tę informację zainteresowanym. Mówił, że może to i owo załatwić dosłownie wszędzie, ale ja wiedziałem, że pieprzy głupoty. Wolałem zadzwonić prosto do sędziego lub kwalifikatora, zamiast bawić się w pośredników. Do celu prowadziły różne drogi, a pieniądze zawsze dzielono tak, żeby wszyscy byli zadowoleni. W tamtych czasach każdego sędziego można było przekupić. Jak była dobra cyfra, zawsze się zgadzali. Cena zależała od ciężaru gatunkowego spotkania. Wiadomo, że jeśli leszcze grały z dużo mocniejszą drużyną, to przekręcić będzie dużo trudniej. Z tego, co słyszałem, największą kwotą za „zrobienie" meczu było pół miliona złotych – albo nawet więcej.

Różne były sposoby na przekupienie arbitra. Każdy klub chciał przede wszystkim bardzo dobrze ugościć sędziego, od tego mnóstwo potem zależało, czyli mówiąc wprost: miało wpływ na mecz. Bo zadowolony sędzia to sędzia, który pomaga drużynie gospodarzy. Do sędziowania pchał się każdy, bo ludzie wiedzieli, że można i na tym zarobić, i napić się gorzały, i dobrze zabawić. Sędziowie lubili się najeść, napić, wyspać w dobrym hotelu. No i najlepiej, żeby była jeszcze jakaś dupa. Albo i dwie, wszystko zależało od możliwości pana sędziego. W każdym razie to, co widzieliśmy w filmie *Piłkarski poker*, to sranie po ścianie – rzeczywistość była znacznie mniej bajkowa. Nie robiło się żadnych podchodów, po prostu ten, kto miał dojście do sędziów, załatwiał sprawę i cześć. Zresztą w dawnych czasach raczej nie ustawiano meczów za pomocą pieniędzy, bo ich nie było. Ludzie radzili sobie inaczej. Na przykład jeśli jechało się na mecz do Dębicy, nigdy nie wracało się bez bagażnika pełnego opon. Chodziło o to, by zapewnić ludziom towar aktualnie poszukiwany. I tak to się kręciło.

Jeśli chodzi na przykład o Amicę Wronki i „darowizny" dla sędziów, to najczęściej towar produkowany przez firmę Amica odbierany był na miejscu, ale zdarzało się też, że kierownik drużyny organizował dowóz dzień lub dwa później. Niekiedy zaopatrywani w sprzęt AGD byli też dziennikarze – by o klubie pisali ciepło, miło i z sympatią. Coś za coś – macie tutaj, najmilsi, dobre jedzenie, picie i dupeczki, ale w zamian oczekujemy pozytywnych artykułów. Byli tacy, którzy zjedliby wszystko i wydupczyli, co tylko się rusza. Jeśli dziennikarz często jeździł do Wronek, to pewne było, że albo liczy na duże zniżki, albo za dobre opisanie tego, co się dzieje w klubie, chce dostać prezent. A to, że brać dziennikarska lubiła dostawać prezenty, nie było niczym wyjątkowym. Zresztą, o czym my mówimy. Sam miałem lodówkę marki Amica.

Organizatorzy meczów ligowych wiedzieli, że jeśli sędzia jest na tyle młody, że jeszcze nie ma problemów z erekcją, to na pewno nie odmówi, kiedy o późnej godzinie jakaś lala zapuka do jego drzwi. Niektórzy sędziowie sami zresztą domagali się dup. Ha, i jeszcze mieli wymagania! Jeden wolał grubszą, inny szczupłą, jeszcze inny rudą... Od trzeciej ligi w górę takie praktyki były normalne – sędzia miał się nachlać i podupczyć. Zdarzali się też tacy, którzy mówili, czego im potrzeba do domu – rzucali się na dywany, pralki, lodówki, taki szajs. Inni zabierali żony na wycieczki zagraniczne i jeszcze dostawali bonusik finansowy. Ale większość od razu zapowiadała, że bez kobitki nawet nie zaczyna rozmowy.

Był taki ciekawy numer, kiedy jeszcze pracowałem w Jagiellonii. Przyjechał do nas pewien sędzia, dostał piękny pokój w hotelu. I kilka godzin przed meczem przybiegł z pretensjami, że panienka go okradła! Okazało się, że gość się nachlał i zasnął na dziwce, a ona się obudziła, wykąpała, oczyściła mu portfel i wyszła. Pewnie rzuciła na odchodnym: „Leż, frajerze". W każdym razie spokojnie oddaliła się z kasą, a klient chrapał nakurwiony. Do niej pretensji być nie mogło, bo swoje zadanie wykonała, więc nie puszczaliśmy za nią psów gończych. Za to sędziemu poradziliśmy, żeby się lepiej pilnował, bo nie będziemy mu stawiać strażników pod drzwiami. Podobnych numerów było kilka – goście tracili wszystko, co dostali, ale mecz musieli poprowadzić tak, jak było ugadane. Panienki były zdecydowanie sprytniejsze niż oni.

Korupcji w polskiej piłce nie wymyślił Fryzjer, ale ludzie, którzy wywodzili się z PZPN-u. Główni decydenci związkowi doskonale wiedzieli, co się dzieje, ale oczywiście wszystko było poufne. Przecież nikt nie latał z kartką, na której napisane jest: „Ja opierdalam mecze i proszę się do mnie zgłaszać". W każdym razie to tam pojawił pomysł na zarabianie dodatkowej kasy przy okazji tego, co dzieje się na boisku. W taki sposób powstał mechanizm, który działał przez wiele, wiele lat i nieustannie był udoskonalany. Maszyna została dobrze naoliwiona i wszystko hulało jak należy.

Głównie chodziło o to, kto ma spaść z pierwszej ligi do drugiej, kto z drugiej do trzeciej, no i w odwrotnym kierunku – kto ma awansować. Rzecz jasna obejmowało to również sędziów. Ustawiało się ich w zależności od zasług. To, że dostawali pieniądze, to jasne, ale mieli też gwarancję, że nie spadną do niższej klasy rozgrywkowej, a czasem za ustawianie meczów byli nagradzani awansami na sędziów międzynarodowych.

Na początku praca w PZPN-ie była mało opłacalna, ale potem ludzie pchali się tam drzwiami i oknami. Na lewiznach, głównie korupcji, można było zarobić kilkakrotność pensji i wszyscy to łykali jak spaniel własne gówno. Jeszcze raz powtórzę – to nie Ryszard z Wronek zbudował mechanizm korupcyjny i trząsł piłkarskim światkiem. Jakim cudem facet, który był fryzjerem, mógł mieć dostęp do informacji, kto ma być wystawiony do prowadzenia konkretnego meczu? Musiałby być ponad prezesem związku, ponad sekretarzem i ponad całym zarządem! Potem oczywiście ludzie ze związku zarzekali się, że nie mieli pojęcia, co dzieje się w sprawie korupcyjnej. Zmieniło się to po tym, jak zatrzymani zostali koledzy Kolator, Żelazko, Diakonowicz.

W czasach, kiedy prowadziłem pierwszą reprezentację, doszło do zabawnego zdarzenia. Wybierałem się na jakąś obserwację i już na lotnisku złapał mnie Jacek Kmiecik. Milutki jak u cioci na imieninach, zagadywał, dopytywał i aż nóżkami przebierał, taki był ciekawy. No to mu powiedziałem:

– Jacek, mecze są u nas, kurwa, tak po chamsku kręcone, że to się w pale nie mieści. Tę ligę to o chuj potłuc. Jak w kolejce są trzy, cztery mecze grane normalnie, to już jest, kurwa, szczyt marzeń.

I on to wszystko napisał, poszło na pierwszej stronie „Przeglądu Sportowego". Wiedziałem, co mnie czeka: nie zdążyłem nawet odłożyć gazety i nalać sobie kropelki na pokrzepienie, a już dostałem wezwanie z Wydziału Dyscypliny PZPN. Grzecznie poszedłem, a tam święte oburzenie: chcieli mnie zawiesić w prawach trenera kadry za to, że nie poinformowałem związku, że wiem o takich niecnych procederach.

– Panowie, znamy się wszyscy doskonale od lat – zacząłem. – I dobrze wiecie, co się dzieje w polskiej lidze. Owszem, mam takie informacje, przyglądam się tej szopce może trochę dokładniej niż wy. Tylko czy gdzieś tu jest napisane, że ten wywiad był autoryzowany? Poproście pana Kmiecika, jak będzie chciał, to przyjdzie i będzie się tłumaczył. Ukłoniłem się, po czym wypiąłem dupę i wyszedłem.

Kmiecik nic nie przekręcił, napisał słowo w słowo to, co powiedziałem, ale chciałem utrzeć nosa tym bucom. Potem odezwał się do mnie pewien prokurator z Poznania, który kręcił się przy piłce. Pytał oczywiście o korupcję w PZPN-ie.

– Panie prokuratorze, przecież wszyscy tam wiedzą, co się wyprawia – zacząłem. – Tylko każdy kłamie, oszukuje, bo, kurwa, nikt nie chce się wystawić. Każdy będzie udawał. A to, co zostało napisane, jest prawdą, ja się nie wycofuję. Jeśli prokuratura podejmie jakieś oficjalne kroki, to oczywiście się wypowiem. Ale teraz jako kto mam się spowiadać? Przecież nie jestem śledczym. Mam pokazywać palcem na przekręciarzy?

I pan prokurator pokiwał główką, po czym więcej się do mnie nie odezwał.

KRĘCENIE W PRAKTYCE

Pierwszy raz spotkałem się z korupcją na dużą skalę, kiedy podjąłem się pracy w Hutniku Kraków. Walczyliśmy ze Stalą Mielec o awans do 1. ligi i wiedzieliśmy, że powinniśmy go uzyskać. Wtedy doskonale zdawałem sobie sprawę, że mecze były robione. Nawet w drużynie miałem kilku takich, którzy nie chcieli wchodzić do pierwszej ligi, bo zdawali sobie sprawę, że stracą robotę, ponieważ są za słabi. Zaczęli wchodzić w układy ze Stalą. To między innymi dlatego ostatecznie nie awansowaliśmy wyżej. Przyszedł taki mecz z Polonią Bytom, przegrany 1:2, który moi piłkarze ewidentnie sprzedali. Co mogłem zrobić? Głowy im poucinać? Dostali kary finansowe i tyle. O tym, że mecz został opierdzielony, dowiedziałem się od sędziów. Moich kochanych handlarzy było czterech, może pięciu, ale to wystarczyło, bo wszyscy oni występowali na kluczowych pozycjach. Gołym okiem dało się zobaczyć, że grają na wstecznym, że odpuszczają. Później dowiedziałem się, że dogadywali się też z kolegami z Bytomia i Mielca. Ile wzięli, nie wiem. Nie miałem okazji ani moczyć ich w wodzie, ani przypalać, by wyciągnąć tego typu informacje. A wtedy chyba by się takie Guantanamo przydało, zeznania byłyby na pewno płynniejsze.

Po Hutniku trafiłem do Jagiellonii Białystok, gdzie też oczywiście zetknąłem się z korupcją. Zapadła decyzja, że Jagiellonię trzeba spuścić z ligi, bo Białystok za daleko i nikomu nie chce się jeździć. Uznano, że choć jest nisko w tabeli, to trzeba mu pomóc, żeby go stamtąd wyjebać. Starałem się walczyć o utrzymanie w każdy sposób. Kiedy dowiadywałem się, że dżentelmen z gwizdkiem może sędziować przeciw nam, od razu starałem się do niego dotrzeć i uświadomić mu, że doskonale o tym wiem. A jeśli to nie skutkowało, wnioskowałem o zmianę sędziego. Oczywiście sami też próbowaliśmy swoimi sposobami przekonywać arbitrów, by stali po naszej stronie. Wręczaliśmy im na przykład zestawy szynek, konserw, fundowaliśmy dobre obiady, zdrową panienkę, a oni chętnie korzystali. Pilnowałem, by sędzia część dostawał przed meczem, a część już po. Ale tak naprawdę nie potrzebowaliśmy poważnego wsparcia, bo i tak goliliśmy frajerów z palcem w dupie. Nie dość, że udało mi się utrzymać zespół, to jeszcze wywindowaliśmy się do czołówki! Z kolei w następnym sezonie już po rundzie jesiennej mieliśmy ogromną przewagę punktową i wszyscy zastanawiali się, kiedy zaczniemy puszczać mecze. Wiedziałem jednak, że jeśli sprzedamy choć jeden, to za nim pójdą kolejne, a to pogrzebałoby sezon. Wpadłem więc na pomysł, by zespoły, którym zależy na naszym zwycięstwie, dodatkowo wspierały nas finansowo. „Proszę bardzo, słucham, jaka jest propozycja? Co oferujecie?", pytałem gagatków, a klientów nigdy nie brakowało. Przyjeżdżał trener, kierownik albo inny działacz. Pieniądze musiał wręczyć zaraz po meczu, w torbie, w walizeczce, w czym tam miał. Przekazywanie odbywało się w klubie, jawnie, bo nie było sensu się z tym kryć.

Informowałem zawodników o moich negocjacjach i pytałem, czy są gotowi przyjąć pieniądze. No i wyobraźcie sobie, że byli gotowi. Nasza przewaga powiększała się, co chyba jasno oznacza, że żadnego handlu nie było. Przeciwnie – laliśmy wszystkich po dupach, bo byliśmy po prostu silni. A czy my kupowaliśmy? Nie było za co, klub był przecież potwornie biedny, a ja nieustannie wypłakiwałem się w komitecie partii, by wybłagać środki na Jagiellonię.

Kiedy pracowałem w silnych klubach, takich jak Legia, rzecz jasna dostawałem liczne propozycje finansowe. Pewnego razu graliśmy z ŁKS-em w Warszawie i łodzianie bali się, że wywiozą worek bramek, więc podpytywali, ile chcielibyśmy za odpuszczenie im meczu. Z miejsca odrzuciłem ich ofertę, bo zamierzaliśmy się bić o tytuł mistrzowski. Czasem rywale chcieli nawet zapłacić za to, byśmy za wysoko ich nie pokonali, żeby było 1:0, góra 2:0. Potem jednak wiedzieli już, że Legia jest rozpędzona i nie ma ceny, za którą można byłoby nas kupić. No, chyba że po ferrari dla każdego z chłopaków.

Gdzie odchodziło największe kupowanie? Legenda głosi, że w Świcie Nowy Dwór, ale to bzdura. W Świcie nie było kasy na takie kręcenie lodów, nie było nawet za co kupić Isostaru czy odżywek dla piłkarzy. Właściciel klubu, Wojtek Szymański, musiałby chyba sprzedać swój zakład z kiełbasami, żeby kupować mecze! My w tym pokerze nie byliśmy nawet dopuszczeni do rozdawania kart.

Każdy może powiedzieć, że Świt kupował mecze na potęgę, a jednak nikt nikomu niczego nie udowodnił. Jakby mógł kupować, to po co byłby mu potrzebny trener Wójcik? Można było załatwić, zapłacić i z głowy. Inna rzecz, że ja się wcale nie wybielam. Przeciwnie – gdybym dysponował większymi pieniędzmi, z pewnością działałbym na znacznie szerszą skalę.

Moi poprzednicy w Świcie, pod przewodnictwem nieżyjącego już Władka Stachurskiego, niewiele jesienią zrobili, a ja na wiosnę dostałem zadanie utrzymania zespołu. Pozmieniałem niemal wszystko: sposób trenowania, obciążenia, skład. Poprzenosiłem zawodników z rezerw, dałem szansę między innymi Wawrzyniakowi i temu małemu Smagaczowi, czy tam Zganiaczowi, co potem trafił do Korony Kielce.

Silne drużyny, jak Legia, były na tyle nie do ruszenia, że nie musiały niczego kupować. Ale na dole tabeli była rąbanina, sieczkarnia.

Jak cztery zespoły w każdej kolejce grały normalnie, to było wszystko. Wygrywał ten, kto był bogatszy, ale też kto miał lepsze układy i lepsze dojścia do sędziów. My nie wyjeżdżaliśmy z tego supermarketu z pełnymi koszykami. Drużynę sponsorował jeden człowiek, Wojtek Szymański, a pomagało mu dwóch innych. Pierwszy handlował pierogami, drugi miał piekarnię. Ten od pierogów, mój imiennik, poprosił mnie na początku mojej pracy w Świcie o umożliwienie kontaktu z kimś z PZPN-u, kto pomógłby załatwić to i owo. Tyle tylko, że on już ten kontakt miał! Znał człowieka, który decydował o przydzielaniu sędziów do konkretnych meczów, i dogadywał się z nim bezpośrednio. Chciał utrzymać drużynę w pierwszej lidze i ratować pieniądze, które z Szymańskim włożyli w klub, więc szukał rozmaitych rozwiązań. On i pozostali nie dysponowali środkami, żeby rywalizować z najbogatszymi, więc rozglądali się za innymi drogami ustawiania meczów. A że teraz mówią, że ja tam z nimi byłem i wszystko widziałem? No skoro byłem trenerem, to i widziałem!

Janusz S. był prawą ręką Wojtka Szymańskiego, czyli właściciela klubu. Z pewnością nie dysponował środkami, dzięki którym można było coś zrobić – musiałby narobić tyle pierogów, żeby zatkać nimi wszystkie sklepy w Polsce! Tym bardziej że czasy, kiedy można było sędziemu nakłaść wędlin do bagażnika albo dać trzymiesięczny zapas pierogów z owocami, minęły bezpowrotnie. Liczyła się kasa, kasa i jeszcze raz kasa.

Nowy Dwór od początku traktowano jako drużynę do odstrzału. Fryzjer powiedział mi nawet podczas jednej z pierwszych rozmów, że „woda po nas została już spuszczona". Świt to był „Jasiu Zielone Ucho", który wśród tych wilków, co latały na dole tabeli, nie miał żadnych szans. Chciały nas ugryźć, a potem zagryźć, byśmy się nie podnieśli. A ja nie miałem siły przebicia. Co, może powinienem wyjąć pieniądze z własnej kieszeni, żeby kogoś przekupić? Albo przystawić sędziom pistolet do łba? Jak wspomniałem, jedynym kontaktem działaczy Świtu, a konkretnie Janusza S., był człowiek, który do dziś pracuje w PZPN-ie.

Nowy Dwór od początku traktowano jako drużynę do odstrzału. Fryzjer powiedział mi nawet podczas jednej z pierwszych rozmów, że „woda po nas została już spuszczona". Świt to był „Jasiu Zielone Ucho", który wśród tych wilków, co latały na dole tabeli, nie miał żadnych szans

To on ustalał składy sędziowskie na każdy mecz. Powiedziałem o tym niedawno Zbyszkowi Bońkowi, który bardzo chciał się dowiedzieć, kto to taki. Nie jestem jednak oficerem śledczym, a Boniek ma swój Wydział Dyscypliny, który to powinien zweryfikować.

ZARZUTY

Wiosną graliśmy z Polonią Warszawa mecz w Nowym Dworze. Zwyciężyliśmy i pojawiło się podejrzenie, że wynik był ustawiony. Sranie w banię! Ja w prokuraturze wyraźnie mówiłem, że Świt był w tej lidze neptkiem, który nie potrafił wygrać nawet ostatniego meczu, decydującego o byciu w pierwszej lidze.

To był pojedynek z Polkowicami, które miały i pieniądze, i układy. Byliśmy od ich zdecydowanie lepsi, ale skończyło się bezbramkowym remisem. Potem zrozumiałem: moi zawodnicy puścili ten mecz. Nam do utrzymania potrzebne było zwycięstwo, im remis, i nagle okazuje się, że mimo zdecydowanej przewagi nasi piłkarze nie potrafią wkopać piłki do pustej bramki! Nikogo nie złapałem za rękę, ale po meczu wpadłem wściekły do szatni i zjebałem tych moich debili z góry na dół: – Nie wiem, czy, kurwa, któryś z was, skurwysyny, nie sprzedał tego meczu. W takich sytuacjach, jakie wam się trafiały, sztuką było nie trafić do siatki. A wyście się wywracali na piłce! Nie wierzę, że ty, ty i ty nie potrafiliście prosto kopnąć piłki. Nie wierzę! A teraz spierdalajcie, kutasy złamane. Nie chce mi się z wami gadać!

Jeden przez drugiego zapewniali mnie, że robili wszystko, żeby ten mecz wygrać. I ja rozumiem, czasem najlepsi piłkarze świata nie trafiają do pustej bramki, ale tych sytuacji było po prostu za dużo. A poza tym sędzia przynajmniej dwukrotnie powinien gwizdnąć karnego dla nas, ale udawał niewidomego.

Moi przemili chłopcy zrobili mi więc psikusa, choć jeszcze niedługo wcześniej zapewniali mnie, że chcą grać w tej pierwszej lidze, bo to większe pieniądze, lepsze kontrakty i w ogóle szczyt hajlajfu.

– Barany jedne, jak spadniecie, to możecie w Nowym Dworze co najwyżej podwórka zamiatać! Jak sobie zabagniliście sytuację, to nie myślcie, że teraz kto inny rozwiąże problem za was – wbijałem do tych pustych łbów, a oni wgapiali się we własne buty jak spłoszone panienki.

Wydawało mi się, że dotarło, ale w ostatnim meczu zdarzyły się rzeczy wprost nieprawdopodobne, a ja w takie przypadki, kurwa, nie wierzę. Bramki, jakie mogły paść, a nie padły, powinno się strzelać po flaszce wódki i w pantoflach, a nie korkach piłkarskich!

Jeden z zarzutów głosił, że miałem zaproponować czwórce zawodników Polkowic – Jackowi Banaszyńskiemu, Marcinowi Jeziornemu, Ireneuszowi Adamskiemu i Tomaszowi Moskalowi – 500 tysięcy złotych za odpuszczenie tego meczu. To niedorzeczne, ci chłopcy w życiu nie widzieli takich pieniędzy, a dostaliby przecież po ponad 100 tysięcy na głowę. Jeśli padłaby taka propozycja, spokojnie by ją przyjęli.

Innym ciekawym przykładem był nasz mecz z Wisłą Płock, który graliśmy na wyjeździe. Prezesem klubu był kolega Krzysztof Dmoszyński, którego przygarnąłem do reprezentacji Polski i z którego zrobiłem dyrektora, kiedy wyleciał z Polonii Warszawa. Marian Dziurowicz co tydzień mówił mi, żebym go wypierdolił, bo się do niczego nie nadaje. Nie wypierdoliłem, a on potem mi się odwdzięczył, oskarżając mnie we Wrocławiu o różne rzeczy. To właśnie tam powiedział, że chcieliśmy ten mecz w Płocku zrobić. A przecież wtopiliśmy 0:2!

Od początku mieliśmy przewagę i wydawało się, że wygramy. Nagle sędzia najpierw wyrzucił z boiska jednego naszego piłkarza, a niedługo później drugiego. Graliśmy dziewięciu na jedenastu i polegliśmy, proszę mi więc powiedzieć, kto tu kogo przekręcił? Jaka w tym jest logika?! Jeśli arbiter byłby opłacony przez nas, to nigdy w życiu nie wyciągnąłby czerwonej kartki!

Graliśmy też z Groclinem Grodzisk Wielkopolski i przegraliśmy 1:3. Prosiłem chłopaków z drużyny, by pogadali z piłkarzami z Grodziska, czyby nas czasem nie oszczędzili. Nie mieliśmy kasy, żeby coś zaoferować, ale liczyłem, że może uda się coś załatwić po koleżeńsku. Rozmowa więc owszem, odbyła się, ale wynik jasno pokazuje, że nic z moich planów nie wyszło. Zawodnicy powiedzieli mi zresztą, że rywale nie zgodzili się na żadną propozycję.

Mówiło się, że podpieraliśmy się w meczu z Amicą Wronki, który skończył się remisem 2:2. Ale jak my mogliśmy się równać do potężnych Wronek?! Przecież finansowo to były dwie różne bajki. Choć przyznaję, to, o czym zawodnicy obu drużyn między sobą rozmawiali, jest dla mnie tajemnicą. Bo że do negocjacji doszło, jestem pewien. Choć my naprawdę nie byliśmy w stanie zaproponować Amice nic takiego, co by ją zainteresowało.

Zarzucano mi też, że chciałem ułożyć się z Legią. To oskarżenie zostało uchylone. Wytłumaczyłem panom prokuratorom, że po pierwsze nie zrobiłbym nic przeciw Legii ze względu na szacunek do tego klubu oraz to, że tam pracowałem. Poza tym nie mieliśmy żadnych szans, by rywalizować z tym zespołem – na płaszczyźnie sportowej i każdej innej.

W tamtym sezonie wygraliśmy z Lechem Poznań 1:0 i prawdą jest, że rozmawiałem o tym meczu z Fryzjerem. Pytałem, czy panowie z Lecha Poznań nie zechcieliby zastosować wobec Świtu taryfy ulgowej. Obiecał, że z nimi pogada, ale zastrzegł, że przekonanie ich będzie bardzo trudne. Stwierdził, że trener nie ma tam nic do powiedzenia, że takie sprawy trzeba załatwiać z ludźmi z zarządu, bo to oni decydują o podziale kasy. Przyznaję, że rozmawiałem na ten temat, ale nie wręczałem żadnych pieniędzy, bo nie miałem do nich dostępu. Mogłem jedynie powiedzieć, że skoro sprawa została załatwiona, to trzeba jechać do tego Poznania i wszystko uregulować. I niewykluczone, że ktoś to zrobił, ale nie mogę tego potwierdzić, bo jeżeli doszło do konkretów, to za moimi plecami.

Kolejny ciekawy zarzut dotyczy mojej rzekomej obietnicy przekazania zawodnikom Górnika Łęczna 75 tysięcy złotych, a następnie, po wygraniu meczu 1:0, wręczenia im 74 500 złotych. Ciekaw jestem, gdzie te 500 złotych wyfrunęło? Przecież gdybym miał chapnąć coś z tych 75 patyków, to wziąłbym chociaż piątkę albo dychę, a nie 500 złotych! Logika, panowie, logika!

WUJO ZA KRATKAMI

22 października 2008 roku. Poprzedniego dnia stałem pod domem i nie dostrzegłem nic, co sugerowałoby, że nazajutrz nastąpi prawdziwe trzęsienie ziemi. Widziałem co prawda, że jacyś młodzi ludzie przechadzają się wzdłuż ulicy, ale nie wzbudziło to moich podejrzeń. Dopiero na drugi dzień rano zobaczyłem, że przed wejściem, tym razem na chodniku prowadzącym do furtki, znów ktoś się szwenda – dwóch mężczyzn, dwie kobiety w średnim wieku. Palili papierosy, kiepy rzucając pod nogi, ale zreflektowali się i pozbierali niedopałki. Cały czas korzystali z telefonów komórkowych. Po chwili odeszli. Ja spokojnie się ubrałem i poszedłem do garażu, by wyprowadzić auto. W tym mo-

mencie podjechał samochód osobowy i zastawił mi wyjazd. Podeszło do mnie dwóch facetów, jeden z nich mignął blachą policyjną i rzucił:

– Policja.

Od razu skojarzyłem, że chodzi o sprawy piłkarskie. Gość poprosił, żebym położył ręce na dachu samochodu, i zapytał, czy mam przy sobie broń. Zaprzeczyłem, choć oczywiście miałem, w teczce. Legalnie trzymałem w domu dwa pistolety – SIG-Sauera i glocka. Była to broń w pełni profesjonalna, półautomatyczna.

Przed domem zrobiło się zbiegowisko, po kilku minutach na miejscu było już kilkunastu dziennikarzy! Kręcili, cykali zdjęcia, zadawali pytania – zrobili z tego prawdziwe *show*. TVN puszczał materiał z mojego zatrzymania przez kilka dobrych dni, jakby dzielne wrocławskie psy pojmały właśnie wierchuszkę Al-Kaidy.

W końcu się wkurwiłem.

– Panowie – powiedziałem do funkcjonariuszy. – Rozgońcie to towarzystwo, nie zgadzam się na pokazywanie mojego miejsca zamieszkania.

Weszliśmy do domu, spokojnie usiedliśmy. W tym czasie pod garaż podjechał drugi samochód, volkswagen, w którym siedziało trzech albo czterech antyterrorystów. Nieco się zdziwiłem – goście wyskoczyli z auta z tak zwanymi pompami, czyli karabinami walącymi ostrą amunicją. Po prostu kryminał! Zatrzymanie szefa mafii w Neapolu!

W sumie do domu weszło bodajże siedmiu mężczyzn. Grzecznie zapytali, gdzie jest broń. Wyjąłem ją z teczki, wysunąłem magazynki i położyłem na stole.

– Nie obawiajcie się. Nie będę strzelał, to nie jest druga Magdalenka. Nie zamierzam walić do was z karabinu maszynowego. Przyjechaliście tu tak zapakowanymi samochodami, jakbyście chcieli odbijać jakiś konwój. Wystarczyło przecież wysłać do mnie kwit z prokuratury, że mam się stawić, i ja bym przyszedł! A nie wydawać pieniądze na tę akcję – tłumaczyłem im.

– Taka procedura. Wiedzieliśmy, że pan ma broń… – zaczęli wyjaśniać, ale im przerwałem, bo mnie w tym momencie szlag trafił.

– I co, myśleliście, że będę do was strzelał? A na końcu walnę sobie w łeb, tak? I może jeszcze wystrzelam całą rodzinę?

– Tak kazano nam zrobić – powtarzali jak mantrę.

Przed domem gromadziło się coraz więcej ludzi. Wszyscy chcieli na żywo zrelacjonować, czy policja zacznie strzelać do Wójcika, czy też Wójcik ostrzela policję. Czekali na wojnę. Tymczasem policjanci przeszukali dom, zabezpieczyli laptopa, telefon i mój notes.

– Panowie, nie czytajcie dokładnie wszystkich moich zapisków, bo tam jest kilka takich nazwisk, że się przestraszycie. Nie chodzi o Fryzjera czy innych frajerów związanych z piłką, ale o tych ze szczytów.

Odpowiedzieli sucho:

– To już nie nasza sprawa.

Wezwano posiłki z prewencji, żeby rozgonić chętnych wrażeń dziennikarzy. Przyjechały dwa albo trzy samochody policyjne, a ja wspólnie z psami zacząłem się zastanawiać, co zrobić, żeby wyjść z domu niezauważonym. W końcu postanowiliśmy, że policyjny samochód wjedzie do garażu, a do nyski, gdzie siedzieli antyterroryści, wskoczy kto inny. Wybrali jednego z policjantów, takiego o budowie zbliżonej do mojej, facet zarzucił kurtkę na głowę i wybiegł do auta. Nie zakuli mnie w kajdanki, po prostu zeszliśmy do garażu jak ludzie i tam dali mi żółtą kamizelkę z napisem „Policja". Siadłem na tylnym siedzeniu z jednym z funkcjonariuszy. Kiedy policjant z kurtką na głowie, który miał przypominać mnie, wsiadał do auta na parkingu, my szybko wyjechaliśmy z garażu. Po drodze jeszcze potrąciliśmy jednego z fotoreporterów.

Ruszyliśmy w kierunku Wrocławia. Na ogonie siedziała nam czarna beemka, w której najprawdopodobniej jechali dziennikarze. Zgubiliśmy ich jednak, bo dzielni funkcjonariusze włączyli syrenę i pojechali pod prąd. Po drodze powiedzieli mi, że ludzie, którzy rano kręcili się pod domem, to funkcjonariusze CBA, a ja byłem dokładnie obserwowany.

Po drodze do Wrocławia zaproponowałem, że może zatrzymamy się, żeby coś przekąsić. Wjechaliśmy do lasu, stanęliśmy koło jakiejś knajpy z kiełbaskami, a antyterroryści zagrodzili drogę do baru. Zjedliśmy, wypiliśmy soczek i ruszyliśmy ku dalszym przygodom.

Gdy dotarliśmy do Wrocławia, policjanci na gorąco zmienili miejsce docelowe, bo w pierwotnym roiło się od dziennikarzy. Koniec końców pojechaliśmy na komendę wojewódzką. Tam uprzejmie i gorąco namawiano mnie, żebym powiedział coś więcej jeszcze przed pójściem do prokuratury. A takiego wała!

– Panie Januszu, tropiliśmy pana ponad rok – usłyszałem.

– Kiedy byłem posłem, też za mną chodziliście? Prawo wam na to pozwalało? – dziwiłem się.

Później poddano mnie badaniom lekarskim. Gdyby nas tak wszędzie badano, to po roku populacja zmniejszyłaby się o jakieś 30 procent. Pan doktor zadawał mi rozmaite kretyńskie pytania. Nie wiem, co to był za lekarz, chyba weterynarii. Burczał tylko coś pod nosem i kreślił jakieś krzyżyki.

Następnie zawieziono mnie do aresztu i wskazano celę. Wyjąłem sobie dres, przebrałem się i położyłem na pryczy. Obok leżał jakiś dżentelmen, ale się do niego nie odzywałem i nie reagowałem na zaczepki. W nocy przywieźli jeszcze jednego misia, ale zobaczyłem go dopiero, gdy wstałem. Spałem dobrze, a rano jak król zasiadłem do śniadania. Kromka chleba, kawa Inka, trochę żółtego sera – no luksusy! Apetytu specjalnie nie miałem. Przynajmniej klawisze zachowali się jak ludzie.

– Jeśli coś panu potrzeba, obiecamy załatwić – zapewnili.

Po śniadaniu zawieziono mnie do prokuratury. Rozpoczęło się przesłuchanie, jak za dobrych stalinowskich czasów – bite 13 godzin zadawania pytań, drążenia i innych rozkoszy. Przez cały ten czas podawano mi tylko wodę. Żadnego jedzenia, ale to akurat rozumiałem, bo to nie kawiarnia.

Po jakimś czasie dojechał mój adwokat i także wziął udział w przesłuchaniu.

Kiedy spytałem, czy mogę pójść do toalety, zgodzili się. Gdy przechodziłem z jednej części korytarza na drugą, usłyszałem głośną rozmowę dobiegającą zza zamkniętych drzwi. Pewien wysoko postawiony prokurator rozmawiał z Warszawą i szczerze żałuję, że go nie nagrałem – miałem przy sobie drugi telefon, który udało mi się zatrzymać.

Dowiedziałem się, że chcą wystąpić o trzymiesięczny areszt dla mnie, choć wcześniej otrzymałem zapewnienie, że nic takiego nie będzie miało miejsca. Chcieli mnie wsadzić do pierdla, żebym zaczął sypać. W sumie im się nie dziwię – podczas przesłuchania ani mi się śniło współpracować.

– Jeśli myślicie, że mnie złamiecie, że zaraz będę opowiadał niestworzone rzeczy, to grubo się mylicie. Jak chcecie, to możecie mnie tu trzymać 24 godziny – zapowiedziałem.

Wreszcie skończyliśmy. Zostałem odwieziony do aresztu. Na drugi dzień mili panowie zadawali mi pytania przez kolejne kilka godzin. Niechętnie, bo niechętnie, ale podali kilka nazwisk.

– Co takiego zrobił pan koledze Dmoszyńskiemu, że tak pana nie lubi?

– Nic mu nie zrobiłem – wzruszyłem ramionami, udając obojętność. – A o co chodzi?

Dowiedziałem się, że był w prokuraturze i opowiadał straszliwe banialuki. Od razu skojarzyłem, w czym rzecz. Wspomniał między innymi, że witałem się przed meczem Polska – Bułgaria w Warszawie z trenerem Christo Stoiczkowem. Znam Stoiczkowa od lat, ale ten as wydedukował, że widocznie go namawiałem, by przekonał swoich piłkarzy do odpuszczenia nam meczu. Było to bzdurą i głupotą. Oczyszczając własną dupę i zmywając z siebie brud, najłatwiej było oczernić kogoś innego, w tym wypadku mnie.

Kolejna sprawa – związana z wygraną w Chorzowie, z Rosją, w meczu towarzyskim. Spotkanie zakończyło się wynikiem 3:1 i zarzucano mi, że je ustawiłem. Nikt nie wierzył, że jesteśmy w stanie nawet zremisować. Pamiętam słowa Mariana Dziurowicza, który powiedział, że jeśli przegram, to mnie zwolni. Wygrałem, więc zaraz po meczu poszedłem zresztą do niego po podwójną premię. W każdym razie posądzono mnie, że ten mecz kupiłem. Cóż, prawdą było, że to dzięki mnie w ogóle doszedł do skutku. Jako że ludzie z PZPN-u byli mocni tylko w gębie, to nie potrafili umówić dobrego rywala na mecz towarzyski. Ja od razu zalecałem, żeby grać z Ruskimi, z którymi miałem znajomości od lat. Często popijałem z nimi wódkę – inni padali, a my twardo siedzieliśmy przy flaszce. W tamtym czasie byliśmy akurat w Szwajcarii, na losowaniu eliminacji do Euro 2000. Spytałem Michała Listkiewicza, gdzie mieszkają Ruscy. Uruchomił swój kontakt w UEFA i szybko się dowiedział. Zadzwoniliśmy do hotelu i poprosiliśmy, żeby nas połączyć z pokojem trenera reprezentacji. Michał przekazał mi słuchawkę.

– Słuchaj, czy można do was przyjechać? Chcę z tobą pogadać, będę z prezesem i sekretarzem – zacząłem.

– Dawaj, Janusz, przyjeżdżaj! – ochoczo się zgodził.

Ruszyliśmy, a po drodze wzięliśmy buteleczkę, żeby łatwiej się rozmawiało. Weszliśmy do pokoju. Jedno, drugie, trzecie, czwarte rozlanie...

– Panowie, zagrajmy jakiś mecz! – zaproponowałem.

I panowie się zgodzili. Sekretarz wyjął kalendarzyk i ustaliliśmy termin. Oczywiście wypiliśmy jeszcze po kilka kolejek, żeby uczcić dogadanie spotkania, w sumie opróżniliśmy ze dwie flaszeczki. Dziurowicz i Listkiewicz zgłupieli, nie wiedzieli, co się dzieje, nie mogli wyjść z podziwu, w jaki sposób to załatwiłem. Dlatego potem pojawiły się głosy, że skoro załatwiłem mecz, to i załatwiłem wynik.

Wróćmy do mojej przygody w areszcie. Kolejną noc w celi spędziłem już sam, bez towarzyszy. Grzecznie poprosiłem strażników o ich wypierdolenie, bo nie dawali spać. Chciałem też kartkę, żeby napisać list do rodziny. Kartkę dostałem, a rano, przy okazji śniadania, moi kochani klawisze postarali się o dodatkowe smakołyki. Chciałem się też umyć.

– Wykąpałbym się – zagaiłem.

– A proszę bardzo.

– Ale słyszałem, że tutaj ciepłej wody nie ma. Mam, kurwa, zapalenia płuc dostać? – zapytałem uprzejmie.

– Panie Januszu, wszystko da się załatwić. Zaraz pójdę i odkręcę panu ciepłą.

Gdy zawołał mnie po kilku minutach, w łazience czekało już mydełko i przyjemnie ciepła woda. Po kąpieli wytarłem się czystym prześcieradłem i po krótkim czasie byłem gotów na trzeci dzień przesłuchania. Pojechaliśmy tym razem do Komendy Wojewódzkiej, gdzie nawet napiłem się kawki. Musiałem jednak przejść do sądu, który był po drugiej stronie ulicy.

– Teraz to musimy założyć kajdanki – zaskoczył mnie dowódca całego bałaganu.

– No, kurwa, naprawdę trzeba?

– Naprawdę. Ale tak założymy i tak schowamy, że nie będzie widać. Będzie luźniutko, nie będzie uwierało – zapewniał.

Było luźniutko i nie uwierało, w ogóle nie czułem, że mam je na rękach. W sumie cały cyrk trwał niecałe pięć minut, od razu po wejściu do sądu zostałem uwolniony. Po drodze przechodziłem przez szpaler utworzony przez policję, która odgradzała mnie od tłumu dziennikarzy.

– Boicie się, że ktoś dźgnie mnie nożem? – zapytałem spokojnie.

– Typowe względy bezpieczeństwa, proszę się nie przejmować.

I w zasadzie się nie przejmowałem.

Na rozprawę oczekiwałem w klatce, takiej jak dla zwierząt. Z każdej strony kraty, a w środku Wójcik. Tam się spotkałem z obserwatorem, kolegą Krzysztofem Perkiem. Zdziwił się, bo jemu zabrali sznurowadła, a mnie nie. Wszedłem na salę, mój adwokat już czekał. Najpierw wystąpił prokurator, potem ja. Zarzuty dotyczyły udziału w procederze korupcyjnym, chciano oczywiście, bym trochę „pośpiewał". Zapewniłem, że jestem gotowy do współpracy i stawię się na każde wezwanie sądu. Potem wypowiedział się mój adwokat, a następnie prokurator wystąpił o trzymiesięczny areszt. Sąd zarządził przerwę. Po niej decyzja – mogę odpowiadać z wolnej stopy. Dostałem za to dozór policyjny i zakaz wyjazdu za granicę.

Prokuratorzy byli rozczarowani, a ja z adwokatem ruszyłem do Warszawy. Pod domem na szczęście nie czekał na mnie komitet powitalny,
dziennikarze nie mieli o niczym pojęcia.

Potem kilka razy byłem wzywany na rozprawy, ale nie mogłem się na
nie stawić ze względu na zły stan zdrowia. Po wypadku (patrz rozdział
16), zanim założono mi implant, mózg miałem niemalże na wierzchu
i biegli sądowi, którzy do mnie przyjeżdżali, nie mogli się napatrzeć.

Dozór policyjny polegał z kolei na tym, że od czasu do czasu musiałem się stawić na komendzie.

– Panie Januszu, po co pan tu w ogóle przychodzi? – usłyszałem któregoś dnia. – Znamy pana, proszę sobie darować i się nie fatygować.

Niebawem sąd zdjął ten nakaz, a także zakaz wyjeżdżania z kraju,
poza tym wysłał do PZPN-u zgodę na wykonywanie przeze mnie zawodu. I wiecie, że te barany pod przewodnictwem Grzegorza Laty w ogóle nie wzięły tego pisma pod uwagę?! Przecież my żyjemy w dżungli,
zapyziałej dżungli. Pismo z sądu, o którym mówię, zostało wysłane
w połowie maja 2010 roku. Od razu po negatywnej dla mnie decyzji PZPN-u pobiegłem jednak do siedziby związku. Nabuzowany jak
woda gazowana.

– Czy ty jesteś jebnięty w łeb? Razem ze swoimi sprzedawczyka-
mi, którym płacisz, by przyjeżdżali na zarząd, upijasz ich i dajesz żreć
w najlepszych hotelach. Nie widzisz, co zostało przesłane przez sąd?
Wy jesteście świętą inkwizycją, decydujecie o tym, co się dzieje w tym
kraju? – zaatakowałem ówczesnego prezesa PZPN-u Grzegorza Latę.

– Janusz, nie denerwuj się, to szybko minie – bronił się.

– A idź w chuj.

Od tamtej pory miałem go już głęboko w dupie.

Cała sprawa miała jeszcze dodatkowy smaczek. Otóż wielu ludzi, dowie-
dziawszy się, że w zeznaniach przewijają się ich nazwiska, przyjeżdżało
do Wrocławia i śpiewało, aż miło. Nie miałbym z tym problemu, gdyby
chcieli się po prostu wybielić, by uniknąć nieprzyjemności, ale takiego

chamstwa, że jawnie wpierdalali w bagno innych, nie wybaczę nigdy. Część z nich działa do tej pory i ma się jak pączki w maśle – prowadzi drużyny w Ekstraklasie czy pracuje w PZPN-ie. To ja się was teraz pytam, ścierwa: pamiętacie, jak wtedy jeździliście do Wrocławia i opowiadaliście swoje dyrdymały między 5.00 a 6.00 rano, żeby nikt ich nie widział? Jesteście tchórzliwymi kanaliami, nikim więcej. Kłamaliście, oczernialiście, byle tylko uratować siebie, oczyścić swoje brudne dupy.

PODDANIE SIĘ KARZE

Na koniec rzecz najświeższa i najważniejsza. We wrześniu 2014 roku dobrowolnie poddałem się karze w procesie o korupcję. Zaraz pojawiła się krytyka, że Wójcik to kawał drania, sprzedawczyk i pierwszy koruptor w Polsce.

Sprawą jednak wygląda inaczej. Otóż moi prawnicy doradzili mi, żeby zakończyć cały ten przedłużający się proces, bo to nic dobrego dla mojego zdrowia. Gdybym nie skorzystał z dobrowolnego poddania się karze, to trwałby jeszcze bardzo długo. Stąd decyzja, żeby zamknąć sprawę właśnie w taki sposób.

Dlaczego wcześniej nie stawiałem się na rozprawach? Tylko i wyłącznie ze względu na zły stan zdrowia, miałem zresztą zwolnienia od biegłych lekarzy. Nie mogłem się ciągle uchylać od odpowiedzialności, boby mnie dowlekli do sądu siłą, nawet chorego.

Dlatego zgodziłem się na udział w ostatniej rozprawie, ale biegły sądowy zadecydował, że może ona się odbyć wyłącznie w obecności ratownika medycznego. Nie wolno mi się denerwować i chyba nikomu nie byłoby przyjemnie, gdybym opuścił budynek sądu w karetce albo gdybym na sali sądowej odwalił tak zwaną kitę. Choć w sumie… Dopiero byłoby ciekawie!

Oczywiście zaraz rozległ się krzyk, że przecież Wójcik winny, ponieważ się przyznał. Ale znacie mnie, ja na to kładę lachę. Jeżeli jednak prokuratura będzie chciała moich dalszych wyjaśnień, to niewykluczone, że wymienię kilka nazwisk. Nie po to, żeby się wybielić – lecz jeśli są tacy, co zamierzają obrzucać mnie błotem, to ja się nie dam! Zajebię między oczy tak, że będą siadać na dupy i prosić o wodę.

Są ludzie, którzy w związku z moim poddaniem się karze odwracają się do mnie plecami, wykreślają mój numer z telefonu, zapominają, że się w ogóle znamy. Łatwo zapominają, co sami robili? Mogę im w każdej chwili przypomnieć.

Podkreślam po raz ostatni: to nie Wójcik rozkręcił w Polsce korupcję. Główni aktorzy tego żenującego spektaklu wciąż cieszą się wolnością. Nie zachowali się tak jak ja, nie stanęli przed sądem i nie poddali się karze. Pamiętajmy o jednym: ten rak nie został do końca wyleczony. I nie wiem, czy kiedykolwiek uda się go wyeliminować.

PZPR

„A na chuj ci, Wójcik, była ta polityka?" – ludzie często zadają mi takie pytanie. I muszę przyznać, że sam też je sobie stawiam od czasu do czasu. Mówią, że polityka bardziej mi zaszkodziła, niż pomogła. Czy żałuję? Tak, można powiedzieć, że to był mój błąd. Mogłem odpuścić, znów wyjechać do jakiegoś muzułmańskiego kraju, założyć turban i spędzić tam kilka lat. Wyszłoby mi na dobre. Nie patrzyłbym na to dziadostwo i nie brał w nim udziału. I pewnie bym już nie wrócił.

Co ja jednak poradzę, że polityka zawsze mnie kręciła? Mimo że w parlamencie poznałem wszystkie towarzyszące jej brudy i przekonałem się, że Sejm to kuźnia nie prawa, a jawnego i bezczelnego bezprawia, to coś nieodmiennie mnie w niej fascynowało.

Od początku byłem związany z lewicą, która za dawnych lat nazywała się PZPR. Należałem do partii i wcale się tego nie wstydzę. Nikogo nie zabiłem, nie zamknąłem, nie wywoziłem do lasu, wręcz przeciwnie – pomagałem ludziom, jeśli esbecy chcieli ich skasować. Byłem w tych trudnych latach odpowiedzialny za sport i edukację. Na Mokotowie mieściło się liceum imienia Rejtana, w którym zdarzały się różne nieciekawe sytuacje, a SB ciągle chciała tam wpadać, żeby kogoś zawinąć. I ja tam jeździłem, by gasić kolejne pożary. Udało mi się uratować mnóstwo osób, uczniów i nauczycieli. Potem wielokrotnie różni pseudopatrioci wypominali mi, że byłem w PZPR, a przecież nie mieli pojęcia, co robiłem w partii. Bo jeśli chcieliby wejść na jakiekolwiek obrady, to po prostu dostaliby kopa w rzyć i wylecieli za drzwi.

Pierwszy raz zetknąłem się więc z polityką, działając w komitecie dzielnicowym, a następnie udzielałem się w komitecie warszawskim. Niedługo później dostałem propozycję z Hutnika Kraków i musiałem wybierać: albo polityka, albo trenerka. To była trudna decyzja, dlatego zabrałem żonę (już drugą) na spacer i szczerze z nią o tym porozmawiałem.

– Powiedz mi, co chciałabyś, żebym robił? – zapytałem, licząc, że podsunie mi właściwe rozwiązanie. Dla niej jednak też to była bardzo trudna decyzja. Wiedziała, że na piłce zjadłem zęby i że zwyczajnie kocham sport.

– Chciałabym, żebyś robił to, co lubisz – odparła.

Z drugiej strony oferta polityczna była niezwykle kusząca. Dostałem bowiem propozycję przejścia do Komitetu Centralnego, czyli najwyższego możliwego szczebla władzy ludowej. Miałem pracować na Wydziale Informacji. Były tam komputery i dostęp do pełnej wiedzy o tym, co się dzieje w państwie. Mimo to, częściowo przekonany przez żonę, a częściowo zdając sobie sprawę, że powinienem iść za głosem serca, zrezygnowałem z dalszej kariery politycznej. Dwa dni później zapakowałem się w mojego malucha i pojechałem do Nowej Huty. Nie żałowałem tego kroku nigdy, ale wiedziałem też, że do polityki zawsze będę mógł wrócić. Jeden z druhów w partii powiedział mi wprost:

– Nie ma problemu, Janusz, jeśli coś ci nie wyjdzie, wracasz do Warszawy i znów jesteś z nami.

Z każdym miesiącem coraz bardziej jednak zapominałem o tym, że mogę wrócić do struktur partyjnych. Myślałem za to o wspinaniu się po szczeblach kariery trenerskiej.

Z czasów partyjnych przypomina mi się pewna historia związana ze świętej pamięci pułkownikiem Marianem Bednarczykiem, moim szefem w Gwardii Warszawa. Działał w PZPN-ie i często spotykaliśmy się w restauracji SPATIF przy Alejach Ujazdowskich, żeby pogadać i wypić drinka. Pewnego razu pan pułkownik trochę za dużo sobie łyknął i trochę za bardzo się podniecił własną opowieścią. Zanim zorientowałem się, co się dzieje, przede mną na stole leżała piękna, błyszcząca spluwa. Nieco wyżej błyszczały jasne oczy pana pułkownika.

– Marian, radzę ci, schowaj to – zacząłem delikatnie, lecz stanowczo. – Po pierwsze, to nie jest miejsce, żeby się chwalić pukawką, a po drugie, jeśli chcesz, to zaraz skontaktuję się z tak zwanym Białym Domem, który jest o tam, na rogu. Albo z komitetem warszawskim. Przyjadą, a ty będziesz miał pełne gacie i narobisz sobie syfu w papierach – ostrzegałem.

Bednarczyk dostał czkawki, próbował coś z siebie wydusić, ale nie był w stanie – i dlatego, że był nagrzmocony, i ponieważ zdziwiła go moja reakcja. Na jego szczęście nigdzie nie zadzwoniłem, ale dostał za swoje, bo przyuważył nas jeden z moich kolegów.

– Chowaj to i wypierdalaj – polecił.

Bednarczyk, posrany ze strachu, porwał pistolet, wepchnął za pazuchę i uciekł chwiejnym krokiem. Inni klienci zaczęli do nas podchodzić i dziękować, a nam z trudem udało się utrzymać powagę.

Inna gruba historia polityczna z tamtych czasów wiąże się już z moją pracą trenerską i z sytuacją, w której musiałem użyć swoich wpływów. Otóż miałem jechać z reprezentacją do lat 18 na turniej do Izraela. Bardzo mi na tym wyjeździe zależało. I podczas którejś wizyty w PZPN-ie poczciwa pani Irenka, jedna z pracownic, zakomunikowała mi:

– Przykro mi, Janusz, ale nigdzie nie pojedziecie.

Co kurwa?!

– Ale dlaczego? – wydusiłem.

– Zawieszono stosunki dyplomatyczne z Izraelem, również na linii sportowej.

– Irenko, a kto wydał taką decyzję? – zapytałem tak spokojnie, jak tylko potrafiłem, choć przed oczami miałem już czerwoną plamę.

– Ministerstwo Sportu.

– Ale przecież Ministerstwo Sportu to nie jest wszystko! – obruszyłem się.

– Ale w tym jeszcze brało udział Ministerstwo Spraw Zagranicznych... – wydukała.

Policzyłem do dziesięciu i, już na osobności, zadzwoniłem do swojego przyjaciela z PZPR, bardzo ważnej persony w strukturach partyjnych. Poprosiłem go o spotkanie.

– Przyjeżdżaj do siedziby partii – zakomunikował. – Nie musisz mieć żadnej przepustki, na bramkach o wszystkim będą wiedzieli.

Kolega zorganizował mi spotkanie z człowiekiem z Wydziału Spraw Zagranicznych. Od razu wyjaśniłem mu, o co chodzi.

– Słuchaj, Janusz, wolelibyśmy, żebyście tam nie jechali – powiedział. Milczałem i patrzyłem mu prosto w oczy. – Tak, widzę, że ci zależy... No dobrze, zrobimy w ten sposób: jedziecie, ale odpowiadasz za tych zawodników własną głową, a po powrocie przyjdziesz do mnie na dywanik i zdasz dokładne sprawozdanie z tego, co się tam działo. I drugi warunek: nie wolno grać polskiego hymnu.

Złapał za słuchawkę i wybrał numer Ministra Spraw Zagranicznych. Szybko wytłumaczył mu, że grupa pod wodzą trenera J.W. jedzie do Izraela, choćby skały srały. O dziwo, minister się zgodził.

– Janusz, załatwione – oznajmił mój odważny sojusznik. – To co, może napijemy się teraz koniaczku?

– Czemu nie! – odparłem, wszak na tego typu przyjemności nie trzeba mnie namawiać.

Wypiliśmy sobie po dwa kieliszeczki, a ja oczywiście obiecałem, że grzecznie zdam relację ze swojego wyjazdu. Następnie wpadłem do siedziby PZPN-u, gdzie już w progu powitał mnie okrzyk Irenki:

– Janusz, Janusz, gdzieś ty był, z kim ty rozmawiałeś?! Wszystko jest odkręcone, jedziecie!

– Widzisz, Irenko – odparłem spokojnie – są jeszcze ludzie ponad tymi, o których mówiłaś, i ja właśnie u tych ludzi byłem.

Zostawiłem osłupiałą Irenkę i poszedłem załatwiać swoje sprawy.

Turniej w Izraelu oczywiście wygraliśmy, lecz przez cały czas byliśmy nieprawdopodobnie pilnowani. Zresztą strona izraelska była zadowolona, że jednak dotarliśmy. Szefową naszej ochrony była siostrzenica Mosze Dajana, legendarnego izraelskiego generała. Zadbała, byśmy się czuli bezpiecznie jak w domu. Muszę też wspomnieć, że ona w moim towarzystwie też czuła się bezpiecznie – dymaliśmy się jak koty na wiosnę! Cóż, nie było jeszcze takiej dziewczyny, która nie uległaby urokowi trenera Wójcika.

Została jeszcze sprawa hymnu, która nurtowała mnie od początku wyjazdu. Pamiętałem, że zabroniono go zagrać, ale postanowiłem rozegrać to po swojemu. Stwierdziłem, że nikt w kraju się nie dowie, jeśli hymn jednak zostanie wykonany, a moje chłopaki będą mieć trochę radości.

– Grajcie, i to najgłośniej, jak potraficie! – zakomunikowałem organizatorom, a chłopakom nakazałem, by śpiewali do zdarcia swoich młodych, zwycięskich gardeł.

Po powrocie karnie poszedłem zdać sprawozdanie, ale nie miałem żadnych obaw. Przywiozłem bowiem ze sobą koniaczek, który był lepszy niż moje opowieści. Wypiliśmy z towarzyszem po kilka kieliszeczków i okazało się, że wszystko było tak, jak trzeba. Pytanie o hymn nawet nie padło.

WUJO W SEJMIE

Jako trener z polityką niewiele miałem wspólnego, cały czas jednak utrzymywałem kontakty z ludźmi z tak zwanej góry – ministrami, premierem, wicepremierem czy nawet prezydentem; bardzo często spotykałem się z Aleksandrem Kwaśniewskim i jego małżonką, szczególnie kiedy byłem selekcjonerem reprezentacji Polski. Wjeżdżaliśmy autokarem na teren pałacu prezydenckiego i byliśmy przyjmowani z honorami. Pan prezydent zresztą znakomicie znał się na futbolu. Kiedyś, gdy urządzał urodziny, powiedział:

– Rozegramy mecz, panowie. Tu, w pałacu prezydenckim!

Uroczystość była mocno zakrapiania, więc bawiliśmy się przednio. Prezydent wpadł na pomysł, żeby podczas meczu ktoś przygrywał na perkusji, która stała w sali kolumnowej. Posadził tam Marka Siwca i ten walił rytmicznie w talerze, żeby podkreślić tempo gry. A ja, jak zwykle pomysłowy, za każdym razem zamiast kopać piłkę do naprędce stworzonych bramek, celowałem w perkusję i jej operatora. I parę razy udało mi się Siwca ustrzelić. W pewnym momencie spierdolił się z krzesła, wpadł w bębny i talerze, robiąc taki huk, że chyba na drugim końcu Warszawy było to słychać!

Graliśmy w garniturach i krawatach, no i oczywiście w lakierkach. Ślizgaliśmy się nieprawdopodobnie na tej posadzce, co chwilę ktoś jęczał, bo przyrżnął zadem o marmur. Nikomu jednak nic się nie stało, bo wszyscy byli po spożyciu, a jak wiadomo, znieczulone ciało jest plastyczne i giętkie.

Już po meczu „zawodnicy" jak dzikie, spragnione stado koni ruszyli do wodopoju. I bawiliśmy się dalej. Świętowaliśmy urodziny wielkiego wodza do utraty tchu.

Aha, i najważniejsze: wygrała moja drużyna, ale to chyba oczywiste.

Do polityki wróciłem, kiedy otrzymałem propozycję wstąpienia do SLD. Początkowo chciałem się dostać do Rady Warszawy i nie mam wątpliwości, że tak by się stało, gdyby nie jedna baba, która zarąbała mi głos i sama wskoczyła na miejsce, na które się szykowałem. Natomiast jakiś czas później zaskoczył mnie Rysio Czarnecki, znany polityk i pasjonat futbolu. Rysiek był też działaczem PZPN-u, ale cóż, jaki działacz – taka piłka. Szanowaliśmy się, ale wiedziałem, że kręci się przy sporcie, żeby sobie robić „fejm".

– Janusz, a nie chciałbyś podziałać w Samoobronie? – zapytał, gdy któregoś dnia spotkaliśmy się w siedzibie PZPN-u.

Przysięgam, myślałem, że robi sobie jaja.

– Rysiek, ja tej partii w ogóle nie znam. Ale co mi tam, jeśli możesz, szepnij wiadomo komu słówko na mój temat – odparłem.

Parę dni później, gdy wylegiwałem się na plaży, dostałem telefon. Po drugiej stronie Rysiek.

– Cześć, Janusz. Jest ktoś, kto chciałby z tobą porozmawiać – rozpoczął, a ja błyskawicznie się domyśliłem, o kogo chodzi.

– Panie Januszu, czy moglibyśmy się spotkać? – Andrzej Lepper nie bawił się w ceregiele.

– W tej chwili nie bardzo, jestem za granicą – odparłem leniwie. – Ale wracam za dwa dni i prosto z lotniska mogę się stawić na spotkanie, proszę tylko podać miejsce.

I Andrzej podał adres – budynek przy Alejach Jerozolimskich, trzecie piętro. Udałem się tam zaraz po przylocie i zaczęła się rozmowa.

– Dacie mi dobre miejsce na liście wyborczej, to wystartuję – zastrzegłem na wejściu.

– Postaram się – rzekł, nalewając nam po kropelce. – A z którego regionu chciałby pan startować?

– Wszystko jedno – wzruszyłem ramionami. – Może być Warszawa, może być Podlasie. Wszędzie tam, gdzie byłem trenerem, bo w tych miejscach ludzie mnie świetnie znają. Wystarczy tylko jakiś plakat powiesić i głosy będą.

– Dobrze, to ja to przedyskutuję ze swoją zastępczynią Genowefą Wiśniowską – obiecał. I nawet nie spytał mnie o poglądy, plan działania czy kampanię wyborczą. Doskonale wiedział, kim jest Wójcik, co uważa i jak trzeba z nim rozmawiać.

Ponownie spotkaliśmy się po dwóch dniach i zaczęły się pierwsze przepychanki o miejsce. Zaproponowali mi nieco dalszą pozycję na liście, ale ja byłem twardy i upierałem się, że chcę dostać jedno z pierwszych. Jedynka była zarezerwowana dla pani Genowefy, drugie dla innego misia, a mnie proponowali czwarte albo piąte.

– Albo pierwsza trójka, albo nie mamy o czym rozmawiać – uciąłem dyskusję.

Na drugi dzień telefon i informacja, że jeśli chcę, to mogę wystartować z trzeciej pozycji. Zgodziłem się, bo wiedziałem, że na Podlasiu dam sobie radę. Nie wstąpiłem do Samoobrony, a tylko startowałem z jej list wyborczych, o czym Lepperius oczywiście nie wiedział. W niczym to jednak nie przeszkodziło, kampania wyborcza została przeprowadzona bardzo właściwie, a ja orżnąłem prawie wszystkich wprost koncertowo.

W Sejmie zawsze działo się mnóstwo ciekawych rzeczy – i groźnych, i śmiesznych. Codziennie widywałem się z Lepperem, a także ze współkoalicjantami z PiS-u i LPR-u. Na mównicy miałem naprawdę sporo wystąpień, poza tym zostałem wybrany przewodniczącym sejmowej Komisji do spraw Sportu i Turystyki. To tam załatwiane były praktycznie wszystkie sprawy dotyczące Euro 2012 – gdzie mają stanąć stadiony, w którym miejscu w Warszawie ma stanąć Stadion Narodowy, tego typu kwestie. Moich argumentów słuchano uważnie, bo szanowano mnie jako człowieka zasłużonego dla polskiej piłki, nie obywało się jednak bez rozlicznych wojenek i podchodów. Niektórzy członkowie komisji z SLD, czyli bratniej partii, podsrywali mnie bez litości, szczególnie po tym jak zatrzymano mnie, gdy prowadziłem pod wpływem alkoholu. Żądali, bym zrzekł się funkcji przewodniczącego. Ani mi to było w głowie.

Jak to było z tym zatrzymaniem? Zacznijmy od początku. W styczniu, dzień przed Balem Mistrzów Sportu, wyjechałem z panią Genowefą Wiśniowską na Podlasie. Służbowym autem. Mieliśmy do obskoczenia kilka miejsc. Wracając do Warszawy, zatrzymaliśmy się w Łomży – pani wicemarszałek została w tym pięknym mieście, a ja udałem się do stolicy, bo miałem iść na rzeczony bal. Odbywał się w Pałacu Kultury i Nauki i okazał się imprezą wszech czasów – można powiedzieć, że udał się aż za bardzo… Natknąłem się tam na rzesze przyjaciół i kolegów, a każdy namawiał, żeby napić się z nim choć kieliszeczek. Alkoholu nie zwykłem odmawiać, więc piłem jak na dobrego druha przystało. Nie była to jakaś oszałamiająca, zwalająca z nóg ilość. Wiedziałem, że na drugi dzień mam wrócić do Łomży i nie mogę się urżnąć do spodu. Gdy wyszedłem z Pałacu, grzecznie wtoczyłem się do taksówki, ale w ostatniej chwili stwierdziłem, że przecież narąbany nie jestem i mogę jechać własnym autem. Tak też zrobiłem – pożegnałem taksówkarza usiadłem za kierownicą swojego wozu, odpaliłem silnik i ruszyłem. Tu ciekawostka: od początku mnie śledzono. Takie mam informacje od kolegów, którzy pracowali w różnych służbach. Już wcześniej mnie ostrzegali, że ktoś chce mnie dojechać, jednak to zbagatelizowałem. Nie czułem się tak najebany, żebym nie mógł prowadzić. Tymczasem zdążyłem oddalić się od Pałacu o zaledwie sto metrów, a dostrzegłem w lusterku, że ktoś za mną jedzie. To była straż miejska, która miała za zadanie zrobić z mojego zatrzymania spektakl dekady. Ci mili chłopcy wymyślili i podali do publicznej wiadomości, że jeździłem po torach tramwajowych i że zrobiłem sobie slalom od krawężnika do krawężnika. Gdy kazali mi się zatrzymać, mogłem ich olać, ale stwierdziłem, że przecież nie jestem tak nadziabany, że nie wiem, o co chodzi. Kiedy zjechałem na pobocze, czym prędzej podbiegli do samochodu. Spokojnie opuściłem szybę. Nie próbowałem wstrzymywać oddechu, więc oczywiście poczuli alkohol.

– Wiemy, kim pan jest – usłyszałem.

„No jasne, że wiecie". Odczyniali te swoje procedury, a niedługo potem pojawili się dziennikarze z kamerami. Hmmm, ciekawe, skąd się dowiedzieli… Zaraz po dziennikarzach na miejsce przybyła policja i dzielni funkcjonariusze odgonili strażników od mojego samochodu. Okazali się bardzo dobrze wychowani, mimo to zdenerwowałem się, kiedy zaproponowali mi pobranie krwi.

– Nie będzie żadnego pobierania. Sami sobie możecie pobrać – odburknąłem.

Pojechaliśmy na komendę, gdzie dmuchnąłem w balonik, i wypuszczono mnie do domu. Na drugi dzień zgodnie z planem ruszyłem do Łomży. Zorganizowałem też konferencję prasową, na której oczywiście przeprosiłem za wydarzenia ubiegłej nocy, ale też podkreśliłem, że historyjki o jeżdżeniu po torach to brednie. To, co powiedziałem, było

Moja wspaniała kadra olimpijska. Wielu chłopców nie zrobiło jednak takiej kariery, na jaką zasługiwało

Podczas ceremonii otwarcia igrzysk

Nawet nie chcę porównywać mojej reprezentacji olimpijskiej do obecnej kadry. Przecież moi chłopcy by ją zmietli z powierzchni ziemi

W Barcelonie najwięcej czasu spędzaliśmy oczywiście w wiosce olimpijskiej. Na plażę, ku naszej radości, były dosłownie dwa kroki

Z Henrykiem Loską (po mojej prawej), znanym śląskim działaczem piłkarskim

Moja Legia Warszawa. Goliliśmy wtedy frajerów, że aż miło! Dobre czasy

Fot. „Przegląd Sportowy" / Newspix.pl

Po meczu z Wisłą, który dał nam mistrzostwo. Potem dziadki z PZPN-u nam je odebrały…

No i wylądowałem w Zjednoczonych Emiratach Arabskich. Zostałem zakwaterowany w luksusowym hotelu w Szardży

Fot. Marek Zochowski / Newspix.pl

Towarzyski mecz Polska – Armenia. Wygraliśmy 1:0. Mecze towarzyskie kadry zawsze chciałem grać na stadionie Legii. Czułem się tam jak w domu

Oj, było wesoło na treningach reprezentacji, było…

Edek (czyli Edward Lorens, pośrodku) niby był płaczliwy i niedorobiony, ale potem zaczął kopać pode mną dołki i robić krecią robotę. W końcu wyrzuciłem go z reprezentacji Polski

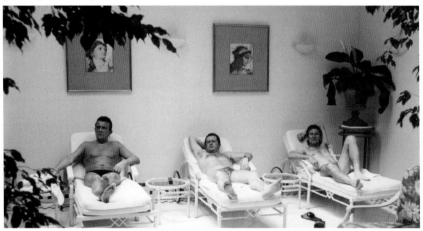

Trening kadry. Po lewej Brzęczek, w środku Łapiński, trzeci z prawej Majak, pierwszy z prawej Wałdoch

Kiedy bawiłem się w politykę, Lepperius stał na pierwszym miejscu w mojej sejmowej hierarchii. To był zacny człowiek i nikt nie wmówi mi, że było inaczej

Przed walką Andrzeja Gołoty w Katowicach. Stoję na ringu obok Dona Kinga i Daniela Olbrychskiego. A Andrzejek, jak to Andrzejek, nie dał poboksować rywalowi. Wygrał w drugiej rundzie

Seniorska kadra na Legii

Z Michałem Listkiewiczem w Cardiff, zaraz po przyznaniu Polsce prawa do organizacji Euro 2012

Spotkanie srebrnej drużyny olimpijskiej po 20 latach

jednak bez znaczenia, bo od razu wszczęto postępowanie. Po kilku dniach spotkałem się z prokuratorem. Szczęśliwie okazał się porządnym człowiekiem.

– Panie pośle, to nieprawda, że jechał pan po torach. Mamy obraz z wszystkich okolicznych kamer. Przejechał pan właściwym pasem – usłyszałem.

Z kolei na samej rozprawie, z której nie robiłem rozgłosu, okazało się, że nie było nikogo ze strony oskarżającej! Policja twierdziła, że przecież za mną nie jechała i w sumie to nic nie wie. Mało tego, nie raczył się pojawić żaden ze strażników miejskich, którzy mnie zatrzymali! Był to jeden wielki kit, którego nie udało się przepchać, bo w centrum miasta było za dużo kamer. Nie wypieram się tego, że prowadziłem pod wpływem alkoholu, więc zostałem ukarany słusznie, a prawa jazdy nie odebrano mi od razu. Istniały okoliczności łagodzące. Nie miałem zbyt wiele alkoholu we krwi, nie stwarzałem żadnego zagrożenia w ruchu drogowym. O, a przy okazji proponowałbym, żeby zbadać tych strażników miejskich, którzy tak bezczelnie łgali na mój temat. Nie będę się jednak o nich rozpisywał, bo szkoda mi czasu, by opowiadać o tchórzach i kłamcach – tacy zasługują wyłącznie na pogardę.

Mówiąc o mojej przygodzie z polityką, nie mogę nie wspomnieć o tak zwanej aferze gruntowej, czyli sprawie tak nadmuchanej, że mało nie pękła. To był jeden z kolejnych zamachów na Andrzeja Leppera. Różne chuje nie wiedziały, jak się do niego dobrać, więc szukały pretekstu, żeby rozprawić się z niewygodnym koalicjantem. Chodziło o to, żeby udupić Lepperiusa. Niewykluczone, że ludzie, którzy tego próbowali, byli podstawieni przez służby.

Ja jako jeden z niewielu wiedziałem, że takie rzeczy się dzieją.

W sprawie afery gruntowej zeznawałem w prokuraturze. Powiedziałem dużo, nawet trochę za dużo, lecz zapewniłem, że jeśli zajdzie potrzeba, dalej będę o tym opowiadał. Ale nikt się nie zgłosił. Nikt nie chciał grzebać w szambie, w obawie, żeby nie wybuchło i nie obryzgało.

Trochę mnie przy okazji wkurzyli funkcjonariusze ABW, bo nastraszyli mocno moją rodzinę. W późnych godzinach wieczornych do domu wparowali przedstawiciele „Abwehry" (tak nazywałem tę wspaniałą organizację). Weszli, wylegitymowali się, ale pojawił się problem, bo mój pies, sznaucer olbrzymi, zaczął na nich warczeć. To wielkie bydlę, gdyby stanął na tylnych łapach, byłby większy od nich.

– Gdzie jest mąż? – zapytali Krystyny.

– Jak to gdzie? W Sejmie – odpowiedziała krótko.

Problem w tym, że mnie już w Sejmie nie było. Byłem za to w innym miejscu, trochę tylko od Sejmu oddalonym, gdzie relaksowałem się z miłymi panami „oficerami" – w siedzibie Agencji Bezpieczeństwa Wewnętrznego na Rakowieckiej.

– Zajęty jestem, załatwiam bardzo ważne sprawy – powiedziałem przez telefon, gdy chcieli mnie tam ściągnąć. W końcu jednak zgodziłem się przyjechać. W „siedzibie zła" posiedziałem dłuższą chwilę. Najpierw rozmawiałem z takim jednym funkcjonariuszem: gadki-szmatki, bardzo miło i sympatycznie.

– Jest szef? – zapytałem w końcu.

– Oczywiście, w gabinecie.

– To niech czeka na mnie z koniaczkiem, chcę z nim porozmawiać – zapowiedziałem.

Po skończeniu rozmowy z jednym dżentelmenem poszedłem więc do drugiego. Zaproponował mi, żebym z nimi współpracował, żebym powiedział więcej, niż mogę. Posiedziałem tam dwie–trzy godziny, potem wsiadłem do samochodu i pojechałem do domu. Na tym koniec. Więcej z nimi nie chciałem rozmawiać.

Jaką ja miałem styczność z tą całą aferą gruntową? Przede wszystkim dowiedziałem się, co było knute przeciwko Lepperowi. I nie tylko przeciwko niemu, bo za Romana Giertycha też się brali. Wszystko odbyło się w taki sposób, jak mi to przekazywano. Ostrzegałem Leppera. Kiedy pewnego razu jechaliśmy razem samochodem, starałem się mu to uzmysłowić.

– Coś złego się dzieje, różni dziwni ludzie się przy panu kręcą – mówiłem.

Tyle mogę powiedzieć, wszystkich rzeczy, które wiem, ujawnić nie mogę. I tak wydaje mi się, że powiedziałem teraz o tym zbyt wiele.

Polityka to nie tylko wystąpienia, afery i sejmowe przepychanki. To także – od czasu do czasu – epicka zabawa.

Po przeczytaniu tej historii niektórzy pewnie powiedzą, że ten Wójcik ciągle opowiada o wódce. Cóż, niestety, kiedy byłem posłem, towarzyszyła mi ona nie rzadziej niż w innych momentach życia. Do dziś pamiętam moje urodzino-imieniny, które odbyły się w Zielonce. Owo pamiętne party organizowaliśmy w zajeździe U Pietrzaków. Do picia były przeróżne trunki, między innymi tak zwany duch puszczy, produkt regionalny, pędzony wyłącznie na Podlasiu. Miał, bagatela, trochę ponad 70 procent, mimo to wchodził jak złoto, zwłaszcza że było czym zagryzać. Działał wprost nieprawdopodobnie! Najpierw odbierał mowę, później pojawiały się kłopoty z równowagą, a następnie zupełnie zwalał z nóg. Dosłownie – goście przewracali się jak zapałki. Przywieźli mi tego parę kanistrów, więc mogłem położyć pół Warszawy i całe Ząbki.

Fakt, że byłem akurat posłem, sprawił, że wokół kręcili się paparazzi, żądni sensacji i ciekawych zdjęć. Moi koledzy, głównie bokserzy, postanowili zadbać, byśmy czuli się bezpiecznie i by nikt nas nie fotografował.

– Janusz, co mamy robić z tymi fotografami? – dopytywali dla pewności.

– Jak to co? Walić w łeb i nokautować, a potem wyciągnąć za nogi i wyrzucić za płot! A na koniec poukładać do snu.

– Będą poukładani idealnie! – zapowiedzieli.

Żeby było weselej, na środku sali postawiono ring, na którym odbywały się walki, a w przerwach tańczyły dziewczyny. Siedziałem przy stole z Rysiem Kaliszem.

– Słuchaj, Janusz, załatwisz mi takie atrakcje, jak będę miał imieniny? – zagadnął.

– Rysiu, jeśli będziesz miał lokal, to oczywiście!

Niestety, później Rysiu trochę przesadził z duchem puszczy i trzeba go było podtrzymywać, a jak wiadomo, nie jest to szczupaczek.

Na imprezę zaprosiłem również kolegę z Jagiellonii Białystok, Wojtka Strzałkowskiego, jedną z ważniejszych postaci w tym klubie. Bardzo zamożny człowiek, wtedy akurat jeździł ferrari i miał helikopter.

– Przylecę swoim helikopterem – poinformował. – Powiedz tylko, gdzie mógłbym wylądować.

– Nie mam pojęcia, bracie, ale nie bój nic, znajdę ci jakieś lądowisko – obiecałem.

Zadzwoniłem do burmistrza i komendanta policji. Poinformowałem, że o konkretnej godzinie w mieście będzie lądował helikopter, i zapytałem, gdzie może to zrobić.

– Najlepiej to na… rynku – odpowiedzieli niezależnie od siebie.

– Jak to na rynku?! Przecież to ludziom łby pourywa!

– Dobra, kiedy będziemy wiedzieli, że nadlatuje, wyczyścimy teren – zapewnił dobry pan burmistrz.

I rzeczywiście, wszystko zostało ładnie załatwione, Strzałka zostawił helikopter na rynku i dotarł na imprezę. Wszystko było cacy, ale tak napierdolił się duchem puszczy, że nie było mowy, by wrócił swoją maszyną do Białegostoku. Gdy on i pilot obudzili się następnego dnia, dosłownie się przewracali. Ja spokojnie zjadłem śniadanie, już rześki, i głowiłem się, co by tu z nimi zrobić. Musiałem działać szybko, bo śmigłowiec cały czas stał na rynku i stał się atrakcją turystyczną. Dzieci i dorośli dotykali go, wchodzili do środka, robili sobie zdjęcia… No kurwa, wspaniale!

– Kiedy oni odlecą? Tu ludzie nie mają jak przechodzić! – pieklił się komendant.

– Teraz nie odlecą, bo są lekko niedysponowani – tłumaczyłem. – Ruszą zaraz jak tylko wytrzeźwieją. A ludzie to niech lepiej omijają ten helikopter.

– Dobrze, to dajcie znać, kiedy dojdą do siebie. Wtedy usuniemy mieszkańców, żeby nikomu nic się nie stało.

Po kilku godzinach Strzałka już kontaktował, w dużej mierze dzięki naszemu specjalistycznemu antykacowemu leczeniu (którego szczegóły niech pozostaną tajemnicą, nie ma tak łatwo, musi was głowa poboleć, gagatki!). Pilot jednak wciąż nie nadawał się do niczego.

– Strzałka, wsiadajcie do tego helikoptera i wracajcie, nawet, kurwa, pijani. Przecież zaraz wam go rozkręcą, śmigła wyniosą! Za chwilę zostanie ci sam kadłub! – postraszyłem.

Wojtek zadzwonił do Białegostoku po nowego pilota. Ten przyjechał po paru godzinach, zapakował dwóch ludzi i odleciał. Sensacja się skończyła. Ale w pamięci pozostała na zawsze.

Nie dajcie się jednak zwieść zabawnym historyjkom. Polskie środowisko polityczne jest zgniłe i zepsute do cna, pełne mend i szumowin. Oczywiście, Wójcik nigdy nie bał się frajerów z Sejmu, ale po jakimś czasie po prostu straciłem ochotę na ich oglądanie. Niebawem jednak możecie się zdziwić, kiedy znów zobaczycie mnie w wielkiej polityce. Ktoś chyba musi zrobić z tym bajzlem porządek. A jak Wujo złapie za szczotkę, to pozamiata skurwieli.

ZNICZ PRUSZKÓW
I ROBERT LEWANDOWSKI
2007–2008

Do Znicza Pruszków trafiłem tuż po samorozwiązaniu Sejmu, kiedy przestałem być posłem. Dostałem telefon od ludzi z klubu i oczywiście zgodziłem się na spotkanie. Do miłej rozmowy doszło w hotelu Novotel przy Okęciu. Zaproponowano mi pracę i dogadaliśmy się praktycznie w dziesięć minut. Nie szalałem z wymaganiami, bo miałem sentyment do tego klubu, lubiłem pracujących tam ludzi. Moje zadanie miało polegać przede wszystkim na utrzymaniu zespołu w pierwszej lidze. Sytuacja w tabeli była cholernie trudna, ale przecież nie takich rzeczy się dokonywało... Oczywiście się udało, nie zawiodłem pokładanych we mnie oczekiwań, ale nie o tym chciałbym wam tu opowiedzieć. Bo praca w Pruszkowie to dla mnie właściwie tylko jedno wspomnienie – prowadzenie pewnego piłkarza, którego dziś oglądamy na pierwszych stronach gazet. Zacznijmy jednak od początku.

Pierwszy trening poprowadziłem zaraz na drugi dzień po porozumieniu się z szefostwem Znicza. Przyglądałem się zespołowi i od razu zauważyłem kilku naprawdę utalentowanych chłopaków, między innymi Roberta Lewandowskiego i Bartosza Wiśniewskiego. Wszyscy w klubie zachwycali się tym drugim, liczyli, że zarobią na nim gigantyczne pieniądze. Poprzyglądałem się obu zawodnikom i zaledwie po tygodniu treningów wiedziałem, na którego z nich warto postawić. Wziąłem na bok dżentelmenów z zarządu.

– Weźcie, panowie, tego Wiśniewskiego – rozpocząłem bez ceregieli – wyślijcie do pobliskiej masarni i przeróbcie na kotlety. Na nic więcej się wam nie przyda. Za to Lewandowskiego zostawcie bezwzględnie, będziecie mieli z niego pożytek. To po prostu piłkarz, bardzo dobry piłkarz. Jeśli pojawi się oferta za Wiśnię, sprzedawajcie bez zastanowienia, bo to „stracone złudzenia Balzaka". Ja utrzymam ten zespół w lidze z Lewym – zapewniłem.

Szok i niedowierzanie! Jak to z Lewym? Przecież Wiśniewski taki wspaniały... Pieprzenie dyletantów. Zamierzałem chronić Lewandowskiego, i przed tymi władzami, i przed piłkarzami, którzy lubili podokuczać młodszym kolegom.

Na jednym z treningów, jeszcze przed rozpoczęciem zajęć, nakazałem przenieść bramkę w ustalone miejsce. Do przodu wyrwali najmłodsi, w tym Lewy. Starsi tylko stali i się patrzyli.

– Lewy, chodź no tutaj, gdzie idziesz? – zawołałem go.

– Ale panie trenerze... – zająknął się.

– Chyba coś ci, kurwa, powiedziałem? Do mnie! Biegiem!

Posłusznie ruszył w moim kierunku, a zapierdalał jak sprinter.

– Masz tu stać i ani kroku w stronę tej pieprzonej bramki – nakazałem, po czym zwróciłem się do starszyzny. – A wy, kurwa, na co czekacie?

– Ale panie trenerze, no... – bąknął któryś, a ja tylko na to czekałem.

– Co „no"?! Brać tę bramkę i przenosić gdzie trzeba, sru!

– A młodzi to co?

– Młodzi? O kim mówicie? Może o Lewandowskim? Jakby jego nie było, tobyście, kurwa, nie mieli po co chodzić do kasy! A kiedy Lewy strzela, to i wy wypłaty dostajecie! Bez niego moglibyście w kasie najwyżej podłogi szorować. Bierzcie się do roboty, czekam! – zakomenderowałem, a panowie szlachta oczywiście wzięli się do roboty. Gdy tak zapierdalali z tą bramką, ja nagadałem Lewemu: – Jak, kurwa, jeszcze raz tam pójdziesz, to się zesrasz, jak cię przegonię dookoła boiska. Zobaczysz.

Nakręcałem go, a on oczywiście spuścił łeb i uważnie słuchał. A że był przyzwyczajony do innych układów w zespole, to bardzo się zdziwił, że teraz przy noszeniu bramki będzie pracowała inna zmiana. Lewandowski miał wiele zalet, ale jedną ceniłem szczególnie. Kiedy tylko piłka zakręciła mu się koło nogi, od razu walił na bramę, jak z armaty. I bez znaczenia, czy było to na hali, czy na boisku. Miał to we krwi. Od razu mi się skojarzył ze słynnym Francuzem Jeanem-Pierrem Papinem, który też ładował z każdej pozycji. Bardzo mi się to podobało i wbijałem Robertowi do łba, żeby robił to jeszcze częściej. Miałem też taką metodę treningową, która polegała na tym, że za sprawą odpowiednich poleceń doprowadzałem do uwydatnienia i ośmieszenia braków technicznych poszczególnych zawodników. Oczywiście tak samo postępowałem z Lewandowskim. On był jednak zawziętą bestią, bardzo ambitną. Widać było gołym okiem, że wszystkie nieudane zagrania ćwiczył w czasie wolnym i coś, co jednego dnia stanowiło problem nie do przejścia, następnego wykonywał z zamkniętymi oczami. Z każdym dniem stawał się coraz lepszy. Uważnie słuchał moich poleceń i brał je sobie do serca. Jeśli było trzeba, opierdzielałem go równo, ani mi w głowie było faworyzowanie zdolnego gówniarza. Gdy w trakcie meczu popełnił błąd, zaraz z ławki dostawał artylerię. Ale najczęściej grał świetnie. Dlatego po paru tygodniach pracy w Zniczu przeprowadziłem kolejną rozmowę z szefostwem.

– Pilnujcie tego Lewandowskiego, dzięki niebu zarobicie kupę kasy. Sprzedacie go za ciężkie pieniądze, a on prędzej niż później trafi do reprezentacji Polski. Te barany z Legii, które powiedziały, że Lewy nie umie grać w piłkę, powinny pójść do najbliższego lasu i się powiesić. Albo i nie, bo szkoda sznurka. W każdym razie tacy ludzie tylko szkodzą polskiej piłce – stwierdziłem.

Patrzyli na mnie jak cielęta, ale widziałem, że coś im zaczyna świtać. Spotkałem się zresztą z Trzeciakiem i tłumaczyłem mu, że popełnił błąd.

– Mirek, kogo wy żeście wzięli zamiast Lewandowskiego? Do Corridy z tym Arruabarreną, czy jak go tam zwać, a nie do piłki nożnej!

Oglądaliście go w ogóle? Widzieliście tego chłopaka na żywo? – pytałem, oczywiście retorycznie.

Trzeciak milczał.

Prywatnie często porównuję Roberta z Wojtkiem Kowalczykiem. To zupełnie różne osobowości: Lewy jest spokojny, wyciszony, Kowal zaś to jego przeciwieństwo, istna szalona dusza. Chociaż nawet Wojtek, gdy się czasem zablokował, zaczynał się jąkać i nic nie dało się z niego wydobyć. Z Lewandowskim nigdy nie miałem żadnych problemów. Szanowałem go za profesjonalne podejście do zawodu. Koledzy z drużyny też bardzo go lubili. Dawał im zarobić, więc go ubóstwiali.

Byłem pewien, że jeśli pójdzie grać do dobrej drużyny, prędzej czy później trafi do reprezentacji Polski. Przy takim stosunku do sportu, jaki prezentował, i takich zdolnościach nie mogło być inaczej. Wiedziałem też, że jeśli dalej będzie strzelał tak, jak strzela, to przyjadą z zagranicy i go kupią za ciężkie pieniądze.

Lewandowski nie był i nie jest facetem, który łapie piłkę, ogrywa czterech po kolei i biegnie jak pomiędzy słupami, a potem wjeżdża do bramki. Strzelając swoje cztery gole Realowi Madryt w półfinale Ligi Mistrzów, został świetnie obsłużony przez kolegów. Oczywiście trzeba jeszcze umieć wykorzystać sytuację i jemu się to udawało, ale nie zapominajmy, że to nie jest Messi, który w pojedynkę potrafi załatwić spotkanie. Mecze reprezentacji pokazują to idealnie – Lewy biega, stara się, walczy, a jego koledzy zamiast porządnie wykonywać swoją pracę, to srają ryżem.

Nie mogę powiedzieć, że to najlepszy piłkarz, z jakim pracowałem – wówczas umniejszyłbym talent chłopaków z reprezentacji olimpijskiej. Gdyby oni zaraz po igrzyskach poszli taką drogą, jaką teraz podąża Lewy, być może zaszliby równie daleko albo jeszcze dalej. Nie miał jakoś specjalnie ułatwionej drogi do wielkiej kariery, ale miał za to coś ważniejszego – wielką ambicję. A na przykład wspomniany wcześniej Kowal – nie mniej utalentowany od Roberta – miał wrodzoną szybkość, nadzwyczajną koordynację, zachwycał skocznością, tyle że był z niego taki „misio-rozrywka" i nieszczególnie skupiał się na piłce. Chciał się cały czas czuć jak taki konik polny, który bryka sobie po trawie i robi, co chce. Taki trochę dzikusek. Gdyby był tak wstrzemięźliwy i konsekwentny jak Lewy, to zrobiłby taką samą karierę, ale nie uznał za stosowne skorzystać z tego, co mu Bozia dała. To samo Andrzej Juskowiak – chłopak na ogół zdyscyplinowany, ale mający tendencje do rozmaitych hopsztosów. Albo Rysiek Staniek – piłkarz kompletny, nieprawdopodobnie utalentowany, któremu niestety nie sprzyjał los i okoliczności. Nie miał tego szczęścia, co Lewandowski. Rysiek Staniek niczym nie ustępował piłkarsko Robertowi. Był gorszy jednak pod innym względem – brakowało mu charakteru, zawziętości, boiskowej zadziory. Nie potrafił też odmówić sobie uciech życia w postaci browarków.

Lewandowski nie miał takich zdolności jak Kowal, Juskowiak czy Staniek. Ale dziś to właśnie on jest gwiazdą futbolu, a taki Wojtuś może mu tylko pozazdrościć. Ja natomiast mogę być dumny, że pracowałem z zawodnikiem tej klasy co Robert. Cieszę się, że w jakiś sposób mogłem przyczynić się do tego, że dziś mówi o nim cały piłkarski świat. Mam nadzieję, że wciąż pamięta, że kiedyś dzięki trenerowi Wójcikowi nie musiał dźwigać ciężkiej bramki. Bo on jest od noszenia ciężaru zwycięstwa, a nie jakiegoś żelastwa. Tym niech zajmują się inni, którzy nie mają szans przejść do historii polskiego sportu.

„BÓJTA SIĘ WÓJTA!"

Chyba każdy trener ma takiego zawodnika, który powoduje u niego palpitacje serca. W moim przypadku był to Bartosz Fabiniak, gagatek co się zowie. To bramkarz, który miał z dumą strzec naszej bramki, a okazał się piłkarską niedorajdą.

Od niego, trochę niechronologicznie, rozpoczynam opowieść o mojej przygodzie z Widzewem. W zasadzie chyba mało kto by pamiętał, że przez krótki czas pracowałem w tym klubie, gdyby nie pewne nagranie, które w internecie długo robiło furorę. Nagranie ze mną i Fabiniakiem w roli głównej. Pewnie większość z was doskonale zna ten kilkuminutowy film. A tym, którzy jeszcze go nie widzieli, chętnie o nim opowiem.

Był to mecz z Groclinem Dyskobolią rozgrywany w Grodzisku. Groclin radził sobie w lidze bardzo dobrze, ale my liczyliśmy na zwycięstwo, więc od razu zapowiedziałem piłkarzom, że nie mogą sobie pozwolić na wpadkę. Okazało się jednak, że nasz bramkarz, który według Józia Młynarczyka (o którym opowiem trochę później) miał być talentem stulecia i podporą Widzewa, wystawił na pośmiewisko i siebie, i mnie, i wszystkich swoich kompanów. Talent to on może miał, ale do żarcia i opierdalania się. Puszczał takie bramki, że ręce opadały, i miałem ochotę zadusić go jeszcze na murawie. Facet, który miał być filarem zespołu, stał się normalnie terrorystą, który podłożył bombę pod własną drużynę.

Rozpoczął się mecz i już wiedziałem, że następne 90 minut będzie drastyczne. Szybko puściły mi nerwy i dosłownie wychodziłem z siebie. Nie wiedziałem, że telewizja, która ulokowała się tuż za moimi plecami, włączyła mikrofon, więc jechałem po całości. Jebałem Fabiniaka jak burą sukę, gdybym tylko mógł, podbiegłbym pod tę bramkę i nawrzucał mu z bliska. Mimo to doskonale słyszał wszystkie ciepłe słowa, jakie słałem pod jego adresem. Podobnie jak Michał Listkiewicz i inni działacze, którzy siedzieli za moją ławką.

– Zobaczcie, kurwa, co on gra! To jest siatkówka! – darłem się wniebogłosy, krzyczałem też do samego Fabiniaka: – Co ty robisz?! Weź się, kurwa, może połóż w tej bramce! Leż! Po co wstajesz, baranie jeden?! – jechałem równo z trawą.

Wkurwiałem się zresztą na całą drużynę. Chciałem błyskawicznie dokonać zmian i postanowiłem wpuścić Stefano Napoleoniego.

– Dawaj tego Włocha, sruu! Już nie można na to dalej patrzeć! Szybciej! – wykrzyczałem w kierunku ławki rezerwowych.

Przyszła przerwa. Najpierw opierdoliłem obrońców, którzy grali jak połamani. Dorwałem Ukaha.

– Jak masz tak, kurwa, grać, to lepiej wracaj do dżungli! Biegaj między drzewami, a nie na boisku! – wykrzyczałem, ale czarny siedział cicho, bo wiedział, że lepiej się nie wychylać.

W szatni oczywiście jeszcze dołożyłem Fabiniakowi. Oj, jak ja mu dołożyłem! Gdy wyrzuciłem już z siebie wszystkie joby, ten wirtuoz stania na bramce zakomunikował:

– Na drugą połowę nie wychodzę.

Aż oczy przetarłem ze zdumienia. Tylko mnie to rozsierdziło. Fabiniak popełnił w tym momencie poważny błąd. Poważniejszy niż wszystkie na boisku.

– Dobrze. Nie wyjdziesz. Ale po meczu będziesz zapierdalał w tym stroju za autobusem. Bo z nami nie wrócisz. A jak będziesz chciał złapać

„Zobaczcie, kurwa, co on gra! To jest siatkówka! – darłem się wniebogłosy, krzyczałem też do samego Fabiniaka: – Co ty robisz?! Weź się, kurwa,
może połóż w tej bramce! Leż! Po co wstajesz, baranie jeden?!" – jechałem równo z trawą

Fot. Andrzej Monczak / Agencja Gazeta

stopa albo pojechać pociągiem, to mówię ci, kurwa, w ubraniu bram-
karskim. Będziesz robił za pajaca. Takiego, jakiego zrobiłeś z siebie, idio-
to, w bramce. I wszyscy będą się z ciebie śmiali – podkręcałem go.

Oczywiście delikwent się wystraszył i potulnie wyszedł na drugą połowę. Zesrał się dokumentnie. Mecz przegraliśmy 0:3 i po wszystkim,
w szatni, poprawiłem Fabiniakowi i Ukahowi, ale kogo trzeba było po-
chwalić, pochwaliłem. Dopiero jakiś czas później dowiedziałem się, że
z moich popisów pod ławką wyszedł prawdziwy bestseller internetowy.
„Bójta się Wójta", mówili kibice i eksperci. A niech się, kurwa, boją!
Pamiętam tylko, że na ławce wszyscy, z ryżawym Stokowcem na czele,
siedzieli tak, jakby im ktoś cementu do gęb nakładł. To był ogień. Wul-
kan, jakiego świat nie widział.

A co z Fabiniakiem? Oczywiście go odstawiłem. Nie mogłem na niego patrzeć. Zacząłem stawiać na młodego Jakuba Hładowczaka, wiel-

240   WÓJT. JEDZIEMY Z FRAJERAMI. CAŁE MOJE ŻYCIE

kiego chłopa, o którym może i nie mówiono, że jest utalentowany, ale przynajmniej mnie nigdy nie zawodził. Zresztą wolę, by młody i głupi popełniał błędy, a przy okazji czegoś się uczył. Nie toleruję tych niby wielkich gwiazd, które nie mają jaj i tylko się przewracają o własne nogi.

WSPÓŁPRACA Z WIDZEWEM

Warto jeszcze wspomnieć, w jaki sposób trafiłem do Widzewa. Otóż wszystko zostało załatwione właściwie w trakcie jednego dnia. Do pracy w łódzkim klubie namówił mnie jego właściciel, biznesmen Sylwester Cacek. Spędziliśmy przemiły wieczór w jednej z warszawskich restauracji, nazajutrz na spotkaniu z radą nadzorczą domknęliśmy sprawę.

Widzew znałem doskonale i sam również byłem tam znany. Kojarzyli mnie wszyscy, od sprzątaczki po wierchuszkę, bo przecież często tam przyjeżdżałem, w różnym charakterze. Oczywiście gdy objąłem posadę trenera, musiałem poznać zawodników, bo ci nieustannie się zmieniają. Spotkanie z piłkarzami przebiegło bardzo fajnie, ale byłem zdziwiony tym, jak przyjął mnie Józio Młynarczyk, trener bramkarzy. Od początku miał do mnie negatywne nastawienie, w zasadzie nie wiem dlaczego. Pewnie się bał, że skrzywdzę jego ulubieńca Bartosza Fabiniaka. Tego, jak się później okazało, od gry w siatkówkę, a nie piłkę nożną.

– Józiu, rozumiem, że dalej będziesz trenował bramkarzy? – zapytałem go spokojnie po masakrze w Grodzisku.

Zaczął się jąkać. Autentycznie włączyła mu się pełna jąkała. A ze mną tak się nie da: jeśli ci się coś nie podoba, to mów wprost albo wypierdalaj. Nie mogliśmy dojść do porozumienia, więc Józio odszedł z Widzewa, a ja zacząłem budować sztab na własnych zasadach. Moim pierwszym asystentem został Rafał Pawlak, wieloletni zawodnik Widzewa. Jako drugi asystent trafił się – tu niespodzianka – Piotr Stokowiec, czyli ten, który nie miał ze mną lekkiego życia w Śląsku Wrocław. Tu przydawał mi się głównie do tego, żeby polecieć po piwo, ewentualnie zapojkę, kiedy sączyło się coś mocniejszego. To akurat bardzo dobrze mu wychodziło. Bo trenerski orzeł to nie był.

W momencie, kiedy zaczęliśmy treningi, od razu pojawiły się niejasności związane ze sprowadzaniem nowych zawodników. Między innymi Włocha Stefano Napoleoniego i czarnego, czyli Ugochukwu Ukaha. Napoleoni dobry był do tego, żeby pograć sobie na treningu, ale podczas meczu bywało gorzej. Z kolei Ukah to taki zdrowy cham – gdybym mu powiedział, żeby kopnął w słupek, toby to zrobił i jeszcze się cieszył. I oczywiście go złamał. Wirtuoz piłki to niestety nie był, do Tomka Łapińskiego brakowało mu lat świetlnych. Obaj byli zawodnikami sprowadzanymi z Włoch przez Zbyszka Bońka. Umiarkowanie mi to pasowało. Od razu zapowiedziałem, że z włoskich tematów to wolę wino, piosenki i kobiety, a nie pseudopiłkarzy wciskanych przez menedżerów.

Kolejne mecze Widzewa były drogą przez mękę, bo skład był słaby – taki skład węgla i papy. Wyglądało to tak, jakby do bramkarza Fabiniaka dobierano podobnych mu nieudaczników. Oczywiście było kilku bardzo dobrych, rokujących chłopaków, ale nie wystarczająco wielu, żebym mógł myśleć o czymś poważnym. I pojawiły się problemy: klub był na tyle słaby, że niestety zajęliśmy przedostatnie miejsce w Ekstraklasie i spadliśmy do pierwszej ligi. Po tej porażce rozstałem się z Widzewem.

Ogromnie lubiłem Łódź, mimo że w Warszawie traktuje się ją jak odwiecznego wroga. Ale taki los trenera – jest najemnikiem i pracuje tam, gdzie go chcą i gdzie mu dają dobre warunki. Chociażby na Kamczatce. Oficjalnie współpracowałem z Łodzią tylko raz, ale wcześniej zdarzało mi się pomagać temu klubowi z tylnej kanapy. Kiedy trenerem Widzewa był Grzegorz Lato, Andrzej Pawelec i Andrzej Grajewski prosili mnie, bym go wsparł, bo Grzesiowi, choć się starał, w ogóle nie szło. Jeździłem na zgrupowania, przeprowadzałem dodatkowe odprawy, starałem się utrzymać wszystko w kupie. I tutaj ciekawostka: w 1999 roku Widzew grał w eliminacjach do Ligi Mistrzów z bułgarskim Liteksem Łowecz. W pierwszym meczu przegrał na wyjeździe aż 1:4 i wizja awansu do elity zawisła na włosku. Poproszono mnie, bym jakoś uratował sytuację. Przyjechałem więc na dwa dni przed meczem i zakasałem rękawy. Na pierwszy ogień poszło ustalenie składu i oczywiście zmotywowanie zawodników.

Podczas meczu usiadłem sobie za ławką rezerwowych. Jeden z kierowników drużyny był ze mną w stałym kontakcie telefonicznym i ja mu na bieżąco tłumaczyłem, jakie ma wydawać polecenia. Grzesiu Lato siedział na ławce jak kukiełka – oczywiście o wszystkim wiedział, ale nic nie mógł zrobić, szczególnie że drużyna ustawiona przeze mnie grała bardzo dobrze. Widzew rozbił Bułgarów 4:1 i po rzutach karnych awansował do kolejnej rundy eliminacji. Ja zaś dumnie przechadzałem się po Łodzi i zbierałem pochwały, a tym, którzy coś do mnie mieli, mówiłem: „Wy to się bójta Wójta!".

WÓJCIK PRYWATNIE

SZCZENIACKIE WYBRYKI

Jestem warszawiakiem z dziada pradziada, a dzieciństwo spędziłem na starym Mokotowie. Matka, Janina, była łączniczką podczas powstania warszawskiego, ojciec, Henryk, również wychował się w stolicy. Oboje trzymali mnie krótko, bo byłem dość niesforny. Nie stroniłem od bójek i na podwórku szybko dałem się poznać jako zawadiaka – na przykład wyskakiwałem przez okno, żeby pograć w piłkę z kolegami mojego starszego o osiem lat brata. Brat pomagał zresztą rodzicom mnie wychowywać. A w piłkę rżnęliśmy cały czas. Gdy trochę podrosłem, mówiłem do kolegów:

– Słuchajcie, dupki, nauczę was grać, ale będziecie musieli mi za to płacić. Darmo nic nie ma.

I kiedy zapłacili, to zabierałem brata i jego kolegów na lody. A parę lat później na alpagę.

Wszystko fajnie, jednak za takie wybryki nie raz, nie dwa dostawałem od ojca taki wpierdziel, że aż mi łeb odskakiwał. Nie było wychowania poprzez spokojne tłumaczenie. Myślę jednak, że to dobrze, bo nie wiem, na kogo bym wyrósł, gdyby ojciec mnie nie lał. Kiedy się wkurwił, łapał, co tylko miał pod ręką, i zaczynał się siwy dym. Kiedyś, gdy przed nim uciekałem, przyrąbałem głową o mur i odłamałem wielki kawał tynku. Matka myślała, że się zabiłem. Zabrali mnie na prześwietlenie czachy, bo wyglądało to naprawdę nieładnie. A o co była cała awantura? Otóż jacyś idioci zrzucili mi na łeb – z trzeciego piętra! – szklaną butelkę. Przecież mogli mnie ukatrupić. Musiałem się zemścić, więc zaczaiłem się z masywnym drągiem na delikwenta, który to zrobił. W końcu wyszedł – przyjebałem mu z całej siły w gębę, tak że wybiłem mu wszystkie zęby. Pobiegł do domu, przyjechała karetka, matka cała we łzach. Wielkie, kurwa, dramaty. Przybiegł do moich rodziców na skargę no i tatuś postanowił wymierzyć sprawiedliwość… Oczywiście zacząłem uciekać. Wiele razy ganialiśmy się tak po domu, niestety częściej to ojciec był szybszy… Jeśli było okno otwarte, to mogłem jeszcze uciec, ale jeśli było zamknięte, to ptaszek nie miał jak wyfrunąć i dostawał wpierdol. Takie było moje życie.

Całe szczęście dziadek, Szczepan, szanowany w Warszawie murarz, a przy okazji potężny mężczyzna, zawsze stawał po mojej stronie. I kiedy ktoś przychodził na mnie naskarżyć, bo coś zmalowałem, wychodził i po prostu stawał z założonymi na piersi rękami, a napastnicy spierdalali w podskokach! Wiedzieli, że jak dziadzio złapie, to zadusi. Kiedy z kolei sam wymierzałem sprawiedliwość, mężnie zagrzewał mnie do walki i nakazywał, żeby tłuc jeszcze mocniej. Oczywiście brałem sobie do serca jego słowa. I tak, byłem mściwy. Wyczekiwałem okazji, żeby komuś dołożyć.

Mama, kobieta niezwykle spokojna, zawsze stawała w mojej obronie, choć zdawała sobie sprawę, że byłem po prostu niedobry. Nadpobudliwy. Nie pozwalałem sobie włazić na głowę, niestraszne mi były wszelkiej maści bójki i rozróby, i na podwórku, i w szkole. Zazwyczaj wyglądało to tak: zlać kilku klientów? Żaden problem.

Pewnego dnia do mojego liceum, przy Okopowej, przyszło kilku takich krewkich uczniów, którzy sądzili, że będą trzęśli całą szkołą. Szybko jednak wraz z kilkoma kolegami wytłumaczyliśmy im, kto tu rządzi. Parę razy spuściliśmy im takie manto, że na drugi dzień nie mieli sił przyjść do szkoły. Lubiłem to. Nie tylko dla adrenaliny, ale i dla samego boksu.

Często też wagarowałem. Razem z kumplami uciekaliśmy ze szkoły przez okno i po piorunochronie, a potem pędziliśmy na Stare Miasto. Tam przesiadywaliśmy długie godziny, oczywiście pijąc alpagi. Z utęsknieniem wypatrywaliśmy kogoś, komu można by spuścić wpierdziel. I czasem się udawało – ileż było radości!

Ojciec był wzywany do szkoły głównie właśnie z powodu bijatyk, ale również dlatego, że pyskowałem nauczycielom. Kiedy grałem w Gwardii Warszawa, chodziłem do technikum imienia Konarskiego. Rodzice bali się, że nie zdam egzaminów wstępnych, ale ja na przekór wszystkim postanowiłem się dostać, no i się dostałem. Zbliżał się wyjazd na zimowe zgrupowanie Gwardii, a wiosną czekała mnie matura.

– Nigdzie nie pojedziesz. Nie puszczę cię, bo nie zdasz matury! – grzmiał dyrektor szkoły. To samo mówił mój ojciec, zupełnie jakby się zmówili.

– Jeszcze się przekonamy... – mruczałem pod nosem. Bez jaj: miałbym odpuścić zgrupowanie z powodu matury?!

Pojechałem na Gwardię, do moich opiekunów, panów oficerów, w tym pana Henia Celaka. Zakomunikowałem, że dyrekcja nie chce mnie puścić na zgrupowanie. Kilka dni później trzech dżentelmenów z klubu, odzianych w stylowe czarne skóry, udało się do szkoły.

– Gdzie dyrektor? – zapytali mnie, a ja szybko pokazałem im drogę.

– Poczekaj tu na nas, młody, zaraz wrócimy.

Weszli do gabinetu, a ja przyłożyłem ucho do drzwi. Rozmowa była krótka.

– Panie dyrektorze, Wójcik ma jechać na to zgrupowanie, po prostu, nie ma dyskusji.

– Ale ja nie gwarantuję, że zda maturę.

– Wójcik pojedzie na zgrupowanie, i to całe. A pan zagwarantuje, że maturę zda.

I tym sposobem na zgrupowanie pojechałem, choć nie na całe. A maturę rzecz jasna zdałem. Pisałem z języka polskiego, matematyki oraz z przedmiotów technicznych. Byłem na kierunku obróbka skrawaniem, chodziło o obrabianie różnych metali. Potem w pracy trenerskiej obrabiałem już tylko zawodników. W zawodzie nie przepracowałem ani dnia.

KOBIETY

Oprócz tego, że jako szczeniak lubiłem się bić, lubiłem też kobiety. I zostało mi to na całe życie. Zresztą w szkole średniej poznałem moją pierwszą żonę, Wisławę Janas. Chodziliśmy za rączkę, wygłupialiśmy się... Byliśmy parą, ale też kumplami, przyjaciółmi. Młodzieńcza miłość kwitła, zaczęliśmy nawet snuć plany na przyszłość. Dzięki grze w piłkę byłem w stanie samodzielnie się utrzymywać, miałem nawet etat milicjanta na jakimś komisariacie. Oczywiście był on fikcyjny, chodziło o to, bym mógł grać w piłkę w milicyjnym klubie – Gwardii Warszawa. Potem poszedłem na studia, na AWF. Wisława i ja chcieliśmy wziąć ślub, ale jej rodzice wyjechali na placówkę dyplomatyczną do Pakistanu i ona ruszyła razem z nimi. Stwierdziliśmy więc, że pobierzemy się na Dalekim Wschodzie. Moi starzy byli niepocieszeni – ja się żeniłem, a oni nie mogli przy tym być. Jakoś to jednak przełknęli.

Małżeństwem byliśmy ponad siedem lat. Dzieci nie mieliśmy – może pojawienie się potomka scementowałoby nasz związek, do tego jednak nie doszło. Poza tym, cóż, nigdy nie stroniłem od kobiet, a fakt, że jestem żonaty, nie stanowił dla mnie specjalnej przeszkody. Byłem mężczyzną aktywnym i towarzyskim, lubiłem się zabawić i poprzytulać. Jednym słowem – byłem normalnym, zdrowym facetem, który chciał korzystać z życia. A w moim małżeństwie wszystko tak naprawdę zaczęło się sypać, kiedy teściowie wyjechali na placówkę do Kanady. Wisławą interesował się taki jeden tamtejszy dupek. Trudno mi powiedzieć, czy do czegoś doszło, ale między nami właśnie wtedy zaczęło się psuć. Żyliśmy na odległość, bo każde z nas mieszkało w innym mieście. Żona nieustannie narzekała, że nam się nie układa, a jej mamusia ochoczo podpuszczała ją przeciwko mnie. Twierdziła, że nie jestem odpowiednim facetem dla jej córki, że jestem zwykłym misiem Yogi, a przecież oni to niemal arystokracja. Potem zresztą Wisława przyznała mi rację – zdała sobie sprawę, że matka miała na nią zbyt duży wpływ. Rozwiedliśmy się w pokoju, bez orzekania o winie. Pamiętam, że to był tłusty czwartek i po rozprawie razem pojechaliśmy na pączki. Mimo rozstania przez długie lata utrzymywaliśmy bliskie kontakty. Wspólnie spędzaliśmy święta, ona często odwiedzała moją matkę, która bardzo ją lubiła. Ja z kolei załatwiłem jej posadę w kolegium sędziów PZPN-u. Pracowała tam, dopóki nie przyszedł Boniek i nie pozwalniał ludzi. Z perspektywy czasu uważam, że to moja pierwsza żona sprawiła, iż złagodniałem i odpuściłem sobie większość szczeniackich zachowań. Byłem chłopcem, a dzięki niej stałem się mężczyzną.

Mimo że moja pierwsza żona poniekąd wyprowadziła mnie na ludzi, po rozwodzie zacząłem szaleć, i to ostro. Byłem wolnym ptakiem i korzystałem z tego z fantazją i przytupem. Kiedy na przykład pracowałem na AWF-ie, na wydziale biomechaniki, i grałem w Hutniku Warszawa, balowałem na całego. Janusz Wójcik – człowiek impreza. Koledzy przychodzili na te zabawy ze swoimi panienkami, przeważnie były z nich zajebiste dupy. Pewnego razu jedna spodobała mi się szczególnie, a ja spodobałem się jej. No i potem kilka razy spotkała się z panem trenerem… Obracałem ją tak, że nigdy nie miała dosyć, ale po jakimś czasie mi się znudziła, więc jej poradziłem, by jednak wróciła do swojego partnera. Było jej żal, ale co miała robić – wróciła, a on ją przyjął.

Nie będę zresztą owijał w bawełnę – znacie mnie i wiecie, że od kobiet nie stroniłem w żadnym momencie mojego życia. Lubiłem się z nimi spotykać, pić kawkę, rozmawiać, flirtować. A że czasem przy okazji coś się wydymało, to inna sprawa. W każdym razie, jeśli chcecie nauczyć się bajeru, przyjdźcie do Wuja!

Mojemu urokowi nie mogły oprzeć się kobiety na całym świecie. W Polsce – to wiadomo – ale też na Bliskim Wschodzie, w Ameryce i wielu innych miejscach. Na przykład w Bangkoku rozkoszowałem się urodą i powabem pięknych Tajek. Kruczoczarne włosy, oczy jak węgielki, ciała aksamitne niczym jedwab… Wspaniałe, usłużne kobiety, polecam wszystkim. Niestety, na Tajkach można się też nieźle przejechać. I nie tyle na Tajkach, co na... Tajach. Posłuchajcie.

To był rok 2007, uniwersjada w Tajlandii. Poleciałem tam jako przewodniczący Sejmowej Komisji Sportu, a ze mną spora grupa parlamentarzystów, którzy chcieli zobaczyć kawałek świata. Pewnego wieczoru lekko się nudziliśmy, a że Wujo nudy nie znosi, po krótkim namyśle zakomunikowałem moim towarzyszom:

– Panowie, idziemy na masaż!

Kolega Boguś aż podskoczył z radości, tak cholernie mu się ten pomysł spodobał.

Akcja była błyskawiczna. Walnęliśmy jeszcze po kieliszeczku, każdy wziął szybki prysznic i po kilkunastu minutach byliśmy gotowi do drogi. Gdy dotarliśmy do naszego „pałacu rozkoszy", wnętrze lekko nas zaszokowało. Nie był to bowiem zwykły salon masażu, taki, jakie możecie spotkać w Polsce. Tu wszystkie światła były jaskrawoczerwone, w wystroju przeważał kolor różowy. Pani na recepcji bardzo miła, ale wpatrywała się w nas z wielką uwagą. Oczywiście, zdawaliśmy sobie sprawę, że w obcokrajowcach widzi trochę świeżutkich dolarów. Ale my za dobrą usługę byliśmy w stanie zapłacić więcej niż trochę!

Dostaliśmy „menu". Wodziłem palcem po lekko już wyświechtanej kartce, na której królował angielski i te ich przedziwne szlaczki. Opcji było mnóstwo i miałem problem, by na coś się zdecydować. Tu masaż w jakimś olejku, tu same stopy, jeszcze gdzie indziej ramiona. Ale co tam, Wujo w delegacji, pójdzie po całości.

– Boguś, bierzemy masaż całego ciała! – uśmiechnąłem się od ucha do ucha, a mój przyjaciel wyszczerzył się i skinął głową.

Sympatyczna recepcjonistka zaprowadziła nas do odpowiedniego pomieszczenia. Czekały na nas dziesiątki zapachowych świec i niezliczone ilości kwiatów, a na środku – dwa zasłane błyszczącą tkaniną łoża: jedno dla mnie, drugie dla Bogusia. Panował nastrojowy półmrok.

– Proszę się rozebrać, położyć i chwilkę zaczekać – poinformowała panienka z recepcji, po czym oddaliła się z gracją.

Szybko zrzuciliśmy z Bogusiem ciuszki i zajęliśmy miejsca. Przymknąłem oczy i zacząłem sobie wyobrażać, co to za chwilę będzie się działo. Już za moment jakaś piękna Tajka tak mnie wymasuje, że będę wyć z rozkoszy. Mmm... Po kilku minutach otwarły się drzwi. No wreszcie, nasze Tajki! Wpatruję się jednak, przyglądam, szukam wzrokiem tych długich, czarnych włosów. I własnym oczom nie wierzę! Żadnych drobnych Tajek nie ma, są za to... postawni Tajowie! Masować ma nas duet skośnookich gogusiów.

– No, tośmy się, Boguś, wpierdolili... – powiedziałem zrezygnowany. – Ale teraz nie ma co wychodzić, niech nas wymasują. Niech pokażą, co potrafią.

I, kurwa, pokazali. Mój masażysta najpierw muskał mnie po nogach, potem ramionach. Ale mało mu było. Przesuwał dłonią coraz niżej, aż w końcu złapał mnie za... jaja! Aż się wzdrygnąłem. Odsunąłem te obleśne, tajskie łapska. Mój towarzysz kompletnie nie wiedział, o co chodzi, bo jego masażysta aż tak się nie spieszył.

– Boguś, kurwa, gdzieś ty mnie przyprowadził?! – krzyknąłem. – Do pedałów?! Nie będzie mnie jakiś fiut skośnooki za jaja łapał. Zaraz mu przyjebię, przysięgam.

– Dobra, to wychodzimy natychmiast – odparł wystraszony kolega Bogusław.

– Podziękuj swojemu skośnookiemu Adonisowi i spierdalamy, bo zaraz nam z tyłków jesień średniowiecza zrobią.

Pospiesznie i nie do końca grzecznie się pożegnaliśmy, po czym wybiegliśmy na zatłoczoną ulicę. O tym, co się stało, nie wspomnieliśmy słowem. Do dziś zresztą, kiedy sobie przypomnę te żółte łapska na moich klejnotach, to zbiera mi się na wymioty. Nigdy więcej żadnych tajskich masaży. Nikt Wuja macał nie będzie!

No dobrze, skończmy już te frywolne opowiastki i przejdźmy do rzeczy naprawdę istotnych.

Drugą żonę, Krystynę, poznałem u Ewy, żony mojego serdecznego przyjaciela pracującej w jednym z wydawnictw. Zobaczyłem, że siedzi sobie taka ładna blondyneczka, i aż mnie skręciło.

– Nie poszlibyśmy na kawkę? – zagadałem do obu.

– Bardzo chętnie, wpadnij do mnie – odparła Krystyna. – Kawkę wypijemy, a i do kawki coś będzie.

– Spokojnie, dziewczynki. Ja wiem, że wy lubicie, ale pomalutku – zażartowałem.

Niedługo później oczywiście znów odwiedziłem dziewczyny. Porozmawialiśmy, pośmialiśmy się, było bardzo miło. Zaoferowałem, że odwiozę panią Krysię do domu. Zgodziła się, a w drodze zaproponowałem herbatę u siebie. No i ta herbata się trochę przedłużyła... Tak zaczęła się dłuższa znajomość, zwieńczona ślubem.

Jesteśmy małżeństwem już prawie 30 lat. W 1985 roku w Warszawie urodził się mój syn Andrzej. Oczywiście Krystyna miała do mnie pretensje, bo nie byłem przy jego narodzinach, są jednak pewne priorytety – w tym czasie przygotowywałem bowiem Hutnika Kraków do sezonu i nie mogłem ot tak wszystkiego rzucić. To prawda, więcej czasu poświęcałem zawodnikom niż żonie, co ją niezmiernie wkurzało.

Któregoś dnia Krystyna przyjechała do mnie do Krakowa. Odebrałem ją z dworca i ruszyliśmy w kierunku mojego mieszkania.

– O, popatrz, kochanie, tutaj stoi pomnik Lenina – powiedziałem, kiedy dojechaliśmy do Nowej Huty.

Żeby było weselej, zrobiłem pięć kółek wokół tego pomnika, mimo obecności patrolującej teren milicji. Wyskoczyli spod filaru i zaczęli mnie gonić – oczywiście się nie zatrzymałem i pomknąłem przed siebie swoim wysłużonym maluchem. Krystyna była skonsternowana i trochę wściekła, ale udało mi się ją ugładzić.

Przez te 30 lat bywało między nami różnie, jak to w każdym małżeństwie, zdarzył się nam też jeden bardzo poważny zakręt. O co się kłóciliśmy? Przede wszystkim o to, że prawie nie bywałem w domu, cały czas pracowałem. Poza tym – i to był główny powód – podczas moich wojaży poznałem pewną kobitkę. Romans kwitł w najlepsze, a ja nawet się z nim nie kryłem. Informacja o moich hopsztosach oczywiście dotarła do żony. Nie wybaczyła mi zdrady i postawiła sprawę na ostrzu noża, przez długi czas było niemal pewne, że się rozwiedziemy. Myślę zresztą, że do dziś mi nie zapomniała tego epizodu, bo takie rzeczy nie ulatują z głowy ot tak. Czy żałuję tego, co zrobiłem? To niewłaściwe słowo. To są sprawy silniejsze od nas, po prostu wszystko potoczyło się tak, a nie inaczej. Nie mogę więc powiedzieć, że żałuję. Szkoda tylko, że wyrządziłem krzywdę bliskim mi osobom. Rozstanie z tamtą kobietą też było dość burzliwe, mocno to przeżyła.

A jeśli chodzi o Krystynę, to po tamtych wydarzeniach często zdarzały się nam ciche dni. Unikaliśmy się wtedy, w ogóle nie rozmawialiśmy. W końcu podjęliśmy decyzję o separacji. Ten stan nie zmienił się do dziś, choć wciąż razem mieszkamy. Czasem przypomina mi o tym, co zrobiłem. Syn, który miał wówczas już ponad 20 lat, stanął oczywiście po stronie matki.

– Tato, tak się nie powinno dziać, tak się po prostu nie robi! – krytykował mnie.

– No, masz rację, Andrzej. Teoretycznie masz rację... – odpowiadałem, nie chcąc ciągnąć tematu.

Synowi przy okazji też należą się dwa słowa. Chciałem oczywiście, by został piłkarzem, ale nigdy nie miał do tego smykałki. Chciał, ale nie wychodziło. Kiedy jeszcze pracowałem w Emiratach Arabskich, załatwiłem mu treningi z drużyną młodzieżową. Niby coś tam grał, ale potem przychodził z płaczem i skarżył się, że koledzy go kopią i że już nie chce z nimi grać.

– Wiesz, co masz zrobić? – instruowałem młodego. – Przywal jednemu i drugiemu w łeb, a ja załatwię resztę.

Do dalszej gry w piłkę jednak go nie zmuszałem. Nic na siłę. Nie byłem tak radykalny jak mój ojciec, ale oczywiście parę razy Andrzej dostał porządny wpierdziel. Zresztą nie był w dzieciństwie tak żywiołowy jak ja, więc nie trzeba było go tak dyscyplinować.

ALKOHOL

Spotykałem na swojej drodze wiele kobiet, które łączyło jedno. Otóż wszystkie mówiły, że dla mnie liczą się tylko piłka, pieniądze i alkohol. I miały rację, choć alkohol na trzecim miejscu to chyba pomyłka. Pieniądze oczywiście lubiłem i lubię, jak każdy. Jeśli podpisywałem jakiś kontrakt, to po to, żeby dobrze zarobić. Kasa, misiu, kasa.

Zanim opowiem, jak wyglądało picie w naszym polskim grajdołku, podzielę się z Wami historią z grubej rury. Bo Wójt, wyobraźcie sobie, pił wódeczkę z największymi tego świata. Rzecz działa się w Portugalii, podczas Euro 2004.

– Trenerze, a może byśmy na imprezę do Romana Abramowicza wpadli? – zagaił mnie Jurek Kopiec, menedżer piłkarski i mój przyjaciel. W otoczeniu rosyjskiego multimilionera znalazł się dzięki swojej pracy i szybko zawarł stosowne znajomości.

– Dwa razy pytać mnie, Juruś, nie musisz! Idziemy! – wykrzyknąłem. Cóż, Wujo kocha bankieciki miłością szczerą, gorącą i bezgraniczną.

Abramowicz wraz ze swoją świtą przypłynął do Portugalii własnym statkiem – tam zresztą miała się odbyć impreza. Wystroiliśmy się jak stróż w Boże Ciało i ruszyliśmy.

Kiedy zobaczyłem statek rosyjskiego miliardera, zaparło mi dech – a wiecie, że na mnie trudno jest zrobić wrażenie. Ten statek był kurewsko kosmiczny! Wcześniej nigdy takiego nie widziałem, tylko jachty moich przyjaciół szejków w jakiś sposób mogły mi go przypominać.

Przed wejściem na pokład trzeba było przejść selekcję. Abramowicz miał taką ochronę, o której prezydenci i premierzy mogą tylko pomarzyć. Dwóch goryli, którzy pilnowali bramki, było tak wielkich, że nawet Grzesiek Szamotulski z Alkiem Kłakiem nie daliby im rady! Odszukali na liście gości nasze nazwiska i w milczeniu wskazali drogę.

Ach, jaki tam był przepych! Trzy osobne, potężne pokłady, piękne sypialnie z osobnymi łazienkami, pozłacane klamki, kryształowe kinkiety… Już po chwili zobaczyłem jego – człowieka z bródką, Romana

Abramowicza. Ubrany był zwyczajnie – w białą koszulę, czarne spodnie i jakieś pantofle. Sprawiał wrażenie miłego, normalnego, spokojnego faceta.

Od razu przedstawiono mnie drogiemu gospodarzowi, podobnie zresztą jak każdego, kogo gościł po raz pierwszy. Właściciel Chelsea Londyn doskonale wiedział, kim jestem, orientował się, że w przeszłości prowadziłem piłkarską reprezentację Polski.

Pewnie zastanawiacie się, czy porozmawiałem z Abramowiczem. A jakże! Pogadaliśmy, aż miło – jak Ruski z Polakiem – a potem przeszliśmy do najważniejszego, czyli bankietowania.

Najpierw Roman zarządził toast szampanem. Umoczyłem usta – wszystkie szampany, jakie piłem do tej pory, w porównaniu z tym wydały mi się gazowanymi szczynami. Coś wspaniałego!

Potem poczułem się bardziej swojsko, bo Abramowicz nakazał polać gościom wódkę. „No, swój chłop! Napijemy się białej, od razu towarzystwo się rozkręci", uśmiechnąłem się do siebie. Bum, bum – poszło! Koledzy Rosjanie nawet się nie skrzywili, wyglądali tak, jakby właśnie przełknęli syrop dla dzieci.

Na bankiecie u Abramowicza było wszystko, czego dusza zapragnie. Żadne tam schaboszczaki, a wykwintne jedzenie, o którego skosztowaniu niektórzy marzą całe życie, wszystko porozkładane na błyszczących talerzach – gdyby jeden zbić, to pewnie tak, jakby zniszczyć dobrej klasy samochód. Poza tym ten alkohol… Było wszystko, każdy rodzaj napitku, jaki człowiek wymyślił. Ja, jako znany koneser, spróbowałem wszystkiego po kolei.

Po dwóch, może trzech godzinach opuściłem statek, najedzony, zadowolony i napity, aż miło. Abramowicz zrobił na mnie bardzo dobre wrażenie. Na zdrowie, Roman!

No, pochwaliłem się, to mogę wrócić do głównego wątku. Wódki po raz pierwszy napiłem się jako 22-latek. Pojechaliśmy do węgierskiej restauracji Budapeszt, serwowali tam pyszne placki. Oczywiście daliśmy czadu, tak że było nas słychać na całym placu Konstytucji. Kilka dni później prezes Gwardii zwołał zebranie. Obecność obowiązkowa.

– Siadajcie i podajcie mi tę teczkę – zaczął.

Wyciągnął wielką kopertę, a z koperty zdjęcia. Były to fotografie z tamtej imprezy, porobione przez szpicli. Chuje uwieczniły wszystko – jak wznosimy toasty, jak do siebie przepijamy, jak coraz bardziej pijani rozkręcamy party stulecia. I jak słaniamy się na nogach, ukurwieni jak nieboskie stworzenia. „No to przejebane", pomyślałem.

– Tak się przygotowujecie do ważnych meczów? – prezes zwrócił się do Rysia Szymczaka, kapitana drużyny.

– Tak, panie prezesie, przygotowujemy się najlepiej, jak umiemy! – wypalił Rysio.

– Ale wy pijecie wódkę!

– Panie prezesie, czy mogę coś powiedzieć?

– Mów, Rysiu, oczywiście.

– Nie będę, kurwa, mówił za kolegów, powiem za siebie. Oni pewnie przyznają to samo: a więc piłem, piję i będę pił! I nic więcej nie mam do powiedzenia!

Prezes ukrył twarz w dłoniach, a my uznaliśmy, że nie ma sensu przedłużać kłopotliwego milczenia, i podreptaliśmy na trening. Rysio został bohaterem dnia.

Spróbowałem w życiu chyba wszystkich alkoholi świata. I, jak pewnie zdążyliście się już zorientować, za kołnierz nigdy nie wylewałem. Okazji do sączenia miałem co niemiara. Piłem z najrozmaitszymi ludźmi, prywatnie i oficjalnie, gdziekolwiek nie poszedłem, od razu otwierano barek. Kiedy wchodziłem do Ministerstwa Spraw Wewnętrznych, to jeśli nie obróciliśmy trzech, czterech flaszeczek, spotkanie uznawano za nieudane. Czy to był UOP, czy inne służby MSW – pić było trzeba, takie były czasy. Szczęśliwie miałem mocną głowę. Nawet gdy popiłem naprawdę porządnie, nie robiłem bydła, po prostu wstawałem od stołu. Wielu ma tak, że dopóki im się film nie urwie, to walczą za dwóch. Cel główny: spaść z fotela i się nie obudzić. Mnie to nie interesowało, poza tym byłem dobrym zawodnikiem. Kiedy inni kończyli już swoją zmianę, ja wciąż mogłem dzierżyć pałeczkę i biec dalej.

W polskiej piłce każdy pił, nigdy nie spotkałem działacza, który stroniłby od wódy. Nikt nie odmawiał i jeśli któryś z sędziów czy kwalifikatorów się krzywił, pozostali myśleli, że sobie robi jaja. Od razu nazywano go trefnym. Członkowie PZPN-u byli wybitnymi specjalistami w zakresie znietrzeźwiania się. Gdy zbliżało się posiedzenie zarządu, to dwa dni wcześniej zaczynała się biesiada, podczas której ustawiało się wybory. W pokojach hotelowych stały wazy z rosołem, którym popijano wódkę. Gorzała lała się strumieniami, aż do zwały. Była biała, ale też whisky i czasem swojski bimber dla najmocniejszych. Kozakiem był Marian Dziurowicz, który jak narzucił tempo, to inni zeza dostawali. Z kolei małolitrażowy był Michał Listkiewicz. Chciał pić, ale nie mógł. A kiedy jakiś działacz zapragnął puścić pawia, błyskawicznie wysyłano go do łazienki. Tam się regenerował i potem wracał do gry.

Dobrym agentem był Kazio Górski. Uwielbiał alkohol! Do tego stopnia, że najpierw pił naftę, a potem popijał ją piwem. Twierdził, że wódka ma odczyn zasadowy kwaśny, a piwo – tylko zasadowy, browar miał więc łagodzić działanie gorzały. Czasami jak go zawoziłem do domu, to był ledwo ciepły, ale najczęściej dobrze się trzymał.

Czy miałem problem z alkoholem? Nigdy. Nie musiałem się z tego leczyć. Nie zdarzyło mi się, bym codziennego kaca musiał leczyć za pomocą wódy. Oczywiście, często wypijałem duże ilości wódki, ale miałem nad tym kontrolę. Nigdy mi się na przykład nie zdarzyło, żebym kompletnie narąbany prowadził trening. Na lekkim cyku – to inna bajka. Czasem wypiło się łyskaczyka i prowadziło zajęcia, ale na pełnej świadomości. Zdarzało się, że rano przed treningiem ktoś przyjechał, to się walnęło małą whisky, ale nigdy tak, żeby zionęło ode mnie na kilometr.

Kiedy jednak siadaliśmy do stołu na poważnie, to trudno było mnie przebić. Kiedyś przekonali się o tym pewni Francuzi. W Pile moi chłopcy, kadra U-18, grali z Francją właśnie, a po meczu odbywał się bankiet. Żabojady, swoim zwyczajem, popijały winko. Wydoili butelkę i mówią, że spróbowaliby polskiej wódeczki. Jak im polaliśmy, to okazało się, że panowie Francuzi, z trenerem na czele, z pomieszczenia nie wyjdą inaczej niż na czworakach. Kompletne dętki, zniszczyli się dokumentnie.

– Odprowadźcie te psiaki do pokojów, pootwierajcie im drzwi – nakazałem swoim kompanom.

Całe szczęście, że mecz był późnym popołudniem, więc zdążyli się podleczyć, może coś sobie strzelili dla zdrowotności. W każdym razie myśleli, że wygrają z polską wódką, a nie wyrobili na zakręcie.

Czasy się zmieniły i teraz, po kilku operacjach, mam zakaz picia alkoholu. Grozi to atakami epilepsji i śmiercią. Oczywiście, czasem mam ochotę sobie walnąć, ale wtedy nie mogę brać prochów. Czasem wiadomo, jak pierdzielnie się szybkie trzy bomby, to przychodzi ochota, by wsiąść na rower i pojechać dalej w Tour de France, ale nie ma co nawet porównywać starych czasów z obecnymi. Nie to zdrowie, nie ten Wójt.

SAMOCHODY

Oprócz kobiet zawsze pociągały mnie samochody. To równie uzależniające hobby, choć znacznie bardziej niebezpieczne – można przez nie stracić życie, a w najlepszym razie, jeśli ma się pecha, solidnie się poharatać. Jadąc swoim pierwszym autem, maluchem, miałem potężny wypadek.

Wracałem akurat z Grodziska do Warszawy i zamierzałem się spotkać z Wisławą, bo byliśmy umówieni do teatru. Już prawie byłem na miejscu, gdy nagle, na ulicy Łopuszańskiej, facet jadący żukiem, skręcając w lewo, wymusił pierwszeństwo. Jak mnie pieprznął, to samochód przeleciał przez rów i dosłownie przekoziołkował parę metrów. Siedzenie było zmiażdżone, karoseria po lewej stronie właściwie przestała istnieć. Gdybym jechał z kimś, toby mnie zmiażdżyło. Dobrze też, że nie miałem zapiętych pasów, dzięki czemu przeleciałem na stronę pasażera i wypadłem na zewnątrz. Rozbita głowa, żebra stłuczone, złamana kość łonowa… Odniosłem bardzo ciężkie obrażenia. Choć byłem w szoku i mocno zmasakrowany, słyszałem głosy gapiów.

– Wyjmijmy go, bo ten samochód zaraz wybuchnie! – krzyczeli jedni.

– Zostawcie go, on już pewnie nie żyje! – odpowiadali drudzy.

Niedługo później przyjechał ambulans. Nie chciałem położyć się na noszach, jak zwykle zgrywałem twardziela. Sanitariusze wzięli mnie więc pod ręce i wpakowali do karetki. Pojechaliśmy do szpitala, tam z głowy powyjmowano mi kawałki szyby. O dziwo, do domu wypuścili mnie szybko, o transport musiałem jednak zatroszczyć się sam. Przyjechał po mnie brat, maluchem. Chyba chcieli mnie dobić.

Nocą dostałem wysokiej gorączki i znów znalazłem się w szpitalu. Okazało się, że podczas pierwszych badań nie sprawdzili, czy kość łonową mam całą, a tak się złożyło, że za cholerę nie miałem. Jeszcze jedna noc i bym się przekręcił. Lekarza, który pełnił wtedy dyżur, zwolniono dyscyplinarnie. Mimo że wiedziałem, że jest ze mną kiepsko, ani mi było w głowie gnicie na szpitalnym łóżku. Załatwiłem sobie wypis i już parę dni później, w Grodzisku Mazowieckim, prowadziłem reprezentację U-16! Siadłem sobie z zabandażowaną głową na ławce i ustawiałem drużynę jak zwykle, żałując jedynie, że nie mogę poszaleć przy linii tak, jak lubię. Nie mogłem też wykonywać gwałtownych ruchów, bo istniało podejrzenie, że kość całkiem przebije pęcherz. Zawodnicy mieli więc taryfę ulgową.

Wróćmy do moich samochodów. Po maluchu miałem fiata 125p, którego dostałem w nagrodę od ministra budownictwa za wyniki uzyskane w Jagiellonii. Potem FSO sprezentowała mi poloneza. Wywalczyłem zresztą, że jeśli drużyna olimpijska zdobędzie medal na igrzyskach, to wszyscy zawodnicy mają dostać nową furę. I dostali! Mój polonez był wyjątkowy, wyglądał jak rajdówka. Na drzwiach, dachu i masce były olbrzymie napisy „Janusz Wójcik". Gdzie się nie ruszyłem, każdy wiedział, kto jedzie. Ludzie do mnie machali, pozdrawiali mnie. Nawet na noc czasami go nie zamykałem, bo któż by ukradł tak pomalowane auto? Dobrze mi się nim jeździło. Z FSO byłem zresztą tak dogadany, że w razie jakiejkolwiek awarii miałem dostać nowy egzemplarz. Żyć, nie umierać!

Gdy czasy się zmieniły, zaczęła się prawdziwa samochodowa ekstrawagancja. Następną moją bryką było bmw 525. Białe, z czarnymi skórami w środku, wypasionymi felgami... Jeden taki samochód w Warszawie. Głównie jeździła nim moja żona, bo ja miałem swojego poloneza z napisami. Nawet jak walnąłem bombkę albo dwie, to spokojnie mogłem nim jechać. Niestety, w końcu mi tę beemkę ukradli. Złodzieje, uzbrojeni, zwinęli mi auto z parkingu strzeżonego. Najpierw powiedzieli ochroniarzowi, że wujek prosił, by odprowadzić samochód w inne miejsce. Kiedy im nie uwierzył, sterroryzowali go i parę razy przywalili w łeb, po czym wsiedli do mojej beemki i odjechali. Na szczęście całe wydarzenie obserwował jakiś facet. Ruszył za skurwysynami, a po jakimś czasie zauważył, że moje bmw eskortuje fiat 125p. Przytomnie spisał numery rejestracyjne.

Gdy Krystyna zadzwoniła do mnie z informacją o kradzieży, byłem akurat w siedzibie Legii, moim ówczesnym miejscu pracy. Od razu wziąłem się do roboty – uruchomiłem wszystkie swoje kontakty i zaczęło się poszukiwanie. Policja ustaliła, że złodziejami mogą być chłopcy z Pragi. Siedziałem jeszcze przez jakiś czas na komendzie przy Malczewskiego, ale potem stwierdziłem, że nie spędzę tam przecież całej nocy. Poprosiłem, by funkcjonariusze odwieźli mnie do domu i informowali o wszystkim na bieżąco. Wsiedliśmy do suki i tak sobie jedziemy, a tu nagle niespodzianka.

– Zaraz, zaraz. Panowie, zatrzymajcie się. To chyba moje auto! – wypaliłem.

– Pan sobie z nas jaja robi, panie Wójcik.

Ale rzeczywiście! Okazało się, że złodzieje połapali się, z kim mają do czynienia, i odstawili samochód! Zaraz wezwano pirotechników, by wykluczyć podejrzenie podłożenia ładunków wybuchowych. Pirotechnicy zabrali bmw na lawetę i zawieźli na testy, a potem odstawili na Malczewskiego.

Fot. Mieczysław Świderski / Newspix.pl

Wywalczyłem, że jeśli drużyna olimpijska zdobędzie medal na igrzyskach, to wszyscy zawodnicy mają dostać nową furę. I dostali! Mój polonez był wyjątkowy, wyglądał jak rajdówka

To niejedyny raz, kiedy skradziono mi auto. Kilka lat później zarąbali mi audi A4, które przywiozłem z Dubaju. Super autko, robione na zamówienie. Byłem selekcjonerem reprezentacji i pewnego dnia na Torwarze miałem spotkanie z Marianem Dziurowiczem. W samochodzie zostawiłem między innymi dresy reprezentacyjne. I wychodzę z Torwaru, a auta nie ma! Od razu pojechałem na Wilczą, na komisariat. Dogadałem się z funkcjonariuszami, wziąłem głośnik z policyjnego radia i ryknąłem:

– Mówi Wójcik, Janusz Wójcik. Te dranie, które zarąbały mi audi, niech słuchają uważnie: auto ma wrócić, bezwzględnie! To samochód selekcjonera reprezentacji Polski! Postawcie je dokładnie w tym samym miejscu, inaczej zmienię wasze życie w piekło!

Nie dalej jak dwie godziny później samochód znów stał pod Torwarem, tyle że po drugiej stronie!

– Panie Januszu, a może coś się panu pokręciło? Może to pan go tam postawił i zapomniał…? – nie dowierzali policjanci.

– Panowie, co to, zabawka? Myślicie, że mogłem zapomnieć, gdzie auto zaparkowałem? – denerwowałem się.

Kolejnym moim samochodem był volkswagen passat, ale nie polubiliśmy się. Potem jeździłem już tylko merolami. Często je zmieniałem, bo miałem bardzo dobry układ z szefem mercedesa na Polskę. Kiedy wchodziła nowa S-klasa, to ją brałem. Nieraz było tak, że w moim garażu stały jednocześnie cztery samochody.

Z jednym z mercedesów, akurat wypożyczonym, wiąże się niesamowita historia. Wybrałem się do marketu, po wyjściu włożyłem zakupy do bagażnika, ale zapomniałem o teczce – odjechałem, zostawiając ją na parkingu. Było w niej 300 tysięcy złotych w gotówce i dwa pistolety. Na ulicy Grójeckiej zorientowałem się, że nie mam walizki. Zatrzymałem się na środku drogi, blokując cały ruch, wyskoczyłem i rzuciłem się do bagażnika – no, kurwa, nie ma.

– Została na parkingu, ja jebię! – wykrzyczałem sam do siebie.

Wskoczyłem z powrotem za kierownicę i przepierdoliłem się przez tory tramwajowe. Pędziłem, ile fabryka dała, w dupie mając takie drobiazgi jak narażanie życia swojego i bliźnich. Pod marketem wjechałem pod prąd i zderzyłem się czołowo z innym samochodem. Jak się okazało, prowadził go mój kolega.

– Jedź do tego a tego hotelu, wszystko pospisujemy, ale teraz muszę coś załatwić, bo tragedia się stała – rzuciłem i nie oglądając się za siebie, popędziłem dalej.

Wreszcie wjeżdżam na parking przed marketem, znajduję miejsce, w którym stałem. Nie ma. Kurwa, nie ma. Zajebał ktoś. Po chwili wychodzi facet ubrany na czarno i macha do mnie. Okazało się, że to ochroniarz. Albo nie mogli teczki otworzyć, albo ją prześwietlili i zobaczyli, że są tam dwie spluwy, więc się wystraszyli, w każdym razie oddał mi walizkę, życząc dobrego dnia. A mnie w ciągu tych kilkunastu minut przybyło mnóstwo siwych włosów. I prawie serce stanęło.

BROŃ

Podobno najlepszy sposób na samobójstwo to strzał w skroń – jedno pociągnięcie za spust i po wszystkim. Wyjąć broń, przystawić, odpalić i po sprawie. Pokój we krwi, zwłoki na podłodze, koniec. Zabić chciałem się raz w życiu, kiedy doszczętnie zawalił mi się cały świat.

Zacząłem inwestować pieniądze w spółkę Interbrok. Na początku przynosiła zyski, byłem zadowolony, a jej właściciele zachęcali, bym inwestował jeszcze więcej. Tak robiłem, a oni zapewniali mnie, że zarobię. Dużo zarobię.

Po pewnym czasie wszystko zaczęło się psuć. Okazało się, że ta firma to jedna wielka mistyfikacja, a moje pieniądze owszem, trafiały na jakieś konta, ale nie zarabiały na siebie i miałem ich już nigdy nie zobaczyć. W sumie straciłem ponad cztery miliony złotych.

Miałem trzy pistolety, zawsze nabite. Wszystkie posiadałem legalnie. Jeśli trzeba byłoby kogoś jebnąć, nie byłoby problemu. To samo z samobójstwem – 20 sekund i po sprawie. I właśnie wtedy, kiedy tak potwornie popłynąłem z kasą, chciałem się zajebać. Strzelić sobie w łeb i zakończyć całą tę farsę. Zostałem z niczym, oszukany, upokorzony, wypłukany do cna. Oszczędności mojego życia poszły psu w dupę.

Miotałem się po domu, w końcu wsiadłem w auto i koniecznie chciałem coś zrobić – choćby i rozbić się gdzieś na drzewie. Stwierdziłem jednak, że nie tak prędko: pojechałem do jednego z tych dyrektorów z bożej łaski, którzy zarządzali Interbrokiem. Spluwę oczywiście wziąłem. Przysięgam, chciałem go zapierdolić.

Drzwi otwarła żona delikwenta i widząc mnie, dosłownie zamarła.

– Pan Wójcik… tylko proszę nic nie robić mężowi – szepnęła.

– Gdzie on, do chuja, jest?! – nie zważałem na to, że tak wulgarnie odnoszę się do kobiety, było mi wszystko jedno.

Wparowałem do domu i rozejrzałem się w poszukiwaniu oszusta. Starał się ukryć, tchórz i pierdoła. Złapałem go za fraki.

– Oddawaj, skurwysynu, moje pieniądze albo cię zajebię! – wykrzyczałem.

Nic nie odpowiedział. Nie miał już tej kasy, przepadła, wiedziałem doskonale. Stracił wszystko. Tyle że były to m o j e pieniądze, urobek życia. Mogłem go zajebać jednym strzałem w głowę, jednak co by mi to dało? Przecież forsy i tak bym nie odzyskał. Poszarpałem nim trochę, patrząc, jak sra pod siebie ze strachu, splunąłem mu pod nogi i wróciłem do domu.

Dziś on i inni, którzy mnie oszukali, siedzą w pierdlu, ale co mi z tego? Pieniądze straciłem bezpowrotnie.

Wtedy do niego nie strzeliłem, nigdy zresztą nie oddałem strzału do człowieka. Ale w powietrze – jak najbardziej. Pamiętam taką groźną sytuację, gdy wraz z Krysią mieszkaliśmy u teściów na Bemowie. Byliśmy w sypialni na piętrze, a była już późna noc, więc wszyscy spali. Usłyszałem, że na dole coś się dzieje, więc po cichu zszedłem po schodach. Na wszelki wypadek wziąłem spluwę. Postanowiłem, że jeśli natknę się na złodziei, to będę walić jak do kaczek. I faktycznie, jakieś gnojki obrabiały dom! Jeszcze dzieciaki, mieli góra po 20 lat.

– Wypierdalać!!! – ryknąłem, ale broni jeszcze nie wyjmowałem.

Gówniarze się wystraszyli i rzucili się do okna. Wtedy wyjąłem pistolet i ruszyłem w ich stronę, celując w plecy. Tak im się spieszyło, że część skradzionych rzeczy pogubili w ogródku. Pobiegłem za nimi na taras i oddałem strzał w powietrze, żeby szybciej spierdalali. Przeskakiwali przez płot z prędkością światła. Później trochę żałowałem, że za wcześnie zdradziłem swoją obecność. Powinienem był bezszelestnie zejść na dół i kazać im kłaść się na ziemię. „Ani drgnąć, bo powystrzelam" – tak bym powiedział. Wtedy oddaliby nawet to, co przynieśli ze sobą. A gdybym kazał im zdjąć gacie, toby z gołymi dupami chodzili. Trochę się jednak obawiałem, że także mogą być uzbrojeni.

Opowiadam wam tu o kobietach, wódzie, autach i broni, ale właśnie wokół tego obracał się mój świat. Zdaję sobie sprawę, że moim życiorysem można by obdzielić trzech różnych facetów, a każdy czułby się jak bohater filmu sensacyjnego. To jednak dla mnie codzienność i chybabym oszalał, siedząc za biurkiem. Czy czegoś żałuję? Mnóstwa rzeczy. Czy gdybym mógł przeżyć swoje życie znów, bez tych wszystkich przygód i zawirowań, tobym na to przystał? W żadnym razie. Święty spokój jest dla frajerów, a z frajerami to wy wiecie, co należy robić!

WYPADEK

To była środa. Jeszcze ciepła, wrześniowa. Zwyczajny dzień. Tego właśnie zwyczajnego dnia otarłem się o śmierć.

Szykowałem się do snu, ale postanowiłem jeszcze pójść na chwilę na dół, do pokoju kominkowego, gdzie był telewizor. Zszedłem ostrożnie po schodach, ale nie chciało mi się zapalać światła. Przechodząc po ciemku przez hol, zahaczyłem o tak zwany pomocnik arabski, czyli nieduży stoliczek o wysokości około 30 centymetrów. Straciłem równowagę. Runąłem na ścianę, odbiłem się od niej i upadłem tak nieszczęśliwie, że nadziałem się na arabski kącik (bardzo wiele rzeczy przywoziłem sobie z krajów Bliskiego Wschodu). Uderzyłem skronią w wazę z brązu, mającą przykrywkę z mosiądzu w kształcie stożka. Stożek wbił mi się w głowę, przewróciłem się. Całe szczęście trzask zbijanej wazy narobił takiego hałasu, że obudził Krystynę. Przybiegła, zawołała syna, natychmiast wezwali karetkę. Wymusili na sanitariuszach, by zawieziono mnie do szpitala MSWiA przy Wołoskiej, żadnego innego. To uratowało mi życie, do dziś zresztą z pełnym przekonaniem twierdzę, że gdybym nie trafił na Wołoską, nie dożyłbym do rana.

W szpitalu stwierdzono pięć złamań kości podstawy czaszki z ostrym stłuczeniem mózgu i rozległym krwiakiem w okolicy ciemieniowej z prawej strony. Zajęli się mną neurochirurdzy pod przewodnictwem ordynatora Bogusława Kostkiewicza. Podjęli decyzję o konieczności niezwłocznego przeprowadzenia operacji, ponieważ mój stan pogarszał się z minuty na minutę. Oceniali go jako krytyczny. Operacja, czyli misterna dłubanina w mojej głowie, trwała w sumie osiem godzin. Wycięto mi fragment czaszki z prawej strony mniej więcej na szerokość i długość dłoni. Mój stan był tak fatalny, że w ciągu tych ośmiu godzin podobno trzy razy odjeżdżałem do Abrahama. Reanimowali mnie, ściągali mnie za nogę na dół, na szczęście za każdym razem skutecznie. Mówią, że kiedy jest się blisko śmierci, widzi się jakiś tunel z białym światłem, ale u mnie była kompletna ciemność. Żadnych odczuć czy wrażeń, tylko głucha cisza. Kiedy operacja dobiegła końca, zostałem wprowadzony w stan śpiączki farmakologicznej i przewieziony na OIOM. Podłączono mnie pod niezliczone, superskomplikowane maszyny. W śpiączce byłem w sumie ponad trzy tygodnie, a mój stan codziennie oceniano jako krytyczny. Rodzinie przekazano, że powinna przygotować się na najgorsze. Tymczasem któregoś dnia, ni stąd, ni zowąd, obudziłem się. Akurat siedzieli przy mnie bliscy, żona i syn. Niespodziewanie otworzyłem oczy i wypaliłem:

– No ileż można na was czekać?

Zgłupieli. Przez dłuższą chwilę nie byli w stanie wydobyć z siebie słowa. Nie wiedzieli, czy powiedziałem to w stanie nieświadomości, czy rzeczywiście się wybudziłem. Oto człowiek, któremu coś wbiło się w mózg na głębokość ponad dziesięciu centymetrów i żegnał się ze światem, właśnie ma pretensje, że za długo czekał na odwiedziny. Myślałem, że zaraz pomdleją i tym razem to ich trzeba będzie reanimować. Dziś właściwie im się nie dziwię – przecież za każdym razem, gdy pytali lekarzy, kiedy mogę się wybudzić, słyszeli:

– Jutro, za tydzień, za miesiąc, za rok… albo wcale.

Żona płakała codziennie. Kiedy odwiedził mnie brat, również nie potrafił ukryć wzruszenia. Oczywiście fotoreporterzy za wszelką cenę chcieli dotrzeć do mnie i porobić trochę zdjęć, ochrona szpitala dbała jednak, żeby nie dopuszczać do mnie nikogo. Udało im się zrobić tylko jedno, na szczęście dopiero wtedy, gdy już odwożono mnie do domu.

W każdym razie sprytni byli niemiłosiernie. Dwóch nawet przebrało się za lekarzy, by dostać się do sali, w której przebywałem. Zdradziły ich wystające spod fartuchów dużych rozmiarów obiektywy. Ochroniarze to dostrzegli i od razu wyrzucili ich ze szpitala.

Kości, które wyciągnięto mi z głowy, umieszczono w okolicach jamy brzusznej, że tak powiem, „na przechowanie". Za jakiś czas z powrotem miały zostać wstawione na miejsce. Niestety wdał się stan zapalny i musiały zostać usunięte, przeszedłem więc kolejną operację. Już się nie nadawały, żeby je zamontować w głowie, można je było tylko wyrzucić – nie tknąłby ich nawet pies.

Zabawa ze stawianiem Wójcika na nogi trwała dalej. Wykonano mi szczegółowe pomiary głowy, bo puste miejsce trzeba było czymś wypełnić. Mogłem wybrać implant sztuczny, krajowy, ale odrzuciłem takie rozwiązanie – słyszałem historię o człowieku, któremu wszczepiono taki szajs i pożył chyba tydzień. Wybrałem implant organiczny firmy Johnson & Johnson. Po dokonaniu wszystkich badań i pomiarów przygotowano go dla mnie we Włoszech. Cała impreza kosztowała ponad 30 tysięcy złotych, więc korzystając ze wsparcia szefa Rady Trenerów Andrzeja Strejlaua i trenera Henia Kasperczaka, zwróciłem się z prośbą do PZPN-u, by dofinansował spłatę należności za implant. W końcu to i owo dla polskiej piłki zrobiłem... Moją sprawę omawiano na posiedzeniu zarządu w jednym z luksusowych warszawskich hoteli. Jeden pobyt całego zarządu w takim miejscu to wydatek rzędu 150–200 tysięcy złotych. Na zarządzie przegłosowano niejednogłośnie, że z powodu trudnej sytuacji finansowej związku dofinansowanie mojego leczenia nie będzie możliwe. Powiedzcie sami: śmiać się, płakać czy tłuc głową w ścianę?

– Janusz, to nie zarząd ma rozpatrywać takie kwestie. Twój wniosek powinien podpisać sekretarz generalny, a związek miał psi obowiązek wypłacić całość należności za implant, a nie tylko go częściowo dofinansować – powiedział mi później były prezes PZPN-u Michał Listkiewicz.

Sekretarzem był wtedy Zdzisław Kręcina, a prezesem Grzegorz Lato. Obu doskonale znałem. W każdym razie podczas głosowania kilku członków zarządu było za dofinansowaniem, a kilkunastu – przeciw. Zastanawiałem się wtedy, co trzeba zrobić, żeby móc związek o cokolwiek poprosić – zostać mistrzem świata, mistrzem Europy, mistrzem olimpijskim? Cała sprawa była przykra tym bardziej, że w przeszłości członkowie PZPN-u dostawali pieniądze na różne operacje, na przykład kolan.

Wówczas dobitnie przekonałem się, że to zgraja oszustów, dla której nie warto robić absolutnie niczego. Dla kibiców – tak, ale nie dla tych cynicznych krętaczy. Pieniądze na ten implant zapewniały mi możliwość normalnego funkcjonowania. Kiedy potem przychodziłem do siedziby związku, wielokrotnie głośno wypowiadałem swoje zdanie na ten temat.

– Chcieliście, żebym się wykończył, tak? – grzmiałem. – Wysłalibyście delegację, żeby znicz zapaliła albo położyła jakąś nędzną wiązankę? Tylko o to chodziło, żebym wam już więcej nie przeszkadzał. Byłem jak cierń wbity w tyłek. Marzyło wam się, żeby się mnie pozbyć.

Pieniądze na implant zdobyłem z innego źródła. Kolejna operacja, znów na otwartym mózgu, trwała siedem i pół godziny. Następnie zostałem poddany skomplikowanej rehabilitacji neurologicznej. Po pierwszej operacji miałem niedowład lewej strony ciała, codziennie więc bardzo intensywnie ćwiczyłem – po dwie godziny, czasem dwie i pół. Potem odpoczywałem, ale wiedziałem też, że nie mogę przesypiać całych dni. Odwiedzali mnie znajomi. Ci, na których mogłem liczyć, okazali się przyjaciółmi na śmierć i życie. Z PZPN-u absolutnie nikt nie zainteresował się, czy jeszcze żyję, czy też może już wywieźli mnie w skrzynce.

Rodzina bardzo mocno przeżyła ten wypadek, dlatego teraz ani żona, ani syn nie chcą do niego wracać. Przecież otarłem się o śmierć. Przez kilka tygodni żyli ze świadomością, że każdy dzień może być moim ostatnim, że w każdej chwili mogą dostać telefon z informacją: „Z przykrością zawiadamiamy, że o tej a o tej godzinie pan J.W. zmarł". Chyba nawet nie umiem sobie wyobrazić ich cierpienia.

Kiedy się obudziłem i okazało się, że jestem w stanie samodzielnie usiąść i rozmawiać, nie dowierzali nie tylko Krysia i Andrzej, ale również lekarze.

– To, że przezwyciężyłeś to wszystko, jest dla mnie ewenementem. Takiego zdrowego chama to nie miałem jeszcze na oddziale! – powiedział mi półżartem ordynator.

Z kolei inny doktor mocno mnie zirytował.

– Gdyby nie my, już dawno wąchałby pan kwiatki od spodu – wypalił.

– Zapewniam pana doktora, że jeśli ja miałbym wąchać, to pan razem ze mną – odgryzłem się, a bliscy, którzy siedzieli obok, wyglądali na zażenowanych moim zachowaniem.

Nie żałuję jednak, bo na chamówę trzeba odpowiadać jeszcze większą chamówą. To był zresztą jedyny zgrzyt, generalnie jestem bardzo wdzięczny za opiekę, jaką otoczono mnie w szpitalu. Tym bardziej że jako pacjent dawałem do wiwatu – byłem niesforny, trudny do upilnowania. Regularnie podłączano mnie pod jakieś maszyny, kroplówki i inne cuda, a ja wszystko to sobie wyrywałem. Nie wiem nawet z jakiego powodu. Może dlatego, że miałem dosyć pobytu w szpitalu i było mi wszystko jedno? W każdym razie, żeby mnie dożywiać i podawać leki, przywiązywano mnie do łóżka pasami, jak w domu wariatów. Oczywiście z miejsca zacząłem kombinować, jak by tu załatwić sobie scyzoryk…

Nigdy nie byłem specjalnie chorowity, może tylko jako mały chłopiec. Moja świętej pamięci mama narzekała, że w dzieciństwie miałem problemy z gardłem, ale później byłem już „twardziocha". Nigdy nie płakałem, kiedy poobijano mnie na meczu, bo wiedziałem, że tak musi być. Ba, to ja z reguły spuszczałem łomot jako pierwszy! Później, gdy grałem w piłkę zawodowo, na skutek kontuzji musiałem przejść dwie operacje kolan. Z jedną z nich wiąże się ciekawa historia. Miałem wtedy chyba 17 lat. Musiałem przejść operację łąkotki, ale nie chciałem denerwować mamy. Wyszedłem więc z domu późnym wieczorem, mówiąc niby od niechcenia:

– Niedługo wracam, odezwę się, na razie.

Szpital mieścił się jakieś 400 metrów dalej – wystarczyło przejść przez podwórko i już mogłem zameldować się na oddziale. Operację miałem mieć dwa dni później. Zadzwoniłem do domu i powiedziałem, że jestem w szpitalu, ale nie wspomniałem nic o zabiegu. Przyznałem się dopiero po powrocie.

Rok później znów miałem operowaną łąkotkę, tyle że w drugim kolanie. Nie mam wątpliwości, że choć oba te zabiegi uniemożliwiły mi kontynuowanie kariery piłkarskiej, to sprawiły, że stałem się silniejszy i z większą łatwością zdołałem przejść kolejne. Dziś rodzina mówi, że po tym, jak cudem wylizałem się po urazie czaszki, powinienem na kolanach iść do Częstochowy. Że dostałem wyraźny znak z góry, coś na zasadzie: „Na razie cię tu nie chcemy, bo narobisz nam za dużo bałaganu".

FRAJERZY I BOHATEROWIE

Przez wiele lat kariery poznałem mnóstwo ludzi – jedni okazali mi życzliwość, inni mocno dali mi się we znaki. Oto parę osób, które napotkałem jako piłkarz, trener i polityk i które wyjątkowo zapadły mi w pamięć. Z pewnością znacie każdą z nich, ale ode mnie dowiecie się o nich czegoś nowego. I pewnie nieźle się zdziwicie.

HENRYK APOSTEL

Wieloletni działacz PZPN-u i jeden z niewielu uczciwych ludzi w tej organizacji. Zawsze był mi bardzo życzliwy. Dlatego uważam, że należy mu się wspomnienie w tym „alfabecie". Sądzę, że mógł zajść znacznie wyżej, gdyby okazał się bardziej stanowczy i dynamiczny. Był za grzeczny i pierdołowaty, nie potrafił walnąć pięścią w stół. Szanowałem go, ale był niestety zbyt miękki, co w PZPN-ie niemiłosiernie wykorzystywano.

Lubił czerwone wino i koniaczek. Zdecydowanie wolał trunki delikatne, w kochanej w PZPN-ie wódeczce nie gustował. Chętnie grał w golfa, ale zwykle średnio mu to wychodziło. Przynajmniej ze mną zawsze przegrywał.

RENATA BEGER

Kurwiki w oczach posłanki Begerowej doprowadziły do tego, że o Samoobronie mówiło się potem, że to ekipa dzikich byków rozpłodowych, które nic innego nie robią, tylko atakują każdą kobitę, żeby ją wydupczyć.

Mieliśmy bardzo dobre stosunki – ale podkreślam, tylko te klubowe. Bardzo mnie lubiła, choć na nią nie poleciałem. Nie ta waga. W każdym razie fajna, miła babka była z tej Reni, choć z polityką za dużo wspólnego nie miała. Błyszczała swoimi oryginalnymi tekstami zamiast pomysłami politycznymi. Niczym ciekawym się nie zasłużyła, poza organizowaniem blokad drogowych i wysypywaniem owsa na ulicę razem z Andrzejem Lepperem. Była zresztą wierną przyboczną Lepperiusa. Potrafiła czasem przypierdolić taką wypowiedzią, że nie wiadomo, „czy go w dupę, czy go w oko". Nie wiadomo było, jak na to wpadła. Ale dzięki temu błyszczała. Cóż, dziś to już historia i gdyby nie gadanie o kurwikach, to nikt by już dziś o niej nie pamiętał.

ZBIGNIEW BONIEK

Mieliśmy ze Zbyszkiem taki *love-hate relationship*. Raz wściekłość i mało się nie pozabijaliśmy, innym razem zgoda, buzi-buzi i wszystko cacy. Mamy trochę podobne charaktery, obaj jesteśmy dość agresywni i zawzięci, ale też różnimy się w wielu kwestiach. Było między nami kilka spięć – szczególnie po tym słynnym meczu z Łotwą, kiedy Zbyszek dostał w dupę i przegrał 0:1. Po meczu pojechaliśmy do hotelu Victoria i tak się tam pokłóciliśmy, że ludzie musieli nas rozdzielać, byśmy się nie pozabijali. Rzucaliśmy mięsem, wyzywaliśmy się od najgorszych. On wytykał błędy mnie, ja jemu. W pewnym momencie stwierdził, że był gwiazdą piłkarską, z czym jeszcze mogę się zgodzić, ale i również gwiazdą trenerską!

– Zbyszek, z ciebie taki trener jak ze mnie chirurg – odparowałem. – Ty jesteś gwiazdą trenerską, ale w komiksie jakimś!

– A z ciebie co za trener? Do Arabów wyjechałeś pracować, bo tu cię nie chcieli?! – ripostował.

Zbyszek był wściekły i rzucał się, a ja byłem przygotowany, że będzie trzeba kolegę Bońka rzucić na glebę. Na szczęście do najgorszego, czyli mordobicia, nie doszło. Sprawa została załagodzona, a później długo na siebie się nie boczyliśmy – wypiliśmy po kieliszeczku i wszystko było już jak dawniej.

Często porównuję go do prezesa Mariana Dziurowicza. Dziura byłby najlepszym prezesem w historii, gdyby nie narobił głupich błędów, przede wszystkim w kwestii korupcji, której nie potrafił, bądź nie chciał, ukrócić. A Boniek? Cóż, był świetnym piłkarzem, ale jako trener się nie popisał. Jego największy błąd to brak wyników reprezentacji. Jeśli chodzi o inne aspekty jego pracy, to uważam, że za bardzo chciał pokazać, jaki to on nie jest stanowczy i bezwzględny. Zaczął zwalniać ludzi, jednego za drugim: czy ktoś był winien, czy nie – wywalał. Na PZPN padł blady strach, każdy bał się, że prędzej czy później przyjdzie czas na niego. To był taki pokaz siły, „bójcie się mnie, pokażę, jaki jestem mocny". Oto właśnie cały Zbysiu Boniek.

MIECZYSŁAW BRONISZEWSKI

Trener Mietek to mój dawny znajomy, z którym nieustannie mieliśmy jakieś konflikty. Nie podobało mu się na przykład, że to ja wziąłem reprezentację, a jemu przeszła koło nosa. Ale największe pretensje miał do mnie po tym, jak pod koniec lat 80. wpadł na „przemycie" podczas odprawy celnej na lotnisku, kiedy miał lecieć z reprezentacją juniorską na jakiś turniej do Izraela. Towarzyszył mu niejaki towarzysz Bednarczyk z warszawskiej Gwardii, który był jednocześnie naczelnikiem BOR-u i działaczem PZPN-u. Mietek myślał więc, że z tak wysoko postawionym gościem będzie mógł wnieść na pokład samolotu wszystko, i do worów ze sprzętem napakował grzybów i wódki. Najlepsze jednak było to, że próbował – oczywiście na polecenie jakiegoś misia z Izraela – przemycić w skarpetce jakąś drogocenną monetę, której nie można było wywozić z kraju. Jak się nietrudno domyślić, włączył się alarm, a celnicy bez trudu odnaleźli zakazane fanty. Bednarczyk jakoś się z problemu wywinął, a wszystkie oskarżenia spadły na Broniszewskiego. I poczciwy Miecio postanowił oskarżyć mnie, że go podpierdzieliłem do służby celnej, bo chciałem go udupić i pozbyć się rywala w walce o najciekawsze stanowiska trenerskie.

– Mietek, a skąd ja mogłem wiedzieć, co ty w swoim Karczewiu wkładasz do skarpety? Przecież ja przy tym nie byłem – tłumaczyłem mu. A Bednarczykowi radziłem: – Weź mu jebnij kolbą karabinu, może to biedaka otrzeźwi.

Popierdoliło mu się w głowie dokumentnie. Potem zresztą odjebało mu jeszcze bardziej, bo powiedział, że gdyby on prowadził reprezentację olimpijską, to w Barcelonie zdobyłby złoto. Niestety, żal mu dupę ściskał. Teraz nie mamy dobrych relacji. Ciągle uważa, że doniosłem na niego i przeze mnie zatrzymali go na granicy. Cóż, choroba przeżarła mózg i tyle.

LUCJAN BRYCHCZY

Wielka piłkarska sława. Poznałem go w Legii Warszawa i błyskawicznie się porozumieliśmy, we wszystkich sprawach, zarówno zawodowych, jak i prywatnych. A jak się ładnie wspólnie relaksowaliśmy! Po treningu wysyłaliśmy kierownika drużyny na Torwar po kotlety mielone, parę kwaszonych ogórków i odprężaliśmy się przy „białej".

Z Luckiem żyłem w zgodzie, zawsze stawał po mojej stronie. Ale nie każdy w klubie był za nim. Pytano mnie, czy może by go nie zwolnić ze względu na wiek. Protestowałem. Brychczy był mi bardzo potrzebny, z piłką potrafił zrobić wszystko. Często zdarzało się, że po treningu strzelał na bramkę z 20 metrów. Mówił Zbyszkowi Robakiewiczowi albo Maćkowi Szczęsnemu, w który róg będzie strzelał, a on walił prosto w okienko, tak że musieli się schylić i wyjąć piłkę z siatki.

– Co wy, kurwa, robicie, żadnej piłki nie możecie wybić? I wy chcecie grać w pierwszej lidze?! – darłem się na nich, oczywiście w żartach. Bo tych strzałów Lucka nie obroniłby żaden bramkarz na świecie!

– Nie bronimy dalej. Po co mamy tu stać, skoro nie pozwolicie nam złapać żadnego strzału – denerwowali się i rzucali rękawicami. A na ustach Lucka zawsze pojawiał się szelmowski uśmiech.

RUDOLF BUGDOŁ

Kolejny prominentny działacz związkowy. Za czasów Mariana Dziurowicza szara eminencja w PZPN-ie, taki uniżony sługa i adiutant Dziury. Czasem prezes tak go opierdalał, że aż wióry leciały. Jechał po nim jak po burej suce.

Bugdoł zawsze był tym od finansów. Żyłem z nim bardzo dobrze, to był taki typowy śląski chłop. Czyli: rozmowa, bania, bania, bania, rozmowa, bania, bania, bania. On nawet jak jest trzeźwy, to wygląda tak, jakby był pijany.

Bardzo ciepło wspominam wspólnie spędzony czas. Ludzi takich jak on w polskim życiu publicznym bardzo brakuje.

WOJCIECH FIBAK

Znam Wojtka jeszcze od czasów, kiedy grał w tenisa i był jedną z gwiazd tego sportu. Zawsze mieliśmy bardzo dobre relacje. Kiedy byłem na przykład na obserwacji mistrzostw świata we Francji, spędziliśmy razem trochę czasu w Paryżu. O czym rozmawialiśmy? Zwykle o ładnych obrazach, bo Wojtek uwielbiał sztukę, a także o ładnych kobietach, które kochał nie mniej.

Wojtek jest koneserem damskiej urody. Było przecież głośno o jego dodatkowych zajęciach, w które na początku nie wierzyłem. Dopiero później pojawiło się potwierdzenie. Ale o co mamy mieć do niego pretensje? Że rozprowadzał kobitki? Przecież burdelmamą nie był. Koło Wojtka zawsze kręciło się dużo kobiet. Co w tym złego, że mężczyźni dzwonili do niego, by skontaktował ich z jakąś miłą dziewczyną? Takie praktyki były, są i będą. Nie doszło przecież do żadnej przemocy czy gwałtów, a pannom nie podawano narkotyków. Burza w szklance wody, a Wojtek to świetny facet.

WALDEMAR FORNALIK

Pamiętam go jeszcze z czasów, kiedy grał w piłkę w Ruchu Chorzów. Moim zdaniem to zdecydowanie lepszy zawodnik niż trener. Na boisku dał się poznać jako człowiek zawsze agresywny, zdecydowany i do bólu zawzięty. Nigdy nie odpuszczał.

Biorąc pod skrzydła reprezentację, wpadł w mętną wodę i od razu mówiłem, że będzie miał problem, żeby się z niej wynurzyć. Praca z kadrą narodową go przerosła. Ulegał różnym podpowiedziom i naciskom, w ogóle nie był samodzielny. Nie brał na siebie odpowiedzialności, nie miał swojego zdania. Kiedy ogłoszono, że będzie selekcjonerem, zadeklarowałem, że jeśli będzie potrzebował podpowiedzi czy rady, zawsze może do mnie zadzwonić. Nigdy tego nie zrobił. Widocznie myślał, że sobie poradzi. A jak sobie poradził, każdy widział.

ANDRZEJ GOŁOTA

Andrzejka znałem już od jego młodzieńczych lat, kiedy zaczynał karierę bokserską. Bardzo nieufny człowiek, trudno było się wkraść w jego łaski, ale mnie oczywiście się to udało. Kiedy wyjechał do USA robić karierę, nasze drogi troszkę się rozeszły, ale potem wielokrotnie walczył też w Polsce i za każdym razem witał mnie bardzo serdecznie. Często odwiedzałem go jeszcze przed walkami, w szatni.

– Andrzejku, daj trochę pooglądać, nie znokautuj go wcześniej niż w czwartej czy piątej rudzie – żartowałem, czym rozbawiałem całe towarzystwo.

Pamiętam walkę Gołoty we Wrocławiu z Timem Witherspoonem. Była dość wyrównana, ale Andrzej wygrał ją na punkty. Tuż po gali pojechaliśmy wszyscy oblewać ten triumf. Wraz z towarzyszami wszedłem do ładnego klubu we Wrocławiu, umiejscowionego pod ziemią. Czekaliśmy na Andrzejka. W końcu chłopcy dali sygnał: „Przyjechał!". Podbiegłem, przywitałem się z nim na misia i dla żartu uderzyłem go otwartą ręką w twarz. Plask!

– Przestań, kurwa, tak mnie wszystko boli, że łeb mi zaraz oderwiesz! – zdenerwował się Gołota.

– Jędruś, przepraszam, wiesz, że to z miłości. Gratulacje – odpowiedziałem.

– Dobra Janusz, ale już nie klep mnie. Boli jak cholera – skrzywił się.

Po tym krótkim przywitaniu przeszliśmy do zabawy i hulaliśmy aż do świtu. Andrzej popił zdrowo, ale cały czas miał wszystko pod kontrolą, nikt nie musiał go wynosić. Zresztą przy jego wadze byłoby to dość karkołomne zadanie. Przy Gołocie cały czas była obstawa, nikt nie mógł go ruszyć. Tylko jeden człowiek podczas tej imprezy walnął go w twarz. I był to Wujo.

WIESŁAW IGNASIEWICZ

Przez długie lata kierownik techniczny reprezentacji Polski. Super facet. Do dziś twierdzi, że takiego trenera jak ja nigdy później nie było. „Cieszcie się, że nie ma Wójcika, on by wam pokazał, jak się trenuje", mówił reprezentantom z kolejnych pokoleń.

Pamiętam pewną humorystyczną historię związaną z Wieśkiem. Graliśmy jakiś mecz na wyjeździe. Ignasiewicz wydał sprzęt piłkarzom przed treningiem, ci ruszyli na boisko, a ja za nimi. Po zajęciach wróciliśmy do szatni, ale Ignasiewicza nie było.

– Wiesiu, Wiesiu! – wykrzykiwałem, ale nie słyszałem żadnej odpowiedzi.

Obszedłem cały budynek klubowy. Faceta wcięło. „Kurwa mać, zasłabł czy co…" – mocno się przeraziłem i postanowiłem szukać go, póki nie sczeznę.

Po jakimś czasie coś mnie tknęło i otworzyłem metalową skrzynię, w której Wiesiek trzymał sprzęt. Patrzę, a tam… Wiesiek właśnie! Okazało się, że położył się na miękkich koszulkach i uciął sobie drzemkę.

– Wiesiek, kurwa, spać tu przyjechałeś?! – naskoczyłem na niego.

Błyskawicznie się obudził, a ze skrzyni wyskoczył tak, jakby faraona wypuścili z sarkofagu.

– Co się stało? Co się stało? – powtarzał przerażony.

– Nic się nie stało, baranie. Wlazłeś do skrzyni i zasnąłeś. Czyś ty zgłupiał?

– Poszliście na trening, myślałem, że długo was nie będzie, i postanowiłem się zdrzemnąć. A noc była ciężka, więc miałem co odsypiać – uśmiechnął się pod nosem.

Jeszcze lepszy numer odwalił tuż przed meczem z Luksemburgiem w eliminacjach Euro 2000.

– Wiesiu, no wydawaj ten sprzęt – ponagliłem go, bo się ociągał. A ten czeka. Stoi i się patrzy jak cielę.

– Kurwa, no sięgaj i wyjmuj! – ryknąłem.

– Panie trenerze, niech pan zobaczy… – powiedział przerażony i wyciągnął czarną koszulkę.

Zdębiałem.

– Czyś ty zwariował? Co to jest? Dla kogo ta koszulka?

– Taki sprzęt nam dali. Innego nie mieli.

– Jak to nie mieli? Wszyscy wiedzieli, że mecz jest, że mamy grać! – wkurzałem się.

Okazało się, że producent uszył właśnie takie stroje, czarne jak, kurwa, noc, a Wiesiek choć wiedział, to nie powiedział, i wręczył nam je w dniu meczu. Chłopcy nie chcieli w nich grać, i wcale im się nie dziwiłem. Zaraz jednak po tym, jak opierdzieliłem Wiesia, kazałem im założyć te wdzianka na dupy i tradycyjnie ogolić frajerów. Bo frajerów można golić, nawet gdy się jest ubranym jak do trumny.

A na Ignasiewicza nie złościłem się długo – bo na niego złościć się po prostu nie dało.

ANDRZEJ IWAN

Znam go z czasów jego gry w Wiśle Kraków, poza tym to mój kolega z boiska. Graliśmy przeciwko sobie w ogólnopolskiej spartakiadzie młodzieży, ja w reprezentacji Warszawy, on – Krakowa. To człowiek orkiestra. Naprawdę super facet, potrafił się bawić jak mało kto. Bardzo dobrze grał w karty, wśród piłkarzy był mistrzem. Ograłby każdego i puściłby w slipach!

Pewnego razu spotkaliśmy się w dawnym hotelu Forum w Warszawie i oczywiście daliśmy mocno w palnik. Kiedy już mocno zakręciło nam się w główkach, postanowiłem pojechać do domu. W tym samym czasie doszło do przepychanki – jakieś wały zaczęły atakować członków naszej imprezy. Zdołałem jakoś dotoczyć się do windy, a na dole ruszyłem do taksówki. Spojrzałem jednak, a pod hotelem walka trwała w najlepsze! Oprychy biły Andrzeja i naszych towarzyszy, ale chłopaki wcale nie odpuszczały. Nagle jeden ze zbirów podbiegł do mnie i spróbował uderzyć mnie w szyję. Zasłoniłem się – na całe szczęście, bo jak potem zobaczyłem, on w tej ręce miał… brzytwę! Odwdzięczyłem mu się, jak tylko mogłem: uczciwie zajebałem w ryj, a potem sprzedałem kilka kopów. Kiedy leżał, pobiegłem do taksówki i odjechałem. Na drugi dzień zadzwoniłem do Andrzeja.

– Nasłałeś, kurwa, na mnie jakichś nożowników! – krzyczałem do słuchawki.

– Januszku, co ty opowiadasz? To bzdury! – tłumaczył się.

– To dlaczego mnie nie odprowadziłeś do taksówki, dziadzie jeden? Na dole już czekali na mnie z brzytwą! – atakowałem, ale oczywiście wiedziałem, że tak naprawdę to nie jego wina. A oprychów nigdy nie znaleźliśmy, choć gdybyśmy chcieli, to ktoś „życzliwy" utopiłby ich w Wiśle.

LECH KACZYŃSKI

Z panem prezydentem poleciałem na mecz mistrzostw świata Niemcy – Polska w 2006 roku. Wybraliśmy się oczywiście specjalnym samolotem, z rządową delegacją. W trakcie lotu Kaczyński zaprosił mnie do siebie.

– Panie Januszu, jak to dzisiaj będzie? – dopytywał.

– A co ma być, panie prezydencie. Niemcy nas pukną i tyle – przewidywałem.

– Może jednak jakoś się wybronimy… – łudził się.

Wylądowaliśmy. Na lotnisku przywitał nas prezydent Niemiec i ruszyliśmy na stadion. Lech Kaczyński od razu zaprosił mnie do swojej loży VIP, byśmy razem mogli obejrzeć ten mecz. Niemcy atakowali.

– Nic z tego nie będzie, panie prezydencie. Zaraz nam strzelą. Ten mecz się nie skończy 0:0. Mogę się z panem założyć, że damy dupy – powiedziałem. Dosłownie.

– Nie, na pewno co najmniej utrzymamy ten remis! – mówił z pewnością w głosie.

– Zakład?

– A o co?

– Kto przegra, nalewa zwycięzcy drinka – wymyśliłem.

Prezydent zapalił się do pomysłu:

– No dobra!

Podaliśmy sobie ręce i wyczekiwaliśmy końca meczu. Już w doliczonym czasie gry padł gol dla Niemców. Dupy dał Paweł Janas, który zdjął lewego obrońcę Michała Żewłakowa i wpuścił za niego Dariusza Dudkę. I ten matołek dał się ograć szybkiemu jak cholera murzynkowi z Niemiec, Odonkorowi. Ten kundel dograł do środka, a tam Oliver Neuville stał niepilnowany i wpakował piłkę do siatki. Przegraliśmy 0:1.

– Idę do nich do szatni – rzekł zrezygnowany, acz honorowy Kaczyński. – Panie trenerze, może wybierze się pan ze mną?

– Panie prezydencie, a po co ja mam tam iść? Mam ich opierdolić? Trener od tego jest. Niech pan im powie, co myśli na ten temat. Ja już w trakcie meczu stwierdziłem przecież, że będzie w łeb – przypomniałem.

– Oj, miał pan rację. Ale blisko było…

– No było. Ale pośliznął się dróżnik i wpadł pod pociąg.

– Nic, to ja pójdę im polać…

– Dobra, dobra. – Machnąłem ręką. – Niech prezydent już nie polewa, łykniemy sobie coś przygotowanego przez barmana. Tylko mam jedną prośbę: proszę ich tam dobrze opierdolić!

– Oj, to dziękuję bardzo. Ale muszę przyznać, że nosa do futbolu pan jednak ma.

Kiedy prezydent wrócił od naszych połamańców, trzasnęliśmy po jednym malutkim, a potem wsiedliśmy do samochodów i ruszyliśmy na lotnisko.

Fot. Kuba Atys / Agencja Gazeta

Do dzisiaj minister sportu Andrzej Biernat wspomina, że o mojej klasie trenerskiej najlepiej świadczy fakt, że prowadzona przeze mnie reprezentacja poselska wygrywała mecze, mając w składzie takiego Kalisza czy Grzegorza Schetynę, którzy nie mają pojęcia o grze w piłkę. Ba, oni nawet w piłkę wodną grać nie potrafią

Bardzo polubiłem pana prezydenta. Do dziś nie mogę odżałować, że nie ma go już pośród nas...

RYSZARD KALISZ

Z Rysiem Kaliszem spotykałem się regularnie – w pałacu prezydenckim, na meczach, na rautach, bankietach i zwykłych popijawach. Kiedy wchodziliśmy razem do naszych ulubionych restauracji, kelnerzy nawet nie pytali o zamówienie, od razu biegli po odpowiedni napitek, czyli mazucik.

Rysiek to nieprawdopodobnie dowcipny i fajny człowiek. Zawsze świetnie się ze sobą bawiliśmy. Próbował grać z posłami w piłkę nożną, ale zanim kopnął, to zwykle dwa razy się wywrócił. Proponowaliśmy mu, żeby się lepiej przyglądał, bo jego wydolność była niezmiernie krucha, ale chciał grać bez względu na wszystko. Dlatego powoływałem go do reprezentacji sejmowej.

Do dzisiaj minister sportu Andrzej Biernat wspomina, że o mojej klasie trenerskiej najlepiej świadczy fakt, że prowadzona przeze mnie reprezentacja poselska wygrywała mecze, mając w składzie takiego Kalisza czy Grzegorza Schetynę, którzy nie mają pojęcia o grze w piłkę. Ba, oni nawet w piłkę wodną grać nie potrafią.

– Panie trenerze, niech pan nas motywuje jak piłkarzy. Niech pan z nami ostro jedzie w szatni – prosił Rysiu jako przedstawiciel poselstwa.

– Mogę jechać. Najwyżej od chujów was powyzywam – stwierdziłem. – A ty, Rysiek, dwa okrążenia wokół boiska. Raz, raz!

– Już się robi, panie trenerze!

Stukał podeszwami aż miło i toczył się przed siebie jak wielka, napuchnięta szynka.

ANDRZEJ LEPPER

Kiedy bawiłem się w politykę, Lepperius stał na pierwszym miejscu w mojej sejmowej hierarchii. To był zacny człowiek i nikt nie wmówi mi, że było inaczej.

Kiedy go poznałem, z jednej strony wydawał mi się bardzo prosty, ale z drugiej strony dziwnie tajemniczy. Oczywiście swoimi sposobami dowiedziałem się o nim kilku rzeczy, więc wiedziałem więcej niż inni. Zawsze był po mojej stronie. Kiedy organizowałem urodziny (tak, te z „duchem puszczy"), przestrzegał mnie, bym uważał, bo wszędzie kręcą się paparazzi i dziennikarze. Ale mnie to, szczerze mówiąc, pierdoliło – niech sobie robią zdjęcia, jeśli nie mają nic innego do roboty.

Nigdy nie miałem z nim żadnych spięć czy utarczek, może oprócz dyskusji na temat godziny spotkań.

– Spotkajmy się jutro o szóstej rano – zarządzał.

– Panie, ja jeszcze o tej godzinie śpię! – protestowałem.

To jego wczesne wstawanie to w gruncie rzeczy nic dziwnego. Lepper to przecież człowiek ze wsi, a tam nie śpi się do dziesiątej, tylko od samego świtu dogląda gospodarstwa. My w mieście jesteśmy do tego nieprzyzwyczajeni. Kiedy rolnik się budzi, my często dopiero odchodzimy od stołu.

Kiedy Lepper coś mówił, wszyscy pukali się w czoło i nazywali go wariatem. To jednak nie był głupi facet i swoje wiedział. Jeśli mówił, że w Polsce są więzienia CIA, to śmiano się, że dostał kota. Ale przecież to fakty! Innym razem wyszedł na mównicę sejmową i prosto z mostu walił w znanych polityków – Grzegorza Schetynę czy świętej pamięci Jurka Szmajdzińskiego. Dostało się także niejakiemu detektywowi Rutkowskiemu, który zdaniem Leppera spotykał się z różnymi oprychami.

Lepper wykorzystał to, że państwo było w kryzysie, stworzył mocną organizację i nazwał ją Samoobrona. Mówił o sprawach, które dotykały zwykłych ludzi, a były pomijane przez grupę rządzącą. Trafiał w ludzkie potrzeby. Dzięki temu Samoobrona rosła w siłę. Wszystko jeszcze dodatkowo podkręcał tymi blokadami dróg, wysypywaniem zboża na ulicę. Rolnicy go pokochali, bo widzieli w nim swego przedstawiciela, obrońcę. Dzięki temu Samoobrona bez problemów weszła do Sejmu i została koalicjantem.

Lepper miał bardzo dobre kontakty na Wschodzie – w Rosji, na Ukrainie, na Białorusi. Ciągle tam jeździł, a czasem zabierał mnie ze sobą. Przyjmowano nas jak członków rodziny cara, z pełnymi honorami. Nie wykluczam nawet, że Samoobrona w części była finansowana z białoruskich pieniędzy, to jednak moje przypuszczenia, w kwitach nie grzebałem.

Lepper miał też bardzo bliskie kontakty z ludźmi biznesu, nauki. Wiedział o różnych rzeczach, które robiono na niekorzyść państwa polskiego. A o tym się teraz w ogóle nie mówi. Jakaś Unia, srunia, dupunia, że Tusk to, tamto, owamto… A Lepper otwarcie mówił, w których segmentach Polska ma problemy, niczego się nie bał. To ludziom nie pasowało.

Oficjalnie Andrzej Lepper się powiesił ze względu na długi i problemy osobiste. To kompletny nonsens, bo wystarczyłoby słowo, a Aleksander Łukaszenka udzieliłby mu wszelkiej pomocy finansowej. Śmierć Leppera utwierdza mnie w przekonaniu, że dobrze zrobiłem, opuszczając politykę.

MICHAŁ LISTKIEWICZ

Człowiek, który mógłby opowiedzieć o PZPN-ie dosłownie wszystko, od A do Z. Bardzo inteligentny facet, z szerokimi znajomościami i układami w UEFA i FIFA. Dla polskiej piłki był i jest niezwykle pożyteczny.

Kiedy prezesem PZPN-u był Marian Dziurowicz, o wielu rzeczach decydował Michał, właśnie dzięki tym swoim znajomościom. Dziurę to denerwowało i starał się Michała odstrzelić, ale nie wiedział jak. W końcu kończyła się kadencja Dziurowicza i doszło do wyborów. O fotel prezesa rywalizowali Dziura, Listkiewicz i Zbyszek Boniek. Już na sali obrad, po pierwszych dyskusjach, wiadomo było, że Dziurowicz ma małe szanse na reelekcję. Na placu boju została tylko dwójka.

– Michał, obiecaj Bońkowi, że jak odda ci głosy, to zrobisz go wiceprezesem – poradziłem Listkiewiczowi.

– Janusz, a mógłbyś ty z nim o tym porozmawiać? – poprosił.

Zgodziłem się i pogadałem ze Zbyszkiem. Niedługo później Boniek wszedł na mównicę i ogłosił, że rezygnuje z kandydowania, a wszystkie swoje głosy przekazuje Listkiewiczowi. Michał dotrzymał słowa i dał mu stanowisko wiceprezesa.

Popełnił jednak poważny błąd – otóż na najważniejszych stanowiskach obsadził sędziów, oczywiście poza Bońkiem. Dzięki temu ci poczuli się mocni i postanowili podoić trochę kasy. Korupcja oczywiście istniała już wcześniej, ale dzięki temu mieli okazję działać praktycznie bezkarnie, skoro sami zarządzali PZPN-em.

Jeśli chodzi o pracę na stanowisku prezesa, Listek zdecydowanie przewyższał Dziurowicza i Grzegorza Latę. W jednym jednak z Dziurą przegrywał – nie był tak twardy jak on. Bo Michał Listkiewicz to taki pozytywny, ciepły misiaczek. Z Dziurowiczem nie było dyskusji, a z Listkiewiczem owszem, zawsze można było podyskutować i przepchnąć własny pomysł.

ADAM NAWAŁKA

Poznałem go w tym samym czasie co Andrzeja Iwana. To porządny facet i normalny chłopak, niczym nie wyróżniał się na tle rówieśników. Lubiliśmy się, ale potem nasze losy się rozjechały.

Jestem dość umiarkowanym fanem Nawałki jako selekcjonera, ale należą mu się słowa uznania za zwycięstwo 2:0 z Niemcami – co prawda byli osłabieni, ale w końcu to mistrzowie świata. Wykorzystaliśmy tak zwaną „niemoc niemiecką". Goście mieli w tym meczu dużą przewagę, stworzyli więcej sytuacji, ale liczy się to, kto zdobędzie więcej goli. A zdobyli Polacy i za to im chwała! Duże gratulacje, panowie, kiełbachy były w górze! Pokonaliście wspaniały zespół, a nie jakichś frajerów, brawo! Niestety, na „niemoc niemiecką" w meczu rewanżowym raczej nie ma co liczyć. Na miejscu Nawałki bardziej koncentrowałbym się na takich meczach jak ten ze Szkocją, przygotował się też do spotkań z Irlandią czy z Gruzją. Szkoci pokazali w Warszawie, że będą trudnym przeciwnikiem w walce o Euro 2016. Skoro Polacy, naładowani energią po sukcesie z Niemcami, nie mogli ich pokonać, to znaczy, że w kolejnym pojedynku mogą im ulec.

Co by jednak nie mówić, chłopcy Nawałki zaliczyli dobry początek. A trener na razie ma nosa do piłkarzy. Fajnie na przykład, że postawił na Sebastiana Milę. To chłopak, który potrafi zorganizować grę w środku pola. Nawałka zaryzykował, ale osiągnął spodziewany efekt. Brawo, Adam, bo trafiłeś z tym Milą, za to masz u mnie plus. Ale pamiętaj: droga do Euro 2016 jest długa i bardzo wyboista.

MIROSŁAW OKOŃSKI

Kiedy Okonek grał w Lechu, bardzo często jeździłem do Poznania i się z nim spotykałem – najczęściej w kasynie, bo Miruś bardzo lubił sobie poobstawiać. Podchodził do mnie z wielkim szacunkiem, ze dwa razy nawet cmoknął mnie w rękę.

Okoński był niekwestionowanym królem Poznania. Wszyscy go uwielbiali. Kiedy się bawił, to cały Poznań razem z nim. Był przy okazji talentem czystej wody, genialnym piłkarzem. Nikt w Polsce w tamtym czasie nie miał takiej lewej nogi. Mimo to nie wykorzystał w pełni swojego potencjału – hazard i wóda zabrały mu wszystko.

Jeśli nie liczyć tych jego słabości, to bardzo dobry człowiek. Do dziś wspominam, jak bardzo mi pomógł. Otóż byłem z reprezentacją olimpijską w Grecji, rozgrywaliśmy mecz towarzyski. Spotkanie wygraliśmy, a wieczorem puściłem drużynę na miasto, ostrzegając, by za bardzo nie narozrabiali. Rzeczywiście, po kilku godzinach wszyscy wrócili do hotelu. Ale do mojego pokoju zapukał Jurek Brzęczek, jakiś dziwnie przerażony.

– Trenerze, nieszczęście – zaczął.

– Jureczku, co się stało? – Od razu udzieliło mi się jego zdenerwowanie.

– Tomek Wałdoch zgubił paszport, albo mu ukradli. Wszędzie sprawdziliśmy, nie ma – oznajmił.

Okazało się, że może nie jest to nieszczęście, ale dość poważny problem. Bez paszportu Wałdoch za cholerę z tej Grecji by nie wyleciał. Zastanawialiśmy się w gronie kilku osób, co robić. W nocy zadzwoniliśmy do ambasady, która jednak na szybko nie była w stanie niczego załatwić. Wtedy wpadłem na pomysł, by skontaktować się z Okońskim, wówczas zawodnikiem AEK-u Ateny.

– Mirek, ratuj, mamy problem – rozpocząłem, po czym opowiedziałem mu, w czym rzecz.

– Janusz, nie ma sprawy. Zaraz będę u was w hotelu i pokombinujemy, co zrobić – obiecał, a we mnie wstąpiła nadzieja.

W dniu wylotu na lotnisko pojechaliśmy z Mirkiem. Ustaliliśmy, że on zajmie celnika, podsunie mu jakieś reprezentacyjne pamiątki, a w tym czasie Wałdoch przemknie przez odprawę. Tak zakręciliśmy facetowi w głowie, że już nie wiedział, kto został sprawdzony, a kto jeszcze nie. Rozglądał się, patrzył zaniepokojony na chłopaków.

– Dawaj, kurwa, idźże i się schowaj – naskoczyłem po cichu na Wałdocha, a ten stanął na samym końcu korytarza.

Wkrótce wsiedliśmy do samolotu i było po sprawie. W Polsce takich problemów już się nie spodziewałem – na Okęciu porozmawiałem z takim jednym znajomym.

– Jeden z naszych nie ma paszportu – oznajmiłem mu.

– To jak żeś go przez granicę w Grecji przeprowadził? – dopytywał.

– Waszymi, kurwa, sposobami!

Tomek potem posiedział w gabinecie z 15 minut, coś tam podpisał i normalnie mógł z nami pojechać do hotelu. A Okoniowi jestem wdzięczny do dziś.

MAREK PAPAŁA

Śmierć Marka, oficjalnie Komendanta Głównego Policji, a prywatnie mojego przyjaciela, porządnego człowieka i prawdziwego profesjonalisty, jest wielką hańbą dla wszystkich tych, którzy od wielu lat usiłują znaleźć winnych jego zabójstwa. Tropy, które podejmują, nie mają nic wspólnego z tym, co się wydarzyło. Marek został zabity, bo po prostu nie pasował. Zbyt dużo wiedział o różnych niewygodnych sprawach i został zlikwidowany. To nie było żadne przypadkowe morderstwo dokonane przez złodziei samochodów, ale zaplanowane i z zimną krwią wykonane zabójstwo. Stali za nim profesjonaliści, to nie był żaden przypadek. Jego śmierć, tak jak śmierć Sławka Petelickiego, to wstyd dla wszystkich, którzy byli w ich otoczeniu. Przecież wiadomo było, że to ważne osoby, na ważnych, strategicznych stanowiskach. Tacy ludzie nie giną w przypadkowy sposób. Tego jestem pewien. Śmierć Marka jest dla nas wszystkich nieodżałowaną stratą.

SŁAWOMIR PETELICKI

Sławka Petelickiego znałem szmat czasu, byliśmy bardzo dobrymi przyjaciółmi. Spotykaliśmy się przy różnych okazjach i darzyliśmy się ogromną sympatią. Informacja o jego śmierci była dla mnie szokiem i ani trochę nie wierzę w to, że popełnił samobójstwo. To był człowiek bardzo silny wewnętrznie, poza tym wiadomo doskonale, gdzie pracował. Wysoki rangą oficer służb nie strzela sobie w tył głowy w garażu, pomiędzy samochodami. Takie rzeczy po prostu się nie zdarzają, nie przyjmuję tego do wiadomości. Rozmawiałem potem z wieloma jego współpracownikami. Wysłuchali mnie, przyjęli do wiadomości mój punkt widzenia. Do tej tragicznej śmierci jest wiele zastrzeżeń i ja również je mam.

FRANCISZEK SMUDA

Kiedy został trenerem reprezentacji, wydawało mi się, że podoła temu zadaniu, że wprowadzi kadrę na wyższy poziom. Strasznie się jednak przeliczyłem.

Pamiętam, jak przed rozpoczęciem mistrzostw Europy pojechałem do hotelu Hyatt, gdzie rezydowały chłopaki z kadry. Było to w przeddzień meczu otwarcia z Grecją. Siedliśmy z Frankiem i spokojnie porozmawialiśmy. Smuda aż się trząsł, taki był zestresowany.

– Czym ty się denerwujesz, Franuś? Przecież oni to wszystko czują! Co ty taki roztrzęsiony? – pytałem. – Oni jutro mają wyjść na boisko, opierdolić tych Greków i pogonić ich na pastwisko, a ty trzęsiesz gaciami!

Milczał, więc kontynuowałem.

– Idź na górę, do pokoju, walnij ze trzy sety i popij piwkiem. Rozluźnij się. Bo piłkarze widzą, że jesteś posrany.

– Boję się pić, bo zaraz mi zrobią zdjęcie i puszczą do gazet – bronił się.

– Franek, chuj z gazetami. Idź i się napij. Bo będzie dupa z tego wszystkiego.

– Janusz, zapraszam cię po meczu. Przyjedź, pogadamy, wypijemy.

– Ty masz złapać moc TERAZ, a nie po meczu! Widzę, że jesteś totalnie zesrany. Nie nadajesz się do poprowadzenia drużyny – zakończyłem, a Smuda zawinął się i poszedł do pokoju.

Postanowiłem, że jeszcze trochę w Hyatcie posiedzę. Pogadałem chwilę z moim dobrym znajomym Wieśkiem Ignasiewiczem.

– Paru chłopaków chciałoby z trenerem dwa słowa zamienić – poprosił w ich imieniu.

– Nie ma problemu, Wiesiek, niech przychodzą – odpowiedziałem bez wahania.

Jak się później okazało, ustawiła się do mnie cała kolejka. Od razu wiedziałem, że to konsekwencja zachowania Smudy. Brakowało im człowieka, który ich wesprze. Jednym z tych, którzy chcieli porozmawiać, był Adrian Mierzejewski. I dosłownie płakał mi w rękaw.

– Trenerze, Smuda w ogóle nie daje mi szansy. Stawia tylko na Obraniaka. To niesprawiedliwe – żalił się.

Nie chciałem ani krytykować Smudy, ani w żaden sposób pocieszać Adriana. To nie moja robota, i cześć. Co więc powiedziałem Mierzejewskiemu i innym piłkarzom? To proste. Żeby, kurwa, ogolili tych greckich frajerów!

Sam siebie jednak oszukiwałem. Widziałem, że zespół jest rozbity i trudno będzie mu pokonać Greków. To się sprawdziło. Najpierw odbyła się stypa w Hyatcie, potem na Stadionie Narodowym. A później podczas całego tego nieszczęsnego „polskiego" Euro.

ROBERT SOWA

Nadworny kucharz reprezentacji. Byłem z niego bardzo zadowolony, dlatego robiłem wszystko, żeby świat o nim usłyszał. I w jakimś stopniu mu pomogłem. Później Robert napisał książkę, założył też własną restaurację.

Kiedy zaczynaliśmy współpracę, oczywiście odpowiednio go wyprostowałem – po to, by chodził jak w zegarku. Sowa więc nie mruczał, tylko robił, co do niego należało. Zawodnicy bardzo go lubili. Kiedy mieli wolne i byli w Warszawie, przyjeżdżali do jego restauracji, żeby coś im upichcił.

Na poważnie pracę z reprezentacją zaczął od wyjazdowego meczu z Bułgarią w Burgas. Zabraliśmy go tam, bo woleliśmy nie jeść tego, co nam podadzą gospodarze. A działacze PZPN-u, darmozjady, już się dopytywali, co takiego będą żarli.

– Czym nas uraczysz, Roberciku? Nie dostaniemy rozwolnienia? – wypytywałem.

– Mam przygotowaną szarlotkę – stwierdził.

– No dobra, to przynieś ją – zgodziłem się, ale zdziwiłem się trochę, że zamiast zaserwować porządny obiad, upiekł nam ciasto.

Po krótkim czasie Sowa wrócił. Ale dziwna sprawa – zamiast brytfanny z ciastem niósł jakieś butelki. Okazało się, że to sok jabłkowy i… gorzałka. Taką to nam szarlotkę przygotował! Wszyscy byli zadowoleni z tej niespodzianki, a dzięki miksturze Sowy byliśmy świetnie przygotowani do walki z Bułgarami. I wygraliśmy.

Z Robertem Sową do tej pory mam świetne relacje. Wielokrotnie zapraszał mnie do swojej restauracji w Warszawie Sowa & Przyjaciele. Po ostatnich wydarzeniach i aferze podsłuchowej trzeba jednak być ostrożnym i uważać, co się tam mówi, ale Robert tak gotuje, że mam to gdzieś!

JAN TOMASZEWSKI

Janek, czyli człowiek, który zatrzymał Anglię. Szkoda, że siebie również. Próbował robić karierę trenerską, oczywiście bezskutecznie. Często spotykałem się z nim w PZPN-ie. Mieliśmy zupełnie inne poglądy i nie mogliśmy się dogadać. W ogóle trudno było z nim wytrzymać, na co dowodem niech będzie fakt, że każda kobieta, z którą próbował się związać, szybko uciekała.

Miał kilka bardzo poważnych wyskoków. Myślał, że jeśli będzie obrażał ludzi jako ten, który zatrzymał Anglię, to wszyscy będą tego słuchali i nikt nie zareaguje. Parę razy doszły mnie słuchy, że i na mój

temat wypowiada się nieciekawie. Zadzwoniłem więc do niego i zjebałem jak kundla.

– Jak masz ochotę, to ja się teraz wezmę za ciebie – zagroziłem.

Miałbym co opowiadać, dlatego niech się Janek zamknie. Powinien
dać sobie spokój, wyciszyć się. Bo on myśli, że jest jedyny na świecie
sprawiedliwy. A więc oświadczam: Janku, tak nie jest i nigdy nie będzie.
I zamilcz łaskawie.

INNI O WÓJCIE

WOJCIECH KOWALCZYK

39-krotny reprezentant Polski. Podopieczny Wójcika w reprezentacji olimpijskiej, Legii Warszawa, reprezentacji A i Anorthosisie Famagusta.

W Legii piłkarze nazywali cię „synkiem Wójcika". Powoływał cię do reprezentacji olimpijskiej, potem tej dorosłej, a na koniec zabrał na Cypr. Byłeś jego pupilem?
Jest w tym trochę prawdy. Janusz zawsze miał zawodników, z którymi trzymał sztamę. Kiedy wyjeżdżał z Legii do Emiratów Arabskich, powiedział mi z tą swoją swadą: „Wojtuś, spokojnie, ja tu wrócę. Obejmę reprezentację Polski, a ty będziesz w niej grał. Czekaj na mnie". Ale żeby też nie było tak słodko, to trzeba powiedzieć, że moje pierwsze spotkanie z trenerem było trochę... szorstkie. Pojechałem na zgrupowanie reprezentacji juniorskiej do Spały, a Wujo od razu pokazał mi, kto w tej kadrze rządzi. Od razu jednak wiedziałem, że to będzie bezproblemowa współpraca.

Skąd miałeś tę pewność?
Byliśmy mieszanką wybuchową. On władający drużyną silną ręką, a ja charakterny młody piłkarz. Po pierwsze, pasowałem mu do koncepcji, a po drugie – byłem w drużynie jedynym zawodnikiem z Warsza-

wy. Jako człowiek ze stolicy chciał mieć jakiegoś warszawiaka w ekipie. A fakt, że byłem niepokorny, tylko go utwierdzał w przekonaniu, że warto na mnie postawić. Powoływał mnie do dorosłej kadry nawet wówczas, gdy grałem w drugoligowym Las Palmas. Wiedział, że przyjadę i dam z siebie wszystko, chociaż występowałem tylko w hiszpańskiej II lidze. Takich piłkarzy potrzebował. Uwielbiał gagatków. Dla niego najważniejszy był charakter piłkarza. Wiedział, że jeśli ktoś jest charakterny, na boisku da z siebie wszystko.

Piłkarze krnąbrni, niepokorni, trudni w wychowaniu mieli u niego dużo łatwiej?
Zdecydowanie. Ale z drugiej strony na kapitana potrzebował człowieka opanowanego i poukładanego, więc w reprezentacji olimpijskiej dał opaskę Jurkowi Brzęczkowi. Jemu najbardziej się należała, bo dzięki swojemu opanowaniu potrafił utrzymać w ryzach cały zespół. Ja tam się na kapitana nie nadawałem i Wujo doskonale o tym wiedział.

Czym najbardziej zaszedłeś mu za skórę?
Młodzieńczych występków w moim wykonaniu nie brakowało, ale to pasowało Wójcikowi. On sam był kontrowersyjny, dużo przeklinał i w taki sposób nas motywował. Ale rzeczywiście, ze mną miewał trochę kłopotów.

Na przykład?
Pamiętam, jak nie dotarłem na sesję fotograficzną drużyny przed wyjazdem na igrzyska olimpijskie. Byliśmy wtedy zakwaterowani w warszawskim hotelu Solec i szykowaliśmy się do wyjazdu na ostatni przed turniejem obóz w Buku. Niestety, minusem zgrupowania w Warszawie było to, że miałem i mam tu wielu znajomych, więc trochę się zawieruszyłem. Wszyscy zrobili sobie i zdjęcia indywidualne, i grupówkę, a potem zapakowali się do autobusu. Niestety, Kowalczyka dalej nie było. W rezultacie zabrakło mnie na przedolimpijskiej fotce. Autokar, beze

mnie na pokładzie, ruszył do Buku, a na poszukiwanie Kowala udał się Paweł Janas. Znalazł mnie, wziął do samochodu i ruszyliśmy. Drużynę dogoniliśmy gdzieś na trasie i spokojnie dołączyłem do kolegów.

Wójcik był wściekły?

Wręcz przeciwnie! Nic nie powiedział, a nawet... czuł lekką satysfakcję. Wiedział, że przysoli mi dużą karę finansową. A jeśli była kara finansowa, to Janusz Wójcik był zadowolony (śmiech).

Wyobraź sobie następującą sytuację: jest przerwa w meczu, przegrywacie, do szatni wpada Janusz Wójcik. Jak się zachowuje?

To zależy, jak wysoko przegrywamy. Kiedy w Danii [baraż o awans do igrzysk – przyp. aut.] dostawaliśmy do przerwy 0:5, to nic nie mówił, bo już nic by nam nie pomogło. Przecież sześciu goli byśmy nie strzelili. U Wójcika największa bomba motywacyjna była przed samym meczem. Jak ktoś nie dostał od niego plaskacza w gołe plecy, to było święto. Takie ciosy naprawdę się odczuwało, a zawodnik od razu był mocno wkurwiony na trenera, co przekładało się na agresję już w trakcie meczu. W reprezentacji olimpijskiej, jak wychodziliśmy na mecz, to patrzyliśmy na przeciwników, jakbyśmy chcieli ich zagryźć, a potem zjeść. Od razu chcieliśmy pokazać, kto rządzi na boisku.

A jak Wójcik motywował was przed olimpijskim finałem z Hiszpanią?

W sposób piorunujący. Czyli jak to on, kazał nam ogolić frajerów (śmiech). Tym mocniej motywował, że nie byliśmy faworytami tego meczu. W hiszpańskiej drużynie grali piłkarze, którzy już byli gwiazdami europejskiego futbolu. Na papierze byli lepsi. Z trybun dopingował ich król, poza tym wiadomo, że gospodarzom zawsze pomagają i ściany, i czasem sędzia. Hiszpanie od początku nas zaczepiali, podszczypywali, rzucali dziwnymi uśmieszkami. Chcieliśmy im na to odpowiedzieć agresją i walką na boisku. Czyli tak, jak chciał Wujo.

W Barcelonie, poza finałem, szliście jak burza. Jak Wójcik reagował na te sukcesy?

Szczerze? Sam chciałbym wiedzieć. Nie bardzo mieliśmy z nim kontakt, bo widzieliśmy się tylko na treningach, a i to nie zawsze (śmiech). Kiedy mecz się kończył, to mogliśmy go zobaczyć jeszcze w drodze do wioski olimpijskiej, a potem słuch o nim ginął. Co wtedy robił? Można się łatwo domyślić. A jeszcze łatwiej – z kim. Ministrem sportu był wtedy przyszły prezydent Aleksander Kwaśniewski, który przebywał z nami w wiosce. Zawsze mieli razem wiele spraw czy to do załatwienia, czy do opicia. Ale my nie narzekaliśmy, że trenera nie ma. Nawet się cieszyliśmy, bo dzięki temu mieliśmy trochę wolnego czasu.

Co najbardziej go denerwowało, czego w zachowaniu piłkarzy nie akceptował?

Słabość na boisku. Miękki charakter. Dlatego nie dziwi fakt, że Darek Gęsior na igrzyskach grał tylko pierwsze 45 minut, a potem nawet nie powąchał murawy. Wójcikowi nie podobało się to, że brakuje mu boiskowego charakteru, że nie robi wślizgów. Był za miękki. Za Darka wszedł Marcin Jałocha, który praktycznie nie wstawał z tyłka. Ciągle wślizg, wślizg, wślizg. Tym kupił Wuja, takich ludzi Wójcik potrzebował. Charakternych, nieobawiających się nastawić głowy, przywalić komuś łokciem. Jego drużyna musiała najpierw składać się z 11 wojowników, a dopiero później z piłkarzy.

Metody motywacyjne i teksty Wójcika na stałe zapisały się w historii. Które powiedzenia trenera zapadły ci w pamięć?

Ma być grzecznie?

Nie musi, trener Wójcik nie zawsze był przecież grzeczny.

No to: „Biało-czerwona na maszt, kiełbasy do góry i ładujemy frajerów w kakao!". To wersja bez wulgaryzmów (śmiech), innych nie da się cytować. Nigdy nie było tak, że grzecznie tłumaczył nam, jak grać.

A to, że przeklinał? Co z tego! Po pierwsze byliśmy już pełnoletni, a po drugie – sami nie mówiliśmy jak poeci. W każdym razie takimi powiedzonkami Wójcik sprawiał, że wychodziliśmy na boisko pełni ambicji, czasami wręcz nienawidziliśmy rywali. Uwielbiał, kiedy już w pierwszej minucie jego piłkarze wykonali ze dwa ostre wślizgi, po których rywale wylatywali w górę jak z katapulty. Mieliśmy już od początku pokazać przeciwnikowi, kto rządzi na boisku.

Podobał wam się taki sposób motywacji?
Na pewno bardzo nam pomagał. Byliśmy młodymi chłopakami, potrzebowaliśmy tego. A poza tym byliśmy zupełnie inni niż dzisiejsi młodzi piłkarze. Wychowywaliśmy się na podwórkach, nie mieliśmy żelu na głowie, playstation i wypasionych komórek. Potrzebowaliśmy takiego twardego ojca, a Wójcik sprawdzał się w tej roli idealnie. Stąd moim zdaniem sukces olimpijski.

Takiego sposobu motywacji, jaki preferował Wójcik, dziś trochę brakuje polskim piłkarzom?
Tak. Ale tylko w reprezentacji młodzieżowej. Bo moim zdaniem w dorosłej piłce, i w Legii, i w kadrze, taka motywacja by się teraz nie sprawdziła. Starsi zawodnicy nie bardzo chcą słuchać, że mają kogoś tam zgwałcić na boisku. Z kolei rozkapryszonej młodzieży bardzo by się to przydało, bo ona w Polsce prezentuje się bardzo źle. To są chłopcy, dla których najważniejsze jest oglądanie wystaw w galerii handlowej, te całe Facebooki, Twittery… Za dużo laptopów i słuchawek na uszach, a za mało ognisk i imprez integracyjnych.

Wam te imprezy pomagały?
Na pewno scalały zespół. Pamiętam, jak po ciężkim zgrupowaniu w Buku, na trzy dni przed wylotem do Barcelony, Wójcik zrobił ognisko dla drużyny i sztabu szkoleniowego. Ale takie, że dogaszaliśmy je nad ranem. Nas nie trzeba było integrować, my byliśmy jedną wielką

rodziną. Teraz tak nie ma. Zastanawiam się, czy naszym młodym nawet Wójcik by pomógł. Bo co, zabrałby im laptopy? Gdyby mieli trenować u Wójcika, to połowa zespołu po pierwszych zajęciach trafiłaby do szpitala. Teraz każdy z zawodników idzie na siłownię i robi, co mu się podoba. A kiedyś brało się piłkę lekarską i z nią trzeba było skakać, robić przewroty, rzucać z autu. To była ścieżka zdrowia Wójcika. Pewnie nie do końca profesjonalna, ale nie było siłowni, a moc trzeba było złapać. Więc radziliśmy sobie w taki sposób.

Wójcikowi nie brakowało też szalonych pomysłów. Podobno kiedyś dzięki specjalnemu szyfrowi dostał się do pokoju w hotelu, w którym imprezowaliście.

Była taka sytuacja. I to nie tylko ja z Krzyśkiem Ratajczykiem tam się bawiłem, ale jakieś trzy czwarte drużyny! Wójcik wcale nie był zdziwiony, wiedział, co się święci. Przecież tak było przy okazji każdego zgrupowania! Kiedy drużyna spotykała się w hotelu Sobieski, to pierwszy wieczór był mocno integracyjny. Jeśli trener zapukał, to otwieraliśmy, żaden w tym problem. Czasami popatrzył, coś powiedział i wyszedł. Ale zdarzało się też, że siadał i dołączał do biesiady! Zdawał sobie sprawę, że piłkarze lubią się zabawić, a przecież sam nie był abstynentem. Nigdy nie miał z nami problemów, wiedział, że na drugi dzień na treningu będziemy w świetnej formie. Ale jeśli komuś coś nie wyszło, nie trafił w piłkę albo się pośliznął, to trener od razu przypominał wieczorną nasiadówkę.

Sam też zapewne kilka numerów wam wykręcił…

Jedną historię pamiętam do dziś. W Pile mieliśmy grać mecz młodzieżówek z Francją. Na jednej połówce trenowaliśmy my, a na drugiej Francuzi. Ćwiczyliśmy przez kilka minut, kiedy nagle pojawił się dobrze „zrobiony" Wójcik. Dopisywał mu humor i – jak się okazało – miał szalone pomysły. Kazał każdemu usiąść na piłce i rozpoczął wykład. Jak wiadomo, we francuskich reprezentacjach nigdy nie brakowało czarnoskórych piłkarzy. Gdybyśmy więc posłuchali przemowy Wuja dzisiaj, toby się to skończyło wielkim skandalem. Byliśmy w szoku. „Nie patrzcie na to, jak grają, ale na to, jak wyglądają!", zarządził Wójcik. Chodziło o to, żeby wyzwolić w nas dodatkową motywację. Oni mogą być wyżsi, szybsi, silniejsi. Ale nie możemy się ich bać. Bo po pierwsze tak trzeba, a po drugie – Janusz miał kilka promili i trzeba go było słuchać. Aha, dodam tylko, że mecz zakończył się remisem 1:1, a gola dla Francji strzelił niejaki Zinédine Zidane.

Wójcik przez lata trzymał się tych samych współpracowników. W reprezentacji olimpijskiej i Legii byli to Paweł Janas, asystent, i Zbigniew Korolkiewicz, masażysta. Jak wyglądała ich współpraca?
Czasem bardzo… procentowo. W hotelach whisky z colą – czyli jak to mówił Wójcik: „mazucik" – przygotowywał Paweł Janas. A na meczach Wujo zawsze miał specjalny bidon z odpowiednim roztworem. Czekał na niego na ławce rezerwowych, a Janusz regularnie uzupełniał płyny. Zwykle szykował go nieżyjący już niestety Zbyszek Korolkiewicz. Kiedy Korol złamał obojczyk, bo wywalił się podczas wyścigu z Wójcikiem na 50 metrów, to trener strasznie rozpaczał. Wygrał wprawdzie zakład z masażystą, ale martwił się, kto mu teraz będzie bidony szykował!

Zdarzyło się, że piłkarz przez przypadek złapał taki bidon?
W Legii. Trwała druga połowa jakiegoś meczu, byliśmy mocno zmęczeni. W trakcie jednej z przerw w grze Leszek Pisz podbiegł po picie. Korolkiewicz podrzucił mu bidon, ale pomylił się i wybrał ten z wódką! Pisz oblał się nią, a potem wziął wielki łyk. Aż nim zatrzęsło! Zakasłał, zakrztusił się, ale pobiegł z powrotem na boisko. Potem mieliśmy z niego mnóstwo śmiechu.

Trudno się oprzeć wrażeniu, że anegdot związanych z Wójcikiem jest tyle, że możesz nimi strzelać jak z karabinu maszynowego.
Tylu anegdot, ile można opowiedzieć o trenerze Wójciku, nie dała cała historia piłki nożnej! Na przykład taka opowieść. Wracaliśmy ze stycz-

niowego przedolimpijskiego zgrupowania w Emiratach Arabskich, ale po drodze mieliśmy jeszcze przystanek w Grecji, gdzie zagraliśmy jakiś mecz towarzyski. Wszyscy zapakowali się do autokaru, którym mieliśmy pojechać na lotnisko. Ale rozejrzeliśmy się i stwierdziliśmy: nie ma Wójcika! Okazało się, że pięć minut przed wyjazdem poczuł się już nieco gorzej i przysnął. Od czegóż był jednak Paweł Janas! Wierny asystent ruszył po szefa i błyskawicznie go wybudził. Po chwili z drzwi hotelu wyłonił się Janusz, na tych swoich charakterystycznych, prostych nogach, ale idący nieco przyspieszonym krokiem. Przyciemnione okulary, lekki uśmieszek. Od razu wiedzieliśmy, o co chodzi. Kiedy dotarł już jakimś cudem do autobusu, próbował się do niego dostać, ale zaszedł od strony, gdzie nie było drzwi! W ogóle mu to jednak nie przeszkadzało. Krzyczał, walił w karoserię, szukał wejścia tam, gdzie go nie było. Próbował tak z dobrą minutę, drużyna miała ubaw po pachy. W końcu ktoś wyszedł z autokaru i poprowadził wyraźnie zmęczonego trenera do wejścia, a potem posadził na fotelu. Kochany trener wydał komendę: „Jedziemy". I ruszyliśmy. Kabaret.

Wójcik tak cię polubił, że po latach zabrał cię na Cypr, byś grał w prowadzonym przez niego Anorthosisie Famagusta.

Tam to już była jazda bez trzymanki. Czasami z Radkiem Michalskim i Sławkiem Majakiem musieliśmy uciekać przed naszymi trenerami, czyli Wójcikiem i Andrzejem Czyżniewskim. Niekiedy udało się pójść gdzieś w *stricte* piłkarskim gronie, ale zdarzało się też, że trener przychodził do nas do domu i zaczynały się „nocne Polaków rozmowy" (śmiech). Wesoło było też na samym początku, kiedy dopiero zabierał mnie na Cypr. Wszystko było już klepnięte, Wójcik przyjechał po mnie do Warszawy. Anorthosis akurat miał zgrupowanie w Austrii. „Kowal, jutro widzimy się na lotnisku, zabieram cię ze sobą, będziesz grał z nami", powiedział. Dwie godziny przed lotem byłem już na Okęciu i spokojnie sobie czekałem. Oczywiście bilety i wszystkie dokumenty miał Wujo. Minęła godzina – nie ma go. „Wójcik, jak to on, jak zwykle lekko się spóźni", pomyślałem. Ale kiedy do odlotu zostało 15 minut, lekko już zrezygnowany postanowiłem zadzwonić do trenera. Nie odebrał. Bombardowałem go telefonami, odezwał się dopiero na pięć minut przed odlotem.

– Wojtuś, spokojnie będę za 15 minut – zakomunikował.

– Ale trenerze, za pięć minut mamy lot! – denerwowałem się.

– Bez nas nigdzie nie odlecą!

Co się okazało? Po tychże 15 minutach Wujo wyszedł z taksówki, oczywiście w ciemnych okularkach. „Chodź", powiedział. Ruszyliśmy. Minęliśmy odprawę bagażową, potem celną. Przemieszczaliśmy się bocznymi przejściami. Jacyś ludzie podwieźli nas pod samolot. Kiedy weszliśmy, pasażerowie patrzyli na nas z wściekłością. Przecież musieli czekać na dwóch spóźnionych gości! To był cały Wójcik, zdolny zatrzymać całe lotnisko. A spóźniał się notorycznie. Całe szczęście, że nie miał wpływu na początek meczów, bo kilka mogłoby się opóźnić.

Te spóźnienia jednak zawsze uchodziły mu płazem. Dlaczego?

Bo miał niesamowitą siłę przebicia, ludzie go lubili, przez pewien czas był niemal gwiazdą. Miał poparcie najważniejszych dziennikarzy i polityków. W hotelu Sobieski ciągle ktoś go odwiedzał. A jak Polak odwiedza Polaka, to czym się to może skończyć? Przecież nie kawką i ciasteczkiem (śmiech). Miał znajomości wszędzie, mógł załatwić sobie, co tylko chciał. „Panowie, pewni ludzie w pewnych sprawach widzą, słyszą i wiedzą" – tak nam odpowiadał, kiedy pytaliśmy o jego dziwne znajomości. Domyślam się, co to byli za „znajomi", ale nigdy nie poznałem ich nazwisk. Wystarczy jednak spojrzeć na to, kto wtedy rządził, i będzie jasne. Bo Wójcik zawsze przyjaźnił się z tymi, którzy akurat byli ważni. Wszędzie miał ludzi, którzy donosili mu, co robią piłkarze. Nawet jednak kiedy się zabawiliśmy, pretensji nie miał. Wymagał tylko jednego – profesjonalizmu na boisku. Można o nim mówić dobrze, można źle. Ale jednego odmówić mu nie sposób: osiągnął taki sukces, jaki powtórzyć będzie cholernie ciężko.

TOMASZ HAJTO

62-krotny reprezentant Polski. Podopieczny Janusza Wójcika w reprezentacji w latach 1997–1999.

Jakie miał pan relacje z Januszem Wójcikiem?

Bardzo dobre, choć trener Janusz Wójcik na początku do wszystkich podchodził bardzo sceptycznie. Kiedy jednak już zobaczył, że ktoś chce oddać mu serce, walczyć i umierać na boisku, to wtedy stawał się piłkarzowi bardzo przychylny. Pamiętam mnóstwo historii związanych z Wójcikiem. Czasem śmiesznych, a niekiedy wręcz kuriozalnych. Starał się motywować nas na przeróżne sposoby – nawet słabemu piłkarzowi był w stanie wmówić, że jest dobry. Niejednokrotnie przekraczało to jakiekolwiek realia piłki nożnej, to były takie piłkarskie anomalie. A o odprawach Wójcika do dzisiaj wszystkim opowiadam. To było coś nieprawdopodobnego.

Jak wyglądała taka przykładowa odprawa?

Nie brakowało oczywiście przekleństw (śmiech). Do dziś pamiętam odprawę przed meczem z Anglią w Warszawie, w którym zremisowaliśmy 0:0 po bardzo dobrej grze. Mogliśmy ich nawet ograć, bo mieliśmy wręcz kapitalne sytuacje, setki znakomitych okazji zmarnowali Juskowiak, Gilewicz czy Siadaczka. To był chyba najlepszy nasz mecz pod wodzą trenera Janusza Wójcika, i to w dużej mierze dzięki niemu oraz jego oryginalnej odprawie tak dobrze zagraliśmy. Pamiętam, jak przed meczem przyszedł do szatni i z zaciekawieniem przyglądał się każdemu z nas.

– Który ma największą szparę między zębami? – zapytał.

Zaczęliśmy się rozglądać, patrzeć po sobie zdziwieni. A Wójcik kontynuował poszukiwania. Ten nie, tamten nie.

– O, Tomek Iwan! Ty masz dużą szparę w zębach! – zatriumfował. – Posłuchaj mnie. Kiedy będziecie wychodzić na boisko, podejdź do Davida Beckhama i siknij na niego śliną przez tę szparę! Kiedy na ciebie spojrzy, powiedz: „All people fuck your wife!". Wtedy już będziemy ich mieć! – przekonywał, a potem odwrócił się w moim kierunku.

– Gianni, a ty głośno krzycz, wal rękami w bramę! Niech się boją! – polecił.

Nie ma się co oszukiwać: taka motywacja bardzo nam pomogła – zremisowaliśmy z wielką Anglią. A pamiętajmy, że to była Anglia pełna gwiazd. W tej drużynie grali Pearce, McManaman, bracia Neville, Shearer, Paul Ince, Scholes i LeSaux.

Z pana opowieści wyłania się obraz trenera Wójcika z głową pełną szalonych pomysłów.

Taki pomysłowy Dobromir (śmiech). Kolejny przykład to odprawa przed meczem z Czechami. Trener wpadł do szatni wściekły jak chmura gradowa.

– Pamiętacie, jak jeździliśmy do nich na zakupy? Nie chcieli nam sprzedawać orzeszków arachidowych! A ja pamiętam, że kiedyś tam byłem i chciałem kupić jarmilki dla dzieci do skakania na gumie. I oni mi tego nie sprzedali! Te pepiki pierdolone! Brać się za nich od początku! – motywował.

Taki był właśnie Wójcik. Drugiego takiego trenera już nie będzie.

Taki sposób prowadzenia drużyny to relikt przeszłości czy przeciwnie – trener Wójcik mógłby się odnaleźć we współczesnej piłce?

Zmieniły się czasy, realia, poziom rozmowy. Wszystko poszło w trochę innym kierunku.

A gdyby dziś Wójcik wszedł jako trener do szatni reprezentacji Polski i zaczął motywować piłkarzy swoimi metodami?

Patrzyliby na niego jak na kosmitę. Dawny sposób polemiki, motywowania zespołu, bardzo się różnił od tego, co obserwujemy teraz.

Miał jakieś oryginalne zwyczaje?

Mnóstwo. Najgorzej było, kiedy pod koniec treningu przyjechała telewizja z kamerami – zajęcia automatycznie przedłużały się o pół godziny. Trener zarządzał sprinty, starty, przewroty. Było bardzo wesoło. Posiadał też specyficzny dar przekonywania.

W jakim sensie specyficzny?

Przed meczem z Rosją dowiedzieliśmy się, że jeśli przegramy, to trener Wójcik zostanie zwolniony. Ja wtedy strzeliłem dwie bramki, wygraliśmy 3:1 i bardzo się cieszyłem, że trener zostanie. A także z tego, że wszyscy na nowo uwierzyli w tę reprezentację. Niedługo później postanowił powołać mnie na dziesięciodniowy wyjazd na mecze towarzyskie w Ameryce Południowej.

– Nie jadę, mam już urlop. Muszę wypocząć – powiedziałem. – To są mecze testowe, niech trener sprawdza zawodników ligowych. Przecież dobrze wie, jak ja gram.

Po pewnym czasie dzwoni kierownik drużyny Krzysztof Dmoszyński.

– Tomek, muszę porozmawiać z Januszem, bo on powiedział, że cię wypierdoli z kadry – przekazał.

Twardo obstawałem przy swoim:

– Trudno, jak chce, to niech mnie wyrzuci. Takie wyjazdy planuje się trochę wcześniej. Po ciężkim sezonie potrzebuję odpoczynku, by potem znów móc grać na najwyższym poziomie.

Wójcik chciał, żebym jednak przyjechał do Warszawy i na żywo porozmawiał z nim o sprawie wyjazdu na zgrupowanie. Oczywiście wsiadłem w samolot i stawiłem się w stolicy. Do wyjazdu pozostało jeszcze kilka dni.

– Dam ci za ten wyjazd cztery tysiące – zaproponował.

– Trenerze, tu nie chodzi o pieniądze. Gdybym mógł, naprawdę bym pojechał.

– Dobra, dam ci osiem.

– Trenerze, naprawdę nie chodzi mi o pieniądze!

– Dobra, piętnaście.

– Trenerze, nie wezmę, nie mogę pojechać!

– Dobra, dwadzieścia pięć, ale to moje ostatnie słowo.

Niesamowity miał ten dar przekonywania. W końcu nie pojechałem, bo wolałem odpocząć, a pieniądze nie były dla mnie najważniejsze. Ale tę historię zapamiętałem do dziś.

Balangi i imprezy na zgrupowaniach u Wójcika to mit czy prawda?

Zdecydowanie mit. W ciągu tygodnia u Wójcika na pewno nikt nie balował. Zgrupowanie zaczynało się w poniedziałek, przez kilka dni trenowaliśmy, a w sobotę był mecz. Jeśli ktoś wracał do klubu dopiero po weekendzie, to mógł się napić z kolegami, to był jego prywatny czas. Ale w trakcie zgrupowania – na pewno nie. A to, że sztab trenerski imprezował, to inna sprawa. Ale oni przecież nie musieli grać w piłkę, więc mogli sobie pofolgować. Nie pamiętam za to sytuacji, żeby Wójcik był pijany na treningu. Zajęcia odbywały się zwykle po południu, a przecież w ciągu dnia nie pił. Jeśli łyknęli coś sobie wieczorem, podczas omawiania taktyki, to już inna sprawa. Ciągle ktoś trenera odwiedzał w hotelu. Śmialiśmy się, że trzeba mocniejszy silnik do drzwi obrotowych zainstalować, bo jak kadra stacjonuje w Sobieskim, to ciągle ktoś przychodzi i wychodzi.

Zdarzyło się, że trener wywinął wam jakiś numer?

Niejeden. Graliśmy z Bułgarią na wyjeździe. Spaliśmy w hotelu należącym do Christo Stoiczkowa, a w dniu meczu udaliśmy się na poranny rozruch. Trenera Wójcika z nami nie było. Wchodzimy na boisko, zaczynamy rozruch, a tu nagle wpada policja i wyrzuca nas za ogrodzenie! Okazało się, że nic nie było załatwione, gospodarze stadionu nie wiedzieli, że mamy przyjechać. Kuriozalna sytuacja, zważywszy na to, że to była pierwsza reprezentacja Polski!

Bułgarów pokonaliście wtedy 3:0, ale ostatecznie do mistrzostw Europy drużyna Wójcika nie awansowała. Dlaczego?

Eliminacje przegraliśmy w Warszawie, kiedy zremisowaliśmy z Anglią, którą spokojnie mogliśmy ograć. Poza tym przez całe eliminacje sprawę trochę zawalili nam bramkarze, którzy popełniali błędy. Prowadziliśmy, a potem padały kuriozalne gole i traciliśmy punkty. Warto też powiedzieć, że nie pomógł nam PZPN, w którym działy się prawdziwie niepojęte rzeczy. To był jeden wielki kryminał.

Jak z perspektywy czasu wspomina pan Janusza Wójcika?
Tylko dobrze. Jak mogę wspominać źle człowieka, z którym świetnie się rozumiałem? Nie ma ludzi idealnych, każdy ma jakieś felery, ale grunt, żeby się dogadać, by osiągnąć założony cel. Szkoda, że ostatecznie nie udało się awansować, choć było strasznie blisko. Wielka szkoda.

KALENDARIUM

1953 – w Warszawie na świat przychodzi Janusz Wójcik, syn Janiny, łączniczki w powstaniu warszawskim, oraz Henryka, rodowitego warszawiaka i pracownika straży pożarnej Warszawskich Zakładów Mechanicznych Delta WZM.

1967–1970 – rozpoczyna karierę piłkarską jako zawodnik warszawskiej Agrykoli.

1970–1974 – piłkarz Gwardii Warszawa, w barwach której rozegrał jeden mecz w Ekstraklasie.

1974 – na krótko wiąże się z Ursusem Warszawa.

1975–1989 – wstępuje do Polskiej Zjednoczonej Partii Robotniczej. Legitymację wręcza mu Edward Gierek w Hucie Warszawa. Ma etat w Komitecie Dzielnicowym Warszawa Mokotów w wydziale organizacyjno-propagandowym. Odpowiada za oświatę na Mokotowie, od przedszkoli do szkół wyższych. Potem zostaje członkiem Komitetu Warszawskiego (wydział organizacyjny).

1975–1976 – dołącza do drużyny Hutnika Warszawa.

1976–1977 – wyjeżdża do Rawalpindi (Pakistan), gdzie kontynuuje karierę piłkarską.

1976 – żeni się ze swoją wieloletnią sympatią Wisławą Janas.

1979 – kończy studia na Wydziale Trenerskim Akademii Wychowania Fizycznego w Warszawie.

1979–1980 – wraz z żoną wyjeżdża do Kanady, gdzie gra w zespole Toronto Falcons. Równolegle pracuje w fabryce okien. Przed powrotem do kraju podejmuje decyzję o zakończeniu kariery piłkarskiej.

1980–1981 – obejmuje funkcję drugiego trenera reprezentacji Polski U-16 (u boku świętej pamięci Władysława Stachurskiego).

1981–1982 – jako pierwszy trener prowadzi Pogoń Grodzisk Mazowiecki.

1983 – rozwodzi się z Wisławą, mimo to pozostają w dobrych stosunkach.

1983–1984 – zostaje trenerem Huraganu Wołomin; równolegle trenuje reprezentację Polski U-16.

1984 – ponownie zawiera związek małżeński, tym razem z Krystyną Zielińską.

1985 – zostaje ojcem – rodzi mu się syn Andrzej.

1984–1985 – obejmuje drużynę Hutnika Kraków.

1986–1987 – pełni funkcję szkoleniowca Jagiellonii Białystok. Pod jego wodzą drużyna zaczyna odnosić sukcesy – w 1987 roku awansuje do I ligi – a Wójcik staje się znany w świecie polskiej piłki.

1988 – trenuje reprezentację Polski U-18.

1989–1992 – obejmuje olimpijską reprezentację Polski. Rozegrawszy szereg spektakularnych meczów, drużyna dochodzi do finału igrzysk w Barcelonie, gdzie zdobywa srebrny medal.

1992–1993 – trenuje Legię Warszawa, z którą zdobywa mistrzostwo Polski. Później tytuł został klubowi odebrany przez PZPN i przyznany Lechowi Poznań.

1994–1996 – wyjeżdża z kraju, by zostać selekcjonerem olimpijskiej reprezentacji Zjednoczonych Emiratów Arabskich. Zyskuje ogromną popularność na Bliskim Wschodzie po niespodziewanych zwycięstwach nad mocną drużyną z Iranu.

1996–1997 – trenuje zespół Al-Khallej w Zjednoczonych Emiratach Arabskich.

1997–1999 – obejmuje funkcję trenera i selekcjonera reprezentacji Polski. Jego zespół remisuje ze złożoną z gwiazd kadrą Anglii. Mimo to Polakom brakuje jednego punktu, by zakwalifikować się do baraży w eliminacjach do Euro 2000.

2000 – zostaje menedżerem Pogoni Szczecin.

2000 – gościnnie występuje w filmie *Chłopaki nie płaczą* Olafa Lubaszenki, gdzie gra gangstera.

2001 – na krótko obejmuje drużynę Śląska Wrocław. Odchodzi na skutek nieporozumień z władzami klubu.

2001–2002 – wyjeżdża na Cypr, gdzie trenuje Anorthosis Famagusta.

2001–2003 – wznawia działalność polityczną i zostaje członkiem Sojuszu Lewicy Demokratycznej.

2003 – znów opuszcza kraj – tym razem udaje się do Syrii, by pełnić funkcję selekcjonera tamtejszej reprezentacji.

2003–2004 – trenuje Świt Nowy Dwór Mazowiecki; działalności w tym klubie dotyczyć będzie większość postawionych mu w 2008 roku zarzutów o korupcję.

2005 – startuje w wyborach parlamentarnych z list Samoobrony. W okręgu białostockim uzyskał 4236 głosów, które zagwarantowały mu mandat poselski. Posłem był aż do 2007 roku. Wówczas w przedterminowych wyborach uzyskał 630 głosów i nie zdołał dostać się do Sejmu.

2006 – 8 stycznia po Balu Mistrzów Sportu zostaje zatrzymany, gdy prowadzi samochodu w stanie nietrzeźwym (ma 1,48 promila w pierwszym badaniu i 1,30 w drugim). Poddaje się karze dziesięciu tysięcy złotych grzywny i dwuletniemu zakazowi prowadzenia samochodów.

2008 – odchodzi z Samoobrony i kończy karierę polityczną.

2007–2008 – trenuje Znicz Pruszków. Jednym z jego podopiecznych jest późniejszy reprezentant Polski Robert Lewandowski.

2008 – zostaje trenerem Widzewa Łódź.

2008 – 22 października zatrzymuje go policja w związku z aferą korupcyjną w polskiej piłce nożnej.

2012 – w związku z aferą korupcyjną Komisja Dyscyplinarna PZPN wymierza mu karę w postaci czteroletniego zawieszenia praw pełnienia funkcji trenerskiej.

2014 – przyznaje się do winy i 9 października zostaje skazany za przestępstwa korupcyjne na karę dwóch lat pozbawienia wolności z warunkowym zawieszeniem jej wykonania na okres pięciu lat próby oraz na karę grzywny.

2014 – w listopadzie nakładem Wydawnictwa SQN ukazuje się jego autobiografia: *Wójt. Jedziemy z frajerami! Całe moje życie*, napisana wspólnie z dziennikarzem sportowym Przemysławem Ofiarą.

TO JESZCZE NIE KONIEC.
CIĄG DALSZY NASTĄPI!

Spis treści

Podejrzewaliśmy, że praw do organizacji mundialu się nie wygrywa, tylko kupuje, a dziesiątki skorumpowanych działaczy bezkarnie napychają sobie kieszenie milionowymi łapówkami.

Teraz mamy pewność.

Czy jesteś gotowy, aby poznać prawdę?

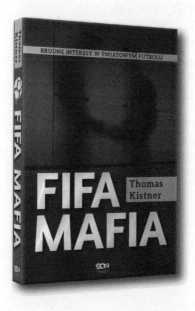

Szukaj w dobrych księgarniach i na
www.labotiga.pl

www.wsqn.pl

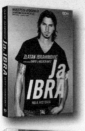